P9-DCX-827

ALSO BY KRISTEN BRITAIN:

Green Rider
First Rider's Call
The High King's Tomb

KRISTEN BRITAIN

THE HIGH KING'S TOMB

DAW BOOKS, INC.
DONALD A. WOLLHEIM, FOUNDER
375 Hudson Street, New York, NY 10014
ELIZABETH R. WOLLHEIM
SHEILA E. GILBERT
PUBLISHERS
http://www.dawbooks.com

Cover art by Donato.

DAW Book Collectors No. 1420.

DAW Books are distributed by Penguin Group (USA).

Book designed by Stanley S. Drate/Folio Graphics Co., Inc.

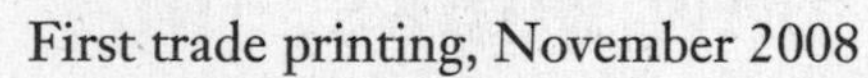

First trade printing, November 2008
2 3 4 5 6 7 8 9 10

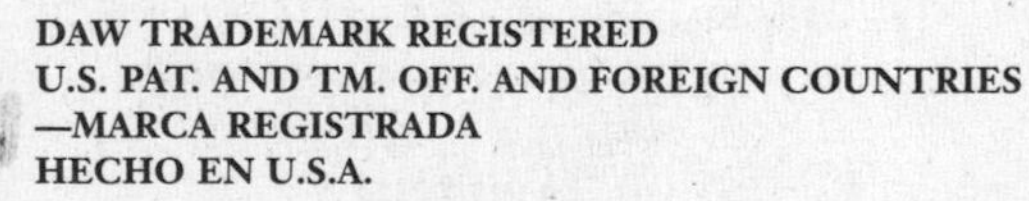

DAW TRADEMARK REGISTERED
U.S. PAT. AND TM. OFF. AND FOREIGN COUNTRIES
—MARCA REGISTRADA
HECHO EN U.S.A.

PRINTED IN THE U.S.A.

ACKNOWLEDGMENTS

Thank you to my readers for their support and enduring the long waits. (It's been a long wait for me, too!)

Thank you to Julie Czerneda, who deserves meadows full of irises for putting up with me, and Ruth Stuart also for listening, reading, and traveling.

Many thanks to the Peninsulans, past and present, for hearing the thing through: Chris Barstow, Annaliese Jakimides, Cynthia Thayer, David Fickett, and Paul Markosian; and welcome to Martha Todd Dudman.

As always, thank you to my editors, Betsy Wollheim and Debra Euler, and the whole DAW crew, as well as my agents, Anna Ghosh and Danny Baror.

Thank you to my web mage, MT O'Shaughnessy, for keeping up www.kristenbritain.com—*Baaah!* and Todd Edgar for assistance with the machine and some graphics stuff—Meow!

Thank you to Donato Giancola for the gorgeous painting which graces the cover of this book.

There are a number of "characters" who taught me many lessons in life, and I'd like to acknowledge them here: Fox, Carefree, Tommy, Seymour, JackO, Roman, Virginia, and so many others. Most, if not all, are gone now, but forever remembered.

Thank you to those who offered support and information that have aided with the progress of this book (i.e. suturing and sidesaddle riding), and any of those whom I've failed to mention. I appreciate your help.

Finally, thank you to my personal managers, to whom a percentage of my earnings go: Percy and Gryphon. You make my monitor hairy and ensure I am walked regularly. Couldn't have done this without you guys.

Onward to the next book . . .

In memory of Batwing
my nasty boy, my true miracle
for whom reams could be written
about the power of love
and the will to live,

—and—

In memory of Earl Grey
my sweet boy and manuscript cozy
a bright spirit
who shone so brilliantly
for too short a time.

I miss you, boys. I really miss you.

CROWN OF FLAME

In the autumn season, hawks, falcons, and eagles followed an ancient path through the sky on their journey south for the winter, the same path their ancestors had flown since the first took wing in ages long dark to memory. Their route swept down from the northlands, along the great frothing river that flowed from the glaciers to the sea, and over a cluster of small mountains. These were the Teligmar Hills of Mirwell Province, located on the western border of Sacoridia.

Perhaps the raptors were relieved when they saw the hills bulging on the horizon, for they were landmarks that helped guide the way, and the rising north wind gave loft to wings that had many hundreds of miles yet to fly, easing the toil of the journey. They hovered on updrafts over the rounded, weathered summits, resting on air currents and keeping an eye out for prey, maybe a stray songbird intent on its own imperative to migrate, or an unwary rodent.

This year, the raptors, with their sharp vision, spotted something new and curious among the mountains: humans. Numerous humans had taken up residence on one of the summits. There were clusters of tents and other structures among the trees and rocks, wood smoke wafting in the air, voices carried by the wind, and metal glinting in the morning sun. The raptors sensed a strange power down there, something their small bird minds could not grasp, but definitely *something* that ruffled their feathers.

Whatever it was, the concerns of the raptors rested with their own journey south, not with the affairs of humans. They left behind the Teligmar Hills, and would soon leave the land of Sacoridia to its winter, the Earth wheeling beneath the trailing edges of their wings.

As soon as the woman stepped out of her tent, she was greeted by the excited voices of children. They clustered around her, all chattering at once, tugging on her skirt for attention, showing her where a baby tooth was newly missing, asking her to play games or tell stories. She laughed and patted heads, the crinkles around her eyes and mouth deepening.

It was a mild autumn morning, but the cold breezes swept over the top of the small mountain's summit as they always did, tumbling leaves about her feet in whorls, and loosening a lock of steel gray hair from her braid. She tired of the wind, but the children didn't mind it, and she'd seen plenty of hawks using it as they passed south. The mountain her people camped on was aptly named Hawk Hill.

"Now, now, my children," she said. "There will be time to play games and tell stories later. Right now I need to see Ferdan. Ferdan? Where are you?"

A towheaded boy raised his hand and the woman waded through the children to reach him. His face was drawn, with circles under his eyes and a smudge of dirt on his chin. His shirt was not buttoned correctly, as if he had dressed himself.

"How is your mum today?" she asked. She knelt to rebutton his shirt and straighten it out.

"Not too good," the boy said. "Coughing real bad."

When the woman finished with his shirt, she stood and pressed a pouch fragrant with herbs into the boy's small hand. "Tell her to take this with her tea, a pinch thrice daily, no more, no less. It will help clear her lungs. Keep water steaming in a pot nearby for her to breathe. It will make her easier. You understand? Be careful not to burn yourself." When Ferdan's expression of worry did not alter, she tousled his hair and said, "I'll be along to visit her this afternoon. Now you go and see that your mum has some of that tea."

"Yes, Grandmother," Ferdan said, and he darted off to a lean-to draped with a stained blanket used both for privacy and to keep out the weather, the pouch clutched to his breast.

She would see to it his mother pulled through. It was a tragedy that any child should lose their mum. She shook her head and turned her attention to the rest of the children. "Isn't it time you went to your lessons with Master Holdt?" There was whining and groaning from the children, but no real rebellion, and she shooed them away, chuckling.

Only one child remained after all the others left, a little girl who was the woman's true granddaughter, Lala. Lala was too simple in her mind for lessons and she did not like playing with the other children. Nor did she talk. So most of the time she shadowed her grandmother or played by herself.

While the woman was Lala's grandmother by blood, she was also known as Grandmother to all her people in the encampment. She birthed their babies, provided them with medicines when they were sick, cared for their wounds, and counseled them on matters of marriage and family. She also led them in their spiritual beliefs. When it came time to flee Sacor City and seek safe haven, it was her they had looked to; it was her they followed on the grueling journey across the country all the way west to Mirwell Province, sometimes traveling along roads, but more often than not making their way through the unforgiving wilderness of the Green Cloak Forest. It had not been easy, and not all survived the journey, but those who did expressed their gratitude for her foresight and wisdom.

She was a simple woman, glad to be of comfort to them and honored by their trust. Leaving Sacor City had meant a great deal of upheaval and sacrifice. They'd left behind trades, businesses, respectable posts in the community; farms, homesteads, and houses. She had worried most about the children in the beginning, but learned over the ensuing months just how resilient the young ones were. This was a grand adventure for them, camping and hiding out in the wilds of the countryside, and the older boys liked to play "outlaw," which usually involved the "king" and his men running after the "outlaws" of Second Empire, and ending when the outlaws slew the enemy with the sticks they used for swords. The empire always prevailed, the lads cheering with gusto.

The hiding and camping tended to be harder on the adults, who recognized what they had given up and left behind forever. Yes, they had lost much, but they still possessed their freedom and their lives, and here they could wear their pendants or tattoos of the black tree unhidden. One day, Grandmother believed, the black tree of Mornhavonia would bloom again, but in the meantime they would not be at the mercy of king's law.

When the king discovered the existence of Second Empire over the summer, the sect in Sacor City began to collapse almost immediately with the capture of their leader, Weldon Spurlock. It was not Weldon who had revealed them, but another of their group, Westley Uxton. Names had been given, which led to more arrests and someone else giving additional names, and so on. Grandmother managed to escape with little more than a hundred of the faithful.

Others chose to remain in Sacor City on the chance they'd not be discovered, and so had those who were too elderly or unfit to travel. Some took their own lives lest they be used by the king to acquire information, and a few were operatives who knew how to evade capture.

The refugees from Sacor City occupied one side of the gray granite summit, where children recited lessons with Master Holdt and their parents washed laundry, repaired household goods, tended chickens and goats, and prepared for stalking game along the flanks of the mountain. The soldiers camped across from them, where they currently sharpened blades, practiced swordplay, and ate breakfast. Their tents and sturdy lean-tos were tucked into clusters of boulders and against outcrops.

The soldiers were not children of the empire, but had been equally persecuted by the king. Some were bandits, mercenaries, and deserters, but most were loyalists of the old Lord Mirwell, who had attempted to depose the king two years ago. The loyalists had been forced into hiding to avoid arrest and the inevitable execution.

Grandmother was convinced it was God who had brought her people and the soldiers together, unlikely allies though they may be. Her people required protection, and she needed to start building an army, and blessing be, she found the leader of the soldiers at a crossroads during their exodus. She had no gold to pay the soldiers with, no position in life with which to reward them—at least not yet—but she had been able to give them purpose, for they shared a common enemy: the king and Sacoridia.

When the time was right, she would expand their ranks with the devout of Second Empire. Already some of the men and older boys of her sect trained with the soldiers. Others remained embedded with their units in provincial and private militias, as well as the king's own military. When she called, they would come to her well trained and ready to attend to whatever task she set before them.

Her ancestors had been wise to melt into everyday Sacoridian society, spreading a network of sects across the provinces and into Rhovanny as well. They had infiltrated not only the military, but the trades and guilds. They ran farms and sold wares. They lived as any Sacoridian did, but secretly awaited the time when the empire would rise again.

One day they would rule over those who had been their neighbors, control all trade and the military. The empire would finally conquer this land of heathens. This was the dream of the five who founded Second Empire in the aftermath of the Long War, and Grandmother did not think the fruition of that dream far off.

Such thoughts always warmed her, made her proud of her people. Over a millennium they had endured, keeping their secrets, and waiting ever so patiently. Their day would come.

The officer who commanded the soldiers made his way across the summit to where she stood taking in the morning and halted before her. They had an appointment.

"Lala, dear," she said, turning to her granddaughter, "fetch my basket, please."

The little girl ducked into the tent they shared, and reemerged almost instantly with a long-handled basket that contained skeins of Grandmother's yarn.

The soldier awaiting her pleasure was tall and broad-shouldered and moved with the grace of any well-trained, disciplined warrior. He wore tough fighting leathers and a serviceable longsword in a scarred sheath on his right hip. His flesh also bore the scars of battle, notably a patch over his eye and the hook on his right wrist that replaced his missing hand. He had once been a favorite of the old lord-governor's, and proved experienced and highly capable. Grandmother liked him very much.

"Good morning, Captain Immerez," she said.

"Morning." His voice was low and gravelly. "We're ready for you."

She nodded and followed him across the summit. Without looking, she knew Lala tagged along carrying the basket. The girl was always interested, or perhaps *entertained,* by her grandmother's activities, whether it was healing the sick or punishing transgressors. Since Lala did not speak or show much in the way of emotion, it was hard to say what she thought about anything. Still, she was biddable, and her silence did not bother Grandmother in the least, for she was used to it. She had cut the girl from the womb of her own dead daughter nine years ago, and even then, though the baby had survived, she uttered not a sound when she emerged into the world, and had not made a sound since.

The captain led them to a corner of the encampment where the prisoner sat bound beneath the watchful gaze of his guard. The man was a wreck of welts, bruises, and gashes. No doubt there were broken bones beneath abused flesh.

"Jeremiah," Grandmother said, "I am disappointed in you."

At the sound of his name, the prisoner looked up at her. One of his eyes was swollen shut.

"Captain Immerez tells me you were seen and overheard

talking to some king's men down in Mirwellton. You were starting to give them details about us. Is this so?"

Jeremiah did not answer, and Grandmother took this as confirmation of his guilt.

"Thank God the captain's men stopped you before you ruined us," she said. "Exposing our secrets is one of the highest acts of betrayal you could commit. Why? Why would you do such a thing?"

Bloody saliva oozed from Jeremiah's mouth. Many of his teeth had been smashed during the interrogation. It took him a few moments to get any words out, and when they came, they were a wet whisper. "I do not believe. I do not believe in the destiny of Second Empire."

Grandmother schooled herself to calmness, though his words made her want to cry. She'd known Jeremiah since he was a toddler, had taught him with the other children in the ways of the empire, and she loved him as she loved all the others.

Before she could speak, he continued, "I like . . . like my life in Sacoridia. Do not need empire."

Grandmother wanted to cover her ears at his words, but she could not deny the truth of his betrayal. It had happened to others, other descendents of Arcosia who adapted to life as Sacoridians so well they gave up on the empire, turned their backs on it. Whole sects had faded away; others had watered down bloodlines so much by marrying outside the society they were shunned. Those of the blood who turned away but did not seem likely to expose Second Empire were left alone in the hope they would return to the fold. Others, like Jeremiah, who had actively tried to betray them, were dealt with.

"You would turn away from your heritage and all it means?" She shook her head in disbelief and he did not deny her accusation. "You would have destroyed us—your family, your neighbors, your kin."

"Just want to farm," Jeremiah said. "Didn't like leaving my land. Have peace. Nothing wrong with Sacoridia. Don't need empire."

Grandmother closed her eyes and took a deep breath. "You know what this means, Jeremiah?"

"I do."

Yes, he would know. Every one of them knew the consequences of betrayal. Second Empire had remained hidden for so long because of the doctrine of secrecy it adhered to. Punishment against transgressors was harsh to protect that secret.

"Jeremiah," she said, "I have no choice but to pronounce you a traitor."

He did not protest, he did not say a word.

"Was anyone else involved in this heresy?" she asked the captain.

"The king's men he talked to were ambushed and killed," the captain replied. "There was no one else. We were thorough in our questioning."

She nodded. The evidence of their thoroughness sat before her. "You have brought this upon yourself," she told Jeremiah.

He bowed his head, accepting his doom.

Grandmother beckoned Lala forward and took her basket of yarn from the girl. "Now be a good girl and go fetch my bowl. You know the one."

Lala nodded and trotted off.

Grandmother gazed into her basket at her yarn. There were skeins dyed deep red, indigo, and an earthy brown, and a small ball of sky blue. She chose the red, drawing out a strand about the length of her arm, and cut it with a sharp little knife that hung from her waist. She set the basket aside.

Jeremiah rocked back and forth at her feet, mumbling prayers to God. Even if he betrayed his people, at least he had not assimilated so far that he had abandoned the one true God in favor of the multitudes the heathen Sacoridians worshipped.

From then on she ignored Jeremiah and concentrated on the strand of yarn, which she started tying into knots. Intricate knots, knots that had been taught to her by her mother, as her mother's mother had taught, and down the maternal line of her family through the millennia. Only since summer, however, had she been able to call the true power to the knots.

As Grandmother worked, sparks flew from her fingers, though they did not ignite the yarn. Cook fires around the encampment dwindled and sputtered as though the life had been sucked from them.

"Feed the fires," she instructed Captain Immerez. She barely registered him passing the order along to his subordinates.

With each loop and tug of the yarn she worked the art, speaking words of power that were Arcosian in origin, but not of the Arcosian language. She bound the power as she tightened each knot.

The energy of the cook fires flowed through her and into the knots. She did not see red yarn woven about her fingers, but a golden strand of flame. It did not burn her.

When she finished, she held in her hands what looked a mass of snarled red yarn to those not gifted with the art. To Grandmother, it was a crown of fire. She placed it on Jeremiah's head.

"Safir!" she commanded, and it blazed.

There were easier, more direct ways to execute traitors, it was true, but this was uniquely Arcosian, and thus fitting. The annals of her people told of the crown of fire as one form of punishing a traitor. It also provided a graphic example to others who might harbor secret thoughts of rebellion. They could not help but recognize her power and authority when they witnessed nothing more than a harmless bit of yarn bring about an excruciating death.

Jeremiah's hair smoldered and crackled, then burned away. The yarn sank into his skull, greedily feeding on flesh to fuel its flame of power. When Jeremiah began screaming, the captain stuffed a rag into his mouth that a soldier had been using to oil his sword.

Smoke rose from Jeremiah's head and his body spasmed, his back arching. The skin of his face and skull blackened and bubbled with blisters as the flames burned from the inside out. With a final muffled scream, Jeremiah heaved over and died.

"I must be quick now," Grandmother said, feeling fevered herself. "Lala? There you are. The bowl, please."

The bowl was made of nondescript earthenware, the spiderweb crackling of the glaze stained a rusty color. The vessel had always been used for the purpose for which Grandmother now employed it. It had been handed down her maternal line like the knowledge of how to tie the knots. Lala set the bowl in place.

"Good girl," Grandmother said. She crouched beside Jeremiah. He may have tried to betray his people, but now he could give back and maybe God would forgive him, allow him into the eternal meadow. Really, she had done the young man a kindness—he now could sin no further and perhaps had not lost all chance of gaining entrance to paradise. She thrust her knife into the artery of his neck and held the bowl to catch his blood.

Captain Immerez hovered nearby while his men stayed clear of the grotesque scene of the bleeding of Jeremiah with his blackened, smoking head. "I've news for you, but thought it better to wait till this task was completed."

Grandmother glanced over her shoulder at him. "Go ahead."

He nodded. "I've had word that the parchment has been located."

Grandmother grinned. "How wonderful!"

"Yes. Events have been set in motion in Sacor City just as you wished, and we should obtain the parchment very soon."

Saddened as Grandmother was by Jeremiah's betrayal and the necessity of his death, Immerez's news buoyed her spirits.

It also pleased her that Jeremiah's blood would not go to waste, but would aid her cause. Her ordinary looking bowl would keep the blood warm and fresh till she needed to use it. Her happiness grew even as crimson liquid filled the bowl to the brim.

THE BLUE DRESS

Tall grasses whipped against the Green Rider's legs as he ran. He cast terrified glances over his shoulder, his breaths harsh and ragged, and punctuated by the thud of hoofbeats behind him. He caught his toe in a hole and plunged to the ground. Desperately he tore at grass stalks to pull himself upright and continue his flight.

And still the hoofbeats followed at a steady, measured pace, never faltering, never slowing, coming inexorably, unrelentingly behind him.

A strangled cry of triumph erupted from the Rider's throat as safety appeared just ahead. He hurled himself between the rails of the fence, sprawling at his captain's feet.

"Well, that didn't go very well, did it?" Laren Mapstone said.

On the other side of the fence, the source of Ben's terror gazed down at him with big brown eyes and snorted.

"And I suppose you're pleased with yourself," Laren told the gelding.

Robin flicked his ears and shook the reins, then dropped his nose into the grass to graze.

Laren gazed down at Ben who labored for breath, more from fright, she thought, than exertion. One day he'd have to get over his irrational fear of horses—he had to! What was a Green Rider without a mount? A Green Pedestrian? She had no idea from where the young man's fear originated. As a mender, he tended the messiest and goriest of injuries without hesitation, but healthy, intelligent horses inspired terror in him. Most Riders *loved* horses.

Karigan strolled across the pasture, following Ben's path and plucking at the tips of grasses as she went. When she reached Robin, she grabbed his reins and jerked his nose out of the grass. Green slobber dripped from his bit.

"We did better today," Karigan said. "Ben actually got his toe in the stirrup to mount."

Laren supposed it was progress, but she didn't feel as optimistic as Karigan sounded. She was getting used to having Karigan around to help out while Mara, her recently promoted Chief Rider, continued to recover from the horrific burns she had received when fire had destroyed Rider barracks during the summer. Karigan took care of Rider accounts and scheduling, and lent a hand with settling in the new Riders that seemed to be appearing on her step weekly now—Laren couldn't help but smile at the thought of more Riders to help fill their ranks.

"We were doing fine," Karigan continued, giving Robin a stern look, "until this one decided to knock Ben off balance."

Robin stamped when a fly alighted on his shoulder, his expression guileless. Laren squinted at him, not believing it for an instant. He looked like he had enjoyed himself while "chasing" Ben.

"I think you're done here for the day," Laren told Ben. "You may go report to Master Destarion for the afternoon."

Ben's relief was palpable. "Yes, Captain." He patted some dust off his trousers and strode toward the castle, where he was due for a shift in the mending wing.

"What are we going to do with him?" Laren wondered, watching him go.

Karigan stroked Robin's neck. "Give him time, I suppose. He dedicated himself to a life of mending the sick and injured, and he's trained for years, only to have a wrinkle thrown into his plans, unforeseen and unasked for."

Laren eyed Karigan sharply, knowing what a struggle it had been for her to leave behind her life as a merchant to answer the Rider call, and how much she had resented it. But Laren could find no resentment in Karigan's demeanor now. She was merely stating fact.

Something behind Laren caught Karigan's attention. Laren followed her gaze to find two finely dressed gentlemen approaching, one bearing packages wrapped in linen and secured with strings.

"We seek Karigan G'ladheon. Might you be she?" the first man, a stout fellow, asked. It was clear the other was a servant, for though his clothing was fine, it lacked the ornamentation of the lead fellow's.

"What is he up to now?" Karigan muttered under her breath. She cleared her throat and said more loudly, "I'm Karigan G'ladheon."

The stout fellow, out of breath from the short walk across castle grounds, assessed Karigan for a moment with a raised eyebrow, then placed his hand over his heart and bowed. "Good day, mistress. I am Akle Mundoy, of Clan Mundoy, from the guild, at your service."

Laren frowned. He could only mean the merchants guild. The "he" Karigan wondered about had to be her father, Stevic G'ladheon, one of the premier merchants of Sacoridia.

Karigan copied Mundoy's bow. "And I'm at yours."

Mundoy nodded. "I bring you a message from your esteemed father, and one from Bernardo Coyle, of the Coyle merchanting family in Rhovanny."

Karigan stared in disbelief at the two envelopes Mundoy passed her, one sealed with a blue and purple ribbon Laren recognized immediately, having opened enough letters from Stevic G'ladheon herself.

"And there are gifts," Mundoy added, gesturing at his servant. "My man Reston will bear them to your chambers, if you like."

"Er, chamber," Karigan corrected. "Thank you, no. I'll—" Then she glanced at Robin.

"Let me take him," Laren said, and Karigan gratefully handed over the reins and slipped through the fence rails.

Laren sensed some undercurrent here, that this merchant, Mundoy, was making judgment on Clan G'ladheon based on Karigan's appearance and circumstances. Why was she uniformed? Where was her servant? Only one chamber?

Appearances must be just as important to merchants as to nobles. If Karigan appeared anything less than prosperous, rumors would spread across the lands, perhaps damaging the clan's image.

"You've a servant to convey these?" Mundoy asked.

Karigan retained a pleasant expression, though Laren could tell it was forced. "I will see to the packages personally." She addressed the servant rather than his master.

"They are an armful, but not overly heavy, mistress," Reston assured her.

Karigan took them into her arms and Mundoy said, "Reston will return tomorrow for your reply to Master Coyle's message. Good day."

Mundoy struck off, his faithful servant close on his heels, Karigan glowering after the pair.

"Fish merchant," she muttered. Then she turned to Laren. "May I be excused?"

Laren nodded her assent and Karigan trotted off toward the castle. Absently she stroked Robin's neck. "What do you suppose that was all about?"

"I can't believe it," Karigan fumed a few hours later. She held the dress up to her shoulders so Mara could fully see it. It was made of deep, sapphire blue velvet patterned with leaves. Depending on the light and fold of the fabric, it took on the hue of midnight blue. The sleeves were puffed and slashed to reveal blue silk, and silver thread glistened in the sunlight beaming through the narrow window.

Mara, propped against a pile of pillows on her bed, smiled. "It brings out your eyes. It's gorgeous."

"But—" Karigan frowned, realizing how petty she must sound. It was deceptive to stand here next to Mara, for her near side appeared unchanged and unmarred, but when she gazed at Mara straight on, half her face looked like melted, puckered wax, and the hair on that side of her head grew back in crazy, curly patches. Much of the right side of her body had been burned. Only Ben's intervention, the use of his magical healing ability, had helped Mara survive the wounds and her ensuing illness. In fact, the speed with which she was recovering was remarkable, and Ben's ability had diminished some of the disfigurement.

"Yes, it's gorgeous," Karigan admitted. Her father had spared no expense on this dress and had sent along additional funds so she could have it properly fitted. It was more the intent behind the gift than the actual dress that concerned her. She fell into the chair next to Mara's bed and let the dress blanket her legs.

"And so who is this Braymer Coyle?" Mara asked. "Is he handsome?"

Karigan sighed. "I've no idea. We were children last time we met. His father, like mine, is a textile merchant, but from Rhovanny; in fact he's one of my father's leading competitors. Braymer is the heir to the family business."

Mara raised an eyebrow that no longer existed. "I see. So this is about more than two old friends getting their children together."

Karigan nodded. "Yes. It's about two middle-aged men concerned about their legacies and expanding their textile empires." She rolled her eyes. "If Braymer and I get along, they are undoubtedly hoping for a–a marriage alliance."

"And here I thought nobles were the only ones who worried about such things."

"It isn't the first time my father has tried to find a suitable match for me, though he'd never force it on me the way some would. But this—" and she rumpled the dress in emphasis "—this is *serious*."

An amused smile formed on Mara's lips, and there was humor in her eyes Karigan had not seen in a long while. "Much more serious than adventures in Blackveil and visitations by spirits of the dead?"

"Thank you for putting it in perspective for me."

"My pleasure. I should think an afternoon out in that

beautiful dress, and on the arm of a wealthy man, a nice change of pace for you from cleaning out the new Rider wing. New faces, different sights."

Karigan took Mara's unburned hand into her own. "I'm sorry—I'm not thinking. Who am I to complain?" Mara had not left the mending wing since the night of the fire, and rarely left her room as she healed.

"Karigan G'ladheon, don't be silly. Your visit here brightens my day, and gives me things to think about other than my treatments. Don't worry about me—I'll soon be out of here, and Captain Mapstone is already keeping me busy with paperwork." She patted a pile on her bedside table. "You went through so much this summer, and you have seemed so sad of late. You deserve a rest day, an afternoon out, and I want you to come back and tell me *everything*."

So Karigan hadn't been able to hide anything from Mara after all. Yes, she had been sad, and angry, but for reasons she would never explain. Not even to Mara. "I can't expect it will be very exciting. We're going to a tea room down on Gryphon Street and then to the Sacor City War Museum."

Karigan left the mending wing for one of the main castle corridors, the bundle of velvet dress spilling over her arms. Not so long ago all she had desired was to follow in her father's footsteps as a merchant and she had resented the Rider call for changing the course of her life. And now she resented her father for trying to draw her back?

She thought he had finally understood that for the time being, she served as a Green Rider, a king's messenger, and it left no room in her life for a role as a merchant. And now he was trying to marry her off? Not in so many words, of course. The pretense was that she was to welcome Braymer Coyle on his first excursion to Sacor City. This was reinforced by a polite request from Braymer's father that she show his son the city, and the gift that had accompanied it—a delicate silver necklace that matched the silver threads of her new dress.

She snorted. Their fathers had been in cahoots.

Well, she would take Mara's advice and just relax and enjoy the change of pace. A quiet change of pace, she decided. No uniform, no sword, no enemies.

And Mara was right: she had been sad.

Her progress was hampered by a gaggle of young noblewomen clogging the corridor. With the announcement of King Zachary's betrothal to Lady Estora, Coutre relations had descended upon the castle from all directions and were still coming, undoubtedly emptying the whole of Coutre Province.

The women were laughing and in high spirits. Karigan marveled at how the announcement of a wedding could turn people into ninnies. The fact that it was the *king's* wedding didn't help matters—the foolishness extended across the entire country.

Moving at the core of the finery and laughter was one who outshone them all, with her sweep of golden hair and statuesque figure. Lady Estora Coutre did not come across as silly or foolish—far from it. Rather she was serene, and while others giggled, she gave only a distant smile. It was almost as if she moved in a different world than they did.

Lady Estora was reputed to be the greatest beauty of the lands, and many anxious suitors had come and gone, had been turned away by her father who had settled for nothing less than the high king as the bridegroom for his firstborn daughter.

At that moment, Estora turned, as if sensing Karigan's gaze, and caught her eyes. Karigan clutched her dress to her chest and sucked in a breath.

"Karigan?" Estora said.

Some of the gaggle paused to see whom she addressed.

Karigan exhaled, turned on her heel, and struck off in the opposite direction.

"How rude," one of the noblewomen loudly commented. "What do you want with a commoner of that ilk anyway?"

Karigan never heard Estora's reply. They had been friends, but ever since the betrothal announcement, Karigan had been unable to speak with her, or even to face her.

She took a long, circuitous route through the servants' quarter of the castle, bypassing cooks and laundresses and runners. Here she felt comfortable and inconspicuous among her own kind. There was no chance she would run into Estora again, and there was especially no chance of encountering King Zachary.

She'd not gone before King Zachary since . . . that night. The starry night he had expressed his love for her atop the castle roof. He had chosen to tell her his feelings even as the ink on the marriage contract with Lord Coutre was drying.

Why had she fallen for her monarch, one who was unobtainable for the likes of her? His timing had been abysmal, and even as she yearned to be held in his arms, she wished he had said nothing to her at all. Maybe then she could have gotten through this whole marriage ordeal without hurting so much. If he truly cared, he would have kept his feelings to himself.

It was next to impossible not to feel pain with all the reminders of the betrothal around the castle; all the talk she overheard about wedding plans, of the children Zachary and Estora would produce. Even Karigan's fellow Riders were caught up in the excitement.

It drowned out more important matters. It wasn't so long ago that the lands had been threatened by a presence in Blackveil Forest which had been no less than the shadow of Mornhavon the Black, an old and deadly enemy. Had everyone forgotten already, amid all the wedding foolishness, that sometime in the future he would be back, and angry in the extreme?

She was grinding her teeth by the time she reached the lower sections of the castle. It didn't help that Alton, whom she considered a dear friend, had decided he hated her for some reason she couldn't fathom. She would never understand men. They were incomprehensible, and she did not hold out much hope for Braymer Coyle.

Karigan sighed as she stepped into the Rider wing. It was part of a more ancient section of the castle, and here the stonework was rougher, the walls closer, and the arched ceiling lower. Long abandoned by the Green Riders, and by everyone else for that matter, it had cleaned up nicely, but it would never replace the old barracks that had housed the king's messengers for two hundred years before fire demolished it.

Someone had seen to hanging bright tapestries along the corridor walls. She would have liked to enlarge the arrow slits that served as windows in each of the tiny chambers, but was unable to for reasons of defense. Overall, despite the improvements that had been made, it was still a dark, gloomy place, but she had to admit that it was getting better. Especially with all the life the new Riders brought to it.

Even now, Ty Newland stood with arms folded, overseeing Fergal Duff, a new Rider, and Yates Cardell, a not-so-new Rider, move an awkward and rather heavy wardrobe down the corridor. The two grunted with effort and sweated profusely, their rolled-up sleeves revealing tautly corded muscles. Ty in contrast, looked as cool and impeccable as usual. The others called him "Rider Perfect" behind his back, but Karigan suspected that if he knew, he'd be rather pleased.

"Good afternoon, Karigan," Ty said.

"Hello."

Fergal, upon seeing her, straightened, which shifted the load of the wardrobe onto Yates, who issued a garbled expletive.

"Hello, Rider G'ladheon," Fergal said, oblivious to Yates' strain.

He was maybe all of fifteen years old, and full of the bright innocence of one who had not been a Green Rider long. It amazed her how eager the novice Riders were about their new lives and the prospect of meeting danger in the course of their work. As part of their training, they heard about the legends and history of the king's messengers—the little that was known, anyway. Quickly becoming part of the recent history were accounts of Karigan's own exploits. She had caught more than one wide-eyed gaze cast in her direction from among the new Riders. Several even paused in their own weapons practice to watch her train with the fearsome Arms Master Drent.

Another male not high on Karigan's happy list. He had insisted on continuing to train her, and unfortunately, Captain Mapstone agreed.

"Fergal!" Yates cried in a strangled tone. "Pay attention!"

"Yes, sir." The young Rider again took on more of the weight of the wardrobe.

"Sir?" Karigan asked Ty.

"The young are impressionable, and at the moment, Fergal's deference is keeping Yates cooperative."

Karigan shook her head and ducked into her chamber. It just wasn't the same as her old room at the barracks that had overlooked the green of pasture and grazing messenger horses, but it was quiet.

"Ow!" Yates howled. "That was, and I put the emphasis on *was,* my toe!"

Mostly quiet, she amended. She shut the door and hung her dress in the dark depths of her own monstrous wardrobe. Garth had found this, and other royal castoffs with which to furnish the new Rider wing, in a storage room somewhere in the castle.

The rich blue and tailoring of her dress looked odd hanging among all the green of her uniforms, like something from another place, another world. And she supposed it was. Her world was now that of the Green Riders, not that of a merchant, and certainly not that of a young woman caught up in more ordinary pursuits, such as attracting a profitable marriage alliance.

The world of the Green Riders was a dangerous one. Riders were not particularly long lived, and Karigan had come close to losing her own life more than once. She had lost count of how many Riders died violent deaths since she had been called. Her own brooch once belonged to a Rider she found impaled with two black arrows and dying in the road.

If she survived her tenure as a Rider, she knew that other

world would be out there waiting for her, and that she'd have incredible tales to tell her grandchildren.

The bell down in the city rang out four hour, and she sat on the edge of her narrow bed, gazing into the open wardrobe. The silvery threads of her dress did not sparkle as brightly as the gold threads of the winged horse insignia on the sleeves of her uniform.

Not one to seek sanctuary, Karigan found it now in the dim light that filtered into her room through her narrow window. Here she heard no words about weddings, nor did she have to look upon preparations. No one was trying to kill her at the moment, and she hadn't even seen the hint of a ghost in a couple months. More important, there was no sign of trouble at the wall. So far. Perhaps her days of danger were over, and some future Rider would deal with Mornhavon the Black. Maybe Alton would fix the wall before Mornhavon returned.

A sort of contentment blanketed her, and she fell asleep, dreaming of walking through a garden in a deep green velvet dress, which sparkled in the sunshine with threads of golden fire.

GRYPHON STREET

"Look at you," Tegan said in a hushed voice. "Beautiful!"

She tilted the mirror so Karigan could get a better glimpse of herself, but it was too small for her to see a full view. She decided she'd just have to take Tegan's word for it that she wasn't about to embarrass herself.

Karigan had needed a great deal of help getting ready—this was not the simple attire of her girlhood, but a complicated system of undergarments, padding, layers of skirts, and the laces necessary to hold it all together. The worst part was the dratted whalebone corset Tegan had cinched tight, squishing all of Karigan's innards and making the scar tissue of a not-so-old stab wound throb. It plumped up her unremarkable bosom into something . . . miraculous. Fortunately the seamstress in town had altered the bodice, with its swooping neckline, to perfection. A slight error in measurement would have been far too revealing.

What was her father thinking by sending her a dress like this? Well, obviously he wanted to impress Braymer Coyle with her, um, feminine wiles. Or maybe, just maybe, he didn't see her as a little girl anymore.

Encased in the dress and its various trappings, Karigan found she could not breathe or bend, and that the layers of skirts felt like they weighed a hundred pounds. Her shoes, comprised of silk brocade dyed to match the dress with narrow wooden soles, were clasped to her feet with silver buckles. The contraptions produced dainty-looking feet but pinched her toes and made walking a treacherous endeavor. She glanced with longing at her supple leather riding boots standing at attention next to her wardrobe and hoped she'd survive the day without breaking any bones.

As the daughter of a merchant, she had always worn all the finest, latest fashions, but throughout her childhood she had admired the sophisticated women attired in their elegant dresses as they paraded about Corsa's most exclusive shopping district and attended socials. At the time, she could hardly wait to be of an age to join them, and she had fantasized about dresses just like the one that now held her captive. What *had* she been thinking?

"I feel like a puffy blue blob," Karigan said, stroking the patterned velvet with a gloved hand. Even her head felt funny with her hair piled up on it and held in place with an armory of pins, combs, and ribbons. She figured the hardware equaled the weight of her saber.

"The blue is wonderful." Tegan's eyes feasted on Karigan's dress. She came from a clan of dyers and knew quality when she saw it. It was even possible the dye had come from her clan. "Oh, we must not forget your necklace," she said. She opened the ornate porcelain box it came in and drew out the silver chain with a crescent moon pendant hanging from it.

Karigan was surprised a Rhovan would choose the symbol of the god most Sacoridians worshipped, Aeryc, as a gift. Rhovans preferred to worship the goddess of the sun, Aeryon. Perhaps Braymer's father thought she was of a religious disposition and that this would please her. Or maybe the Coyles were religious and her father had exaggerated some facts about Clan G'ladheon to impress them. It wouldn't surprise her in the least if he had.

Tegan clasped the chain around Karigan's neck. The only other piece of "jewelry" she wore was her Rider brooch. It had been something of a challenge to figure out where to pin it. Ordinarily it was attached to her uniform above her heart, but presently there was not enough cloth in that region to hold it, so she had clasped it close to her shoulder. It was an awkward placement, but by the brooch's special nature, its true form would remain invisible to everyone except other Riders.

Tegan helped wrap a matching shawl around Karigan's shoulders and handed her a little drawstring purse. She then made Karigan turn all the way around.

Tegan clapped her hands together. "You are . . ." she paused, as if words failed her. "You are utterly transformed. You . . . you outshine even Lady Estora."

"Don't exaggerate, Tegan."

"Truly, you are stunning, my dear. A noble lady."

"Oh, my." Karigan smiled faintly, knowing how her father would react to *that* comment. Stevic G'ladheon was not fond of aristocrats.

"It's getting late," Tegan said. "You should probably head for the castle entrance."

Karigan grimaced. "I'm not sure I can move." The walk to the castle entrance suddenly seemed daunting though normally she wouldn't have thought twice about it. She sucked in a breath and wobbled out into the corridor.

Everything in the corridor stopped. Riders who had been chatting fell silent. Others striding by halted. Anyone going about their business came to a standstill and gawked. Particularly the males.

Tegan squeezed through the doorway around Karigan's skirts. "It's my pleasure to introduce Her Ridership, Lady Karigan."

The Riders hooted and clapped, some of the females oohing and aahing over the dress. Karigan, taken aback, did not know what to say or do besides blush profusely.

Yates pushed his way forward and bowed with a mischievous grin, then offered her his arm. "Might I have the honor of escorting Her Ridership to the castle entrance?"

Ordinarily Yates might receive a sarcastic retort for such an offer, but this time Karigan was actually relieved, and she took his proffered arm. The challenge of walking in the blasted shoes would be easier now that she had someone to lean on.

How does Estora manage this every day? Actually, this was beyond an everyday dressing affair for most anyone, even Estora, who could make rags look elegant.

Yates was the perfect gentleman as he escorted her through the castle corridors. There were many rumors about Yates and his exploits with women, and while their veracity was uncertain, she was sure having half the castle population observe them together would send tongues wagging, something that would not displease Yates in the least.

During the seemingly endless journey to the castle entrance, men—soldiers and courtiers alike—bowed out of her way. She felt their lingering looks on her long after she had passed them by, and warmth blossomed in her cheeks. The glances she received from women were more critical and appraising. Some of these people had seen her a hundred times before as she went about her regular duties, but now they seemed not to recognize her. Maybe it was because when uniformed, she was just another servant, insignificant and common and easily overlooked. She bit her bottom lip in discomfort, suddenly feeling like she was trying to masquerade as someone she wasn't.

As it turned out, there was a goodly number of courtiers dressed in their finest and glittering with precious gems heading in the same direction.

"There's a garden party being held down in the noble quarter today, in honor of King Zachary and Lady Estora's betrothal," Yates explained.

Just what she needed to hear.

They wove through the ever thickening crowd of nobles to reach the entrance, some of whom seemed to have drenched themselves in heavy perfumes. Karigan gasped on the stench, expelling what little air she could get into her lungs, which were crushed by the hellacious corset.

Finally they broke free and walked out onto the front steps of the main castle entrance, into the fresh air. Karigan blinked in the sunshine, praising the gods it wasn't raining. She didn't think the velvet or her ridiculous shoes would fare well in wet conditions. It was a fine, mellow autumn day, neither too hot nor too cold. Another blessing.

Lined up along the drive were numerous shining carriages with pairs of matching horses, all their harness leathers and brasses gleaming. Grooms and drivers stood ready to aid their noble passengers into their carriages.

"Uh oh," Karigan said.

"What's wrong?" Yates asked.

"I don't know which belongs to Braymer. I don't even know what Braymer looks like."

Then a stylish black carriage pulled by matching black horses bypassed the others. It bore a small but obvious sun banner of Rhovanny. The passengers were two finely dressed gentlemen.

"Could that be him?" Yates asked, pointing out the carriage.

Karigan shrugged. "It could be some Rhovan noble come to join the festivities."

"But everyone's heading out, not in."

"True."

The two gentlemen disembarked from the carriage, one older, one younger, and both appearing to be at a loss as they gazed upon the gathering of folk at the entrance. Just as Karigan had no idea of what Braymer looked like, he had no way of knowing what she looked like.

"I think that must be him," she told Yates, indicating the younger of the two. She started forward, but Yates' hand on her arm forestalled her.

"Allow me," he said.

Before she could say otherwise, he hopped down the steps to the drive and hailed the two gentlemen. Even from this distance, she could see Yates looking the younger of the two up and down, assessing him as a protective older brother might. Karigan had to suppress a laugh.

Presently Yates returned with the two men behind him. Braymer had turned out rather well, she thought. He was dark haired and complexioned, as many Rhovans were, with smooth handsome features and brown eyes. His frock coat of jet and cream-colored silk waistcoat held an understated elegance. He was plainly rich, but not ostentatious. Some merchants had a knack for flaunting their wealth in gaudy colors and jewels, but she was glad to see that the Coyle family was not of this ilk.

He grinned broadly as he approached and she decided she liked his smile. He moved easily up the steps and presented himself to her in traditional merchant fashion, with a hand over his heart and a deep bow.

"Greetings, Karigan G'ladheon. I am Braymer Coyle, at your service." His command of the common tongue was flawless.

For one panicked moment, Karigan was caught between bowing and a more ladylike curtsy. A bow might send her off balance and headlong down the steps. Maybe Braymer or Yates would catch her. Thinking it better to avoid a spectacle, she compromised between the two, dipping and curtsying.

"And I'm at yours," she said.

He then took her gloved hand in his and kissed it, and rather suddenly, she was quite caught up in a fancy of being a princess, and he her prince. Even the people around them bowed and curtsied.

Bowing? Curtsying? She glanced around, her heart fluttering, only to discover King Zachary and Lady Estora, flanked by somber Weapons in black, joining her on the top step.

Something withered inside her. The castle grounds grew uncommonly quiet, except for the stray scrape of a hoof down on the drive and the shuffle of feet. For a long-drawn-out moment, everything stilled until Karigan regained enough sense to curtsy for her monarch.

The man who had told her he loved her.

Braymer, still holding her hand, fell to his knee upon realizing he was in the presence of Sacoridia's high king.

King Zachary filled her vision with his autumn colors as the sun struck the fillet that crowned his head of amber hair. They stared at one another as though stunned by the light of day.

It was Lady Estora who broke the silence. "Karigan!" She strode over—with ease, Karigan noted—and clapped her hands together. "Your dress! You! Absolutely beautiful!"

It took a moment for Karigan to unglue her gaze from the king and to give Estora more than a passing glance, and she nearly snorted, for Estora was her usual radiant self, the great beauty of Sacoridia, with her hair of spun gold. Karigan, by comparison, was a peasant girl in rags.

"Karigan?" the king said as if disbelieving his eyes. "I mean, Rider G'ladheon?"

Her cheeks and neck were burning, and she'd probably gone blotchy across the exposed portion of her chest.

The king cleared his throat. "I–I did not know you would be attending Lord Meere's garden party this afternoon."

Karigan tugged on Braymer's hand so he would rise. "*We're* not, sire." She glanced significantly at Braymer.

The king drew his eyebrows together, bemused, and he stroked his beard.

Yates, sensing undercurrents ebbing and flowing, but not knowing exactly what or why, interceded. "Excuse me, Your Highness, but if any of the carriages are to move, we must get Master Coyle's out of the way first."

It wasn't entirely true, but Karigan blessed his quick thinking.

The king, as if stunned by the sight of Karigan in anything other than green, made a weak gesture. "Of course. Proceed."

With another bow, Braymer led Karigan down the steps and over to his waiting carriage, the older gentleman, his servant, falling in step behind them. Karigan was relieved, with that audience looking on, that she hadn't floundered too badly in the idiotic shoes, or fallen. The carriage driver and Braymer made her ascent into the carriage as effortless as possible.

When all were seated, the driver snapped the reins and the horses stepped out smartly. Karigan glanced once more at the king watching them from atop the steps. He must wonder why she was dressed up, where she was going, and who the young man was that accompanied her.

Good, she thought, not without a certain amount of spiteful satisfaction.

The carriage ride proved stiff and awkward with Styles, Braymer's manservant, watching Karigan down his nose. He queried after Karigan's chaperone, for surely the young lady must be accompanied by one, and when she informed him that she indeed had none, he grunted with an expression of displeasure, and spoke in rapid Rhovan to Braymer. Braymer's reply was sharp.

Karigan did not know much Rhovan, but she caught the gist of the discussion. Rhovanny was a far more conservative country in regard to its beliefs and customs, and a woman's place in society, than Sacoridia. The women might toil in the fields, bear endless children, or manage a husband's lands and household while he attended to "business" elsewhere, but it was rare for a woman to own a business, and unheard of for a woman to serve the king in a uniformed capacity, as Karigan did. Women bearing swords were considered immodest; those who admitted to such aspirations were regarded as ill of mind, and were treated as such.

Rhovanny tolerated the larger role women played in Sacoridian society. It had to if it wanted to participate in commercial and political endeavors with its neighbor. Rhovanny also knew Sacoridia's history: women, and even children, had taken up arms during the Long War to defend the decimated country from the legions of Mornhavon the Black when so many of the menfolk had been slain on the field of battle. It had widened the role of women forever after, and though women could choose to continue on in traditional roles or to operate businesses or to serve the monarchy in many capacities, those who chose to carry swords remained in the minority.

Rhovans were polite about Sacoridia's perceived oddities, but they didn't necessarily like them or approve of them. Styles certainly did not, and Karigan was sure the absence of a chaperone placed her in the category of "loose women" as defined by Rhovan culture. She wondered what

Styles would think if he saw her in uniform with her saber girded at her side. She smiled at the image that came to mind, and thought that this was going to be an interesting afternoon.

The carriage rumbled over cobblestones off Sacor City's main thoroughfare, the Winding Way, onto Gryphon Street, one of the city's more artistic districts. Here bookbinders and jewelers practiced their crafts, and sculptors and painters exhibited their work, hoping to attract the attention of wealthy patrons. Music wafted from an open, top story window, floating down to the street below. Fine harp music it was, music of the heavens, followed by a clamorous clash of strings and a wail.

"It is rubbish! Everything I compose! Absolute rubbish!"

Karigan winced at the anguish in the harpist's voice. The music had sounded nice to her.

Gryphon Street was lined with bookshops and the workshops of luthiers, tailors, weavers, and potters; pubs, tobacco shops, and the occasional fortune-teller. It was also said that no less than forty poets lived in rooms above the shops. Karigan could not verify this, for she did not follow the trends in poetry.

A man leaned in the doorway of his music shop playing a jaunty tune on a pipe for passersby while two men beside him argued philosophy.

The scents of spicy foods drifted into the street from tiny eateries and mingled. There was a growing population from the Under Kingdoms now residing in the city, bringing with them the sounds of their ringing accents and the flavors of their exotic foods.

The horses skittered around an oblivious fellow who crossed the street with his nose in a book. A man and woman, gaudily dressed and painted, juggled rings and balls for a collection of youngsters and their parents.

The colors, smells, and sounds of Gryphon Street were an enlivening feast for one who had been spending far too much time on castle grounds. Mara was right: it was good to get out and see something different. When Mara was well enough, Karigan vowed to bring her here to Gryphon Street, and maybe to other parts of the city as well. There was so much to see, but it seemed like she never had the time. Until today.

Along the way, Braymer spoke little. Perhaps he was shy, or maybe just content to absorb his surroundings, looking from side to side as the carriage rolled down the street. Karigan supposed that if she were playing more the part of a lady, she'd engage him in some meaningless conversation, or flirt, or *something*. She just didn't feel like making the effort.

Presently the carriage pulled up to a bright storefront under the sign of the teapot and cup.

"Ah, this is the place," Braymer said, an expression of delight on his face. "Mistress Lampala's Tea Room. I understand it is very good."

Fortunately, when one was in "lady mode," the gentlemen were quite willing to assist one in disembarking from the carriage. They even opened doors!

Karigan teetered on the uneven cobblestones. "Ridiculous shoes," she murmured to herself. Only Braymer and Styles prevented her from falling face-first into horse droppings. No wonder some perceived women as weak—it was the clothes!

She had to admit that the solicitous attention was nice. She rarely received such courtesy when in uniform.

The tea room was dark after the bright sunshine on the street, the sound muted. There were eight tables inside, mostly occupied by couples. One young woman sat alone by a window scrawling furiously on a sheaf of papers, crossing out most of what she had just written with dramatic sweeps of her pen, and pausing only to sip from her teacup. One of Gryphon Street's forty poets?

The aroma of delicious baked treats drifted in the air, mixing with something more exotic. *Kauv.* Kauv was a hot, bitter drink imported from the Cloud Islands that was all the rage among the nobles.

The tea room was not the fancy, formal place Karigan feared it might be, the type of place where noble matrons nibbled on sweet dainties and gossiped the afternoon away. Rather, it catered to the artistic denizens of the neighborhood, as well as a healthy mix of everyone else, from the common laborer to a pair of stylish aristocrats.

Just as Karigan's feet began to go completely numb in the bloody shoes, a voluptuous woman burst from a back room, seeming to suck in the energy from all those around her.

"Hello, hello, my dears," she said.

This would be Mistress Lampala no doubt, Karigan thought.

"Be seated, be seated." She swept them to an open table, Styles scowling all the way.

Judging from Mistress Lampala's accent and deep bronze skin, she hailed from the Cloud Islands, a likely connection that allowed her to serve kauv in her tea room. Not only did the beans that made kauv grow on the islands, but so did sugarcane, and in Karigan's opinion, one needed lots of sugar to make kauv palatable, otherwise it tasted rather like burned bark. It was a winning situation for Mistress Lampala who charged an exorbitant price for both, but currency was of no consequence to the wealthy Coyle family, and Braymer ensured there was plenty of kauv, sugar, cream, and sweet treats to go around.

Braymer smiled tentatively at Karigan while she sipped her kauv, but seemed unable to find anything to say. Styles sighed with a roll of his eyes and said something in Rhovan to his ward who straightened his posture and cleared his throat, and then said in a stiff, formal way, "You are very lovely."

Karigan nearly spewed her kauv, but swallowed hastily, only to have it scald the back of her throat and induce a most unladylike fit of coughing. "Thank you," she rasped, more amused than flattered. The deadpan way in which he had delivered his compliment made it obvious he had practiced the words many times in front of a mirror.

Styles rolled his eyes again.

"What have I done wrong?" Braymer asked, his forehead crinkled.

Styles spoke quietly to Braymer again in Rhovan, and the young man reddened. "I . . . I am sorry. I am recently come from the monastery, and I find this awkward."

Karigan raised both eyebrows in surprise. "Monastery?"

"Yes. My elder brother, you see, was to take over the business from my father, but he, alas, disgraced the family by running off with a harlot and getting her with child."

Styles groaned and dropped his face into his hands.

"What have I said now?" Braymer asked, clearly bewildered.

"The lady! An indelicate subject—the family embarrassment."

Karigan's mouth twitched as she fought laughter.

Braymer glanced from Styles to Karigan. "M–my apologies. You see? I was given to the monastery at a very young age, and I've not been outside for many years and certainly . . . certainly not among," and here he whispered, "young women." He blushed madly. "Silence was the rule of the monastery. We spoke only in prayer, and now I do not know what to say."

Awkward was an understatement. To save Braymer further embarrassment, Karigan decided she'd better redirect the conversation. "Perhaps you could tell me about your life at the monastery."

Styles brightened and nodded.

Braymer, seeing his approval, smiled in delight. "Of course." What started as an initially interesting description of the daily life and rituals of the monks in the service to the goddess Aeryon turned into an endless torrent of one-sided conversation. It was as if his years of silence had been uncorked and all the words bottled inside cascaded out.

The torrent lasted all the way from Mistress Lampala's to the Sacor City War Museum. Karigan hoped the change of venue would dam the constant stream, but it only seemed to open a whole new freshet. Apparently both the monastery and the Coyles owned vast libraries, and Braymer had done his share of reading about Sacoridia and its wars.

Karigan drifted away from Braymer, who seemed not to

notice, he was so engrossed in a display of heraldic emblems. The stone exhibition hall had high vaulted ceilings and a marble floor causing Braymer's voice to echo to all corners. If he said anything of importance, she would hear it. At this point, she didn't care what Styles thought of her, and he seemed to have given up on his ward himself, after a few interjected instructions about polite conversation went unheeded.

The museum covered the war history of Sacoridia but was devoted largely to arms and armor. There were racks and racks of spears and swords, and numerous suits of armor stood stiffly along the walls. Frankly, she had seen better specimens in the castle. Until, that is, the armor had magically come to life and the king ordered it locked away. She had noticed of late, however, that some of the suits were slowly repopulating the castle corridors, which had seemed strangely empty without them.

Glass cases contained more fragile items, such as documents and bits of uniforms, with cards labeled in hard to read cramped script. She gave up trying to decipher the writing and gazed at the objects with only cursory interest.

Among the artifacts that did interest her were those the museum claimed had belonged to the Arcosian Empire, which tried to crush and enslave Sacoridia a thousand years ago. There were some fragile scraps of parchment with faded, foreign script on them, some rusted weapons and bits of twisted metal that looked like articulated pieces that had once fit together. The label could only tell her: *Metal pieces excavated on shore of Ullem Bay, believed to have originated in Arcosia.*

There was a belt of silver links embossed with gold, pitted and discolored, with a lion's head on the buckle. Here the label was more explanatory: *Officer's belt, elite Lion Regiment, Arcosian Empire.*

Karigan had traveled to the time of the Long War and saw some of the empire's forces firsthand. One of her ancestors, in fact, had hailed from Arcosia, a brutal man intent on subjugating the Sacoridians who had, in the end, betrayed

Mornhavon to stop the war and suffering. It was difficult to believe that all that remained of the Arcosian occupation were these few rusted artifacts. Considering the alternative, she supposed it was a good thing.

She glanced Braymer's way and caught Styles yawning while his ward examined some shields mounted on the wall. There were a few other visitors poking about, gazing into cases, and an attendant making sure no one touched anything.

Karigan slipped into a side hall, hoping to find a more interesting display, only to come face-to-face with King Zachary, his bared sword held high.

THE MAN IN THE SILK MASK

Karigan's compressed lungs emitted only a squeak upon the menacing sight. She backed away, her hand on her heaving chest.

There was a soft chuckle beside her, and she whirled to find a red-coated attendant there.

"Lifelike, isn't he?" he asked.

Karigan swallowed hard and looked upon the king again, feeling rather stupid. It was a wax figure made to look like the king. The effect was hauntingly realistic, from the silver fillet crowning its head of amber hair to the sword it gripped, a replica of the king's own.

The figure was part of a tableau with banners hanging on the wall behind it, and the traitor Lord-Governor Tomastine Mirwell kneeling at the block, a basket ready to receive his head. Mirwell was as Karigan remembered him on that day, an old, crusty man with a bear pelt draped over his shoulders, who had needed the aid of servants to hobble onto the platform to meet his end. Certainly a piteous sight that was, perhaps, even worse punishment for such a proud man than the execution itself had been.

The figure of the king was attired in black, just as the real king had been the day of the execution. It had been a terrible thing to witness, and she knew it had lain heavily on King Zachary for a long time. As far as Karigan was concerned, old Mirwell got what he deserved. He had nearly succeeded in handing over the kingdom to Zachary's villainous brother, Prince Amilton. Unfortunately, some of their conspirators were still at large, concealing themselves well enough to evade king's law.

"Originally the artists set up the scene for just after decapitation," the attendant said, "but too many people had not the stomach for it. Too realistic."

Karigan gave him a sidelong look. He sounded disappointed.

He moved off to chat with a couple gazing at other figures in the hall. She turned her attention back to the "king," and shuddered. His expression was wrong. He looked crazed, when all she could remember from that day was resolve. And remorse. Gazing more closely, she noted other inaccuracies. His chest and shoulders, for instance, were not the breadth to which she was accustomed, and his hips—

When she caught the direction in which that line of thought was heading, she silently cursed herself and tore her gaze away from the wax figure, forcing herself to look at the other tableaux. There were likenesses of other kings and queens, various heroic knights and warriors from Sacoridia's past, and a pair of aristocrats dueling for a lady's favor. There was no way of knowing if these visages were accurate, since she had never met those whom the figures represented, with the exception of the first high king, Jonaeus.

He sat on a thronelike chair, sunshine streaming on him from an arched window above. Though the label claimed this was King Jonaeus, the figure was all wrong. It certainly looked kingly with its crown and strong features, but it wasn't at all as she remembered. King Jonaeus had been a grizzled, wearied warrior with gray in his beard. Even the clothing was inaccurate. She couldn't imagine him having access to finely tailored silks, a luxury unheard of during the time of the Long War. In life, he was a man of hard leathers, coarse wool, and iron. There was no way the artists could have known his true appearance, she reminded herself, the way she had. They could only make guesses and create a representation.

She shrugged and was about to move on to the next tableau when glass shattered and someone screamed. Startled, she grabbed her skirts and hurried out to the main hall as fast as her daintily-shod feet would carry her. A surprising sight greeted her. A man wearing a black silk mask stood in the center of the hall fending off attendants and museum patrons with a rapier. In his other hand he held a document taken from a smashed case.

"Priceless!" an attendant sobbed. "Please, I beg of you! Please don't take it."

No one else moved. Ladies clung to their escorts, faces pale. Gentlemen stood frozen as if a spell had been worked upon them. Braymer looked his usual bewildered self, but was silent for once, with Styles bravely splayed in front of his young ward.

"Priceless to you maybe," the masked man told the attendant, "but eminently useful to me." Then to the rest he added, "My apologies for interrupting your afternoon. Good day." And he saluted them with his sword.

Braggart, Karigan thought with distaste. She sighed. If no one else was going to do anything to stop him, perhaps as a representative of the king she should.

"Halt!" she cried after him as he turned to flee. "In the name of the king!"

Everyone stared at her in surprise, including the thief, whose eyes sparkled behind his mask.

"You are breaking king's law," Karigan said. The thief took two steps toward her and halted. She felt his eyes look her up and down in crude fashion. She blushed.

And he laughed. "Yes, and what do *you* plan to do about it, my lady? Certainly nothing to muss that hair so nicely arranged on your head."

"Oh, good heavens," she murmured in disgust. She grabbed her skirts and bustled to the nearest wall of weaponry. She yanked a sword from its mount.

"Y–you're not supposed to t–touch the artifacts," the attendant cried, fretting at his handkerchief. She glared at him, stifling further argument.

The masked man laughed. "I feel so threatened."

Karigan rolled her eyes. Grabbing a bunch of skirt with

her left hand, she started toward the braggart with the sword held before her. Braymer suddenly came to life and darted to her side, clutching her arm.

"Mistress Karigan, what are you doing? Don't worry, I'll protect you from this villain, I'll—"

She yanked her arm loose and brushed him aside. He fell back several steps, perhaps not expecting her strength. The thief watched with apparent interest.

Though Arms Master Drent had trained her thoroughly in all manner of fighting techniques and scenarios, she had never fought in a dress. She was hoping it would not come to an actual fight.

"Leave the document and go," Karigan said. "That artifact belongs to the people of Sacoridia."

"And you will stop me, my lady?" There was much amusement in the thief's voice, and an upturn to his lips suggested a smile.

Karigan sighed. "If I must." She shifted the sword in her grip. It was a longsword, much heavier than what she was used to.

"Perhaps you should return to your needlework, my lady." He turned dismissively and started to stride away, but Karigan shoved the blade between his legs and tripped him. Quick as a cat he rolled and was on his feet again. He tucked the document into his frock coat and gazed at her, this time without the smile.

"Mistress Karigan, is it?" Steel tinged his voice. "You would do well not to anger me."

"I wouldn't anger you if you'd simply return the document and leave."

"And how would that be worth my time?"

"It might be worth your life."

"That's a very unladylike threat."

"And this is the only needlework I know." She raised the sword to eye level.

The thief barked out a laugh. "You are an intriguing lady, Mistress Karigan. Now let's dispense with this nonsense, shall we? I'll be on my—"

Karigan engaged him and their quick exchange of blows rang throughout the expansive halls of the museum. In retrospect, she realized she had done it again; had gotten herself into a fight when she could have just as easily pretended to be helpless and let the thief make off with the document. It was the responsibility of the constabulary, really. She always seemed to act first and think later, a dangerous failing on her part. In this first exchange, the thief revealed his rapier wasn't just a pretty ornament he wore at his side—he knew how to use it. He was no ordinary thief, this masked man, and she might be in for more than she bargained for.

But she wasn't helpless, and she hated standing around when she might be able to prevent a treasured artifact from being stolen, and in full daylight no less. And she had to admit, it was a bit of a response to Braymer and Styles, and their conservative Rhovan ways. Let them see what a Sacoridian woman was capable of.

"I see you have practiced your needlework," the thief said. "A little."

Karigan scowled.

"Tut, tut, don't frown," he said. "It ruins your pretty face."

Karigan closed in again, and he met her blow for blow, his sword work elegant and nimble compared to her own which was made ponderous by the weight of the longsword. She had to use it two-handed, which left her skirts dragging about her feet and seriously hampering her footwork. He glided about, his other hand set on his hip, his back held erect, his bearing aristocratic.

Karigan thrust, and he slipped aside. Her sword hissed at his neck, and he danced away. The smirk on his face revealed he thought it all a great joke. She brought the sword down in what should have been a crushing blow, but he flitted out of the way. Blow after blow was casually deflected, and when she threw herself into one particularly powerful thrust, he simply stepped aside. Her center of gravity was thrown forward and she had to hurry her feet back under her before she fell on her face.

Her lungs strained against the corset for breath. Sweat

trickled down her neck and temples. The thief remained cool and impeccable, awaiting her next move. It infuriated her.

She whirled and their blades clanged together and slid hilt to hilt. They were very close, almost nose to nose. She could look right into his light gray eyes.

"I'm enjoying this dance," he said in a silken whisper, "and I think you are, too."

Karigan shoved him away with a growl. For a moment their hilt guards caught and she thought she might be able to tear his sword from his hands, but he deftly untangled it and backed away.

He shrugged off her blows one by one, she growing increasingly weary and light-headed because of the corset. She stepped on the hem of her dress and nearly bowled right over.

Their fight carried them out of the main exhibition hall into the wing with the wax figures. She was struggling now, struggling to remain standing, struggling to breathe, struggling just to lift the sword, which seemed to gain pounds with every blow he parried.

They locked together again.

"So enjoyable," he said, "to dance with a lovely woman. I wonder if you would be this feisty in my bed."

She jerked her knee up between his legs, but her skirts foiled the blow. He broke away, chuckling at her. She swung wildly, but he turned aside, the momentum of her blade chopping off Lord Mirwell's head. It plopped neatly into its receiving basket.

The thief hooted. "Well done!"

Karigan rounded on him, her breathing harsh now. Some hair had come loose from a comb and hung in an annoying strand down the middle of her face. She stared at him, puffing, the sword valiantly held before her in hands trembling from fatigue.

With one swift blow he knocked it from her grasp and sent it clattering across the marble floor. She fell to her knees, too robbed of breath to do anything else. She was going to burn the damnable corset the first chance she got. If the thief didn't kill her first.

The tip of his rapier flashed to the hollow of her throat. It pricked her skin as she swallowed, warm blood trickling down her chest.

The thief smiled, his gaze intent. "Ladies should not play with swords. The steel type, anyway." He lowered the rapier tip to the top lace of her bodice and toyed with it. "But you've provided me with a most interesting diversion."

Karigan wanted to tell him a thing or two that would burn his ears from the inside out, but she hadn't the breath to speak.

"Thank the gods!" someone shouted from without. "The constables have finally arrived!"

Karigan had forgotten about all the others, and so had the thief, so immersed in their swordplay had they been.

"Time to go," he said. With a flick of his wrist he sliced the lace of her bodice, then wrapped the chain of her necklace around the blade and yanked it from her neck. "To remember you by," he explained. He unwound the necklace from the rapier and dropped it into his pocket.

Karigan grabbed at her gaping bodice. "You—you—" But she had so many things to say, they bottled up in her throat.

The thief backed toward the end of the exhibit hall at the sound of approaching feet. He paused and tugged off a velvet glove that matched the deep wine color of his frock coat. He kissed it and tossed it to the floor before her. "For you to remember *me* by."

"You—you—*you*." The venom in her voice made him wince, then grin broadly. He hopped onto the arm of King Jonaeus' throne.

Karigan pulled off one of her useless shoes and threw it at him. She missed, knocking off King Jonaeus' crown instead.

Armed constables rushed into the hall. "Stop, thief!"

"Good day," he said, and he climbed up onto the casement of the window above King Jonaeus, kicked out the window, and vanished, but not before another well-aimed shoe clobbered him in the head.

"Ow!" came his cry from the street below. "That hurt, my lady!"

"You clobbered him in the head?" Mara asked incredulously.

"I was angry."

"Karigan, you are the only person I know who can turn a pleasant excursion to a museum into a swordfight."

Karigan sighed. Dressed now in her green uniform, she sat with her feet tucked under her in the chair next to Mara's bed. It had been a huge relief to pry the corset loose from her body. It felt like her rib cage was still trying to spring back to its normal profile, and the whalebone ribbing had left deep indentations in her flesh.

Mara rubbed her chin. "Good aim with the shoe, though."

Karigan had been very pleased with the throw herself, and felt no remorse over the loss of the shoe. What she hadn't liked was how vulnerable she felt when at the mercy of the thief, which, she realized, was most of the time. She had not been able to defend herself while trapped in the dress, and he could have killed her at his pleasure. Her fingers went to the hollow of her throat where his rapier nicked her, and felt the scab. She never wanted to feel that vulnerable again. Ever.

Mara pushed back into her pillows, her gaze distant. "He sounds like the Raven Mask."

"Who?"

Mara smiled. "The Raven Mask, a stealthy gentleman thief who prowled Sacor City some years ago, stealing select items like rare paintings and precious jewels. It's said he especially favored entering the chambers of ladies to steal their fine jewels even as they slept in the night. He would leave some token for those he favored." She glanced significantly at the velvet glove Karigan had dropped on the bed. "Some ladies were said to leave their windows wide open with gems sitting on their dressing tables in hopes he would come to them in the night, and they'd offer him other, ahem, favors. If caught and confronted, he was always polite, but he always managed to escape. He was known as a master swordsman."

"He . . . the thief, he was good." Karigan said.

"It was believed the Raven Mask retired, or was finally killed by an enraged husband, but more rumors point to him retiring to some country estate and a manor house filled with the riches he had accumulated throughout his career. Come to think of it, he'd be an elderly fellow by now."

"This fellow was *not* elderly." His hair had held no gray, but his mask hid too much of his face for her to otherwise judge his age. He certainly moved like a younger man.

Mara shifted her position on her bed. "What was the document he stole? Did you ever find out?"

"Something from the Long War days written in Old Sacoridian. The museum attendant called it 'priceless,' but apparently it has little market value among collectors. It only has value to historians I guess, though the attendant said they never made much sense out of it."

"If it was the Raven Mask who took it," Mara said, "it must have some value."

Karigan thought back to the thief facing the museum patrons and attendants, holding his rapier in one hand and the document in another. "He called it 'useful.' "

Mara chuckled. "Maybe it's directions to a secret treasure. Sounds like the sort of thing the Raven Mask would steal."

Karigan did not know, nor did she really care to, and if she ever encountered the man again, she wouldn't give him a chance to explain. No, she wouldn't kill him, but she would overcome him, and he could do all his explaining to the constabulary.

"And how did Braymer Coyle and his stern chaperone react to this eventful end to your outing?" Mara asked.

Karigan groaned. Braymer had become very solicitous, and had continually stolen looks at her nearly exposed bosom even as she spoke with the constables about the theft. "Let's say that Braymer has probably set aside his monastic vows for good." Yes, he had been much more interested in her after the eventful museum visit, in a most clinging and annoying way, as if he suddenly discovered she was female. Her sword work seemed to have excited him.

"Master Styles was unhappy." During the carriage ride back to the castle, it was almost as if the man had turned to stone. He had refused to speak to her, or even to look at her. "No doubt his report to Braymer's father will not prove favorable."

"You don't sound displeased," Mara said.

Karigan smiled smugly. "I'm sure the Coyles will find a gentle Rhovan lady more to their liking for Braymer." As for her father's stake in this? Served him right. The whole set-up had been a disaster from its inception.

She stood and stretched, reveling in her freedom from corset and dress.

"Leaving so soon?" Mara asked.

"Thought I'd see to some chores before dinner."

Mara picked up the glove from her bed and extended it to Karigan. "Don't forget this."

Karigan frowned. "No, you keep it. I don't want to see it again." It reminded her too much of her vulnerability.

In the late hours of night, long after the lights in the homes of Sacor City's more respectable citizens had winked out, two men met in a seedy inn in a rundown section of the lower city. They sat apart from the other patrons, away from the sooty lamps and the hearth fire, allowing shadows and the haze of smoke to obscure their features.

A third man sat in the darkest corner by himself, a tankard of ale before him and a hood drawn over his head. His back was to the two men who sat opposite each other at a rickety table, but if he listened closely, he could discern their conversation over the drunken carousing of the inn's other patrons.

"My master has obtained what you seek," Morry said. He

was an older man in common garb, but his refined speech revealed he was more than he appeared.

"Hand it over," said the second man in a gruff, no-nonsense voice. He wore scarred fighting leathers and a plain cloak, a serviceable sword girded at his side. Like Morry, there was nothing exceptional about him, but those who were keen observers knew that by the way he carried himself he was a soldier, or had been at one time. A soldier with no device, no sign of allegiance.

"Tut, tut," Morry said. "Show me the payment."

There was a grunt and the thud and clink of a bulging purse dropped on the table. The man in the corner smiled and sipped his ale.

"Here is what you seek, as requested," Morry said, followed by the sound of the leather folder scraping across the rough surface of the table. Many moments of silence followed while the soldier examined the document within.

Another grunt. "Excellent. This is the one we wanted."

"A satisfactory transaction, then," Morry said.

Leathers creaked and the man in the corner imagined the soldier leaning across the table. "I was instructed to arrange more work for your master upon the acceptable completion of today's assignment." He strained to hear the soldier's lowered voice. "It will be risky, but there will be commensurate reward if he is successful."

"Tell on," said Morry, "and I shall convey your wishes to my master."

The soldier outlined the proposal. The man in the corner listened avidly. "Risky" was an understatement. It was much more than simple theft, much more, but the man had to admit he was intrigued by the challenge and by the revival of the old and once-honored custom it represented.

Morry must have been just as flabbergasted, for it took him a long while to respond. Presently he said, "I shall tell my master all you have said. You mentioned he would be rewarded commensurately?"

"Of course." The soldier named an outrageous sum, then

added, "Half up front, half upon successful delivery. We need to know his decision as soon as possible."

The man in the corner toyed with the silver moon necklace sparkling on the table before him, a thrill of excitement making his heart pound harder. He already knew the answer to the proposal. Yes, he certainly did.

THE WALL SPEAKS

From Ullem Bay to the shores of the dawn, we weave our song through stone and mortar, we sing our will to strengthen and bind. We shield the lands from ancient dark. We are the bulwark of the Ages. We stand sentry day and night, through storm and winter, and freeze and thaw.

From Ullem Bay to the shores of dawn, we weave our song in harmony for we are one.

We are broken.

From Ullem Bay to—

Losing rhythm.

We shield the lands—

Broken. Lost. *Despair.*

Hear us! Help us! Heal us!

Do not trust him.

We do not trust. We forbid him passage.

ALTON AND THE WALL

The stone facing of the wall changed aspect with the passing light of the sun. One moment the stone was a bright gray-white, reflecting the sunlight back into the world. In another instant, its rough texture emerged in relief, dimpled by shadows that revealed every contour of its topography; every pit, every crag, every fissure. It looked primal, as if risen from the Earth, formed by the forces that built mountains and divided canyons, or perhaps shaped by the hands of the gods themselves. Yet the simpler truth was that it had been built by mortal men, desperate mortal men, who had deeply feared what lay on the other side. As the sun drifted farther to the west, the wall clad itself in shadow, megalithic, mysterious, and threatening.

Alton D'Yer vowed to uncover the secrets locked in the wall so that which had withstood the assault of time and weathering for over a thousand years would not crumble and unleash the evil it had been built to hold at bay. Yet the wall would not give up its secrets so easily.

"That should do it," Leese said, tying off the last of the bandage she had wrapped around his hand. Then in a tone that was simultaneously light and pointed, she added, "I trust you won't start banging your head against the wall next."

Alton glanced at both hands, now swaddled in linen, and frowned. "Thank you."

The mender sighed and picked up her pack of supplies. "If you need me again, you know where to find me."

Alton nodded and watched her as she strode off toward

her tent. She had moved down to this secondary encampment by the Tower of the Heavens after he had raged at the wall one too many times. The first time had left him with a broken toe. This time he had banged his hands bloody against it, and though he'd struck with mindless force, he'd managed not to break anything, which, he supposed, was a good thing.

Frustration brought the rages on, rage he never knew he possessed. It had been a couple months since last he stood within the tower, one of ten situated along the vast expanse of the wall. The towers once housed keepers, ancestral members of his own clan, who watched over the wall's condition and the enemy beyond. All too acutely he remembered the fateful day when he had stepped out of the tower with his fellow Green Riders, never knowing he'd be forbidden access the next time he tried to enter.

He had traveled to Woodhaven to report to his father, the lord-governor of D'Yer Province. Swift orders had come to Woodhaven from the king that Alton should return to the tower and learn what he could about the wall and repairing it by speaking to Merdigen, a magical presence that resided in the tower.

The orders were a formality. Alton had planned to return to the wall with or without them. The wall obsessed him, crowded his dreams and his waking thoughts. Now was the time to fix the breach that weakened it, now was the time to strengthen it. Now, before Mornhavon the Black appeared in Blackveil Forest again.

Only the wall wouldn't let him pass. No matter how he bent his mind to it, no matter how he pleaded with the guardians who inhabited the wall, they refused him. And it brought on the rage.

The tower had admitted him and the other Riders before. Why would it deny him now?

He knew the soldiers, even those at the main encampment near the breach, gossiped about him, about his obsession. Had he gone mad like his cousin Pendric, who now existed as a guardian within the wall?

The wall's shadow swallowed his camp and the forest, and soon all would be submerged in darkness. Now that it was autumn, the hours of daylight were shrinking, and it made him feel as if he were running out of time. No one knew how far into the future Karigan had taken Mornhavon the Black. No one knew when their time line would merge with his, and his presence would again threaten the world. This was why Alton had to find the answers *now.* He had to take advantage of the time Karigan secured for him, and for everyone.

Before thoughts of Karigan could cloud his mind, he pushed them out—forcibly—and traced the contours of the stone wall with his fingertips.

"I will understand," he promised the wall. "I will enter the tower, and I will understand, and nothing will hold me back."

Sometimes the fevers came on Alton during the night like a sudden gale as the residue of poisons racked his body. Leese guessed that the poisons would eventually seep out of his blood and he'd return to normal, but he wasn't so sure. He hadn't given himself enough time to fully heal after his ordeal in Blackveil, and now he writhed in his bedding, the dark forest haunting his dreams. Sickly black branches snaked out of the shifting, ever present mist and stabbed at his flesh. He heard the calls of creatures that hunted him. And he dreamed of *her.*

He remembered her in the ivory dress, and how her long brown hair had fallen softly about her shoulders. He recalled the blush upon her cheeks, and the paleness of her neck, of her throat. She had spoken, but he could no longer hear the words, nor could he remember the sound of her voice. She had betrayed him. Karigan had betrayed him into nearly destroying the wall with false promises.

Traitor!

A need came upon him, even as he slept, to send a message to King Zachary and Captain Mapstone to warn them there was a traitor in their midst. Then as morning broke, and so did his fever, he would remember that Karigan was the one who risked herself to move Mornhavon into the future. Maybe it had really been a trick she played, part of some nefarious scheme. Maybe . . .

Birds squabbled in the trees outside his tent, and the crisp morning air flowing through the entry flap chilled the sweat clinging to his skin. He shivered violently, pulled his blanket over his shoulder, and laid there for some minutes, trying to work things out in his mind. Karigan confused him. He remembered so clearly that she had come to him in the forest, had soothed him and helped him find his way into the tower, yet was it really her? He'd been so very ill. Probably delirious. The power of the forest could have manipulated things, could have made him believe he was seeing and hearing things that were untrue.

He sighed. That had to be it. He could not imagine Karigan . . . No, she would not betray him, or her country. The forest had given him lies. He closed his eyes, remembering how angry he had been with her when they parted and she had not understood why. He could still see her bewilderment and her hurt. She had wanted to talk to him, but he had refused. What must she think of him?

They had been friends, though Alton had once hoped for more. He had probably ruined even the friendship.

He started to drift back into sleep as the blanket warmed him. His night had not been a restful one, and now peace lulled him. But just as the morning sunshine beating through the canvas walls of his tent and the bustle of camp faded away, a new clamor jolted Alton awake.

Outside, soldiers raised their voices in cheerful greeting. "Rider!" one exclaimed.

Alton rolled off his cot and, wrapping his blanket about himself, peered through the flap of his tent.

A Rider, indeed. He grinned.

Garth Bowen handed off his mare, Chickadee, to a soldier when Alton stepped out of the tent and called to him. The big man waved and sauntered over. "Alton, well met!" He reached out to shake with Alton, but Alton ruefully held up his bandaged hands. Garth swept an assessing gaze over him. "I would say you are looking well, but I'm afraid I cannot."

Alton could only imagine how bad he looked. Then a breeze carried to him a whiff of eggs, sausages, and bread frying over a nearby fire. His stomach growled. "Have you had breakfast yet?"

"Just some hardtack on the road."

Alton caught hold of one of his servants and requested food be brought to his tent. One of the benefits of being the lord-governor's heir was having servants in attendance, even at an encampment. Once inside the tent, Garth's considerable self took over one of the campaign chairs. He stretched out his legs before him and slumped comfortably in his seat.

Alton, meanwhile, pulled on a rumpled shirt and a pair of trousers that had seen much wear.

"Have you brought news from the king?" Alton asked.

"Not exactly, no. I'm here because the king and Captain Mapstone are anxious to know what progress you've made with Merdigen and the wall."

Alton dropped into the chair opposite Garth's and frowned. "None."

"None?"

He shook his head. "I can't even enter the tower. It's like . . . it's like it's gone deaf on me."

Garth stroked his upper lip and looked like he was about to say something when Alton's servant entered with heaping platters of sausage rolls, sweet bread, and scrambled eggs. Another servant followed bearing mugs and a pot of tea. Garth rubbed his hands together in glee before tucking in. Between mouthfuls, he caught Alton up on some of the news in Sacor City.

"Several new Riders have come on," he said. "I've never seen the captain so happy—she's practically bouncing."

Alton smiled at the improbable image. "Why so many new Riders now?" For years beyond count, the call had brought in so very few.

"She thinks the First Rider's horn has somehow awakened them to the call."

"Ah." When Tegan came to Woodhaven with the king's orders, she had told him of the Rider artifacts Karigan had found. He wished he could see them, but for now he had more important business to attend to at the wall. "New Riders—that's good to hear."

"Ty is in his glory, taking the new ones on, while the rest of us are left to sweep and scrub more rooms in the Rider wing." Garth rolled his eyes. "Happy I am to get away from the dust, cobwebs, and mouse turds. Oh, and all the wedding euphoria."

"Wedding euphoria?"

"That's right," Garth said. "You can't have heard yet. King Zachary announced he is marrying Lady Estora Coutre."

Alton dropped his slab of sweet bread in shock. "What? Really?"

Garth nodded. "King Zachary saw the necessity of appeasing Lord Coutre, what with the uncertainty of the wall and all."

Alton laughed as he fumbled after the sweet bread. So Lord Coutre had turned down the D'Yer proposal that Alton wed Lady Estora. He found it amusing, and enormously freeing. So all along, crafty Lord Coutre had turned down every other lord in this land and others, taking a chance he'd win the ultimate prize for his daughter: the high king of Sacoridia himself.

No longer was the prospect of marriage being held over Alton's head, at least for the moment.

"All of court is atwitter in anticipation," Garth continued. "Heralds and some Riders have been sent to spread the news among the populace. Noblewomen are buzzing about it and all they can talk about are wedding gowns and flowers, and even the elder ones among them giggle and blush like girls."

"Has a date been set?"

"The king has the moon priests working on a forecast for an auspicious date. Won't be before spring, I don't expect."

Alton leaned back in his chair considering the suitability of the match, a mug of tea warming his hands through the bandages. "I wonder what took so long for the king to agree, for surely Coutre put his bid in some time ago."

"Gossip has it there was some other woman he had his eye on—a commoner of all things. Fortunately he's come to his senses and is marrying a proper lady as he ought."

"And strengthening his ties with the eastern lords." Secretly, Alton sympathized with the king if the gossip was true. Hadn't he himself desired Karigan, a commoner? Expressing that desire, however, would have displeased his clan. It was bad enough, they thought, that he served as a Green Rider and not, say, as an officer in the elite light cavalry. He had since explained to them about the Rider call, and because his clan had been founded on an alchemy of stonework and magic, they were more accepting of Rider magic than others would be. Especially if it meant his own special ability would help him mend the D'Yer Wall.

As the mound of sausage rolls and eggs disappeared, mostly into Garth's mouth, their conversation came back to the purpose of the Rider's visit.

"So what's the problem?" Garth asked. "Why can't you enter the tower?"

"I wish I knew. The wall—it won't talk to me."

"That's odd," Garth said, scratching his head. "I thought you had it all figured out—talking to it."

"I do. I mean, I did, but it's ignoring me now. It's just like dead, cold . . . stone." Alton knew how bizarre it sounded, but for a brief time, he had lived within the wall, within the stone, and had learned its stories, had heard and felt the pulse of the song that bound it together, aware of the presences of the guardians who also resided within. To him, the stone was anything but dead.

Garth sipped his tea with a thoughtful expression on his face. "I wonder . . ."

"What?"

Garth cleared his throat and straightened in his chair. "I assume if the wall doesn't allow you into the tower, that it won't let me in either, but it might be worth trying."

Alton had long ago come to the same conclusion as Garth that the tower had closed access to all but, as the

Rider suggested, it was certainly worth seeing if it were in fact true.

The two men polished off breakfast and left the tent for the outdoors. The morning sun was quickly warming the air and burning off dew. It cast a bronze glow onto the face of the wall. When they reached the tower, Garth craned his neck looking up and up and up . . . And he could keep looking up till he snapped his neck. The magic of the wall made it seem to stretch all the way to the heavens, when in fact the actual stone base of it stood only ten feet high. Yet the magic portion of the wall was as durable as stone, and looked just like it. There was no distinction between the two.

The Tower of the Heavens possessed no windows, not even any arrow loops, to break up its impassive facade. And there was no door.

"Let's try it," Garth said in a hushed tone.

He grasped his gold winged horse brooch, emblem of the Green Riders and the device that enhanced their magical abilities, and reached with his other hand through stone *into* the tower.

Alton's heart thudded. The stone molded around Garth's wrist as though he reached into nothing more innocuous than water.

"I'll be back in a moment," Garth said, and he plunged all the way into the tower leaving nary a ripple to indicate he had ever existed.

Alton was flummoxed. How in five hells had the wall admitted Garth so easily when it wouldn't even respond to his touch? Maybe something had changed overnight—maybe the wall would let him pass now.

He fumbled for his brooch, the gold warm and oily smooth beneath his fingers, and pressed his other hand against the rough unyielding stone. He willed the wall to open for him, to allow him to enter the tower. He called upon his Rider magic, but to no avail. The tower remained impassible.

He found himself with fist clenched to hammer against the wall and stopped, recalling himself and the soreness of his bandaged hands. It wouldn't do any good to injure himself again.

It was not easy waiting for Garth to return, and Alton paced madly. More than a moment had passed, much more, before the Rider poked his head out of the stone wall of the tower looking absurdly like a hunter's mounted trophy. All Garth needed was a pair of antlers.

"Well?" Alton demanded.

"I've been speaking with Merdigen." Garth rolled his eyes. "He's been wondering why we abandoned him again—he's been waiting for us to return and didn't we know that the wall is growing more unstable as each day passes. When I told him you were trying, he checked with the guardians himself." A strange expression fell over Garth's face. "After he did so, he told me that the wall doesn't like you very much. It doesn't trust you."

Alton stumbled backward, realizing how much sense it made. While under the influence of Mornhavon the Black, he had almost destroyed the wall, though at the time he believed he was strengthening it. And his cousin Pendric, his cousin who hated him, had merged with the wall and became a guardian. Could Pendric have influenced the other guardians against him?

"Damnation," Alton muttered. How was he supposed to mend the wall if it wouldn't trust him?

PATCHWORK PRIDE

Lady Estora Coutre slipped quietly into the corridor and eased her chamber door shut behind her, overcome by a sudden giddy sense of freedom. The morning was early yet, and none of her attendants had risen, nor had her mother or any of her numerous cousins, aunts, or siblings who had traveled over sea and land to be present during this momentous time in her life. The other unrelated noble ladies who clung to her like limpets to a rock would be abed for hours yet. They had not been born and raised on the sunrise coast as she had, where the days started much earlier.

Alone. She was finally alone.

Except for the Weapon who peeled away from the wall and followed her. She was growing rather accustomed to her shadow-clad guardians, and while their presence might jangle the nerves of her relations who were unused to them, to her they had become almost invisible. They stayed out of her way and remained silent unless addressed directly. They would not report her early morning sojourns unless she ordered them to, which, of course, she would not.

Trained to safeguard members of the royal family to the death, their code of honor held discretion sacred. It was not their place to comment on or question the actions of their wards, but to protect. She found it inconceivable, however, that they didn't have the odd conversation or two among themselves about what happened in the course of their workday. In any case, she doubted she had given them much to gossip about thus far.

She drew a shawl over her head and walked along the corridor, hoping none would awaken and note her passage, or insist they accompany her, or try to redirect her, or fill her ears with inane chatter. It had been almost too much to bear these last couple months. Was this how her life would be from here on in? She feared it would be so.

Fortunately no one burst through a doorway to ruin her morning. It was as if the castle itself slumbered. The air did not stir and the corridors were dusky and quiet. Peaceful. Soon enough it would awaken, brimming with people hurrying from here to there on errands, appointments, and meetings, and there would be much tiresome activity. Best to enjoy the solitude while she could.

Zachary must be well used to always being in the company of others, though she sensed he liked it no more than she. In fact, the two of them were so constantly surrounded by others that they were rarely able to speak with each other, and certainly not privately. They would never get to know one another until their wedding night. If even then the throngs let them alone . . .

In their brief exchanges, Zachary had been kind and courtly, but distant, just as she supposed she had been herself. This matchmaking of nobles was an awkward tradition. It was, her mother informed her time and again, the way things had been done for hundreds and hundreds of years. Her mother hadn't even looked upon her father until their wedding day. Over time her parents had grown fond of one another, and had even found mutual respect and love in their lengthy partnership. It would be the same for Estora and Zachary, her mother assured her.

Estora had always known it would be this way. She had known since she was a little girl that she would be paired with a man not of her choosing. The knowing, however, was not the same as the reality.

Choice was never a part of my life.

No, this is what she had been born and bred for: to be the wife of some highborn man and to bear his children. Nothing more. Had she been born mindless, the outcome would have been the same.

Do any of us really have any choices, or are we all pieces on an Intrigue board, moved to action by someone else's will?

The thought brought to mind a conversation she had with Karigan not so long ago. The two of them had been sitting together in the inner courtyard gardens and she had just revealed to Karigan that the king signed her father's contract of marriage. Then without thinking, she had told Karigan that she envied her for her freedom, the freedom to do as she wished, and to marry whom she wanted.

It had been a mistake. Estora should have known better. No one *chose* to be a Green Rider, one was *called* to service. A magical calling, as she understood it. An irresistible, unyielding call that could break your mind if you failed to heed it. It did not matter what you were doing with your life—the call made you drop everything and come serve the king as one of his messengers. Choice was not involved.

She paused at an intersection of corridors, deciding she would head for the outdoors to listen to birds and breathe the free air. She turned down the corridor that led past the kitchens and to a servants' entrance.

She tugged her shawl closer, and passed a servant pausing along the corridor to yawn. He rubbed his eyes and forged on in the opposite direction.

Pleased he hadn't even noticed her, she continued on her way. It was odd, but the more people crowded around her, the lonelier she felt. The only reason they flocked to her was because she was to be queen with all of that rank's attendant power, not because they cared about her as a person. Since that day in the garden, Karigan had behaved the opposite of everyone else by avoiding her, and it hurt. She'd turn in the other direction if by chance they met in a corridor, and she even declined formal invitations to join Estora for tea. Karigan had been the one person who offered Estora genuine friendship with no conditions attached, and she missed it.

If only F'ryan were still alive, she would not be so alone. She felt his loss as keenly as if it had happened just yesterday and not two years ago; and in the deep of night, when she was most lonely, she still wept for him. Wept for her lost love, wept for the emptiness in her heart. She held on to her memories of him as if they were the only things anchoring her to Earth; memories of his laughter, his touch, and the light shining in his eyes.

"Oh, F'ryan, I miss you," she murmured.

It made Karigan's avoidance of her all the more hurtful, for Karigan had been the last to see F'ryan alive and had taken his place among the Green Riders. She was, in a sense, Estora's last connection to F'ryan.

Activity picked up near the kitchens. Cooks and bakers would have already been at work for hours now, and she smelled luscious breads and pastries baking. Bright lamplight spilled through the arched entryway of the kitchens, and cooks and servants bustled within, clattering dishware and chattering boisterously among themselves. The kitchens were cavernous with numerous ovens, hearths, and preparation tables. Feeding a castle full of soldiers, administrators, nobles, servants, and visitors was a huge undertaking, which the kitchen operations reflected.

Estora smiled and continued toward the servants' entrance only to discover a certain Green Rider there with a pair of bulging saddlebags thrown over her shoulders and her hand on the door handle.

"Karigan?"

The Rider swung around, startled. Panic flickered across her features when she saw who addressed her.

"Good morning, my lady," she said with a quick bob. "I've two Riders needing these provisions, so I must—"

"Oh, no, you don't!" Estora strode forward and stood squarely before Karigan. "You will not run off on me again."

Karigan opened her mouth as if to speak, but Estora cut her off. "I know I upset you in the past, but is it really a reason to avoid me each and every time I see you? I apologize if that will help. But really, avoiding me is not the most adult reaction."

At first, unsettled emotions rippled across Karigan's face, but then she took a deep breath, steadying her expression. It was not the open, friendly face Estora was accustomed to but closed and set.

"It may be perceived," Karigan said, "as improper for a commoner to associate with the future queen in such a familiar manner."

Where had that come from? Estora had to double-check that this was Karigan she was talking to. Never before had Karigan adopted so formal a tone with her.

"Karigan, I am still Estora, the same person as before. My marriage to the king changes nothing."

"It changes everything, my lady."

"Don't be ridiculous. I—"

"I am a lowly messenger," Karigan said without meeting her gaze. "Your servant. You are to be queen, and that is a barrier between us that cannot be casually crossed. I will serve you and the king to the best of my ability, and as duty requires, but the friendship we enjoyed in the past would be inappropriate for one of your station. That is all there is to it."

No it wasn't, Estora was sure of it. She narrowed her eyes, trying to discern what Karigan was hiding. Why was she pushing her away? "Let's talk this out. Maybe—"

"As your future subject, I will talk with you if you command it, my lady, but I fear it would not change our circumstances. I do not believe we can continue to be friends."

It was as though Estora had been struck in the face. Never had she known Karigan to be so cold, and her formal tone made it all the worse. All at once she realized what it meant to be queen—she'd never be regarded in the same light again, even by those she had counted among her friends. What came with being queen was a terrible power as well, a power to punish any who displeased her. That explained, at least in part, Karigan's careful and proper choice of words, and it saddened Estora that Karigan would even consider her capable of carrying out a punishment against her. The worst part, however, was what lay beneath the words: utter rejection of their friendship, utter rejection of Estora.

Overcome by a sense of loss—loss of who she once was, and of Karigan's friendship—tears filled her eyes. "You can't mean it."

"If you require nothing further of me, my lady," Karigan said, "I need to take these saddlebags to Riders who must depart on the king's business." She bowed, turned on her heel, and strode out the door.

Estora blinked against the morning light that splashed across her face as the door opened and closed. After a moment's hesitation, she flung the door open and rushed out after Karigan into the chill morning. She would shake the truth out of the Rider if she had to.

But Karigan was already halfway across the castle grounds making a straight line for the Rider stables. Estora lifted her skirts and followed the steps down to the pathway. She wanted to scream and cry. What had come over Karigan? Certainly their exchange in the gardens couldn't have made Karigan *hate* her. What had she done to deserve such cold treatment?

Nothing.

Karigan's behavior was so unusual, so unlike herself, that there must be some greater issue at hand, and it was just beyond Estora's grasp. Still, this inner knowledge did nothing to lessen the hurt. She sniffled.

"My pardon. I simply thought the lady might like a handkerchief."

Estora turned to find her Weapon blocking the approach of a gentleman.

"I thought I was the only one out and about this early in the morning," he said, "only to find a beautiful face stricken with sorrow." He waved the handkerchief like a sign of surrender.

Estora nodded to her Weapon that it was all right to allow the man to approach. She accepted his handkerchief and dabbed her eyes. "Thank you."

He smiled, which made his well-chiseled features all the

more handsome. Black hair was drawn back in a ponytail, and he wore the clothing of a noble, though it showed some wear. The colors were slightly faded, the cuffs frayed, and there were signs of meticulous mending.

"It's my pleasure to be of assistance," he said with a bow. "If there is anything else I can do to further diminish your tears, I am at your service." He magically produced a white rose from his sleeve.

Estora laughed in delight, and accepted it.

"See!" he said with a grin. "The sun is shining again. But now I fear I must be off for a breakfast appointment with my cousin, though I find your company more enjoyable."

With another bow, he lightly trotted up the steps and through the kitchen entrance. She watched after him bemused, wondering if he were a kitchen servant, but despite the wear of his clothing, it was too rich for a servant and not far enough gone to be cast-off. And most servants did not leave behind fancy handkerchiefs with their initials embroidered on them.

X.P.A. Who is he? she wondered. And she brought the rose blossom to her nose, delighting in its scent.

Karigan was still shaking later that morning as she trudged toward the practice grounds for weapons training. Her confrontation with Estora left her feeling sick to her stomach, and she thought she'd lose her breakfast.

Wouldn't Drent love that . . .

Severing her friendship with Estora was one of the hardest things she ever had to do, but the alternative seemed so . . . difficult. How could she continue a friendship with a woman who was to marry the man she . . . she loved? How could she pretend nothing had passed between her and King Zachary? How could she pretend not to be jealous? And worst of all, how could she bear the inevitable conversations friends shared, with all the intimate details?

Distancing herself from Estora also meant distancing

herself from King Zachary. It simplified matters, kept her feelings from twisting like a knife within her. It was *safe.*

When Karigan arrived at the practice grounds, she found Arms Master Drent waiting for her there with his meaty fists on his hips. The glower on his gargoylelike face emanated severe disapproval.

Uh oh. Her tangled thoughts of Estora evaporated and a tremor of fear quaked through her even though she knew full well Drent used sheer physical presence to intimidate his trainees. She wondered what sort of abuse she was in for today, and why.

"I've been training you these past months," he said in an icy voice that was all the more frightening because it was not his usual bellow, "even though there was no reason I had to. I did it because I thought you showed promise in the weapons arts. And yet I hear all that training was for naught."

"W–what?"

"The museum."

Karigan's mouth dropped open in surprise. How had he heard? "I—"

"Silence! I will not waste my time on trainees who lack the good sense not to confront a superior opponent over a trivial scrap of parchment. And if the confrontation takes place, the trainee should have fared better in the fight. No trainee of mine makes such a poor showing."

"But—"

"You will no longer report to me for training. I will not waste my time with you."

Karigan could only stare at him, flabbergasted.

"Dismissed." He turned his back on her.

She watched that broad back as he marched away toward other trainees on the practice field going through daily exercises and clattering wooden practice swords together in bouts. She knew she should be jumping up and down for joy—no more brutal sessions with Drent. Sessions that had left her spent, blistered, and bruised, her ears ringing from his abusive ranting. Yet she only felt irritated, insulted, in fact. She could have bested that swordsman yesterday if she hadn't been wearing that blasted dress. How would Drent fare against an expert swordsman were he attired in a corset and dress?

The image made her sputter with laughter. She left the practice grounds and headed for the castle, suddenly wondering what she would do with the novelty of free time.

By the time she entered the Rider wing, however, she was filled with a sense of failure. It was an honor, so she was told, to be chosen to work with Arms Master Drent. It was he who trained swordmasters and judged if they were worthy of becoming Weapons, and she had rather liked being classed among such elite warriors, even if she hated the training sessions themselves.

Drent wouldn't even hear her side of the story. Instead of turning her away, he should have shown her how she could have done better. That's what a good teacher would have done.

Just then, Tegan emerged from her room, and Karigan was struck by an idea.

"Hello, Tegan, do you have a few minutes?"

"Certainly."

When Karigan returned to the practice field, she strode right up to Drent, or at least as best she could with Tegan's slightly too small shoes rubbing blisters into her heels. They didn't match the dress, but this was not about wearing the perfect ensemble.

When Drent saw her, he started to bow, then he realized who she was. Oh yes, she had Tegan cinch up the corset again and arrange her hair. Remarkably Drent's cheeks bloomed with color and he cleared his throat, glancing away and shifting his stance.

"Your training has fallen short of my needs," she announced. Her attire inspired a tone of arrogance in her voice that pleased her. "You have trained me on equal ground with others similarly equipped and prepared to fight. Yesterday, as you can see, I was not properly equipped or prepared to face an expert swordsman, yet I did so because I felt an artifact of Sacoridia's history worth rescuing, an artifact held priceless by some. It may have been poor judgment on my behalf, but had I been attired differently, the outcome may have proved more favorable." The corset left her breathless, but she concluded, "I demand you to train me to fight when formally attired."

Drent's mouth worked like a fish's, and he ran his hand over the top of his short, spiky hair. Karigan had never seen him at a loss for words before. Several of his trainees stopped what they were doing to peer at the unusual scene of a coiffed and dressed-up female staring down their hulking, fearsome arms master.

"Of course, my la–la—" He choked on words he had not meant to expel.

Karigan smiled darkly. She had won.

Drent growled and bristled, trying to look his usual mean and hideous self. "I see your point. Ordinary sword work is not necessarily the best option thus attired, but it does present opportunities. We'll begin with your hair."

Her hair? Was he going to teach her to strangle someone with her tresses? He made her remove the various pins and combs that held her hair in place atop her head.

"These," he said, turning them over in his huge, calloused hand, "can be lethal, used to gouge out an assailant's eye, for instance, during close combat. And if sharpened, they can be like tiny daggers."

He returned them to her and looked her up and down. "Weapons of various sorts can be hidden elsewhere. Lift your skirts."

"What?"

Drent blushed and swallowed. "Er, just to your knees."

Under different circumstances, even this would have been scandalous, but she did as he asked.

The arms master grunted. "Sheaths for throwing knives can be fitted to your calves and, uh, elsewhere if you wish. They'd also fit in your boots when you are being a Green Rider."

Karigan raised an eyebrow. "Being" a Green Rider?

She'd like to know what Drent thought she was "being" right now.

"I don't know how to throw knives."

"It can be taught."

"And you will teach me."

He sighed, still unable to look her in the eye. "Aye, I will teach you. Today we will start with close combat; knife throwing tomorrow."

He made Karigan insert the combs and pins back into her hair. Without a mirror or Tegan to help her, she could only guess at how ridiculous she must look.

Drent couldn't bring himself to attack her, so he enlisted the aid of one of his students, the one the others called "Flogger." He was almost as big as Drent, and just as ugly, and he seemed to like the idea of attacking a lady. He licked his lips in anticipation.

Drent had him creep up from behind and grab Karigan in a stranglehold. She bashed the back of her head into his face and skimmed his shin with the edge of her shoe. Flogger howled and hopped away clutching his bloody nose.

Flogger was then instructed to grab her arm. She broke his hold by grasping his thumb and bending it backward until he was on his knees whimpering. Those who paused their own bouts to watch hooted and hollered, chivvying Flogger good and hard.

When Flogger tried another grab around her waist, she pulled a pin from her hair and jabbed it into the meaty part of his forearm. He fell away swearing. She wiped the blood off on her skirts and reinserted the pin into her hair. Apart from being breathless courtesy of the corset, she hadn't even perspired during Flogger's attempts.

"My father's cargo master taught me such skills of defense," she explained to Drent. "The thief at the museum, however, had a rapier and did not attack me in that manner."

Drent scratched his head and ordered Flogger to fetch a pair of practice swords. Karigan took hers with trepidation when she saw the malice creeping into Flogger's eyes. His expression seemed to say he'd pay her back for the bloody nose and the humiliation he suffered in front of his fellows.

"We'll have a bout," Drent said, "and see what we can do to help a *lady* defend herself should the situation ever arise." He rolled his eyes probably doubting that a *true* lady would ever find herself in such a situation.

Karigan and Flogger stepped into a practice ring and tapped swords. As Karigan predicted, the humiliation was hers within minutes. Sword moves she had been trained to make hundreds of times were hampered by her skirts and corset, and Flogger did not hold back, battering her relentlessly. As before, she grew light-headed from lack of air, and the weight of the skirts dragged her down. Flogger slammed his sword into her gut for kill point, and she crumpled to her knees in a cloud of dust, sputtering.

Flogger beamed proudly, but his fellows cast him disgusted looks and shook their heads. He had taken advantage of the "lady."

"A little excessive, Flogger," Drent commented.

Karigan could only stay on her knees gasping and retching, attempting to suck air back into her lungs. She had asked for it.

When she could breathe again, a guilty looking Flogger pulled her to her feet.

"Again," Drent said.

And they went at it again, Drent yelling instructions at her on how she should move her feet to cope with the restricting skirts, and how she might conserve her breath. Flogger still managed to "kill" her several times over before Drent finally declared the session over.

Karigan stood before him panting, sweat slicking her face and neck.

"A suggestion," Drent said, still not quite able to look her dead on. "That thing you're wearing . . ."

"Thing?"

"Aye, the thing under your . . . the thing women wear to—" He stopped as if biting his tongue.

Karigan's mouth quirked into a half smile. "The corset?"

Drent made a garbled noise. "Aye, the corset. If you weren't so unreasonably adherent to fashion, you could, uh, loosen it. Make it easier to breathe."

Karigan limped back to the castle past the wondering looks of others, her hair in total disarray, her face grimed with dirt and probably bruised, and her fine dress ripped and coated with dust, but she held her chin high. Dresses could be fixed, but pride was more difficult to patch back together.

She may never see her love for a certain man fulfilled, and she may have lost a friend today, but by the gods, she still had Drent.

A NEW ASSIGNMENT

In the days and weeks that followed, Karigan had to reassess her sanity for wanting to continue her training sessions with Drent. He took her desire to learn how to fight in fancy attire to heart. He didn't make her wear corset and dress, but he found other ways to simulate the difficulties presented by restrictive garments. He made her strap on a forty pound pack to represent the weight of her skirts, then ordered her to run around the practice grounds and participate in weapons practice while wearing it.

To train her in footwork, he buckled modified horse hobbles around her ankles to limit her movement as skirts would. He used the device, he said, on his swordmaster initiates to teach them economy of movement. Swordmastery, he said, was not about jumping around and flailing the sword through the air. It was about making each action count. There was an elegance and efficiency in simplicity.

Karigan agreed for she had seen such skill at work among swordmasters and Weapons during practice bouts and in battle. It turned brutal conflict into beauty in motion; deadly beauty.

Trying to make that economy of movement work for herself, however, proved to be another matter entirely. She could not keep count of the many times the hobbles tripped her up and she spilled unceremoniously out of the practice ring and hit the ground hard enough, thanks to the weight of her pack, that dust rose up around her. Her opponents won automatic kill points each time she fell, and while she couldn't keep track of the points, she knew Drent and his assistants did. The points were posted at the field house at the end of every week, and competition was fierce among the trainees to attain the most points, a matter of pride and honor and desire to win Drent's approval. Invariably Karigan was at the bottom of the list.

Her sessions left her bruised, exhausted, cut up, limping, and discouraged, but slowly, ever so slowly, she noticed her strength improving and her swordplay becoming more precise.

If trying to fight while hobbled made her feel ridiculous, knife throwing humiliated her even further. She realized, to her chagrin, that clobbering the thief at the museum with her shoe had not been a matter of skill, but of luck.

"Retain your line of sight," Drent said during one such session. "Focus and see the knife in the target."

Karigan squinted at the straw-stuffed dummy hanging from a wooden frame some yards away. The weight of the knife felt good in her hand. It was specially balanced for throwing. When she first received the pair, she had been quite impressed with herself and showed them off to her fellow Riders, wearing them around in her new boot sheaths. However, when Drent saw how abysmal she was at throwing, he decided to hold onto them when she wasn't training so she wouldn't endanger herself or others, which resulted in a good deal of ribbing from her friends.

She licked her lips and concentrated. She held the tip of the blade in her fingers just as Drent had shown her. As soon as the other trainees saw her with a knife in her hand, they scattered out of throwing distance. One wild throw had nearly killed one of them during her first session and now only Drent had the nerve to stand anywhere near her.

She would hit the target this time. She would show them. She stared hard at the dummy's "heart" imagining the knife sticking through it. A bead of sweat trickled down her lip and she tasted salt.

Her expression set and determined, she flung her arm back for the throw, but the blade slipped from her fingers and flew over her shoulder. Someone yelped from behind. Grimacing at what she might find, she slowly turned around. The knife was planted in the ground between the feet of a Green Foot runner.

"Oops," Karigan said. She snuck a glance at Drent whose veins were popping out on his neck.

"Oops?" he repeated quietly. Too quietly.

Karigan flinched in anticipation of the storm that was about to blow over her, but it never came. Drent passed his hand over his spiky hair, nostrils flaring. "You are hopeless," he said, his voice full of despair. "Absolutely hopeless." And he wandered away shaking his head and mumbling to himself.

Karigan blinked in surprise, then turned her attention to the runner who had not moved, as if still shocked by her close call with death. "Sorry," Karigan said. "I, um, I didn't meant to—" She gestured at the knife.

"Ung . . ." The girl shook her head, her eyes bulging. Moments passed before she was able to focus on Karigan and speak. "Um, the captain would like you to join her and the king in his study."

Chills prickled along Karigan's nerves at the girl's words. "Thank you," she managed to say.

The runner nodded and took off at a trot. Karigan pulled her knife from the ground and slipped it into the boot sheath, wondering what this summons might be about. She avoided the king as much as possible for all the pain and desires he stirred in her, but she knew that in the course of her duties she could not avoid him indefinitely. And now she had been summoned.

She glanced in Drent's direction. He was busy bellowing at a pair of swordsmen across the practice field. She shrugged off the weighted pack and informed one of his assistants that she must leave, and she hurried to the castle, stopping in her own chamber in the Rider wing just long enough to change out of her work tunic and pull on a fresh shirt and shortcoat and to splash water on her face. It would not do to appear before the king covered in dust and sweat.

When she arrived at the king's study, the Weapon at the door let her in.

"Thank you, Travis," she murmured.

He nodded in reply, more acknowledgment than most would receive from one of the king's stern guardians.

Sunlight glared through the study's many windows that faced the courtyard gardens. The room had once been a queen's solarium, and Karigan wondered if, when the king married, it would be restored to its original use and become the domain of Estora. She took a deep breath to help resist the bitter thoughts *that* conjured.

The king sat at his desk, its white marble surface glowing in the sunshine, reflecting onto his face, making him appear ethereal, a creature of light, while all else around him fell into shadow. His hair and beard blazed with fine gold and copper strands instead of the more subdued amber, and contrasted with his rich brown eyes.

He sat there with his hands folded before him, and the light brought to sharp relief how strong they were as it outlined muscles and tendons, his fingers adorned only by simple gold bands. Hands that wielded a sword, hands that wielded a scepter, hands that wielded power. How she wished, how she desired, those hands of light to unfold and caress her in tender strokes. Karigan shivered.

His face, however, told another story. As king, he had acquired the skill of concealing his thoughts and feelings from others, an advantage when he did not want enemies, or politicians, or supplicants to know what he was thinking. He now donned that mask, and it staggered Karigan that he should use it in her presence. She supposed it was for the best, for it gave them distance. She would wear a mask of her own as well, that of a dutiful Green Rider.

She bowed to the king. "You summoned me, sire?"

"We did."

He was not using the royal "we," she knew, for he never did. Someone cleared her throat and Karigan squinted toward the windows to find Captain Mapstone seated there, with legs crossed. The sun glared around her, making her a silhouette, but Karigan recognized her shape and the flare of red hair at her crown.

"Good morning, Karigan," she said.

Karigan opened her mouth to return the greeting when a third person barreled out of the shadows at her with his arms thrown wide open.

"Garth!" she cried.

He wrapped his arms around her in a bear hug and lifted her off the floor. How could she have overlooked his presence when she entered the study? Garth was hard to miss!

"Welcome back," she said, her voice muffled by his chest.

His laugh rumbled against her face, and he patted her on the back before setting her down. She staggered a little when he released her.

"Good to be back," he said, grinning.

"Please be seated," the king said. His mask remained intact, unmoved by Garth's boisterous greeting.

After the two Riders settled in chairs next to Captain Mapstone's, the captain cleared her throat again and gazed at Karigan.

"As you know, Garth was on an errand to the wall to check on Alton's progress there."

Yes, Karigan did know. She glanced anxiously at Garth, hoping to convey in that one look how much she wanted to speak to him after this meeting adjourned.

"To our dismay," the captain continued, "Alton has been unable to make any progress whatsoever."

Karigan's mouth dropped open.

"It's true," Garth said. "The wall rejects him—won't let him in. It refuses to trust him."

"Doesn't . . . trust him?" Karigan's echoing him must have sounded idiotic, but Garth's words overwhelmed her. Over two months had passed, and there was no telling when Mornhavon the Black would reappear in Blackveil Forest. And if Alton could not communicate with the wall and fix it, how much more time would be lost before a way was found?

"You more than most understand the gravity of the situation," the king said, "which is why you've been chosen for a new assignment."

"To go to the wall?"

"No," Captain Mapstone said. "Dale is actually heading that way."

"Dale? But how?" The Rider had been gravely wounded during the battle at the breach in the wall and remained in Woodhaven to mend.

"She wanted to go," Garth said, "and I really thought one of us ought to be at the wall to help Alton communicate with Merdigen. She was tired of being cooped up in the mending hall at Woodhaven and Lord D'Yer's chief mender deemed her fit to travel, so long as she did not participate in strenuous activity and rested frequently."

"I don't understand. How could Dale communicate with Merdigen if Alton can't?"

"We," and Garth jabbed his thumb at his Rider brooch, "can enter Tower of the Heavens even if Alton can't. The wall still trusts *us*."

Karigan shook her head in incredulity.

"With each passing day," the king said, "we chance the return of Mornhavon. We must use well the time you've bought for us." For a moment, the mask slipped from his face, and she saw in the depths of his eyes his concern, not just for what could lie ahead, but for her and all she had already endured. Karigan averted her gaze.

"What's my assignment?"

"It's actually threefold," Captain Mapstone said. "We are sending you west, first to Selium."

Karigan managed to refrain from jumping out of her chair and cheering. In Selium she'd get to visit with her friend Estral Andovian but she was curious to know what Selium had to do with the wall.

"One of our most frustrating issues," the captain continued, "is our lack of knowledge, or rather, our *loss* of knowledge concerning the arcane arts and ancient craft, such as that used to construct the D'Yer Wall. Why or how we lost it, who can say?" She shrugged. "If certain knowledge were to fall into the hands of the enemy? Then perhaps it was deemed necessary to destroy anything that documented important creations like the wall to safeguard them. There is a chance, however, that one document has survived through the ages. Merdigen told Garth he had a dim recollection of a book kept by one of the mages who helped build the wall, a log of sorts that may offer Alton clues as to how he can bypass the guardians and begin restoring the wall."

"You believe this book is in Selium?"

Captain Mapstone sighed. "We don't know. Chances are it no longer exists at all, but if it does, the one person who might know something about it is the Golden Guardian."

"Ah." The Golden Guardian, Aaron Fiori, was Estral's father. He was, in a sense, the lord-governor of Sacoridia's arts, history, and culture, and he oversaw the school of Selium and the city of the same name that surrounded it, though more often than not he was traveling the countryside collecting stories and songs, playing music, and seeking talented children to bring to the school. Actual day-to-day management of the city and school was left to the lord-mayor and the dean.

"Lord D'Yer is already having his people turn their archival collections upside down for the hundredth time," Captain Mapstone said, "and Dakrias Brown and his clerks will be doing the same here."

Karigan smiled when the captain named the king's newest chief administrator. Recognizing the immensity of the undertaking, she didn't envy him his task, though he might receive aid from a ghost or two.

"It may be that the book is under some spell of concealment," the king added, "which is why it has not come to light before. If Lord Fiori can search for it with this in mind, it may guide him. You will bear a message directly to Lord Fiori, personally written by me so he understands the urgency of the matter. And if he is on one of his travels, then I suppose you will have to approach Dean Crosley."

There was a knock upon the door and the king's secretary, Cummings, poked his head in. "Pardon me, Your

Majesty, but the Huradeshian delegation is awaiting you in the throne room."

The king nodded and stood, all three Riders rising with him. On his way out he paused in front of Karigan, no longer an ethereal being of light, but an ordinary man, his king's mask slipping again. "May your journey be a safe one, Karigan," he said. "And may it prove successful."

Karigan could not meet his gaze. "Thank you, sire," she murmured, but he had already left the room, the door sweeping shut behind him.

She tore her gaze from the door only to find the captain watching her closely. Then with a blink of her hazel eyes, the captain shifted her attention to Garth.

"You may be excused," she said. "The rest concerns Karigan's other errands and I'm sure you've much to catch up on now that you're back."

"Thank you," Garth said. On his way out, he squeezed Karigan's shoulder and said, "We'll talk later."

Karigan nodded and smiled at him as he departed.

"Now then," the captain said, settling back into her chair, "shall we continue?"

"Yes, Captain."

"As I mentioned, the errand is threefold. Your first and most urgent errand is to Selium. If Lord Fiori should produce this book we're looking for, or if he should know something of it, you are to return immediately and report, and disregard the other two errands. They are of lesser importance, understood?"

"Yes."

"The likelihood of the book existing is slim in any case, so should nothing come of your visit with Lord Fiori, the king is permitting me to send you on two additional errands while you are in the west."

"These are not king's errands?"

"They're Rider business. As you may have noticed, we've more Riders than horses these days." Here the captain smiled, as she often did when the subject of her new Riders came up. "I need you to visit with the man from whom we purchase our horses and tell him our needs. I'm afraid we aren't likely to get the horses till spring or summer, but it will have to do.

"The horse trader's name is Damian Frost and his farm is located on the outskirts of the town of Aubry Crossing."

Karigan searched her mental map. "The border with Rhovanny?"

"Yes, and also where the boundaries of Wayman and Mirwell provinces meet as well. It's something of a crossroads as the name implies." The captain unrolled a map that had been lying across her lap and spread it over the king's desk. She planted her forefinger on a speck in western Sacoridia. "Aubry Crossing's small. People mainly use it to travel between Rhovanny and Sacoridia. There's a garrison of boundary guards there, a few shops and outfitters, and a couple inns, and that's about it. You'll have to ask around for directions to Damian's place. Everyone knows him. And if anyone else tries to sell you horses, we buy only from Damian."

The captain told her how many head she had in mind. "We'll give you an official certificate that Damian can redeem for currency at the garrison—much safer than carrying around purses of king's gold. Damian will receive the rest of his payment when the beasts are delivered. Don't worry about haggling for a price; that comes later, and it will probably be Hep closing the deal anyway." Then she rolled her eyes. "Not that Damian has any competition, and he knows it. We just try to keep things fair."

Karigan nodded, a trifle disappointed that she wouldn't be able to flex her merchanting skills.

Captain Mapstone then gazed out the window and into the gardens with a whimsical smile. "I rather envy you getting to visit with Damian. He's . . . well, he has a way with horses."

And Rider horses were special, very intelligent. Karigan found herself looking forward to meeting the man who supplied them.

"My third assignment?" Karigan asked.

"Lord Mirwell," Captain Mapstone said.

An image of gruff old Mirwell with his bear hide draped over his shoulders flashed through Karigan's mind before she remembered he was dead. The captain meant his son, Timas, who had made Karigan's life unpleasant during her school years at Selium. Now he was a lord-governor and she knew he would love the fact that she was a lowly messenger who must grovel before him no matter what abuse he chose to heap on her. Maybe he'd matured since those days. Maybe he wouldn't even remember her. But how could he forget how she humiliated him in front of all their classmates that day during a bout of swordplay?

"Actually," the captain said, "Lord Mirwell is an excuse. You'll deliver him some innocuous message from the king. I'm more interested in you contacting Beryl. We haven't heard from her in a good while, which leaves me a little concerned."

Beryl Spencer was a Green Rider whose special ability allowed her to portray a role and convince others of it, which made her an ideal operative for the king. Placed in the Mirwellian militia, she had quickly earned rank as a major and gained the old lord-governor's confidence. He had handpicked her as his aide, never suspecting her true allegiance till she helped to bring about his downfall. Afterward, Beryl returned to Mirwell Province to resume her role in the militia and as an aide to Timas, keeping an eye on him lest he decide to follow in his father's footsteps or was approached by any of his father's fellow conspirators who had escaped king's law.

"If you can't see or meet with Beryl," the captain said, "make some careful inquiries, but nothing more. If something untoward has happened to her, do not get involved. Return to report immediately. I don't want you endangering yourself. Most likely she is out on maneuvers with the militia—it would not be the first time we've had silence from her because of this." Then she gave Karigan a penetrating look. "Are you clear on this? You are only to observe, not to get yourself in trouble."

"Clear," Karigan assured her. She had already had

enough adventures to last a lifetime, and steering clear of potential trouble was fine with her. "Is that all?"

"Actually, no," the captain said. "There's one more thing. I'm sending Fergal Duff with you."

"But he's new—"

"Precisely why I'm sending him with you. As horses become available, I'm pairing up other Riders in hopes our new people can get a feel for being on an errand before actually having to do a solo run."

Karigan clamped her mouth shut. It had been part of her training, too. She had accompanied Ty on several errands, but none so far afield as this one. She would be stuck with Fergal for quite some time.

"You will leave in two days. I'll brief Fergal myself." The captain rose from her chair and smiled again. "I'm sure you'll leave Rider accounts in good shape so Mara can handle them—until you return."

Karigan suppressed a groan. It appeared her least favorite aspect of the merchanting business would haunt her forever.

She found Garth in the Rider wing in the large chamber they had converted into a common room. With a long oaken table that was a gift from the king, some comfortable chairs, and a warm hearth fire blazing, it wasn't too bad. Shelves even began to collect new books and games, replacing those that had been lost in the fire.

Garth's bulk overflowed a rocking chair beside the hearth. He held a teacup that looked ridiculously dainty in his hands, and a book lay open across his knees.

She crossed the room and dropped into a chair opposite him, relieved no one else was around. Most senior Riders would be out on message errands and the new Riders were at lessons. Some were learning to ride, others were learning to write and figure, and still others would be at weapons practice with Arms Master Gresia.

"How did the rest of your meeting go?" Garth asked.

Karigan outlined her assignment and Garth let out a low whistle. "That should keep you busy for a while."

"I haven't been on a long-distance errand since forever. I hope it doesn't snow." She shuddered and gazed into the hearth fire. Avoiding snow was unlikely now that it was mid-autumn, and she briefly thought about all she'd have to pack to stay warm.

"At least the Grandgent won't be frozen," Garth said.

"True." If they were unable to use the ferry crossing, it would lengthen the journey by weeks. She shook off thoughts of her impending travel and said, "How's Alton? Did he mention me at all?"

Garth blew on his still steaming tea before sipping. "I'm sorry, Karigan, but he refused to talk about you. I tried, I really did, but he just wouldn't talk."

"Then I suppose he didn't respond to my letter."

"I'm afraid not."

A silence fell between them and the fire popped. Crestfallen, Karigan could only look at her knees.

"Alton hasn't been well, Karigan," Garth said. "The mender down there tells me he's still fighting the forest's poisons in his veins. He doesn't look very good. And the wall is frustrating him. He's more than frustrated. You would hardly recognize him."

"Probably not," she mumbled.

"Be patient with him. He'll come around—he's had a hard time."

Karigan frowned. And she hadn't? Who had borne the consciousness of Mornhavon the Black within her? Who had been assaulted, stabbed, and manipulated? Why did Alton get to have excuses when it was his behavior that had been execrable? Abruptly she stood and strode out of the chamber.

"Karigan, wait!" Garth called after her.

She kept walking and did not stop till she reached her own chamber. She stepped inside and heaved a long breath. Without a hearth fire to warm her room, it was cool, which in turn helped to cool her temper.

To her surprise, she discovered a white cat sitting in the middle of her bed, staring at her with pale blue eyes.

"Hello," Karigan said.

The cat stood and stretched, then leaped off her bed, darting past her legs through the doorway. Karigan peered into the corridor, but there was no sign of it.

"Strange," she murmured. Either the cat was phenomenally quick or she was seeing ghosts again. Ghost kitties? That was all she needed.

She shrugged. The comings and goings of the castle's mousers, supernatural or not, were the least of her worries. She would sit down and list all the things she would want along with her for her impending journey. It would help her keep her mind off both Alton and King Zachary.

KING ZACHARY'S TREASURE

The Huradeshian dancers wove circular patterns to the beat of drums and rattles, a strange stringed instrument whining in the background. Their dance was not dance as Estora and other Sacoridians knew it; a refined meeting of ladies and gentlemen moving in time to harmonic orchestral music. No, this was something quite different, their dance like a story unfolding in a foreign language that required interpretation. Sacoridians had no point of reference from which to understand it, and watching it proved disconcerting in its alienness, even uncomfortable.

The dancers wore animal masks decorated with feathers, antlers, and fur, some representing specific creatures, others without any semblance at all to the natural world. Many of the masks were nightmarish, sporting huge eyeballs and teeth, some slashed through with scarlet, like blood.

The male dancers wore little more than loincloths in addition to their masks. Even their feet were bare, leaving Estora to speculate whether or not they were cold on the stone floor. As they contorted their oiled bodies as though in the throes of some madness, the ritual tattoos of birds, serpents, and animals emblazoned across their chests and down their backs rippled to life across flexing muscles, and it occurred to Estora that maybe it was the tattoos that they were trying to make dance.

The ceaseless giggling and whispering of the ladies surrounding Estora was ignited by the sight of half-naked men. Evidently they were not put off by the masks or tattoos.

Some of the matrons had acquired a high color in their cheeks and were fanning themselves.

Her mother, in contrast, and other ladies of Coutre, had gone stiff, disgusted by the exposure of bare flesh. Her mother, in fact, had grabbed the hand of Estora's littlest sister and marched her out of the throne room the moment the Huradeshians began their dance, and gave her into the care of her nanny. Her mother then returned to her chair, disapproval etched into her features as if into stone, and sat. She remained, Estora knew, only because she was there at the king's invitation and did not wish to offend him.

The eastern provinces tended to hold to a more conservative view of life, their values rather strict and restricting. Estora had heard her father and others mutter about the decadent standards of those in Sacor City, and she was sure that King Zachary only confirmed their notions by allowing the Huradeshians to perform in such a "depraved" manner before decent people. A glance at her father sitting next to her mother revealed a stony countenance of dismay. Meanwhile, non-Coutre members of the audience appeared unoffended by the show of flesh, and even seemed to be enjoying the spectacle.

The female dancers were attired more modestly, wearing rough woven dresses dyed with colors so dazzling they overwhelmed Estora's eyes. They seemed to have taken on bird-type roles and fluttered about the male dancers, mirroring them, shadowing them, teasing them.

Tribal leader Yusha Lewend sat in a chair adjacent to Zachary's throne. Lewend and the other men of importance from his tribe wore a melding of traditional Huradeshian costume and Sacoridian attire: velvet frock coats with fine stitching over multihued shirts, trousers that matched the frock coats, their feet shod only with sandals. The ensemble was topped off with cloths wound around their heads and tied in intricate knots. One of Zachary's advisors, Colin Dovekey, explained that each of the knots was symbolic, but what they symbolized, he could not say.

"Barbarians," muttered Estora's cousin Richmont Spane, seated to her left.

"Handsome barbarians," said Amarillene, another of Estora's cousins, who could not stop ogling the dancers.

Richmont murmured something disparaging under his breath.

Lewend's escort of Huradeshian warriors stood near the far wall, their arms crossed over bare, brawny chests. They wore bright scarlet head cloths and long, curved blades hung at their sides. Their clothing, or lack thereof, deeply contrasted with the black cloth and leather of the king's Weapons, but astonishingly their watchful attitudes and stern expressions were nearly identical.

"Is it true," Amarillene asked Richmont, "that Chief Lewend offered the king a gift of fifty slave girls?"

Richmont shook his head. "Only twenty."

Amarillene squealed. "Did he accept them?"

Marilen, her older sister, nudged her. "Don't be ridiculous. Slavery is against king's law."

"*Did* he?" Amarillene persisted.

Richmont rolled his eyes. "No. To do so would have been scandalous to say the least."

Estora permitted herself a tiny sigh, wondering if the Huradeshians likewise considered the Sacoridians barbaric and strange. She wished the ladies behind her would stop their incessant giggling. It was most undignified. And annoying. Some elder Coutres passed the ladies looks of displeasure, but the hint went ignored.

She glanced in Zachary's direction. His expression was pensive as he watched the dancers. Did he even see them? She didn't think so, for his gaze seemed far away and she wondered what thoughts occupied him, but when the dancers finished and the music abruptly halted, he straightened and clapped along with everyone else. The dancers and musicians left the throne room at a trot.

Yusha Lewend rose from his chair and made a long speech in his own language. Since Estora understood none of it, her attention wandered. To her surprise, near the throne room doors, she saw the man she had met on the kitchen steps the morning she had exchanged unhappy words with Karigan. He was dressed in the same clothes as before, but from this distance she could not discern their flaws. He cut a sharp figure, angular and athletic, no excess to be found on his frame.

Estora placed her hand on Richmont's wrist and he bent toward her.

"Do you know that man?" she asked, pointing him out.

"Distant relative of Zachary's, I think. The name's Amberhill. Small landowner, impoverished. I suppose he's come around to ask his cousin for charity." With that, Richmont returned his attention to Yusha Lewend.

Amberhill. The name was unfamiliar to Estora, but that was hardly surprising, considering how many counted themselves among the ranks of nobility. It seemed like most of them had paraded through the castle to meet her since the betrothal announcement. Amberhill perceived her gaze and returned it, nodding at her with a smile.

Embarrassed that she had been caught staring, she returned her attention to Yusha Lewend. An interpreter had come forward, probably a merchant versed in a number of languages, and spoke in impeccable common tongue: "Most gracious king, we are honored by your hospitality. You have further honored us by recognizing our importance in your trade."

The interpreter droned on, interrupted periodically by Yusha Lewend to add some comment in praise of the king. Bored by the ostentatious speech, Estora's gaze strayed back to Amberhill, and when their gazes intersected, he mimed an exaggerated yawn. Estora stifled a laugh.

". . . and your fair queen-to-be," the interpreter said.

Estora blinked in surprise and found many pairs of eyes looking her way. She wondered what she had missed; what had been said about her. Did they notice she hadn't been paying attention?

"Sacoridia is certain to flourish with such beauty in its midst, and assuredly the king will soon find many children playing at his feet. May Methren, our goddess of fertility, embrace you."

Twittering from behind Estora made her cheeks warm.

Yusha Lewend then said something in his own tongue directly to King Zachary, and followed it with a hearty laugh. His people laughed as well.

The interpreter licked his lips and looked a little nervous. "Uh," he began, "Yusha Lewend believes you will not, uh, need much of the goddess' help to make children with your beautiful queen." Yusha Lewend slapped the interpreter on the back and barked something at him. The interpreter turned red. "Yusha Lewend wishes me to tell you exactly what he said, sire. May I approach the throne?"

Zachary nodded.

The interpreter did so hesitantly, and spoke in such low tones that only Zachary could hear. A mortified look actually crept over his features and his ears turned scarlet. Yusha Lewend laughed uproariously at his great joke, obviously something of a rather lewd nature.

"Please inform Yusha Lewend," Zachary said to the interpreter in a cool tone, "that this kind of talk is not acceptable in my court, not even in jest. I value all members of my court, including the women, and I would like that considered in all conversation."

An uncomfortable silence followed as the interpreter relayed Zachary's words. When he finished, Yusha Lewend looked baffled, but unoffended, and shrugged his shoulders.

"I don't see why Zachary has decided to entertain these crude beasts," Richmont murmured. "Instead of negotiating trade with them, he should just send some soldiers over and claim whatever it is he wants from them."

Estora sighed. Conquest was Richmont's answer to everything. "The ways of the Huradeshian people are not our own."

"That's because ours is a cultured, moral society."

"Our differences do not necessarily mean we are better than they, nor that we should start a war with them."

"War? Who said anything about war? We could just take what we need."

Estora shook her head. Her cousin would never see things in any other light, so there was no use in arguing with him.

During the reception that followed, servants wove among the guests offering food and wine. As usual, Estora was hemmed in by clinging ladies asking questions about wedding plans that she had grown heartily weary of answering. She did not feel like responding at all, but her mother had trained her well, and she maintained a smile—though it did not reach her heart—and responded to the questions with courtesy.

"What color will the gown be, my dear?" old Lady Creen asked.

"Cobalt, for the clan," Estora said.

"A harsh color for a bride." Several ladies nodded in agreement with Lady Creen.

"It is tradition in Coutre Province," Estora said. From the corner of her eye, she saw Zachary near the throne, his attention dominated by Yusha Lewend and a group of gentlemen. They were all staring at the ceiling. It was an almost comical sight until she realized he must be explaining the significance of the portraits of his predecessors painted there. Soon she too would sit there, beside Zachary on a queen's throne, with the rulers of the past peering down on her as if in judgment. Would she meet their approval? She shuddered.

Actually, she was more worried about what Zachary would think on their wedding night when he realized she wasn't—

"—picked a day yet?" Lady Creen inquired.

Estora brought her attention back to those who encircled her. "No, though the moon priests are leaning toward the summer solstice, Day of Aeryon."

There was much murmuring and nods of approval among the ladies. Again from the corner of her eye, she glimpsed the man Richmont had named Amberhill roving among loose groupings of people, a goblet in his hand, and a charming smile on his face as he greeted those he knew.

The ladies were discussing the advantages and disadvantages of a solstice wedding when Estora politely extricated herself and edged through the crowded throne room in a path she hoped would lead to Amberhill. Courtesy required her to pause and exchange greetings with those who wished to speak to her, but with a deftness acquired over a lifetime of banquets and receptions in her father's manor house, she was able to keep moving while appearing to be attentive to all she encountered. As she went, she overheard snippets of conversation.

"The price of silk has—"

"—heard that the council in D'Ivary has already chosen a successor—"

"I want to leave now."

"Rumor has it that the Raven Mask has returned to burgle—"

"—filthy barbarians coming half naked before decent folk."

Estora forged on, keeping her eye on Amberhill, but somehow he always managed to slip farther away. Then she came to a clearing near the fringes of the crowd, and she hurried, without seeming to, to approach him. He was currently engaged in conversation with two elderly ladies who were giggling and fanning themselves like schoolgirls. He had a devilish glint in his eyes as he regaled them with some tale.

Estora paused to consider why she was pursuing him like this. She supposed it was to thank him for his kindness that morning when Karigan upset her so. But inside, she knew it was more, that she was drawn by the mystery of who he was. His kindness and handkerchief would be an excuse to speak with him and learn more.

She lifted her skirts to approach him when someone touched her arm. "My lady?"

Estora turned to find Zachary beside her, accompanied by Yusha Lewend, his interpreter, and the most wrinkled crone she had ever seen. The crone gazed at her with one sharp green eye. The other was opaque with blindness. She clung to Yusha Lewend's arm, and was dressed in a more subdued fashion than the other Huradeshians, in somber grays. A round emerald stone tied around her neck with a leather thong was the only adornment she wore. The emerald matched her eye. Was this Yusha Lewend's mother? Estora curtsied.

"Yusha Lewend wishes to meet you," Zachary said, "and the lady is Meer Tahlid, a wisewoman of the tribe."

Estora nodded respectfully, which made the wisewoman smile broadly. Gold teeth glinted in the late afternoon sunshine that streamed through the tall windows. Yusha Lewend started rattling off something in his own tongue, and Estora glimpsed Amberhill on his way out of the throne room. Somehow aware of her gaze on him, he smiled at her before passing through the entrance.

"Yusha Lewend expresses that such beauty is rare and he is honored to be in its presence. A gift of your sun goddess, no doubt."

Estora jerked her attention back to those who stood before her. Astonishingly, Meer Tahlid started weaving back and forth, muttering, a hand held to her forehead and the other grasping her emerald. Both Zachary and Estora looked at her in alarm, but Yusha Lewend appeared unconcerned.

"The wisewoman can see many things ordinary souls cannot," the interpreter explained. "These seeings sometimes come on her suddenly."

Then, in a high-pitched voice, Meer Tahlid spoke in a rush. Both Yusha Lewend and the interpreter glanced at Estora. When the woman stopped weaving and speaking, she smiled again like a benevolent grandmother who had no idea of what just transpired.

The interpreter and Yusha Lewend conferred for a moment before the interpreter finally said to Zachary, "Meer Tahlid has had a seeing, Your Highness. She said you must guard your treasure well, for men are greedy and will want what does not belong to them."

"My . . . treasure?"

The interpreter gazed significantly at Estora. "Meer Tahlid saw that one would try to steal your lady from you."

Zachary gazed at Estora as if seeing her for the first time. "I will not permit that to happen."

Long after most of the castle's human inhabitants settled into their beds for a night of rest and dreaming, and most lamps along the corridors were extinguished or turned down to a low ambient glow, a white cat emerged from the dusty, unused corridor that joined the section being reinhabited by Green Riders.

At first all the activity had frightened the cat, who had watched from the shadows, around doorways, and from behind suits of armor, but being a cat, his fear was soon overcome by curiosity and so he investigated, over the course of weeks, this intriguing new world created by the Riders. Not only was it a feast to his senses of smell and hearing, but it was warm. If there were embers still burning in the common room's hearth and no Riders in sight, he'd settle down before it on the hearth rug, stretched out to his full length.

Tonight, however, there was another sort of warmth he sought.

When he arrived at the door, he found it slightly ajar. He butted it open with his head and slipped inside, pausing, his tail in a low sweep from side to side as he looked around. A candle next to the bed was close to sputtering out, and the human was sprawled under a blanket breathing deeply, an open ledger and some papers scattered atop her chest.

The cat rubbed his full body length against the corner post of the bedframe, then lightly jumped up, walking so carefully, as only cats can, that he did not rumple the papers or inadvertently awaken the human. He curled up on the human's long brown hair, which was splayed across the pillow. His brethren might catch more vermin down below and have full bellies by morning, but he preferred sleeping with the warm living humans rather than the cold husks of the dead.

The cat's eyes were beginning to close when suddenly he felt a tingling along his whiskers and down the fur on his back. A spirit was present in the room. Cats were very adept at sensing spirits, and this one regularly saw them wandering the castle and tombs, the living humans remarkably ignorant of their presence. How could they fail to notice something right in front of them? Humans were, the cat decided, very limited.

Sometimes the cat saw the spirits as solid entities, and sometimes only as mere points of light. This one materialized as a smoky figure that wavered in spectral air currents. A gold brooch gleamed on his chest and he carried a bow in his hands. There was some armor and other weapons, and a horn slung at his hip. He had the look of a Green Rider, but the cat really didn't care about any of that. To him, it was just another spirit among the many that inhabited the castle.

The spirit drifted in the air for a time, gazing down at the human in her bed, who snored away as obliviously as any of her kind in the presence of a ghost. What this one's purpose was, the cat could not divine. What prompted any spirit to haunt the living world when they could be resting peacefully instead? It was a mystery, but not one the cat wasted time puzzling over. To his mind, it was more imperative to find his next meal and decide where to take his afternoon nap.

But then the Green Rider ghost did something unusual, something none of the other spirits had ever done: he spoke to the cat. *I think,* he said, *you know what she is.*

The cat's eyes widened in surprise, but as the words faded, so did the spirit, its smoky form seeping away until the cat's whiskers no longer tingled.

The cat, of course, could not speak the human tongue, nor did he understand most of it, so the words of the spirit came to him as gibberish. That a spirit addressed him? Now that was curious, but not likely to change his life overmuch.

He yawned and stretched, more interested in sleep than the inscrutable ways of humans or their ghostly counterparts. All he knew was that he chose to sleep with this particular human because, though she was alive, there was something about her that was not so far removed from the dead, which made him feel right at home.

DEPARTURE

Karigan's breath fogged upon the crisp autumn air as she strode across the castle grounds toward the Rider stables with her saddlebags thrown over her shoulder and a bedroll and greatcoat tucked under her arm. Frosted grass crunched underfoot. The frost would melt off quickly as the morning sun rose above the castle walls.

She couldn't wait to ride, to escape the castle grounds, to move toward a goal and leave behind all the talk of wedding preparations. Distance would make everything easier. Distance would remove her from King Zachary and all the feelings he made roil within her. She would go away, and by the time she returned, she would be over him.

And maybe, just maybe, Alton would have come to his senses by then.

Now she wouldn't have to concern herself about either man. She had a journey ahead and tasks laid out before her. Each task would carry her farther away, and the day-to-day needs of her journey would occupy her thoughts. She never knew what a relief a message errand could be.

She rolled her shoulders to loosen the tension in them, her stride never slackening till she reached the Rider stables. Outside she found Connly helping Fergal Duff strap his saddlebags to the saddle on an older gray mare retired from the light cavalry, who stood dozing with eyes closed and nose sinking toward the ground.

"Morning, Karigan!" Fergal cried.

Though it wasn't terrifically early in the morning, his enthusiasm grated on her. "Morning," she replied, more subdued.

Connly straightened and slapped the mare on her neck. "Sunny's all ready, Fergal. Good luck on your first errand."

"Thank you, sir!"

"What brings you out this morning?" Karigan asked Connly.

He shrugged. "Just thought I'd help see you off. Since you've been filling in for Mara, someone has to fill in for you."

"True." The job of helping Riders off on message errands belonged to the Chief Rider, but since Mara was confined to the mending wing, the task had fallen to Karigan.

"Condor's all tacked up inside," Connly said, jabbing his thumb over his shoulder toward the entrance to stables.

"Thank you."

"Don't thank *me*," he said with an enigmatic smile. "I'm not the only one who came out this morning."

Curious, Karigan headed into the stable. It took a moment for her eyes to adjust to the gloom, but when they did, she found Condor hooked up to cross-ties in the center aisle, all groomed and tacked. Captain Mapstone cradled one of his hooves in her hands, inspecting it. Condor gave Karigan a perky whinny of greeting, and the captain released his hoof and straightened.

"Hello," Karigan said in surprise. It was unusual for the captain to see off any of her Riders. Usually she was too busy attending the king or sitting in on meetings.

The captain dusted her hands off on her trousers. "Good morning!"

"His hooves all right?" Karigan stroked the big chestnut's nose and he bobbed his head.

"Perfect. He's in fine fettle, and seems anxious for his journey to begin. Speaking of which . . ." And the captain smiled. "You wouldn't happen to have some space to spare in one of your saddlebags, would you?"

Karigan did not, for she had packed extra layers of clothes to contend with the colder weather, but she'd make room, for she could guess why the captain asked.

"Certainly," she said.

The captain's smile brightened. "Wonderful." She walked over to a bale of hay sitting against the wall and picked up a package bound in paper and string, as well as a message satchel. "Just a few things for Melry. Er, don't get it too near a campfire—there's some chocolate in it from Master Gruntler's."

Karigan chuckled. Melry, or Mel as the captain's adopted daughter preferred to be called, would be thrilled. Master Gruntler was the premier confectioner in Sacor City, and Mel often spent any currency she earned in his shop. Currently, Mel was attending Selium, and Karigan would be sure to visit with her there. She took the package from the captain and rummaged through one of her saddlebags to make room. She then hitched the bulging pouches to Condor's saddle and lashed on her bedroll.

The captain handed her the message satchel. The leather was well scarred and worn, but the emblem of the winged horse punched into its flap remained unmarred. Karigan crossed the strap over her shoulder so that the pouch fell comfortably against her right hip, opposite her saber.

"There's a letter for Melry in the satchel," the captain told her, "as well as the messages for lords Fiori and Mirwell, and the certificate of purchase for horses, which you will present to Damian Frost. Along your journey, Arms Master Gresia has asked that you run through some sword exercises with Fergal."

Karigan nodded.

"He's also written and mathematical exercises to keep him occupied during the evenings. Ty says he's coming along fine, but he should keep practicing. He'd like you to assist as you can."

Karigan resisted the impulse to sigh. While she knew this would be a training journey for Fergal, she hadn't expected to play the role of instructor. She reminded herself that most Riders, unlike herself, came to the messenger service without an education of any kind. If they were to bear the king's messages, they needed to learn courtly etiquette; to read, write, and figure; and to ride and fight. It was a lot to learn all at once, and Karigan had been fortunate to have good schooling behind her when she had finally answered the call. As she thought about it, it occurred to her that she knew nothing of Fergal's background, not even where he was from. She supposed she now had time to find out.

"Any questions?" the captain asked.

Karigan mulled it over for a moment. "I don't think so, but . . ."

"But?"

"If something should happen, if Mornhavon should return and magic were to become unreliable again . . ." The thoughts ran continuously in the back of her mind. *When* would he return? What would they do?

"The king and I trust your judgment, Karigan. If something does go awry, whether it's Mornhavon or something else entirely, and you feel it necessary to abort your mission and return, we will support your decision. Never fear that."

Karigan nodded, pleased by the implicit trust in her words. She unhitched Condor from the cross-ties and started to lead him out when the captain stopped her with a hand on her arm.

"One more thing. I realize you've been involved closely with all that has happened with the wall and Blackveil, but I don't want you to think of it as your personal responsibility. You've done this kingdom an astonishing service by securing us the time to prepare for Mornhavon's return. Free your heart of the weight of such concerns. If Mornhavon returns, he returns, and we will cope with it best as we can. In the meantime, you are a Green Rider with tasks set before her. Think only of those tasks, for others are shouldering the responsibility of coping with the threat Mornhavon poses."

It was an unusual speech from the captain, and only after hearing it did Karigan realize how much of the problem of Mornhavon and ending the threat he represented she had taken upon herself. The captain's words reassured her she wasn't alone, easing the burden. She could be an ordinary

Green Rider for once with delivering messages as her sole duty. And looking after Fergal, of course.

"Thank you," she said.

"It was never really yours to worry about in the first place—it's the responsibility of your king and his advisors. Trust me, one day when you're an officer, you'll have more than enough to worry about."

Karigan couldn't tell from the captain's expression whether or not she was joking. It had never even occurred to her to contemplate becoming an officer . . .

"You'd better get going," the captain said, gazing through the stable doors. "Fergal is mounted and looks ready to ride off without you."

Karigan led Condor outside where, indeed, Fergal sat astride Sunny, and in his eagerness, was trotting her around in circles.

"Leg up?" the captain offered.

Karigan dared not refuse the honor, and with the captain's help, swung up into the saddle.

"Safe journey," the captain said. "May Aeryc and Aeryon watch over you."

"Thank you," Karigan said, "and . . . and good-bye."

She reined Condor away from the stables and onto the pathway that led to the gates of the wall that surrounded the castle and its grounds. "Let's go," she told Fergal.

"Let's go" translated to Fergal as "let's gallop." He whooped in delight and dug his heels into Sunny's sides. The old cavalry horse's head jolted right up and she sprang down the path as though to charge the enemy on the field of battle.

"Oh, dear," the captain said behind Karigan.

Oh, dear was right. Karigan ground her teeth, and with a final wave to the captain and Connly, she urged Condor into a slow jog after Fergal. One did not gallop across castle grounds under any circumstances except in a dire emergency, and her first duty as Fergal's mentor would be to explain this to him. Or maybe the guards at the gate would chew him out for her. With that pleasant thought in mind, she smiled, pleased to be finally on her way.

Laren watched thoughtfully after Karigan and Condor. It seemed almost a waste to send one of her most capable Riders on so simple an errand, but the potential was there for it to turn out to be more complex than either she or the king anticipated, and they wanted Karigan on the errand because of her experience. If anything came up, she was confident Karigan could handle it, and look after Fergal, too.

And there was another reason she wanted Karigan to go on a long distance errand, one she hadn't mentioned to Zachary. Her gaze picked out a solitary figure atop the wall that surrounded the castle grounds, his cloak billowing out around him. He watched Karigan's progress, she knew.

Over the course of the summer, she had pieced together that the "mystery woman" who had been distracting Zachary from his kingly duty of signing Clan Coutre's marriage contract was one of her very own Riders and not some nameless mistress tucked away in the countryside of Hillander Province.

She didn't care if Zachary had a dozen mistresses, just so long as love did not divert him from doing the right thing: marrying Lady Estora and producing heirs. And just so long as one of those mistresses wasn't one of her Riders.

From what Laren could tell, the attraction was dangerously mutual, and she had observed Karigan struggling with herself. For Karigan's sake, it was best to send her away; a kindness. It would also give Zachary a chance to settle into his role of future husband to Lady Estora.

The country could not afford Zachary to be distracted by his love of a commoner—it could wreak havoc politically, and prove dangerous for Karigan. There were those who would stop at nothing to protect the Hillander-Coutre alliance. Were a commoner to interfere, there was no telling what harm could come to her no matter what her position in the king's court. Laren would do all in her power she could to keep them apart.

Then, if that wasn't enough, there was another matter she must address with Lady Estora—the secret they shared. The secret the Riders kept. It put Laren in an awkward position, caught between the wishes of her slain Rider, F'ryan Coblebay, and the trust of her liege lord.

She shook her head, wondering why everything had to be so bloody complicated.

TO THE HAWK'S TAIL

After Karigan and Fergal passed through the outermost city gate, Karigan reined in Condor and turned in her saddle to look behind her. While the nearness of the city wall blocked much of her view, the castle stood high enough on its hill, a small mountain really, that she had no trouble seeing its facade of bright stone against the morning sky. Tall and impregnable it stood, built by the same stonemasons who created the D'Yer Wall. The shingled roofs of the city stood gathered beneath its shadow before disappearing behind the wall.

"Be well," she whispered, unsure of whom she addressed. The city would take care of itself, she knew, and very suddenly she felt bereft, exiled from her friends. Now outside the gates, she might as well be a hundred miles from them.

She sighed and turned away from the city only to find Fergal watching her expectantly. Being shouted at by the guards at the castle gates had not diminished his enthusiasm in the least. Karigan had informed him that not only did one not charge one's horse across castle grounds, but there was generally no reason to rush through town, especially with all the traffic. She refused to let him trot, more out of perversity than anything else, so he challenged her order by urging Sunny into a fast walk, constantly nosing her ahead of Condor.

Sunny now had an annoyed look in her eye and shifted her stance with a definitive swish of her tail. She was probably wondering what she had done to deserve this young wiggly creature on her back instead of a highly trained cavalryman. If Fergal kept kicking her and yanking on the reins, he might get himself bucked off. The thought did not dismay Karigan in the least.

Carts rumbled around them toward the city bearing goods for market day. Farmers carried the last of the season's harvests, including whole cartloads of bright orange pumpkins, ripe apples, and milled grain.

"You know," Karigan said, watching another cart roll by, this one full of wine casks, "if you hadn't been so eager to hurry out of the city, I could have shown you some shortcuts that would have gotten us here much sooner."

The Winding Way, the main thoroughfare through Sacor City, roped around the city in lazy turns from the gates all the way up to the castle, intended by the engineers to foil the progress of an invading army. The Riders, and most city dwellers, knew how to cut down travel time by using side streets and alleys. While invaders could potentially use those same side streets, their narrowness would cause an entire army to jam up.

"Oh," was all Fergal said.

Karigan pursed her lips. They were not off to a good start. For some reason Fergal just rubbed her the wrong way. Maybe she resented his eagerness, or maybe she just wasn't meant to mentor new Riders. This was the sort of thing Ty was good at, not her.

She took a deep breath. "This is the Kingway," she said, indicating the road ahead, "and we'll follow it all the way to Selium."

"Wahoo!" Fergal cried, and he and Sunny were off in a cloud of dust.

Karigan rolled her eyes and decided she would sit and wait until he realized she hadn't followed him.

It was quite a while before Fergal realized he was alone, for the bells in the city rang off two cycles before he returned at a trot, Sunny's neck all lathered. Karigan sat beside the road chewing on a stalk of grass, her back against a maple and her legs stretched out before her. She had loosened Condor's girth and replaced his bridle with a halter so he could graze.

Fergal's cheeks were flushed, but that could have been from the exertion of the ride and not contrition.

"Where were you?" he sputtered.

No, not contrition.

"Why weren't you with me?" he demanded. "I had to come all the way back."

Karigan pushed herself up from the ground. "Dismount."

"What?"

"Dismount," she said evenly, "and that's an order."

Perplexed, Fergal obeyed.

"Loosen Sunny's girth."

"But—"

"That's an order, too."

He complied, but still did not understand. "Why?"

"All I can figure is that you've ignored everything Horsemaster Riggs has tried to teach you," Karigan said. "Being a messenger isn't about galloping off into the horizon. Yes, it's about the efficient delivery of the king's messages, but not at the expense of your steed. You've already spent Sunny. Look at the lather on her neck! Now you must walk her to cool her off."

"But—"

"If you can't follow basic orders, orders that have been repeated to you, and if you can't put to use what you've learned, then I'll have no choice but to escort you back to the castle where you can explain yourself to Captain Mapstone. Perhaps you will even have to go before the king to tell him why his messages were delayed."

Fergal blanched. "But I thought—"

"Doesn't matter what you thought." Karigan almost hoped he gave her reason to return him to the castle. "Your horse is your lifeline, not just a . . . a slave to bear you from here to there. As a messenger, you've entered into a partnership with your horse, and first consideration must go to your mount."

"But she's not a real messenger horse—"

Karigan looked from Fergal to Sunny, and back, and restrained an impulse to swat the lad. "She's carrying a messenger, isn't she? Looks like a messenger horse to me."

"But—"

Karigan guessed he had heard a good deal about how special Rider horses were, how greathearted they were, and of the special bonds that developed between Rider and horse. He clearly saw Sunny as something inferior. She stepped over to Sunny and rubbed her above the eye. The mare leaned into Karigan's strokes.

"No, Sunny did not start out life as a Rider horse," Karigan said, "but she is highly trained, and gave her heart to her work, as I know she will on this errand if you treat her well. She's seen battle, and is seasoned and reliable. You can't ask for much better than that. Respect your horse, and she will respect you."

For once Fergal had the sense to keep his mouth shut, but he looked miffed.

"Foolishly setting off at a gallop for no reason will exhaust your horse sooner, maybe make her pull up lame, and shorten your day's travel. How does that help you serve your king?"

Fergal looked down at his feet. "Sorry," he mumbled.

"Don't apologize to me," Karigan said. "Apologize to Sunny."

She could see Fergal's reluctance, but he patted the mare on the neck, though half-heartedly.

"Now, shall we return to Captain Mapstone, or are you ready to go about this the right way?" she asked.

"You would actually do that? I mean, make me go back?"

"Yes. You're compromising the errand."

Fergal shifted his eyes nervously and Karigan sensed the shame he'd feel in returning. "I'll do things . . . right. I swear."

Karigan suppressed a sigh. She wasn't sure her point had been driven home, but she was stuck with him for the time being. "All right, now we walk." She took Condor's lead rope and started strolling down the Kingway. Fergal just stood in place, staring after her, mouth open as if to protest, but at

Karigan's stern look, he drew Sunny's reins over her head and fell in behind.

As Karigan followed the road through the small collection of cots a short distance outside the city gates, she wished she had known more about Fergal before setting out. The glimpses she'd had of him in the castle were of an eager boy ready to please. What she saw now was one with a rebellious streak she didn't understand. Some of it was the excitement of being on his first errand, and some of it could just be his age. She hoped he'd prove more sensible for the duration of their journey.

A journey barely begun. She gave a preoccupied wave to some of the farmers at work in their fields. Not that she had always made sensible decisions in her own life. One of those decisions landed her in the messenger service. That and the call, of course. She strode on with a chuckle.

For the remainder of the day, Fergal was in a sullen mood, speaking little and riding behind her. Karigan put his behavior down to adolescence and shrugged it off. If he didn't want to talk, that was just fine with her. She would enjoy traveling in the company of her own thoughts.

She paced their ride with long stretches of walking interspersed with trotting. Fergal did not attempt any more gallops, not even a canter. Maybe his lessons with Riggs, and her reprimand, had finally sunk in. If they were to make any headway, maintaining the endurance of their horses was of the utmost importance.

Fortunately, the Kingway was an easy ride, a well-maintained road of level stretches and gentle rises. Trees shaded it, and they passed through villages where they watered the horses in public troughs. Villagers politely requested the latest news from the city, mostly about the king's betrothal, much to Karigan's chagrin. The brief rests also gave the Riders a chance to stretch and stamp out their stiff legs. If the prolonged riding was causing Fergal discomfort, he did not complain.

Villages and woodlands were interspersed with rolling

farmland bordered by stone fence lines. Most of the crops had been hauled in by now and many activities centered around winter preparations: a pair of boys cutting through logs with a cross cut saw, their father splitting the wood with his ax while girls stacked the firewood in a neat pile near their little cot.

At another farm with many apple trees, children jostled the red fruit from the upper branches for their mother who caught them in her apron. Upon seeing the Riders, the farmwife and children presented them and the horses with some delicious samples.

Fergal's sullen demeanor softened with the gift, and the children chattered at him in their excitement to see a real Green Rider. He gave them rides on Sunny, while Karigan traded predictions with the farmwife about the winter to come.

Farther on, others tended livestock and repaired shingles on roofs while a lucky hunter rumbled by with a stag in his cart. Squirrels scolded the Riders from the branches above and it seemed at times they purposely dropped spruce cones on their heads.

Karigan liked autumn, she decided, while crunching a tart apple. The air was sharp and fresh, not too warm and not too cold, and the sky clear. The deciduous trees of the countryside were afire with bright yellows, oranges, and reds, contrasting with the deep greens of spruce and pine. Blueberry bushes, now past their fruit-bearing season, were clumps of crimson along the road's edges. The horses' hoof falls were softened by rusty pine needles and colorful leaves matting the road.

Dusk was settling in by the time they reached the village of Deering. Despite Fergal's transgressions of the morning, they made acceptable time. The village was carved out of the forest, this the southern fringe of the mighty Green Cloak. Mostly it served wayfarers and woodsmen with a mercantile, a farrier's forge, a pair of inns, a wheelwright's shop, and a humble chapel of the moon made of stone.

"We usually stay at the Hawk's Tail," Karigan said. The

other inn, the Red Pony, was a little rougher, primarily serving woodsmen, while the Hawk's Tail received more custom from wayfarers.

The Hawk's Tail was a homely house with a sign hanging over the front door featuring a red-tailed hawk with open beak. Lanterns hanging outside on posts, and lamps lit within, made a cheery welcome that was augmented by the mixed scents of good things cooking and baking inside.

"Why don't you check if they have rooms for us," Karigan told Fergal, "and then you can meet me in the stables."

Fergal's eyes widened in surprise that she would allow him such a responsibility. She dug into her message satchel and passed him a seal bearing the winged horse insignia of the messenger service. Riders didn't carry enough currency to pay for every lodging or each supply purchased, but instead sealed documents that the proprietors could present at tax time for redemption.

Fergal glanced at the seal in his hand, then clenched his fingers around it. He dismounted and clambered up the inn's front steps and went inside. Karigan led both horses behind the inn and into the stable's courtyard. A stablehand pointed out a couple stalls she could use. First she untacked the horses, and then started rubbing down Condor with her currycomb. He groaned with pleasure and leaned into her circular strokes. Soon the grime worked out of his hide and the sweat marks left by his saddle disappeared. She had kept their pace at a walk for the last mile or so, so they wouldn't be overwarm when they reached the inn.

Next she checked up and down Condor's legs, examining him for any signs of swelling or lameness. None. Then she picked out his hooves and inspected them. All was well, and she let him loose into the paddock for a good roll.

She turned to Sunny who gazed expectantly at her. Where was Fergal? He should have been out by now to tend his horse.

Karigan made a disparaging sound and started caring for Sunny as she had Condor. Once she released the mare into the paddock and instructed the stablehand on their feeding, she burdened herself with both her saddlebags and Fergal's and entered the inn.

The innkeeper, Jolly Miles, greeted her courteously and said, "Your lad is in the common room."

By now fuming, she clattered into the common room. A friendly fire crackled in a big stone hearth. Some merchants sat near it, smoking pipes and playing at Knights. Fergal sat at another table with a man and was sawing away at a hunk of bread to dip in the gravy slathered over his mutton and potatoes. He looked to be on his second tankard of ale.

Without a word she strode over to his table and glared down at him. A ripple of shame, and maybe a little fear, moved across his features. Karigan dumped his saddlebags at his feet. The noise made Fergal flinch and drew the attention of the merchants from their cards.

The man sitting with Fergal, who was quite drunk if his blurry eyes and red nose were any indication, elbowed Fergal. "Hooz this un, young Ferg'l? Sweet she is." And he sniggered.

"Um . . ." was all Fergal said.

"Rooms?" Karigan demanded.

"Upstairs," he said, pointing vaguely behind him.

"I know they're upstairs. The only rooms here are upstairs."

The sullen look crept back into Fergal's face.

"What's wrong with you? I told you to meet me at the stables." The drunkard sniggered again and she glared at him. *"To tend the horses."*

Fergal shrugged. "I was thirsty is all."

"Horses first," she said. "Horses *always* first." His indifference grated on her. Why had he been called to be a Rider when he held so little regard for his office?

The drunkard hiccupped. "Whassa matter, honey, this li'l boy not man enough for ya?" He smiled and staggered to his feet, opening his arms wide. "I can show ya what a real man's like."

Karigan ignored him. "Fergal, grab your bags and come upstairs."

When he just sat there glowering into his ale, she said,

"Now." When this failed to produce results, she grabbed his collar and hauled him out of his chair.

"Let go!" His voice held a whiney tone to it.

The merchants were laughing at him. Flushing, Fergal straightened his shortcoat and grabbed his saddlebags.

"Ya need a man, not this runt," the drunkard proclaimed.

"Shut up, you stupid ass," Fergal muttered.

"Leave it," Karigan said. "There's no use in—"

"Whad ya say?" the drunkard demanded, grabbing Fergal's elbow. "Whad ya call me?"

"Stupid ass, or are you deaf, too?"

"Fergal!" Karigan said in dismay. Some drunks were harmless, and some weren't. She didn't think this man was the former.

"I'll teach ya to be more polite, boy." Unsteady on his feet, the drunk rolled up his sleeves and drew both hands into fists. "Come in here with yer fancy uniform an' all, thinkin' yer better than anyone."

"Fergal," Karigan said in low warning, "come on."

"Li'l runt," the drunk said.

Fergal's expression darkened and his body went rigid.

"Oh no," Karigan murmured. She went to grab him, but he threw his saddlebags down and launched himself on the drunk. Both went crashing to the floor. Innkeeper Miles rushed in at the clamor, and both he and Karigan stepped in to pull the combatants apart. Karigan hauled on Fergal's shortcoat, and he rose still swinging, his nose bloody.

Miles pushed the drunk away, speaking placatingly to him.

"I'll kill you!" Fergal cried.

"Try it, runt!"

Fergal surged in Karigan's grip, and when she shook him, he turned on her, swinging.

THE KNACKER'S BOY

Karigan sat on the edge of the bed and dabbed the wet cloth at the bulging welt on her temple and winced. Fergal had slugged her hard and her whole head throbbed. When she pulled the cloth away, there was a spot of blood on it. Fergal sat in a chair opposite her, staring morosely at his knees. His nosebleed had cleared up quickly, and though his nose would be puffy and red for a couple days, it didn't look broken. He was lucky.

"Would you care to explain yourself?" Karigan's voice sounded tired even to herself.

"No."

"That was an order, Rider. Not really a question."

Fergal glanced at her and quickly averted his gaze. "He—he made me mad."

Karigan waited for more, but Fergal offered nothing. "That's it?"

He nodded.

Karigan sighed and started to stand, but it increased the throbbing in her head, so she stayed her seat. "You do realize we're lucky that Innkeeper Miles hasn't cast us out tonight, don't you?"

Fergal nodded.

"Look, I don't understand what is going on with you, but you are a king's messenger now. When you wear this uniform, you are acting on his behalf, you are his voice. Do you think you represented the king well tonight?"

Fergal shook his head.

"There were some merchants who viewed this whole spectacle, just a few of them, but merchants travel and they gossip. I should know." She had been the brunt of such gossip herself. People still pointed her out as the girl who rode her horse naked all the way to Darden—never mind she had been wearing a nightgown at the time. "The story of a Green Rider attacking a drunkard will undoubtedly get passed around, and the story will change and grow. Who knows what they'll say? In any case, it will not reflect well on other Riders or the king. At this point I don't care if you'd have been beaten senseless, except that you were in an official capacity as a Green Rider."

Fergal's shoulders slumped.

"Furthermore," Karigan continued, feeling supremely old after delivering so many lectures in one day, "you failed to return to the stable to assist with your horse. I'm not sure what I have to do to drive it into your head that your horse is your first priority."

"She's just meat."

"What?" Karigan wasn't sure she had heard him correctly. Maybe hc had rattled her brain when he hit her.

"Meat."

"Meat?"

Fergal nodded.

Karigan's head was throbbing more than ever, and an absurd image of Fergal saddled up on a giant prime roast came to mind. She shook her head—the evening had become surreal. "And here I thought you were riding a horse."

Fergal shifted uncomfortably in his chair. "You wouldn't understand."

Karigan rinsed her cloth in the bowl of cold water, listening to the drips and splashes, trying to gather her thoughts. "Perhaps," she said, placing the cloth back against the lump, "you could try and explain it. Help me understand."

Fergal's expression darkened and she hoped he wasn't about to explode with another violent outburst. Really, she didn't know what to expect from him with these mood swings. Had Captain Mapstone known what he was like when she assigned him to her? Had any of them known?

"Fergal—"

"My da's a knacker, all right? I watched him slaughter horses like Sunny all the time. Horses people got rid of quick 'cause they no longer were quite young enough, or pretty enough, or 'cause their owners needed money bad. Might not be anything wrong with 'em at all, and they were brought in every day. Meat. Meat my da used to throw to the dogs just to see them fight." Tears formed around his eyes and he swiped at them with his sleeve.

Incredulous, Karigan didn't know what to say.

"Cav horses ended up at my father's all the time," Fergal said. "Just a little old like Sunny, but nothing wrong with them. They'd end up as bits of meat, bone, and hair." He gazed directly at her. "My da made me work for him."

With that, he stood and ran from the room, slamming the door behind him. Karigan winced as the sound richocheted through her sore head. She pulled her legs onto the bed and lay down, staring at the cracked ceiling, dumbfounded.

How horrible to see that slaughter daily, she mused. *Especially of healthy animals.* She wondered how people could do such a thing to creatures that had served their human counterparts innocently and honestly. *We repay them not with our gratitude, but with the slaughterhouse.*

Would Sunny have been sent to the knacker if the messenger service hadn't needed her? Karigan shuddered. She didn't want to know. Messenger horses retired with their Riders, and it was up to each individual Rider what became of them. Considering the close partnership between horse and Rider, she could not imagine any messenger horse dying at the knacker's. When the time came for retirement, she would provide Condor with the most comfortable life possible.

As for Fergal, at least she now understood his regard, or disregard, for Sunny. He had taught himself not to grow attached to animals because the only end for them he ever saw was slaughter. Karigan could not imagine growing up in such an environment.

* * *

The next morning Karigan ate a hearty breakfast of sausages and fry cakes in the inn's common room, Fergal nowhere in sight. No matter, today they would return to Sacor City. She had thought it over through the night and decided Fergal was not yet ready even for a training run, that he was just too volatile and could not yet represent the king properly.

Her decision was reinforced when she saw the sickly bruised bump on her temple in the mirror in the morning light. The bruise had spread in a half circle around her eye and looked just lovely.

She drank the last of her tea and grabbed her saddlebags from the floor. She supposed she would have to ready the horses by herself.

She stepped out into the courtyard between the inn and stables, her stride faltering when she saw two horses standing there, their coats shining in the morning sun. The sight took a moment to register—not only were their coats at high gloss, but their manes and tails were combed out, every snarl, every bit of straw, and every burr removed. Their tack had been thoroughly cleaned and oiled, and the silver polished so that it sparkled. Even the green saddle blankets had had the sweat and horsehair brushed out of them.

Karigan stepped closer and saw that fetlocks and whiskers were trimmed and eye goo wiped away. Condor arched his neck as though a parade horse showing off his good looks, and Sunny had a horsy look of contentment on her face. The intensive grooming had brought a glow to her coat that made her dapples gleam.

Karigan set aside her saddlebags and inspected Condor's hooves. They'd been thoroughly cleaned and picked. She released his last hoof in astonishment.

The stablehand stood watching her.

"You do this?" she asked.

"Nope, the lad did." He nodded his head toward the stable, and Karigan saw Fergal there, standing in the shadows, looking at the ground, hands in pockets. "Been here since dawn bathing and grooming and polishing. Did a good job."

"Yes," Karigan admitted, "he did."

Fergal came out into the sun, still unable to look her in the eye. His shirttails flopped out of his trousers and his chin was smudged with dirt.

"I'm sorry. Last night . . . yesterday. I didn't mean to hit you—I swear. I was just so angry at that old drunk. I'll never do that again." Finally their eyes did meet, and she saw the desperation in his. "Please don't make me go back; please—I don't want to be sent back to my da. I'll do better, I promise."

There was more than desperation in his eyes; there was fear.

Apparently Fergal didn't understand the nature of the Rider call; that he couldn't be forced to return to his father unless it released him. Karigan wasn't sure she wanted to enlighten him, thinking she could use his fear to help keep him in line, if necessary, sparing her further trouble. She touched the tender bruising around her eye and winced, his explosive behavior all too fresh in her memory.

"Have you had breakfast yet?" she asked him. When he shook his head, she said, "Please go inside and get some, and wash up."

She watched him as he shuffled off, looking decidedly beaten. Karigan was not gifted with Captain Mapstone's ability to read truth or falsehood in another person's words, but her years growing up in a merchant clan helped her judge character, a talent even King Zachary had made use of in his dealings with petitioners. As far as she could tell, Fergal was being honest with her and would not repeat his mistakes. That he had apologized unbidden was another point in his favor.

She also admired the amount of work he put into grooming Condor and Sunny. Not only did it result in a pair of gleaming horses that looked more ready for a parade than an ordinary message errand, but his efforts also served as a peace offering. A peace offering to her? To Sunny? *Himself?* Maybe all three. In any case, it was a gesture she appreciated very much.

She patted Condor on the rump. "I guess we're stuck with him."

A SHIMMERING IN THE WOODS

After breakfast when Karigan told Fergal that he was to continue riding west and that she was not going to return him to Sacor City, his relief was so palpable that she almost felt guilty about her previous plans.

He remained quiet as they rode, and followed her instructions to perfection, not pulling any of the previous day's mischief. They continued at a steady rhythm, alternating long walks with long trots. It was a fine autumn day with golden leaves drifting down around them and chickadees fluttering in the branches along the road. Brassy blue jays could be heard bellowing above the clip-clop of hooves.

They encountered a few travelers heading east, the wheels of carts following well-established ruts in the road. During the reign of Queen Isen, major portions of the Kingway had been paved with cobbles, but since the work was left to local authorities, there were long stretches of road between towns and villages that remained dirt tracks through the woods.

By midday, Karigan called a halt so they could rest and have a bite to eat. She found a grassy carriage turn-around next to a stream and they dismounted. Fergal pleased her by immediately turning his attention to Sunny, loosening her girth, and replacing her bridle with a halter so she could graze and drink.

Karigan couldn't say whether he cared for her out of growing affection or duty. She hoped he at least began to view the mare as something more than "meat," but it was probably too soon to expect too much.

She tended Condor, then led him to the stream for a drink. When the horses were all settled, the Riders removed from their saddlebags strips of dried meat and fresh-baked bread Innkeeper Miles had supplied them with, and the apples given to them by the farmwife the previous day.

They sat in silence on boulders, the only immediate sounds that of the gurgling stream and the horses pulling at grass and swishing their tails. Karigan found she could no longer abide the silence, and after sloshing some water down her throat, she asked, "You feeling the long ride? Are you sore?"

"It's not bad," he mumbled.

"That's good." Karigan racked her brain for another way to initiate conversation. "Where are you from?"

"Arey Province."

"That's a long way."

Fergal nodded.

Karigan waited for him to tell her of his travels, how he managed the journey from the northeast corner of Sacoridia and across the Wingsong Mountains, but he volunteered nothing.

She sighed and tore at her bread. It was clear he didn't feel like talking.

They rode in silence until the evening hours set in. This time they were not near a village or an inn, nor were there any Rider waystations nearby. Populations ebbed and flowed over the eons, and Karigan guessed that during the era of waystation construction, there had been villages or farmsteads in the area that could house a Rider, but they had disappeared with time. It left stretches of road without shelter for wayfarers between villages.

Karigan searched the edge of the road for a trail leading to a campsite Ty once showed her. As time went on and she couldn't find the signs, she feared she had missed it completely. Then they came upon a massive boulder with tongues of tripe lichen growing on it that looked like strips of peeling brown paint.

In the boulder's shadow was a cairn of rocks marking the trail. She reined Condor onto it, ducking beneath low-hanging branches. The world muted around them as the woods closed in, the horses' hoof falls muffled by a deep carpet of pine needles and moss. The air thickened with moldering leaf litter and the darkness deepened.

The horses picked their way over tree roots that arced and snaked across the trail, and clipped hooves on the occasional rock. The trail went on at length before opening up at the shore of a lake. The air freshened like a wave falling over them.

Karigan raised her hand so Fergal wouldn't speak, and she pointed at a bull moose wading through the shallows. Water rippled away from his stiltlike legs, lighter lines against water that reflected the darkening sky.

The moose dipped his nose into the water after cattail tubers. The water poured off his muzzle when he raised his head. Chewing on vegetation, he shambled toward shore, a giant bearing a majestic crown, and vanished into the woods, never hurrying; regal despite his ungainly size.

Karigan glanced at Fergal, realizing that moose must be even more common in Arey and he undoubtedly saw them as . . . meat. His features fell in shadow and she could not read them.

"Probably looking for a mate," she said quietly.

"Probably."

They tended their horses and while Karigan collected wood and laid it in a charred stone ring a previous camper had built, Fergal squatted at the edge of the lake staring into it, or so she thought. Suddenly he jerked and pulled and there was much splashing. He whooped in delight. To Karigan's astonishment, he grabbed a large, silvery fish by the gills, pulled it out of the water, and held it up for her to see.

"We will have trout tonight!" he proudly declared.

Karigan was impressed. He showed her his fishing kit of string and odd hooks wrapped with colorful threads, which he claimed looked like the bugs the trout liked to eat. Having grown up on the coast, Karigan's experience with the tools of fishing ranged from heavy deep-sea hooks, to nets, weirs, traps, and harpoons. Not that she engaged in fishing herself, but she had spent enough time on the wharves of Corsa Harbor to have known the men and women who fished for a living. If her father had not fled Black Island when he was a boy to seek his fortune elsewhere, she supposed she would have grown up to be a fishwife. The thought was not an appealing one.

After Fergal caught a second monster of a fish, he chopped off their heads and gutted them with expert, deft strokes, then extracted the bones. When he finished, he rummaged through his saddlebags and produced little sacks of spices which he sprinkled liberally onto the fish. He left them in their skins, and wrapped them in leaves to cook among the coals of the fire Karigan had started.

"Learned to fish when I got sick of horse meat," Fergal said, the flames playing in his eyes as he poked the coals with a stick. "My da thought it was fine when he didn't have to feed me."

Karigan waited to hear more about Fergal's da, the knacker, but he said no more and seemed content to watch the fire. She wasn't going to press him, considering his actions of the previous night.

The trout, when it finished cooking, tasted better than anything Karigan had ever eaten. Or maybe it was just the alchemy of the cold air and the stars shining above that made it taste so good. Whatever it was, she hoped Fergal had opportunities to catch more trout along their journey.

"It was a long way from Arey," Fergal said unexpectedly, as though there had been no intervening time between midday, when she tried to draw him out, and now. Maybe it was the companionability of the meal and campfire that inspired him to speak, or the time had simply come. Karigan dared not interrupt for fear he'd withdraw again.

"I thought I was running away from my da," Fergal continued. "I wanted to often enough, but it turns out I wasn't really running away, but running *to* Sacor City because of the call. It came on me fast, so I didn't take too much with me.

Just the clothes I was wearing and my fishing gear. One minute I'm washing down the floor in the shop, the next I'm running out the door all sudden like. Didn't know where I was going at the time, but I always seemed to want to head west. Slept in barns, under trees, in abandoned cots. Sometimes there was just the stars, like tonight." He laughed. "Good thing it was summer."

He went on to describe how he had worked his way west in exchange for food, and had even hitched up with a merchant's caravan coming over the mountains. Sometimes he'd fished if there was a stream or lake along the route, or built traps with his own hands to snare small animals. Karigan found herself impressed with how he'd made his way, surviving by virtue of his own ingenuity.

"I was hungry and cold some of the time," he said. "It wasn't bad though. Folks were good to me—far better than my own da, but I couldn't stay anywhere long. I had to keep going till I reached Sacor City. And now to be a Rider—that's like heaven!"

Karigan could see that being a Rider was a definite improvement over the knacker's shop. He didn't have to go into detail about his life with his father for her to make guesses about how hellish it must have been. Despite his harsh life, he'd shown himself as resourceful and clever during his journey to Sacor City, which only made sense since Green Riders shared such traits.

"Thank you for telling me about your journey," she told him, and she meant it.

He glanced sharply at her as if expecting to be mocked or lectured, but then nodded and relaxed when she remained silent.

A pair of raccoons hissed at one another over the fish guts, which Fergal had dumped by the shore. Better raccoons than bears, Karigan thought, though they were making enough of a ruckus to be mistaken for bears. Eventually they sorted out their dispute and toddled off with the offal, one casting the Riders a bandit-faced glance, the firelight catching in its eyes before it vanished into the night.

The raccoon reminded Karigan of the masked thief she had fought in the Sacor City War Museum. She had not thought much of him since their encounter—she hadn't had time!—but now her thoughts strayed to him, and she wondered what he wanted with a bit of ancient parchment. It seemed beneath him somehow. She'd expect him to be more interested in jewels and gold. Maybe, as Mara suggested, the parchment gave directions to a hidden treasure.

She shrugged. Sacor City was miles away, and she would never know what value the thief placed on his plunder. That would be for the constabulary to figure out, but somehow she didn't think they'd ever catch him.

With the raccoons gone and Fergal staring into the fire, the night grew quiet, except for the hiss of flames and gentle lap of waves upon the shore. If loons called this lake home, they were long gone, well on their way out to sea for the winter. It made the lake seem desolate, knowing she would not hear their haunting calls this night.

"I'll take first watch," Fergal offered.

"You're welcome to watch if you like," Karigan said, "but unless it's a dangerous situation, there's really no need. Remember, when you're finished with training, you'll be on the road by yourself, and you won't be able to watch all the time. You'll need to sleep."

"Oh."

Karigan smiled to herself as she unrolled her bedding, thinking how nice it was to be on an ordinary message errand, without outlaws pursuing her or supernatural forces influencing her. There was always the chance of encountering a bandit or the stray groundmite, but this far from the border she wasn't too worried.

"I just thought . . ." Fergal began.

"Yes?"

"Well, I just thought it would be more . . . more exciting than this."

Karigan wondered what stories he had heard. "Be happy when it is this ordinary and peaceful. Running for your life is not fun." She sat on her bedding and pulled off her boots.

"Is it true . . . ?"

"Is what true?"

"All they say about you."

"It depends. What are they saying?"

"About how you defeated that Eletian and how you pushed Mornhavon into the future."

Karigan sighed. "I was involved in those things. Look, Fergal, as messengers, our main job is to deliver the king's word, and that can be dangerous enough on its own. Messengers face blizzards and have accidents and encounter cutthroats. Some have their lives cut short by angry message recipients. Others have died in battle." When Fergal appeared skeptical, she added, "Mara lost fingers when some cutthroats tried to rob her and Tegan nearly got caught in a deadly snowstorm. Just this summer, the ship Connly was sailing on went aground on a deserted island. Don't wish anything extra to come down on you—an ordinary errand can be hazardous enough, and remember, we've only just begun this journey."

Karigan drifted off to sleep that night not sure he was convinced. It was the difference, she reminded herself, between a seasoned Rider and a green Greenie.

Maybe it was a cold breeze seeping beneath Karigan's blanket, or maybe it was a quiet whicker from Condor that warned her, but her hand went immediately to the hilt of her saber, which she always kept beside her when she slept. Her eyes fluttered open to a dazzling array of stars piercing the heavens above, the constellations framed by the spires of jagged spruce and pine.

All was still, their campfire burned down to dull, orange embers. Fergal was a dark lump of bundled blankets on the ground across the fire ring. The horses were peaceful enough, though Condor gazed at her with shining eyes.

What woke me up?

Carefully she raised herself to her knees, her blanket

falling away from her shoulders. A shiver spasmed through her body. She looked around, searching the darkest shadows of night, her senses honed to a knife's edge as she tried to discern what had awakened her.

Then a flicker of light among the trees on the far shore caught the edge of her vision. It was gone as quickly as it came. Had she really seen it? Then there was another shimmer, this time closer, and as quick as the blink of an eye.

It was much too late in the season for fireflies.

She waited, tense, forcing herself to breathe. It wasn't the light that came upon her again, but voices in song, achingly beautiful voices singing in a language she did not understand, though enchanting enough that she could guess who sang it: Eletians. Eletians were passing through the woods.

She drew her saber.

Light—many lights—came to life among the trees, flaring between tree trunks across the cove from where Karigan and Fergal camped, glancing on the still surface of the lake. Dewdrops clinging to the tips of pine needles glistened. Figures, some on horseback, some afoot, shone in the silvery glow of moonstones, moonstones held like lanterns on the ends of poles and shrouded by colorful shades. Some Eletians held moonstones on their palms before them, like acolytes bearing candles down the aisle of a chapel of the moon.

The moonstone lights were reflected in the black surface of the lake like stars. Karigan, unable to move from her knees, watched in wonder, a supplicant before these godly beings.

The Eletians' passage was silent but for their song. If they knew of Karigan's presence, none changed course to approach her.

She thought their procession solemn, but discerned laughter amid their singing. Then, with a surge that went through her heart and nearly made her lose hold of her saber, she recognized her name in the song. As she listened more closely, she gleaned some understanding of the words, an understanding in her heart, though the language was foreign.

* * *

Galadheon, Galadheon, far from home,
Galadheon, Galadheon, we've roused you from your dreams,
What far lands shall you roam
Beneath the stars that gleam?

Galadheon, Galadheon, put down your sword,
Galadheon, Galadheon, you must sleep,
You must carry your king's word,
What secrets do you keep?

Karigan drew her eyebrows together. The singing grew more distant and here and there lights extinguished.

Galadheon, Galadheon, save your sword,
For the storm shall come another day,
Now we must be on our way, Galadheon,
East we must go, a-journeying we roam

Put your head down to rest, Galadheon,
Put your head down to rest . . .

Karigan awoke with a start to the golden light of dawn breaking through the mist that had settled over the lake during the night. Eletians. She had dreamed of Eletians passing through the woods. No, it had not been a dream. Or maybe . . . ? She was unsure. Until her eyes focused on the arrow protruding from her chest, an arrow with a white shaft and fletching. She screamed at the sight of crimson blooming across her chest.

Fergal jumped up from a dead sleep, looking wildly around. "What is it? What is it?"

Karigan opened her mouth to speak, but the arrow turned to smoke and drifted away. The blood vanished, too. She pawed at her chest finding no evidence of arrow or wound.

"What is it?" Fergal repeated, blinking blearily.

"I–I . . . dreams," she said, more than a little rattled. Had she merely imagined the arrow, or had one of the Eletians left her a message? Gods, if it had all been real, the Eletians, the faction that wanted her dead, already knew she yet lived.

"Dreams." Fergal yawned. "I dreamed of people laughing at me, and singing 'knacker's boy, knacker's boy . . .' " He shook his head. "I can't remember it too well."

When he rubbed the sleep from his eyes, Karigan noticed it glittered like gold dust as it drifted to the ground. She shuddered.

WALKING THROUGH WALLS

Dale Littlepage's stomach clenched as the wagon bumped along the "road" into the encampment. She closed her eyes not against the sunshine suddenly unfiltered by the forest canopy, but against memory, against black wings.

They had ridden to the wall this summer past, Captain Mapstone and all the Riders she could muster, to gather information for the king. A blast of wild magic from Blackveil Forest had turned life upside down in Sacor City and elsewhere—whole villages had vanished, people had turned to stone in the streets . . . When they arrived, they'd been astonished to discover a swath of forest toppled by the force of the wind and magic that funneled through the breach. Branches had been hurled with such power they impaled tree trunks. Other trees had been uprooted and huge boulders rolled over. They also found a fresh row of graves dug for those who had not survived the maelstrom.

At the breach itself, there had been confusion when a wraith that assumed Alton's appearance tricked them all except Karigan, who attempted to attack him. And it was here that Dale's memory faltered, became shadowed by the wings, and only afterward had she heard about the illusion of Alton melting away to reveal the wraith, and of Karigan racing through the breach into Blackveil. A battle ensued when groundmites poured out of the forest and attacked the Riders, but for Dale, there were only the wings.

Black wings that had shot through the breach and hovered over her like death's shadow. She had been certain she was going to die; she'd heard the hunger in the avian's screech. The wings had closed down on her, their fetid wind roaring in her ears. Talons had hooked into her flesh, and that was all she could remember. The Riders had to fill in the rest for her. Though she did not die that day, others among her comrades had, and she did not understand why. *Why had she been spared when others died?* A whimper escaped her lips.

"Are you well, Rider?"

Clyde's voice drew her back to herself and she opened her eyes to the sunshine again, realizing with a start that the wagon had come to a halt. Voices of men at work and the sound of hammering echoed across the encampment. The soldiers had scavenged in the forest for the fallen trees and used them to build log structures to replace their tents for the oncoming winter. Now they framed out the roof of a cabin.

The rest of the wagon train rumbled by and into the encampment. There were many glad greetings from the guards on duty here, for the wagon train brought not only supplies, but letters from home and relief troops.

"Rider?" Clyde asked again.

Dale turned to the grizzled drover. A gruff fellow, he had taken her into his care during the journey from Woodhaven, ensuring their travel did not harm her mending wounds.

"I'm all right," she told him. The truth was the journey had taken its toll and she was exhausted, but she had only herself to blame, insisting to Garth that she be the one to return to the wall to help Alton. She had tired of "quiet" recuperation and wanted to feel useful again, fully healed or not.

"Let's find Alton." Then, for Clyde's benefit, she amended, "*Lord* Alton." Clyde was a devout clansman and frowned on her casual use of Alton's name, no matter that the nobleman in question was also a Green Rider and her friend.

Clyde nodded and slapped the reins against the rumps of his mules, and the wagon lurched forward. Dale's horse, Plover, trailed behind on a lead rope. She twisted round to watch the mare, who had become frisky at the prospect of a journey, despite the kindness and good care that had been lavished upon her at Woodhaven.

Just as happy to leave as me, Dale thought. But when she glanced at the breach in the wall, she wasn't so sure of her decision. The breach had been repaired again with ordinary stonework, but above the new stonework where the wall was pure magic, there was a cleft that looked as though an angry god had torn out an entire section of the wall.

Clyde asked after Lord Alton and was directed to a secondary encampment a bit of a distance along a path heading east. Here they found no log cabins being built, but crisp rows of tents set up between the woods and the wall, and a tower. Dale's gaze followed it up to the clouds. *Tower of the Heavens.* This was the tower Alton needed her to enter, if her Rider magic was working properly.

"This is the place," Clyde said, hauling back on the reins and setting the brake.

As he had so many times before, he jumped from the wagon and hurried round to lift her down despite her protestations she could manage on her own. She had to admit she felt about a hundred years old when she rose from the bench, all aches and exhaustion, all her joints creaking in protest. Her arm bound to her body did nothing to enhance her balance. Clyde was at least twice her age, but he was strong and possessed boundless energy. Before she knew it, her feet were firmly planted on the ground.

That's better. She stretched and rubbed her back end, glaring at the wagon's bare wooden bench, polished smooth over the years by the buttocks of so many other tortured passengers.

"You wait here," Clyde said. "I'll see to getting you situated."

"Thank you," she said. "Thank you for everything."

He grunted and nodded in his usual taciturn way, then went in search of someone in authority.

Dale stamped out her legs and stretched again, grimacing as her healing flesh was pulled taut. She walked in circles to further loosen up, and soon found herself wandering away from the wagon toward the tower.

Soldiers on guard duty warily watched her approach, but her own attention fell upon a figure in green, his back to her, and his hands on his hips. He stared at the tower, unaware of her approach.

"Alton?" she said.

He turned, and at first she thought she was mistaken, that this scarecrow of a man couldn't be Alton after all, but beneath the shaggy brown hair and stubble on his chin, she recognized him. Garth's description of him had hardly prepared her. He was so thin, and while she felt as though she had aged, he *looked* it.

It took a few moments for him to register who she was. After her own injuries and sickness, and the past several days of travel, she shouldn't be surprised if she looked changed as well.

"Dale!" he said finally, and in three strides he was over to her and hugging her gently so as not to cause her healing injuries pain. Then he put her at arm's length, his eyes searching. "How are you? We didn't think you . . . not at first."

They hadn't thought she would live, she knew he meant to say. "I guess we've both been better. Seems like few of us survived the summer unscathed." Not wishing to sink into dark thoughts again, she continued, "Lord and Lady D'Yer send you their love as well as some packages."

Alton nodded. "And your care, was it satisfactory?"

"With Woodhaven's best menders attending me? And your little brother to keep me company? I couldn't have asked for better."

"Marc? I hope he didn't pester you too much."

Dale laughed. "He tired me out at times, bringing me kittens and games, but he was a welcome sight between all those grim-faced menders."

Alton smiled. "I'm glad." Then he faced the wall. "Welcome to Tower of the Heavens, or *Haethen Toundrel,* as our ancestors called it. It's been the object of my frustration these last two and a half months."

Dale trailed him as he approached the stone wall of the tower. Empty of embellishment, even of windows or arrow loops, it evoked an inhuman countenance.

"No, uh, progress," she said, "with your trying to enter it?"

He shook his head. "No one's been inside since Garth was here." He then glanced eagerly at her, almost hungrily. "Would you like to give it a try, to go inside?"

Dale gazed at the wall of ashlars before her with trepidation. Unlike Garth or Alton, or several of the other Riders, she had never had the chance to enter the tower. Garth had tried to describe what it was like to pass through the wall and emerge within it, like walking through a veil of water, he'd said, but looking upon this bulwark of stone, she was filled with doubt. She raised a trembling hand toward it.

"Don't you dare!"

Dale snatched her hand back and stepped away, wondering what she had done wrong. A woman in D'Yerian blue and gold strode toward them, Clyde at her side. She clutched a letter in her hand, and while Dale thought the sharp words had been directed at her, the woman's gaze settled on Alton, who looked sheepish in return.

When the woman and Clyde halted before them, she waved the letter in Alton's face. "Your father's personal mender has told me the nature and extent of Rider Littlepage's injuries, my lord, and I cannot approve of you putting her straight to work when she's barely arrived after an arduous journey."

"I—" Alton said.

"Yes, I know how terribly frustrating it has been for you to wait, Lord Alton, but really, you must take others into consideration."

"But—"

"I've the right to override your decisions when they relate to health and welfare, and this is one of those occasions."

Alton held up his hands, hands with their own pink, healing injuries on them, and said, "Of course, of course. I wouldn't—I would never—"

"Good then." The woman then turned to Dale. "Welcome," she said, a smile warming her face and her voice softening. "I am Leese, the encampment's chief mender. Tomorrow will be soon enough to begin work, yes?"

Dale *was* tired. She nodded and Leese began to lead her away.

"We've some soldiers setting up a tent for you, and Clyde here has agreed to help you with your things."

Dale glanced over her shoulder only to discover Alton as she found him: hands on hips and his back to her as he stared at the wall. This thin, intense man was not the Alton she remembered.

Once Dale's tent was set up and Leese had examined her, she dropped onto her cot and remembered nothing of the intervening hours until she awoke sometime late the next morning. She had been exhausted, but the rest did her wonders. Not even black wings intruded on her dreams.

Leese came to check on her while she breakfasted, the sunshine on the tent warming the air within to the point it became stuffy. Dale was glad of the inrush of fresh air with Leese's entrance.

"Lord Alton has been pacing a trench between the tower and your tent, waiting for you to wake up," the mender said. "Do you feel up to working with him? If not, I can put him off . . ."

"No, no. I feel good," Dale said.

A little later she slipped through the tent flaps and blinked at the sun in her eyes, and found herself face to face with Alton. He *had* been waiting.

"Uh . . ." he began.

Dale looked him over. He was as disheveled as the day before, and she decided she would have to do something about it. "Good morning."

"Morning. You can come to the tower?"

"Yes, of course, that's what I'm here for." He turned and started walking toward the tower as if expecting her to follow. "But first I want to look in on Plover."

Alton halted and turned about. Was that guilt on his face?

She soon saw why, for when they reached the pickets, Alton's gelding, Night Hawk, was so overjoyed to see his Rider that he nearly yanked his picket stake right out of the ground. Not only had Alton neglected himself, but his horse as well. She watched as he patted the gelding, looking abashed, then she moved on to her own Plover. She checked that the mare was rubbed down, comfortable, and had enough water, and joined Alton where he awaited her on the other side of the picket.

He said nothing, but strode off again, expecting her to follow. She did so, shaking her head. The Alton of old would have asked how she was, joked with her. However, this was not the Alton of old, but a haunted specter of him. She had no idea of what had befallen him while he was trapped in Blackveil. Perhaps with more time, he would come around; if not unchanged, at least more like his old self.

When they reached the wall, Alton took up the stance that was becoming all too familiar—his hands on his hips, and his gaze hard, as if he could break through the stone facade by pure will alone.

"You know about Merdigen?" he asked her.

"Garth filled me in. He's a magical something-or-other."

For the first time, humor lit Alton's eyes. "I wouldn't say that to his face."

"And you're sure he'll be there?"

Alton shrugged. "It's where he exists. Did Garth describe the tower to you?"

Dale paused a moment before replying. Garth described the tower as "impossible," that there were vast plains of grass within, an image she found difficult to conceptualize. "He tried," she said.

"Yes." Alton rubbed the bristles on his chin. "It takes seeing it to understand. Are you ready?"

"Yep. If the tower lets me in, what do you want me to do?"

"Get any information about the wall's condition you can from Merdigen. Ask him if there is a way to circumvent the guardians so I can enter."

"All right." With some trepidation, she approached the tower, the windowless, doorless tower that nonetheless admitted Green Riders. She half listened to Alton's instructions about how to enter, trying to hold her skepticism about walking through walls at bay.

She stroked the cold, rough stone. It felt ordinary enough. Then she patted it soundly. Definitely granite.

"Are you sure this will work?" she asked Alton.

"We won't know until you try."

She took a deep breath, touched her Rider brooch, and sidled toward the tower wall. She stretched her hand out to the wall, expecting to jar it on stone, but it sank right in. She stared incredulously at it, then said to Alton, "Wish me luck."

MEETING MERDIGEN

Passing through the wall was pretty much as Garth had described, like floating through water, a mere moment of breath holding and darkness. But during Dale's passage, voices rasped against her mind; distant murmurs. She could discern no words, but she felt from the voices curiosity and suspicion, a questioning of her presence, and lingering sorrow. So much sorrow . . . She gave a mental shudder and the voices whispered away.

She exhaled in relief when she emerged into the open air of the tower chamber, the wall clinging to her, then snapping away. On impulse she turned and rapped her knuckles on the section of wall she just walked through. *Yep, pure solid granite.* There was no sign of distortion in the stone, no hint of fluidity. She wasn't sure if she believed what she had just done, but here she stood in the tower. The process had been as effortless as Garth claimed, but it nevertheless jangled her nerves. He had said *nothing* about voices. Maybe it had been her imagination.

A source of light that she could not identify dimly lit the tower interior, leaving darkness to fill in the edges of the chamber and the ceiling above. There were no grass plains she could detect, and she wondered if Garth had been imbibing a bit too much when he imagined them. In fact, but for a few details, the place was pretty ordinary. To her right was a big hearth, soot-darkened by many fires, its cooking irons and utensils rusty and strung with spiderwebs.

To her left along the wall was a stone basin with a brass

fish, covered with the verdigris of age, perched on its lip. Garth had told her about this marvel as well, and when she passed her hand under the fish, water spouted from its mouth and poured into the basin. At least this hadn't been a fancy on his part. Dale smiled, letting the water plash into her palm. Her special ability was to find water—specifically water born of the earth. Sometimes she could smell a good rain on the horizon, but her ability was tied groundward.

There were dowsers in her family in Adolind Province, but her ability went deeper. At least that's what she'd found out when it had emerged after her first year as a Rider. She had been on a message errand to an island village on the verge of dying off during a drought. Most of the islanders' wells had gone dry, and the rest were so low they'd turned bad, making countless members of the community ill. Without reliable and safe fresh water, Saltshake Island could not support a permanent population.

As if called upon by the need to save the lives of the islanders, her ability had blossomed to the point where, if she concentrated hard enough, she could feel the vegetation beneath her feet sucking up moisture. Maybe if she had not been called to the messenger service, if she had never become a Green Rider, she would have remained with her family, carrying on the business of dowsing, but as a Rider, her brooch augmented her ability, made her more sure, more sensitive, and most important, completely accurate.

That day on the island she'd discovered a previously unknown spring that would tide the people over till the drought ended. She had also told them where to dig new wells, and how deep. In the end, she had left behind islanders relieved they would not have to be uprooted from the lives they knew and who were well pleased by this emissary of King Zachary's.

The water that now played over her hand came from a deep, deep aquifer that sang of dark earth and pure sand and pebbles, of subterranean streams and falling from the sky. It sang as it drained from the basin, singing as it returned to the earth. Some mage, she surmised, had called the water to flow in this tower when beckoned, and over the millennia, it heeded his call. Such a feat required power far beyond her own meager ability.

Reluctantly she withdrew her hand and shook off the water. She had work to do. She had to find this Merdigen, the magical whatsit. She looked around. A table stood nearby with an unfinished game of Intrigue on it, the pieces draped with cobwebs, but there was no Merdigen in sight.

She turned toward the center of the chamber. Columns stood in a circle, supporting the shadowed ceiling, and on either side archways gaped with blackness. What drew her attention the most, however, was the pedestal in the center of the circle. A gemstone of green gleamed atop it. Tourmaline. If she shifted her gaze just right, viewed it with her peripheral vision, she could almost see something clouded above it, like the greens and blues of grass and sky. It was there, but not, hovering on the edge of her vision.

Still she saw no sign of Merdigen, and she recalled Garth had mentioned using the tourmaline to draw him out. That didn't sound so strange, considering she just walked through a wall of granite.

She strode toward the center of the chamber and between a pair of columns and—

With a yelp she leaped backward, her heart trying to pound its way out of her chest. She took a few moments to calm herself, surrounded by the ordinary chamber. Then, like a swimmer testing the water, she stuck her toe between the columns. When nothing dire happened, she followed with the rest of her body, and found herself amid a grassland.

Sunshine flowed down on her at the same autumn angle she had left outside, and the grasses hissed as a breeze flowed over them. Golden they were, with the season. Oddly though, there were no other structures or signs of civilization, and no D'Yer Wall within sight. All that remained of the tower were the columns standing in their ring, the arches east and west, the table with its dusty game of Intrigue on it, and the pedestal holding its gemstone.

So this was what Garth had meant by there being grasslands in the tower. But was she still in the tower? Her boot scuffed on stones, the same stone floor she had stood upon in the tower. The blocks that formed it looped outward in concentric circles till lost to the grasses beyond the columns, like ruins being reclaimed by nature.

She stepped back through the columns, and found herself surrounded by the stone of the tower chamber. She went back and forth a few times, testing the incongruity. She paused between the columns with one foot on each side to see what would happen. It was like standing in a doorway, she decided. When she looked at the foot outside the columns, she saw the tower chamber like the interior of a house. When she looked at the other foot, she saw the grasslands beyond stretching to the horizon.

Eventually she gave up the game knowing that Alton must be going mad waiting for her to report back. She advanced on the pedestal and circled it. The stone on top was pretty, she thought, sparkling in the sun, and looked harmless enough. What had Garth called it? The *tempes stone.*

She shrugged and put her hand on it. At first nothing happened, then a green glow rose from the stone and between her fingers. Fascinated, Dale removed her hand and surges of energy crackled within the stone, like lightning sealed in green amber.

"Finished playing?"

Dale leaped away from the pedestal as if it suddenly learned to speak.

"Over here."

Dale glanced over her shoulder and discovered an elderly fellow seated at the table, one elbow propped next to the Intrigue board. Long ivory whiskers drooped from his jaw and he wore pale blue robes.

"M–M–Merdigen?"

"Of course I'm Merdigen. Who else would I be?" He rolled his eyes. Then he pressed his hand to his chest and bowed slightly. "More precisely, I am a magical projection of the great mage Merdigen. And who are *you?* You're not the big oaf who was here last."

"Garth—" she began.

"Funny, but that was the oaf's name, too."

"No! I mean the oaf—the Rider who was here last was named Garth."

"That's what I just said."

Dale took a deep breath, feeling less startled, but more exasperated. "I'm Dale Littlepage, a Green Rider."

"So I see." He rose and crossed between the columns to stand before her. He looked her up and down in appraisal. "Well, Dale Littlepage, Green Rider, what have you to say for yourself?"

She fought the urge to jab him to find out if he had substance, or if he were a mere illusion. If he were illusion, what should he care? Still, she restrained the impulse because it just didn't seem polite.

"Alton sent me."

"The Deyer?"

"Alton D'Yer."

Merdigen nodded. "Yes, the Deyer. That's what I said."

Dale put her hand on her hip and frowned. She could see this was going to take more than a little patience. "Right. The Deyer. He sent me in here because the wall won't let him pass."

Merdigen tugged on his beard. "*That* much I know."

"Alton—the Deyer—wants to know the latest on the condition of the wall—anything you can tell him. He also wants to know if there is some way to get around the guardians to let him enter."

"Hah! As if the wall would talk to him even if he got in! Tell me, has the book been found?"

Fortunately Dale knew what book he was referring to thanks to Garth's briefing. "I don't know. I'm sure King Zachary will see to it that it's looked for."

"Zachary of Hillander," Merdigen muttered. "At least another two hundred years have not passed while you people dillydally about, trying to figure out what to do."

"What? Two hundred years?" Dale scrunched her eyebrows together. "Er, no."

"Well, I can only tell you what I told that big fellow, Garth, is that the guardians will have nothing to do with the Deyer. He betrayed them."

"He did no—"

Merdigen raised his hand to silence her. "Knowingly or not, he betrayed them and nearly brought the whole of the wall down in spectacular and utter ruin. As it is, the guardians are in disarray, confused, and even if the wall would talk to him, I could not guarantee his success in calming it down. And there is another thing." He leaned toward her and lowered his voice as if afraid he might be overheard. "There is also a strand of hate and—and . . ." He shuddered. "And madness in the voices of the guardians."

It was all beyond Dale's comprehension. She knew the wall was inhabited by "guardians," what she imagined to be spiritlike presences, and that somehow they wove the magical fabric of the wall together to keep it stable. What she didn't understand was how the guardians accomplished this and what Alton had done to "betray" them. Once she finished with Merdigen, the two Riders would have a lengthy talk.

"Not only is there physical damage to the wall," Merdigen continued, "but I think—I think the other Deyer, the Pendric who is now a guardian, I think it is his despair that is spreading to the others."

Pendric, Pendric, Pendric . . . Then Dale remembered that Pendric was Alton's recently deceased cousin. His name was mentioned in hushed tones in Woodhaven, but his death had not been explained to her, and she didn't pry.

"So what does it all mean?"

"Hope that your king finds the book," Merdigen said, "because if the wall falls into despair and madness, then all is lost."

Alton scrounged up a "nip of something" from his private stores and splashed it into both Dale's teacup and his own.

The concoction scoured Dale's throat as it went down and she had several breathless moments before she could speak, and when she did so, she would not want to be next to an open flame.

"Good tea," she said in a hoarse voice.

Alton grinned. "My aunt, on my mother's side, distills whiskey. Got a couple casks among the packages my parents sent."

That was one aunt, Dale thought, she would like to meet someday. Her tongue tasted the cool, mossy water used in the distilling process, even diluted by the tea. Perhaps it was an extension of her special ability to recognize it, or maybe it was just the taste of good whiskey.

She eased back into her chair, the concoction relaxing her. She was tired, more tired than she imagined she'd be after her trip from Woodhaven and dealing with the tower. Her bones ached and her wound was sore, but the whiskey helped. Her return through the wall was silent, much to her relief. No voices touched her mind, but she felt a watchful presence around her, like thousands of eyes observing her passage.

Alton sat across from her, his legs sprawled out. They left the tent flaps open to allow fresh air to circulate within, and considering the state of Alton's tent and the stale taint that clung to its walls, it was probably a good idea. His blankets were rumpled upon his cot, and uniform parts were strewn about and hanging over the sides of his travel chests. Books were stacked on his table next to a lamp and a nub of a candle, the tent roof stained with a circle of soot. Apparently servants saw to removing his used dishes, and the cleaning of the lamp's chimney, and probably they laundered his clothes, but the place was still shabby and unkempt.

The Alton of old had been meticulous—perhaps not to the extent of Ty's zeal for perfection—but his boots had always shone and he'd worn his uniform without stain or wrinkle. He used to comb his hair and keep his face free of whiskers. Now he possessed the look of someone forgetful of the world around him, and perhaps he was, because of his obsession with the wall.

As they talked, Alton's expression darkened and his tea cooled, forgotten on the table. When Dale finished telling him about her visit with Merdigen, he chucked his tea out the tent opening and refilled his mug with plain whiskey which he swallowed in a single swig.

"I don't believe it," he said at last.

"Which part?"

"All of it. There has got to be some way to make the wall listen to me. I mean, how likely is it that the book will be found? And if it is found, who's to say it will offer any help?"

Dale shrugged. She was just the messenger. She had no answers. "Looks like we're stuck."

The two sat there in gloomy silence, a frown deepening on Alton's face.

Dale fidgeted. "What is this Merdigen anyway? He called himself the projection of the great mage Merdigen, whatever that means. But what is his function? What is he there for?"

"From what I gather," Alton replied, "he's there to help the wallkeepers keep an eye on the wall. He can communicate with the guardians, and in turn relay information to the wallkeepers. When there were wallkeepers, that is."

"Sort of like a messenger himself."

"I suppose."

Dale swallowed her tea, forgetting about the whiskey. She gritted her teeth as it flamed in her throat and made her eyes water. Her expression elicited another smile from Alton.

When she could speak again, she said, "All right, so Merdigen is a messenger of sorts, but he's also not really a live being. An illusion?"

"As far as any of us can tell," Alton said. "No one has really had a chance to question him, and certainly I've not been able to."

"Well, maybe it's time someone did thoroughly question him. Perhaps if we find out more about Merdigen himself, we will learn more about the wall."

Alton straightened in his chair, hope plain on his face. "Surely he must know much about the construction of the wall if he lived during that time."

"There's only one way to find out," Dale said. She was tired, but game. Before she could rise, however, Leese appeared in the tent opening.

"If you don't mind, Rider Littlepage, I'd like to make sure you aren't straining yourself. If we could go to your tent?"

With an apologetic look to Alton, Dale abandoned her cup of "tea," and followed the mender out.

THE GRANDGENT

Karigan held the knife blade before her as she took aim at her target, just as Arms Master Drent had instructed her. She knew she should have returned the throwing knives to him as she had after every session; she knew Drent believed her a danger to herself and others when handling them, but she wanted to perfect the art of knife throwing, and the only way to succeed was through practice, and if she could do so unseen without every other trainee watching her and avoid the humiliation, all the better.

Besides, who could she hurt in the middle of the forest? She ensured Fergal was safely inside the waystation cabin working on the assignments Ty sent with him, and she put the cabin between herself and the paddock where Condor and Sunny munched on hay. Everyone should be safe.

Her target was an old grain sack she found in the cabin that she stuffed with leaves, pine needles, and moss. She tied it to a stout white birch with peeling papery bark. Most of its leaves had yellowed and fallen, its branches crooked bones against the evergreen backdrop.

Squinting at the target in deep concentration, she drew her hand back and threw. The knife whistled tip over butt well wide and high of the target. It clattered somewhere in the upper branches of the pine, arousing the ire of resident squirrels who bounded to the end of a limb to harangue her. The knife thumped to the ground at the base of the tree.

"Sorry," she told the squirrels. So not *everyone* was safe . . .

She drew the second knife from its boot sheath and rolled the well-balanced weapon from hand to hand, considering the target. Then, instead of taking so much time to aim or think about her technique, she swiftly threw it. It nicked the birch above the target.

"Yes!" she cried. She jumped up and down in triumph.

At some point Karigan noticed Fergal watching her display from the front step of the cabin. She froze. Irritated she'd been spied upon, she demanded, "Don't you have some more book work to do inside?"

"Finished."

Karigan grumbled to herself as she went to retrieve her knives. Locating the first knife entailed bushwhacking through undergrowth to reach it. When she returned, she found Fergal where she had been standing, gazing at her lumpy target.

"It's not as easy as it looks," she said, guessing what he was thinking.

"Can I try?"

Reluctantly she passed him one of the knives. "You have to visualize where you want—" Drent's advice barely left her tongue when the knife soared at the target and hit it with a solid *thunk*. Karigan's mouth dropped open. She closed it, and handed him the other knife.

Once again he hit the mark square on. It was no accident.

"How?" Karigan asked.

"My da had lots of knives." Fergal walked over to the birch to extract the blades from the target. "Sometimes I got bored and practiced throwing them. When he wasn't around. These are better weighted though." He tossed one into the air and caught the hilt with ease when it came whirling down. If Karigan attempted such a thing, she'd slice off several fingers. Deflated, she sat down on a tree stump.

When he offered her the knives back, hilts first, she waved him off. "You might as well keep them."

"Really?"

Karigan nodded, and Fergal did a little dance of his own. When he paused, he asked, "Why?"

"You have a better, uh, aptitude for throwing, and if we ever get into a situation where those knives are needed, I'd rather they be in your hands."

"I can teach you," he said.

"Maybe, but in the meantime, I better leave them in your care." She had no idea of what Drent would say to this—if he ever forgave her for taking the knives without permission in the first place.

"There's one thing I'm not so good at," Fergal said.

"Oh?"

"Arms Master Gresia wanted me to practice swordplay. She said you would coach me well."

A smile formed on Karigan's lips. "Fetch the practice blades, then."

Karigan ran him through basic exercises, beginning to see him as any arms master might see the untrained as raw material with much to sculpt; technique to hone and skill to develop. Fergal was right: he was "not so good" at swordplay, and if she felt demoralized by his superior ability in knife throwing, the swordplay restored her self-confidence. She recognized, however, the potential for him to improve, and she resolved to return him to Sacor City a better swordsman than he left.

The wooden blades cracked through the forest as dusk swallowed late afternoon. When it was too dark to see, they retired to the cabin for a simple, but warm, meal.

Preble Waystation was more heavily used than others Karigan had stayed in and so was larger, with three beds instead of one, should chance bring in more than one Rider at a time, and its fragrant cedar closet was filled with more replacement gear than was usual. There was additional paddock space and fodder for the horses as well.

The waystations were for the sole use of Green Riders and had originally been built where no other lodging was available. Over the years, however, the number of Riders had declined, which meant fewer Riders able to stock and maintain the stations, and in some places, the growth of towns had reduced their necessity. As a result, the least used waystations, and those closest to population centers, had been decommissioned long before Karigan entered the messenger service.

Riders welcomed the waystations not only for the shelter they provided along the road, but for their sense of security. They had been built to blend into the landscape and had been warded with spells to keep out unwanted intruders. The wards didn't keep the wildlife out, however, and it wasn't unusual for Riders to have to dislodge squirrel nests from chimneys or chase bats out the door with brooms. On a few occasions, Riders had arrived at a waystation to discover a bear had broken in and made a terrible mess. And then there was Garth's encounter with the Skunk . . . The poor man had been ostracized for weeks.

Even if none of these creatures had taken up lodging in a waystation, their littlest cousins were inevitable residents. Sweeping out mouse droppings was usually the first order of business for a Rider settling into a waystation for the night.

Karigan knew that Captain Mapstone dreamed of her Riders one day being permanently posted not at these simple waystations, but at larger relays built in Sacoridia's towns and cities. Even if all the Rider brooches in the captain's coffer were claimed, Karigan wondered if there would be enough Riders to fulfill her dream. If so, then relay stations would offer a more efficient use of Green Riders and swifter message delivery.

These were some of her meandering thoughts as she sat rocking before the cobblestone hearth, warming her stocking feet before the fire, a mug of tea cupped in her hands. It was, she thought, better to look ahead to a positive future rather than worry about Eletians or the wall. Here she was on an ordinary errand that, despite its rough beginning, was going smoothly and making good time. Of course, they had farther to go and hadn't even reached their first destination. Anything could go wrong between now and then.

"Osric M'Grew was the last one here," Fergal said. He was flipping through the waystation's logbook. "He was here last month."

Karigan nodded, her eyes half-closed as she watched the flames flare and twist. "I suppose you could sign us in."

Fergal did so eagerly. Karigan had seen from his lessons that his handwriting was wobbly and his spelling atrocious, but he could spell his own name. She had to help him with hers. There was some blotting of ink and intense concentration as he recorded the date and wrote, *The weather is nice.*

When he finished, he continued to leaf through the pages, pausing now and then to read. "Pretty boring," he said. "Mostly dates and names."

Karigan restrained the impulse to roll her eyes. "Our entry isn't very exciting either."

"I know." Fergal sounded so disappointed that Karigan did roll her eyes.

She had weighed whether or not to tell him about the Eletians that passed their campsite some nights ago, but for some reason, she felt as though it had been a vision meant only for her. There was also the "personal message" at least one among them left her. Wasn't it her duty to report any unusual sightings in the logbook as a warning to other Riders who passed this way?

She said nothing, did not request Fergal to pass her the logbook. She remained silent about the Eletians because it was *her,* not the other Riders, with whom they were playing games.

A snort from Fergal startled her back to the present.

"What?"

Fergal read slowly and carefully, not quite getting all the words right, an entry from Mara Brennyn: "*. . . I saved myself when my ability emerged for the first time; a ball of flame erupted from my palm and lit the kindling when my fingers were too numb to strike flint. Actually, I almost burned down the forest . . .*"

Several miles north of Preble Waystation, at a campsite along a woods trail, Mara had broken through the ice of a pond in deepest winter. The emergence of her ability to create fire had saved her from freezing to death. Karigan once asked Mara what she had been doing on the pond, and the

Rider blushed. "Ice skating. I carry my blades with me during the winter. I thought the pond was safe."

Karigan learned early on that many of her colleagues had interesting and sometimes eccentric pastimes outside of the messenger service. When Karigan laughed at Mara's explanation, the Rider said, "What? I grew up on a lake, and during the winter skating was the easiest way to reach the village." Karigan hadn't been laughing entirely at the idea of Mara ice skating, but at the fact the accident hadn't been related to some danger of the job, which was most often the case with emerging Rider abilities.

"How far back does that book go?" Karigan asked.

"Seven years. It's almost filled up."

Mara had been called to the messenger service about six years ago. Riders often did not make it to five years, some because an accident befell them, others because their brooches simply abandoned them.

Fergal flipped through a few more pages before growing very still. Though Karigan continued to stare into the fire, she could feel his gaze on her.

Slowly, as though gathering courage, he asked, "When will I come into my magic?"

The plaintive question caught her off guard, but she supposed she should have anticipated it. If she were Fergal, she'd be curious, too. "It's hard to say. It'll make itself known when it's ready to."

"*I know.* That's what Ty said. What does it mean?"

Karigan rocked more slowly. What *did* it mean? Her ability had surfaced before she'd even known or acknowledged herself to be a Rider. She'd never gone through a period of waiting and wondering.

"There's no easy answer," she said. "Your ability will become apparent when it needs to. They seem to require a crisis or some trauma to emerge, something that endangers the Rider or those around him, like when Mara fell through the ice. She'd have frozen to death if her ability hadn't arisen to help her build a fire."

"And like when you were being chased by Lord Mirwell's men," Fergal said.

"Yes." The floorboards beneath her chair creaked as she rocked harder.

"Ty said they almost caught you."

"Yes."

"He said you turned invisible to escape them."

"Yes. Well, more or less." She would have to speak to Ty about how much he told the new Riders. It felt strange to have people talking about her.

"What was it like?" Fergal asked. "How did it happen exactly?"

He meant the emergence of her ability, but it was so tied up with other things, bad memories, that it was difficult to talk about even now. She turned the rocking chair to face him. Despite her reluctance, it was probably better to get this over with now so he wouldn't plague her about it the entire journey.

"It was raining that day," she began, "and a thick fog had settled into the forest. I had in my possession a message the Mirwellians dearly wanted to intercept before it could reach the king. At that point, I really had no idea of what it was all about, and since this was thrust upon me unexpectedly, I certainly knew nothing of the special abilities of Riders."

"F'ryan Coblebay gave you his brooch," Fergal said.

"Yes. I didn't know what it meant at the time." She remembered the dying Rider on the road. She remembered him pleading with her to carry his message to King Zachary and the blood that saturated his gauntlets as he reached out to her. She shook herself out of her reverie. It seemed ancient history, but now that she recalled it, it returned with startling clarity.

"Pursuit followed," she continued, "and their captain found me. Immerez was his name. I was—I was terrified. I was caught, and I didn't know what to do."

"You cut off his hand, didn't you?"

Karigan scowled. She would definitely have to have a talk with Ty. "That was later. This time I managed to escape. I wanted to disappear, I was so scared, and the brooch responded. I vanished from Immerez's sight and that of his men."

"But . . . what was it like?"

Karigan shrugged. "I didn't feel any great change, and it took me a while to figure out what happened. When I became aware of it, I realized it was not so much the fog that dulled my vision, but the use of my new ability. I also get nasty headaches. Most Riders will tell you they suffer some ill effect from using their abilities. It's like having to sacrifice something for the gift."

"I don't care," Fergal said. "I just want mine."

Karigan raised her eyebrows. Why did he make her feel ever so old? Only experience, she supposed, would show him the truth. Telling him of Captain Mapstone's chronic joint pain or of Mara's fevers—the costs of using their abilities—would not convince him there was a dark side to a Rider's magic. He must fancy the idea of being able to walk through walls, or of molding fire in the palm of his hand, or even to fade from view as she could. She would ask him what he thought when his ability finally did emerge and he had a chance to use it.

Even if the subject made her uneasy, she was pleased he was at least willing to talk to her about it. He was looking at the logbook again, then glanced at her and handed it to her.

"An entry from F'ryan Coblebay," he said.

Karigan took the book expecting to see nothing more than a date and his signature, but to her surprise, there was more: *I make good time on the road, yet farther west I must travel, across the Grandgent and skirting Selium northward to Mirwell Province. I know not what I may encounter, but I fear this errand is not without peril. So to you my good Riders, should I fail in my duty, I say ride well for your king and your country; and for she who awaits me and in the garden dwells, watch over her for me. Tell her I love her.*

Somehow he had known. Somehow he had known he would not return from his errand, for this was dated just a month before Karigan encountered him dying on the road.

And the one who awaited him? None other than Lady Estora. She still grieved for him, Karigan knew, but it was a secret grief that must be hidden from all but the Riders lest it become known she had loved a commoner. F'ryan was the bond that had created a friendship between Estora and Karigan. Karigan was the last to see him alive and now wore his brooch, and Estora had spoken to her as if she could bridge some chasm, somehow allow her words to connect with F'ryan beyond the veil of death.

Had Karigan betrayed more than friendship when she pushed Estora away? Had she betrayed F'ryan's wishes? He had come to her after death in the form of a ghost on that long ago journey, and still his words reached her from beyond the grave.

She closed the logbook saddened that the line between commoner and noble, and that between life and death, kept apart those who loved one another. Life was such a fleeting thing, after all.

Over the days that followed, they rode into a stiff northwest wind that froze cheeks and nose tips, and portended the winter to come. Mostly they rode in silence, but it was a comfortable silence. In the evenings they practiced with the wooden swords, providing much entertainment for the children of one village. Fergal was beginning to get a better sense of rhythm with the drills Karigan put him through. When outside the confines of a village, Fergal tried to teach her to throw knives. While her efforts went wild less often, the knives still soared far off target. Karigan had to give Fergal credit for containing both his impatience with her and his laughter.

They encountered more and more farms and villages as they neared the Grandgent River. The Grandgent was the largest river in Sacoridia, and much commerce occurred along its shores. Her father's river cogs sailed its water on trading missions all the way from Corsa Harbor to Adolind Province. Shipyards launched vessels along its banks, and river drivers sent rafts of logs down the currents destined for one of the many sawmills. Hundreds of feet of board then went on to the shipyards for the building of vessels of all sizes and types.

The Kingway split the boundaries of Penburn and L'Petrie provinces as it approached the river, and if Karigan hadn't been duty bound on king's business, she could steer southward to the coast and her home in Corsa. She might even obtain a berth on a riverboat heading downstream. She smiled at the thought of her aunts fussing over her and pushing more food before her than she could ever hope to eat. And of course there were her father's hugs. Then once the initial greetings were over, she knew her aunts would bemoan her "decision" to "join" the messenger service. Even worse, the debacle of her outing with Braymer Coyle would have reached their ears by now via the merchants guild, and she would never hear the end of it. Better that she continue heading west than face the indignation of her strong-willed aunts.

Chicken, she told herself, but the smile did not leave her face.

The road cut through the center of one of the busiest towns on the east bank of the Grandgent, called Rivertown. Here the road was well made, a reflection of the wealth the shipbuilders and timber merchants heaped on their town, and the hooves of Condor and Sunny clattered on broad paving stones. Along the road were grand houses with formal gardens. As they neared Rivertown's center, buildings clustered closer together and there were interesting shops of all kinds, as well as inns and eateries. Despite the neat and clean appearance of the main street, Karigan knew that rougher neighborhoods existed but a block away.

They circled a fountain in the town's center in which a statue of Nia, goddess of rivers, stood. In one hand she balanced a river cog, and in the other, a cant dog, a common tool used by foresters and river drivers. No mistaking what this town was about. And while there were at least two chapels dedicated to Aeryc, Karigan espied a tiny chapel in Nia's service. It wasn't often one found a chapel devoted to the lesser gods these days.

Soon their first view of the river appeared as the street dipped down. Bookended by the facades of buildings on either side of the street, it shone a deep, royal blue with the sun glancing on it, and after the greens, browns, and rusts of the countryside, it proved a delight to the eye.

Karigan halted Condor in front of a mercantile. "This is our last big town before we reach Selium," she said, "so I want to restock our provisions."

Fergal chose to wait for her outside with the horses, and when she returned with her arms full of foodstuffs, she found him fingering his Rider brooch and staring at the river.

"Pretty, isn't it?" she said. "My father always called it the grandfather of rivers, and he's sailed up and down it quite a bit."

"Oh." Fergal tried to look interested in her words, but failed. Something about the river did hold his attention, but whatever it was, he did not say. Karigan dismissed it and they loaded the new provisions into their saddlebags.

She mounted Condor and reined him back onto the street.

"How long until we reach Selium?" Fergal asked.

"If we make good time this afternoon, it should be only a few more days."

They descended the street to Rivertown Landing, and here the scent of dead fish and rotting river weed rose up from the shore and from the marshes across the river. If it weren't so late in the season, they'd see all kinds of birds nesting, hovering, and wading, but the waters and sky were empty and the only bird Karigan espied was a lone gull winging southward.

Even the docks felt abandoned. Smaller boats were pulled up on the bank and turned over for the season, and along the shore, river sloops were on dry dock. Some cogs bobbed at the end of the town pier, but they were few compared to the confusion and congestion the summer trading season brought.

The ferry was tied up where the street met water. It

wasn't more than a barge with rails, large enough to carry horse-drawn wagons and carriages. It was propelled by oars, for a line and pulley system one might find on a smaller river was impractical due to the Grandgent's breadth and the mast height of the vessels that needed to pass through the ferry crossing.

Karigan rang a brass bell that hung from a post beside the ferry and four burly, grubby rivermen emerged from the nearest tavern. These were the oarsmen. An older fellow with gray whiskers and a pipe sauntered out behind them, no doubt the ferry master.

"Weeell," he drawled, "a pair o' king's men if my eyes don' deceive me."

Karigan wanted to tell him that, yes, his eyes did in fact deceive him, but she learned to restrain her sarcasm when on duty. At least most of the time. Now she had the added pressure of setting a good example of Rider comportment for Fergal.

"We require passage across the river," she said.

"O' course ye do," he replied, taking his own time to amble up to her. "Two 'orses and two men. That'll be a silver each."

An internal struggle erupted within Karigan as she attempted to quell her outrage at such an appalling price. What was needed here was a bridge and not this thievery. Her merchant's instinct took hold, and much to her own satisfaction, and to the ferry master's astonishment, she backed him down to two coppers.

"You shouldn't be wrongly charging the king's servants," she admonished him. "It's people like you who take advantage and drive up taxes. The king shall hear of it." It was a bit more heated than she intended, and not that perfect show of comportment she was trying to model for Fergal, but the ferry master blanched in a pleasing manner.

"Sorry, sir, sorry. Don' tell the king! I swear I won' overcharge his men again!"

Sir? Karigan sighed.

The deal was struck and the ramp drawn down so the Riders could lead their mounts aboard. Condor loaded with no problem, having had his share of ferry crossings through his career. Sunny, however, was less sure and balked. She had to look the contraption over carefully before she allowed Fergal to lead her on board. Karigan was impressed by how he remained calm and patient with her, and even patted her neck and offered her praise once she stood solidly on board. He was learning, though she could not say he had warmed up to the mare, and she sensed his good care of her was inspired more by duty than affection. Once Sunny was loaded, he turned his attention back to the river, and fidgeted as they waited for the oarsmen to shove off.

In some places the river was half a mile wide, but in the far north where it originated, born of ice and snow in a jagged line of mountains, the river ran narrow, wild, and white, cascading down the landscape in unnavigable rapids, birthing other rivers that spread across the land like the veins of a hand. Few adventurers traveled that far north for the land was icy and harsh and no one lived there. As the river flowed into Sacoridia, first through Adolind Province, it calmed and widened, though the spring melt created some fast-moving rapids. Here at the Rivertown crossing, the river was wide and comparatively placid.

The oarsmen took up their stations starboard and port, and the ferry master dropped his rudder and tiller into place. With strong, long strokes of the oars, they began the crossing. The northwest wind pushed at the ferry and curdled the surface of the river, but the ferry master leaning on the tiller kept them on course. Poor Sunny braced her legs to stand steady, the whites of her eyes showing.

As the ferry pulled out farther into the river, they left behind a shore littered with rank river weed and fish floating belly up in the shallows among snarled strands of netting and broken barrel staves. Rotten vegetables and refuse added to the stink of dead fish, and a boot was caught in the ribs of an abandoned dory. There was smashed crockery and tangled fishing gear stuck in the mud. The scene, Karigan thought, could belong to any busy harbor town.

The wind lifted spray from the oars in upstroke, which slapped her cheek in icy splashes.

"So's it true the king has got hisself a woman?" the ferry master asked.

Karigan blinked, then almost laughed. It was the first time she had heard the betrothal referred to in such a way. "King Zachary has contracted to marry Lord-Governor Coutre's daughter."

"Aye, contracted. Whore games of the nobles that is."

"Best to watch how you speak of our king and future queen," Karigan warned, though she thought of it in much the same way.

"Well, that's fine," the ferry master said, puffing on his pipe. "Time the old boy took a wife."

Karigan lifted her eyebrows. *Old boy?* King Zachary? She didn't know whether to be perturbed or to laugh. King Zachary was older than she by twelve years, but "old boy"? She glanced at Fergal to see how he was taking the conversation, but he was leaning over the port rail, staring into the river's depths as the ferrymen dipped and pulled on their oars in a hypnotic rhythm, the oarlocks groaning with each stroke.

The harsh wind blew down the river and nearly carried off the ferry master's cap. He caught it in time and pulled it down securely over his head. The craft shuddered against the blast and more spray washed over the starboard side. Karigan shivered and stood in the lee of Condor to cut the wind.

"Aye," said the ferry master when it died down, "it's lookin' like an early winter. Already had some ice floatin' down from the north."

If their business in the west took longer than expected and the river iced over, Karigan and Fergal would have to ride south to the nearest bridge for their return crossing. The river would not freeze smoothly like a lake; no, it would crack and buckle, and the layers would stack up in sharp angles, making the ice impassible.

Karigan was about to comment when there was a loud splash and a strangled cry. To her horror, Fergal no longer stood at the rail. He no longer stood on the ferry at all.

THE GOLDEN RUDDER

Everyone froze. The only sound was the water lapping against the ferry.

"Fergal!" Karigan cried and she dashed to the rail.

At first she saw nothing, heard nothing, then there was another splash and his head bobbed to the surface. He flailed his arms, the current sweeping him down river.

"Keep with him, lads," the ferry master ordered the oarsmen, and he abandoned the tiller to gather a line to toss to Fergal.

"Fergal!" Karigan cried again. "Tread water—hang on!" But Fergal's efforts to stay afloat foundered. He did not know how to swim. Before the ferry master could toss his line, Fergal sank under and did not reappear.

For five heartbeats Karigan hesitated, staring in horror at the bubbles that rose to the surface. She then glanced at the ferry master and oarsmen who seemed unable to move.

Without a second thought, she threw off her message satchel and coat, then unbuckled her swordbelt. It clattered to the deck.

The ferry master's eyes nearly bugged out of his head. "Ye can' go in there, sir, it's cold! Ye'll drown!"

She tore off her boots, ducked under the port rail, and jumped into the river. At first she felt nothing but a space of shock. Then the cold grabbed her.

When Karigan was little, her father teased her that she had the hide of a seal because she loved to play in the ocean. Even at the height of summer, Sacoridia's coastal waters were frigid, fed by rivers, including the Grandgent, that were born of the northern ice. If she waded in the shallows for more than a few seconds, her toes would go numb, then her feet and ankles, making her legs ache all the way up to her knees.

She'd made a game of it, charging in and out of the waves, giggling madly, challenging herself to go deeper and for longer. Sometimes she endured the bitter currents long enough to swim out to a ledge at the mouth of the cove on which cormorants liked to perch and spread their wings.

Karigan had an idea of what she faced when she plunged into the brilliant waters of the Grandgent, but knowing could not fully prepare her. The cold stole her breath. It seeped through her clothes, through flesh, and gnawed into her bones, sapping her inner warmth. Her toes and fingers grew numb. She had not the hide of a seal, nor was this some childhood game of summer days long past. She had only minutes to find Fergal or succumb to the river herself. She took a last glance at the ferry, and saw that the oarsmen were holding it steady, allowing the craft to drift with her and the current. They watched her in disbelief, but would not abandon her.

She took a deep breath and dove beneath the surface. It was a dark world that swallowed her. The cold pressed against her head like a vise and cut off her hearing. It squeezed her lungs and almost forced the air from her cheeks. From the lighter levels of blue near the surface, she kicked into deeper, darker blue, searching in desperation for Fergal. She knew the currents were carrying her swiftly along, and it frightened her.

Sunlight penetrated through bluish-green layers to the river bottom, where she found an otherworldly landscape littered with boulders the size of wagons, and huge logs lying among them that had sunk during river drives. Weeds grew up between the rocks, and she caught sight of a cart wheel and broken jug.

She despaired of finding Fergal in the rocky, shadowy river and had no breath left in her. She swam back up to the surface, the relative warmth of the air stinging her face. The ferry was still with her, and the men shouted to her, but her ears rang so fiercely she could not hear them. The cold had already exhausted much of her strength and her extremities were without feeling, but she couldn't give up if there was a chance she could save Fergal. She plunged again into the river's depths.

This time another unnatural shape appeared among the boulders, a river cog gouged on its port side, debris spilled around it, the shapes of barrels and bottles and jars all coated with a fine silt. In the blue-green light, the cog's tattered sails flowed in the currents with ghostly gestures. Karigan drifted over the figurehead of a fair lady holding a bouquet of flowers, her expression eerily undismayed by her watery grave.

The current drew Karigan on and she thrust upward to avoid becoming ensnared in the sails and rigging, and then she saw him. He was trapped in the rigging, his arms and legs splayed out like a dead man. She swam toward him, the lines groping for her like tentacles. If she got caught in them, they were both dead.

She pushed the ropes away as she swam, aware of darkness flooding the edges of her vision, aware of expending her last breaths, and of feeling weary. So very weary. When she reached Fergal, she found the rigging lashed around his torso and one of his legs. He showed no signs of life. Karigan tugged at the ropes that bound him but they held fast, unwilling to give up their prey.

She drew his longknife. The darkness clouded into her vision as she sawed into the thick rope. The knife was well-honed, something she now came to expect of Fergal, and it slashed through the rigging that anchored him. She dropped the knife and it drifted with silvery flashes toward the wreck.

She grabbed Fergal's collar and thrust upward for the surface. She gasped when her head emerged from the water and she sucked in air. The ferry was not far off and the oarsmen threw her the line. When her numb fingers were finally able to grip it, they drew her in as she tried to keep Fergal's head above water.

When at last they hauled her from the grasp of the river, she fell to the ferry's deck gagging, and for a while after that, she knew nothing more.

Karigan sat by the kitchen hearth of the Golden Rudder shivering uncontrollably even though the cook stoked the fire to inferno proportions to help thaw her out. The ferry master claimed the inn was the best Rivertown had to offer, though she never heard any of her fellow Riders mention it. While it was hard to judge anything one way or another in her current condition, the staff was kindly and attentive. The innkeeper, Silva Early, had helped her peel off her sodden uniform right there in the kitchen and supplied her with a warm, dry flannel nightgown. Now Silva poured more warm water into the basin in which Karigan soaked her feet and thrust a mug of broth into her hands. Her hands shook so violently she almost spilled it.

"Rona is preparing a room for you," Silva said, "but in the meantime, you must drink up."

Karigan tried to smile, but it only made her teeth clack spasmodically. Her hostess was dressed in silks that would impress her merchant father, and her hair was coiled upon her head in a way that would have taken Karigan hours to fashion, even with Tegan's help. Soft colors applied to her face accentuated her eyes, cheekbones, and lips. It was everything Karigan admired about those fashionable women of highborn status she used to see promenading about the exclusive shopping districts of Corsa, and all she failed to be herself. It wasn't just a matter of dressing the part, she knew, but a matter of demeanor. Silva exuded soft, unharried elegance not typical of an innkeeper. For some reason, she made Karigan think of her mother.

As for Fergal, the ferry master told Karigan they'd pumped about half the river out of him and got him breathing again, and when they took him to the mender's house, the other half came gushing out, "With all the fishes, too." It would take the night to see how well Fergal fared.

"I'm g–g–going to k–k–kill him," Karigan said through chattering teeth.

"My dear," Silva said, "if you wished him dead, you could have just left him in the river." She glided away, a rich but not unpleasant perfume lingering in the air behind her.

Still, if Fergal survived the night, Karigan was tempted to throttle him for putting her through this—not only because she had to risk her own life to save him and as a result felt bloody awful, but because of the anguish he caused her. She had visions of returning to Sacor City with his corpse swathed in winding cloths and lashed across Sunny's back. Even if he tried her patience at times, she had to admit she cared. One thing was for certain: she was going to get to the bottom of the incident. No one saw him fall into the river, and until he was well enough, she would not know how it happened. She wanted an explanation, and by the gods, it had better be a good one.

Meanwhile, all she could do was sip the broth. It helped quell the inner cold that made her bones ache, and when she started to sag in her chair and the bustle of the kitchen became a distant thing, Silva gently pried the mug from her hands.

"Nia certainly watched over you this day," she said in a soft voice.

"The room is ready," someone else announced from behind.

"Good. Just in time, I'm thinking. Thank you, Rona. I believe we shall need help getting her upstairs. Could you please fetch Zem?"

Karigan must have drifted off after Silva's order, for a broad-shouldered man stood before her when he hadn't been there just a moment ago. He smelled of soil and decaying autumn leaves.

"Karigan, dear," Silva said, "this is Zem, the inn's gardener. He's going to assist you to your room. I'll be right behind him."

"I don't need help," Karigan said. But she couldn't seem to rise by herself, and when Zem got her upright, she found she did need his help to remain standing.

They progressed slowly from the kitchen to a foyer illuminated by a crystal chandelier that reminded her of ice. She shuddered. The sounds of men and women engaged in sociable conversation drifted out of an adjoining parlor. Zem, with his arm around her to support her, directed her toward a daunting staircase. Step by step they made the ascent till they reached the top landing.

"Room six," Silva instructed from behind.

Karigan's toes curled in the plush carpeting as Zem guided her along the corridor. They passed numbered doors, all closed, but through which trickled the laughter of women and the voices of men.

Karigan was almost beyond recall when Zem helped her into a bedroom with a blazing fire in the hearth. It contained a stately, canopied bed, and when she sank into the down mattress, Silva hurried to pull the covers over her. This was indeed a luxurious inn, Karigan thought, and she wondered just how much it was going to cost the king for her to stay here.

"Is she a new girl?" asked a feminine voice in the corridor.

"No, dear," Silva said. "A guest."

"Oh? One of Trudy's then? Shouldn't someone tell her?"

"No, dear," Silva said more firmly. "This one requires no company."

"Pity, Trudy always likes the ones in uniform."

Karigan's foggy brain could not comprehend the conversation. The bed was blissfully soft, and warmed with river-rounded stones taken from the hearth, wrapped, and placed under the covers with her. The last thing she remembered was Silva looking down at her with a smile and saying, "Rest well, dear."

Dreams plagued Karigan. She dreamed of descending through the blackened depths of the river, descending like a rock, and the harder she tried to swim, the faster she sank.

And there, in the gloom, she saw the sunken river cog. The figurehead watched her as she drifted near, though this was not the wooden figure she'd seen adorning the prow of the real wreck but Lady Estora.

The garden is too cold, she said. *I want it to be summer again.*

"I cannot be your friend," Karigan tried to say, but only bubbles rushed from her mouth.

We are not who we must be.

Then slowly, Estora's body stiffened and took on the grainy texture of wood. The illusion of flesh was no more than paint, her expression one of endless sorrow. She held a bouquet of dead flowers.

The current carried Karigan away over the wreck and again the rigging reached out for her like a live thing. She found Fergal trapped in the ropes, but realized it was not Fergal at all, but King Zachary, his face a sickly greenish-white, a drowned corpse with its eyes wide open.

"No!" Karigan cried, but again, only bubbles exploded from her mouth.

Do not grieve for me, he said with blue lips.

Then the scene changed to night dark instead of river dark. Stars shone in the sky high above and she was surrounded by forest, and he was there. No longer a corpse, he pulled her to him, into his warm arms, warm body, his skin soft as velvet . . .

I want it to be summer again, he murmured into her neck.

She wanted to say, "Me, too," but his mouth covered hers, and there was only his warmth around her, and within her.

Karigan awoke with a groan and found herself clutching her pillow. She willed the dream to be real, but it was not. Overwarm, she released the pillow and pushed back the comforter. It was then she realized she was not alone.

"Shhh," said a female voice in the dusky dark. "We heard you cry out."

As Karigan's eyes adjusted, she made out a slender woman standing at the foot of her bed who was wearing a filmy shift that revealed her curves in silhouette. In the doorway, two others peered in, the lamplight of the corridor gleaming in their eyes.

"Who are you?" Karigan demanded, hauling the comforter back up to her chin.

"Trudy. I work here." She sat beside Karigan on the edge of her bed. "Are you well?"

"Yes, I'm fine, thank you. I will go back to sleep now."

"Would you like company?"

"Would I like *what?*"

"I could help keep you warm."

Then it dawned on Karigan—the luxurious inn, Silva's elegance, the noises she was beginning to discern creeping through the walls of adjacent rooms . . . The ferry master had brought her to a brothel.

"N–no, thank you," Karigan stammered, overcome by the urge to pull the comforter over her head. "I am quite warm."

"Are you now," the woman said softly.

"She's not interested, Trude," said one of the women in the doorway.

"If you change your mind, I'm in room twelve." Trudy stood and left with her companions, closing the door behind them.

A brothel! Well, it explained the one dream, which was beginning to fade away, though it left her with a strong sense of longing.

If her aunts and father ever heard of this, they'd be scandalized. One did not stay at brothels. One did not even go near brothels. That was, at least, the law as handed down by her aunts. Aunt Stace would have a heart attack if she found out!

And Karigan had been *propositioned.* Now she did pull the comforter over her head. "Company" might warm her, but the only "company" she desired was a man miles away in a castle, a man never destined to be hers.

She drifted back into sleep, wishing for some reason, it was summer.

* * *

In the morning, Rona, a matron in her grandmotherly years, and obviously not one of the "ladies" who served the brothel's clients, dragged an oversized hip bath into Karigan's room and filled it with steaming water from a kettle.

"You take a bath like a good girl," she said, "then come on down for breakfast. I'll leave you to it."

After the door closed behind Rona, Karigan slipped into the bath with a sigh. She decided she must find alternate lodging as soon as possible. It didn't look good for a servant of the king to bide her time in a brothel, no matter how fine the establishment, and no matter her reasons for her being there. It was just plain inappropriate.

Her aunts would agree. She remembered accompanying them on a shopping trip to a mercantile that shared the same street with a couple of brothels, although she was young at the time and didn't know what they were. Her aunts had held her hands tight, and when she expressed admiration for the "pretty ladies" she saw, Aunt Stace slapped her, explaining how those "pretty ladies" lived.

Karigan had never been slapped before, and even now she touched her cheek as though all these years later it still stung. She'd been horrified by the things her aunts told her. How could one sell her most precious commodity—her body, her *self*—for currency?

For her aunts, it was a matter of immorality. They had been raised, like her father, on Black Island, where there were no brothels, only a tight-knit community that honored the gods with hard work and attention to family. There was no tolerance outside the islanders' strict mind-set of right and wrong—one of the reasons her father had fled the island. He'd felt stifled, trapped.

Yet, when her aunts also left to join her father in Corsa, they brought with them their islander attitudes, and after Kariny's death, they had much influence on Karigan's upbringing. They could be doting and playful, but also stern and disapproving, imposing their rigid ways on her. Fortunately her father's more indulgent nature had lent some balance to her childhood.

She lathered fragrant lemon soap on her arm, watching steam rise off her skin. After the incident with Aunt Stace, she'd given brothels little thought. They were usually located in neighborhoods into which she rarely ventured, kept out of sight, really, and out of mind. While brothels weren't banned in most towns in Sacoridia, they weren't exactly condoned, either, particularly by the more "upright" citizens of her aunts' disposition.

Some brothels purchased textiles directly from Clan G'ladheon, but for Karigan they were only names recorded in her father's ledgers. They were treated as any other customer so long as they had the currency to pay for their goods.

And yet . . . she could never imagine selling her body, giving away its mysteries to anyone less than the right man, one whom she loved, and one who returned that love, and most certainly not in exchange for currency. She couldn't even give herself over to the casual pairings some of her fellow Riders engaged in, whether among themselves or along the road. Their work was dangerous and often solitary, and she couldn't blame them for seeking companionship where they could find it, fulfilling very human needs. In fact, she'd been tempted herself by more than one offer . . .

Still, while Karigan's own urges were alive and well, they were overridden by her desire for a relationship of deep trust and respect, one that transcended baser needs. She remembered how her mother and father cherished one another, and though Kariny died when Karigan was young, she recalled the tenderness between her parents, the soft touches, the wordplay—even if she hadn't understood it all back then—and the way they gazed at one another. This lesson left an even more indelible impression upon her than Aunt Stace's slap, and it was the standard by which she measured her own life. How could anyone desire anything less?

She sank beneath the water to wet her hair, and

reemerged longing for the kind of love her parents had shared. The way her life was going, however, she feared it might be something she was never destined to experience.

When Karigan finished her bath, she found her uniform laid out for her, clean and dry, and she dressed. Still exhausted from her ordeal in the Grandgent and desiring nothing other than to crawl back into bed, she needed to find out how Fergal fared through the night.

She hurried down the corridor and found Rona at the bottom of the stairs, smiling as if she found something about Karigan amusing.

"I hear Trudy looked after you during the night," she said.

"*What?* No, no. She looked *in.* Not after."

Rona chuckled. "We do try to look after our guests. Cetchum is breaking his fast in the kitchen. You should join him."

"Cetchum?"

"Yes, dearie, the ferry master. My husband."

Oh, so that explained why she ended up *here.* Karigan entered the kitchen and found him tucking into ham and eggs while Silva sat with him looking as regal and perfect as the previous evening. She sipped on a brew that smelled like kauv.

"Come, Karigan, dear," Silva said, "and join us for breakfast."

Hesitantly, Karigan sat at the table across from Silva. "Morning," she said.

Cetchum grunted as he looked her over. "Weeell, yer looking a sight better, sir."

Karigan pinched her eyebrows together, and glanced at Silva who smiled and shrugged. Apparently calling her "sir" was an accepted eccentricity on Cetchum's part.

A cook set a plate of eggs and ham before Karigan, as well as a loaf of bread just drawn from the oven. Cetchum pushed a pot of creamy butter toward her.

Karigan, however, couldn't eat until she heard about Fergal. "How is Rider Duff?" she asked.

"The lad is fine," Cetchum said, maneuvering a mouthful of eggs around his words. "Or will be. Needs his rest, so says Mender Gills."

Karigan closed her eyes in relief. Relief that she would not have to return Fergal's body back to Sacor City.

"The young man will be transferred here for the duration," Silva said.

"Here?" Karigan had not meant to sound so expressive, but she sensed that bringing Fergal into a brothel was like dropping a candle in a hay barn. At Silva's raised eyebrow, she said, "Uh, I am sure your rates are steep for those on king's business."

"Perhaps." Silva sipped from her cup, and her gaze unnerved Karigan. "You are of Clan G'ladheon, are you not?"

Karigan nodded, wondering what this had to do with anything.

Silva smiled. "Stevic's daughter, I daresay, though you must favor your mother."

"You know my father?" Karigan did not like where this conversation was leading.

Silva's smile deepened. "He is a most generous friend and patron. I am housing you and the young man at no expense as a favor to Stevic. That saves explaining to your superiors why you spent the night in a brothel, does it not? It would appear inappropriate, I would guess, for the madam of a brothel to present a Rider seal at tax time for reimbursement."

"My father?" was all Karigan could say, appalled. How in the world did he know Silva? What was he doing visiting a brothel? Well, she knew *what,* but *why?* She knew *why,* too, but–but—*her father?*

"You are mistaken," Karigan said, certain of Silva's error, certain of what she knew of her father. He would never patronize a brothel.

"No, dear, I am not. I hold Stevic in high esteem, and he conducts a good deal of clan business from here."

A blackness flooded Karigan's vision. "No," she whispered. Everything she believed and thought she knew was cast into oblivion; the world was falling out from beneath her.

How could her father betray her this way? Dishonor the memory of her mother? She believed the love between her parents pure and true; thought he'd never remarried or seriously courted another woman because his love for Kariny was singular and infinite. It seemed, however, he'd been *buying* his pleasure elsewhere. *Here.* How could he . . . how could he consort with whores? Had his life with Kariny been a lie?

Suddenly, her father was a stranger to her.

To her disgust, tears flowed down her cheeks. She swiped them away. Everything good she thought her father stood for was false.

Silva watched her with a placid expression on her face. "Never doubt your father, dear. No matter what you may be thinking of him right now, he is a good man and I owe him much. I don't allow just anyone into my house, either, you know; it's very exclusive, and not all the entertainment my guests partake in is what you're thinking." When Karigan said nothing, she continued, "I know of your father's life, of how he tried to raise you in the absence of Kariny—"

"Do *not* invoke my mother's name," Karigan said in a hoarse whisper. "Not in this place."

"As you wish," Silva said, "but I do want you to know that I hold your father in high esteem. He helped me in the past, so this house is always open to him when he is in town, and to his kin, as well." With that, Silva set aside her cup and stood. She walked across the kitchen to leave, but paused by the door. "It saddens me that Stevic's daughter would think less of him for wanting to seek comfort on a rare occasion even though his wife has been gone all these years. Do not think less of him, Karigan, for he never forgets your mother, and he grieves for her still." And she left.

Karigan could only stare at her plate with blurry eyes, yellow egg yokes bleeding into the ham steak.

"A great lady, that," said Cetchum. "Aye, she keeps a goodly house, taking in girls who have lived through the five hells and worse, an' teachin' them their letters and figures. They don' have to stay, and a lot have off and married good gents. And only the most worthy gents come here." And now he whispered, "Why I've seen a lord-governor or two come here. Aye, fair lady Silva is good to all under her roof, including my Rona and me, and especially to the girls who provide the gents with companionship."

Companionship. Trading in flesh. An even worse thought occurred to Karigan: there were brothels in almost every major city and town in Sacoridia, and Rhovanny, too. At how many of these was her father a favored "patron"?

Karigan wanted to fling something across the room. Instead, she would seek lodging elsewhere right this moment, someplace where decent folk stayed, and she would pen her father a letter about all this. She stood hastily, and the blood drained from her head. The world went gray and fuzzy.

Next thing she knew, she was on her back on the floor, staring up at the concerned faces of Cetchum, Rona, and Silva.

"Tsk, tsk," Rona said. "You should've et your breakfast, dearie. Still weak from your dunking in the river, too."

Sweat slithered down the sides of Karigan's face. All she wanted to do was close her eyes and sleep.

"Get Zem and help her back to her room," Silva ordered Rona, "and make sure she stays abed and eats this time."

Trapped, Karigan thought. She was trapped in a brothel.

MIRWELL PROVINCE

Beryl Spencer stepped out into the corridor, the door to Lord Mirwell's library closing soundly behind her. She stood there fuming for several moments, feeling thwarted, annoyed, and perhaps worst of all, betrayed.

More maneuvers? He was sending her out on more exercises with the troops? She had just returned from the last set this week past and barely had time to brush the dust off her boots. One field camp blurred into another.

As she stood there in the corridor, she could not erase the image of that pompous son of a goat, Colonel Birch, standing there next to Timas, handing her her new orders. Somehow he had courted favor with Timas, had insinuated himself into the role that should have been hers, of close confidant and aide, first in Timas' affections; he had outmaneuvered her and she couldn't figure out how. Now she had become just another military officer with no special standing in the lord-governor's eyes.

Beryl tried everything to gain Timas' confidence, from deference, authority, efficiency, and hard work, even to using her femininity, all of which had worked so well on his father. She drew on all the power of her brooch to enhance her special ability to assume a role and convince others she was someone whom she was not, to win him over, but to no avail.

Which naturally made her suspicious.

She struck off down the corridor. Timas didn't appear to be hiding anything; nothing obvious at least, and he was governing the province well despite his inexperience and difficulties compounded by the failure of crops over the summer, and rather odd magical occurrences, like the fire-breathing snapping turtle they'd found in the keep's ornamental pond. Yet he kept sending her away.

Getting me out of the way. Why?

She turned a corner of the keep's corridor, brightly lit for the evening hours. Her stride was crisp, even, and purposeful. Anyone noting her passage would see only the officer, all her medals, buttons, and insignia gleaming on her scarlet shortcoat, her hair severely tied back, and her boot heels sharp on the floor.

Everything about her appearance and carriage was impeccable—it was an image she'd worked hard to cultivate. Most viewed her, as she intended, as a cold, calculating soldier dedicated to the province and its lord-governor. Many of the keep's denizens and members of Mirwell's court feared her, as well they should. During old Lord Mirwell's reign she had been not only his most trusted aide, but his chief interrogator. In the course of her duties, she employed many methods to force confessions of anyone he deemed worthy of his suspicions.

Her boots rapped on the spiraling stone stairs as she descended to the keep's main level. Despite her reputation, she found herself constantly having to reinforce her role. Returning to Mirwellton after the old lord-governor's fall had been risky. There were those who suspected she had betrayed him. Otherwise, wouldn't the king have executed her as well, or at least kept her in prison? Not that anyone would admit they approved of the old lord or his plans to dethrone King Zachary . . . but it did generate her share of enemies among those who remained secretly loyal to the dead man and his ambitions.

She ensured none of these suspicions led to the truth, that no one exposed her real affiliations and compromised her position as an operative of King Zachary's. Her mission was to keep watch on Timas Mirwell, to make sure he did not follow in the footsteps of his traitorous father.

She entered the main hall. Soldiers saluted her and

courtiers spared her a nervous glance before hurrying away. She allowed herself a small, grim smile. If she caught wind of anyone expressing suspicions about her, if she believed they would reveal her true affiliations, her true duty, they quietly disappeared, never to be heard from again.

She was not what one would consider a typical Green Rider.

Beryl contemplated what her next step should be. Timas persisted in assigning her duties that would keep her away, seriously hampering her overriding duty to maintain vigil over him. There were two possibilities: either Timas just didn't like her, or something else was afoot and he couldn't trust her. If it were the latter, it meant her mission was compromised. If the mission was compromised, it meant she'd been exposed and was likely in danger, unless they—Colonel Birch and Lord Mirwell—believed her ignorant of their activities and that she continued to give only positive reports to King Zachary.

She must get to the bottom of it while feigning ignorance, but that was bloody hard when they kept sending her away.

Crossing the main hall and starting down a corridor toward her quarters, Beryl was wondering how she might get out of her latest orders when she heard Birch speaking with someone behind her. She turned about and peered back into the main hall. A runner handed him a folded piece of paper. He opened it and glanced at it before folding it back up and dropping it into his pocket. He dismissed the runner and headed toward the keep's entranceway. Guards hauled open the massive ironbound doors for him, and even before Beryl could feel the draft of chill air against her face, he walked out into the night.

She decided to follow him. If she needed information, this was the way to start: to see what Birch was about. If he and Timas were up to something the king did not approve of, it was her duty to find out about it. And if they were diverting her attention because they knew her real identity and wanted her out of the way, she had to correct the situation.

She paused for several moments before crossing the main

hall. The guards opened the great doors once again at her approach, and she strode out onto the front steps. Torches sputtered on either side of her, so she descended the steps to stand in the deeper gloom of the night to allow her eyes time to adjust to the dark. Across the courtyard she could make out Birch receding into the night.

She glanced about to make sure no one was watching and set off across the courtyard with a determined stride, leaving the torchlit entrance behind. Birch was angling toward the stables. Would she have to follow him somewhere on horseback?

The heavy, cool air subdued the world around her. No breeze stirred the treetops, there was no sound of owls hooting or dogs baying in the distance; only her feet crunching on the gravel walkway.

She slowed as she approached the stable, not wishing to give away her presence. There were no lanterns lit within, just the blackened windows gaping at her. At this hour, the horses were quiet inside, dozing or munching on hay. She hoped her own mare, Luna Moth, would not catch wind of her and call out with a whinny as she sometimes did.

Unsure of where Birch had gotten to, Beryl paused and listened. The damp air carried the nearby sound of voices to her. She judged that Birch and whomever he met with were located just on the other side of the stables.

She stepped off the gravel walkway and onto the grass to conceal the sound of her footsteps. Cautiously she inched forward, closer to the building, sticking to the shadows, hardly daring to breathe, all her senses taut.

As she edged toward a corner of the building, the voices grew louder.

"—taking a chance by coming here," Birch said.

"Don't think so," said a man. "I wanted to deliver this myself."

Beryl peered around the corner. Her eyesight wasn't the best, and though her specs were tucked in an inner pocket of her shortcoat, she didn't dare risk the movement to take them out. So she was left squinting in the dark, discerning a figure that must be Birch standing before a horseman in plain leathers and a cloak. He sat his horse like a trained soldier, but if he was someone she knew, the dark and her nearsightedness confounded her ability to identify him.

"You got it then," Birch said in a pleased murmur.

"Aye, and our thief has agreed to the other assignment as well. He believed our cover story that our 'employer' was a nobleman desiring to settle a matter of honor." The horseman leaned over his horse's withers to hand Birch a document case.

"Grandmother will be most pleased to see this," Birch said.

Grandmother? Beryl wondered. Birch was working with a thief on behalf of his grandmother?

"Thought she would be," the horseman said. "The thief is good, though he met with some resistance at the museum." He laughed. "A lady in a dress of all things! She didn't give him much trouble."

"I should hope not," Birch muttered, gazing at the object in his hands. "When does he think he can deliver on his next task?"

"He said it requires some *cultivation* and planning. He doesn't want to move too quickly, considering the delicacy of the task. I'll return to ensure everything is carried out."

Birch grunted. "Good. Anything else?"

Beryl never heard the horseman's reply. Her nerves jangled when she sensed someone standing behind her. She whirled, her hand on her saber, just in time to see a looming figure swinging at her head with a large rock in its hand. The rock struck her temple and she crashed backward into the stable wall.

Flurries of crackling snow speckled Beryl's vision while hammers banged on the inside of her skull. At any moment, she thought she might disgorge her guts she felt so ill. Through the blizzard in her vision, she made out three figures gazing down at her.

"This one is no Mirwellian officer," said a distantly familiar, abrasive voice, "but a Greenie. She betrayed her old lord."

"I know," Birch said matter-of-factly. "We've been keeping her out of the way till now. She's had nothing to tell the king."

"Should we kill her?" asked the horseman.

When Beryl shifted her gaze to look on him, her stomach lurched. She closed her eyes, but the snow still crackled and popped behind her eyelids. If they killed her, at least it would end her misery.

A silence followed as they decided what to do.

"No," said the rough voice. "We'll let Grandmother decide."

Oh, good, Beryl thought. Grandmother would be kind and gentle. Understanding.

She cracked her eyes open. Starlight gleamed on a sharp hook the gruff-voiced man rubbed against his chin like a finger. She blinked. Yes, it was, in a way, his finger, for he had no hand. Just the hook.

They made her stand. The world reeled and finally she lost the contents of her stomach before passing into unconsciousness.

Grandmother stared at the Mirwellian officer, whom the captain's men dropped like a sack of sand onto the tent platform before they marched back out into the night. The woman had a frightful lump on her head and was, fortunately for her, quite unconscious. Captain Immerez appeared pleased with himself, even more so than a cat who has caught a very fat mouse.

"So this is the spy you told me about," Grandmother said.

"Yes," he replied. "She was Lord Mirwell's closest aide. Her name's Beryl Spencer."

She heard the resentment in his voice. "The old Lord Mirwell, you mean."

He bristled. "The *only* Lord Mirwell. His son is useless.

His father did what he could with the whelp, but all for nothing."

Grandmother gave Captain Immerez a sidelong glance, hearing much more in his words than he spoke aloud, as she always did whenever they discussed the current Lord Mirwell. He was not only aggrieved that the "whelp" sat in the governor's chair in Mirwellton, but he represented to Immerez all he had failed to attain. He'd expected to realize a powerful position in the province through his good standing with the old lord-governor, but Tomas Mirwell was dead, and Captain Immerez's ambitions with him. His bitterness only festered during his two years of hiding. It was, at least in part, what made him malleable to her will. She provided him with a new outlet for his ambition.

Among Captain Immerez's complaints was that the current lord-governor had not seen fit to follow in the footsteps of his scheming father, had not gone against the will of the king and engaged in bloody little wars so the province could wrap itself in the glory of battle. Instead, he attempted to make his province prosper by emphasizing farming and industry rather than the military. She could not fault the young man for serving his province rather than himself, but it made him untrustworthy to the cause of Second Empire.

"We need these hills to hide in," Grandmother said, "and young Lord Mirwell's cooperation has allowed us to do so."

An ugly sneer crossed the captain's face. "Without Birch there, he'd go squealing to the king. And I'm sure your little demonstration has helped keep him quiet."

Colonel Birch was one of her own, born of the true blood of Second Empire, and one who commanded his own following of soldiers within the militia. Not so long ago he'd brought Timas Mirwell to Hawk Hill to meet her and witness a demonstration of her power on some unfortunate beggar the captain's men dragged off the streets in Mirwellton.

"Whelp couldn't keep his dinner down." Captain Immerez's laughter rasped like rusted iron.

The demonstration had proven effective, but she did not wish to persuade Timas Mirwell entirely with threats. She'd reminded him of the historical alliance between his clan and Mornhavon the Great during the Long War. If he cooperated, she would reward him. She would gift him with King Zachary's intended, whom all men seemed to desire, if he wished it, or even better, an important role in Second Empire when it conquered Sacoridia.

In any case, Birch kept Timas Mirwell bent to her will, and she did not interfere with the day-to-day management of the province. Travelers were kept out of the hills with rumors of outlaws preying on the unwary, which was not exactly untrue. The captain had to provide for his men somehow. To Grandmother's mind, it all worked out satisfactorily.

"And you caught this woman eavesdropping?" Grandmother asked. She nudged the slack body with her toe.

"Yes."

"Why didn't you kill her?"

"The king expects occasional contact with her. If she totally vanished, he'd grow suspicious."

"But she *has* vanished," Grandmother countered. "She's vanished to *here.*"

The captain scratched around his eye socket beneath the patch. "We could force her to write a message or something, so it appeared all was well."

Grandmother sighed in exasperation. The spy would be too clever, manipulating any message they coerced her to write into revealing her predicament and Second Empire. It was clear to Grandmother that the captain had another agenda when it came to the spy, a personal agenda of retribution that overrode common sense. If she judged the situation right, the spy's first affront had been becoming the former Lord Mirwell's *closest* aide, dearer to him than Captain Immerez. Her second affront had been betraying the old schemer.

"Birch has been sending her out on maneuvers to keep her out of the way," the captain said. "I suppose he can use that excuse if anyone comes looking for her."

"Very well," Grandmother said. The woman stirred with

a little cry, then fell unconscious again. The captain had told her that the spy was actually a Green Rider, and it was known to Grandmother that Green Riders, at least historically speaking, had minor abilities with the art. "You know, since we do have this one, there is something I believe I'd like to try."

"Try?" Captain Immerez asked in surprise.

"I'd like to see what I can learn about the Green Riders and their abilities."

The captain rubbed the curve of his hook against his chin. "An interrogation would be challenging. She's a master interrogator herself, and would know how to resist any questioning."

Grandmother smiled. "It's not really an interrogation I have in mind, more of a notion of an experiment I'd like to try. Gold chains . . ." Before she could lose herself in envisioning the procedure, the captain cleared his throat. "Yes?"

"I have something for you, carried all the way from Sacor City." He withdrew a document case from beneath his cloak and proffered it to her with a low bow.

Grandmother clapped in delight. "Wonderful. You and your men have served me well." She eagerly opened the case. Within lay a fragile, parchment document, scrawled with faint ink. She held it up, the lantern that hung from the center pole of the tent illuminating it with a deep golden glow. She frowned.

"What is it?" the captain asked. "What's wrong?"

Grandmother sighed and closed the parchment in the case, and handed it back to him. "I can't read it," she said.

"You can't read it?" He opened the case and looked at the parchment.

"Can you?" she asked him.

"N–no. It's in a different language."

"That would be ancient Sacoridian," she told him. "I cannot read it, nor could any of my people here. If Weldon Spurlock were still alive, he might be able to, but he's very much gone. I need a translation."

"I–I see."

"Do you? The parchment is worthless without it. How will you rectify the situation, Captain?"

"I'll—I'll find a way."

"I would not wish for you to fail," Grandmother said. "I am nearly done with the pouch, but I dare not use it until I have this parchment translated." She pointed to the pouch, about the size of a finger, lying atop the skeins of yarn in her basket. She had knit all her different colors into it, the red, brown, indigo, and sky blue.

Immerez hooked his thumb into his swordbelt. "I do not understand why—"

"This parchment contains instructions for reading the book of Theanduris Silverwood. Books of magic sometimes require very specific instructions for their handling and reading. I would hate the book to destroy itself before it can be read because it was improperly handled."

"I see," the captain said. "I think I know where to find you that translation. It may take a while, though." Without another word, he turned on his heel and left the tent.

"Don't take too long," she called out after him.

He was a clever man and she had confidence in him. He would find a way for her to translate the instructions. She put it out of her mind for now, gazing down at the spy, who lay at her feet, helpless and hurt. She could go back to her own fire and work on the pouch, which she could easily finish tonight, or make those booties for Amala's baby that was due in a few weeks. But, when it came down to it, the project that intrigued her most concerned their captive and gold chains.

When she perceived someone watching her, she glanced at the tent flaps and saw light glinting in a pair of eyes. "Come, girl," she told her granddaughter. "You can help me figure this out."

Lala stepped into the tent, gazed down at the spy, then up at her grandmother. Yes, they would figure it out together.

FERGAL'S EXPLANATION

Over the days that followed, Karigan's usual strength returned. She sat in her room and wrote numerous versions of an angry letter to her father, all of which she wadded up and tossed into the fire. There just wasn't any easy way to address his "association" with the Golden Rudder in letter form that did not make her sound insufferable, especially considering the subject matter. No, she'd have to discuss this with him in person. She was sorely tempted to sail down the Grandgent to Corsa while Fergal continued his recovery, but she dared not leave him unchaperoned for too long in the hands of the ladies of the Golden Rudder.

Besides, she was on king's business, not her own, and she couldn't afford the time a detour to Corsa would take. She sighed and crumpled up her latest and last version of the letter and fed it to the flames. She would have to see her father another time, or find another way to write her letter when her words were less fueled by anger.

Everyone seemed to sense her fury and stayed clear of her, even though it wasn't really Silva or the inhabitants of the brothel that angered her. And while she was certainly upset with her father, she directed the worst of her rage at herself for having been so bloody naïve.

Her father had loved Kariny. She knew it with both her head and heart, but she'd been foolish to believe that their love had the power to trap him in time; to believe that memory was enough for him, that it quelled any need he might have for affection and physical release, even after so many years.

How stupid she'd been to expect her father to lead such an ascetic life.

But why, she wondered, did he have to *buy* affection? Why sully himself in such a way? Why disrespect what he had with her mother?

Karigan wasn't sure if it was possible to understand. All she knew now was that she would never look at her father the same way again, and that he had shown her that her own ideals of love were little more than childish fantasies.

The strokes of the town bell drew her from her introspection. It was time for midmorning tea, which Rona made sure Karigan and Fergal enjoyed every day. Karigan left her room and strolled along the corridor, which was quite empty, and no surprise at that due to the nocturnal employment of those who lived here.

Downstairs she found the parlor, too, was empty, though a teapot, breads, cakes, and scones awaited her. She took a seat in a plush red velvet chair with an ornate cherrywood frame. Heavy drapes were tied back from the windows to reveal the dim autumn light on the street outside, and a fire crackled in the fireplace.

All the materials of the parlor were very fine, from the rich carpeting to the porcelain tea service. Karigan couldn't help but check the maker's mark on the bottom of a cup, only to discover it was made by Barden House, one of the finest producers of porcelain in L'Petrie Province, if not all of Sacoridia. There was even Barden porcelain in the king's castle. She had looked.

Fine works of art adorned the walls, including a massive oil over the fireplace of the Grandgent in spring, lupine bursting with color along its banks and a fleet of sailing vessels on its waters. The artist was renowned across the provinces.

Karigan poured herself tea, and when Fergal hesitantly entered the room, she poured a second. For a change he was dressed in his uniform, and not the gentleman's robe Silva had supplied him with. This was a good sign.

Karigan handed him his tea after he sat down. "How are you doing today?" she asked.

"Better."

"Better enough to leave tomorrow?"

He nodded, and blew on his tea.

"Good." Karigan exhaled with relief. The sooner they were away from the Golden Rudder, the better.

They sat in silence for a while, sipping tea and eating the sugary treats laid out before them. Finally Karigan decided to ask him about the incident.

"Fergal," she said, "what do you remember about falling in the river? How did it happen?"

He stared morosely at his knees, a half-eaten scone in his hand.

"It's all right," Karigan reassured him, "we've all had accidents, done silly things. There's no need to feel embarrassed about it. I could tell you a few stories myself." She smiled, hoping her words would make him more comfortable.

"It didn't rescue me."

"What?"

"My Rider magic."

"No," she said, "it didn't. Riders often have accidents and their special abilities don't save them. It depends on the type of accident and the nature of their ability. Dale's ability to find water, for instance, wouldn't help her in a shipwreck." She stopped then, hoping that what she was beginning to suspect was not true. He hadn't jumped into the river on purpose, had he? Surely he wasn't *that* stupid. Surely not. But judging by some of his other antics earlier on this journey . . .

"It wasn't an accident, was it?"

He shook his head.

"You were hoping to force your ability to emerge by attempting to drown yourself."

He nodded, still staring at his knees.

"You endangered your life and mine to do this." Her voice was calm, but as cold as the river itself. "Your behavior also delayed king's business and landed us in a brothel, which, if word ever gets out, will make the messenger service look foolish." Then she laughed harshly. "I guess I'm the fool. I should have taken you back to Sacor City when I had the chance."

Her teacup clattered into its saucer and she stood and strode out, not caring to see or hear Fergal's reaction. She remembered how eager he had been for his ability to reveal itself. Becoming a Green Rider had started a whole new life for him, far from his father and the knacker's shop, and it must have seemed to him he was not a full Rider without his ability. She applauded his desire to serve, but purposely throwing oneself into mortal danger and endangering others—namely herself—was inexcusable. She would not, could not, afford to be forgiving on this. There was plenty of danger in this line of work without inviting it.

She crossed the foyer and cut through the kitchen, brushing past a startled Rona, and headed for the inn's stable and Condor's stall. There she slipped on his bridle and mounted him bareback. She rode throughout the day, away from the brothel, away from Fergal, away from everything. She allayed her anger with exertion, riding hard up hill and down, weaving in and out of trees along woods trails, fording streams, following the river, riding till the sun began to set and her mind cleared like the sky after a storm.

When she returned to the Golden Rudder's stable yard, she found Fergal leading a fully tacked Sunny out onto the street.

Karigan halted Condor. "Where are you going?"

Fergal's face paled when he saw her. "I'm going back. To Sacor City."

"Oh?"

"You want to be rid of me, don't you?"

"What I want seems irrelevant to you," Karigan said. "What I'd like is for you to start acting like a Green Rider." She swung her leg forward over Condor's withers and slipped to the ground.

"I heard you didn't even want to be a Green Rider," Fergal said with heat in his voice. "You don't even care about the messenger service. You tried to leave. I at least want to be one."

She considered him long and hard, the darkness of his eyes, the rings beneath them no doubt from the exhaustion of trying to drown himself and fretting over her reaction. "It's true," she said. "I did not plan to be a Green Rider. Most who end up in the messenger service don't. I grew up expecting to follow in my father's footsteps as a merchant, and that's all I wanted to be, but I hadn't counted on the Rider call. What is untrue is that I don't care about the messenger service. I care about serving the king and doing the best job I can. I care about how Riders are perceived in the world, and most important, I care about the people who serve with me. I have seen far too many of them die."

Silence fell between them as Fergal sorted out her words. "I thought going back to Sacor City would be for the best."

"Maybe for me, but not for you." When he frowned, she continued, "Look, running away doesn't help anything, and I should know—I've done enough of it myself. If you're going to be a Rider, you need to face up to your mistakes and learn from them. Otherwise, you might as well surrender that brooch you're wearing and forget about being a Green Rider. Believe me when I say there are far worse things out there to deal with than me, and if you can't deal with me?" She shrugged.

"I want to be a Rider," he said, fingering his brooch.

"Then," Karigan said, "put Sunny back in her stall and go have some dinner. I want you at full strength tomorrow morning for travel. Then when you're finished, go back to your room and look in your mirror, and perhaps you'll see a Rider staring back at you. If you do, we'll leave together. If not, you can return to Sacor City and explain yourself to Captain Mapstone." When Fergal did not move, she added, "That's an order, Rider, and if you ever attempt to drown yourself again, or anything as remotely idiotic, I shall see you removed from the messenger service so fast you'll be on your way to your father's knackery the day before yesterday." With that, she led Condor into the stable.

These encounters were emotionally fatiguing and she wondered how the captain dealt with so many under her command, guiding their impulses, punishing their mistakes, and handling their personalities. She hated to lie to him about taking away his brooch and returning him to his father, but she knew of no other way of convincing him to behave.

Inside the stable she rubbed Condor down, noting most of the stalls were full, which they had not been when she left. Carriage horses and saddle horses, all of fine lines and breeding, munched on hay or watched her and Condor. The Golden Rudder looked to be busy this evening.

Fergal finally returned with Sunny, to Karigan's relief, and started to untack her.

Good, she thought. *He took time to think things over.* She patted Condor, and without a word to Fergal, left the stable for the inn.

Stepping up into the kitchen she found "busy" to be an understatement. She had to dodge cooks wielding dripping ladles and servants bearing platters of roast beef and boats of gravy, flagons of wine, and boards of cheese. She ducked and danced and back-hopped her way out of the kitchen and into the foyer.

"Whew," she murmured, wiping her hand across her brow. She would see about getting her dinner later when the chaos died down. For now she'd retreat to her room. She paused to listen a moment to the talking, laughter, and clinking of tableware coming from the great hall and thought it could be a party at any grand house, but it was not, for this was a house of a different sort.

The bell jangled at the door and Rona hurried to answer it. Karigan bounded up the stairs two at a time, hoping to avoid being seen. She did not wish it to be generally known that Green Riders were staying at the Golden Rudder, though she suspected it was likewise true for most patrons of any brothel. Her father had kept *his* secret well enough.

When she reached the landing, she careened into the arms of a man who reeked of whiskey.

"Well, my lovely!" he said. "Come to entertain me instead of Loni?"

Karigan tried to extract herself from his embrace, but he only tightened it. "I'm not your lovely," she protested.

He puckered his lips to smooch her, but she twisted her face away. "I *don't* work here."

"I won't tell anyone if you don't," the man said.

Karigan was ready to put into use some of the defensive moves she learned from Drent, but Trudy appeared just in time, striding down the corridor at a great clip, skirts swishing and arms swinging at her sides.

"Master Welles!" she chided. "You must release Karigan this instant—she's a guest."

"But I like her," the man said.

Karigan grimaced as his whiskey-laden breath flowed into her face.

"If you don't release her right now," Trudy declared, hands on her hips, "you know Silva will cast you out and you won't be invited back."

"Aw, all right, all right," he said, but he did not release Karigan without planting a wet smooch right on her lips.

"Master Welles!" Trudy cried.

"Bleah," Karigan said.

The man giggled like a schoolboy, while Karigan scowled in disgust and wiped the residue of whiskey off her mouth with the back of her hand.

Master Welles staggered and put his hand out to the wall to hold himself up. Trudy rolled her eyes.

"Would you help me?" she asked Karigan, taking one of the man's arms. "I want him in room thirteen."

"Um, all right."

Karigan took Master Welles' other arm and the two of them guided the unsteady man down the hall.

"Didya know I'm the harbor master?" he asked Karigan.

"No," she replied.

"Well, I am." He sounded very proud, as he should. The

harbor master was a significant position in any port town. And, Karigan supposed, the harbor master was exactly the kind of important gentleman the Golden Rudder catered to. She wondered what his fellow citizens would think if they saw him now.

When they reached room thirteen, Trudy assisted Master Welles up onto the high bed.

"Loni will come later," she assured him. "Right now you need some rest."

"You could stay with me," he said, patting the bed next to him. "Both of you."

"I'm afraid not," Trudy said. "It would make Loni jealous, you know."

"I s'pose you're right," he said, eyes half closed. "Hate to disappoint her." He rolled to his side and plumped his pillow. With a fading voice, he murmured to Karigan, "That Trudy . . ." And in short order he began to snore.

"I'm sorry about this," Trudy told Karigan, pulling off one of Master Welles' boots, "and I appreciate your help. Silva likes to keep things orderly here, and she really would have barred him from the Rudder if he got rough or unmanageable. Zem isn't just a gardener, you know." She slid the second boot off and draped a blanket over the sleeping man.

Karigan didn't know what to say.

"I realize you're not comfortable here, or around *us,*" Trudy continued. "Particularly around me, I'm thinking."

"Well, I—"

"Never mind," Trudy said. She bustled to the bedside table and lowered the lamplight. "You were raised in a respectable family that loved you. You've no business being near a brothel."

And her father did? Karigan ran her hand through her hair in an attempt to soothe a sudden flare of anger. She was so very tired. The revelation about her father would have been enough to contend with on its own, but the whole incident with Fergal and its aftermath positively sapped her. Not for the first time she wished Captain Mapstone were here to take over the reins, to solve her problems. She wished she'd never heard of the Golden Rudder, much less ended up as one of its guests. But here she was, and without the captain's guidance. She had only herself to rely on. Of course, she didn't think she'd really want the captain in on this little detail of her father's life, though the thought of the captain giving Stevic G'ladheon a piece of her mind on the subject made Karigan smile.

Trudy straightened cushions on a window seat, Master Welles' snoring filling the chamber. She must have taken Karigan's silence as confirmation of her statement, for she continued, "You have a wonderful father, but mine wasn't so kind."

"You know my father?"

"We all do."

Karigan believed Trudy hadn't meant to be cruel, but the simple words were like a knife plunged into her gut. Of course her father knew *all* the ladies of the Golden Rudder.

"We don't all know him in the way you are thinking, but he is very nice to us nevertheless. Brings us gifts and kind words." Trudy set the last cushion in place and took up a rumpled throw, which she began to fold. "No, my father was not so kind. I ran away to hide from his beatings, but the streets were no better." She turned to Karigan, and Karigan could see, even in the dim light, how haunted her eyes were. "There are those on the street who prey on the likes of me."

Karigan shuddered. She knew it was true. There were those who lived in the shadows, those who "respectable" citizens like herself did not see, or *chose* not to see.

"I'm—I'm sorry," she said.

Trudy shrugged. "If not for Silva rescuing me, taking me in and feeding me, keeping me warm, I'd be dead. Or worse. I'm one of the lucky ones. Silva lets me stay even if I haven't many clients."

"Not many—? Oh." Karigan guessed women were less apt to seek out company in a brothel and that Trudy cultivated a more particular clientele.

"I will admit I'm rather in demand as a partner in

Knights," Trudy said with a half smile. "I'm not bad at Triples or Black Queen either. In fact, I win an awful lot. But I also have a few devoted clients."

"Um, oh."

"Is that all you have to say?" There was an amused gleam in Trudy's eye.

"Yes." Karigan had known throughout her life, due to the clan business and its position in society, all kinds of people, including those who favored their own gender in relationships. In fact, there was a pair of gents who owned a highly regarded tailor shop in uptown Corsa who were one of the clan's earliest and most loyal customers, eventually becoming close family friends. Growing up with visits from Joshua and Orlen—or Uncle Josh and Uncle Orry, as Karigan called them—she saw them as little different from anyone else in her life and regarded them with great affection.

Heavens, even her usually conservative aunts had raptures over their visits, delighting over gifts of flowers and scarves and candies. The two men were very disarming and entertaining, and everyone in the clan loved and respected them. Karigan realized hers might not be the prevailing attitude of Sacoridia toward such pairings, but so long as the couples lived as productive and law-abiding citizens, their presence appeared to be more or less tolerated, if not welcomed, by the larger community.

The difference with Trudy was that Karigan had never been approached—propositioned—before. Even just thinking about it caused warmth to creep into her cheeks.

As if Trudy knew how she disconcerted Karigan, she laughed softly. "You should see your expression."

"I'd rather not, thank you." Karigan could only guess. Did she look like a deer staring down a hunter's arrow?

"If anything," Trudy said, more soberly, "be glad of your life and your wonderful father. You know, it could've been you on the streets as easily as me had the gods allotted us different fates. But they didn't, and here we are crossing paths anyway."

The two left room thirteen, and paused in the corridor.

"Remember," Trudy said, "if you want me, you know where to find me. The king's gold is always welcome."

As Trudy strode down the corridor, laughter trickled back to Karigan. In some wicked way, Trudy enjoyed making her squirm. That aside, the young woman had given her much to consider. She headed for her own room wondering about the gods and how different her life was from those who worked in the Golden Rudder, and it made her thankful for her father—truly thankful for the kind of man he was despite his taste for brothels, and even thankful she was a Green Rider when she could have been destined for a far less savory existence.

She did not blame the ladies for the lives they led if their backgrounds, like Trudy's, had forced them into the "trade." She decided the blame lay on those who used brothels. After all, without demand, there'd be no brothels. It was one of the first tenants of merchanting Karigan learned from her father.

Ironically, her father was one who helped create demand. No matter how much she loved him, she resolved to give him her opinion on the matter just as soon as she could manage it.

The next morning, Silva, Rona, and Zem stood in the courtyard between the stable and the inn for Karigan's and Fergal's leave-taking. Fergal said little to Karigan over breakfast, but she assumed he intended to continue the journey west with her and not return to Sacor City. As they led their horses from the stable, Silva stepped forward.

"Remember, Karigan dear, you are always welcome beneath my roof."

"Thank you," she replied in a subdued tone, though she knew she would never willingly find herself this close to the Golden Rudder again. But Silva had been very generous and kind, expecting nothing in return for room and board. "I . . . I appreciate your help."

Silva smiled and nodded. Good-byes were exchanged and

the Riders were leading their horses out of the courtyard when an upstairs gable window flung open. It was Trudy, and she waved a handkerchief at them.

"Good-bye, Karigan! Thank you for the wonderful time!" And she blew a kiss. Laughter issued from behind her and she slammed the window shut.

Karigan's mouth dropped open. "N-no," she started to explain. "N–nothing—nothing happened."

Silva, Rona, and Zem simply regarded her with pleasant expressions. Fergal's was a cock-eyed gaze of reassessment.

She'd let Trudy have her little joke. Trying to deny anything happened to the madam and her servants would only make her sound defensive. And guilty. She pulled on Condor's reins and hurriedly led him out of the courtyard and onto the street. When Fergal caught up, he asked, "Did you—?"

"NO."

A moment passed as he digested her response. "Well, I did."

When she turned her glare on him, his step faltered and his cheeks turned the color of ripe tomatoes.

"You did *what?*" Fire flickered around the coolness of her words. When he opened his mouth to answer, she cut him off. "Never mind. Don't tell me. I don't want to know."

Fergal shrugged, his expression one of contentment. He started to whistle, but stopped when she glowered at him.

This was the last time, Karigan decided, anyone accompanied her on an errand. Captain Mapstone would have a complete report about Fergal on her desk when she returned. Though the whole brothel episode might be difficult to explain, especially if she included the revelation about her father. Well, she wouldn't worry about it for now.

They led the horses to the ferry landing where Cetchum and his oarsmen awaited them.

"Good morning, sirs!" the ferry master said. "I hear ye were *real* well taken care of at the Rudder." He gave them each knowing winks and Karigan just wanted to die.

Fergal thought it was very funny and he exchanged mock blows with Cetchum.

"You know," Karigan mused, "I've been thinking that maybe we ought to tie Fergal down to the deck this time to make sure he doesn't *fall* into the river again."

Fergal sobered immediately.

They loaded the horses onto the ferry and shoved off. It had rained during the night and the sky was still dull, leaving the river a slate blue. The farther the oarsmen rowed them out onto the river, the more relieved Karigan became that the Golden Rudder was being left far behind.

When the ferry scraped bottom on the west bank landing, Karigan gave Cetchum four coppers and a silver. "For both crossings," she explained, "and for your efforts to aid us." She had thought this over hard, and when she decided that not everyone would have helped her in her rescue attempt of Fergal, she saw it was the right thing to do. If nothing else, it might encourage the ferry master to help others in need, as well.

He tipped his cap. "Thank ye, sir. Good speed to ye."

"You're welcome. *Ma'am.*"

Cetchum blinked in surprise and scratched his head beneath his cap. Karigan and Fergal rode off to the sound of the oarsmen laughing heartily at their ferry master.

ELETIANS

One morning, without warning, the citizens of Sacor City awoke to a strange sight before the outermost wall and gate: tents of all sizes and deep coloration had bloomed in a fallow field overnight, like the plantings of a flower garden that suddenly emerge from the soil after having lain dormant all winter. The silken material of the tents rippled in the breeze and their hues called to mind the azure of the summer sky, the new green of spring leaves, and the deep red of roses shining with morning dew.

The sun glowed more golden on the grouping of tents, more warm, more gentle; a light like that of the elder days when the world was new. As if in response, the grasses of the field grew a richer green; too green if one took into account the time of year. The leaves of nearby trees brightened with renewed autumnal fire, and the stream that cut through the field and *beneath* the large blue tent chuckled more gaily and sparkled as though it were made of gems. Birds sang in the trees and hedges like spring reborn.

How odd it was, the city's inhabitants thought. They climbed to the battlements of the outer wall, which was usually reserved for soldiers only, to peer down on the scene. They crowded at the gate to peer out, and the more courageous among them even stepped away from the wall's protection to take a closer look.

This was no circus or fair come to town. There were no jesters, no exotic animals, no tumblers in bright costumes. The tents did not look like the gaudy pavilions of Wayfarers, who sometimes passed by the city to deal in horses and read fortunes.

No one emerged from the tents to pronounce this or that, or to reveal their identity or purpose. No one, not even the guards at the gate, had seen the tents go up. They weren't there one day but appeared the next, revealed with the dawn. The only clue to their identity were banners hung on poles seemingly of ivory and emblazoned with a green birch leaf against a field of stunning, snowy white. Yet the banners told the city folk little, for the device had not been seen by mortals in a thousand years.

Who were the owners of the tents, people wondered. What designs did they hold against Sacor City? Were they hiding a force of invaders come to annihilate the city? Did the tents contain magicians ready to cast evil spells on them? The populace murmured uneasily for the disruptions of the summer were still fresh in their minds.

It was the talk in every quarter of the city, these tents, their mysterious inhabitants, and what they intended. It surpassed interest in the king's forthcoming wedding, and rumors that the Raven Mask was again prowling the fine houses at night. Why, twice this week jewels had been removed from the rooms of prominent ladies!

The guards at the gate sent word at once to the castle. Captains and colonels and generals descended from the castle, trailed by steel-wielding soldiers and accompanied by king's messengers in green.

One by one the officers attempted to parley with the tent dwellers, but none would answer or come forth. When they tried to enter the grouping of tents, they were turned around as though repelled by some unknown force, expressions of surprise on their faces.

"Magic," some whispered, and a pulse of fear quickened through the crowds.

Yet the tent dwellers showed no sign of aggression or evil intent—they simply showed nothing of themselves at all. Even the king came down from his castle and, surrounded by his grim, black-clad bodyguards, called out to the tent dwellers, but none replied.

The king and his guards returned up the Winding Way and he was overheard mentioning to one of his advisors, "The Elt Wood . . ." and the folk of Sacor City spread the rumor that the Eletians had now come forth from their mysterious realm for unknown purposes.

For four days and four nights the soldiers kept vigil over the grouping of tents. They maintained their distance, but surrounded them in a half circle, and a king's messenger was always with them in case a tent dweller should come forth.

On the fifth day, as the novelty of the tents began to diminish and folk of the city went about their daily lives, a flap in the blue tent creased open and a hand emerged to beckon forth the king's messenger. The Green Rider nudged her gelding forward, one hand on the hilt of her saber. This was none other than the Green Rider captain, recognizable by her red hair and the gold knot at her shoulder.

She halted her horse before the tent and sat there for some time conversing with the mysterious visitor within. No one but the captain and the one to whom she spoke knew what words passed between them, but after a short conversation, she reined her horse around and headed up the Winding Way at a swift trot.

The light that streamed through the windows of the king's study was bright, but not the same, not as pure or as authentic, as that which shone upon the grouping of tents outside the city.

Laren Mapstone shook her head trying to keep her attention in the here and now. The king sat behind his desk and they were joined by advisors Colin Dovekey and Castellan Sperren, as well as by General Harborough.

"I don't like it," the general was saying. "They've hidden in their woods these last thousand years and suddenly they're camped out on our threshold?"

"I would not say they've been hiding," the king replied.

"Yes, Your Majesty," the general said, "I remember well the Eletian who helped your brother in his attempt to usurp the throne, and considering that is our experience with these folk, we cannot trust them." General Harborough was not a tall man, but his features and body were stocky and square, his neck thick, and face scarred. He was an excellent commander and oversaw the workings of all branches of Sacoridia's military. Laren knew it was his duty to be suspicious of anything that might threaten his king or country.

"There have been other encounters with Eletians, General," Laren said, "including the aid they rendered to the remnants of Lady Penburn's delegation this past summer. I do not think we can judge all Eletians by the actions of just one." Laren could not say that she totally trusted them herself, recalling some of the interactions Karigan had with them.

"They were our allies of old," Zachary said. "It was their king, Santanara, who united the defenders of the free lands against the might of Mornhavon and his empire. Without them, we'd be enslaved to the will of Arcosia."

The general crossed his arms. "That was still a thousand years ago."

"Which they remember as yesterday."

"It seems," Colin Dovekey said, "we finally have the opportunity we sought with Lady Penburn's delegation: to speak with the Eletians and learn their intentions; to find out what has stirred them from the Elt Wood."

"Skulking about our country as though they have every right," the general grumbled.

"Our borders are guarded," said crusty old Sperren, "but not closed."

"Still, it does not give them leave to—"

The king raised his hand for silence. "I appreciate your words of caution, General, but they have come to parley. If they intended harm, I suspect we'd have known it by now. I have every intention of speaking with them."

The only one who protested was the general, but the king was adamant. "Laren," he said, "you may tell them that I accept their invitation, that I will visit with them on the appointed day, but the time will be of my choosing."

Laren smiled. The Eletian she had spoken with had specified the day after tomorrow, but the king was showing he would not dance according to their whims by choosing the time. "Very well, sire."

"You will not go without your guards," the general said.

"Never fear," Zachary replied, "I will come to no harm."

The appointed day came with a cold misting rain that made Laren's joints ache. Dressed in her formal uniform, she passed the morning in her office shuffling reports, awaiting the king's word that the time had come to descend the Winding Way. But the day wore on, the bell down in the city tolling away the hours, and still the king's word did not come. She loosened her stock and collar.

Eventually she gave up on trying to accomplish any work, and unwound her waist sash and took off her longcoat, and propped her feet on her bed and tilted her chair back, a cup of tea warming her achy hands. The pains came on her more fiercely than ever since the summer when the awakening of Mornhavon wreaked havoc with her special ability, its voice clamoring in her head, constant and unrelenting, which drove her to the brink of madness and suicide.

In the end, one who possessed her brooch two hundred years before her came to her in spirit form and helped her regain control. And after Mornhavon had been banished to the future, thanks to Karigan, the chaos his awakening caused settled down. No longer were there reports of villages vanishing or people turning to stone, and those that had were restored. All her Riders agreed their special abilities were functioning properly, as was her own.

Still, the pain in her joints hurt more than ever when she used her special ability in service to Zachary, but she spoke to no one about it, and swore Master Mender Destarion to secrecy about her need for willowbark tea. He wasn't happy, but he provided her with what she wanted, and it gave her some measure of relief.

She supposed a lifetime of accidents and abuses to her body, and the fact she was entering her middling years, contributed to the pain. She just wasn't able to recover from injuries as she had in her younger days. It was rare for one to remain a Green Rider as long as she had. Most either died in the course of their duties or their brooches abandoned them, releasing them from the call. The gods must have some purpose in mind for her, keeping her bound to the messenger service for so long. Even so, she tried as best as she could to prepare her Riders for the eventuality when she would not be there for them, a day when someone else must assume the role of Rider captain.

The bell tolled two hour and the light and shadows of her quarters shifted with the movement of the cloud-shrouded sun. If the king did not proceed soon to meet the Eletians, they'd be going in the dark, and she did not think that for the best.

She had not seen much beyond those tent flaps when beckoned forth to receive the word of the Eletians, nor when she delivered to them the king's reply. A woman stood there in the shadows of the tent flaps, nothing to be revealed in the darkness beyond, and yet . . .

There was the sense of vast space and movement, like trees in a wood, the rustling she heard not the tent walls only, but a breeze through the boughs of limbs and leaves. She had an inexplicable feeling of an entire world beyond her sight, or maybe of a dream just on the rim of memory.

As she sat there considering it all, a knock came on the door. Laren rose and opened the door to find a Green Foot runner there, his hands clasped behind his back.

"The king says it is time to make ready, ma'am," he said. "He plans to leave castle grounds in half an hour."

"Please inform Lieutenant Connly as well." Laren thanked the boy and hastened to tighten her stock. It was of the blue-green plaid like that worn by the First Rider so long ago, and so was her waistcoat. The present day Riders had adopted the colors into their uniforms to connect them to their heritage. She knotted her gold sash back into place and buckled on her swordbelt. Over her shoulder she slung the horn of the First Rider.

Before she left her quarters, she removed from a corner the ancient banner of the Green Riders, wrapped carefully about its staff, which had been presented to the First Rider by King Santanara of Eletia a millennium ago. Laren hoped these reminders of long ago friendship would not be overlooked by the Eletians.

The members of the delegation, for that's what it was, had been handpicked by the king. He brought with him two of his most important advisors: Laren and Colin Dovekey. Castellan Sperren remained on duty in the castle to take charge if anything went awry. General Harborough, as top commander of the military, also joined them, as well as Lord-Governor Coutre to represent the interests of the provinces and that of the future queen.

Their ranks were filled out by standard bearers and armed guards, including no few Weapons who surrounded the king. All branches of the military were represented, even the navy, but the most impressive, most stunning banner of all was that borne by Connly, of the gold winged horse on a field of green rippling with life, even in the mist and against the gray sky. It was bordered with gold, and the gold embroidered with Eletian runes, which Laren had not yet had translated.

Raised highest and foremost, however, was the silver and black banner of Sacoridia, of the firebrand and crescent moon. Right behind it came Zachary's clan banner of a white Hillander terrier on a field of heather. Slightly lower was the cormorant banner of Clan Coutre.

Folk on the Winding Way parted to the sides of the street to gawk at the grand procession making its way through the city. All members of the delegation were attired in their formal and best, the steel of weapons, buckles, and mail polished bright. The king wore black with the firebrand and crescent moon embroidered with silver threads upon his chest, a long black cloak flowing off his shoulders, and he wore the silver fillet upon his brow. Colin, too, wore black, as was his right as the chief of the Weapons. Lord Coutre was attired in the cobalt of his clan.

A shining group they were, as they rode in formation and silence down the street, the hooves of horses ringing upon the paving stones. There was scattered cheering and applause from the street, and waves of bowing citizens as the king passed by. Laren decided it was high time the citizens got to see some pageantry, which occurred too rarely during Zachary's reign. She knew it was reticence on his part, but the populace needed to be reminded now and then of the glory of their homeland.

She looked fondly upon Zachary who, when he was a boy, was like a little brother to her. Now he was a man full grown who had truly come into his kingship, every inch of him, his expression grave and his chin set.

When finally the delegation exited the city and came upon the encampment, they found it as quiet and empty as before, but here the drizzle became less penetrating and the sky lighter, the colors around the tents richer.

Neff the herald rode forth and his voice rang out against the city wall: "His Excellency King Zachary, lord and clan chief of Hillander Province, and high king of the twelve provinces, from the eastern shores to the plains of the west, from the forests of the north to the islands of the southern coast; leader of the clans of Sacor and bearer of the firebrand, supplicant to the gods only, comes forth to meet with the lords of Eletia."

Silence. Nothing moved among the tents, no beckoning hands appeared, no Eletian heralds emerged to welcome them. Was it the intention of the Eletians to mock them? Were they insulted the king refused to come at the time *they* designated? Did they hold such contempt for those other than themselves that they would ignore the presence of King Zachary and his folk?

Just as General Harborough began to whisper his disgust to the king and Colin, the flaps of all the tents parted nearly in unison. Eletians emerged bearing wreaths of flowers and laurels, and trailing garlands that were presented to members of the delegation. As Laren received a garland of lilies and roses and columbine, she marveled to see such flowers in bloom at this time of year, and so fresh and fragrant. General Harborough's stunned expression at receiving a wreath of white flowers from a slim Eletian girl with golden hair almost made Laren laugh.

When the flowers were all handed out, a tall, slender woman emerged from the large blue tent. Her flaxen hair was pulled back into many braids, snowy feathers bound into them. Her simple dress was of ocean colors, of foamy blues and greens. She bowed slightly to the king.

"We greet you, Firebrand, great lord of the Sacor Clans," she said in a voice that rang like music. Laren was certain this was the woman to whom she had spoken before. "If you would bring those closest to you, we may meet within." She gestured to the blue tent.

The king chose Laren, the general, Colin, Lord Coutre, and Fastion, one of his Weapons, to accompany him. When the general argued he should take more bodyguards, Zachary said to him, "I have no need if you are there to protect me."

General Harborough could only scratch his head, unable to come up with a response.

The chosen companions of the king followed the woman into the tent.

KING AND PRINCE AND FUTURE QUEEN

Laren followed Colin and upon entering the tent, stared in wonder. It was as though they entered a forest glade. Great white-skinned birches with golden leaves arched above them, supporting the canopy, and the space felt too vast for the confines of a tent. The trees were lined up in rows like a great hall of living boughs. Tall, emerald grasses wavered as if touched by open air, and before them, the stream that passed by the city gate gurgled through the tent-glade.

The tent walls rustled, their coloring that of the sky, and the more Laren gazed, the more the walls and ceiling lost definition and did become open air, as though the king and his companions had not stepped into a tent at all, but were somehow transported to another place where it was still warm, still spring, or at least the warmer days of autumn extended.

A narrow path lay before them, winding away through the grasses and beneath the boughs of the birches.

"Be welcome," their guide said, "and follow."

Laren glanced at her companions and saw their expressions of surprise and awe, even on the face of the Weapon, Fastion. Her own must look much the same.

"I presume you are taking us to see someone in authority," Zachary said, "but to whom? I should like to know before we are presented."

The Eletian woman paused, the white feathers bound in her hair drifting about her head. Laren thought she detected surprise, as though the Eletian expected complete compliance from her guests and no questions whatsoever.

After a moment's hesitation, she nodded. "You will meet one among us that your folk would call a prince. We name him Ari-matiel, for he is Jametari, our northern star, Santanara's son, and my brother."

Laren exchanged a significant glance with Zachary.

"Perhaps you have heard his name before," the Eletian said.

"Yes," Laren replied. "He held one of my Riders prisoner."

Now the Eletian looked annoyed, though she tried to conceal it. "The Galadheon. She was no prisoner."

"That's not the way it sounded to me," Laren said.

General Harborough flicked his gaze from the Eletian to Laren. "I thought you said these people were to be trusted."

"I never said that," Laren replied. "I believed, however, and still do, that they would not dare harm us."

"We intend you no harm," the Eletian said, "nor did we come so far to quarrel over an insignificant encounter of this summer."

Before Laren could protest, Zachary said, "To you, perhaps, it was insignificant. To us, it was not, and you would do well to remember that in dealings with my people. But we agree we did not come here to quarrel. Please lead on."

The Eletian hesitated, a look of displeasure on her face, but said no more. She turned and guided them into the verdant depths of the tent. Laren took a deep breath, thinking that Karigan's description of some Eletians and their haughtiness was not far off the mark.

They followed the meandering path through the birch grove, crossing the stream using strategically-placed stones that did not wobble when stepped on. The path wound on longer than seemed possible, as if the tent had no end, but Laren could not swear they were still in a tent.

"How can this be?" General Harborough murmured, glancing up at the roof of entwined tree boughs.

Laren did not provide an answer, for she had none,

though she did know that to Eletians, magic was second nature, or rather it was their nature, and perhaps this tentless tent was an expression of it. Without magic, the Eletians would fade from the world. This was one of the bits of information Karigan had gleaned from her "insignificant encounter" with Prince Jametari this past summer.

Laren glanced at her other companions. Zachary looked intrigued, and maybe even delighted, by his surroundings, and she saw no fear in him. Lord Coutre was grim with his heavy white brows drawn over dark eyes. If Laren could judge his thoughts, it was that he refused to be deceived by the Eletians. He was as suspicious of their motives as General Harborough.

Colin's expression was neutral, though his gaze darted about as if expecting some assailant to leap out from behind trees. His years as a Weapon made such habits die hard. Fastion's demeanor was much the same—edgy and alert.

Eventually they halted before a group of Eletians standing within a semicircle of birches, and here the stream trickled again into the tent—or wherever they were, and beyond the birches and out of their ken.

The Eletians were simply clothed in the hues of nature, and none wore weapons or armor. Laren did not doubt that despite the seeming lack of armament, the king's group was keenly watched by those who would defend their prince. But if there were watchers, they were well concealed.

One very like their guide in stature and coloring stepped forward, and this Laren took to be the prince, brother to their guide. He wore startling white, a long over-tunic belted with silver and green gems, and embroidered white on white with a leaf design. He wore loose white trousers long enough to partly cover his sandaled feet.

"Welcome," he told them. "I am Jametari."

Zachary stepped forward, his posture erect, and held out his hand in greeting, which Jametari clasped. "You and your people are welcome in Sacoridia." General Harborough did not appear pleased by his words.

Jametari nodded graciously, then to his servants he said, "Seating for our guests."

The Eletians brought each of the king's company chairs made of woven tree boughs. Laren didn't think they could possibly be comfortable, but to her surprise, hers was. The only one who refused a chair was Fastion, who stood in a watchful attitude behind the king.

Jametari sat facing them while the other Eletians receded into the shadows of the trees. Refreshments were brought forth, drinks and golden cakes that melted like honey and cream on the tongue. The drink was clear and cold with the distant tang of dew-laden berries. It refreshed Laren, lifted her cares and awakened her. She felt it to the roots of her hair, and all the aches and pains that had bothered her throughout the day subsided. Whatever the drink was, it was more efficacious than willowbark tea. If she had a chance, she would find out what it was.

Zachary and Jametari made light talk over their refreshments, sizing up one another. Zachary was asking their host about his travels.

"We followed ancient paths," Jametari said. "Paths long ago frequently traveled by my folk as they journeyed across the lands. Time has changed the landscape, but the paths recall us."

Any other time, and uttered by anyone else, such a statement would sound absurd.

"And many years," he continued, "has it been since last my folk came willingly among the Sacoridum. Once we dwelled in all these lands before the coming of men. Alas, it is a time even before my reckoning, but ever smaller has our territory grown as a result."

"I hope you have not come all this way," Zachary said, "to seek recompense for wrongs committed generations upon generations ago by forgotten ancestors."

"No, we have not, though there are Eletians who have not forgotten."

His words hung there between them, between mortals whose time on Earth was but the blinking of an eye and those who lived eternal lives.

"We also do not forget the alliance of men and Eletians

during the Cataclysm," Jametari said, and then glancing at Laren, he added, "and it seems you have not either, for the banner of the Green Riders you bear was woven by the hands of Eletians and presented to Liliedhe Ambriodhe on the eve of the decisive battle. It is threaded with words of justice and victory, and of friendship between our peoples. In common purpose, our peoples defeated darkness and unjust conquest."

"We do not forget," Zachary said, "especially in these days when darkness has returned."

"And it has returned, though *Kanmorhan Vane* sleeps for the moment," Jametari said, using the Eletian name for Blackveil Forest. "When it awakens again, it will be with vengeance at its heart. I fear the D'Yer Wall will not hold against the onslaught."

Zachary shifted in his chair. "The old ways of making the wall strong are lost, but we are attempting to relearn them."

"There may not be the time."

"We do not know how much time we have."

The golden leaves stirred above and the boughs of the birches creaked. Laren thought she saw a ripple in the tent-sky. The stream gurgled unabated and it felt like ages passed. Zachary and Jametari regarded one another like lords carved in stone carrying on some mental conversation.

"You sent a delegation northward," Jametari said, "to seek us out, to know our mind, to find out if the old alliance still holds true. That delegation failed, ambushed during its journey. And now I have come forth in turn, to take the measure of this king and his people, to see for myself the strength or lack of foundation for an alliance."

"If you are an enemy of the darkness to the south," Zachary said, "then I would say a rekindling of the alliance sounds promising."

"Mornhavon is our mutual enemy. His conquering of Argenthyne and the depredations committed against our people are evils that shall never be forgotten. Now that the wall is failing and Mornhavon awakened from his banishment, I must decide what is the best course for my people."

Laren noticed he completely circumvented a commitment to an alliance. To take the measure of king and country? What would it mean if he did not care for what he saw and refused to reestablish the alliance? Then she remembered Karigan telling her there were factions of Eletians who wanted to see the wall fail and release all the wild magic pent up in Blackveil, whether or not it was tainted by Mornhavon. Some Eletians felt it would return raw magic to the world.

Laren could only shake her head in wonder that they would turn their backs on an entire people in that way and wish them ill. It was no better than the conquest of Mornhavon the Black. How prevalent was that feeling among the Eletians? How deep did their bitterness delve? They had all of eternity for it to stew.

Zachary laughed. Everyone, both Sacoridians and Eletians alike, stared at him in astonishment.

"And so you will judge our worthiness," he said. "My worthiness in my own realm. Or perhaps you wish to delay, for the politics of your court are attempting to sway you one way or another. Trees will bend to and fro," and he gestured at the birches, "but in a storm, they can snap."

He stood then, tall and regal, and Laren and the other Sacoridians stood in unison in his wake. "Judge us as you will, prince of Eletia, but I've no time to play your games. The time to act is now, and we have been acting. Not spying, not playing games, not waiting. While you may be content for the tide to rise to crisis point, I am not. Whether you are with us or against us, we of Sacoridia will forge ahead as we always have. But know this, if in your self-interest you choose to do nothing at all, then you are against us, and we shall consider you our enemy in league with the powers of Blackveil."

Stunned silence met the king's speech, but he did not wait for a reaction. "I will take leave of you now." He nodded toward Jametari, and without pausing or waiting for an escort, he turned on his heel and headed back through the grove. His companions followed, and Laren brought up the rear. Glancing back at the prince and his people, she found they remained unmoved, still in shock.

Estora flew from the chamber and slammed the door shut behind her before any of her cousins, aunts, sisters, ladies, or more important, her mother, could protest or follow her out. She glanced about the corridor only to discover one surprised servant who curtsied and scurried away. She even managed to leave her Weapon behind and, to her dismay, close a swath of her skirts in the door.

She cracked the door open and yanked them out. A deafening chatter poured from the room; the women oohing and aahing over materials merchants had brought up from the city and designs for the wedding gown drawn by tailors. A baker had brought samples of cake and other dainties, and vintners bottles of their best wines. The ladies, it seemed, had tested enough of the wines to not even note her departure, or care, and the volume of their voices rose to fevered pitches as swatches of cloth and frills flew through the air. She saw her poor Weapon attempting to make his way across the room through the melee, his expression grimmer than usual, especially when some lace was flung into his face.

Estora closed the door again, shutting away the clamor. If they enjoyed all the wedding planning on her behalf, she would leave them to it. If they made any decisions that displeased her, she could simply command that changes be made and no one would dare question her. She was to be queen, after all, wasn't she? She could request what she wanted, and when she wanted it.

She daydreamed that on the eve of the wedding she decided she didn't like the gown and demanded it be remade. The tailor would have no choice but to comply. It could mean his head! Not that Zachary would allow such a punishment, of course, and not that she would actually consider it, but she was only now beginning to recognize the power she was marrying into; the power she could wield over others.

She emitted a tiny little hiccup and covered her mouth and blushed though no one was there to witness it.

I've had a little too much wine as well.

She quelled an abrupt giggle and fled down the corridor, barely noticing that her Weapon, looking uncharacteristically harried, emerged from the chamber and followed her.

Estora stepped out into the central courtyard gardens, breathing free at last. The chamber, her mother's parlor while in residence, had been crammed with so many bodies that the air was stuffy and stale. This was much more the thing, this clean autumn air. It was sobering.

She walked the gravel pathway, drawing her shawl about her shoulders. The mist that permeated everything had subsided, but the sky was still heavy and the air smelled of wet earth and moldering leaves. The garden had gone to dull yellows and browns, the flower beds already mulched against frost and the coming winter. It was a sparse scene, with only a few of the trees holding onto their leaves.

If Estora thought things unbearable now, winter would only be worse, cooped up in the castle with all her relatives and nowhere to escape. The gardens would be snowy, icy, cold. She shivered at the mere thought. Spring would prove no better, for then would be the wedding.

It didn't help that Zachary did not have a moment to spare for her. She knew the realm must come first, but why couldn't he even involve her in the business of its running? If she was to be queen, she must learn all she could about it. If he didn't have time for her as his betrothed, he should at least spare time for the one with whom he'd be sharing power. She refused to ascend the throne simply to be his brood mare, and if that was all he expected of her, then he was in for a surprise.

The arrival of the Eletians sparked her discontent. The castle, of course, was full of gossip about the mysterious folk and what their visit portended, and she, like everyone else, wanted to see firsthand their encampment, at the very least. Instead, she had to rely on secondhand descriptions of the tents, for both the king and her father had forbidden her to leave the castle grounds. Forbidden her! Was she to be queen, or a prisoner? If the latter, she might as well throw herself off the castle's highest tower at once.

She pulled her shawl more closely about her shoulders. It was not fair. It was not fair that she have no choice in this marriage, and it was not fair that she be excluded from the business of the country she was to help lead. Her father and Zachary treated her as though she were some fine porcelain vase that would crack and break if someone even glanced inappropriately at her.

If only they knew the truth! The truth of her relationship with F'ryan. She felt faint at the very thought of its exposure, for her father's response would be swift, extreme, and devastating. He'd consider her ruined, and cast her from the clan forever, never permitting her near family members again.

Zachary's reaction? That was more difficult to divine, for he was in many ways a mystery to her. How strictly did he judge transgressions of the heart?

She slowed her walk, considering. So far she hadn't given anyone any reason to doubt her virtue. Only the Green Riders knew about her and F'ryan, and they were bound by honor to keep her secret. None of them wanted to see her disowned by her clan, and by safeguarding her reputation, the Riders also honored F'ryan, and his wish that they look out for her.

For this Estora was thankful beyond measure, but she also knew the Riders were oathbound servants of the king. In light of the betrothal, how could they continue to withhold the secret from him?

"And for how long?" she murmured. Long enough that he did not discover the truth till their wedding night?

She paused and picked up a perfect crimson maple leaf from the pathway and twirled it between her fingers. In court, chaste behavior was expected, but what actually happened was another thing. Estora knew of young noble ladies who carried on secret affairs, though it was difficult to say for certain which of these liasons were actually consummated.

Much of it appeared innocent: gifts hidden in niches, soulful poetry read through open windows, romantic strolls through the garden, stolen kisses, all accompanied by an ample amount of swooning and dreamy looks.

It was all a result, she believed, of young people who would soon be faced with arranged marriages, often to total strangers. They saw only a lifetime barren of love ahead of them, a marriage made for alliance and bloodline, not for personal happiness. It pushed forbidden romances to be all the more fiery, passionate. And heartrending. Sometimes driving them to their apex.

Periodically a young woman would be "sent away" from court by her parents for one purpose or another, but everyone knew the real reason. Either it was to separate her from an unsuitable paramour, or, if the young lady in question was not careful enough, to conceal her gravid condition. A family of status, especially a noble family, would not wish their good name besmirched by such a disgrace.

How was it for the others, Estora wondered, bending her leaf between her fingers. How was it for those who weren't so obviously compromised? What did they say and do on their wedding night when their maiden's blood, the mark of their chastity, did not flow?

There were ways to explain it, of course. Some girls "damaged" themselves just horseback riding, but she doubted such claims salved the temper of new husbands expecting virginal wives. Some young ladies might stain the bridal bed with pig's blood to trick their husbands, but most men, she believed, were not stupid enough to fall for it.

What would *she* do?

There was, she supposed, the truth. But just how did one go about telling her intended, who also happened to be the king, that she had been with another man? And what would he do when he knew the truth?

After all, in the end, her fate was in Zachary's hands.

Perhaps he'd be understanding. She did not think he lived the life of a celibate himself, but it was different for men. More acceptable for them, especially men of power, to engage in liasons as they wished. In contrast, if Zachary did not take the truth well, it could destroy her. She would never escape the shame.

Thought of the repercussions dizzied her, made her want to hide in a dark cave somewhere far away, but she could not deny her love for F'ryan, and she would not change it, or the past, for all the world. Soon, however, she would have to find a way to address it with her husband-to-be, and pray his outrage would not lead to her becoming a pariah to her own clan and in turn ruin the peace between the eastern provinces and the west. She would pray, and pray fervently, for strength and courage.

At the sound of footsteps upon the gravel path, she turned to find Lord Amberhill strolling leisurely toward her.

"Good day, my lady," he said with a half bow.

She nodded, trying not to show her surprise. "Good day to you."

"May I offer you my coat?" he inquired. "You look chilled."

"Thank you, no. I'm fine." An awkward moment passed and Estora felt a blush creeping up her neck.

Amberhill bowed his head to her again, a lock of raven hair straying from his pony tail to hang over his temple. "Forgive me for my intrusion then, my lady." And he turned to leave.

Estora took a step after him. "Wait."

He paused and faced her. "Yes?"

Estora wasn't quite sure what impulse drove her to stop him. Discomfited, it took her a breath or two to respond. "I don't believe we have been formally introduced."

"It is true, but I would not pretend to be worthy of your attention."

Estora almost laughed. The words were pretty enough, but she did not believe him so modest, and they exchanged enough covert looks at the Huradeshian reception to dispute his words.

"I expect to know all those who are of blood relation to my future husband."

Amberhill quirked an eyebrow. "Then I am not completely unknown to you."

"Hardly an introduction."

"Then allow me to remedy that." He put his hand to temple and bent into a deep, supple bow, the velvet of his dark blue frock coat rippling across his shoulders. The coat was in good condition, she noted, but of a style from her grandfather's generation, with its puffed sleeves. His linen shirt was yellowed and frayed at the collar.

"I am Xandis Pierce Amberhill. The third. And your servant." When he rose, he stood erect and proud, and gazed at her as if daring her to dispute his lineage.

"And cousin to the king," she added.

"Somewhat removed."

Estora thought it interesting he'd admit such to her. Most would try to emphasize the closeness of the relationship rather than its distance. Since the announcement of her wedding contract, she was sprouting distant relations she never knew existed.

Amberhill gazed into the distance as if in deep thought before returning his attention to her. "I am of Clan Hillander, and my lands, what are left of them, are in the middle of the province."

Her cousin, Richmont Spane, had indicated Amberhill was an impoverished landowner, but she did not pry.

"And what brings you to Sacor City?" she inquired.

"Why news of my cousin's betrothal," he said with a grin. "And other business."

Estora hadn't noticed when they began strolling, but stroll they did along the garden paths. She supposed others would view this as indecent, that she, future wife to the king, was strolling unchaperoned with another man—unless one counted her Weapon, and most did not.

With her thoughts of F'ryan and her sullied circumstances still fresh in her mind, she found herself tired, wrung out by such worries. She dropped her maple leaf, watched it whirl to the ground, staining the earth blood-red.

"Have you been down to see the Eletians?" Amberhill inquired.

"No."

Her answer must have sounded vehement enough that he gave her a startled look.

"They won't let me," she added.

"They?"

"My father and the king."

"Oh, I see. For your protection."

Estora wanted to scream, but she retained her composure and her calm facade. "So they say."

"Well, one knows so little of these Eletians and the dangers they pose," Amberhill said, "and you are worth protecting." Then he paused in the walkway. "The poets have spoken of you and the minstrels sung."

"I am afraid they have created words about an ideal that does not exist."

"I see no flaws."

"I am but an ordinary woman."

"A woman, yes," he said. "I had noticed that. But ordinary? I think not."

Estora should have blushed, but she could only sigh. She had heard it all before, all the flattery from so many men. Only F'ryan ever reached her with his words.

He gazed boldly at her. She had seen the hunger on the faces of men before, from the promise of power a marriage alliance would secure, or raw lust for her body. Amberhill carried something altogether different in his demeanor. Yes, the desire was there, but allied with a cocky self-confidence and a residue of . . . of mockery?

He chuckled and shook his head. "You take yourself much too seriously, my lady."

Estora's mouth dropped open and she did not know what to say.

"I must be off," Amberhill said with surprising brusqueness. He gave her one of his graceful bows. "It's been an honor." He strode off and she could only watch him go, his gait fluid like a cat's, sleek, belying tautly corded muscles ready to pounce.

How dare he? she fumed. And when she realized how much she was admiring the view of him from behind, she turned away, her cheeks warming.

To accuse her of taking herself too seriously and then run off? *How dare he?*

Coward.

She set off along the garden path at a furious rate not caring where her feet led her. Why did she allow him to prickle her so badly? She paused and took some breaths, willing calm to blanket her. He had been playing with her. And perhaps he prickled her because he was right: she took herself too seriously.

She started along the path again, but at a more sedate pace. There was no other way to be. Only F'ryan had lifted her cool introspection from her. He made her laugh like a girl; his lovemaking took her to the core of her being, made her real. He unlocked her true self.

She had been drawn to F'ryan by his roguish charm, his reckless humor, and his bald honesty. With a start, she realized that Xandis Pierce Amberhill exhibited something of F'ryan's roguish nature, and he had been nothing if not honest.

A QUEEN'S PLACE

Amberhill's abrupt departure did little to improve Estora's humor. Feeling rather damp and chilled, she abandoned the gardens for the indoors, but she could not bear to return to the family quarters and her mother's crowded chamber where the women must surely still be sampling the wines and dainties.

She often walked the castle corridors, especially when the weather was inclement, and after so long as a resident, she'd grown to know them well, from the dwellings of servants and the bustling administrative wing to the plush monarch's wing, of which one day she would be an inhabitant.

She made now for the castle library with sure steps. Often it was a quiet refuge that few took advantage of. She could not imagine why, for it contained an impressive collection of books both rare and common, covering histories, herb lore, poetry, fiction, and more. She especially enjoyed leafing through ancient manuscripts, painstakingly lettered by hand and illuminated with bright inks and gold leaf. These eldest of texts were written in Old Sacoridian, so she understood very little of the content, but she was drawn to the artistry. The printing press, with its movable type, made books more widely available and in greater quantities, but they contained little of the visual beauty of their predecessors.

The library was located on the west side of the main castle, not far from the monarch's wing. To her relief, she encountered few people along the way and those who she did simply nodded courteously as she passed by and did not hinder her.

When she arrived at the library, she found the great doors wide open, and bronze light puddling beneath the arched entry. Her silent Weapon slipped by her and into the library chamber to ensure no dangers awaited her. Perhaps a venomous bookworm? A tome of vicious intent overhanging its shelf ready to pounce on her head? She smiled and entered.

Whenever she stepped into the library, she always had a sense of the castle walls falling away, an enormous space expanding around her. The main chamber was circular with marble columns supporting a domed ceiling, which was painted with constellations, accentuating the feeling of vastness. Colorful book bindings lined the walls, starting from the floor and soaring up two stories. The upper levels were accessed by spiraling stairs and narrow walkways that looked over brass banisters to the main chamber below.

On each level, books on high shelves could be reached by rolling ladders. Despite the extensive proportions of the chamber, Estora was not intimidated, but rather seduced, for all the books housed there contained inestimable amounts of knowledge just waiting to be discovered and devoured.

She glanced about in pleasure, as she always did when entering the room, and found Master Fogg, a man of middling years, poised over his desk, scrutinizing a tall stack of volumes. When he noted her presence, he hopped off his stool and bowed to her.

"My lady! Such an honor to see you again. Is there anything with which I may assist you?"

"No, thank you," she said. "I'm going to browse the stacks."

"Very good," he said. "Please call me the instant you have a need."

"I shall."

A fire blazed and flickered in the grand hearth which was tucked into an alcove. A pair of comfortable chairs were situated before it, a Hillander terrier sprawled across one of them, its legs twitching in a dream. With a start, Estora realized that where there was a Hillander terrier, there was likely to be the king. She glanced around again, seeing only a pile of books on one of the tables in the center of the chamber, and a black cloak draped across a chair. If it was indeed the king, then he must be in the long room beyond the main chamber, which was also filled with books.

Estora did not know whether to leave or remain, and while she stood there trapped in indecision, Zachary emerged from the back chamber bearing heavy tomes in his arms, followed by his Weapon, Fastion, who was likewise burdened. It was too late to leave now, for the king had seen her.

Master Fogg leaped off his stool. "Sire! You should have told me—I could have retrieved those books for you!"

"No need; Fastion and I are quite capable of carrying them."

Master Fogg bowed and returned to his desk.

After Zachary set down his load on the table, he nodded to Estora. "My lady."

"Sire," she said with a curtsy. "I didn't expect to see you here. I should leave."

"Nonsense." He rounded the table and approached her. He was dressed formally in black and she guessed he must have just returned from meeting with the Eletians. "I hope my presence won't deter you from enjoying the library. In fact, I was just thinking of taking my tea here. Would you join me?"

Estora hesitated, taken aback. Hadn't she complained that the two of them were so often mobbed they never had a moment for a quiet word? Though they were not precisely alone with the librarian and two Weapons present, this was as close to it they would ever get. Until they were married.

"Thank you, sire, I would enjoy some tea."

The tea was sent for and Zachary scooped up the terrier from its chair and placed it gently on the hearth rug.

"There you go, Brex," he said. The dog licked its paw and flopped back to sleep.

Zachary and Estora settled into their chairs and awaited the tea.

"You are doing some research?" Estora asked.

"I'm looking over what some of the old histories have to say about Eletians—even the legends. I've read most of it before, but I thought I'd go over it again."

"They are a mysterious people."

"And I'm afraid the books do not tell me much. Once there was more openness between our races."

"Did your meeting not go well?" Estora asked.

A slow smile grew on his face. "I am under the impression they have preconceived notions of whom and what they are dealing with, and they know very well their ability to inspire awe in others. When the proper amount of awe is not exhibited?" He shrugged. "I do not fear them, though perhaps I should. It will take time for us to come to understand one another."

Then to Estora's astonishment, he told her in detail of his meeting with Prince Jametari. It was more than she ever hoped to hear about it, for her father would never tell her, and it seemed right that Zachary would. This was to be her role when they married, was it not? To listen and offer support?

Entranced by his descriptions of the Eletians and the world they created within their tent, Estora barely noticed when servants arrived bearing trays of tea and cakes. Zachary called Fastion over to confirm his recollection of events. Most astounding of all to Estora was the ultimatum Zachary had given the Eletian prince to join Sacoridia against Mornhavon, or to consider themselves enemies of the realm.

"Is that not dangerous?" Estora asked. "Will we not have enemies on two fronts?"

"The prince already stated that the Eletian people were ardent enemies of Mornhavon." Zachary paused to sip his tea. "At worst, I think, we can expect no aid from them, but I don't imagine they would have traveled all this way if they had nothing to offer. I believe the prince is caught between factions among his own people, and perhaps came here hoping to find a clearer path to support us. Or not. In the meantime, I shall not give them the pleasure of judging themselves as masters and lords over the will of the Sacoridian people or their king."

Estora had not touched her tea. It no longer steamed and must be lukewarm by now. She had always held esteem for Zachary as her king, and never more so when just over two years ago he stood up to his brother, the would-be usurper of the throne, willing to die for the good of Sacoridia. He put his people and land before himself, and that said much for him as a monarch. And again, in his interaction with the Eletians he showed himself to be made of steel.

He sat there comfortable and at ease, slipping his dog a bit of tea cake. It was simple, she thought, for one to underestimate him, to find him soft and too kind, but it was the sort of mistake one made at one's peril.

"It has been brought to my attention," he said suddenly, "that you may be rather overwhelmed with relatives and wedding preparations."

Estora could not hide her surprise. Who told him? Who had even noticed?

"Soon the gardens will be too cold an escape," he said, "and I see there is no single place you have to call your own and attain true privacy."

She could only stare at him, still unable to overcome her surprise.

"I'm afraid I have a sense of what it's like," he continued, giving her a wry smile. "But at least I have places where others dare not follow, and I have found one for you."

She half rose from her chair, filled suddenly with an impulse to hug him, but her training as a lady tamed it and she sank back into her seat.

"Such a place I would find of great value," she said instead.

He nodded. "I want you to feel at ease here, for this is to be your home. I want it to start *feeling* like home to you, that you have a proprietary sense about it. Shall we go see?"

"Go see?"

He stood. "Your sanctuary." And he held out his arm for her.

She rose to her feet, trembling a little, and laid her hand on his forearm. "What of your research?"

"It can wait for a little while. A rare moment to speak with you without the hordes surrounding us is not to be discarded."

Estora walked with him out of the library, the elderly terrier plodding behind them. They strolled the main corridor and though many tried to speak with Zachary, he waved them off or asked them to seek out his secretary, Cummings. The people bowed away, and others who saw the king and Lady Estora together murmured among themselves.

Eventually they made their way to Zachary's study and halted outside the door.

"I hope it pleases you," he said.

"What?" Confused, Estora glanced from him to the door.

He chuckled and opened it, and led her within. The chamber was light filled, but hollow, for all of Zachary's furnishings and belongings had been removed, including the big marble-top desk. All that remained was a tiny pedestal table on which sat a vase of exotic and fragrant flowers.

Estora could only stand there speechless.

"The flowers were given to us by the Eletians," he said, "but they seem more appropriate here, for you."

"Your study," she finally managed to say.

"It *was* my study, but before it was my study, it was always the queen's solarium, though not used for that purpose since the passing of my grandmother. Now it's yours to use and furnish as you wish, and I believe you will enjoy the access to the gardens.

Estora put her hand to her cheek in disbelief. "It—it's wonderful, thank you."

"My grandmother had other private places," he said, "and here she often sat with her ladies at tea or needlework, gossiping away. They also played games and listened to minstrels, but you may keep the solarium as private or public as you wish. At your word, you may deny anyone entrance, including your mother and father."

"I can? I mean . . . I mean *I can.*"

"Yes," Zachary said. "You are a princess of the realm, soon to be queen. It will be your privilege to command even your family."

Estora thought she would cry. To think this was all hers, and hers alone. Maybe coming to love Zachary as more than her king would not be so difficult after all.

"Inform Sperren of your needs," Zachary said. "Furnish and decorate it however it may please you." He stroked his chin, and mused, "It is as it should be, a queen's solarium once again."

She then took his hand into her own. It dwarfed hers, was solid and strong, and calloused from sword work.

"Thank you," she said. "I cannot express how happy this makes me."

"Your smile tells me much," he replied. "And remember always, if there is some matter you believe requires my attention, no matter how trivial, that you come to me with it immediately. We have been treading separate paths, and it seems to me that we need to know one another better as our paths become one. Otherwise, I fear it will be a longer winter than usual."

Estora's heart fluttered. Was this the moment to be honest with him? To open up to him and reveal her relationship with F'ryan? She closed her eyes and trembled.

"My lady?" Zachary asked, concern in his voice. "Are you well?"

"Yes, I—" she began, but broke off, too terrified to continue. *No, no,* she thought. *There is time yet. I am not ready.* So instead, she said, "My lord, with your leave, I should like to look upon the Eletians myself."

He froze and she perceived the first hint of a frown. "I am sorry my lady, but I cannot permit you to leave castle grounds. The Eletians are still too unknown an entity, and we must not put you in any danger, no matter how minuscule the threat may seem."

"I will not be held here like a prisoner."

"You are no prisoner, my lady, but the future of Sacoridia, thus a treasure to protect for your people."

Now it was Estora's turn to frown. "You believe what that old Huradeshian woman, that seer, said?"

"Whether or not she is blessed with a true gift of sight," he said, "her words are wise. My lady, I must ask you to remain patient until we learn more of the mind of the Eletians, and then, if all goes well, you will more than likely see them up close."

With that as his final word, he took leave of her, left her alone in the room, alone but for the flowers and sunshine. She gazed out into the garden.

I am a prisoner. I am a well-kept prisoner.

It occurred to her that maybe the gift of the solarium was to blunt her feelings of imprisonment, a bribe to keep her happy and distracted from thoughts of the Eletians, and maybe, despite all his kindly words, it was all Zachary intended for her. If this was the case, she despaired of him understanding her past with F'ryan.

THE RAVEN MASK

When darkness shrouded the castle grounds and evening passed into the deep of midnight, and when all was quiet but for the third watch of the guard and those restless souls tossing and turning in their beds, the Raven Mask scaled the wall of the castle's east wing. Dressed in tight-fitting black and dark gray, with soot smeared across his face beneath his silk mask, he blended into the night as he crawled upward like a spider, his limbs splayed as he searched for finger- and toeholds among the ashlars, gutters, cornices, and decorative embellishments of the wall. If Morry knew what he was up to, the old man would probably keel over from heart failure. So Morry had not been told.

Up and up the Raven Mask pulled himself, his fingers seeking the barest of crevices in which to anchor. The tiniest mistake, the least of slips, could culminate in disaster. Even if he survived the fall, his body would be broken and bleeding, and even worse, he'd be caught. He was thief enough to deserve being locked up by the constabulary till the end of his days. What he was doing now could merit execution, though if all went as planned, this would be the least of his deeds.

Despite the frosty chill of the night, sweat slicked his sides. He prayed that the soldiers on duty would not espy him, would not think to look for intruders on the wall. He hoped they all searched for danger outward beyond the castle walls, not inward. The arrival of the Eletians had been a serendipitous event, for everyone, not just the soldiery, was looking outward and paid little heed to what occurred on castle grounds, not taking any special note of one impoverished aristocrat wandering within their walls.

He had used the unexpected diversion well, picking out routes up the wall, and studying the routines of the castle and the habits of its guards. He'd taken time to become friendly with servants and to learn their ways through the warren of service corridors within the castle. There were many more corridors left abandoned that he itched to explore, but though they could be useful, he hadn't the time to figure them all out.

Right arm up, finger-walk to the next seam between ashlars. Left arm. Right foot up, left foot. Stretch the right arm again and—his left foot slipped and he saw it all in his mind's eye, the fall, the long tumble to the ground, the explosions of pain, his body lying broken and helpless.

He dangled there by the fingertips of one hand, his arm stretched taut, the muscles and sinews searing and strained. With a grunt he swung up his left arm and scrabbled for a hold, and when he found it, he worked his toes back into the crevices and leaned into the wall, pressing his cheek against cold stone, his heart pounding.

That was close.

He swallowed hard and worked to control his breathing. When he mastered himself, he continued his climb upward, disregarding the pain in his right arm and shoulder. He crawled until his toes stood securely on a cornice, and certain this was the desired level, he shuffled along it counting windows as he went.

Those three are for the chambers of Lord and Lady Coutre, he thought as he sidled by them. *Two more for the sisters.*

When he came to *her* window, he paused and sat upon the sill, which was flat and wide enough to hold him. No light shone within, but a shred of moonlight illuminated a square of floor and a corner of the bed.

How easy it would be to enter through the window, to steal across the floor and place a kiss upon her brow. He had done it a hundred times before, slipping into the bedrooms of highborn ladies—those who had so much wealth and glittery jewels that they'd not miss just one ring, or one brooch, or one necklace. Some anticipating, if not outright hoping, for his visit into their bedrooms left choice gems in the open for him, especially if they wished him to return certain "favors." Sometimes he did, and sometimes he chose not to.

He thought he'd like to find the bedchamber of the lady who had confronted him at the museum. The thought of climbing through her window aroused all kinds of delicious sensations. He'd made discreet inquiries among the aristocratic circles about "Lady Karigan," but no one seemed to know her. A pity, for he'd enjoyed riling her up, how her color rose. He'd continue to ask around. Who knew, but maybe by mere chance he'd come upon her bedchamber some night. The thought brought him pleasure.

Often he must remind himself that his work was not just for pleasure, but to help his foundering estate from being totally dismantled, leaving him a landless beggar without title. His grandsire, the first Raven Mask, had done as he now did: resorted to thievery to preserve their lands. But then his father, through terrible management and drunken gambling, had lost nearly everything his grandsire attained.

So, Xandis Pierce Amberhill the Third had taken up where his grandsire left off, training as he trained, learning the arts of the stealthy, and stealing from those who could afford to miss a trifle. Slowly he worked to rebuild the family's wealth. His dream was to purchase back all the lands his father had squandered, and it might very well happen sooner rather than later if his latest task succeeded. He would earn a handsome sum.

Morry disapproved of the whole scheme, disliked their co-conspirator, the plainshield, thought the whole thing lacked honor and was too risky. Risky, very risky—Morry was right on that count, dear Morry his cautious manservant, who was so much more: surrogate father, teacher, and the one who had taught him the arts of the Raven Mask, for Morry had served his grandsire as a young man.

It was the servant in Morry who submitted to Amberhill's

desire to partake in this plan, this challenge, this opportunity to regain the wealth of his estate.

His breath fogged the window as he peered into it, discerning nothing. It was not his object this evening to slip into the bedchamber of Lady Estora Coutre and steal her jewels. He would not chance awakening her or her maidservant who must sleep at the foot of her bed. To do so could rouse the Weapon who stood guard on the other side of the door, causing a confrontation the Raven Mask did not desire, and ruining all his plans. It would bring him to no good end. He had risked enough already just by scaling the castle heights to sit on Lady Estora's windowsill.

It was as surreptitiously close as he dared get to her on castle grounds. It was important for him to try, though, important for him to know whether or not this approach, via the wall, might work, but before he had gotten very far, he ruled it out, for he believed there were less perilous ways to accomplish his task.

He gazed out into the night. Distant lantern lights bobbed along the walls that surrounded the castle grounds as guards went about their patrols. Others walked the paths below. Fortunately their light would not reach him.

It wasn't just the desire to restore his lands that drove him to take such risks. No, something about his secret work, about climbing one of the most secure walls in all of Sacoridia thrilled him, made his pulse rush, made him feel alive. It was like stepping on death's threshold, but cheating it. He guessed his grandsire must have felt much the same in his youth, and maybe there was something of a gambler in him, too, like there was in his father.

He was about to begin his descent when light grew in Lady Estora's chamber. He stopped himself and peered into the window again, careful to edge away from view. Lady Estora entered the room, her maidservant behind her bearing a lamp. So she hadn't been in bed at all. He surmised the lady had been wandering the corridors again, which he observed her doing several times. He wondered what she thought about as she walked at night. What had she to concern herself with? Her father and clan were prosperous, and she was about to make the best marriage match in the land.

The servant took away Lady Estora's shawl, folding it and storing it in a wardrobe, then returned to start unfastening the hooks on the back of the lady's dress. At first he watched transfixed as the dress began to fall, revealing pale skin and the corset, then he averted his eyes, blinking in confusion.

He was a gentleman, not a voyeur, he reminded himself. A gentleman who crept into the sleeping chambers of ladies and sometimes bedded them. How different was this? Was it not less invasive? Who would know if he watched?

I would.

He glanced through the window. The maidservant was now untying the bonds of the corset. He swallowed, taking in the curve of Lady Estora's bare shoulders and arms, the plumpness of partially revealed, creamy breasts that had never known harsh sunlight. And again, he forcefully averted his gaze, feeling overheated.

This was his future queen, his cousin's wife-to-be, not some courtesan to toy with. He had gazed in like a hungry animal and it was difficult to withdraw his gaze; it was equally difficult not to peer in again. Most considered her the greatest beauty of the land, and he could not argue, but it made him feel base, a beast unrefined, wild.

He struggled within himself for an unmeasurable time, but his will held out and he did not look in again until he deemed the danger well past. When he did so, he saw that the maidservant had left. Lady Estora sat at her vanity gazing into her mirror without expression. Her white nightgown flowed from her shoulders in elegant folds, pooling at her feet. Her golden hair, now unbound, tumbled down her back in waves that shone in the lamplight. If possible, he found her more lovely than ever, the heat rising in him again.

She then placed her face in her hands, her shoulders trembling as though she wept. This was somehow even more embarrassing to view than her undressing. What sadness afflicted her? Certainly it could not be his cousin, could it? Zachary was a just king and treated her with kindness. It would be beyond the best dreams of most ladies to be marrying one such as he.

He found himself pitying her for whatever sadness assailed her, but in his guise as the Raven Mask, he could not allow himself to get caught up in it. To do so would endanger his task. He drew away from the window and began his descent.

Amberhill crept through the window and into the house as stealthily as he would any he was intent upon stealing from, but his aim wasn't to pilfer jewels. Rather, this was his own house he rented in the noble quarter, and his object was to not rouse Morry.

The house was, by necessity, the smallest in the neighborhood. He could not afford one of the larger, ostentatious manses that dwarfed this one, though by some standards his rental was perfectly spacious and elegant. It also served his purposes well. Tucked back from the street and shrouded by shrubbery and trees planted by an overzealous gardener, it offered the Raven Mask concealment for his comings and goings. Since he often hunted the noble quarter for his trinkets, the location was perfect.

He closed the window behind him and latched it shut. He peeled off his mask and stood there in the library releasing a long, tired sigh and flexing his sore arm. It would be fine in a few days. He just wouldn't scale any more walls in the meantime.

He'd left himself a lamp at low glow and now he turned it up, only to find, to his surprise, his manservant sitting in the shadows by the unlit fireplace.

"Morry!" Amberhill exclaimed. "What are you doing up?"

The older gentleman was in his sleeping clothes and a robe, but quite awake.

"You did not tell me you were going out tonight."

Amberhill ran the silk mask between his fingers. Usually

he told Morry precisely what he was up to when he went out as the Raven Mask, but even so, it rankled that Morry should need to know his every move as if he were still a boy.

"It is not necessary for you to wait up every time I go out," he replied.

"The idea is that I be included in the plan in case there is trouble," Morry said.

"I wasn't anticipating trouble." There easily could have been, but Amberhill wasn't about to admit it.

"Well, then, what treasures did you bring home?"

"Er, none." Amberhill hadn't expected to be interrogated upon his return, and he found himself grasping for an explanation that would not reveal what he'd really been up to. He didn't care to imagine Morry's rebuke if he found out the Raven Mask had been scaling castle walls and peering into Lady Estora's window. "I was out practicing my skills. More of a walk in the shadows, really."

"Is that why your arm seems to be sore?" Morry demanded. "Because you were *walking?*"

Amberhill frowned. Morry would know just by glancing at him that the slightest thing wasn't quite right. Even minor pain could alter a man's posture, and after all these years of training together, Morry knew him as well as he knew himself.

"It is of no matter," Amberhill replied.

A suspicious gleam remained in Morry's eye, but the older gent, as paternal as he might be, was still a servant, and Amberhill knew each of these conflicting roles fought to assert itself over the other. The servant won this time, at least for the moment, and Morry did not pursue the matter.

"I was afraid you'd gone and done something rash," Morry said.

"You know I'm more careful than that. I won't do the job until the conditions are perfect."

Morry shook his head. "I'm not sure the conditions ever will be. It's not a proper sort of—"

"Nothing the Raven Mask does is *proper,*" Amberhill snapped, aggrieved he must always defend his decisions. He strode over to a table that held a bottle of brandy. He splashed some into a glass and downed it in a single gulp, then poured some more.

"Some things are less proper than others," Morry said, undeterred. "Especially when they are traitorous."

"Such things were commonplace centuries ago, and were considered an honorable way for one noble to express disagreement with another, or to show himself as a rival for an intended wife and to benefit from a token ransom as solace."

"I doubt the women involved ever saw it as 'honorable,' " Morry said. "In any case, King Smidhe outlawed the practice of honor abductions long ago because it created disunity among the clans. In some cases it was an excuse for them to commit war upon each other."

"You know as well as I do that honor abductions still go on in remote provinces where the king's law holds less sway. *Coutre,* for instance. And to my thinking, there is still a place for some of the old traditions." It had been a long night already, and Morry's interrogation was not soothing Amberhill's irritation. If anything, it added to it. "Did you always question my grandfather's decisions this way?" he demanded.

"Your grandfather," Morry replied, stroking his chin, "practiced and practiced his art to its fullest, and was well-seasoned before he attempted some of his more dangerous thefts. Such tasks were extensively planned before execution, creating a seeming effortlessness on his behalf that baffled the authorities. That was the art of it—no one knew just how much work went into it. They saw only the results. A man who could melt into shadows and charm the most happily of married women. A man who could steal a highly guarded gem without being detected. An act of seeming ease that was in fact an exercise of great intellect and the culmination of much sweat."

"So you are saying I'm an impulsive whelp."

"That is what *you* are saying," Morry replied. "Your grandfather was a man full grown when I came to serve him, and I was just a boy. He'd been the Raven Mask for several years already. Did I question your grandfather's motives and actions? No. Not at first, but as time went on and I grew in experience, I learned to question him if I thought an endeavor too risky. Usually it turned out everything was so well-planned, I was the one who learned from it. After all those years of serving your grandfather, I should think I have some words of value to share with you. I offer it out of love, and offer it now, especially since you have been the Raven Mask but a short time."

"I've been very successful," Amberhill said, still irked.

"And I do not deny it, for I have trained you well." Morry smiled, but it was fleeting. "You must understand, Xandis, that it is only because of my regard for you, and my concern for the young woman, that I raise questions. And certainly I do not trust the plainshield. He will not reveal to us his liege lord. Who is this noble who seeks an honor abduction of the most prestigious lady in all of Sacoridia? The whole scheme smells rotten to me."

"I will see to the lady's safety myself," Amberhill said. "I swear it."

"Even plans well-laid sometimes go wrong."

Amberhill tightened his grip on the glass, then relaxed. "I've already agreed to this thing, and on my honor, I will finish it. The Amberhill estate will be restored, and the Raven Mask can retire once again."

"What is the greater honor, I wonder," Morry muttered, but before Amberhill could retort, the older man stood and said, "It is late and I need my bed." He started away, but then paused. "Your new boots were delivered today. Good night, sir."

"Good night," Amberhill murmured. He watched Morry make his way from the room and into the dark corridor beyond. He was trim and unbent despite his years, and worked hard to maintain himself, mostly by training with Amberhill. Amberhill loved Morry, but as a son will chafe against a father, so he resented Morry's challenging his decisions.

It is, after all, my *decision,* Amberhill thought. He'd become the Raven Mask with one goal in mind: to restore his estate. And so he would. As an impoverished noble, he couldn't hope to win anything but a wife of mediocre status with a scant dowry, and then he'd never be able to establish the horse farm he dreamed of. He would die wanting, his life unremarked upon.

At one time, his family had been very wealthy and powerful within Clan Hillander, owning vast expanses of land. Now he had but a crumbling manor house and the small acreage it sat upon to call his own, despite the prominence of his ancestors. The gold the plainshield offered would help him reclaim much and launch the horse farm, and he'd manage it all scrupulously to bring the estate back to its former splendor.

No more pinching jewels from the bedchambers of ladies. Unless he felt like it.

As determined as Amberhill was to see this through, the tension between him and Morry hurt. Never did Morry call him "sir," except in public.

He shook off his feelings of guilt and doubt when he espied the package on the large library table. His boots! He set his glass aside and unbound the boots from their protective linen wrappings, inhaling the intoxicating fragrance of new leather.

This purchase represented one of his few extravagances. With the currency the plainshield advanced him, he'd gotten fitted for the boots in the finest shop in all of Sacor City. He chose only the best grade of leather, pliant but sturdy, which he now caressed, the lamplight gleaming off the polished, black finish. He could wear the boots unrolled to his thighs for riding, or rolled down as desired.

The expense was unbelievable, but he grew tired of wearing old things, things his father and grandfather once wore. He owned some garb specifically for thieving as the Raven Mask, but could not wear it when he was being himself, so he had to settle for the old things. He wished he could purchase a whole new wardrobe, but not only did he dare not squander his funds all at once, it would appear suspicious for him to suddenly dress like a well-off aristocrat. Comments would be made, and questions asked. He'd be *noticed.* Too many knew his father had gambled away the family holdings, and questions would lead to guesses about where he'd acquired the funds. He could not take the chance his role as the Raven Mask be revealed.

No, Amberhill dared only make careful purchases for now, and by the time his fortunes were transformed, no one would think to ask questions.

I will tell them I made a profitable business deal, he thought. *And it will be the truth.*

For all that Morry might worry, Amberhill saw only a bright future of opportunity and wealth.

THE WALL SPEAKS

We stand sentry day and night, through storm and winter, and freeze and thaw.
From Ullem Bay to—
The storm batters us.
From Ullem Bay to—
The storm weathers us.
To the shores of dawn we—
are cracking.
Hear us. Help us. Heal us.
Do not trust him. He nearly brought us to ruin.
Hate him!
We cannot trust. We hate him.
Yes, hate him.

THE STORM

Dale's condition delayed Alton's search for answers. He'd tried to hide his impatience from her—it wasn't as if it was her fault. According to Leese, the Rider's slowly healing wounds and the travel from Woodhaven had strained her and hampered recuperation. She'd been allowed to leave Woodhaven too soon, Leese insisted, and Tower of the Heavens would have to wait a few more days for Dale to rest up.

It was true, Alton reflected as he approached the tower. He'd observed dark rings beneath Dale's eyes and that she moved stiffly. She would not admit being tired or in pain, and he chose blindness, not wanting to see what was right in front of him because he needed answers, and he needed them *now.* Leese, however, had other ideas, and Dale was forced to take bed rest and swallow noxious teas that were supposed to help her heal. When Alton left her, he saw her expression of guilt for letting him down.

He could have said something reassuring to her, but he hadn't. He'd just left her tent, bridling with frustration, frustration verging on anger at the delay. Now he stood before the tower, his hands clenched at his sides, needing to vent all he held within.

Delay!

His urgent need to fix the wall rose in him like a fever. He could no longer abide waiting. Every day lost meant another day closer to disaster. As if shadowing his mood, clouds built all morning, blotting out sunshine and turning day to dusk, and now they hung bloated and leaden above, ready to loose torrents of rain. The tips of trees wavered in the growing wind, as restless and unsettled as he felt. The wind carried the tang of the sea. This was a sea storm brewing, the kind that racked the coast in late summer and into fall, and here they were not all that far from the ocean.

He could practically feel the oncoming storm throbbing through him, and when he closed his eyes, he saw winds peeling spray off the crests of waves, layers of waves that plunged and reared gray-green and spewed foam. That turmoil roiled inside him.

Wind *whooshed* through the encampment snapping tent flaps and banners and sending sparks from campfires showering through the air. Columns of smoke bent, coiled, danced. It was as though the Earth had made a great exhalation.

Then everything stilled.

"We're in for a good blow, m'lord," said a nearby soldier on guard duty by the tower.

"Yes," Alton replied, his voice quiet and tight. He gazed up at the sky and the first fat drops of rain fell from the heavens and splattered on his face.

The storm deepened the dark of night, the wind whipping the walls of Alton's tent. He secured his shelter as best as he could with extra lengths of cord, and so far it was holding, but rain battered its way in through any hole it could find, and the wooden poles that supported the tent braced against the force of wind. He thanked the gods the tent was on a platform or he'd be swamped.

When his candle's sputtering and twisting light added to his growing headache, he blew it out and went to his cot, which he'd had to move from beneath a leak, and laid down, pulling his damp blanket over him.

The shriek of wind and groan of tree boughs became voices in his mind as he drifted into uneasy sleep, and the drumming of rain on canvas was the hammer blows of a thousand stonecutters.

It was the voices, though, that bore deepest into his mind, their wailing, their despair. Their hatred. Walls of stone closed in on him and he tossed on his cot. The voices screamed at him.

He turned to his side, breathing hard, fist opening and closing even as he slept.

Go away, cousin, the voices said. *Stay away. Die, cousin, we hate you.*

Alton cried out, his own voice lost in the storm. The maelstrom raged on.

The residue of Blackveil's poison flamed in his blood, bringing on the fever and the dream that haunted him. Karigan came to him in the ivory dress, her brown hair sun-touched with gold. His head rested on her lap and she caressed his temple, her touch warm and soft.

Behind her the limbs of trees swayed and groaned, turned black and snarled, reaching around her for him. Karigan's hair fluttered in the breeze, and she began to transform into a loathsome creature with yellow eyes and claws that scratched his cheeks.

Betrayer! Alton screamed. He launched from her lap, fell from his cot onto the tent platform. A peal of thunder extended his scream.

He knelt there, panting, sweat dripping down his face. He was insufferably hot and the storm without only seemed to fuel the storm within. The wall hated him, and he hated it back.

He stood, kicked over his chair, swept a pile of books off his table. He staggered out of his tent without even donning cloak or pulling on boots, lightning illuminating the way.

Outside rain pelted his face and instead of quelling his fever, it empowered him. As the storm ripped tents from their ties around him and snapped branches, Alton reveled in his own power and screamed at the wall, screamed in fury at Blackveil and Mornhavon the Black.

"I hate you!" he yelled. "I'll find a way! You can't defy me!"

He then cursed the gods and lightning filled the sky above him, but he continued his tirade, no longer conscious of his words or the destruction the storm wrought around him.

Even when Dale rushed out to him, her greatcoat draped over her shoulders, and tried to drag him out of the rain, he didn't stop his cursing or shaking his fist at the heavens.

"Idiot!" she cried at him, and she slapped him.

He hit back.

The world clarified around Alton. He saw the devastation as if for the first time, and all he felt was cold and tired, his inner storm spent. A flash of lightning revealed Dale in the mud at his feet, struggling to rise, but obviously hurting.

"What have I—?" He bit off his own question and helped Dale up, then, supporting her, led her through the rain back toward her tent, its flaps whipping in the wind.

"I'm sorry," he told Dale.

"I know," she replied.

TO SELIUM

A torrent of wind and rain forced Karigan and Fergal to seek shelter at an inn a couple days out of Rivertown. They blew into the courtyard of the Cup and Kettle amid broken branches and deep puddles. The inn's proprietor ushered them into the stable and Karigan sighed in relief to be out of the storm and in the relative warmth and dryness that four walls and a roof provided. She had lived near the coast long enough to recognize a sea-driven storm, even this far inland, and this one was as bad as any she remembered.

They were all soaked to the skin. Condor was one wretched-looking, drenched horse, with his mane and tail hanging limp and straggly, and water runneling down his sides. She slapped his neck splattering drops everywhere. He gave a pathetic, deep-down sigh that made Karigan laugh.

Condor nudged her shoulder with his nose as if to say, "Look at yourself if you want a good chuckle." It only made her laugh harder.

In the gloomy light, she saw Fergal gazing her way with a slight scowl on his face, observing her interaction with Condor. Since the Golden Rudder, he'd been remakably cooperative, and she noted he continued to be dutiful in his care of Sunny.

Dutiful. And that was all. She still saw no growing affection for Sunny on his part, and suspected he put as much energy into horse chores as he did only because it was his duty. He did not do it to please Sunny. He must regard her in much the same way he regarded his boots: He needed them to perform his job, they required some care, but beyond that, they did not inspire love. They were useful, and that was that.

It saddened Karigan, even as Condor playfully nibbled at her braid, that anyone could regard a living, breathing creature as no more than a useful object. She hoped Fergal would grow to—if not love Sunny—at least like and appreciate her.

"Hey!"

Fergal's cry jolted Karigan from her thoughts. He had just removed Sunny's saddle, and the mare was enjoying a full-body shake, showering him with water.

Karigan started to laugh, but stopped dead when she saw the anger on his face. He rammed his saddle down on the stall door, and turned to Sunny and yanked on her reins.

"Stupid animal!" he shouted.

Sunny jerked her head up and skittered backward.

"Fergal!" Karigan's voice rang sharp in the stable.

He loosened his hold on the reins, but his posture was stiff, almost quivering.

"Are you going to *order* me to apologize to her?" Fergal demanded.

"Wipe her down and she won't shake all over you," Karigan said, forcing herself to keep her tone mild. "She doesn't understand your anger."

"I know—she's stupid."

Karigan ground her teeth, keeping an eye on Fergal even as she grabbed a handful of straw to wipe down Condor. He nudged her shoulder again, telling her he knew she was troubled. She rubbed and patted and whispered to him. He was her comfort. If only Fergal could understand how it could be.

Later, Karigan and Fergal sat in front of the hearth of the Cup and Kettle's common room, with mugs of warm spiced cider in their hands. Fergal had been sullen all through supper, speaking little. Karigan did not try to draw him out, guessing she'd only antagonize him. She'd experienced his volatile behavior before and did not want to relive it.

Now that they were warm and dry, and their stomachs

full, Fergal appeared to relax. Karigan opened her mouth to speak, but he interrupted.

"Are you going to lecture me?"

"What do you think?"

Fergal glowered, but then settled. "I was cold, wet, and tired. She made me mad."

"We were *all* wet and tired," Karigan replied. "The horses were drenched."

Fergal stared straight into the fire. "I know."

"Look, Sunny isn't stupid."

"They're dumb beasts," Fergal shot back. "That's what my da always said. That's what the moon priest said. He said the gods gave people dominion over beasts. That's why we can use them, eat them. Ride them."

Did Fergal truly believe it, or was he simply reiterating words that had been pounded into him? It wasn't the first time Karigan had heard such words herself, but in the case of Fergal's da, she thought it only an excuse for him to profit from butchery.

As for the moon priest? Arguing against a belief based on faith, not logic, was generally fruitless, so she didn't even try. What she didn't understand was why the moon priests would preach such things when some of the gods took on animal visages, like Westrion, the Birdman.

Rain lashed windows in sheets. The gloomy weather left the common room subdued, other patrons conversing in muted tones over hot drinks, or playing games. A flash of lightning illuminated the room.

"I'll take care of Sunny," Fergal said quietly in an afterthought, "don't worry on that count, because if I don't, I can't be a Rider."

It was good he intended to provide Sunny with care, but what kind of Green Rider would he be, Karigan wondered, if he could not see horses as more than lowly beasts? As *meat?*

I guess it's not a requirement that he love horses, but she shook her head, thinking such feelings could only render a horse and Rider an ineffective team.

Despite Fergal's attitude, she still held out hope for him. She stole a glance at him as he sat there gazing into the fire, his eyebrows drawn together as he brooded.

It wasn't so much that he hated horses, she thought, but that he feared forming attachments. A lesson learned, no doubt, from his da.

For his sake, and that of any horse that served with him, she hoped he unlearned such lessons. She truly did.

The storm blew itself out during the night, but as brief as it was, once they set out the next morning, they found evidence of its ferocity everywhere. The countryside was littered with broken tree limbs and shingles that had been ripped off houses. A few trees had toppled across the Kingway, which they had to navigate around.

The weather, however, was perfectly calm and sunny by the time the Riders found themselves less than a day's ride from Selium. Whenever Karigan rode this section of the Kingway, she identified a certain spot along the edge of the road that awakened memories of when her life had changed, memories of when she had become more than a mere schoolgirl or merchant's daughter.

The place was just beyond the bend in the road ahead, and Condor's gait slackened perceptibly for he knew it, too. Fergal adjusted Sunny's pace to match Condor's. He asked no questions and appeared unconcerned, probably figuring it was the rate of travel Karigan wished to set and nothing more. He rode on, oblivious to the significance of the place and she chose not to break the silence or enlighten him. This was between her, Condor, and F'ryan Coblebay.

They rounded the bend and Karigan picked out the landmarks: the tree stump scorched by lightning, the boulder with a layer of moss on it, the particular jagged line of trees . . . She almost expected to find F'ryan's body lying there in the road, stiffened in death, his hand outstretched, black hair plastered against a face drained of blood.

Only in memory did she see him, for his corpse had been removed long ago, his presence erased, the blood washed away by seasons of rain and snow. Nothing remained of that day when the dying Green Rider passed on his desperate message errand, and with it his mantle of king's messenger, to a runaway schoolgirl who had no idea of what she was getting into and what dangers lay ahead.

Anyone else riding past this spot would never know or care that a man died here, but Karigan did, and so did Condor. The chestnut gelding bowed his head as they plodded by, and Karigan closed her eyes.

Swear you'll deliver the message, F'ryan's lips whispered in her memory, *to King Zachary . . . for love of country . . .* Though weak, his voice had contained power enough to command. He had made her swear on his sword—the very same one she now wore at her side—to complete his mission. Then he had instructed her to take his Rider brooch. Little had she realized how much this act would change her life.

There had been no time to honor F'ryan properly. Her acceptance of his mission had left her in peril and she'd needed to flee lest those who impaled him with arrows come upon her. So she'd left him on the road without even a blanket to cover him, exposed to the elements and scavengers.

When Karigan opened her eyes, they were well past the place, and Condor's stride quickened with a swish of his tail, his ears pricked forward. No ghostly presence followed, and she left memory behind.

The shadows of the Green Cloak, its southwestern fringe, gave way to farm fields and open sky. As Karigan and Fergal drew closer to Selium, they encountered more villages and people, and with this change in atmosphere, memories of a different nature surfaced as Karigan gazed upon familiar buildings and landmarks.

It was not her first visit to Selium since she ran away that spring day over two years ago. No, indeed. After completing F'ryan's mission, she had returned to Selium to finish her schooling. When she finally answered the Rider call, she had carried messages to Selium on two occasions. More than being preoccupied by difficult school days, she looked forward to visiting with good friends.

Soon the campus atop its hill and the city clustered beneath it rose above the open farmland. Karigan clucked Condor into an easy lope with a smile, the breeze pressing against her face. She slowed to a jog when they reached the gate to accommodate others on the street. She waved to the gatekeeper and continued on through. No one stopped them or questioned them, for Selium was an open city, not a fortress. No wall surrounded it—the gate was merely a marker of the city's boundary.

Almost as well known as the school that was also called Selium were the city's hot springs, which drew tourists and the infirm from afar to bathe in one of the numerous bathhouses that lined the main thoroughfare. Steam vented from rooftops, and signs extolled the healing qualities of the springs and listed prices. There were public baths and private. Some were luxurious, and others less expensive to meet only basic needs. Today there were no lines, not this late in the season. The bathhouse operators would be more dependent now on local patrons. Some simply shut down for the winter.

"Who would wish to bathe in public?" Fergal asked, wrinkling his nose as they passed such an establishment.

"Who would want to throw himself into a freezing river?" Karigan countered, sounding more acerbic than she intended.

Fergal clamped his mouth shut.

Feeling a little guilty, Karigan explained, "The public baths are inexpensive compared to the private ones, and not all who come for the restorative powers of the hot springs are wealthy. Some are farmers and laborers."

"Have you ever used them?" Fergal asked.

"The school taps into the springs. I never had to." Almost as much as Karigan looked forward to seeing her friends, she looked forward to one of those baths. As king's messengers, she and Fergal would be put up in the Guesting House, which, of course, had big tubs that could be filled with hot spring water.

The city felt subdued as they continued on, with only a few students sitting on the steps of the art museum. During the warmer months, outdoor eateries and vendors set up along the street, but now these were also closed for the season. There were some shoppers out and about, but no musicians looking for stray coppers played for them. Most students would be in classes at this hour.

As the main thoroughfare through the city, Guardian Avenue, traveled upward toward the campus, the buildings on either side were of older architecture, with columns and red clay roofs. Older still were the buildings of the school, for the city had grown up around it.

Guardian Avenue led beneath the ancient P'ehdrosian Arch onto the school grounds. The campus itself was an orderly "town" of well-laid paths and academic buildings, residences, and administrative offices. On the far side of campus were fields for athletics and arms practice, and stables with pasture, paddock, and outdoor riding ring.

Immediately inside campus loomed the main administrative building. This was where they'd find the offices of the Golden Guardian and the dean.

Karigan and Fergal rode up to the front steps of the administration building and handed over the reins of their horses to a stablehand.

"I'll see your saddlebags to the Guesting House," he said.

"Thank you," Karigan replied, handing him a copper.

As Condor and Sunny were led away, Karigan turned to the great double doors before her. She straightened her shortcoat and message satchel, and took a deep breath. Fergal waited expectantly beside her. After a second and third deep breath, she pushed open the door and plunged inside.

MASTER RENDLE

They entered a rotunda lined with busts and statuary of deans and scholars and Guardians, their bronze and marble gazes falling coldly upon the Riders. The rotunda no doubt impressed wealthy parents into sending their children here for their education. It also intimidated the students. As one who was not particularly serious about her studies in her early years, and one who had also managed to get into her share of trouble, Karigan ended up having to cross this rotunda several times to face the assistant dean for her transgressions. She loathed the rotunda and the stern faces encountered here.

When she had returned for her final year, she applied herself to her studies and did not have to make this walk even once. Still, despite all she had seen and done since, the rotunda held its power over her.

She lifted her chin and walked across the marble floor resolutely. Even if she felt intimidated, she did not have to show it.

A student, dressed in the maroon of languages with a white apprentice knot affixed to his shoulder, sat at the clerk's desk across the rotunda studying a book. When he saw them approach, he set his book aside and stood. "May I help you?"

"We've a message from the king for the Golden Guardian."

"I am sorry, but he is away from the city. He may be back very soon but . . . it is often hard to know."

Karigan nodded. She expected as much. "Dean Crosley?" she inquired.

The young man frowned. "I fear he is unavailable."

Karigan placed her hand on her satchel and, thinking the apprentice was simply trying to prevent her from disturbing his master, said, "This is a message penned by the king himself. It would not please him for its delivery to be delayed."

"I'm sorry, Rider, but—but Dean Crosley is in the House of Mending."

"What?" Karigan stepped backward. "Is he all right?"

"He lives," the apprentice said, "but I don't know the particulars. He interrupted a burglary and was beaten. His heart is not strong either."

"I am sorry to hear that," she said. Unlike his predecessor, Dean Crosley was a practical and fair-minded administrator. "I suppose the assistant dean has his hands full then."

The apprentice nodded. "Master Howard is helping to sort out the mess with the archivists and trying to figure out what was stolen, if anything."

"The burglary occurred in the archives?" Karigan asked in disbelief.

"Yes, Rider. We think it very odd. There are precious documents down there to be sure, but none of those are missing, or even disturbed."

"Strange," she murmured. Then she faced Fergal. "Looks like we'll be doing some waiting."

Fergal nodded, and Karigan could not tell whether or not he was pleased by this development.

"You could leave your message with one of the masters or trustees," the apprentice suggested.

"Thank you, but my message is for the Golden Guardian or the dean alone. I am hesitant to leave it even with Master Howard."

"I'm afraid I can be of no service then. May I at least lead you to the Guesting House?"

"No, thank you. I am familiar with campus."

As they retreated across the rotunda, Fergal asked,

"What are we going to do now? Just wait around until the Guardian shows up?"

"I'm afraid so. That, or until the dean is well enough to receive the message. You might as well enjoy it—there's much of interest going on here."

Karigan gave Fergal a tour of the campus so he might become familiar with its layout. She pointed out the library, various academic buildings, and the dining hall. When the campus bell rang they got caught in the middle of a colorful swarm as buildings emptied and students hurried to their next class. Karigan remembered herself burdened with books, rushing and dodging to reach her next class before the bell rang again for lessons to begin. In her early days, she had often been late or had not attended at all.

Almost as quickly as the courtyard filled, it emptied, punctuated by another ring of the bell. Fergal looked stymied, as if some magical spell had been cast to make the students vanish. Karigan smiled and led him across campus to the athletics field, hoping to find a certain master at work there.

When they arrived at the arms practice area beside the field house, they found Arms Master Rendle instructing first-year students in basic defensive moves with wooden swords. Karigan and Fergal watched over the fence as the arms master and his apprentice walked among the students, assisting them in finding the correct stances and technique. Some were intent on just swatting one another and smacking knuckles, their voices shrill. All through it, the arms master remained calm, never raising his voice. It struck Karigan as such a complete contrast to Drent's "teaching style," that she felt jealous of the students getting to work with Rendle. Drent, she thought, being the monster he was, would eat these youngsters as an appetizer before breakfast.

Rendle looked up just then, and smiled when he spied them.

"Now class, I'm going to show you what real swordplay looks like." He waved Karigan and Fergal over.

They stepped through the fence rails and the students hushed, regarding the Riders with curiosity.

"These are Green Riders," he told them. "Messengers of King Zachary."

The youngsters gazed at them with even more interest. Riders were a rare sight, especially off main roads and deep in the countryside. A Sacoridian could live an entire lifetime without ever seeing a Rider, or even knowing they existed. Hands darted up and so many questions poured out that Rendle and Karigan could barely keep up with them.

"Why do you wear green?"

"Do you know the king?"

"How old are you?"

"Are those swords real?"

To the last, Karigan answered by sliding her saber from the sheath just enough to give them a hint of the steel that remained hidden. The children clustered around her to touch pommel and hilt.

"That's nothing," one loud boy said. "My father has a jeweled sword used in the Clan Wars. I get to touch it anytime I want."

"Shut up, Garen," the other students said.

When an argument threatened to arise, Rendle raised his hands and commanded, "Enough." Silence fell immediately. "I am sure that the sword of Garen's father is a fine and storied weapon. But these *are* weapons, and their purpose is not glory or decoration, but use in combat. I have no doubt that this Rider saber has seen a good deal of service."

Garen was red faced and looked displeased.

"Have you killed lotsa people?" a girl asked Karigan.

"Um . . ."

Rendle sighed. "That is not an appropriate question for our guest, Nance."

"Sorry, Master Rendle."

He nodded. "Now, if Rider G'ladheon is willing, we shall demonstrate some true swordplay at a level that, if you practice hard enough, you may one day attain. This all right with you?" he asked Karigan.

Karigan felt she could hardly decline after that buildup, but she didn't mind anyway. She passed the message satchel and her swordbelt into Fergal's keeping and picked through a pile of wooden practice swords till she found one that suited her. She and Rendle then moved to a worn ring on the practice field where bouts were conducted. She swept the blade through the air to get the feel of it and loosen her muscles. The apprentice moved the students a safe distance from the ring. If either Rendle or Karigan stepped outside of it, the bout was lost.

They touched swords and initially went easy, each gauging the other. Then they worked through basic moves, the *clack-clack-clack* of their wooden blades the only sound on the field.

As Rendle got a feel for her ability, he increased the speed and difficulty of his technique. Karigan met him blow for blow, enjoying the effort, both physical and mental. The work cleared the presence of the students from her mind, her world now only Rendle and the rhythm of their blades.

Rendle accelerated again and Karigan whirled to block his blow, responding with an undercut that would have disemboweled a lesser opponent. He attempted to hook her sword out of her hands, but anticipating this, she pushed him away. They circled the ring, breathing hard, evaluating, waiting for the other to make the next move.

"You've been training," Rendle said. "Good."

Karigan responded with an advanced sequence that took Rendle by surprise and nearly caused him to stumble out of the ring, but he was a swordmaster and not only saved himself, but reversed Karigan's momentum and put her on the defensive. He scored a touch on her shoulder.

Karigan tightened her defenses. To her it was a dance, movement flowing naturally from repeated practice. They settled into a level of swordsmanship bordering on mastery in which more was achieved with less—more power, more finesse, more sustained action. It was the stealth and stillness of hunting cats that placed swordmasters above all others.

Karigan was unaware of how far she stretched her ability,

for there were only the swords, and they brought to her a sense of peace. Until, quite suddenly, Rendle's sword pressed into her gut.

"Kill point," he said, his voice soft.

Karigan could only stare at his sword as though it had really passed through her belly. Where did it come from? What move had he used?

"I see you haven't learned everything yet." Rendle grinned and withdrew the wooden blade. "Who've you been training with? Has Gresia been teaching you this advanced stuff?"

"I . . ." Karigan was still trying to sort out what he had done. "Drent," she said in a distracted way.

"Drent?"

Karigan remembered where she was and looked around. Rendle's class had been joined by dozens of other students of various ages, all watching her and Rendle.

Rendle cleared his throat and turned to the students. "Now this was swordplay. Swordplay of a very high order."

The onlookers applauded, a much different reaction than what Karigan normally received when she trained with Drent on castle grounds. Drent and his other trainees greeted her efforts with derision, though she believed her skills superior to at least a few of theirs.

Rendle dismissed the students and when some of them lingered to ask questions, he shooed them away. "There will be time for questions tomorrow," he told them. "Go on now." To Karigan he said, "Would you like to see where you went wrong with that last move?"

Karigan did, and they worked it out till dusk, with only Fergal watching. It reminded Karigan of many such sessions when she was Rendle's pupil, his method of teaching supporting her abilities rather than tearing them to pieces as Drent's did. His teaching inspired her to pay attention to her studies as well, and she thought it interesting how far a little encouragement from one whom she respected could go.

When Rendle taught Karigan the intricacies of the technique to his satisfaction, he said, "Try that one on Drent."

Karigan grinned. "I will."

Rendle then became very still. "Has he made an initiate of you yet?"

"A what?"

"A swordmaster initiate?"

"Uh, no," Karigan replied, surprised by the question.

Rendle drew his dark eyebrows together. "If you were still my student, I would."

"Really?"

Rendle nodded. "Your level of swordplay today was borderline swordmastery."

"It was?" Karigan knew her skills had improved dramatically with Drent's tutelage, but she never dreamed of being on that level.

Rendle grinned. "I've been softened by working with beginners all the time, but I know skill when I'm up against it. You've had a natural talent all along, and now you've built upon it."

"I did? I have?"

Still grinning, he patted her on the shoulder. "Felt good to work at such a level. Now why don't you help me clear up this equipment and we'll catch up over some supper."

Fergal, apparently hungry, helped them carry armloads of practice swords to the field house.

"Would you teach me, sir?" he asked.

Rendle halted in the doorway. "Pardon my manners, Rider, but we've not even been properly introduced!"

Karigan remedied the matter and added, "He's trained some with Arms Master Gresia, and I've been working with him during our travels. It seems we'll be on campus for a little while, and if it's no burden, well, we'd both benefit from some training, and be honored by it."

Rendle stepped inside and dumped the practice swords into their storage chest. "I will do so, and schedule you for my advanced class time. You will inspire the students to work harder."

Karigan was pleased, not only for herself, but for Fergal. Maybe Rendle's mild manner would prove an encouraging influence on Fergal, as he had on her.

GREETING FRIENDS

When Karigan stepped outside the field house, she was almost knocked over by someone hurtling out of the dusk and into her arms. She laughed when she realized who it was, and gave her young friend a fierce hug in return.

Mel released her and jumped up and down. "They said a Rider was here and doing swordplay with Master Rendle and I knew it was you!"

"They?"

"My friends, but I didn't hear about it till after." Mel pouted, then laughed and hugged her again.

"Ah," Rendle said, "another of my impertinent but talented students."

"*Another* impertinent student?" Karigan asked, placing a hand on her hip.

"But talented," Rendle said, unflappable as ever.

Karigan scrutinized Mel. She was an inch or two taller than she remembered, and her shape was growing into something more mature. "Anything I need to report to this one's mother?" she asked Rendle.

Mel's eyes widened in mortification and she whipped her gaze to Rendle.

"Oh," he said, "nothing I don't think I can handle. If anything arises, however, I'll be sure to send word back with you."

A protest was about to burst past Mel's lips when she noticed Fergal. "Who are you? Are you new?"

Karigan noted his startled expression and said, "Fergal Duff, meet Melry Exiter, daughter of our captain."

This time it was Fergal's eyes that widened. "I didn't know . . ."

Mel, unaware of his awkwardness, or ignoring it, said, "Yep. I plan to be a Green Rider, too, if the call would call me, if you know what I mean."

By now the sun had set and the dusk covering the practice field was deepening, so they set off together to take supper at the Guesting House. The whole way over, Mel carried on a one-sided conversation telling them about her classes and school gossip, including some about her instructors.

"I don't think I want to hear this," Rendle said. He tugged his pipe from his pocket and proceeded to pack the bowl with tobacco. He clamped his teeth on the stem of the unlit pipe and said no more. Mel carried on with exclamations about this and that, waving to friends as she passed them by, and adding a snippet or two of information about each person.

With some bemusement, Karigan realized Mel was comfortable here and quite popular, a rather different experience than her own had been. Fergal appeared overwhelmed by Mel, but listened politely, almost gravely, to her chattering on.

When they entered the Guesting House, Mel strode right for the common room as though she owned the place and declared, "This will be much better than the dining hall's food. I could eat about ten horses, but I could never eat horses, of course."

Fergal frowned, but Mel did not notice and dropped into a chair at an empty table as though she'd been at hard labor all day and was exhausted.

Karigan excused herself and ran upstairs to wash up and grab the package Captain Mapstone sent with her for Mel. When she returned, Rendle sat at the head of the table, his pipe now lit and sending aromatic smoke up to the ceiling, an expression of bliss on his face. Fergal sat opposite Mel, who was still chattering away. Aside from Mel, the common room was quiet, almost like a library instead of a gathering and dining area. The other guests, visiting scholars by the look of their specs and piles of books, scowled in Mel's direction.

Upon seeing the package, Mel squealed and clapped with delight, driving a couple annoyed scholars from the room. Mel tore the package apart and withdrew a cloak in Rider green lined with the blue-green plaid of the First Rider.

"It's wonderful!" She tried it on and whirled about, causing more scholars to slam their books shut and leave. Those on other business seemed unfazed by Mel's exuberance, and some even smiled as they continued with their meals. "I'm sure to hear the Rider call now."

She returned to her chair, still draped in the cloak, and discovered the chocolate from Master Gruntler's.

"Dragon Droppings!" She popped one into her mouth and rolled her eyes in ecstasy. "They've some good confectioners in town," she said, "but none as good as Master Gruntler."

"There's a letter as well," Karigan said, and she asked Fergal, who still had the message satchel, to dig it out.

Quiet finally descended as Mel set to reading, with only occasional exclamations and muttering. The woman who ran the Guesting House brought them a pitcher of ale and tankards, and some cider for Mel, as well as bread, a tub of butter, and wedges of chicken pie.

Rendle tapped out his pipe and set it aside to eat. He said, "So you are here on king's business, or simply to check in on young Melry?"

"A little of both, I suppose," Karigan said. "We brought a message for the Golden Guardian, which in his absence, was to go to Dean Crosley."

"I see, and with the Guardian away and the dean in the House of Mending, you are stuck."

Karigan nodded.

Rendle chewed thoughtfully on a bite of chicken pie, then said, "It'll be a while before Dean Crosley is well enough to assume his duties. Received a nasty beating, and he being elderly and all. Took us all by surprise, and I think most on campus are unsettled by the crime—at least the faculty is.

There'll be more patrols made by the constabulary, and the faculty will be keeping its own watch as well. If the burglar makes another appearance, he will be dealt with. Firmly." His face hardened, and Karigan knew she'd not want to be that burglar if Rendle caught hold of him.

"The dean is well thought of," Rendle continued. "Much more than his predecessor, I'd daresay."

Karigan silently agreed, having been on the receiving end of Geyer's punishments. Fortunately the trustees had seen how poor an administrator he had been and dismissed him.

Mel's fork clattered to her plate and she slapped her letter onto the table. "What's wrong with my mother?" she demanded.

They all stared at her in astonishment.

"What do you mean?" Karigan asked.

Mel huffed, then jabbed her finger at the letter. "She tells me everything's good, nothing to worry about, new Riders coming in, tra-la-la, then . . . *then* she gets mushy and tells me how much she loves me."

When Mel's outburst produced only blank stares, she explained, "She *never* goes on about that stuff. The love stuff. And there's a whole lot missing from this, it seems to me. *What* happened this summer?"

Three pairs of eyes turned in Karigan's direction. "Uh . . ." she said.

"Yes," said a voice from behind, "I'd like to hear about this summer, too."

Karigan almost knocked over her chair in her haste to stand. "Estral!" she cried, and strode over to her friend to give her a hug.

After enthusiastic greetings, Estral demanded, "And I want to know why no one sent me word of your arrival. Or, were you planning to sneak about the whole time?"

"Sneak about? No! We . . . I was . . ."

Estral laughed and it was a silvery sound. "Never mind, not much gets past me anyway. I have my sources." She grinned and took a chair next to Mel. Estral Andovian, daughter of the Golden Guardian and journeyman minstrel, joined them for tea and a dessert of hot apple crisp smothered in cream. Conversation turned to general topics of the school and of Karigan's and Fergal's journey. Karigan was careful to leave out their "adventures" in Rivertown.

Estral listened with her head cocked and her gaze trained on the speaker's lips, for she was deaf in one ear. Instead of it inhibiting her musical ability, she claimed it made her a much better listener and musician. Children had been cruel to her when she was a student, no matter that she was the Golden Guardian's daughter. She and Karigan had become best friends when Karigan stood up for her against the bullies, in one instance using wharf language so vile it brought her tormentors to tears. It had not made Karigan popular, but she hadn't cared. Estral's friendship made up for it all.

Much had changed since those early school days. Among Estral's duties was teaching students and Karigan suspected she handled many of her father's obligations during his long absences. One day Estral would inherit the title of Golden Guardian and become responsible for Selium and its repositories of history and culture. Hers was a noble station of a sort, though what the Golden Guardian governed was different than that of a lord-governor.

"So you've a message for my father," Estral said. "I am expecting him to return soon, though I couldn't tell you exactly when. I suspect he's had word about the attack on the dean and will hurry home."

"We're planning to wait," Karigan said. "His response to the king's message will determine whether or not we continue on with our other errands."

"Where are you headed?" Rendle asked. "That is, if it's not a secret—"

"No secret," Karigan replied. "We're off to a border town to meet with a horse trader. With more Riders coming in, we need more horses. Fergal here has been riding a retired cavalry horse."

"More horses! Yay!" Mel cried. "I wonder if one will be mine someday."

Karigan glanced at Fergal who looked to be in a continual state of astonishment, if not awe, in Mel's presence. She suppressed a laugh. "After we meet with the trader, it's off to Mirwellton."

Estral gave her a sympathetic look. They'd both been exposed to Timas Mirwell's cruel behavior during their school days. Seeing him was the one part of the errand Karigan dreaded.

"Mirwell ba-a-ad," Mel said.

This time, Karigan did laugh.

"Don't you need to see to your studies?" Estral asked Mel. "It's getting late and soon it will be lights out in your dorm."

Mel pouted. "But Karigan hasn't told me what's wrong with my mother."

Again, all gazes were fixed on Karigan. She squirmed in discomfort. "Your mother is well," she said. "Overworked, but that's not unusual. Connly and the rest of us are trying to help her keep up. Even Mara from her bed in the mending wing."

At Mel's perplexed expression, Karigan realized Mel must have heard almost nothing of the summer's events. A glance at Estral's expression revealed that her friend knew at least something of what had happened. Having been caught in the middle of those events, Karigan forgot that news was sometimes slow to reach outlying areas, and if the captain did not see fit to tell her daughter everything, Karigan wasn't sure it was her place to do so.

"Why is Mara in the mending wing?" Mel asked, her voice uncharacteristically level.

"She got hurt. When Rider barracks burned down."

"What?"

It took them several moments to calm down the agitated girl.

"Perhaps you should start at the beginning," Estral said. "Mel won't be able to sleep with just that information, and I'll see to it she doesn't get into trouble for being out late."

Karigan was trapped, but Estral was right. Worry would

gnaw Mel to death, so Karigan related the summer's events as best as she could, delicately maneuvering around bits she thought better to withhold, including the extent to which the captain had been affected by the disruption in magic. At certain points Rendle and Estral nodded or made affirmative noises when they heard news that was familiar to them.

By the time she finished, she was hoarse, though she left out a good many details, and her companions sat in silence. Mel cried several times during the telling, for Riders had perished and the news hadn't reached her yet. Karigan wished the captain was better at keeping her daughter informed, but she understood the desire to protect her from worry. Better, however, for her to hear the truth of it before rumors reached her.

"That is quite a story," Estral said, her eyes distant. Karigan wondered if she was already forming songs in her head about those events. "I've heard portions of it from different sources. You know, this is the sort of thing the people of Sacoridia ought to hear."

"That's your job," Karigan said.

"It's hard to do when no one steps forward to give us a firsthand account."

"It's not something you just, well, talk about."

Estral chuckled. "You Riders have kept so many secrets for so long that trying to pry information out of you is next to impossible. People should hear of your accomplishments." She then rose and added, "I think it is time for Mel to return to her dorm."

Mel protested, but Estral was firm. With a fierce hug for Karigan, Mel obeyed and left the common room. Estral followed behind to escort her and said in parting, "We'll talk more later."

Later never seemed to arrive. Estral was caught up in classes—both teaching and attending—as well as taking care of any odds and ends left to her in her father's absence. Over the course of several days, the most Karigan saw of her friend was only in passing and over hurried midday meals.

Meanwhile, Karigan and Fergal bided their stay in Selium by working with Master Rendle. Karigan assisted Rendle with many of his classes, while Fergal spent his extra time exploring the city. She suspected he even tried one of the public baths, but he wouldn't admit it. When he wasn't in the city, he followed Mel around, listening in bemusement as she chattered away about this and that. She was proud of her association with the Green Riders, and liked to show him off to her friends. About the only time Karigan saw him was at supper or during his sessions with Master Rendle.

One evening she wandered campus pathways to stretch her legs, remembering school days when she used to sneak out of her dorm to visit Estral. The two would chat deep into the night, Karigan returning to her bed just in time for the morning bell. She'd then spend most of her day drifting from class to class in a sleepy haze.

She smiled and struck off for the Golden Guardian's residence, which lay outside the grouping of academic buildings and looked over the city. She had no idea if Estral would be in, but she yearned for a chat with her friend, just like in the old days.

As befitting the Golden Guardian, the house was large with symmetrical columns lining its front facade. Mellow lamplight filled a few of the windows on the bottom floor. Karigan mounted the granite steps and jangled the bell at the large door, which was embedded with a brass plaque in the shape of a harp.

Presently the door opened and a gentleman, attired in a dark velvet longcoat and high collar wrapped with a silk cravat, peered out at her, a lamp in his hand. "Yes?" he asked.

"Good evening, Biersly," Karigan said. "I'm wondering if Estral is in."

He beckoned her into the entry hall and placed his lamp on a table. "Please wait here one moment." He turned on his heel and retreated down the hall. Karigan shook her head. Biersly knew who she was—she'd been a frequent visitor during her school years, yet he did not seem to recognize her.

The entry hall remained as Karigan remembered. Familiar masterworks of art and tapestries hung on the walls, and the same furniture sat where it always had been. It was both stylish and impersonal, the way the houses of other nobles and officials tended to be. It was the public space for visitors and dignitaries to enter and business to be conducted. The family quarters, with their more personal touches and belongings, were usually located on an upper floor. It was true of this house.

With slow, deliberate strides, Biersly returned. "Mistress Andovian will see you. Please follow me."

Karigan could not help but imitate the butler's lilting gait and serious demeanor as she followed him. To her surprise they bypassed the marble staircase that wound to the upper floor and instead headed for the back of the house toward the kitchen. The house, as they passed through it, exuded silence, and Karigan thought it odd for a place that housed the musically oriented Golden Guardian and his minstrel daughter. Of course, the Golden Guardian was rarely home.

The kitchen, too, was quiet, but they found Estral sitting there at the long, rough table in the spill of lamplight, with papers, pen, and ink before her. Gentle heat radiated from the cook stove behind her. When Estral looked up, Biersly halted and bowed. "Rider G'ladheon to see you, mistress."

Estral smiled. "Thank you, Biersly. You're dismissed for the evening."

"Thank you, mistress." He bowed again and departed.

Estral watched after him, still smiling. "It's gaming night," she said.

"What?"

"All the butlers gather in their favorite pub down in town to dice and such. I think it's just an excuse to get together to gossip about their masters and mistresses."

"Biersly?" Karigan asked. "Gambling?" Then she laughed, envisioning that solemn, proper man with his sleeves rolled up and a tankard of ale at his elbow as he rolled dice.

"I'm glad you came over," Estral said, shoving her papers aside. "We haven't had a chance to visit properly."

They raided the pantry for some gingerbread baked that afternoon, put water on the stove for tea, and proceeded to engage in some gossip of their own, about some of Karigan's old classmates and instructors and Estral's students. Without anyone around to overhear them, the talk was free, and at times loud, accompanied by much laughter.

Timbre, Estral's gray tabby, leaped onto the table and butted his head against his mistress' chin. A typical shipcat, he was huge, his long fur and plumed tail augmenting his size. Estral crumpled a piece of paper and threw it across the kitchen. Timbre clomped to the floor to chase it, and bore it back in his mouth. Shipcats were that way, sort of doglike.

After a few minutes of play, Timbre jumped back onto the table and flopped, purring loudly enough that Karigan swore she felt the table vibrate.

They finished the last crumbs of gingerbread and Estral cocked her head. "So, I assume that, aside from your delay here, your message errand is going well . . ."

Karigan sighed.

"Oh dear," Estral said, passing her hand through Timbre's luxurious fur. His purring grew louder. "That good, eh?"

Because of Estral's sympathetic ear, Karigan opened up and the details of her journey tumbled from her mouth. It was a relief to tell her about Fergal's intentional plunge into the Grandgent, and about the brothel and her father's association with it.

"You have had a trying time of it, haven't you?" Estral said.

"There are times when I want to throttle him."

"Fergal or your father?"

"Both, I suppose, but at the moment Fergal is closer at hand."

Estral propped her chin on her hand. "He seems terribly eager to prove himself, and judging from what you've said of his past, it's no surprise. I do notice him in Mel's company an awful lot."

Karigan sighed. "I've noticed as well. I might be more amused if Mel weren't the captain's daughter."

"Seems harmless enough. Look, Karigan, you can't expect to control Fergal's every move. People are, well, people, and they all have their own quirks and will do whatever they want to no matter what *you* would like them to do. At some point they are responsible for their own actions. You have created very high standards for yourself, but not everyone is going to adopt them just because you want them to. Don't be so hard on yourself."

Karigan gazed at her friend, stunned. "And when did you become such a wise one, Old Mother?"

"Teaching. Teaching a hundred Fergals. Well, maybe not as challenging as your Fergal, but challenging nonetheless. Somewhere I've acquired vast amounts of patience." She rolled her eyes. "It appears to me you've been doing your best with Fergal. He seems good-hearted, and I should think he's learned quite a lot from you so far." Estral paused, and chuckled. "I *do* sound like an old mother, don't I?"

Karigan didn't feel as confident about her ability as a mentor as Estral sounded. She was certain that if she were more patient, more instructorly like Ty, Fergal wouldn't even have thought of jumping into the Grandgent, much less done it. But she wasn't Ty, and she could only continue to do her best. Then she laughed.

"What's so funny?" Estral asked.

"My high standards, as you called them," Karigan replied, barely able to contain herself. "How did I get those? Surely not by skipping class and starting fights and—"

"By learning," Estral said, "and by having a good heart. Like Fergal."

Karigan stopped laughing, stilled by sudden revelation. "Oh, my," she murmured. "I was a difficult child at times." If she were to mentor a younger version of herself, her younger self would drive her current self batty. Fergal couldn't hold a light to that! "I was . . . I was a *brat*."

Estral patted her wrist. "Yes, at times, but we love you anyway, and you've turned out just fine."

"Er, thanks."

"My pleasure."

Timbre, tired of being ignored, pawed at Estral's pen and papers. She rescued the pen, but the papers fluttered off the table.

"You're a big help," she muttered at the cat, and she retrieved the papers, arranging them into a neat pile. "Exams I'm grading." She then lifted Timbre onto her lap. He draped himself across her thighs in boneless fashion and resumed purring.

"So when does the journeyman go journeying?" Karigan asked her.

Estral grimaced. "I suppose I'll have to do so by next year, but truth be told, I . . . I don't feel inclined to travel much."

"What? A minstrel who doesn't want to travel?"

"I like teaching." Estral stroked Timbre. "That's a good thing because Selium will always need teachers. But to teach more than the youngest children and assist with some of the other classes, I have to become a master, and to become a master, I have to do my year of wandering." Her expression grew mournful.

"Good thing you weren't called into the messenger service," Karigan said.

"I know."

Estral's response was so earnest they both laughed. Annoyed, Timbre jumped from Estral's lap and slinked away to sit by the cook stove and lick his paw. Then he froze in mid-lick as if frightened by something, and darted out of the kitchen into the darkness of the house.

"What's with him?" Karigan asked.

Estral shrugged. "He's a cat."

Then Karigan heard something, a stealthy noise somewhere in the house. The creaking of floorboards, which now, to her sensitized ears, was excruciating in the silence.

"What is it?" Estral asked.

Her voice low, but just loud enough so her friend could hear, Karigan replied, “Someone’s in the house.”

They looked at one another, Estral’s expression stricken, the break-in at the archives and assault upon the dean fresh in their minds.

THE GOLDEN GUARDIAN

"It can't be Biersly," Estral whispered, "he'll be gone for hours still."

"Shhh . . ." Karigan strained to listen, the silence complete and ominous. Had she imagined it? Then there it was again, a creaking floorboard, a shuffling noise. She had come to Estral's house unarmed, believing there was no need to bring her saber on a friendly visit. She gazed about the kitchen and spotted a poker next to the cook stove. She stood as quietly as she could and grasped it.

"What are—" Estral began, but Karigan gestured her to be quiet.

She crept out of the kitchen, motioning for Estral to stay put. She attempted to move as noiselessly as possible. It was likely the intruder would head for the kitchen once he saw the lamplight. Biersly left a lamp burning in the entry hall, making it obvious the house was occupied, and if an occupied house was not enough to deter the intruder, then Karigan must assume he was willing to harm those within, especially if it was the same person who broke into the archives and injured Dean Crosley.

The hall outside the kitchen fell into shadow and Karigan paused several moments to allow her eyes to adjust. It would do no good to go blundering into the intruder because she was light blind. She tamed her breathing and she listened. A door moaned open deeper in the house.

She set off slowly, poker clenched in her hand, aware of Estral hovering in the kitchen door behind her. She wished she knew the layout of the house better to help compensate for the darkness. She moved at a turtle's pace, navigating furnishings and straining to hear the movements of the intruder. She should have told Estral to leave by the back entrance and seek help, but she hadn't thought of that in time. Maybe Estral would think to do so herself.

Karigan licked her lips and pressed on. When she reached the front entry hall, Biersly's lamp twisted and flickered wildly. The front door had been left ajar and the cold wind curled in and around Karigan's ankles. She shivered.

Thunk.

The noises were concentrated toward the far end of the house. Karigan crept on, step by step. In daylight this walk would have taken mere seconds. Now it felt like a hundred year journey. In the parlor she smacked her knee into a chair. She covered her mouth to stop a stream of curses and hopped madly on one foot. When the pain subsided, she limped on, her senses raw to telltale sounds and to furnishings that might impede her way.

She rounded a corner in a side hall and found lamplight emanating from a doorway. The glow of light dimmed and brightened as someone moved around it.

If Karigan remembered correctly, this was the library. It made sense. If the thief couldn't find what he wanted at the archives, then perhaps he'd find what he was looking for in the Golden Guardian's personal library. She eased her way to the door and peered in. At first the light was too much after her eyes had become accustomed to the dark, but soon she could make out the scene.

The Fiori library was full of deep mahogany hues and rich fabrics on upholstered furniture. It was not a large library, but was filled to capacity by leather-bound volumes and scrolls. A marble-framed fireplace gaped dark and dormant. In the center of the room was the library table where a figure in a gray cloak bent over an open book. Saddlebags were strewn on the floor at his feet. Timbre the cat sat in the center of the table looking down at the open book as if he could read it, then he glanced at her with his green, slitted eyes and thumped his tail on the table. The cloaked intruder stiffened.

Karigan adjusted her grip on the poker. "Put your hands out to your sides where I can see them and turn around slowly."

An agonizing amount of time passed in which the intruder stood where he was, unmoving. She wondered if he was considering his options, thinking of plans of attack and escape.

"In the name of the king—" Karigan began.

Immediately his stance relaxed. He obeyed and put his hands out. Hands empty of weapons. He turned around. The hood of his cloak shadowed the upper portions of his face. His chin was unshaven and golden bristles glinted in the lamplight. He was about to speak when something behind her caught his attention.

Karigan whirled and raised her poker just in time to turn a swordblade cutting out of the dark. How stupid she'd been to assume there was only one intruder in the house. A quick exchange of blows ensued, the assailant's blade sparking against the coarse iron of the poker. She could not see him, caught as she was between the light of the library and the dark of the house. The assailant was also dressed in black and was absorbed by the formless shadows beyond.

The poker proved a crude sword, awkward to handle, poorly balanced, and lacking a guard to protect her hand. Her assailant was an expert swordsman and she knew she was in trouble with her clumsy weapon.

Clang-clang-clang-cling-clang!

Her best defense was to move quickly, to leap out of the way, to— She collided into a small side table and it smashed beneath her. She found herself sprawled atop the broken wood with a swordtip pressed against her neck. Desperately she groped for the poker, but it had rolled out of reach.

"Karigan?" the assailant said in disbelief.

"Master Rendle?"

The sword retracted into the shadows and a hand

emerged in its place to help her rise. The side table was in shambles and Karigan felt rather bruised. Gratefully she accepted the hand up.

"Then who—?" She gestured at the man in the library.

She perceived Rendle's sword up at guard more than saw it.

"My good Rendle," the cloaked intruder said, "this is a fine way to welcome me home."

The swordtip dropped to the floor. "My lord! I had no idea!" And Rendle knelt in obeisance, Karigan too startled to move. Their intruder was the Golden Guardian?

If there had been any question, it was dispelled by Estral, who flew from the darkness that Karigan had only inched through, and threw herself into the man's wide open arms. "Father!"

When Estral broke away from him, the dark gray hood fell back and he undraped the cloak from his shoulders, revealing a lean man with faded blond hair and the same sea-green eyes as his daughter. Fine lines crinkled around his eyes as though he squinted too much in the sun or laughed a lot. Despite the lines, his age was difficult to determine, much the way it was with the Eletians. It was said that Eletian blood had intermingled with the Fiori line long ago, and Karigan believed it.

Aaron Fiori, Golden Guardian of Selium, cast them all a brilliant grin.

"If I didn't know better, it would seem there was some conspiracy afoot—an arms master and a Green Rider sneaking about my house."

"I'm . . . I'm sorry, sir," Karigan said. Her bow was jerky, for she was still startled. "I didn't realize—I didn't—"

His laugh was a deep sound that resonated around them, breaking the spell of silence. "That's what I get for trying not to disturb anyone. At this hour I expect my daughter to be abed."

"You wouldn't have awakened me to let me know you were home?" Estral asked.

"Morning would have been soon enough, eh? But since

you are up, hug me again." And she did. "Come, come," he said, beckoning his accidental visitors into the library.

Karigan winced as she gazed down at the table she had crushed. "Sir, I—"

"Never you mind that. It's only Second Age, by one of the lesser known craftmasters."

Second Age? That meant it was hundreds of years old and now she was more than sorry—she was mortified.

"Come," Lord Fiori insisted. Then more gently he added, "I would never blame anyone who thought she was defending my daughter and home." He placed his hand on her shoulder and guided her to a comfortable chair in front of the cold fireplace. When she was settled, he placed kindling on the hearth. Removing steel and flint from the mantel, he struck them together to spark a blaze. Timbre trotted over and planted himself on the hearth rug. After a few quick licks to his shoulder, he rolled and curled, his eyes fixed on the Golden Guardian.

"We are relieved you are back, my lord," Rendle said. "There has been some trouble on campus."

Lord Fiori leaned against the mantel, a stick of wood in his hand, his expression serious. "Yes, even from afar I heard news of the attack on Dean Crosley and of the theft."

"The theft?" Karigan said. "Has it been determined what was taken?"

"Nothing of seeming significance," Lord Fiori said. "But who is to say what significance it held for the thief?"

Apparently this was news to Rendle as well. "What was it?"

Lord Fiori placed the wood onto his growing fire. "A translation key for Old Sacoridian. We've more than one copy, and the one that was stolen held no special value. Yet it was worth enough to the thief to steal it and harm someone in the process."

"We've been keeping an extra watch on campus should the thief make a reappearance," Rendle said. "That's what I was up to tonight, and when I saw a suspicious person enter your house, I feared for Estral."

"So I surmised." Lord Fiori slid into an overstuffed chair.

"And I am grateful for everyone's vigilance. While I doubt the thief will return, it would not be imprudent to continue the faculty patrols for a while just to be on the safe side."

Rendle nodded. "We will do so."

While the two men spoke softly of school business, Karigan thought about the theft anew, which brought to mind her ill-fated outing with Braymer Coyle at the Sacor City War Museum and the appearance of the Raven Mask.

Lord Fiori gazed at her curiously. "What are you thinking about?"

"There was a theft at the Sacor City War Museum not all that long ago," she said. "It may be coincidental, but the thief took a scrap of old parchment."

"Yes," he said, "I heard about it." He smiled. It was a knowing smile. Karigan couldn't get over how he knew so much of the news of the land. He traveled extensively and must hear much on the road, but surely not any more than a Green Rider would. Or would he? Maybe folk were freer with their conversation around a minstrel than a uniformed representative of the king, and she doubted he flaunted himself as the Golden Guardian, but instead traveled in the humbler guise of an ordinary minstrel. What conversations must he overhear in the common rooms of inns and pubs between ballads and rousing drinking songs? What stories did folk tell *him* that they wouldn't tell a Green Rider?

Then there were all the other Selium minstrels who were wide-ranging in their travels and constantly acquired news. The Golden Guardian was their chief, and they must report everything of interest to him.

"Yes," he said, "I heard about the theft and that some brave lady tried to prevent it. You wouldn't happen to know who she was, would you?"

Heat crept up Karigan's neck and into her cheeks.

"You're teasing her, father," Estral said. She had heard a full account of the incident from Karigan.

"So it was Karigan." Lord Fiori nodded as if confirming it for himself. "I did not make it to Sacor City on this journey, but I overheard the remarks of some Rhovan merchants and the name G'ladheon though one of the fellows, an older gent, used a less kind word than 'brave' to describe the lady. There was the occasional mention of the incident elsewhere with no name attached. Are the two thefts coincidence? It's difficult to say. Other than these being documents, what ties them together?"

"There are hundreds of thefts across the kingdom each year," Rendle said.

"Yes, but how many of those thefts are of objects of seemingly little worth?" Lord Fiori shrugged. "I find it curious. What do you think, Karigan?"

Karigan thought he was testing her and she shifted uncomfortably in her chair, wishing she was the cat who was now sprawled on his back with paws in the air, absorbing the warmth of the fire and purring away, unconcerned.

"I think," she began, "there were two different thieves."

"How so?"

"The thief at the museum, who may have been the Raven Mask, or was impersonating him, made the theft in full daylight and in front of witnesses. He didn't seem to want to hurt anyone unnecessarily." She remembered his swordtip at her throat. He could have easily killed her. "My understanding is that the thief here came stealthily in the night and showed no such concern for Dean Crosley."

"Very good reasoning," Lord Fiori said, his tone full of approval. "I believe you are correct. However, it is possible that more than one thief was working toward the same goal. We may never know the answer. The sad part is that had someone wanted to view the translation key, the archivists most likely would have helped him."

"Unless the thief planned to translate something nefarious—something he didn't want anyone else to see," Rendle said. The pipe was out and lit, and he pulled deeply on it.

"True," Lord Fiori said.

"There is something else," Karigan said.

"Yes?"

"I remember the museum attendants saying that the parchment the thief stole was in Old Sacoridian."

Lord Fiori scratched his chin. "That sounds like more than coincidence. A document in Old Sacoridian is stolen, but it needs to be translated, so a translation key is stolen from the Selium archives. Do you know what the document contained?"

"The museum attendants didn't seem to know," Karigan replied, "and I never heard any more about it."

"That is unfortunate," Lord Fiori said. "I'm afraid we'll learn little more unless either of the thieves is apprehended, which seems rather unlikely."

The group sat in silence until Estral, unable to sit still any longer, burst out, "Where have you been, father?"

"West mostly," he said. "West into Rhovanny and beyond, trying to get a feel for the mood of the people beyond Sacoridia's borders. They appear to have been spared the reach of Blackveil Forest this summer past, but rumors of magical oddities here reached even as far west as Dunan and the folk are uneasy. Though I did not venture east this journey, the land was full of tales of passing Eletians, Eletians wandering east, a very bright company of them. I understand they are now encamped outside the gates of Sacor City."

At the mention of Eletians, Karigan straightened in her chair. "They've gone to Sacor City?"

"So it appears," Lord Fiori said.

"What do they want? What do they plan?"

"I wish I knew," Lord Fiori replied. "I have not heard."

Karigan's knuckles whitened as she gripped the arms of her chair. She wanted to ride back to Sacor City to find out what the Eletians were up to. She did not trust them, not entirely.

"I should think their intentions are peaceful," Lord Fiori said, as if sensing her turmoil. "I heard nothing of them traveling as a war party. The land told no such tale of danger, only wonder and joy at their passing."

Wonder and joy . . . His words soothed her but little. Yes, the Eletians were magical beings, but they were also quite possibly a threat. A threat to herself, and a threat to her people. It was difficult to sort out the Eletians' intentions. On one hand they were willing to save mortal lives, as in the aftermath of the massacre of Lady Penburn's delegation. On the other, they were willing to allow all to be destroyed.

Song murmured in the back of her mind. The Golden Guardian sang, his voice growing and distracting her from her worries, bringing her back to the present. His voice arose from the deepest of places within, not just from himself, but from his listeners, and encompassed the entire room, filled the spaces between books and shelves, flowed into the fireplace and up the chimney with the smoke, and arched over them like the ceiling itself. Karigan felt the song vibrate within her. The room was music. He sang:

"The music of the stars mourns
their passing, their passing,
from the shining Land of Avrath
from the shining Land of Avrath

"Will they return?
Will they return to the bright woods,
to the cerulean sea,
home to Avrath,
the Shining Land?"

When he stopped, it was like being dropped out of a dream. The song was a lament and saddened Karigan, but it held great beauty in its mourning.

"I haven't heard that one before," Estral said, breaking the spell of the song.

"I shouldn't think so," Lord Fiori murmured. "I have heard it sung among the Eletians, and this is but a rough translation."

"What is this Shining Land?" Rendle asked. "This Avrath?"

Lord Fiori rose to toss another log on the fire. "It is," he said, "their highest spiritual place, the place from whence they came and to where they aspire to return. Or so I gather."

"Like the heavens," Rendle said.

The fire hissed and sparked as it consumed the new log. Lord Fiori returned to his chair and spread his long legs before him. "Perhaps that is so, but I do not know. It may be a physical place, or a layer of the world. It may even be a state of mind. I do know the Eletians believe their presence on Earth is a time of exile."

Exile. Karigan turned that over in her mind. Hadn't the Eletians always dwelled here? If it were a literal exile from a place called Avrath, maybe the divisions among the Eletians went deeper than anyone could imagine. What would cause them to be exiled from their "Shining Land?" And why were some of them so adamant about cleansing this land of mortals? To re-create Avrath on Earth? She yawned and thought the late hour was leading her to unlikely conclusions.

"I assume it is not by chance that one of the king's own messengers is here in Selium," Lord Fiori said, gazing at her.

"No, sir. I've a message from the king." She patted the message satchel at her side. She had not been willing to leave it unattended at the Guesting House. She removed the message and passed it to Lord Fiori.

He raised his eyebrows. "Addressed in the king's own hand—I recognize his scrawl. I trust this will require a response." He glanced up at Karigan. "Seek me out tomorrow." When the campus bell rang out the early morning hour, he amended, with a smile, "Later today."

Karigan took that as a dismissal and she was more than ready for her bed. She walked out with Master Rendle and he said, "Good fight. Too bad about the table."

He went off in his own direction with a hearty chuckle trailing behind him. Karigan smiled and shook her head. It had turned into an interesting evening, and she had much to think about, not the least of which was her technique with the poker.

INTO THE ARCHIVES

Karigan arose from bed much later than she intended, but it couldn't be helped. After she made it back to her room in the small hours, it was a long time before she was able to sleep with all the chatter in her brain about thieves of documents and Eletians camped outside the gates of Sacor City. She had gone over everything Lord Fiori said again and again, but no great revelations had come of it; her mind was too busy just trying to sort it all out.

When she could no longer ignore the sunshine glaring through her window, she dragged herself out of bed and ate a late breakfast alone in the common room. The angle of the sun and the campus bell told her she'd let most of the morning slip by. The Guesting House staff were busy in the kitchen preparing the midday meal.

It took her some time to track down Lord Fiori, for he wasn't home, nor was he in his office in the administration building. A helpful clerk suggested she check the archives, which were located in the catacombs beneath the library. She'd used the library as a student, but never had call to visit the archives, which were off limits to most students anyway.

From the curatorial office on the main floor, a clerk led her down a corridor lined with old portraits then to a thick, heavy door that opened onto a stone staircase. As they descended, Karigan thought it looked like it belonged to a construction older than the upper levels, but no scent of mustiness or decay met her as they descended. The updrafts were cool and clean without a hint of moisture.

When she reached the bottom step, she found herself in a low-ceilinged stone chamber held up by rough granite pillars. A labyrinth of shelves laden with tomes and manuscripts and scrolls and crates extended deep into cavernous shadows where no lamp was lit. Muffled voices emanated from somewhere beyond rows of shelves.

"I'll see if I can find Lord Fiori for you," the clerk said.

While he set off on his search, Karigan hopped onto a stool at a worktable, which was covered in curling maps. They looked to be ancient and fragile, so she did not dare touch them, but the top map, mottled brown with age, showed Sacoridia divided into small chunks, illustrating not provinces, but clan territories, and there were plenty of them, far exceeding today's twelve provinces. The landscape had changed little over time, but those who claimed it and drew boundaries on maps came and went with the politics of the day.

The return of the clerk, accompanied by both Lord Fiori and Estral, drew Karigan's attention from the map. The ceiling was so low that the top of Lord Fiori's head brushed it. She slipped off her stool and bowed, and the clerk excused himself.

"We wondered when you'd be up and about," Estral said, smiling.

"It took me a while to locate you."

"And so you've found us," Lord Fiori said. "What do you think of our archives?"

Karigan didn't really know what to say. The archives were not precisely what she expected. They contained the breadth and depth of Sacoridia's history and culture, a precious collection she expected to be displayed in some magnificent hall surrounded by the best works of art. Not buried in this . . . this root cellar. Well, the floor was smooth marble and not quite dirt, so maybe not a root cellar.

"It's . . ." She groped for words. "It's interesting."

The archives boomed with Lord Fiori's laugh. "Not what

you expected, eh? Perhaps you will be more impressed to know the vaults were constructed by Clan D'Yer. They are not beautiful to look upon, maybe, but ingeniously built to protect documents stored here from light, flame, and damp. We hold that more important than fancy surroundings. The object is to preserve the documents for generations to come so they can be learned from; not to show them off."

It made sense, but all the same, with Sacoridia's history buried in what amounted to little more than a cellar, albeit a well-constructed cellar, didn't it obscure the country's past with it hidden from the view of ordinary citizens?

"I am honored," she said, "that I get to view them."

Lord Fiori laughed again. "I see you've learned to be quite the diplomat during your time as a king's messenger. Speaking of which, I read the king's message after your departure last night." He removed it from an inner pocket of his waistcoat, the seals broken. "I've heard of this book the king seeks, though not recently, mind you. More a rumor of the book." He rubbed the bristles on his chin, his gaze distant. "It's been many a year, and if ever it existed, it vanished long ago. Alas, Selium contains only a rare volume or two related to works of magic. Most such documents were destroyed after the Long War. The collection of Selium, such as it was in those days, was plundered and cleansed."

"Cleansed?" Karigan asked.

"Magic in all forms was suppressed by those who held a dim view of it after the atrocities committed by Mornhavon the Black. They did not distinguish between that which was neutral or good in nature, and that which had been tainted by darkness. Thus, our archives lack valuable information, including anything that could help us repair the D'Yer Wall. I'm afraid it may never be recovered."

"So the book we're looking for may have been destroyed after the Long War," Karigan said.

"Destroyed or fallen into obscurity, and most assuredly not to be found in any of our collections. To make absolutely certain, however, I've our chief archivists and curators checking into it, and they will round up some idle journeymen to conduct a thorough search." He grinned at Estral, who frowned in response. "The search will no doubt take months, so you should not further delay your other errands by waiting on us. I will pen the king a message telling him as much as I've told you, and should we come up with anything during our search, I will send along one of my own messengers with the news."

With that, he set off to find his archivists and curators, leaving Estral and Karigan in silence.

Finally Estral said, "I guess this means you'll be heading out soon."

Karigan nodded. "Our orders are to go on with our other errands if the book can't be found here. I suppose we'll leave first thing tomorrow morning."

"Seems as though you just got here. I wish you could stay longer."

"Me, too."

As if to set aside the depressing news, Estral asked, "Would you like a tour while you're down here?"

"Of course," Karigan said, especially if it meant spending more time with her friend.

"We've only just been getting things back in order," Estral explained, "after the renovations. When we were moving things, we came across some real gems that hadn't been looked at in a couple hundred years—made it hard to pay attention to the work at hand. And there is always new stuff coming in—new songs and compositions, documents acquired from other collections, and the like. Keeps the archivists busy. Looking for that book may provide an opportunity to update the inventory. Which I'll probably have to help with. I suppose it'll be a good winter project."

Estral did not look thrilled by the prospect, but as they delved into the depths of the archives, illuminated only by the single lamp she carried, the journeyman minstrel's voice brightened and her step quickened as she pointed out various documents.

"These crates contain the correspondence of all the

Fioris," she said, "all the way back to Gerlrand, though there are only a few pieces from his time." Pointing to an opposing section of shelves, she said, "These are the folk songs of Sacoridia as copied down over the last one hundred years. Each shelf below it goes back another hundred years. Some of it is gibberish as far as I'm concerned."

And on she went, down the darkened row of shelves. Karigan glimpsed briefly the crates or sheaves of paper or parchment laid flat as Estral's lamplight rolled over them. She made out spiderlike strands of faded ink on some of the documents, but that was all.

Deeper and deeper they went, Karigan growing more impressed by the immensity of the chamber. It had been difficult to discern its size from the entrance, and she no longer thought of the archives as a root cellar but as a tomb. A tomb for old documents. Now that she thought of it, entering the archival vaults had that same feel of entering the tombs sheltered beneath the king's castle, with its clean air, low ceilings, lack of damp, and ability to *preserve,* though what the tombs preserved was a bit different . . . Clan D'Yer must have used similar construction techniques in both the tombs and the archives.

By the time they reached the end of the chamber, Karigan felt as though she'd been on some long subterranean journey. The dark hovering on the edges of Estral's lamp and the silence around them held such a dense quality that it was hard to believe it was daylight above and the campus was alive with the comings and goings of students.

The chamber ended at a room framed by a broad arched entryway. It contained a worktable and a couple sections of shelving that were mostly empty. The lamplight glistened against a seam of crystalline quartz that jagged through the smooth granite of the back wall like a streak of lightning. Inset into the wall was an alcove with a manuscript displayed in it.

"This was the area we discovered during renovations," Estral said. "It was all walled off and we had no idea it was here." She walked past the table to the alcove. "And it was here we found some old manuscripts, but only the one remained intact."

Karigan followed Estral into the barrel-vaulted chamber and over to the alcove. She looked down on the manuscript. It was yellowed and stained. She knew what it was without Estral telling her. This was why Estral had brought her on the "tour," to show her this one thing: the *Journal of Hadriax el Fex.* Her ancestor, the murderer.

Her fingers hovered just above the fragile title page. She could not read the scrawl on it, for it was written in the imperial tongue, but she knew the translation: *My Voyage from Arcosia to the New Lands; the Country There and Its Resources; My Adventures Among the Heathen Inhabitants; Our Settlement of Morhavonia; and the Long War that Ensued. Journal of Hadriax el Fex, Count of Fextaigne.* Then in Old Sacoridian, he had written: *Hereby known as Galadheon.*

"The paper must have been from Arcosia," Estral commented, "and of a very high quality to last all these years. Our ancestors had nothing like it."

Sacoridian ancestors, she meant. Karigan's ancestor was of Arcosia. "I sent my father the copy you made for me," she said. "But I don't know if he's bothered to read it."

Her fingers trembled and she withdrew her hand without touching the manuscript. Though she could not read the words, words in her ancestor's own hand, they seemed to speak to her, reach out and resonate. She turned her back on it.

Why was it that everything she had once thought to be true, like her father's fidelity to her dead mother, had been turned upside down? It wasn't enough that she had become a Rider instead of the merchant she had always planned to be, but even those things she had thought incontrovertible, like her heritage, had been swept out from under her feet. Everything that had been the foundation of who she was turned out to be nothing but lies. She swiped away unexpected tears.

"Karigan?" Estral's voice held a tinge of concern. "What's wrong?"

"Everything and nothing." She strode down the aisle between shelves but did not get far before she stood in darkness. Estral had not followed. She turned and saw her friend standing at the alcove gazing at Hadriax el Fex's journal. After a few moments, she left it behind, her lamplight pushing the dark down the aisle and revealing piles of scrolls on the shelves to either side of them.

"Is it something to do with Hadriax?" she asked.

Karigan took a shuddering breath. "My people were fishermen, or still are, I presume." Her father had never taken her to Black Island where he grew up. There was little love between him and his father, the grandfather she'd never met. "Simple Sacoridian fishermen. They're not supposed to be descended from imperial murderers."

Estral cocked her head the way she did when listening very closely, or turning something over in her mind. "It was war, and atrocities were committed on both sides, by Arcosians and Sacoridians both. Karigan, you aren't your ancestor. Hadriax el Fex is long dead and gone to dust. Besides, he was courageous enough to renounce Mornhavon in the end and aid the League. If he had not, the outcome of the war might have been far different.

"As for your family on Black Island, they are not the simple folk you think. Your grandfather holds a good deal of prestige among the islanders and owns several fishing vessels."

"I–I didn't know." Karigan scrunched her eyebrows in consternation. It was not fair that Estral knew more about her family than she did. "I know only the stories my father and aunts told me. Seems my father has kept a number of things from me."

"I'm sure he had his reasons," Estral said. "Your family was poor when your father left the island, and though they are not exactly prosperous by some accountings, they are, for fishermen, doing well enough for themselves."

"How do you know?"

"Our minstrels voyage out to the Night Islands from time to time, where they are eagerly received, for news is sparse and visitors rare, especially visitors gifted in music and tale telling. The minstrels watch and listen, and learn the affairs of the communities around them."

I should have guessed, Karigan thought.

She had never been overly curious about her extended family out on Black Island. She knew they fished, and that her grandfather was a horrible enough tyrant that her father left the island to seek his destiny elsewhere. She had grown up absorbing her father's antipathy toward the island G'ladheons. She'd had enough love and support from her father and aunts, other mainland members of the family, and even the household staff, that she never felt anything was missing. Just her mother who had died so young. Her mother's side of the family, also from Black Island, was an even greater mystery to her. Maybe one day she'd venture to the island and see for herself what her family was all about.

"Nothing is ever what it seems anymore, and nothing is what it should be," Karigan said.

Estral's eyes glinted in the lamplight as she gazed at Karigan. "I'm sorry things haven't gone the way you've expected, or have turned out differently than you've always known them to be. It does seem like you're adjusting to Rider life, though."

"Yes, I suppose I have. It's an honor to serve the king."

"And not just because you're in love with him?"

"WHAT?" Karigan rocked backward as if struck.

"As I thought," Estral murmured.

Karigan placed her hand on a shelf to steady herself. "Five hells! How can you—"

"Something in your face, your eyes, changes when he is mentioned, and your reaction confirms for me how you feel about him; that it goes beyond duty and respect for your monarch."

Karigan sagged. "Do you have some time?"

"I've no classes today," Estral said, "and we'd better sit. I'm tired of holding this lamp."

They returned to the chamber with the alcove and sat on stools at the worktable. "This is not song fodder for your minstrels," Karigan said. "It is between you and me."

"You have my promise I'll keep it to myself," Estral replied.

Karigan let flow all the feelings she had kept inside, her blossoming realization of her feelings for the king; his expression of love for her one night on the castle rooftop. She told Estral how he had attempted to present to her an all-too intimate gift even as his signature was drying on the marriage contract with Clan Coutre. She railed against the divisions between nobility and common blood.

"I'm so stupid," she said. "To even think—to even hope."

Estral, who remained silent through the entire thing, said, "Love is not stupid. It's just difficult when it happens this way. I think you're doing the right thing, trying to get on with life and beyond something that can't happen. I've no wisdom to offer, I'm afraid, just sympathy for my dear friend. It is hard that the matter of birth to one bloodline or another determines our path in society, but we have no say in to whom we are born, just as we have no say in who our distant ancestors are."

Estral may claim to lack wisdom, but her words quieted the conflict inside Karigan. Estral was right: one did not have control over the matter of one's birth, and to be angry and frustrated about it was futile. It would change nothing. Maybe if she were more accepting of life as it was, as she now accepted being a Green Rider, it would ease her heart.

Telling someone about it all also relieved her. She had not realized the weight she had carried by keeping it all inside her, how miserable these feelings for King Zachary had made her. Telling Estral freed her as telling another Rider friend could not. The Riders were bound to the king's service, too close to him, and revealing her secret to them would be humiliating.

"Well, Old Mother," Karigan said, her spirits lighter, "it's chilly down here. Shouldn't we go into town for some tea and sweets?"

Estral slowly smiled. "My inner wisdom tells me this is a very good idea."

And laughing, they left behind the darkness of the archives.

* * *

Before the pair headed into town, Estral needed to speak with one of the assistant curators on some business for her father. She promised she'd be quick.

Karigan waited for her in the corridor outside the curatorial office, not exactly pacing, but strolling its length with her hands clasped behind her back. Portraits lined the walls—portraits of old school masters, she assumed. Maybe patrons or administrators. In any case, persons not important enough to be exhibited in the major halls.

All of them looked out from canvases with stern and stuffy visages, all dressed in the finest fashions according to time period, including powdered wigs for more than a few of the men. Ordinarily Karigan would pay the portraits scant attention, but at the moment there was nothing else to do as she waited, so she took a closer look.

Some of the portraits were of a primitive style, as though very old. Proportions were off—sometimes a head was too big or arms too skinny. The paintings lacked depth, the shading poorly executed and the pigmentation of the colors weak, yet there was an inexplicable charm about them. Many of these older oils were crackling, attesting to their great age.

Others were more masterfully painted with rich detail and depth. The persons depicted looked ready to step out of their gilded frames. Karigan paused to gaze at a matron whose clothing and accoutrements were detailed with high realism. The intricacy of her lace collar fascinated Karigan, as did a gold pendant that looked real enough to touch. She leaned closer to see how the artist achieved the effect.

Liiibraaary . . . , a voice wheezed behind her.

She jumped. "What?" She looked all around, but no one else shared the corridor with her. Except for the portraits.

"Must have imagined it," she muttered.

She turned back to the portrait she'd been studying. The woman's pendant was the shape of a lion's head with ruby eyes. Delicate brush strokes created dimension and the metallic gleam of the gold.

Liiibraaary . . .

Karigan whirled. "Who said that?"

A clerk froze in an office doorway, eyes wide. "R–Rider?"

"Did you say something?" Karigan demanded.

"N–no, Rider." The clerk smoothed her tunic. "I was just on my way to do an errand for Master Clark."

Karigan scratched her head, and an awkward silence fell on the corridor. "I—" she began.

A screeching, scraping sound interrupted her. A painting on the opposite wall slid on its mounting till it hung askew.

The clerk sighed and strode over to the painting. "I'm always having to fix this one," she said. "The frame is heavy and off balance, I think. Fitting, I suppose."

Karigan joined the clerk to help her straighten it. Like all the others, the painting was displayed in a massive, ornate frame, in this case a rich mahogany carved with a leafy pattern interspersed with berries. A bunchberry flower was carved into each corner. The portrait was of a distinguished gent with long gray side whiskers and a walrus mustache. He was dressed in white robes.

"Why should it be fitting that this portrait be off balance?" Karigan asked, as she helped shift it into position. It *was* heavy.

"This fellow," the clerk replied, stepping back to make sure the painting was level, "was known for being a bit peculiar. Maybe it's because he was so brilliant. Some of our masters can be a wee bit eccentric, you know. But this fellow?" The clerk shook her head, then whispered as if afraid someone would overhear her, "He collected objects of the arcane sort, or so it's said. He traveled far and wide to find objects of a magical nature. It is even said he tried to learn how to *use* magic."

Aloud she added, "The Guardian of that time, and the trustees, did not like his activities and pretty much drummed him out of Selium."

Shivers trailed down Karigan's spine. "What . . . what was his name?"

"Erasmus Norwood Berry. *Professor* Erasmus Norwood Berry. He was a master of many disciplines, which is why he wore white, rather than the color of a single discipline, like the maroon of the language arts."

Karigan knew, had known even before the clerk supplied his name, who he was. She had once met his two daughters, now elderly, living at Seven Chimneys, a fine manor house located in the northern wilds of the Green Cloak.

"When was he—?" Karigan started to ask, but the clerk was already halfway down the corridor, off to carry out her task.

Karigan turned back to the professor. Under all those whiskers, not to mention the impressively bushy eyebrows, it was difficult to see the resemblance between him and his daughters, except for his blueberry blue eyes. Those eyes pierced right into her.

"I can't believe it," Karigan said. Sometimes she wondered if meeting the Berry sisters those two years ago had been real, or the mist of some dream, yet here was the portrait of their father as clear as day on the wall of this Selium corridor: Professor Berry, the master of many disciplines.

The sisters had told her of his predilection for collecting arcane objects—Karigan had handled some of them in his library, including a telescope that looked into both the past and future. She had gazed into it and, sure enough, saw many disturbing images. Miss Bayberry's words now trickled back to her like a whisper of memory: *Remember, child, your future is not made of stone.*

The sisters also told Karigan how their father possessed no natural talent for magic but had attempted to learn how to use it anyway. One experiment had ended badly when he'd accidentally turned all the household servants invisible. He was unable to reverse the spell.

Liiibraaary . . . , the voice whispered near her ear. She peered around the corridor but saw no one. Were Selium's ghosts now wanting to speak to her? Library ghosts? Made sense since this was the library building. She gazed hard at the portrait of Professor Berry, and he gazed back at her as only a picture could, unmoving and two-dimensional.

"I liked your house," Karigan said, not sure why she did, but feeling compelled to do so. "And your daughters were wonderful. They helped me." She remembered how homey and magical Seven Chimneys was, and how odd but sweet Miss Bay and Miss Bunch had been.

Her words elicited only silence in the corridor, silence almost as complete as that in the archives below. Nothing so much as moved.

She stepped back from the portrait and planted her hands on her hips. "Well, good. It was my imagination after all."

"I'm ready to go," Estral said, startling Karigan as she emerged from the curatorial office.

Karigan cleared her throat. "Yes. Good."

"Who were you talking to?"

"Er, myself."

"I always get the crawlies walking down this hall," Estral said. "All those old teachers glaring at me as if I don't measure up." She chuckled.

They started down the corridor, and from behind her, Karigan heard the now familiar screech of a frame scraping the wall. She did not look back, but redoubled her pace so that Estral had to hurry to keep up.

Like Estral, the corridor was giving Karigan a serious case of the crawlies, and to her mind, she had already dealt with enough supernatural occurrences elsewhere that she didn't need to add Selium's population of ghosts to her list.

The next morning Lord Fiori hosted a farewell breakfast in honor of Karigan and Fergal. The great hall of the Golden Guardian's residence brimmed with guests, several masters who had once given up on Karigan as a student during her early years at Selium among them. Now they treated her as a peer, asking her about her life as a Rider, and Karigan was startled to realize that the last vestige of master and student was gone from her life. She was now an adult among other adults.

Master Rendle attended, accompanied by Master Deleon, Karigan's old riding instructor. Estral sat beside her father, and Karigan was glad she'd had time to spend with her friend yesterday. With all the chatter, clinking of tableware, and music, it was nearly impossible to carry on a conversation. And yes, there was music, much music, performed by minstrel students playing their best to impress their listening masters, and especially Lord Fiori. It was the liveliest breakfast Karigan ever attended.

Fergal sat quietly beside Mel, who chattered on to all those around her, whether they could hear her or not.

When the festivities came to a close and most guests filed out to teach classes or attend them, Lord Fiori handed Karigan his message for the king. It was sealed with gold wax imprinted with a harp.

"My message to the king as promised," he said. "If we find the book, I shall send it to him directly."

"Thank you, sir."

Lord Fiori gave her a dazzling smile. "May your journey bring success, and no doubt we shall be seeing you in song."

"What? *What?*" But he had already moved off to speak with one of the remaining masters.

Rendle came forward then with two messages of his own. "This first is to Captain Mapstone on behalf of all of Melry's instructors."

Mel overheard and her eyes widened. For once she was speechless.

"And this other," Rendle continued, "is for Arms Master Drent." He did not explain further, but he said, "May the gods bless your journey. I'll miss your help with my classes, and I enjoyed having Fergal here, too. Keep working with him—he's learned much during his short stay."

Fergal stammered his thanks, and Rendle squeezed his shoulder.

Before Karigan could stuff the new messages into her satchel, Mel gave her a letter to her mother as well.

"You couldn't let me see what Rendle's sending her, could you?" she whispered.

Karigan *tsked.* "You of all people should know better. A Green Rider would never open a message intended for someone else."

"I know, I know," Mel grumbled. "Not allowed to break the seal and all that."

Karigan laughed and hugged her. No doubt Mel would pester Master Rendle for details about the messages for days, if not weeks.

On the front steps of the Golden Guardian's house, Karigan bade everyone farewell, and gave Estral a final hug.

"Never fear," Estral whispered, "your secret will remain safe with me."

"Thank you."

Karigan and Fergal mounted their horses and set off, leaving the Golden Guardian's house and the campus behind. As they rode through the streets of Selium, Karigan speculated that perhaps the most pleasant part of their journey was now over.

TYING KNOTS

Grandmother sat beside the fire tying knots, the insistent winds numbing her fingers and the cold sun providing absolutely no warmth at all, but she could not pause, not even to warm her hands. Hawk Hill was no place for her or her people to be with the winter coming, and soon they'd have to disperse into the countryside. Some would seek shelter with members of other sects of Second Empire, and the rest would move into one town or another to start their lives over. Captain Immerez and his men may have survived winters up here, but families with little children were another thing.

Grandmother's pouch had been done for a while now and it lay in the basket at her feet. She struggled with this new piece, and tried to block out the sound of hungry wails from Amala's baby in a nearby tent so she could concentrate on her knots. He was a strong, healthy little boy and his parents were justifiably pleased. He had Amala's eyes and the roundness of his father's face.

Concentrate, old woman, she chided herself.

This was delicate work. She chose the brown yarn for it, because it was the color of the earth, and the spell would be used underground. The words she spoke as she knotted were ancient, dark, almost freezing upon her lips. She had not dared attempt the spell at night, when that which was already dark deepened in the shadows. The time was now, in daylight.

The yarn fought her, tried to slip the knots and her mastery. She used all the authority she could muster, drawing on the voices of her ancestral mothers to tame the yarn.

She tightened a knot for *awakening*.

The end of the yarn tried to wriggle free from her fingers.

A knot to *call*.

A loop slipped around her index finger and tightened in an attempt to cut off circulation.

And a knot to *rise*.

A force flung her hands apart so she could not finish the complex sequence, for her spell was one that perverted the natural order of the world, but she bore her whole will into it, and as she tied off the last knot, wind blasted the summit, bending trees and ripping needles and leaves off limbs, and sending sparks and ashes from Grandmother's fire into her face. Tents braced against the wind and her people hid their faces from it. An angry wind, it was, and she fought to control the knotted yarn in her hands that came alive, distorting, growing, and shrinking as she murmured still more words of power.

As she spoke, the power sipped the life out of dormant plants around the summit. A hare, its fur mottled in the midst of its change from summer brown to winter white, dropped dead in its tracks. The heart of a stag browsing somewhere below the summit stopped. These little lives fed the knots.

The power she worked crept about the summit, and she fought to keep it out of the encampment. It took the life of a fox in its den. Ravens flushed from a pine as they sensed the power's encroachment, but the last was not fast enough. Needles of the tall, strong pine they had perched in yellowed and dropped, swirling in the wind.

The power oozed closer to the encampment, voracious in its need. She fought to ward it off, to redirect it. A clutch of chittering squirrels silenced and plummeted from a tree to the ground. A grouse fell limp, never to thrum for a mate in the spring again. Raccoons, a stand of aspen, sheep laurel . . .

Grandmother built shields to protect her people, but it was like trying to grasp a wave with her hands. The power could not be tamed and it leaked through her commands. It slithered along the summit, seeking only one more life, and it knew which it wanted.

"No!" Grandmother whispered, and she tried to avert the power once more, to make it at least take an adult, one of Immerez's men, or their Greenie prisoner, but the power sought something more innocent, new.

The power washed past Grandmother's shields and the incessant crying of Amala's baby stilled.

There was only silence but for the wind that roared in Grandmother's ears. "No!" she screamed.

The knotted thing wriggled and burned in her hands. The power had fed, and was now satiated. The baby's cries were replaced by Amala's wails.

Grandmother squeezed her eyes shut. When she opened them, she found Lala beside her. The girl touched her sleeve, gazing at her with that inscrutable gaze of hers.

Hovering over Grandmother's blistered hands was a black sphere that gleamed like glass. It gently descended till it rested on her palm. It was smooth and cold. She shuddered.

"Child," she said to Lala, her voice a croak, "please bring Captain Immerez and Thursgad to me."

The girl nodded and trotted off.

There was one more thing Grandmother needed to do to complete the binding of the sphere. She rolled it off her palm into the bowl that preserved Jeremiah's blood. The sphere bobbed on the surface for a moment, then sank to the bottom with a solid clink. The blood began to steam and boil, then quickly evaporated until there was none left. The black sphere remained on the bottom of the bowl, an unnatural gleam upon it.

She hesitated to touch the sphere, but had no choice. It felt heavier than before, heavier with the accumulated weight of souls. Little souls, innocent souls, and that which was once verdant with life. She spoke one last word of power and breathed on the sphere, turning it silver. Suddenly it started to draw the breath from her, sucking it out of her lungs. She looked away and gasped for air, feeling faint. Hastily she tucked the sphere into a leather purse and drew the strings closed.

Chills surged through her and she pulled her cloak tighter about her shoulders. The gray of stone, the weak sun and biting wind, not to mention the exhaustion of working the art, left her feeling forlorn and empty. It did not help that Amala's unquenchable grief and weeping buffeted her in stormy waves. Some of the encampment's women clustered at the entrance to Amala's tent, murmuring among themselves. Tears gathered in Grandmother's eyes, and she kept telling herself the sacrifice had been necessary.

Presently Lala returned with Captain Immerez and Thursgad. Now that their parchment had been translated, it was time to take action. As Grandmother hoped, it had contained the instructions for the handling and reading of the book of Theanduris Silverwood. When she first informed the captain a week ago that she wished to utilize Thursgad in her plan, he was incredulous and asked, "Why *Thursgad?*" He did not think much of his soldier, despite the fact the young man had remained loyal to him and had even joined him in exile.

The only response Grandmother could conjure at the time was, "He's a good boy." And he was. Of all of Captain Immerez's soldiers, which was really a band of criminals and thugs, intuition told her Thursgad was the most likely to complete the task she laid out before him. He had soldierly training, but more than that, he'd been raised in the country with simple values, including the loyalty he showed Captain Immerez, and a good dose of honesty. He would do as he was told.

"Are you prepared to leave?" she asked Thursgad.

"His horse and gear are being readied for him," Captain Immerez answered for him.

"Good, for he will have to leave immediately." She picked up the purse with the solid weight of the sphere in it and passed it to Thursgad. "Protect this well, for it is dangerous. Break it only when your business in the tombs is finished, no sooner. Do not even look at it or handle it until the appointed time. Do not let anyone else near it, not even Gare or Rol. Do you understand?"

Thursgad's face paled, and that told her more than his nod that he understood very well.

"Now," she said, "in order to find the book, I'm making a seeker to guide you. Once you have the book, you are clear on what to do?"

Thursgad nodded.

Captain Immerez jabbed him in the ribs with his elbow. "*Tell* her."

"Aye, sir. Aye, Grandmother. I understand. When I find the book, I am to take it to Sacor City."

"Correct," Grandmother said. "And?"

"And I find Gare and Rol at the Sign of the Red Arrow and show them this." He pulled a pendant of the black tree out from beneath his shirt. It bore in white paint the heart sigil for "friend of Second Empire" on it. "Then I tell them what is to be done. From that point they will take the lead."

"Very good, Thursgad," Grandmother said. "You will make me proud. I know you will." She affirmed her words with a smile. He smiled back, albeit tentatively.

"I will now make the seeker," she said, "and you must not waver in your pursuit of it."

"I won't, Grandmother."

"I know, my boy." She took the knitted pouch from her yarn basket. The use of all four colors, and the knots and gaps and hanging strands looked as if it had been knitted by a madwoman, but each stitch, each knot, wove together the spell to conjure and direct the seeker. From her pocket she removed the finger bone of Theanduris Silverwood. The story of how one of her far distant ancestors acquired it was lost through the veil of time. In those days, the practice was to cremate the remains of mages, to enhance the flames with magic to such a heat that every last bone was burned to ashes, and then the ashes were scattered across vast areas. Bones held power, and Sacoridians did not want that power to get into the wrong hands.

Grandmother's ancestors had had the foresight to steal and hold onto this finger bone, somehow knowing that it would one day be required for a then unknown task. That task was now apparent, and Grandmother was humbled that it should happen in her time. In order to find the book of Theanduris Silverwood, she needed something of his essence, and the finger bone would serve perfectly.

It was the full finger, the joints held together with faded, knotted yarn, the bone smooth ivory. She slipped it into the pouch, used the word of power, and flung it into the fire. The yarn of the pouch wiggled like glowing worms and the bone itself tried to probe its way out of the pouch, out of the fire, but it was trapped. The pouch melted into the bone until it all became one molten lump among the coals.

Grandmother was tired. Making the sphere had drained her, but she gathered what energy remained and blew on the coals. The flames leaped, and from them rose another sphere, a tiny orb of red-gold flame that wafted in the air.

"Lead Thursgad to the book of Theanduris Silverwood," she commanded it.

The seeker floated through the air and slowly circled around Thursgad's head. He licked his lips and a bead of sweat rolled down his temple.

"It will lead you along the most direct route," Grandmother said.

Captain Immerez beckoned forth one of his soldiers, who waited with Thursgad's horse and gear. Without a word, Thursgad mounted, his gaze cocked to the seeker.

"Go with my blessing," she told him.

"Aye, Grandmother," he said, and the seeker flared and sped to the east.

"What are you waiting for, idiot?" the captain yelled at Thursgad.

Thursgad spurred his horse after the seeker.

Captain Immerez muttered inaudibly as he watched Thursgad vanish from sight, then said, "I impressed upon him that he was not to fail. He isn't the sharpest nail of the bunch, you know."

Grandmother sighed. "I do know, but he will not fail me."

The captain seemed about to walk away, but hesitated. He rubbed the curve of his hook against his chin the way he always did when troubled or in deep thought. "Grandmother, that other thing you made . . . What was it?"

"Just something to keep the king and his men busy. Yes, a little bit of yarn to shake the castle's foundation." But it was much more than that. So much more.

When it was clear nothing else was forthcoming, the captain left her, striding toward his side of the encampment.

Grandmother inspected her red and blistered hands, and before she knew it, Lala was at her side with a pot of healing salve without even being asked.

"Such a good girl," Grandmother said. "I'm tired to the bone, but as soon as we take care of my old hands, we should help lay out Amala's baby."

Lala rubbed the salve into Grandmother's hands, then helped her rise to get her aching bones moving. Grandmother hobbled toward Amala's tent from which so much grief emanated.

"Her child died for the empire," Grandmother murmured. "I will make her see that and she will be proud."

MERDIGEN'S TALE

The storm hadn't done any of them good, Dale reflected, except possibly Alton. It seemed to ease some turmoil within him; that is until he realized he was beset by yet more delays, namely having to deal with the devastation in both encampments. As the man of rank, it was his obligation to oversee recovery efforts.

The wind had peeled roofs off new cabins in the main encampment and trees had flattened tents. Every single person worked to secure shelter, rescue supplies, and tend the injured—even Dale, though Leese made her rest frequently.

Being struck by Alton and falling into the mud had not helped Dale's injury, but it wasn't so much the physical pain or telltale bruise on her cheek that hurt most. It was more the wound to her spirit. Rationally she knew he hadn't meant to hurt her, that he'd been caught up in some inner battle the way he'd shaken his fist at the storm and yelled who-knew-what at the gods. He'd looked a madman in the flashes of lightning as the wind and rain lashed him.

She remembered how the moon priests used to talk about the demons that occupied the hells and how at times they escaped their imprisonment and infested the souls of people and changed their behavior. At their worst, the demons could provoke people to commit vile acts like murder. She didn't think Alton struggled with actual demons, but it was a good metaphor for what he seemed to be battling.

In the days following the storm she'd heard the whispers circulating among the soldiers, laborers, and servants of the two camps, who thought him cracking just like his cousin had. Alton must have overheard the talk, too, for he'd worked dawn to dark to restore order, reshingling roofs, clearing broken boughs, mending tents. She believed only the thinnest of veneers, however, held his frustration and anger at bay.

Yes, rationally she knew he wasn't himself when he'd hit her, but no matter how often he apologized, hurt lingered inside. He had not been able to stop himself from hitting *her,* his friend and fellow Rider.

Presently the sun beat down on her shoulders as she stood before the tower wall. She could not reconcile the day's serenity with the howling tempest of that night, but the debris still strewn about the encampment was sufficient evidence of what had happened.

At breakfast, Alton declared enough work had been accomplished that he could once again focus on the wall and Tower of the Heavens, and now she sensed his presence behind her like a physical force urging her to pass through stone.

She sucked in a breath, touched her brooch, and without looking back or speaking to him, she sank into Tower of Heavens. The passage was not as fluid as she remembered, but jarred her with sharp edges and the texture of stone scraping her flesh. The voices were there, scratching at her mind, and restless. When she fell out of the wall into the tower chamber, she exhaled in relief, a little disoriented.

"Back so soon?" The sarcasm in Merdigen's voice was unmistakable. "At least a hundred years or so haven't passed this time."

She found him sitting at the table and combing out his beard. A couple long white whiskers drifted to the floor and disappeared.

"Um," she said trying to organize her thoughts, "there was a storm."

Merdigen grunted.

Dale joined him at the table, brushing off what must be several hundred years' accumulation of dust from a chair before sitting on it. Merdigen sneezed at the cloud she raised. "Do you . . . do you really need to sneeze?" she asked.

Merdigen paused his beard combing. "Usually the polite response to a sneeze is an offering of blessing. You raised dust, therefore I sneezed. You've returned for a reason?"

"We had more questions."

"I see. Then ask them. I haven't all day."

Dale wanted to know what on Earth could possibly compete for his time, but she held her tongue. "Alton—the Deyer—and I felt there was much you might tell us."

"As I've said before, I have no idea of how he might pass into the tower, and the guardians want nothing to do with him."

"We believe there are other things you might be able to tell us," Dale said, "beginning with very basic information. Over the centuries, a lot of history about the wall has been lost. The more we can find out about it, the better we might understand how to fix it, and we believe there is much we can learn from you."

Merdigen eyed her with a skeptical gaze. "Tell me what you do know, then we shall see."

"We know that the wall was built over generations, toward the end of the Long War, to contain Blackveil Forest, to prevent it from spreading out into the world, and that Mornhavon the Black, his spirit or whatever, was also contained behind the wall. We're aware there are . . . presences in the wall—guardians—that keep it bound together with song." Dale frowned realizing how odd it sounded when spoken aloud. She tried to remember if there was more she and Alton had discussed. "Oh, and then there's you. You're a sort of tower guardian who can speak with the presences in the wall. That's all we know."

"That's it?"

Dale nodded.

"Seems it's true you've lost a good deal of knowledge." Merdigen set his comb on the table and it evaporated into nothingness. "One of the greatest works of humankind is the wall, yet its creation is all but a mystery. And still, I shouldn't be surprised."

"Why is that?"

"Tell me, Dale Littlepage, what you know of the days following the end of the Long War."

Dale thought hard. "There was sickness, the Scourge, which passed among the people. Many who survived the war died of disease, and it was a long time before the country could rebuild to become what it is now. Otherwise there was peace."

"The Scourge a sickness? I suppose it could be called that." Merdigen shook his head. "And peace? It depends on how you define peace. The end of fighting Mornhavon? Yes. Tranquility among the people? Hardly. Though I was not present in the world for all that occurred, I will tell you what you are missing, Dale Littlepage, and you may conclude for yourself whether or not it is useful."

Dale nodded, intrigued now that the peevish Merdigen had quieted, become so serious.

"The Long War encompassed many long years indeed, but my order, which lived aloof from our fellow Sacoridians high up in the Wingsong Mountains, refused to participate in it. We did not believe in using our powers to kill. Even as Mornhavon's forces committed unspeakable crimes against our people, we remained solid in our determination not to participate." His expression became downcast. "Whether we were wrong or right not to defend our homeland, we didn't believe we had been gifted with powers to be used in violence. They were too great a weapon.

"Unfortunately, Mornhavon's mages did not share our reverence for life as they lay waste to one village after another." Merdigen looked down at his knees, his expression one of sorrow. "On our side, there were other great mages who felt that using their powers against the enemy was not murder, but the preservation of Sacoridian life. Even a few among my order abandoned the mountains to join the fight, though a core group of us held out.

"There came a time when, after many years of fighting had elapsed, the people proclaimed that one of their valiant leaders must be high king of the land. His name was Jonaeus, and he sent to us a messenger."

"A Green Rider?" Dale asked.

"What? No, of course not. The Green Riders were too busy on the field of battle. He sent an eagle."

"An *eagle?*"

"A great gray eagle, a denizen of the mountains. They had befriended us over the years, but they also helped in the efforts to repel Mornhavon."

Then Dale remembered the tale of how a gray eagle had once helped Karigan defeat a creature from Blackveil. It was, until now, the only instance she heard of the eagles helping anyone, but perhaps in the far distant past they'd not been so aloof.

"The eagle came to us from the king," Merdigen continued, "who said that if we did not join in the war effort, we would be cast into deeper exile than we had ever known, sent away where Mornhavon could never find us and use us as weapons of his own." He sighed deeply. "We refused to fight, of course, but promised to help with reconstruction after the war."

Dale shifted in her uncomfortable chair. "So what happened?"

"We were dispersed and sent into exile, carried off by the great eagles. Where each of us went, no one knew. I was deposited on some nameless rock of an island in the Northern Sea Archipelago, far from civilization. The king isolated us so that if Mornhavon's forces found one of us, he would not find all. As it turns out, we were hidden well enough that we were never discovered. My only visitors were the eagles who brought news and meager supplies. Not even the occasional ship on the horizon dared approach the island, for the currents and reefs about it were deadly.

"Many, many years passed while I lived alone on the accursed island. Island of Sorrows I called it, for my loneliness and hardscrabble life." Merdigen thrust his hands out, palms up, and above them formed a picture in the air of a rocky island, its shore lashed by greenish blue waves with terns skimming their crests and gulls wheeling above. A figure with a snarled beard and wearing tattered robes picked his way among the rocks, turning over the smaller ones, and peering into tide pools. "I tried to survive day-to-day through the storms of all seasons, gleaning what sustenance I could from land and sea to supplement the scanty and all too infrequent supplies sent by the king."

The figure in the vision suddenly squatted down and seized something from a pool. He lifted it up to the light. It was a crab snapping its claws at the air. Then the vision dripped away like a painting splashed with water. Merdigen shook his head.

"It was some years after Mornhavon was defeated that the eagles carried us to the king's keep on the hill in what is now Sacor City. In those days it was not much of a city. The streets were little more than muddy cow paths and the people lived in dilapidated huts with vermin underfoot. The population looked starved and beaten, and I realized their lives had been more wretched than mine on my island. There were few elders among them and I remember thinking there were only children left, children who appeared older than their years with their wizened gaunt faces; children bearing their own pale weak babes. Children missing limbs. Children who were the veterans of many battles."

Merdigen fell into silence, seemingly lost in memory. No sounds of the outside world intruded on the tower, and for all Dale knew, riveted as she was by his story, the outside world no longer existed.

"I will never forget how they stared at me," Merdigen said, "me with my wrinkles and white hair. Me who evaded battle. They said nothing, just stared at me with their haunted eyes."

Dale tried to imagine Sacor City as Merdigen described it but found she could not. All she could see were the well-made streets brimming with shoppers and travelers and the good neighborhoods with flowers growing in the window boxes of well-kept houses and shops. How fortunate she was to live in the time she did.

"We had been summoned to the king," Merdigen continued, "but before we heard him speak, my companions of the order and I could not help but rejoice to be together again. A family we had been, then separated for so many years.

"The king looked weary beyond all reason, and little did we know at the time how many concerns lay upon his shoulders. We, perhaps, did not care for we were back together again, and jubilant.

" 'You offered to help in reconstruction after the war,' the king said. 'That is true,' I replied. 'We will help in any way we can.' 'Do not be so eager to offer,' said he, 'until you have heard me out.' He told us of the great wall being constructed along the border of Blackveil Forest and its purpose. Major portions had already been completed."

Merdigen flung his arms wide as if to illustrate the expanse of the wall. "The entire thing was an engineering marvel, and Clan Deyer was at the height of its powers. The king then told us it was not only the expertise of the Deyers who made the wall what it is, but the sacrifices of thousands. Thousands who possessed magical abilities."

"Sacrifices?"

"Mages who shed their corporeal forms to join with the wall, to bind it together with their collective powers. Their spirits and their powers merged with the wall, and exist within it to keep it strong. They are not precisely dead, nor are they precisely alive. They exist within the wall and sing with one voice. We were told their sacrifice had been voluntary."

The air in the tower seemed to constrict, then ease like a mournful sigh.

Dale drew her shortcoat closer about her. How could so many be willing to . . . to become part of the wall? She could think of no greater torture but to exist within stone for a thousand years. What must it be like? She did not want to know.

"The king then told us of the towers that had been built," Merdigen said. "Towers to house wallkeepers who could maintain perpetual watch on the wall as well as ensure that Blackveil in no way encroached past the barrier. Ten towers that needed guardians who could communicate with the wall as well as the wallkeepers. 'We've few mages left,' the king said, 'and none with your quality of power.'

"At the time, this did not seem too great a request especially in comparison with the sacrifices made by others. We would be among people again, and able to communicate with one another, and of course practice the art, perfect our technique. We'd also be helping our country—not by spilling blood, but by adding to its protection so the great evil would not cross the border ever again. But then the king brought in one of his counselors, a great mage by the name of Theanduris Silverwood."

Silverwood, Silverwood, Silverwood . . . The name undulated against Dale's mind in a faint, but angry, echo.

Merdigen gazed about the chamber as if looking for ghosts. "You hear that? The guardians know the name. Indeed, they know it all too well."

Dale shuddered, but Merdigen plunged right back into his story. "Noble and silent was Theanduris Silverwood as he glided to the king's side. He bristled with power, his robes flowing behind him. Black uniformed guards surrounded him."

"Weapons?" Dale asked.

"They had many weapons," Merdigen replied, looking annoyed by the interruption.

"No, I mean were the guards Weapons, er, what we call Weapons? They guard the king. Mostly."

"Oh, I see. Yes, I've heard them referred to as such, though back then we knew them as Black Shields, an order of warriors created after the war and new to us. We did not know at the time if they were guarding Theanduris or if they were protecting others from Theanduris. Later we discovered it was a little of both.

"Tucked beneath his arm was a leather-bound book, quite ordinary really, except that we mages, who valued knowledge above all else, and who had seen neither page nor parchment, book nor scroll for so long, stared in wonder at it. Theanduris ignored our interest and would not share its contents with us. I came to understand later that this book was the journal in which he documented the building of the wall, perhaps including notes about the spells cast for the binding. This is the book I told the Garth fellow about."

"Ah," Dale said. "But you never saw the actual contents?"

"Only blank pages, I'm afraid, and those on a visit during an otherwise benign conversation. Theanduris indicated what information it held, but that's all I ever saw or heard of it."

And this was all, Dale thought, with apprehension, they were basing their hopes on, that the book might solve the mysteries of the wall. If it could even be found.

Before Merdigen continued with his tale, a mug of frothy ale appeared in his hand. First he sipped cautiously from it, then he took great gulps. "Aaah, that's good. Throat is getting dry with all this talking." He took a few more swigs before setting aside the mug and wiping his mouth with the back of his hand.

"Where was I?" he muttered.

"Theanduris and his book."

"Yes, yes. Well, Theanduris obviously did not think much of us, young whelp that he was, only a hundred years old or so."

"Only?"

"Working the art can sometimes extend the years," Merdigen replied. "When my companions and I were placed in exile, we were well past a hundred years old. This is why we are known for our wisdom: all those years of learning, research, and knowledge."

"Like Eletians," Dale said.

"No, no." Merdigen chuckled. "The lifetimes of Eletians are without end. The same cannot be said about great mages." As if this was nothing out of the ordinary, he went on with his tale. "And so we considered Theanduris a young whelp. His age, as well as his haughty demeanor, put us off." Merdigen flung his hand out and from a ball of light grew the figure of a man with a beard of steel gray and wearing long white robes. He loomed over them, his expression arrogant as he gazed down at them.

"No doubt he regarded us as without honor for having chosen exile over participation in the war, though that exile had been no easy thing to endure. In truth, many a time I had considered abandoning my principles and sending a message to the king to tell him I would join the fray—just to be among human beings again—but I could not betray my beliefs.

"And so Theanduris put before us a choice: to become keepers of the towers or to return to our order's lodge in the mountains. We should know, he added, that we'd be left to ourselves if we returned to the mountains, and should not expect the king's protection. Well, we never had a king's protection before, so the words meant nothing to us. Little did we understand the significance of his comment." Merdigen frowned and the menacing image of Theanduris disappeared with a *poof.* "If we decided to become guardians of the towers, it would be for all time."

"I can see what choice you made," Dale said.

Merdigen raised a snowy eyebrow and gazed hard at her. "Can you now? Would it surprise you if I told you we chose to return home before we made our final decision? I will not forget the knowing gleam in Theanduris' eyes when we told him of our plan to return to the mountains, and immediately I grew suspicious that there was something he was not telling us. But I let it pass, for the eagles arrived to once again carry us back to the Wingsong Mountains.

"When we arrived, we found our lodge burned to the ground. Odd and angry symbols had been scrawled on signposts and stuck around the borders of our land, along with wards against evil. The rotting carcasses of animals were hung amid the remains of our lodge. It was clear its burning had been no accident. Some among us burst into tears, remembering the vast library it once housed—all that knowledge burned to ashes. And it had long been our home.

"A few of us walked to a nearby village for help. The folk there had always been friendly to us. We purchased their goods, hired their people to do jobs around the lodge and work our land, taught their children to read, and had any number of beneficial interactions with them. Yet when we arrived, people ran into their houses and slammed their doors shut. We could not coax anyone to help us, and a man who had been a stablehand at the lodge as a boy, and who was now a man grown old, met us with a pitchfork and demanded we remove our dirty, evil selves from the village and never return. Bewildered, we walked back to the remains of our lodge where our brothers and sisters were knocking down the signposts. The carcasses were long gone, thank the heavens.

"There was nothing to do but make camp before nightfall. Nights in the mountains are chilly no matter the season. We discussed all that had come to pass, especially the attitude of the villagers. If a new lodge were to be built, we realized it would have to be done with our very own hands. We'd also have to start fresh, start collecting a new library and the equipment necessary in the practice of the art. Some of the knowledge in the library was irreplaceable, but we were determined to start again. We hoped the villagers would eventually come to accept us as they once had and develop the agreeable relationship we previously enjoyed. What we did not expect was murder in the night."

SACRIFICES

Dale leaned forward, eager for Merdigen to continue, but the mage slumped in his chair as if in pain.

"What happened?" she prompted.

"Some of the villagers came during the dark of night while we slept and started killing us." His voice was muffled. "They killed us, though we had never used our gifts of magic for ill, never for violence."

"Why?" Dale asked, horrified. "Why did they do it?"

He lifted his head and gazed at her. His face looked awful, gray and shadowed. "Tell me," he said, "why there is a spell of concealment over your Rider brooch."

"What?" Dale's fingers went to the gold brooch, touching its angles and contours, reassured by its familiar shape and texture. And she shrugged. "It's always been this way. I was told that it was a way of identifying a true Rider from those who were false." As she said it, it suddenly did not seem like an adequate explanation.

"Do the mundanes, er, the non-Riders around you, know of Rider magic?"

"No. It's not something we discuss. The king and his advisors know, of course, and I suspect the Weapons do as well."

Merdigen shuddered. "Yes," he murmured, "the Black Shields would. Now tell me why you do not openly discuss your abilities."

"Because," Dale said, "its . . . magic isn't accepted. People don't like it. It reminds them of the terrible things Mornhavon did during the Long War."

"Hmph. Once those badges of office were worn proudly and unhidden, but things changed. Imagine the atmosphere just after the war—the fear, the anger, the hatred of all things magical."

Dale had not lived through that time as Merdigen had, nor was her knowledge of the history great, but she began to understand. It didn't take much to imagine the fear and suspicion of people who had endured a hundred years of war led by one endowed with enormous powers, powers that were used as a weapon that took lives, leveled towns, and created monstrosities. If magic was held with suspicion today, back then it must have been despised.

The League may have defeated Mornhavon, but the Sacoridians had been a beaten people, reduced to the very lowest levels of humanity able to survive and carry on. She could only imagine how King Jonaeus had fought to retain his control over the ragged country. Opportunists must have swooped in like carrion birds to wrest power from him: warlords, mercenaries, his own subjects. In this environment, something had to take the blame for all the woes that troubled the land.

"Your brooches were known in those days for what they were: devices to augment your innate abilities. Those who were against all magic demanded the brooches be destroyed, along with many other artifacts of magic. Under great pressure from these powerful individuals, the king had no choice but to acquiesce."

"But—" Dale gripped her brooch all the harder.

Merdigen's lips curled into an ironic smile. "And thus it was believed the brooches were destroyed. The real brooches, however, received a spell of concealment and the Riders retained their abilities, but they've remained a well-kept secret, and for good reason."

Dale wondered what kind of danger her ancestral Riders had been in simply because they possessed minor magical abilities that emerged only when coupled with the brooches. The opponents to magic must have judged the Riders harmless once their brooches were amputated from them. And this after all the Riders had done against Mornhavon in the service of their country.

"Yes," Merdigen said, "they came for us, those who feared and hated us. You referred to the Scourge as a disease, a disease that started taking lives at the end of the war. True, there was plague that spread among the population and claimed lives, but there was another that selectively culled those with magical talents, or those suspected of having them. It was not that they sickened, but that they were persecuted; persecuted by those who had not slaked the hatred in their hearts during the war. They believed magic to be the root of evil, and its elimination the remedy to every ill. Things would improve once the evil magic was cleansed from the land—the cleansing, they believed, would end starvation and poverty and the country would arise from the devastation. The fanatics spoke with bold voices and the promise of better days easily bought by the elimination of magic. Many rushed to their cause, and across the land thousands were murdered."

This was a part of history Dale had never learned, not even during her Green Rider training. She had always heard of the Scourge in terms of illness and plague, not in terms of persecution. She had always thought the end of the Long War brought celebration and light, but now she saw just how devastated her ancestors had been. Peace was not something to celebrate, but something to survive.

Merdigen conjured himself another ale and looked weary. He drank deeply from his mug and said, "A very bleak time, and all the while the king struggled to hold the country together. Perhaps that was a greater battle than those he fought in the Long War. Though I might have railed against him and cursed his name during my exile on the Island of Sorrows, I began to see him for the leader he truly was. But that is jumping ahead in the tale."

"The attack," Dale said. "How did you escape the attack at your lodge?"

Merdigen looked into his mug, and could not meet her gaze. "For all my years, I never used my powers against another soul. Never. I suffered a long exile for my beliefs, but that night as the members of my order, who were my only family, were murdered in their sleep, I used my powers and killed. Killed to defend us. Killed every last marauder." A strained silence gripped Merdigen.

"What then?" Dale gently prodded, both horrified and fascinated.

"In the morning the eagles came to us. They had seen the light of my powers from their eyries, so vicious had my assault been. In the daylight we found the charred husks of the villagers, including the one whom we identified as our old stablehand. Among our own we lost thirty of our order to the slaughter, and two were very near death, including Daria, the one true healer among us. We tried to aid them, but could not."

A tear dripped down Merdigen's cheek into his beard.

"After we burned our dead, the eagles took us aloft before more villagers could organize a reprisal." Merdigen created a vision of the remains of the lodge amid a mountain meadow and smoke rising from pyres for Dale. She could almost smell the stench of scorched flesh. The scene dwindled from view, grew smaller and smaller, as if she watched from Merdigen's eyes as an eagle lifted him away, until the scar on the mountain blended into its surroundings and the Wingsong Mountains opened in a white-peaked panorama framed by clear blue sky. Merdigen waved his hand and abruptly the scene dissipated like smoke.

"They carried us to the eyrie of Venwing, lord of the eagles. His eyrie was a mere ledge among the clouds in the mountains, the air sharp and thin. We clustered together, those of us who survived—ten of us as it would happen—lost in grief and shivering with cold.

" 'Thus it has been across the lands,' Lord Venwing said, 'the killing does not end.' I crumpled to my knees, feeling the weight of the lives I had taken."

"You were defending your people!"

"So I was, and for that reason I was not executed immediately. But what right had I, or anyone else, to cause a life to end?"

"You were trying to preserve the lives of your people."

"And such was the rationale of those who went to war." Merdigen shook his head. "But I only proved the fearful stories of those villagers true. I was a user of magic, and used it to kill. I gave those who had not died that night reason to persecute us. The taking of a life, for some, is a heavy burden. For others? It is little more than the swatting of a fly."

Dale leaned back into her chair, thinking of the battles she had engaged in, of the lives she had taken. Yes, it was a burden, but one she could live with. There were gray areas in Merdigen's extremes.

He continued his tale. "Lord Venwing told us, 'Yes, across all the lands it has been happening, the attacks on those gifted with magic.' That was when we began to realize the extent of the persecution. If it was happening in our remote mountain location, one that was little touched by the war itself, then it must be so widespread that nowhere was truly safe. 'They seek to end all magic in the world,' Venwing said. 'But to end all magic is to end life.'

"You see," Merdigen explained, "what those who attempted to eradicate magic did not know is that magic is a natural force. It is in the air we breathe and the water we drink. By killing those with the ability to work magic, they were not killing the magic itself, just those who were attuned to it and could use it. From what I understand has happened on the outside world, magic has lain dormant, or so it would seem, with so few possessing the ability to work it. I fear the eradication of magic users proved much too successful"

Dale rubbed her upper lip. "When Mornhavon awoke, all manner of strange magic occurred on our side of the wall, and the special abilities of some Riders became unreliable."

"Interesting," Merdigen said. "He created a flux in the natural order, and it must have flowed through the breach."

"So what happened next?" Dale asked. "Did the eagles return you to the king?"

"Yes. And once there, Theanduris Silverwood could not

hide his gloating. He knew what would befall us, the ingrate. We were offered sanctuary only if we committed ourselves to the towers."

"Which you did."

"Yes. We'd little choice, for the world was no longer safe for us. It was only after we were stationed in our towers that we learned the truth about the wall guardians, that they'd been coerced into joining with the wall with threats of torture against them and those they loved. For the magic haters, this accomplished two things at once: the elimination of thousands of magic users and the strengthening of the D'Yer Wall against the influence of Blackveil."

Merdigen released a deep sigh. "Life in our towers was not bad. The wallkeepers kept us company and updated us on the news of the world. In the beginning we were visited by members of Clan Deyer, the occasional Green Rider, and . . . Black Shields. Over the years these visits waned, then ceased altogether. I slept and no one woke me for two hundred years, until your friend, the Deyer, stumbled into the tower." Merdigen fell silent, bemused, then softly added, "If no one has entered the other towers, I suppose my companions still slumber."

Now that Merdigen had concluded his tale, Dale decided to ask the question she had been dying to ask from the beginning. "Merdigen, what are you?"

"I am a magical projection of the great mage Merdigen."

"Yes, but what does it mean?"

"It means I am Merdigen, his personality and memory, though his corporeal form long ago ceased to exist."

"So you are illusion—"

"No. *This* is illusion." Merdigen flashed his hand out in a wave and a black bear suddenly appeared rearing over Dale, swiping its claws through the air, its growl resonating through the chamber. Dale was so surprised she almost tipped over backward in her chair.

"It has no personality, no soul, and it's certainly not self-aware," Merdigen explained. With another wave of his hand the bear vanished, much to Dale's relief. It might have been an illusion, but it sure seemed real. "Unlike the bear," he continued, "the spirit of Merdigen exists within the tower. I am a projection of it."

"A ghost?"

"No, no, no. Ghosts are shadows of the dead. I guess you could say I am a shadow of the living. I am not unlike the guardians of the wall with my spirit anchored in place, but unlike the guardians, I exist as an individual."

Dale still didn't completely understand it, but she supposed it didn't matter. Aside from the history lesson, interesting though it was, all she really learned was no, Merdigen had no additional information about the wall that could help Alton unravel its mysteries.

"Merdigen," she said, "can any of the wall guardians help us understand the wall?"

His comb had reappeared in his hand and he stroked it through his beard again. "No. They are no longer individuals. They are song. They bind the magic of the wall together. They've no memory, except the memory of stone, and of the song they must sing." He paused his combing and became reflective again. "Theirs was a much greater sacrifice than ours. Perhaps the lack of memory is a mercy for them."

It was not something Dale could conceive of, this sacrificing of one's spirit to the wall and existing only as song.

The interview over, she took leave of Merdigen to report back to Alton, who must surely be going mad by now to hear what she had learned. She was afraid he was going to be disappointed. She stepped into the wall, but somehow it felt even worse this time, less fluid around her, almost rigid. Crackling chimed in her ears, a primordial sound, if she knew it, of a time before people, a time before light brightened the Earth; before time itself was measured. It was a sound of liquid rock cooling and fracturing, and forming crystals; a sound heard, had there been anyone to hear it, when the Earth's bedrock formed.

The wall was solidifying.

Through the chiming she heard the voices, voices in

lament, despairing, and others chanting, *Hate, hate, hate* . . .

Blinded in the darkness and seized by panic, she thrust forward, hardened rock abrading her flesh, crushing the breath from her body, crushing her. Like one who is submerged and drowning, she could only scream within herself.

THE WALL SPEAKS

From Ullem Bay to the shores of dawn, we are—

Cracking.

Hear us!

Never forget his betrayal.

Help us!

Do not trust him.

Heal us!

Hate him.

Yes, hate . . . hate . . . hate . . .

The voices of the guardians are tinged with uncertainty and conflict with one another, and now the one on whom the Deyer depends moves through the wall as she has many times before. Can they permit this trespass to continue? If she is affiliated with the Deyer, is she not tainted by his evil? Yes, *some say.* No, *say others. They must sing with one voice, but they have splintered, lost harmony, their rhythm gone astray.*

Do not trust! Capture, crush, turn to stone. Hate!

We hear. We hate. We obey.

Merdigen seeps into the wall, filled with alarm, for Dale is caught between, and the guardians are behaving erratically, driven by the hateful commands of the Deyer's cousin, the Pendric. Merdigen must intervene. "Release her!" *he cries.*

We must stand sentry, capture, crush, turn to stone.

"She has done you no harm."

Do not listen.

A void of silence surrounds Merdigen, and this is almost more frightening than the disarray of the guardians' voices.

"She seeks only to help heal you!"

We sacrifice as we were sacrificed. We must stand sentry.

"She cannot be one of you," *Merdigen insists.* "You cannot make human flesh stone."

Her blood holds magic.

"It is meager, not worthy, not enough to heal you. Hear me! She seeks only to help you. You must trust her—let her go!"

Do not listen.

Once again silence envelops Merdigen as the guardians consider his words. He is overcome by their fear, their confusion. He wants to help them, but he hasn't the power. Everything they were, everything they should be, is unraveling and the Pendric has a strong voice that turns them against reason. Merdigen must find a way to convince them to release Dale or she will die.

MERDIGEN SETS OFF

Alton paced furiously before Tower of the Heavens. What was taking Dale so long? He could only hope that Merdigen was providing her with mountains of information that would lead to the repair of the wall.

He paused and took a deep breath, trying to remain calm. The day was fine, the fevers hadn't afflicted him as severely as the night of the storm, and if Dale was taking a long time to gather information, it was all for the good, right?

And then there was the guilt that he'd actually struck Dale to the ground that night. How could he have done such a thing? What had possessed him? The fever had crazed him, had stoked his anger at the wall and his inability to fix it.

Dale's forgiveness had made him feel all the more guilty. He did not deserve it. Somehow he would make all this up to her. Somehow . . .

"Lord D'Yer!" one of the guards shouted. He pointed at the tower wall. "Look!"

A distortion rippled in fluid waves along the wall's facade. He approached cautiously, not daring to avert his gaze, apprehension gnawing at his gut.

A hand punched through the wall. He jumped back in shock. It was not a hand of flesh and blood, but a hand of granite. Apprehension turned to dread that filled his belly with ice.

"Dale? *Dale?*"

A bulge protruded above the hand; a face pressed against

the inner surface of the wall, a face of familiar features. Dale's, molded in stone.

"Dale?" Alton's voice was scarcely a whisper.

The undulating ripples of the distortion calmed and receded, until they died out altogether and the surface of the wall smoothed to its normal state.

And solidified.

"No!" He grabbed at Dale's hand, but it was cold, grainy, hard. He pummeled the wall, tears streaming down his face. "No! You can't have her!"

Soldiers and laborers trotted over to see what the matter was and stopped in horror. "Gods!" one of them gasped. Several of them made the sign of the crescent moon.

Ours, ours, ours . . . came the voices into Alton's mind.

"Let her go!" Blood splattered the wall as Alton pounded, soaked into the pores of granite. "She's not yours! Let her go!"

All at once the wall around Dale warped and ruptured. It disgorged her and she spilled to the ground, a shell of granite that encased her crumbling from her body, a body of flesh and blood, not a statue. Alton dragged her clear of the wall and Leese pushed through the crowd with her apprentice and fell to her knees beside the lifeless Dale.

Alton watched as they examined her, blood running down his fingers, dripping off fingertips, and soaking into the ground. Was she alive? He couldn't see her breathing. Leese worked on her for a few moments more and suddenly Dale's body jerked and she coughed and gagged, fighting for air. When the fit passed and her breathing eased, Dale grabbed Leese's tunic and pulled her close to whisper to her.

When Dale released the mender, Alton demanded, "What? What did she say?"

Leese looked over her shoulder at him, her expression unreadable. "She said something about knowing what it's like to be a fossil."

Alton paused outside Dale's tent with his bandaged hand raised to knock. It was a measure of his anxiety that he forgot there wasn't really anything solid to knock on. A stiff, cold breeze ruffled his hair and bowed the tent walls inward. Fallen leaves rushed around his ankles. He cleared his throat to announce himself.

"I know you're out there," Dale said before he could speak. "Come in."

He parted the tent flaps and stepped inside. Through the gloom he could see Dale seated on her cot, rubbing oil into a boot that lay across her knees.

"Have a seat," she said.

He dragged a stool over next to her cot, watching her while she worked. Her one arm was still bound to her side from the old injury, but he could discern no new hurts from her alarming passage through the tower wall. He would not forget her hand of stone reaching out, reaching toward him. Even in his dreams he could not forget and just thinking of it made him shudder. According to Leese, Dale had come to little harm, but he needed to make sure of that for himself.

He also wanted to find out what she learned from Merdigen. That and . . . He hated himself for having to come to her after all she endured, for having to ask her to risk her life all over again and return through the tower wall. One guilt layered upon another. If only the wall would let *him* through.

Dale paused her oiling and looked up at him, her mouth a narrow line. "You may stop feeling guilty. I'm fine. Whatever happened in there rattled my bones and frankly scared me to all five hells, but I am alive."

Alton opened his mouth and shut it.

"I can see it in your face. Your guilt."

He nodded and stared at his feet.

"You want me to go back in, don't you." Dale's voice was flat.

"How . . . ? Have you become a mind reader?"

"Like I said, I can see it in your face. For a noble, you're utterly transparent. You might want to work on that."

"Uh . . ."

"Of course you want to hear about what Merdigen and I chatted about all that time first," Dale said, "but you also need me to find out what went wrong when I tried to come back, which means I have to go back and talk to Merdigen, because I sure as five hells don't know."

"Yes."

Dale did not respond, but she scrutinized him from head to foot, eyes narrowed. He squirmed in discomfort. "Your boots look terrible. What would Captain Mapstone say?"

"What? I—" He glanced down at his boots. They were caked with dry mud, scuffed, and dull. Clearly they were unacceptable, but there had been more urgent matters demanding his attention. Clean boots just hadn't seemed all that important in comparison.

"The water's still warm." Dale tapped her toe against a bucket on the floor beside her. "And I've a cake of saddle soap." She tossed it to him and it spurted out of his grasp, and when he reached after it, his stool tipped over sending him sprawling across the tent floor. He lay there feeling undignified, the amber soap at rest next to his face. Dale looked as though she was desperately trying to suppress laughter.

"Here," she said, reaching to give him a hand up.

Alton settled himself back onto his stool, and before he knew it, he was unwinding the bandages from his hands and pulling off his boots. He scrubbed at the grit accumulated in the creases of the leather, foamy lather dripping to the tent floor as he worked. The soap and water stung his abrasions, but the effort of cleaning worked the stiffness out of his hands and fingers. It was somehow peaceful, this task, a diversion from the worries that so often plagued his every waking thought. This was something he could accomplish, something in which he could achieve results. It was a simple act, this cleaning of boots, but satisfying to see them transformed.

Really, he thought, he should take better care of his gear, but life seemed too complicated to worry about its condition. When it came time to oil the boots, the leather drank it up as if parched. He frowned. If he had let it go any longer, he'd have cracks, and that was no good with winter coming on.

While he oiled and shined the leather, Dale recounted her conversation with Merdigen. It was disappointing. Merdigen had provided no new insights on how to fix the wall, and Dale had risked her life for nothing. And now he wanted her to do it again.

When he finished with his boots, he looked them over, well pleased with his efforts. They were black again, their shine restored. Even Captain Mapstone would have nothing to complain about. Except the boots now made the rest of him look a mess. Then he noticed Dale watching him.

"Yes," she said.

"Yes? Yes what?" Dale was, he decided, in a very perplexing mood.

"I'll go back into the tower to ask Merdigen what happened."

"I don't know. It's not safe." The guilt returned full measure. As desperate as he was to acquire information from Merdigen about the status of the wall, he would not forgive himself if something happened to his friend again.

"Since when," Dale asked, "has our job been safe?"

It was true Green Riders did not have long life expectancies. Even Alton had come close to death. All Riders were aware of the dangers and accepted them. Yet what right had he to ask her to risk herself again?

Dale hopped to her feet. "All right. I'm ready."

"Right now?"

She nodded, her expression set.

Alton followed her out of the tent. "Are you sure about this?"

"Yes, as I've told you already." She gave him a sidelong gaze as they walked between tents and toward the tower. "Do me a favor?"

"Anything. You know that." Alton couldn't read the look that appeared in her eyes, and suddenly he was suspicious. What had he just agreed to?

"Plover needs exercise," she said. "I've not been able to ride her since—since—" She indicated her bound arm.

"While I'm with Merdigen, could you exercise her? You could ride Hawk and lead her."

"I—" He came to an ungainly halt before the tower, surprised by the simple request. He had been expecting something more devious. She and Tegan were the terrors of Rider barracks, playing practical jokes at every chance. This was different, and he could only imagine how frustrated she was at being unable to care for her own horse. Keeping a messenger horse in top condition was of utmost importance. "Of course I will, but—"

Before he could finish the sentence, she stepped up to the tower wall and passed into it. He clenched and unclenched his hands, staring at the blank wall, reluctant to leave his post. What if something went wrong again? Couldn't the exercise wait? But he'd promised. Then with a shake of his head he realized that Dale did not want to worry about him worrying about her. She was keeping him busy.

He resigned himself to honoring her request. It was the least he could do. He assigned a pair of guards to keep watch on the spot and to find him immediately at the first sign of trouble. With that, he turned his back on the tower and headed toward the pickets, realizing how long it had been since he last exercised Night Hawk. Captain Mapstone would not be happy with him. Not at all.

When Dale passed into the tower without incident, she sank to the floor in relief so profound she nearly cried. She was not as brave as she had sounded when she told Alton she'd return. Her nightmares of black wings had been replaced by the sensation of her bones being crushed and pulverized and her soul forever imprisoned in stone. The only way for her to restore her courage was to face what she most feared, like climbing back into the saddle after a fall from her horse. It was the only way.

Fortunately this passage had been as easy as her very

first—no resistance, no solidifying of the wall around her. No crackling in her ears, not even any voices at all. Perfectly normal, as though nothing had ever gone wrong.

Inside the tower chamber, she fought to control her breathing and she trembled from all the fear that had been bound up in her. When finally she opened her eyes, she found Merdigen looking down at her.

"You came back," he said in a soft voice. "I did not think you would after—"

"I didn't think I would either. Do you know what happened? Why the wall trapped me?"

Merdigen fingered his beard. "The guardians have grown more unstable. I argued on your behalf to make them release you. Fortunately they weren't entirely unreasonable when I convinced them you represented no harm. I should think they'll give you safe passage . . . for the time being. I wouldn't trust them entirely."

Well, that's reassuring, Dale thought.

Merdigen stood in silence for a while, gazing at nothing. When he sprang back to life, he startled Dale. "I must arrange for the care of my cat!"

"What?"

"I am going on a journey. It could be perilous, it could be fruitless, but I think it's necessary and I can't put it off any longer."

"You're *what?*"

Merdigen strode across the chamber and between a pair of columns into the center of the tower. Dale rose to her feet and followed. She'd never get over the transition from stone chamber to open grasslands. Above, heavy clouds that reminded her of winter scudded across the sky.

Merdigen rubbed his hands together. "It is time the tower guardians all woke up. We will need a council. We need solutions! I shall first contact the towers eastward."

Dale watched in amazement as he withdrew a dove from his sleeve and whispered to it. He tossed it into the air, and with a fluttering of white wings, it circled them once, twice, and then darted through the east archway, flying madly till it became nothing but a speck in the sky and was at last beyond her sight. He repeated this five more times.

"One of them should be willing to watch the cat," Merdigen said.

"Cat?" was all Dale could say.

But now Merdigen was pulling other items out of the air. First a warm cloak he threw over his shoulders, then a pack that bulged with provisions . . . illusionary provisions? What could he possibly need? The last object he snaked out of his sleeve was impossibly long—a walking staff.

"The way to the west is broken," he said. "There are three towers that have been cut off from us by the breach. I cannot send a message the conventional way."

"Conventional . . . the doves?"

"I will seek bridges," he continued, "and hope I find the right ones. I should have dared this when I was first aware of the breach, when the Deyer first awakened me, but I hoped he could repair it. Now I only hope it's not too late and the towers have not been sundered from us." He adjusted the straps of his pack on his shoulders. "Check in now and then to see if I've returned, or if any of my colleagues have arrived. If a long time as you reckon it has elapsed, well, we can assume I've crossed a bad bridge."

"Bad . . . bridge?" Not that Dale expected an explanation.

"Don't despair," he said, "I shall be very prudent. No unnecessary risks. Farewell, Rider Littlepage." And he set off.

"You're *leaving?*"

He halted and turned back to her, his cloak billowing around him, and she thought she saw in him not the peevish illusion to whom she'd grown accustomed, but a vestige of the great mage of old with unthinkable powers at his disposal. "My dear child, results sometimes command immediate action, no matter the danger that may lay ahead. To not leave could condemn us to even greater peril."

Dale watched as he strode through the west archway. She kept watching as he trudged through hip-high grasses, becoming smaller and smaller until he vanished against the horizon.

A RIDE IN THE COUNTRY

"I'm sorry, my lady, but His Majesty's instructions were clear." The Weapon put his hand on the stall door to block her.

Estora drew herself up. "You must let me go. I command it."

She could see the discomfort in his face no matter how he tried to conceal it. "I'm sorry, my lady, but we're responsible for the safety of your person, and His Majesty has not deemed it safe to allow you off castle grounds."

Only years of training to retain a calm facade prevented Estora from screaming her frustration. She hated feeling so trapped, so . . . so kept. All she wanted was a ride in the country and a peek at the Eletian encampment. This morning she had dressed in her black riding habit and made for the stables, determined to take a ride no matter what obstacles arose. The ubiquitous Weapon Fastion had dogged her every step and now barred her way. Her hunter was so close, almost within reach.

"What danger is there if you're with me?"

"I'm sorry, my lady."

If she heard him say he was sorry one more time, she really would scream. And short of her being able to pick up the man and move him aside, she was not going to gain access to Falan no matter how determined she was. She flexed her riding crop in her hands. If only she were a Green Rider! Then she could ride away from this place and her keepers, but such was not her fate in life.

She turned on her heel and left the stable, the sound of

Fastion's boots close behind. She strode out onto castle grounds. There was only one person who could release her from this prison and she intended to see him *now.* She did not care what he was in the middle of.

She was so intent upon her goal, the skirts of her habit flaring out behind her, that she did not see Amberhill till she was almost upon him. He appeared to be strolling in a casual manner, hands clasped behind his back, gazing at the castle heights, or maybe at the leaves twirling down from trees. He was the epitome of an idle noble with no responsibilities to fill his day.

He grinned when he saw her and swept into a low bow. "My lady, you are in a hurry today."

Yes, she thought, *and you best not hinder me.* "I'm on my way to see the king."

"Oh," he said. "By appearances you look rather ready for a ride."

She sighed. "That is what I wish to discuss with him. This one—" and she pointed her crop at Fastion "—won't let me take a simple ride in the country."

Amberhill barely gave the Weapon any notice. "I see. It is most unfair, though I know Zachary has your best interests in mind."

"*His* best interests," Estora muttered.

Amberhill rubbed his chin. "Yes, I can see how the restriction chafes at you. Perhaps I can put in a good word on your behalf?"

His words calmed her. She had no idea if this young noble had any influence with his cousin, but she appreciated the offer of help and wasn't about to turn down an ally.

"Would you care to accompany me?" she asked.

He bowed again and offered her his arm. "It would be my honor."

He kept her laughing all the way across the castle grounds and into the castle itself and she almost forgot her troubles. A page informed her she would find Zachary in his new study in the west wing. By the time they reached his door, her mood had altered favorably, but now she must face Zachary.

"I wish to see the king," she told the Weapon at the door.

He bowed, "I'm sorry, my lady, but he's meeting with—"

"I am very tired of hearing 'I'm sorry, my lady,' " she said.

"But—"

Bolstering her resolve with a deep breath, she reached past the Weapon, knocked on the door, and admitted herself without waiting for permission to enter. Zachary and his counselors stared and met her with flabbergasted silence. Colin Dovekey was first to respond and rose from his chair with a bow, followed by Captain Mapstone and Castellan Sperren.

"My lady," Zachary said. "And Xandis?"

Amberhill swooped into a bow, a roguish smile on his face.

"I'm sorry, my lord," said the Weapon at the door. "I tried to—"

"It's all right, Willis. Carry on."

"Yes, sire."

Willis and Fastion withdrew into the corridor, closing the door behind them. Zachary sat on the edge of his desk, waiting expectantly for Estora to speak. She glanced around, trying to collect her thoughts, her resolve turning to embarrassment. The chamber was barren but for the necessary furniture. Zachary's possessions from his old study had not yet been unpacked.

"What is it, my lady?"

He asked politely enough and she could not read whether or not he was annoyed by her intrusion. Her gaze darted to his counselors, her determination flagging even more in front of this audience. She supposed she ought to get used to this trio, for they were his closest advisors, and if they were a part of his life, they were to be a part of hers as well.

She cleared her throat. "I wish to go for a ride into the country," she said. "I need off castle grounds or—or I shall go mad."

Zachary nodded slowly. "Yes, and as you understand from our previous conversation, we are as yet unsure of what threat, if any, our Eletian visitors pose. I do not wish to place you at risk."

"If I may intercede," Amberhill said, placing his hand over his heart, "the Eletians have been here a while and have not proven aggressive toward you or your people. They are carefully watched by your soldiers, and my lady is well guarded by your Weapons. It seems unfair to stifle the lady's desire to ride into the countryside that she will soon be ruling jointly with you. What will the people think if they perceive her to be hiding in the castle?"

A silent hurrah rose up within Estora, for Amberhill stated what was in her heart and she found herself grateful for his presence and persuasive voice. His was a logical argument, as opposed to the emotional one she was sure to have used. He made her plight sound not a trivial complaint, but a matter of importance to the welfare of their country.

Their audience followed the exchange with interest, especially Captain Mapstone who, with a smile on the edges her mouth, appeared amused by the situation Zachary now found himself in, and maybe not displeased that Estora chose to assert herself.

Zachary shifted against his desk. "Lady Estora is our future queen and her safety is not to be taken lightly."

"If it would ease your mind, assign her additional guards, and I will personally vouch for her safety and accompany her." Amberhill bowed again.

"I will think on it," Zachary said. He was not pleased, but he also sounded like he had run out of arguments. "I'll have an answer for you in the morning."

It was clearly a dismissal, and when Estora and Amberhill stepped into the corridor and the study door was shut after them, Amberhill said, "Be ready in the morning, my lady, for if I read my cousin right, we shall be cleared for a long day's ride in the countryside."

He sounded as eager as she felt.

Amberhill took his leave of Lady Estora as swiftly as courtesy permitted. He must head down into the city and warn

Morry of what was afoot. Then Morry must make contact with the plainshield. Plans and possibilities engulfed his thoughts as he strode through the castle corridors. This was the opening the Raven Mask had been waiting for.

In the morning, Amberhill walked to the stables attired in riding breeches, snug where it counted, his supple black boots unrolled to his thighs. He wore one of his better long-coats of rich blue velvet with matching gloves. Underneath was his canary waistcoat and a new linen shirt with a black silk stock. His hair was tightly drawn back with a black ribbon that blended into his hair. His hand rested casually on the hilt of his rapier.

He knew very well what effect the ensemble had on women. He knew how their gazes followed him, lingered on him, young and old, poor and rich. Some men would regard him as foppish, dismiss him as less than manly or incapable of using a sword. He preferred they underestimate him.

When he arrived at the stables that housed the horses of the nobility, including his own steed, he was not surprised to find numerous other courtiers milling in the stable yard, mostly ladies, including Lady Estora's sisters. Word of her ride into the country must have spread quickly through the noble wing. Once the word was out, it would have been impossible for her to leave castle grounds without an entourage, whether she desired one or not. Nobles rarely traveled alone, and for someone of Estora's rank to travel without an entourage would have been shocking.

In addition to all the courtiers, he picked out six Weapons and six cavalry officers who were Lady Estora's guards for the excursion.

Interesting.

Some were mounted and others sipped tea and brandy while awaiting grooms to bring out their horses. Lady Estora sat sidesaddle atop her mare, the skirts of her habit splayed across her horse's flank. Black was a harsh color on her, but he did not disapprove. The cut of Estora's habit and surcoat had a military style to it, like that of many of the other ladies, but hers was filled out with enough brocade and frills to make it eminently feminine. Her golden hair was tucked and pinned under a hat that was decorated with long trailing pheasant feathers.

While his stallion, Goss, was readied, Amberhill made the rounds, greeting the assembled, making matrons blush and Estora's sisters, both younger, giggle. The girls were pretty, but not of the same rare beauty as their elder sister. One still retained the roundness of prepubescence.

He counted fifteen additional nobles, accompanied by almost as many servants. Not a huge party, for which he was glad, but enough to permit confusion. Zachary, thank the gods, had not joined them.

Horses stamped and shook their manes and steam rose from their nostrils. It was a cold morning with a hard frost, but good riding weather. There wasn't a single cloud in the sky.

A groom led Goss out to Amberhill and the stallion's dark bay coat shone in the morning light. He mounted and soon the company rode off castle grounds, hooves clattering over the bridge at the gates, and onto the Winding Way. Three Weapons ranged ahead while the other three dropped behind to guard from the rear. The cavalry officers were more intent upon looking handsome in their uniforms and flirting with the ladies than performing guard duty. Lady Estora rode at the head of the nobles, conversing with Lady Miranda, and clearly enjoying herself. Last of all trailed the servants.

Amberhill stayed near Lady Estora, keeping watch on her. Townsfolk gathered to observe the company ride by, and to gaze upon the one who was to be their queen. She waved and smiled to them, and her greetings were returned with enthusiasm, and, it appeared, gratitude. Amberhill suspected she was going to make a popular queen.

When the party rode through the main city gates and emerged before the Eletian encampment, Lady Estora reined her horse to a halt. The colorful tents billowed in the breeze, their colors intense beneath the sun. As was usual, there was no sign of the Eletians astir in their camp, but if this disappointed Lady Estora, he could not tell. She just seemed glad to be free of the castle grounds, her features less taut, happier.

He edged Goss up beside her. "What do you make of it, my lady?" he asked.

"Eletian," she said. Then she laughed.

"Truly," and he couldn't help but smile. "Do you have a particular course in mind for today?"

She laughed again and it made him think of the joyful girl she must have been before the world began to press its problems on her. "I did not think beyond this point."

Those nearby who overheard began suggesting their favorite rides. Most were easy courses over rolling farmland, and well-traveled.

"I've another in mind," Amberhill said, "perhaps a little more challenging, a little wilder, through the woods west of here. It is a trail most often used by hunters and woodsmen, but clear enough for those mounted. I daresay there will be logs to jump and streams to ford."

Lady Estora looked uncertain, so he added, "There is a fine lake by which we may picnic. We are apt to see moose there, and waterfowl."

"Oh, I know that place," said Lord Henley. "It is as our Amberhill suggests, more challenging, but exhilarating. Most enjoyable."

"Let us try it then," she said. "I will not be put off by a little challenge, and today is all about different scenery."

Amberhill fought to conceal his relief. If she had ignored his suggestion and taken some other route, it would have complicated his plans. He gestured down the road. "This is the way, my lady." He reined Goss onto the Kingway and headed west.

Fields became apple groves, a sweet scent arising from fallen apples pulverized beneath hooves. Soon the apple groves turned to overgrown meadows with trees still clutching onto brightly hued leaves, and finally they entered the darker, more primal forest, all sounds subdued and the ground soft with pine needles and moss.

They had galloped and cantered over open land, jumped hedges and old stone fences, laughing and scattering birds and a fox from the fields before them. But now in the forest they quieted for a time, absorbing the feel and woodsy smell. Now and then a hoof clacked on a rock or a horse snorted.

Goss was turning out to be something of a nuisance. The run got his blood rising and he was all too interested in Lady Miranda's mare, who must be in heat. He arched his neck and pranced, his ears perked straight ahead.

"This is not the time," Amberhill murmured to his stallion. Goss tossed his head, uninterested in anything his master had to say.

Then, without warning, Lady Estora kicked her horse into a quick trot, then into a canter, and they were off again, careening through the trees, ducking beneath low limbs, clods of dirt flying up from hooves. They came upon a series of old rotted logs lying across the path and leaped them. Goss refused the trees and paced in a circle until Lady Miranda's mare went before him.

Amberhill leaned forward and said into his horse's ear, "Before the day is done I will see you gelded!" It was an empty threat, for he'd intended to use Goss as the foundation stud of his horse farm.

But Goss did not pay a whit of attention to him anyway, all his senses focused on the mare, his nostrils flared. Amberhill growled. He needed to be up front, closer to Lady Estora, but Lady Miranda, a more timid rider, hung toward the back. The trail was a narrow track, and it would not be easy to thrash through the trees to get to the front, and they were nearing the place . . .

In a moment of inattention, Goss snapped at Lady Miranda's mare above the tail. The mare kicked and Goss sidestepped with a snort.

"Idiot!" Amberhill slapped Goss with his crop, causing the stallion to half-rear and circle. While he struggled to control his horse, he was passed by the servants. A Weapon on a steed as black as his uniform gave him a sympathetic glance as he cantered by.

"I will feed your bones to the dogs!" Amberhill told his unimpressed horse.

When Goss realized the mare was out of sight, he whirled and charged down the trail, Amberhill barely maintaining his seat. By the time Amberhill caught up with the party, it was too late.

FOG

An unnatural fog crept through the woods, tumbled across the trail, obscured everything farther than a few feet ahead. Panicked whinnies and shouts echoed through the woods. A riderless horse galloped back down the trail, dragging its reins. Then silence.

Goss seemed to run in place even as Amberhill laid his whip into him. "Damnation," he muttered. The fog must be some trick of the plainshield's. At its edge, he pulled Goss to a halt. He could not gallop heedlessly where he could not see. Goss pranced and snorted, but Amberhill held him in, trying to decide what to do.

A voice rang out somewhere ahead. "My lady, you will come with me."

It was Morry. Amberhill imagined him sitting tall upon his sleek horse attired as the Raven Mask, the silk obscuring his features. The plan was going ahead even without Amberhill in his place.

Morry, as the Raven Mask, was supposed to present Lady Estora to the mysterious noble who was behind the abduction. Amberhill was then to pretend to be held at bay by the Raven Mask while the noble made his terms for Lady Estora's release known. Then they'd go their separate ways, the noble with Lady Estora to whatever estate he held, Morry into the woods with his payment, and Amberhill back to the city to report the honor abduction and pass on the noble's demands.

In an honor abduction, the captive wasn't supposed to be

placed in danger, and was required to be treated well by her captors. Nobles understood what was expected, for this code of honorable conduct had ancient and revered roots among the Sacor Clans. The demands would be met, maybe a grievance aired, and the captive returned unharmed, and the realm could go about its business.

The unnatural fog, however, heightened Amberhill's sense of foreboding. Anxiety knotted in his gut. Morry had warned him that the best of plans could go awry. Morry hadn't liked this plan from the beginning . . .

Amberhill urged Goss into the wall of fog. It was like entering another world, or maybe one of the five hells. Horses thrashed this way and that, limbs of trees reached out of nowhere to grab at him. Goss leaped over an unhorsed servant cowering beside a rock. He glimpsed Estora's youngest sister clinging to her horse's mane as it bucked in fright.

He heard swords slide from sheaths. The Weapons would be moving forward to protect Lady Estora. His gut clenched at the whine of a crossbow bolt and the scream of a horse as it crashed to the ground. Goss reared and Amberhill fought him down.

"No!" he cried.

More bolts whined through the fog. Now there were human cries among the trampling hooves and the squeals of terrified horses.

"No." This time it came as a whisper.

Goss planted his hooves, sweat foaming on his neck. Amberhill dug his spurs into the horse's sides and Goss leaped forward. Deeper into the fog he found the dead horse lying on a dead or unconscious Weapon. He found a cavalry officer with a crossbow bolt through his neck, his eyes wide open.

"It wasn't supposed to happen like this," Amberhill said.

Lord Henley was draped across a log, his body twisted at an impossible angle. Another Weapon with a bolt in his stomach writhed on the ground, blood bubbling from his mouth.

A third Weapon appeared out of the mist beside him like a ghost. "Sir, you are all right?"

Amberhill nodded. "Yes, yes."

He worked Goss along the trail, the fog wisping before him like layers of veils, revealing in only small increments the scene around him. Lady Miranda knelt on the side of the trail weeping, another dead cavalryman sprawled across a boulder.

Goss' nostrils flared and he champed on his bit as they picked their way down the trail. Lady Estora's other sister helped a Weapon with a bolt in his leg. The Weapon struggled to rise, holding onto a tree. With a scream of pain and frustration he fell back to the ground.

The sister looked up at him then, her face pale. "Someone has taken Estora."

He did not answer, but nudged Goss forward and forward until the fog revealed a man lying prone on the ground on a bed of moss, a bolt in his back. A mask concealed his face.

"Morry!" Amberhill dismounted and knelt beside him. "Morry . . ." Gently he peeled away the mask, revealing the older man's gray face.

Morry's body quivered. "Betrayed," he whispered. "Bad business, my boy. Bad men. Betrayed us. Not . . . not an honor abduction."

"Morry?" A sob caught in Amberhill's throat.

Morry's mouth opened and at first nothing came out, then he whispered, "Remember honor, Xandis. Remember *true* honor." He did not speak again.

Amberhill sat back on his heels and rubbed his face with his hands. All his fault. He moved his foot and his toe struck something that jingled. A bulging purse of gold. A mocking gesture from the men who had betrayed them.

He gathered Morry into his arms. At first Goss shied away, but then the stallion allowed him to place the dead man across his back. Amberhill took the purse of gold and led Goss through the fog.

He would not let Morry be found and the blame laid on him. He would find a place for him to rest until he could return his body to Hillander for a proper burial. He deserved no less.

All my fault.

Morry had been a devoted servant, had raised him when his own father was incapable. Had trained him in the ways of the Raven Mask. Now he was gone. Morry had said he didn't trust the plainshield. Morry hadn't thought the scheme worth any amount gold. He was right.

I did not listen.

It was one thing for the Raven Mask to steal jewels and trinkets, or even a piece of parchment from a museum, and quite something else to deal in human lives. He knew that now. Morry's final lesson.

Without looking back, Amberhill led Goss out of the fog into the brightness of day. He would find a temporary resting place for Morry, then pursue the plainshield and his cohorts. When he caught up with them, he would make the plainshield eat the gold, one coin at a time.

"If you do not find my daughter, if any harm comes to her, the eastern lords will march on this city and see your crown removed."

Lord Coutre's face was so red Laren feared his heart would burst. Zachary sagged in his throne, rubbing his temple.

"You are under great strain, my lord," Castellan Sperren said. "Do not use this time to make threats you will later regret. Under other circumstances, we would take your words as treason."

Lord Coutre's face only grew redder, his white eyebrows standing out in sharp contrast. "I shall say what I want! It's my daughter who's been abducted! What were you thinking by allowing her a ride in the country with the Eletian threat?"

"It was not the Eletians who took her," Colin said. He displayed the crossbow bolt on his palm. It was common enough looking, and not of the sort of weapon Eletians were known to use.

Lord Coutre dismissed him. "What are you going to do about it?"

Zachary looked up and Laren wondered what thoughts flowed through his mind. Certainly he worried for Lady Estora's welfare, but her abduction raised so many other questions: Who dared such a brazen act? Could it have been the Eletians? She didn't think so, but she knew he must consider the possibility. If not, who else wanted the future queen? Some group, no doubt, that wished to destabilize Zachary's power. Second Empire came immediately to mind.

There were likely other groups and individuals out there with all kinds of grievances. Enemies of Coutre, perhaps, who did not wish to see the clan rise to such prominence with Estora's marriage to Zachary. Enemies they couldn't even begin to imagine.

These possibilities and more must occupy Zachary's mind. What enemy was he facing? Would Lord Coutre follow up on his threat if Lady Estora were harmed? It was not a complication he, or any of them, needed right now.

"We will find her," Zachary said, his voice gruff. "I've a phalanx of Weapons assembling. And I will lead them."

"No, you won't," Laren and Colin said simultaneously.

"They likely wish to draw you out," Colin added, "so they can capture you, too, or worse."

Zachary stood and upon the dais he towered over them. "I will not stay. I cannot just sit here and do nothing."

Lord Coutre grunted. "Better that than you endangering the mission to rescue my daughter. Send your Weapons—they'll do their job better if they don't have to worry about you."

They all looked at Lord Coutre in surprise, and Laren applauded his reasoning.

"I wish to go, too," he added, "but I am an old man and would only hinder your Weapons. Wisdom is knowing when to go and when not to. I have a wife and children to comfort, so I will leave you now. But I want word sent to me the moment you know anything."

They watched him as he made his way down the throne

room runner. He moved slowly, was more bent than Laren remembered. Zachary sank back into his throne chair.

"I'll send Ty and Osric with your Weapons," Laren said. "They can bring word back."

Zachary gave her the barest of nods. She called a Green Foot runner over to deliver her instructions.

"We've wasted so much time," Zachary murmured.

"Necessary," Colin replied. "The abductors may have a strong lead on us, but our Weapons shall be tireless in their pursuit. When the Weapons catch up with them, they shall be sorry they chose such a course."

Such a fervor had grown in Colin's voice that Laren could tell he longed to partake in the pursuit himself.

"Meanwhile," he continued, "we shall bring up Weapons from the tombs to take their place and guard you. The gods only know what other acts these villains have planned."

"My cousin did not return," Zachary said.

"No," Colin replied. "Willis said he was not among the dead or injured, and was fine when last he saw him. We can only conclude he went in pursuit of the abductors immediately."

What Zachary thought of this he did not say. "The fog Willis mentioned, it sounds like magic."

"He said it was *unnatural,*" Laren recalled. "I agree."

"The Eletians will have to be questioned."

Laren thought that would be an interesting discussion.

Neff the herald rushed through the throne room doors and down the runner. He dropped to his knee before the dais. "Eletians, my lord, from the encampment. Three have come to speak to you."

Laren and Zachary exchanged glances, stunned by the uncanny timing.

"Send them—" Zachary began, but the Eletians had already entered the throne room and were gliding down the runner.

They came unarmed, but the guards in the throne room moved in closer to their king, hands on the hilts of their swords. The Eletians did not appear intimidated in the least, their stride unflagging, their features unperturbed. Leading them was the one who had been their guide in Prince Jametari's tent that day, his sister. She wore a gray-green cloak about her shoulders. But for a few thin, looping braids, her pale hair was unbound and flowed to the small of her back.

The other two Eletians, males, followed behind her, and were similarly attired in gray-green. Sunlight slanted through the throne room windows and played across their hair and brightened their faces as though pulled to them.

The woman in the lead knelt before Zachary, followed in turn by her companions.

"Greetings, Firebrand," she said. "My brother bade us speak to you in this troubled time."

Zachary indicated they should rise. "And what troubled time does Prince Jametari think this?"

"Little passes without our notice, especially that of our Ari-matiel. We are aware that your lady has been taken from you."

Zachary's eyes narrowed just a hint. "We have only just heard the news ourselves. How is it the Eletians know so much?"

"We have different ways of knowing," the woman replied. "We hear the voice of the forest carried along the stream that flows through our camp. We felt a small surge of magic in the woods west of us, and the tale is told to us by limb, by leaf, by breath of wind."

Old Sperren, leaning on his staff of office, quaked to life beneath his cloak. "How do we know you did not take Lady Estora yourselves?"

"*He* knows," the woman said, gazing at Zachary. "Deep inside he knows the truth of it. We have nothing to gain by seizing this land's future queen and everything to lose. There is another power at work in the lands. You may ask your Green Rider captain if we speak truth."

Laren's eyes widened. How did they know the nature of her special ability?

"Laren?" Zachary said.

She brushed her fingers over her brooch. It warmed to her touch, and she felt nothing but harmony, no sense of falsehood or deception. Only peace. The voice of her ability fairly hummed with truth. Astounded, she nodded to the king.

Zachary relaxed perceptibly. "What is this other power you speak of?"

"It is something we've been aware of since summer," the Eletian said, "when so much was awakened and stirred up. However, when all else settled, this did not. We know not its shape or intent, only that it lies westward, and that it was behind the surge of magic we felt in the woods. We feel that your rescue party will track the abductors westward toward the source."

Colin called one of his Weapons over and spoke quietly to him. The Weapon trotted out of the throne room.

"And this is what brings you forth from your encampment?" Zachary asked.

"We had no desire for blame to be mislaid upon us, and wish for you not to fear us as a threat. That was your line of thought, was it not?" She eyed them each in turn. "And our Ari-matiel sends words, for he is one gifted with foresight, and you may use his words as you will. Telagioth?"

One of the men stepped forward and put his hands before him, palms upward. Laren expected some enchantment to arise from them, at least some glow of light, but it did not. He simply spoke: "Ari-matiel Jametari says, 'The golden lady shall find safety only in green. A time shall come when black shrouds green, and among the dead a voice shall speak of stone.' "

Silence followed until Sperren sputtered, "What in the five hells is that supposed to mean?"

"We do not know," the woman said, "though we assume 'golden lady' refers to the one who was taken. Our Ari-matiel does not interpret his words. Often he does not remember their speaking. It is up to the recipients to find the meaning."

"Worthless," Sperren muttered.

"Perhaps, perhaps not," the woman said.

With that, and without seeking leave, the Eletians bowed and departed. Once they exited the throne room, everything was cast into its ordinary gloom and felt tired, as though the sun had moved behind the clouds.

Later that evening, Laren mulled over the day's events as she wandered down to the Rider wing of the castle. The company of Weapons and her two Riders had set out in pursuit of Lady Estora hours ago, and there was much to think on. The parameters of the situation staggered her. Possible civil war with the eastern provinces, loss of confidence in Zachary by his people. If he could not protect their future queen, how could he protect them? If anything happened to Lady Estora, she could see only disaster, and who knew what was brewing in Blackveil. They could all be caught up in internal fighting when suddenly the threat of Blackveil descended on them.

She found the Rider wing quiet. Many of her Riders were out on errands, several paired with new Riders-in-training. The empty corridor and closed doors left her feeling desolate, but she walked on.

A blur of white fur streaked past her feet. She jumped aside, her heart clamoring in her chest. The creature—a cat?—darted through a doorway standing ajar and into the room beyond. Laren peered in, and realized the room was Karigan's. Two globes of gold-blue gazed back at her. She opened the door all the way and the corridor's lamplight revealed the cat nestled in a clump on Karigan's bed. It watched her every move, tensed to leap away if she came too close.

"Huh." Laren left the door cracked open, and headed on to the common room where she found Connly, his heels upon the hearth and a mug of tea cupped in his hands.

"Captain!" He stood in surprise and she gestured he should sit. She pulled up a rocking chair to sit next to him.

"Since when did Karigan take in a cat?" she asked him.

Connly snorted. "I don't think she knows she has. It

sleeps there on her bed most every day. Sometimes we find it here at the hearth. We leave it scraps and water. We think it lives in the abandoned corridors. It's not bothering anyone."

"I suppose." Laren's thoughts were already plunging back into the realm's troubles. She rocked absently, only half listening as Connly updated her on the doings of the Riders.

She had approved of Lady Estora confronting Zachary yesterday. She had approved of her spirit, and had thought Zachary was being overprotective. It surprised her, really, for he had done little else to recognize her status. Giving over his study to her had been a compassionate move, which Laren had applauded, and there had been the obligatory appearances at state and social events, but otherwise he had reached out very little to her.

Should this crisis pass and Lady Estora return unharmed, she planned to have a long talk with him no matter how unhappy it made him. If Lady Estora was to share power with him, he must bring her in on meetings, have her sit beside him during public audiences. She needed to hear the voices of the common folk and their troubles, to see the mechanics of her country at work.

Then there was the conversation Laren intended to have with Lady Estora herself, the one about revealing the secret. She had not yet approached the young noblewoman, thinking there was plenty of time, and she'd had so many other immediate concerns—duties to attend to, meetings to sit through, problems to be solved. Now she was sorry she'd never gotten a chance to speak with her.

Until Lady Estora returned to them healthy and unharmed, it was all moot anyway.

"—and I don't see us making any progress with Ben and the horses," Connly said.

She shifted in her chair becoming aware of where she was again. "Ben," she said.

Connly glanced sideways at her. "You haven't heard a word I've said, have you?"

"You were talking about Ben and horses."

Connly laughed. "Yes, at the very end. Don't worry, there wasn't anything terribly important. Not like the other news of the day."

"Could you tell me again? Tell me what my Riders have been up to?"

Connly started over and this time she listened, and listened closely and engaged herself in the routine and the mundane. It was a relief from the day's greater, more threatening events.

AUBRY CROSSING

The Green Cloak's sheltering growth was a distant memory for Karigan and Fergal as they forged ahead into stiff winds that swept out of the arctic lands in the far north and cut through the Wanda Plains and into western Sacoridia like a scythe of ice. Only patches of trees, stripped of their leaves, lent some protection, but the farther north and west they traveled, the more the land opened up, and the more fierce the wind became.

The horses didn't seem to mind the cold in the least. Their coats had fluffed up almost overnight. Both Riders, had donned their fur-lined greatcoats against the chill and wrapped scarves around their faces. There were, fortunately, adequate inns along the way to provide them shelter from the cutting wind and a chance to warm up.

Karigan halted Condor beside a signpost, its arms pointing east and west along the road, a third arrow pointing northwest toward a narrower dirt track. The sign boards creaked in the wind.

"Ten miles to Aubry Crossing," Karigan told Fergal.

"What?" he shouted.

Karigan fought to not roll her eyes. She pointed to her ear.

"Oops, sorry," Fergal said, and he pulled tiny wads of linen he used to block the wind from his ears, which he said made his ears ache.

"I said," and Karigan pointed at the signpost, "ten miles to Aubry Crossing."

"Oh." He appeared unaffected by the news and stuffed his ears again.

Now Karigan did roll her eyes. She for one was relieved to be closing in on their next destination. She'd be glad to get out of this wind for a while. She reined Condor onto the spur leading northwest and nudged him into a leisurely jog, Fergal and Sunny following close behind.

Aubry Crossing was a minor border town between Sacoridia and Rhovanny. To the south was Lecia, the primary border crossing between the two countries.

Aubry Crossing was, as Captain Mapstone described, a small town with a few inns and outfitters. There were some rough houses on either side of the road, and that was about it, except for the barracks at the boundary gate.

Karigan stopped at an outfitter's and asked for directions to Damian Frost's place. When she rejoined Fergal outside, she patted Condor's neck and said, "Well, that was a bit convoluted."

Fergal cupped his hand to his car. *"What?"*

"Oh, never mind." She waved him off and mounted, hoping she could keep the directions straight.

After the yellow house down the main street she was to head due north on a path. She somehow missed the yellow house. Up and down the street they went, Karigan muttering to herself and Fergal following with an oblivious expression on his face. No yellow house was to be found. The proprietor of the outfitter shop must have observed them going back and forth for he emerged on the street and pointed to a ramshackle cottage that was weather-beaten to a dull gray.

"That's the yellow house," he said.

Karigan rounded her lips into an O and thanked the man. On closer inspection she discerned a few faded flecks of yellow paint the wind hadn't peeled away.

"Yellow house. Right. Hope the rest of his directions are more clear."

"What?" Fergal demanded.

Karigan urged Condor past the "yellow" house and onto

a trail. It passed the back side of a tiny chapel of the moon and the town's burying ground with its cairns and carved stone markers. Other paths branched off from the main trail to homesteads and farms. She was not to turn off until she came to the "big rock." The proprietor of the outfitter shop assured her she could not miss it. She hoped not, for large rocks were plentiful along the trail.

When she came to it, she had to admit the rock was rather obvious. It was a behemoth of a boulder that looked as though the gods had planted it in place. It dwarfed everything around them, including the horses, and was a finer grain of rock than others in the landscape. Deer moss grew like a furry cap atop it and splotches of blue-green lichens spread across weathered carvings. Karigan had seen the ancient picture-writing elsewhere on other travels, and it did not surprise her to see it on this boulder that was such a major landmark.

There were more recent markings as well—initials scratched over the pictographs, some with dates. People were always wanting to announce their existence to the world in a way that would surpass the ages, creating some sort of immortality. For all Karigan knew, the more ancient carvings were just another incarnation of such an urge.

She almost missed the horse carving, it was so faded and matted with lichens. Elsewhere she had taken the image to represent Salvistar, steed of the god Westrion, who carried souls to the heavens. Legend had it that Salvistar was the harbinger of battle and strife. But in this location the carving of a horse could be far more simple in its symbolism.

The path forked at the boulder, and Karigan reined Condor left. The trail narrowed and rambled through thicket and field and under the crooked boughs of apple trees. Trying to remember the shop proprietor's directions was not easy. She reined left again at the "broken oak," straight at the "old wagon wheel," right on the path at the stream.

Very soon their daylight dwindled. Karigan paused to recall what their next landmark was, the stream rushing and swirling beside her, and aglow with the last gleam of day.

Fergal rode Sunny on ahead, quickly disappearing into the dusk.

At the stream, there was something important she was supposed to remember. As soon as she heard the sounds of thrashing in underbrush and a shouted, "Stupid horse!" from Fergal, she did.

She moved Condor out at a swift trot, and in moments they reached Fergal, who was digging his heels into Sunny's sides in an effort to convince her to cross a bridge over the stream. He'd broken a branch off a tree and was using it like a whip. Sunny, the whites of her eyes flashing in the dark, placed a tentative hoof on the bridge, pushed as she was by Fergal, then whirled away on her haunches in terror.

Fergal hauled on the reins and swatted her with the branch. "Idiot!" he hollered.

Before he could raise the branch again, Karigan and Condor were there. Karigan ripped the branch from his hand and Condor pivoted, placing himself between Sunny and the bridge.

Karigan and Fergal stared hard at one another, each breathing hard. Fergal pulled out the wads of linen from his ears and looked ready to shout something angry at her. Karigan beat him to it.

"*Never, ever* use a stick on this horse or any other," she said, barely restraining the full force of her anger. She threw the branch clattering into some trees. "If I ever see you mistreat Sunny again, you will be walking back to Sacor City and I'll see to it you wished you never even heard of the Green Riders."

It was hard to read Fergal's expression, for his face was shadowed. Karigan trembled with fury.

"There is only one idiot here," she continued, "and it's not Sunny. She may have just saved you from a bad accident. She may have even spared you your life."

At Fergal's snort of disbelief, Karigan dismounted and walked onto the bridge. It looked fine and sturdy in the dark, crossing the deep, strong stream flowing between steep embankments. It would be difficult, if not foolish, to attempt fording the stream without a bridge.

But, according to the shop proprietor in town, this was not the bridge to cross, and Karigan felt it the moment she stepped upon it. It swayed with her weight and the planking creaked beneath her feet. It would never support a horse.

"That shopkeeper warned me it might be in bad shape," she said, "especially after that storm we had." Some of the planking was soft beneath her foot, and she stomped on it, breaking through rot. Pieces of wood splashed into the stream below.

"Sunny sensed this bridge was not safe," Karigan explained. "Instead of beating her, you should have listened to her warning. Call horses stupid if you must, but they're more intelligent than some people."

Fergal made no reply, but his head was bowed.

Karigan left the bridge and mounted Condor, reining him upstream where there was supposed to be a better bridge. Fergal and Sunny followed.

Karigan could have sworn she heard Fergal say he was sorry, but if he did, the words were not meant for her. Some of her tension eased, but it seemed maybe her hopes for Fergal moving beyond mere duty in his care of horses were never to be realized. Maybe with his background, he'd never be able to genuinely care for horses, never allow himself to care. And with his cruel knacker father as his model? Karigan shook her head.

And yet Fergal had been called. He had been called to be a Green *Rider,* which necessitated riding horses. Perhaps whatever higher powers existed in the world knew something she did not.

Was it just coincidence Fergal was chosen for an errand that included visiting the man who supplied the Green Riders with their horses? Definitely ironic, but coincidental?

She'd experienced too much in her own life to believe in pure coincidence. Maybe, just maybe, this visit to Damian Frost would be just the thing to help Fergal see beyond duty. Maybe he'd learn to care. Or it could be too much, too overwhelming, and there was a chance it might drive him to reject horses altogether.

It was out of her hands, she decided. Only Fergal could determine how it would all turn out.

"Wait," Fergal called to her.

Karigan halted Condor, and Fergal nudged Sunny up beside them. He kept the mare on a long rein, was gentle with the bit.

"Yes?" Karigan asked. Was that the shine of tears on his cheeks? It was too dark to tell.

"It won't happen again," he replied. "I–I don't want to disappoint Captain Mapstone or the king."

Or you, he might have added.

"I know Sunny's not stupid," he continued. "It's just . . . I don't know how to be."

"Listen to your heart," Karigan said.

"I just hear my da."

"He's far, far away, Fergal. He can't tell you how to think or feel now. You are a Green Rider, and we are your family. You don't have to be the knacker's son if you don't want to be."

Fergal fell into thoughtful silence and again they set off, at last coming to a sturdy bridge Sunny did not balk at. Karigan noted Fergal patting the mare's neck as they crossed, and the last of her tension eased, allowing her to settle into a kind of peace.

In the dark, Karigan feared she would miss the last sign, a cairn at a junction of three trails. She need not have worried, however, as the pile of stones was enormous and it was topped by a flat-faced rock with a horse painted in white and an arrow pointing the way.

"We're almost there," she said.

"Good. I'm starving." If Fergal continued to feel remorse for his earlier behavior, she could not hear it in his voice, unless he sounded just a little too chipper.

As they continued on, Condor's step picked up and he bobbed his head. Was it possible he retained memories of his first home? With messenger horses, anything was possible.

The farther down the trail they went, the friskier Condor became, prancing and whisking his tail, snorts steaming from his nostrils. Karigan began to think she was riding some young colt rather than her staid, experienced messenger horse. Sunny, sensing his spirits, picked up her gait and bobbed her head as well.

"What's wrong with them?" Fergal asked.

"Condor is going home," Karigan said.

THE FROST PLACE

They rode out of a thicket to the top of a ridge. The land rolled away from them, open to the sky and the sharpness of stars. Below them, golden light spilled from the windows of a long, low building. There were other buildings near the main one, but the dark claimed their shape and size. The breeze shifted and Karigan smelled wood smoke.

"I think we've found Damian Frost's place," Karigan said.

Though Karigan did not completely give Condor his head, she allowed him to canter down the ridge, tail swishing all the way. When they arrived at the front porch of the place, Karigan had to check Condor so he didn't climb right up the steps onto it and through the door. He pranced and bucked at the command.

"Settle," she told him.

He shook his head, rattling the reins in rebellion.

Before she could dismount, the door swung open and a wiry fellow stood there silhouetted by the lamplight.

"It's about time," he said. "I've been expecting you for weeks now."

Before Karigan could ask how he knew, or say anything for that matter, Condor launched up onto the front porch, taking her by complete surprise. She did not duck in time and smacked her head on the eave of the low, overhanging roof. She spilled off Condor's back, over his rump, and hit the ground.

There were only the stars above, like a great spangled black quilt over her. Her body took its time to sort out the pain, the worst of which was the growing throb above the bridge of her nose.

Suddenly the night sky was framed by heads—two human, two horse. Fergal and Sunny stood to one side of her, and the wiry fellow and Condor on the other. Actually, Condor stood behind the man, peering at her around his shoulder. His ears wilted as if in apology.

"Chicken," she said.

"What's she saying, lad?" the man asked Fergal.

"She called you a chick—"

"I was addressing the horse," Karigan said. "The one hiding behind you."

The man reached over his shoulder and patted Condor's neck. "Aye, a little overexcited. S'posed to protect his Rider, not dump her."

Condor's ears wilted even more.

"He sometimes has a mind of his own."

"Aye."

Karigan ungloved her right hand and reached up. "I'm Karigan G'ladheon, and my companion is Fergal Duff. May I presume you are Damian Frost?"

The wiry man bent to his knee and grasped her hand to shake it. His hand felt rough and gnarly, like old tree roots, and his grip was firm. "I am Damian. Welcome, Riders." He reached across Karigan to shake Fergal's hand.

"You have any broken bones, lass?" Damian asked.

Karigan felt more undignified sprawled on her back than hurt, though she was sure that would change when her body realized what happened.

"I don't think so," she said. She rose gingerly to her elbows. Her head throbbed anew and her neck felt the strain. Tomorrow she'd really be in for it.

Damian and Fergal helped Karigan rise to her feet, the world tilting, and she patted dust off her trousers and adjusted her swordbelt to conceal her unsteadiness. Condor still hid behind Damian.

"Gus! Jericho!" Damian hollered into the house, making both Karigan and Fergal jump.

Two hulking youths emerged from the house. "My sons," Damian said, jerking his thumb in their direction. They dwarfed their father. "Lads, take these horses out back and settle them in for the night."

"Aye, Pop."

Condor and Sunny were led away and Damian said, "Lady is just putting supper away, but I 'spect there is enough left over to warm two Rider bellies. Hungry?"

"Yes, sir!" Fergal said.

Damian laughed and slapped him on the back. "Still growing, aren't you, lad? Just like my boys, the young giants they be." He sprang onto the porch and bellowed, "Lady, my lady, we've got us some hungry guests!"

Fergal followed him eagerly into the house, Karigan coming along more slowly, trying to make her limbs work again, but each step sent a jolt of pain up between her shoulder blades and through her neck.

"The horse is dog meat," she muttered.

Fergal glanced back at her in surprise. She scowled at him.

When she entered the Frost house, however, it was difficult to feel dark. Lamps bathed the walls and heavy timber rafters in a warm glow. The cooking area was to their immediate right, dominated by a long farm table that was lined with benches. The wood was smoothed and darkened by the touch of many hands over the years. A bowl of apples sat in the middle.

Beyond the table was the cooking hearth, counters, and cupboards. Dried herbs and flowers hung from the rafters by the thousands. As dazed as Karigan was, it was like looking at an upside down garden.

At the center of it all bearing a ladle was a woman attired in a homespun dress of vibrant blue with intricate designs of horses sewn onto it with crimson thread. As fine as the workmanship was, Karigan was drawn to the woman's pure white hair and eyes of ice blue.

Damian Frost danced around her and gave her a twirl. "Lady, my lady, the Riders have come, on Condor and a war horse all dapple and gray."

Lady Frost—Lady? Was her name really Lady, or were they faced with some unknown noble living the rustic life?—smiled, and despite her icy colored eyes, she did not seem at all cold.

"Welcome, Riders. If my husband would stop dancing 'round me, I would bring you ale and stew and cornbread."

"Of course!" Damian said. "Where are my manners? Please be seated, Fergal and Karigan, and supper will commence immediately."

Fergal wasted no time in seating himself on a bench. Karigan followed more slowly, and felt rather befuddled as Damian and Lady bustled around the kitchen as though performing an orchestrated dance. Damian held bowls while Lady ladled steaming stew into them and added a dollop of cream and he bore the bowls to the table and placed them before his guests with the gentility of a footman. Next came a basket of golden cornbread and a warmed crock of molasses to spread atop it. Damian lifted a trap door to the root cellar and descended with a stoneware pitcher. When he reappeared, foam oozed over the pitcher's lip and he poured the ale into mugs for Karigan, Fergal, and himself. At some point Lady had brewed herself a cup of tea and now stirred it.

The stew, of course, was excellent and took the cold out of Karigan's limbs and the ale warmed her cheeks. Her stomach, however, was uncertain about retaining the food, as though her fall off Condor had shaken it up. She sipped at the stew's broth and avoided the larger bits of vegetables and beef. She could not drink more than half her mug of ale.

The Frosts asked the Riders about their journey and Karigan let Fergal do the talking around mouthfuls of food. The conversation became a distant noise to Karigan, like wind in the trees or the breeze brushing across vast grasslands. She imagined the plains and a dark horse surging through the grasses like a ship plowing through the sea, his mane and tail long and wild. He ran toward her.

"Red?" Fergal said.

Karigan shook herself as though awakening from a dream. She blinked at the lamplight.

"Aye," Damian said, "young Red Mapstone."

"The captain?" Fergal's tone was incredulous.

Damian clapped his hands. "Aye, the captain. Usually she comes herself when the need for horses arises. Is she well?"

"Well, but overwhelmed," Karigan murmured, surprised to hear herself answer.

"Nothing new there, I s'pose," Damian said.

Damian continued to question Fergal, but Karigan found Lady gazing at her, unblinking, the teacup poised before her lips.

"You've hardly touched your stew," Lady said.

Her voice was quiet, but Damian nonetheless heard and turned his attention to his wife. "What is it, my lady?"

"Oh, Damian," she said with a roll of her eyes. "Sometimes you lack even the wits of your horses." She reached over and patted Karigan's hand. "I will give you a soothing tea and let you go to bed directly." She turned back to her husband. "Honestly, you could have told me she's hurt."

"Hurt? Oh, the fall. Well, she didn't complain . . ."

"Honestly."

Before Karigan knew it, she was hustled off to a small guest chamber and settled into bed with a mattress stuffed with sweet grasses. Lady brought her tea, a compress for the bridge of her nose, and a hot water bottle for her neck.

"I'm not too bad," Karigan said.

"Honestly. You Riders are as stubborn as my husband. A few falls from a horse and it knocks the sense right out of you. You drink that tea, young lady, then waste no time in trying to sleep."

"Th–thank you."

Lady left and Karigan sighed in contentment, the water bottle easing the ache in her neck. The tea was herbal and heartening, and had a soporific effect, for no sooner did she finish it and set the mug aside on a night table than she fell asleep, dreaming she stood alone in a vast, empty grassland. No great, dark horse surged across waves of rolling grasses, only the wind. She thought she could discern it speaking, but the words were unintelligible.

Then she discovered she was not alone after all. A man trudged toward her, his back humped with a pack and his long white beard swaying with the motion of his stride. He bore a long walking staff.

As he came closer, she recognized him.

"Merdigen?" she said. Why wasn't he in his tower?

He paused and peered around as if he couldn't see her at first, then he narrowed his eyes and gazed directly at her.

"What are *you* doing here?" he demanded.

"It's *my* dream," she said. "There should be a horse."

Merdigen huffed. "It's always about horses with you Riders. Horses, horses, horses. You shouldn't be here. Go away!" He trudged past her grumbling to himself. "This happens and I haven't even crossed a bridge yet."

Karigan watched him stride on till he disappeared into the horizon. When she turned around, she saw another figure watching her, a man standing off in the distance, the grasses undulating toward him in waves. Even this far away she discerned details. He was dressed in the ancient garb of the Green Riders, his brooch glowing golden in the sunshine, and his mail gleaming. He wore a sword and bow across his back, and a horn slung at his hip. His hair streamed away from his face in the wind.

From a world away, his voice came to her. He asked, *Do you know what you are?*

Karigan wanted to speak to him, to ask him what he meant, but he vanished, and the plains with him, leaving her dreams to drift into the realm of the vague and unmemorable.

DAMIAN'S HERD

The next morning Karigan awoke refreshed with no memory of her dreams but for a lingering sense of some question left unanswered. Since she couldn't remember the question, it was going to stay unanswered. She shrugged it off, ready to begin the new day.

When she stepped out of bed and stretched, she was pleased to feel little achiness from her fall, even in her neck. Whatever herbs Lady brewed in her tea, they worked miracles. She discovered little bruising or swelling on her forehead as she gazed into the round mirror above her washstand. Maybe she hadn't hit the eave as hard as she thought or maybe Lady's tea possessed properties that went beyond simply alleviating pain. Maybe Lady herself possessed abilities in mending that went beyond the ordinary.

Cobwebs still clouded Karigan's brain and she deemed it too early to speculate about Lady or her tea. She was just grateful to be spared the pain.

She washed and dressed, then went looking for people, but the house was quiet and empty. Across from her room was a large bedchamber that must belong to Lady and Damian. Down the short hall was a common living area with a fireplace. The furnishings were ingeniously made of stout branches and the cushions covered in soft hide. Deer antlers hung above the mantel. She had missed all this last night.

Adjoining the common room was the kitchen, where she found a note from Lady saying she should make herself at home and eat breakfast, then join them in the stable out back.

Karigan was tempted to skip breakfast and just go out, but her empty stomach made her think better of it. She found a kettle still warming over the banked coals in the large hearth and a jar of tea and a mug awaiting her on the table. She sniffed the crushed tea leaves, wondering if they held any special properties like last night's brew, but though they smelled pungent and fresh, they seemed like an ordinary blend. Then she noticed the neatly written label: *Breakfast Tea.* She shrugged and spooned the tea leaves into her mug then poured hot water into it.

On the table was also a loaf of bread, crock of butter, and a second crock of blueberry preserves. If she looked further she would have found more, but she was embarrassed enough by having overslept that she made do with the tea and two helpings of bread slathered with butter and jam.

When she finished, she drew on her greatcoat and stepped outside. It was cold enough for her to see her breath on the air, and the weather dissipated any remnant cobwebs in her head. She strode off the front porch and rounded the house. What she had not been able to see in the dark the previous evening was a series of outbuildings and enclosures. Damian Frost's place was a proper farm with gardens now dormant, chickens pecking the ground around their henhouse, a lean-to occupied by pigs, and a shed housing goats and a pair of cows. Beyond was a barn that Karigan assumed stabled the horses.

She set off for the barn, thinking that something was missing from the scene. The gardens, pens, and outbuildings were right, and there were a sled and wagon situated outside the barn, but something wasn't in place. As she approached the barn, walking a well-worn path beaten by hooves and boots, she realized what it was. There was no paddock or fencing of any kind for holding horses.

Just as she began to doubt the barn served as the stable, Condor poked his head out a window and whinnied at her as if to hurry her up. Karigan did just that.

The large double doors were wide open and she stepped inside, wondering if she'd find some enchanted scene before her wrought by Damian Frost, the man who provided the Green Riders with their extraordinary horses, and by his wife who apparently possessed unknown healing skills. She found nothing out of the ordinary, however, unless one counted Fergal pitching manure out of a stall into a wheelbarrow.

The stable was airy and clean, with eight box stalls, all empty but for those occupied by Sunny and Condor. Sunny was contentedly pulling at hay from her hay rack, and Condor bobbed his head over his stall door and nickered. Karigan walked over to him and caressed his nose.

"Morning," Fergal said.

"Morning. Where are the Frosts?"

"Here we be, lass." Damian emerged from a doorway, carrying two Rider saddles, with matching bridles draped over each shoulder. Beside him walked a brindle wolfhound about the size of a pony. It padded to a pile of fresh straw, yawned, and heaved over, raising a cloud of dust. It dropped its head onto its front paws, settling in for a nap.

"That's Ero," Damian said. "Runt of the litter."

Karigan decided Ero's littermates must then be the size of horses.

Lady was a few steps behind Damian, bearing another bridle and a covered basket over her arm. "So glad to see you up and about," she told Karigan.

"Uh, yes, thank you. Your tea—it worked wonders."

Lady responded with a pleased smile.

"Come get your gear, my Riders," Damian said. "Riding I'm going, riding with Riders!"

Karigan and Fergal collected their tack from him.

"I've brushed and curried your Condor, lass, and picked his hooves clean. No need to fuss, just saddle up."

While Karigan did so, she wondered what Damian was going to ride, then began to listen to the debate developing between him and Lady.

"What about Abby?" Lady said.

"She's resting. I rode her yesterday."

"How about Uncle?"

"No, no, not today."

"Sea Star?"

Damian grimaced and rubbed his back end as though remembering some unpleasant experience. "No, definitely not Sea Star."

Karigan tightened Condor's girth, watching the couple over his withers. Lady gazed up toward the rafters as if in deep thought. "Seymour, perhaps?"

"Too slow," Damian said. "He'd never keep apace of Condor."

"Jack?"

"Jericho has Jack today, and Gus has Rose."

Karigan wondered where Damian hid all his horses.

"I know! Gracie!"

"Heavens, no. She's absolutely bats."

"Then who?" Lady demanded. "The dog?"

Ero lifted his massive head as if alarmed by the suggestion. Karigan giggled into Condor's neck.

"How am I supposed to know what to sing?" Lady asked.

Sing? What did singing have to do with anything?

"Who do we have left?" Damian started counting on his fingers, muttering to himself. "I know, I'll ride Cat."

Lady shook her head. "My dear, you sold Cat two weeks ago to old Tom Binder."

"Oh, I forgot. That leaves Fox."

"Fox it is, then," Lady said. "I shall sing him in." Basket still hanging from her arm, she walked to the stable entrance and peered out. Glancing back at her husband, she said, "They are far off this morn."

Damian shrugged.

Lady sighed, then loosed a deafening holler that nearly knocked Karigan off her feet. "*FOX!* Fox, Fox, Fox, *FOX!*"

That was singing?

But then Lady did sing, and in normal tones: "*Come Foxy, come Fox, from your grazing and phlox. Your master seeks you and needs you to ride among the flocks. Come Foxy, come Fox!"*

The song went on at some length with its nonsensical lyrics, but pleasant tones, and Karigan expected the song's subject to trot into the stable at any moment. Lady's song faded to an end. All watched and waited. Still nothing. Lady looked vexed.

Damian stepped up beside his wife and put his arm around her shoulders. "You're right, Lady, my lady and love. They're far off." He then stuck two fingers in his mouth and whistled a note so shrill Karigan clenched her teeth and poor Ero whined.

When the whistle died, they waited again. This time Karigan heard hooves pounding the ground—many hooves.

Damian and Lady stepped away from the entrance and even Ero rose to his feet and lumbered to the safety of the tack room. A veritable herd of horses crowded into the stable. They were of all proportions and colors and markings. They milled about poking their noses into Condor's stall, lipping at stray bits of straw, bumping into one another, their hooves scraping loudly on the cobble floor. In the crowded confines there were a few nips and kicks, but no serious altercations.

"Fox!" Damian yelled. A horse somewhere in the throng whinnied. "Fox, it's you I'm wanting—the rest of you clear out. Get on with you, back to pasture!"

As if the horses understood his words exactly, they flowed out of the stable as quickly as they entered, but for a shaggy bay gelding who remained behind.

"That's the trouble with whistling them in," Lady said, "it's not very specific. They were just too far off to hear my song."

Karigan had never heard of singing a horse in and was sorry the demonstration had not worked. She did know a Rider or two who could summon their individual horses with a whistle, but an entire herd? She was impressed.

"Could you teach me to do that, sir?" Fergal asked, apparently impressed as well.

"Why sure, lad." Damian stood beside the bay, scrutinizing him. He was a stocky specimen with a star between his eyes, and he was coated in dry mud. "It will have to be later though. My foxy Fox here needs curry and comb, and brush and pick before we ride. Gave himself a mud bath, he did, and us a delay."

Karigan leaned against the stall door, Condor resting his chin on her shoulder as she watched Damian work on Fox. The gelding stood there unmoving without cross-tie or halter. He half closed his eyes in contentment as Damian stroked him with the currycomb. Damian must have trained his horses well to enjoy being groomed, for Karigan had known some in her life that were intolerant of it, or at least had sensitive areas that when touched, incited a kick or bite.

In the meantime, Fergal further surprised her that morning by grabbing a shovel to pick up piles of manure left behind by the horses.

"Damian is taking you out to the plains to look over the herds," Lady told her.

"That . . . wasn't them?" Karigan asked.

"That lot? That was our domestic stock. No, he's going to take you to see where the wild ones run. That is, after all, the stock from which he picks Green Rider horses."

"Wild horses," Karigan murmured. "I didn't know."

"There are wild horses," Lady said, her gaze distant, "and then there are wild horses."

"True enough," Damian said. Without a word or even a tap on the leg, Fox lifted a hoof for him to pick out. "I don't choose just any horses for my Riders."

In no time, Fox's coat gleamed and his tail and mane were combed neat and unmatted. Damian slipped the bridle over his nose. It had no bit. "Fergal, lad," he said, "give me a leg up if you would."

Fergal did so and Damian sat upon Fox bareback. "Thank you, Fergal. Used to be able to vault right up, but I'm not as young as I once was, am I, Lady."

"You are ancient," she told him and they laughed as though this were a cherished joke. She brought him her basket and placed the handle over his wrist. He leaned down and they kissed. "Now don't be too late in coming back, Master Frost. I'll have supper waiting."

"Oh ho, I shall not be late for that!" He turned to Karigan and Fergal and said, "Mount up my friends. It's time we went riding." He squeezed Fox's sides and they plodded out of the stable. A whistle issued from without—this time a quick, sharp tone—and Ero the wolfhound emerged from the tack room and trotted outside to join his master.

Karigan led Condor out of his stall and as she prepared to mount, Lady said, "If you are lucky, you might even see the patron of your messenger horses." Without explaining, she left the stable with a wave and an, "Enjoy your day!"

With that intriguing comment to gnaw on, Karigan placed her toe into the stirrup and swung up onto Condor's back.

WILD HORSES

As they rode, Damian wanted to know the fates of some of the horses which he supplied to the Green Riders over the years. Karigan found herself passing on the sad news of those who died in the line of duty, horses and Riders both. Tears glistened in Damian's eyes. She told him also of Crane, who lost his Rider, but chose Ty as his new partner.

"Is Crane still the fastest?" Damian asked.

Karigan chuckled. "Ty does not believe racing is befitting for a Green Rider. That said, they've not lost a single race yet."

Damian rocked on Fox's back with laughter. "And I know who'd not take any nonsense about not racing—that Red, she's a wicked one. And mind you, a devious gambler."

Karigan smiled at the thought of her captain as "wicked," and found she could not disagree.

Damian grew serious again. "I rarely meet the Riders who become partners with my equine friends. Old Condor there, he's seen some action by the look of those scars on his hide. And I know you are not his original Rider."

"No, I'm not," Karigan said. "F'ryan Coblebay died a couple springs back."

Damian nodded. "Usually it's Red who travels here to deal for new horses, though I met Crane's Ereal once. I'm sorry for her loss, and for that of the others."

Karigan closed her eyes but doing so only brought back the nightmare memories of two arrows arcing through the night, thudding into Ereal's body one after the other.

She cleared her throat, wanting to steer the conversation in a less painful direction. "How long have you supplied Riders with horses?"

"Oh, all my life, as my family has down the generations. Since Captain Faraday Hartwood Simms led the Riders some eight hundred years ago or so."

"Really?" Karigan, knowledgeable in the ways of trade as she was, was shocked. "Your family must be extraordinary traders."

Damian flashed her a disarming smile. "You will soon see why you Riders come to us for horses, lass, and I can assure you, it has little to do with our prowess in trade. We must step smart now, we have some ground to cover."

On loose rein, and without any perceptible command from Damian, Fox picked up into a fast, ground-eating trot. Ero loped ahead, his nose periodically poking above the brush as he paused to make sure everyone was coming along, then he'd dash off again, tail wagging. That tail, Karigan thought, could probably fell a tree. He had no trouble keeping up with the horses and appeared to take joy in running ahead or alongside them.

The trail they followed was well beaten and churned by horse hooves, leading Karigan to believe that it wasn't only the Frosts who used the trail, but the herd as well.

Thickets of trees turned to low-growing scrub and, after some miles, the scrub became mere islands in an expanse of rolling grasslands. The tips of the grasses, now golden brown with the season, brushed the soles of Karigan's boots as she rode along.

Damian slowed Fox to a walk and the three of them rode shoulder to shoulder instead of single file. "We are technically in Rhovanny," Damian said. "And this is the southernmost finger of the Wanda Plains. There are many herds of wild horses that roam the plains. Mine tend to call this area their own territory."

"Why are there so many wild horses here?" Fergal asked.

"It is passed down through my family that the plains horses are descendants of warhorses who lost their riders during the last battle of the Long War, which took place on the central plains. Sacoridian horses, Arcosian horses, Eletian horses, Rhovan . . . Those horses escaped the bloodletting and ran free, becoming as feral as their own ancestors in the time before humankind first domesticated them. They mixed their bloodlines in a way their human counterparts could never hope to. Horses have more sense than people, I often think." Damian paused and rubbed his chin, his gaze far off.

"The horses do well enough here, despite the harsh winters. Those in the north plains find it more difficult. Not only are the winters tougher, but there are more predators—wolves, big cats, and the groundmites that den in the region. Our family has always kept wolfhounds, and that has helped stave off the predators, though Ero here is as like to invite a wolf to play as to attack it. All in all, the plains and the original mix of horses have yielded a very sturdy beast."

Karigan patted Condor's neck, wondering about his ancestors and the bloodlines that must flow through his veins. Were his ancestors of Eletian origin? Or, like her, of Arcosian descent? If so, she was comforted by the thought. If anything Arcosian could lead to a horse like him, she herself couldn't be all that bad. She smiled.

"We still have a little way to go," Damian said. "We keep shelter in some old ruins, and we'll find Gus and Jericho there."

He picked up their pace again, this time easing into a lope. Condor's ears were at attention and his step lighter than she ever recalled. This was his home and she tried to imagine him as a foal running among spring grasses, kicking up his hooves and nudging close to his mother. *What did she look like?* Did he resemble his dam more, or his sire?

The sun continued to climb and the grasslands spread around them as their horses beat across the land in a hypnotic rhythm. Ero bounded through the grasses, eyes bright and tongue lolling in evident delight.

If only every day could be like this, Karigan thought.

Soon a knoll rose above them, crowned by unnatural shapes jutting from the earth. Damian reined Fox to a jog, then a walk.

"Here is our shelter," Damian said, pointing up the knoll.

The ruins were made of stone, and were round and jagged like broken teeth. As they neared the ruins, she saw that these were remnants, just foundations, as though some great hand had emerged from the sky and knocked the structures over, except for one that looked to be partially rebuilt. Smoke issued through a hole in its conical, thatched roof.

Ero bounded off, pausing only to lift his leg here and there. Slabs of cut stone, most too large for a single man to lift, littered either side of their path. Whatever force toppled the buildings had been cataclysmic.

"What are these ruins?" Fergal asked.

"Tradition holds," Damian said, "that this was easternmost Kmaern. If so, this was but one village destroyed by Mornhavon the Black."

Though it was by now midday and the sky clear, a shadow seemed to pass over them and just briefly Karigan thought she could hear lost voices carried on a breeze and away. She shuddered.

"They lived in towers," Damian said. "They were the greatest stoneworkers in all the lands, and it was from them the D'Yers learned their craft. Mornhavon despised them and obliterated them. Even their towers could not withstand him, except for the very foundations that are rooted to the Earth."

"Didn't any of them survive?" Fergal asked.

"Hard to say, lad. Hard to say. Kmaern, at any rate, is dead."

Dead, dead, dead . . . the wind seemed to say as it passed over the ruins.

Gooseflesh spread across Karigan's skin.

At Ero's bark, one of Damian's sons emerged from the shelter and waved. He played with Ero until they reached him. Karigan had no idea if this was Jericho or Gus. It had been too dark last night to distinguish between the two.

"Well, son," Damian said as he drew Fox to a halt by the shelter, "I assume Jericho is out watching?"

"Aye, he is. The wind has changed and the herds are joining."

Karigan and Fergal exchanged glances.

"Jericho can see the patron," Damian said.

"I can't. Not yet, anyway," Gus said, with a downcast look.

"Sounds like he may make an appearance for us, for some of us at least," Damian said. "But first things first—food!"

How could someone see the patron—whoever or whatever he was—and someone else not, Karigan wondered. She doubted she'd get a straight answer from Damian.

They dismounted and set the horses to grazing. Damian assured Karigan that Condor and Sunny would not stray too far, and she believed him. Condor, relieved of his tack, ran and bucked like a young colt, then found a place to roll in the deep grasses. It pleased her to see him so happy, and she was sorry she'd have to take him from the plains of his birth once their business with Damian Frost was completed. She decided not to think about it for now.

Gus and Fergal were already rummaging through Lady's basket when Karigan entered the shelter. She found a small fire crackling in the center of the floor, with a couple of crude benches pulled up to it. There was also a pair of pallets with gear strewn about that must belong to the boys.

While Damian made tea, Gus and Fergal produced sausage rolls, bread, apples—with extras for the horses—and a crock of goat cheese.

"Save some for Jericho," Damian reminded them.

The cold air and morning ride had awakened their appetites and they ate, barely pausing to speak. When they finished, Damian packed the remnants of the meal into the basket, then with a whistle, called upon their horses to return. True to his word, they had not strayed far. The Riders tacked their horses, took leave of Gus, and rode through the ruins to the open plains, Ero trailing behind.

"There is a particular place the horses like," Damian said. "A valley with a stream that offers some protection from the wind. I 'spect we'll find Jericho there and the wild ones. It's not far."

By Karigan's calculations, the valley was but a few miles off. They found Jericho sitting cross-legged in the grass gazing into the valley below through a spyglass. Ero announced their arrival by bouncing over to him and licking his ears. Jericho laughed and ruffled the fur atop the wolfhound's head. Karigan realized another reason why she had trouble distinguishing between the two boys—they were twins.

Jericho rose to greet them, tucking the spyglass under his arm. Damian handed him the basket and slid off Fox's back. "How goes it, son?"

"Good, Pop. Three bands have merged."

While Karigan did not know a whole lot about wild horses, she said, "That's unusual, isn't it? Bands merging?"

"These are not your usual wild horses," Damian replied. He took the spyglass from Jericho and walked over to the edge of the ridge to look into the valley below.

Karigan dismounted and once again untacked Condor. His ears were erect and his flesh quivered. She wondered if he wanted to run down into the valley to join the wild ones, but when he was loose, he and Sunny simply ambled off along the ridge to graze. She shrugged and joined Damian and Fergal. Behind her, Jericho ate the leftovers from the basket and played with Ero, who rolled on his back with legs up in the air.

Big puppy, she thought.

The valley sloped gently beneath them, the grasses interspersed with scrub. At the bottom of the valley, a stream of silver-black meandered among reeds and cattail stalks, and some trees found shelter enough from the winds to grow. It was at the far end of the valley that Karigan saw the bumps in the landscape that were the horses.

"Three bands," Damian murmured. "Jericho was right. The stallions are watchful and dare not mingle, but the mares and youngsters have merged." He handed the spyglass to Fergal.

"Why would they merge?" Karigan asked. "I don't get it."

"It's a sign the patron is expected," Damian said. "This year past he's been appearing more often. There is more than horse sense at work here—maybe you'd call it god sense. Anyway, when he is expected, the bands merge so he can come among them again. It is how I also knew to expect Green Riders on my front porch. He seems to sense when messenger horses are needed."

"What is this patron?" Karigan asked.

"A stallion like you've never seen before, lass."

A breeze plucked a strand of hair from Karigan's braid and tickled her face. She tucked it behind her ear. "And the stallions just tolerate this interloper among their harems?"

"Aye," Damian said. "He is, in a sense, their king. They bow down to him."

Karigan wanted to ask if they literally bowed, but then Fergal passed her the spyglass and left her and Damian to go sit with Jericho and Ero. Just as she wondered how a horse trader came to possess a very expensive spyglass, she noted an inscription right on the brass tubing: *To the Family Frost, with appreciation for generations of dedicated service, Her Royal Highness Queen Isen Hillander.* A gift from King Zachary's grandmother! There must be quite a story behind the gift, but that would be for later. Other business was at hand.

She put the spyglass to her eye and focused, finding the view fine and clear, attesting to the superior grade of glass used for the lenses. Her gaze followed along the stream to where the bands of horses grazed and drank. Some leggy foals rested on the ground, their heads just visible above the tips of sun-touched grasses. The mares were alert, but not anxious. Karigan counted twenty-five to thirty in all, chestnuts, bays, grays, duns, roans, and blacks, some with markings, some without. A couple were spotted over the whole of their bodies, and there were a few paints, but she could find no definite pattern of lineage from horse to horse.

The three stallions kept their distance from one another and their harems, putting their noses to the wind, watching for predators, and occasionally grabbing a mouthful of grass.

One was gray, another dun, and the third a bay with one white sock. Their manes and tails grew long and untamed, their forelocks falling over an eye, giving them each a rakish look. The spyglass presented her with no more detail than that at this distance.

"So this is the stock that Green Rider horses come from," she murmured.

"A special few are born true," Damian said. "They've that spark of intelligence 'bout them."

Karigan took the spyglass from her eye. "How do you know which to choose?"

"How do you know your Condor isn't the same as other horses?"

"He's pretty smart."

"Just smart, lass?"

Karigan knew it was more than that. She and Condor shared a rapport as with no other horse she'd known. It was as if he sensed sometimes exactly what was on her mind, and could understand her words, not just commands. He'd saved her life a time or two when other horses would have bolted in terror. He wasn't just well-trained; he wasn't just smart.

"Down the line of my family," Damian said, his eyes squinting as he gazed into the valley, "it has always been told that these certain horses are god-touched, and that the patron is the bearer of that touch."

"Salvistar?" Karigan asked in incredulity.

Damian shrugged. "If you believe it, maybe it is so. He has never walked up to us and told us his name." He laughed and slapped his thigh. "That'd be the day! Westrion's steed speaking to us. Imagine that."

"This stallion," Karigan pressed, not yet willing to accept the idea he was a god-being, "he's the sire of the messenger horses?"

"No, not the sire, lass, except maybe in spirit. He has an influence, or at least an *interest,* we don't rightly comprehend. Maybe it's the plains that produce our special horses. With all the magic gone amok in the final battle of the Long War, I shouldn't be surprised if there weren't some remnant of it left behind, like the ruins of the Kmaernians, that somehow has some effect on the horses. Still . . ." Damian stroked his chin. "Still, I've never heard of any of the other scattered herds producing horses quite like mine, nor have I ever heard of one such as our patron passing among them. Whatever the truth of it is, I consider it a blessing. A joy for me it has been to be among such fine beasties."

Karigan glanced over her shoulder at Condor happily munching away at the grass, his tail whisking in contentment. He was not a particularly attractive horse, ill-proportioned as he was, but he was special. Special enough that he was the chosen of the death god's steed? Or the product of remnant magic? She shook her head.

One question always led to a hundred more. If she saw this "patron" of Green Rider horses, would it answer questions or prompt more? The breeze tugged her hair loose again and fluttered it in her face. She pressed it back.

"It is an oath spoken centuries ago," Damian said, "that my family swore to stand steward over these special steeds, and that they were to go to Green Riders only, and it is an oath we will never break. The horses would accept no one else anyway. Why this is so, I cannot say. The others who are not god-touched? Why, they are fine beasties, too, though rather ordinary, and my family supports itself on their trade. Let's move a little closer."

"They won't run off?"

"Naw. We've never treated them ill and they are accustomed to me and the boys. We won't crowd them."

Damian started off along the ridge, and when Ero followed, Jericho called him back. Fergal looked content to remain with Jericho and Ero, but Damian glanced back at him and beckoned. "C'mon, my lad, let's see how they take to you."

Karigan didn't think Fergal would care to take a closer look at the horses, but to her surprise, he sprang immediately to his feet, appearing pleased by the invitation. He strode through the grasses beside Damian and the older man put his arm around his shoulder, spinning some tale or telling secrets. Karigan couldn't discern which.

She trudged after them thinking maybe Damian didn't have a way with just horses, but with the sons of knackers as well.

SHAPER OF WIND

Damian didn't stay atop the ridge but angled downward, closer to the herd, though not threatening the position of the bay stallion on the closer side of the stream. He was wary of them, but issued no challenge and bugled no warning to his band.

Wading through the grasses, letting her hands float across their tips, Karigan began to wonder if whatever mending Lady had done was wearing off, for she felt a pressure mounting in her head, in the air, like a storm building. She forced herself to take a deep breath, but it did not ease the sensation. The breeze kicked up again, whispering across the grasses, whipping the hem of her greatcoat about her legs, and dislodging that very annoying strand of hair from behind her ear again. She thrust it back, deciding she'd have to rebraid when they stopped, wild horses or not.

At about a good stone's throw from the horses, Damian motioned for her and Fergal to halt, while he continued on. The horses noted their progress all along, raising their heads from grazing to glance at them and to sniff their scent on the air. Still no alarm was given.

Damian approached the herd slowly and one by one the horses stopped what they were doing to turn to him. A few ambled toward him, and a couple of fearless youngsters trotted right up to him and nudged at his pockets. He laughed and produced an apple which he split with his thumbs and fed to them. More members of the herd overcame their reticence to investigate, some crossing the stream to do so.

Soon all the horses stood around Damian, tails flicking. There was no kicking, biting, or shouldering of one another. Each appeared intent on Damian in some silent rapport.

"I thought they were supposed to be wild," Fergal said.

Karigan had been thinking much the same thing, but as Damian said, these were not ordinary wild horses. Damian himself was no ordinary horse trader.

One by one the horses peeled away from the group to resume grazing. A couple of foals lingered, poking Damian's pockets again. He patted them on their necks, said something to them, and they dispersed. Damian shook his head and returned to Karigan and Fergal, falling to the ground with his legs spread out in front of him.

"What now?" Karigan asked.

"We watch and wait," Damian replied.

A breeze tickled Karigan's nose and she rubbed it, only to realize she had fallen asleep. She blinked her eyes wide open to the grass stalks that surrounded her, the smell of the crushed greens filling her nose. The nap, unfortunately, did not relieve the sense of pressure in the air. She rolled to her side and leaned on her elbow, discovering Fergal had also fallen asleep. Not only that, but a foal was nosing Fergal's toes. He was a handsome fellow, creamy in color with a flaxen mane. He'd probably darken to a lovely golden palomino as he matured.

Just beyond Fergal, Damian sat cross-legged in the grass, grinning.

The colt continued to whiffle along Fergal's legs, lipping at his greatcoat. Karigan dared not move lest she spook the colt and ruin the moment.

The colt reached Fergal's head and nibbled hair.

Fergal, still more asleep than awake, swatted blindly as though ridding himself of a fly. The colt jerked his head up, hair caught between his teeth. Fergal's eyes popped open and he screamed. The colt jumped straight up from a standstill. Karigan had never seen anything like it and she could not help but laugh. The poor colt bolted off and hid behind his mother, poking his head under her belly to watch the humans from safety.

Fergal rubbed his head. "Wha–what happened?"

Karigan was laughing too hard to answer.

"The young ones are curious," Damian said. "Seems one took a liking to you."

From the gleam in Damian's eye, Karigan took it to mean that Fergal had found more than a "friend." It was odd the way the world worked. Fergal wanted nothing to do with horses, but now as a Green Rider he must depend on them, and one may have just chosen him to be his Rider partner.

Fergal's face hardened. "Well, my da would have liked these horses, too," he said, "but for other reasons." He rose and stomped back up the ridge in the direction of Jericho and Ero.

"Oh, no," Karigan muttered, fearing Fergal may have just rejected horses for good.

"A wounded spirit," Damian said as he watched after Fergal, "but not broken. As time passes, he will mend."

Karigan hoped so, for the sake of the young colt, and for Fergal's own.

"Has he ever told you," Damian asked softly, "about the first animal his father made him slaughter?"

Karigan shook her head, certain she did not want to hear about it now, as she found the entire subject distressing.

"It was a gentle draft horse named Randy that pulled the knacker's wagon," Damian said. "Old Randy was probably Fergal's best friend in the whole world—someone he could tell his dreams and secrets to. Someone who loved him no matter what, and who would not hurt him. Fergal certainly wasn't getting much affection elsewhere, except maybe from some kind folk in the village who took pity on him. He sure wasn't getting it at home."

Damian sat in silence for a few moments, the sunlight playing across his weathered face and deepening wrinkles and crags in bold shadows. "When Fergal's father decided it was time his boy was old enough to learn the family trade, he used his own horse for Fergal's first lesson. Claimed

Randy was getting on in years, wasn't pulling his weight anymore."

Karigan wanted to cover her ears against the painful tale. Damian didn't have to tell her what this must have been like for Fergal—she could imagine it, all the horrid details. She just had to substitute herself and Condor for Fergal and Randy, and she knew. She *knew.*

"His father beat him for crying," Damian said.

"Enough," Karigan pleaded. "Please don't tell me anymore. I–I don't want to hear it."

"I know, lass," Damian replied, not unkindly, "but think of Fergal not just hearing it, but *living* it. He learned from his father very early on not to grow attached to animals. And certainly not to cry." He paused and scratched his head. "He never stopped caring, though. That much I can see. He just buried it real deep so it wouldn't hurt so much. He's a resilient lad, and becoming a Rider has done much toward healing him. He has a new family now, eh?"

Karigan nodded and pulled at some grass. She was both relieved and jealous Fergal had chosen to open up to Damian instead of herself. *Mostly relieved,* she had to admit. They must have spoken during the night while she slept and dreamed of . . . of grasslands?

It was not surprising Fergal chose to talk to Damian, she reflected. She was so wrapped up in her own life she hadn't been overly patient with him at times, and Damian possessed a well of compassion a hundred fathoms deeper than her own. She could tell just by the way the horses, including Condor, responded to him. She thanked the gods Fergal had been able to meet men like Rendle and Damian, so different from his father, especially since she'd fallen short a time or two in her duty as mentor.

And Damian echoed her own belief that the Riders were a family, or maybe even better than a family. Fergal would find friendship and respect among them. The Riders watched out for one another, cared for one another, and sometimes even squabbled like true siblings. Karigan smiled as she imagined herself as Fergal's grouchy, older sister.

A stiff breeze funneled into the valley, plowing down the grasses before it, tousling the manes of horses, tugging yet again on that bit of hair Karigan had forgotten to rebraid. Damian took to scanning the valley, his back erect.

"What is it?" Karigan asked, her hand going to the hilt of the saber. Could it be predators he was worried about, or maybe even groundmites?

The horses all faced into the wind, their ears perked.

"Damian?" Karigan said. She glanced up the ridge. Jericho stood in a watchful attitude as well.

She started to draw her saber, but Damian leaned over and stayed her hand with a touch. "No, lass. It's the patron. He comes."

Karigan released the saber's hilt, but remained suspicious. "Where is he?"

"He comes." Damian rose to his feet and she followed suit.

"Well *I* don't see him."

"Not here yet."

Karigan asked, "Then how do you know he comes?"

"The wind, lass," Damian said. "The wind precedes him, and the wind follows. He is Eolian."

"Eolian?" Was it some exotic breed of horse she had never heard of before?

"Shaper of wind," Damian said.

Karigan sighed. The more Damian tried to explain, the less she understood.

"There," Damian said, pointing toward the mouth of the valley. "There he is."

Karigan squinted trying to see, but no horse was visible to her. Then her vision blurred and there was a flutter of motion . . . She blinked and her eyes cleared. She couldn't have seen anything; just a trick of the eye, the wind tossing grass and brush around . . .

Then she was met with the absurd sight of the horses bowing their heads. Up on the ridge even her Condor did so. Damian had meant it literally when he said the horses bowed to their king.

She gazed at the valley anew. Maybe her eyes had not been playing tricks on her after all. The pressure in her head, in the air, continued to build, swell. She rubbed her temple.

"Do you see him?" Damian asked.

"No."

"Do not look with your eyes."

It was one absurdity after another. She closed her eyes and saw only the back of her eyelids. What did Damian mean? Her Rider brooch flashed in warmth. She touched it, felt a throb through her fingertips, like the rhythm of hoofbeats. When she opened her eyes, the world had gone gray—the land, the horses, Damian, everything.

"You've faded, lass, like a ghost!" There was consternation in Damian's voice.

Karigan smiled. It was fair play to perplex him this time. Her special ability worked better in darkness and shadows in which she seemed to vanish completely. In direct sunlight like this, the effect was less successful, making her a living wraith.

Something in the air had prompted her to use her ability, so she gazed across the valley anew, and there he was, the stallion, practically pulsating in her vision with blackness against desolate gray. He pawed the earth, each muscle rippling beneath a hide smooth as ebon silk. He negated light, was made of its absence, like the night sky, the heavens; and when he moved, the grasses around him swirled like a dervish, though his long mane and tail remained undisturbed.

"Eolian," Karigan murmured.

He raised his head, tossing aside his forelock, as though deigning to take notice of the more earthly creatures around him. He snorted and trotted over to Fergal's little colt and his dam. The colt's legs folded beneath him—or buckled—and he lay on the ground looking up at the god-being that was his patron.

If not a god-being, Karigan thought, what else could the stallion be?

The dam bobbed her head and, incredibly, nibbled just above the stallion's withers, and he reciprocated by nibbling at the base of her tail. This friendly grooming went on for a short while and gradually others among the horses came to touch noses to the stallion or offer grooming. He flicked his ears as they came and went, chasing none off. The only ones who did not approach were the other stallions, who remained at their watchful distance.

Once again the black stallion raised his head to the sky, curling back his upper lip.

"Our turn," Damian said. "He's taking our scent."

"Wouldn't we have . . . I mean, shouldn't he have been concerned about us sooner?"

Damian chuckled. "And what could *we* do against him if he thought us a threat? No, lass, he knows we're no threat. And he's familiar with my scent."

The stallion left the herd and approached them, head lowered, each stride self-contained power. He halted and gazed at them through his long forelock. A breeze pulled on Karigan's hair and this time she didn't push it away.

Beside her, Damian knelt to one knee. "Greetings, Eolian," he said.

Karigan's own knees trembled, for she believed she looked upon something greater than a king, something not of this world. When she gazed into his eyes, she saw beyond simple intelligence, saw chaos and the infinite. The blackness of his eyes absorbed her, consumed her, and in a vision she saw the star-draped universe, and amid the constellations galloped the stallion, muscles flowing in midnight hues. Upon his back rode a winged warrior whose helm was the beak and visage of a raptor. Westrion, the Birdman, god of death.

All at once the vision was drawn from her and she felt empty inside, but the stallion still stood before her.

"Salvistar," she whispered.

He blew through his nostrils and a great gust of wind knocked Karigan right off her feet. When she hit the ground, she could feel the throb of hoofbeats rise up through the earth. When she sat up, the stallion was gone, and all was as it had been before.

WIND DREAMS

"You all right, lass?" Damian asked.

"I'm—" Karigan wiggled her fingers and toes to make sure she was whole. She dropped the fading and at once the world became awash with color. Unfortunately, a wicked headache pounded in her skull, the result of using her special ability. She rubbed her temple. "I'm all right."

Damian hooked his thumbs in his belt and did a good job of looking unconvinced. "I hope so, or my Lady will let me have it. Gave me a scare, you did."

"You mean the fading?"

"Though I'm aware of Rider magic—now don't give me that look, lass—that was strange enough for my old eyes. But no, that wasn't it. You completely *vanished* for a few minutes. Thought you were gone for good."

Karigan rose to her feet, feeling shaky. The pressure in the air was gone and she could breathe easier. The saber stabs of pain in her head ought to subside soon—she hoped so, anyway. Jericho and Fergal descended the ridge, Ero running before them. When the wolfhound reached her, he sniffed all around her feet, then with a bark, reared up and planted his massive paws on her shoulders, nearly knocking her over. He gazed down his muzzle into her face, his dark eyes deep and unfathomable, as if trying to look into her soul. After a moment of this, he bathed her face with several slobbery kisses. By the time Jericho and Fergal joined them, she was laughing too hard to fend off Ero's show of affection.

When all four of Ero's feet were firmly planted on the ground once again, Karigan wiped her face with her sleeve, and caught Fergal staring at her with a glower.

"Well?" he demanded.

"Well what?"

"What was all *that* about? The vanishing?"

She scratched absently behind Ero's ear, not really certain herself. "I saw the stallion—the patron."

"You had to vanish to do it?"

"I guess. I don't know. For part of the time."

Fergal continued to frown. "I didn't see him at all."

"It's all right, lad," Damian said, squeezing his shoulder. "Only a few do. You heard Gus say he doesn't, though I 'spect that'll change with time, and your captain never has."

Fergal brightened. "She hasn't?"

Damian gave him a solemn shake of his head. "And something more important happened today." He gestured over Fergal's shoulder, and there was the colt, taking tentative steps from his mother toward them.

Karigan watched as Fergal's face rippled from surprise, to anger, to uncertainty. He glanced to Damian for guidance. Damian reached into his pocket and found a piece of apple.

"Was saving this for my foxy Fox," he said, "but I think you should offer it to that young one and make a truce of sorts."

Fergal took the apple, and with a serious expression on his face, marched toward the colt.

"Softly, lad," Damian called after him. "Go softly. No sudden moves."

Fergal modified his pace, but even so, the colt retreated behind his mother. When Fergal glanced over his shoulder, Damian called, "Be patient."

Fergal stood in one place, and it wasn't long before the colt grew curious, first peeking around his mother's rump, then stepping away from her protection. Fergal stood his ground and Karigan wondered what was going through his mind, what thoughts were at war there. Would the colt win him over?

The colt moved forward, halted, took a few more steps,

then halted again. He must be as unsure as Fergal. Fergal held the bit of apple in his palm before him.

It took a few more steps before the colt came close enough to stretch out his neck and reach the apple with his lips. Fergal still did not move. Karigan wished she could see his face.

The colt lipped the apple into his mouth and crunched into it. In moments he swallowed it down and was inspecting Fergal's hand for more. With a movement as tentative as the colt's had been, Fergal reached with his other hand and stroked the colt's neck. The colt did not flinch or run, too interested in the lingering scent of apple on Fergal's hand. With more assurance, Fergal continued to stroke him.

"Now that's a vision," Damian said in a soft voice.

Karigan couldn't agree more—her cheeks ached from smiling so hard. As stunning as her vision of the stallion had been, this was the more miraculous sight.

They let Fergal and the colt get to know one another until the shadows began to lengthen and a frosty chill descended on the valley. The colt's dam hovered nearby, tail swishing, as if to say it was time for junior to end play and come home for the night.

Damian walked over to Fergal and put a hand on his shoulder. "You've got a good friend there, and no mistake, but now it is time to take our leave, for it will soon be dark and my Lady awaits us for supper."

When Fergal hesitated, combing his fingers through the colt's brushy mane, Damian added, "Not to worry, Fergal, lad, I'll bring him to you in the spring, and you'll have a long summer of training ahead of you. For now, trust in Sunny. She is as fine a beastie as one could wish for."

Fergal gave the colt one last stroke down his nose before turning away, Damian's hand still on his shoulder.

Lady greeted them in the doorway, lamplight gleaming around her. Her arms were crossed and she held a ladle. Aromatic scents of roasting meat and apple pie wafted past her into the night air.

"It's about time," she said.

Damian danced up the porch steps. "Lady, my lady, my dear, but we've had an eventful day on the plains among the wild ones."

She rolled her eyes and stepped aside. "If you find my roast tough tonight, you may blame yourself."

Karigan and Fergal went to their respective rooms to clean up, and when they returned to the kitchen they found Gus and Jericho already seated at the table, and Ero sprawled in front of the hearth. Damian carved a roast of lamb and as the juices flowed from it and the cutting revealed pink meat, Karigan did not expect it would be tough. Her stomach rumbled in anticipation.

Lady, trying to work around the hearth, placed her hands on her hips and declared, "Ero, you are *not* a hearth rug."

Ero's only response was to yawn and stretch his long body even longer. Lady shook her head.

Everyone ate as though famished. Ero abandoned hearth duty to sit beside the table. He was more than tall enough to rest his chin on the tabletop and gaze longingly at food as it was consumed by his people. Damian and the boys slipped him some scraps.

Meanwhile, Damian recounted to Lady the day's events.

"Did you see the patron, too?" Lady asked Karigan, her blue eyes intense.

"Yes."

Lady nodded as though she had expected all along that she would.

"I didn't," Fergal said.

Lady reached across the table and patted his wrist. "Maybe another time. You are both welcome to visit whenever you want."

Fergal brightened. "Really?"

"Really," she said. "As your duty to the king allows."

When dinner was finished and Karigan stood up to help clear the table, Damian motioned her to remain seated. "We have business, you and I."

Karigan nodded in understanding and excused herself to retrieve her message satchel from her bedchamber. By the time she returned, most everything had been cleared, and Lady was directing the boys to take a bucket of scraps out to the pigs. Karigan sat next to Damian at the quietest end of the table.

She removed a packet of papers and handed them to Damian, waiting while he inspected them.

"Ah, a letter from your captain." He read along, then, "Hee hee." He glanced up at Karigan. "I am to remind you not to drive a hard bargain. I had not realized you were from an important merchanting clan."

"We don't trade in horses," Karigan said with a smile, remembering the captain's admonition that she agree to whatever Damian asked for anyway.

"Heh, I guess that's lucky for me."

He read on, and when he got to the documents of trade, both he and Karigan signed in the appropriate places, and Karigan dripped wax on the document, which she imprinted with the winged horse seal of the Green Riders.

"Delivery will be late spring, early summer most like," Damian said. "There'll be some yearlings in the mix, including Fergal's little colt, as well as older beasties, which the boys and I will gentle over the winter so they are ready to train for service with their new Riders. The Riders will have to see to the overall gentling of the yearlings themselves beyond some halter training, but that's nothing new."

It was all new to Karigan. She wondered who would be in charge of training.

"I'll write Red a letter to confirm it all. It'll be ready by the morning."

The business concluded, the Frosts surprised Karigan and Fergal by entertaining them with music. Jericho fetched a beat-up fiddle and Gus took a pipe out of his pocket. Damian, muttering to himself, searched through the kitchen till he stood triumphant holding two silver spoons.

"Damian!" Lady cried. "My mother's good spoons!"

He grinned. "They make fine music."

Lady sighed and shook her head, and the music began. While the Frosts did not possess the finesse of the students of Selium, they played well-known, rollicking tunes to which all could sing. Lady's voice was a lovely counterpoint to Damian's gruff baritone and even Fergal sang well. Karigan, tone deaf as always, sang quietly, content herself to enjoy the others and clap to the rhythm.

The last song of the evening was sung solo by Lady, with only Jericho accompanying her on the fiddle. The song was slow, full of long notes textured by a haunting melody. The lyrics took Karigan back to the plains, past the broken towers of Kmaern where the wind blew in mournful voices. She returned to the valley with its trickling stream, and farther beyond the song led, to the wide open and lonely expanses, touched by lightning and blanketed by blue-black storm clouds. Then came winter and sheets of blizzard snow shrouding the scene, a band of wild horses trudging through it, heads bowed against the wind, their coats plastered by snow and ice. Then it was spring again in the valley, newborn foals taking their first shaky steps.

On the song went, through a full cycle of seasons and from life to death. When Lady stopped singing and the last note on the fiddle sighed to fading, Karigan sagged on her seat, exhausted. No one spoke and everyone looked as though they were awakening from a dream. Except Ero who snored by the hearth.

It was no wonder Lady could sing the horses in, considering the spell she'd put them under.

Karigan regretted that in the morning she and Fergal would have to take leave of the Frosts to continue on their journey.

After the music, Karigan stepped outside for some fresh air. Wrapped in her greatcoat against the piercing cold, she sat on a weathered plank chair that faced the nothingness of night. The porch roof obscured much of the sky, but just below the eave hung a few stars.

Legs stretched out before her and hands tucked beneath her armpits for warmth, she wondered about her day, about the wild horses, and about the stallion. Had she really seen what she thought she saw? Had it been some sort of dream? And if not, could it have been Salvistar for real?

She'd never felt one way or the other about the gods, mostly because her father hadn't. He supported Corsa's chapel of the moon, but mainly to enhance his standing in the community. No one had made her attend chapel, not even her aunts, and the prevailing G'ladheon wisdom seemed to be, "We don't bother the gods, so they don't bother us." That wisdom held, until now.

Karigan was torn. Part of her wished she'd been made to attend chapel so she could better grasp what she'd seen, or hadn't seen, this afternoon. The other part felt that she'd rather not invite god-beings into her everyday life by invoking them in chapel. No good could come of drawing the attention of gods to oneself. And yet it may have happened anyway.

The front door creaked open and in the flash of lamplight, Karigan saw Lady draped in a heavy shawl.

"May I join you?" she asked.

"Of course."

The door closed and all was darkness again. There was a scraping as Lady pulled a bench near, then a groan of old wood as she settled onto it. At first neither of them spoke, and silence reigned but for the sigh of the wind and an owl hooting somewhere in the distance. They were content enough in one another's company that they did not have to fill the night with chatter.

After a while though, Lady did break the silence. "I can only guess what you are thinking about, but I should not be surprised if it's about what you saw on the plains today."

"Yes."

"I thought so. The plains are not just grass and sky, though it may seem so on first appearance. They are different, powerful, dangerous even. I have always believed that some echo of the war magic used during the last great battle of the Long War remains in the land. The land does not easily forget the death and suffering, the blood that was spilled onto it, and sometimes I can feel it through the soles of my feet, the power that still remains in the soil. There are the lost Kmaernians, too, whose cries I sometimes hear in the wind."

Karigan could make out Lady's shape, but not her features. "You don't think it's just the wind?"

"I choose to believe that I hear more than the wind," Lady said. "I think Damian does, too, but he will not speak of it readily, for the cries are full of despair. We both have faith in our perception of things, you understand. Damian's gift of perception, and his trust in himself, makes him the horseman he is."

The bench squeaked as Lady shifted her position. Starlight gleamed in her eyes. "Maybe we are crazy old coots, Damian and I. Maybe we've lived on the plains too long. Some say the plains can play tricks on you, like the desert lands where you see mirages shimmering in the sun. Maybe it's just the wind on the grass making you see a horse running there, or storm clouds building castles on the horizon. Wind dreams, I call them, those things you think you see."

Yes, wind dreams, Karigan thought. She preferred to believe her vision of the black stallion had been nothing more. Maybe they were all mad, sharing in the same delusions. It was easier to accept than to believe she came face-to-face with a god-being.

"There are wind dreams," Lady continued, "but I choose to believe that not all you see out there can be discounted as such. Much happened on the plains and the land does not forget. And there are many layers of the world. It makes sense to me that in some places those layers are thin, or even intersect. Maybe that great battle of ancient times changed the natural order of things, thinning the layers, making them merge."

Karigan shuddered, and it was not from the cold. She did not think she'd like to live anywhere near the plains. Too many shadows, too many ghosts. Yet her beloved Condor came from the plains.

She turned her thoughts to Lady's words about choosing

to believe her perceptions. Karigan wondered if she chose *not* to believe her vision of Salvistar, the experience would cease to exist. Somehow, she didn't think it would work.

"Does your perception," Karigan asked, "aid your skill in herb lore?"

Lady chuckled. "You are right to call it skill, for it has been taught down a long line of the women in my family. Well, some of the men, but mostly the women. I have no daughters to pass it on to, but Gus has taken a little interest, though both boys are more apt to chase after their father in pursuit of wild horses. Perhaps I'll take on an apprentice one day, or one of my sons will give me a granddaughter."

"Then it *is* skill," Karigan said, feeling awkward. "I mean, after my fall, you helped me heal."

"Skill, knowledge, and *knowing,*" Lady said. "My grandmum started teaching me when I was just a bitty thing. Born in the lake country of Rhovanny, I was."

Karigan heard no Rhovan accent in her speaking, and so was surprised.

"My father was Sacoridian and a farmer, and when I was young, we moved here to the western edge of Sacoridia. My mum continued to teach me all through my growing up." Lady paused. "Are you worried I have more than mere skill?"

"Not worried, precisely," Karigan said. "Wondering. We've a Rider . . . well, he doesn't ride—"

"He *what?*"

"He's afraid of horses."

"Oh, my!" Lady said. "I've never heard of such a thing. Damian will be most interested."

"Yes, well, when he became a Rider, his special ability was to enhance the mending skill he already possessed." Karigan didn't feel she was betraying anything by discussing Rider magic since Damian already showed himself well aware of it. She assumed Lady must know as well. "I was wondering if maybe . . . if maybe you had that kind of ability."

Lady did not respond immediately and Karigan thought

she'd offended her hostess, but when Lady at last spoke she did not sound upset, just thoughtful.

"There are the seen and unseen. Skill and that which goes beyond skill. And that is all I can tell you."

Lady suddenly declared herself chilled and rose to enter the house. Before she did so, however, she added, "Not all is certainty in our world, Karigan. If it were, there'd be no opportunity for faith, and then it would be a very dull existence."

Lady left her confounded in the darkness. She had not received a definitive answer. The seen, the unseen, perceptions . . . She groaned. Maybe she was better off not mulling over such things and should just accept each day for what it was.

Problem was, if she really saw Salvistar, it could only mean trouble. Like Karigan, the death god's steed was a messenger, but he brought only one message: strife, battle, death.

THE WALL SPEAKS

From Ullem Bay to the shores of dawn, we weave our song in—
Disharmony.
From Ullem Bay to the shores of dawn, we—
Discord.
He is there. We feel it.
From Ullem Bay—
Can he hear us?
Do not seek his help. Do not trust.
Hear us. Help us. Heal us.
He does not hear.
See him. He betrayed us.
We see.
Look well. He is evil.
We watch.
Do not trust.
We see.
We watch.
We are blind.

PATTERNS

Ever since his experiences in Blackveil, Alton had slept poorly, if he was able to sleep at all. There were the fevers and nightmares, and those were augmented by the anxiety that glutted his mind with what-ifs and visions of everything ending in catastrophe. If he tried to sleep, the entire wall failed and Mornhavon rose above the rubble like a vengeful god who would bring all of Sacoridia to heel.

Often Alton was up before dawn pacing in his tent, the platform boards creaking beneath his feet, or he'd try to devise possible solutions in his journal, but the entries always ended in more frustration. He'd broken dozens of pen nibs by stabbing the pages.

Sometimes he went to the tower, the encampment as quiet as a sickroom, the third watch the only souls up and about. However, battering his will at the wall had proved just as futile as scheming in his journal had, so he decided to try something more productive. Sometimes he split wood for the cook fires; mindless repetitive work that allowed him to use his feelings of aggression productively. Grateful cooks made sure he received an extra hearty breakfast for his efforts.

Other times he saddled up Night Hawk to inspect the wall in either direction. He wrote his observations in his beat-up journal, and all of this before Dale had even rolled out of her cot.

The early morning sojourns did make him feel as if he were contributing something. The soldiers regularly patrolled along the wall but they were watching for more obvious signs of encroachment from Blackveil, such as monstrous creatures finding their way through the breach.

Alton focused more on the wall itself, particularly the cracks on either side of the breach. He measured and recorded their growth, which was often minute, and while he could not ascertain how deep into the stone these cracks bore, he had to assume they went all the way through the thickness of the wall. He was not reassured by his observations, for the cracks did progress, but at least he was doing *something,* something that was potentially useful.

As a side benefit, he knew Night Hawk enjoyed the excursions, and the gelding eagerly greeted Alton on the mornings he went on inspection rides. Riding Night Hawk, the companionship and the movement of his steed's strides, soothed him.

One morning Alton stood at the site where tendrils of the cracks terminated, somewhere midway between the breach and Tower of the Heavens. The rising sun dimpled the granite facade with gold as he finished up his measurements and recorded them in his journal, the sound of Night Hawk pulling at grass somewhere behind him.

When he looked up from his writing, he almost dropped the journal. Maybe it was the change of light, but it looked like . . . it looked like the cracks had formed a pattern.

He stepped back a few paces and changed the angle of his gaze, thinking it would either clarify or erase the pattern, but there it remained: a pair of large eyes, formed by the cracks, staring back at him. No matter which way he moved, the eyes seemed to follow him.

He strode rapidly along the wall, gazing at the cracks along the way, and more eyes watched him. The more he looked, the more eyes he saw, and he began to make out whole faces etched into stone. Sad faces, angry faces, tormented faces. All faces of despair.

He halted, trembling, then backed away from the wall ready to bolt, but Night Hawk had followed him and Alton had only to reach out to touch the gelding. It grounded him.

What do they want? he wondered.

He could not tolerate their stares for they seemed to accuse him of something, of everything, stripped him naked, their gazes abrading his soul. He mounted Night Hawk and urged the gelding toward camp at a canter.

LIBERATING THE ARM

Each day Dale checked the tower as she had promised Merdigen she would, despite the tremors that assailed her whenever she passed through the wall. Every heartbeat she believed her last and that she'd be sealed in granite for all time, only to emerge breathless in the tower chamber and find it empty, its silence and stone walls oppressive. She did not linger, and the wall guardians did not hinder her passage, but she felt them observing her.

When she returned through the wall to the encampment, Alton awaited her as always. There he stood, watching her intently, hands clenched at his sides. He was looking better. It wasn't just the polished boots, but his hair no longer stuck out at angles, and he took pains to neaten his uniform, shining the buttons and cleaning stains, mending tears and frays, and attempting to press out wrinkles.

Dale smiled, pleased by Alton's overall appearance. It was an improvement, though he still fell into gloomy silences and remained intense about the wall. Some things, she reckoned, she could not influence. The place, with its forbidding wall and nightmarish forest beyond, had the tendency to suck the life out of one. What they needed was a party. A party would lift everyone's mood, maybe even Alton's.

"Merdigen?" he asked.

"Not back yet."

"What was he thinking?" Alton demanded. "He can be of no help to us if he's haring off to wherever—wherever illusions go!"

"He said he'd return," Dale reminded him.

"How do we know?"

Dale sighed. "How do we know anything? Sometimes you have to accept a thing on faith."

Alton opened his mouth as if to retort, but then closed it. "There's something I'd like you to see," he said.

He took her into the encampment where a servant stood waiting with a mule hitched up to a wagon.

"I know you can't ride yet," Alton began.

"Not *allowed* to ride," Dale corrected.

Alton smiled. "Not allowed, so we're using the wagon."

He helped her up onto the bench, then climbed up himself and collected the reins. To her surprise, instead of heading toward the makeshift road that led to the main encampment at the breach, he slapped the mule with the reins and whistled it toward the wall, then turned so they headed west, in the direction of the breach. Alton's uncle, who had been in charge of the encampment before his death, initiated clearing along the wall, the soldiers and laborers under his command chopping down trees and burning brush to a distance of several yards. When Alton came to the encampment, he ensured his uncle's work continued.

It was in this clearing between wall and forest that Alton guided the wagon. It was bumpy and hard going over stumps, rocks, and uneven ground, and it jostled every single bone in Dale's body. She would have had an easier time on horseback, but Leese wouldn't allow her to ride. Alton remained silent throughout, not explaining what this little excursion was about. His hands seemed to shake, though it was hard to tell with the jarring ride. Something was eating at him, that was for sure.

The wagon pitched and swayed as roughly as any boat in an unrelenting sea storm, the wall always oppressive and cold at their left. Dale was never so relieved when, miles later, Alton reined the mule to a halt and set the brake. He came around to her side of the wagon and helped her down. Her old drover friend Clyde would approve.

She followed Alton to the wall. "What do you see?" he asked.

Dale withheld a sarcastic reply and examined the granite expanse before her. She did not know exactly how far they had come in the wagon, but there were cracks feathering the surface. She knew they were spreading all the time, no matter how minutely, evidence of the weakening of the wall.

"I see cracks," she said.

Alton nodded. "Yes, cracks. Anything . . . odd about them?"

"No," Dale replied.

Alton narrowed his brows and stared hard at the wall. "You sure?"

Dale glanced at the cracks again, seeing nothing different about them from others she'd observed closer to the breach. "I am sure. Why?"

"It's just that—" Alton scratched his head. "It's just that I think I see some sort of pattern in the cracks. Or at least this morning I thought I did."

Dale glanced uneasily at him, and back at the wall. Sure, she could see patterns, like watching puffy clouds passing overhead that looked like birds, faces, ships, and any number of things, but she did not say this to him. She wondered just how deeply his obsession was affecting him.

He shrugged. "My imagination." He helped her up into the wagon for another torturous ride back to their encampment, during which he fell back to brooding.

Dale scarcely touched ground in the encampment when the mender Leese approached with a wave.

"Rider Littlepage," she said, "just the one I wanted to see."

"Uh oh," Dale said under her breath, but she smiled. Leese no doubt wanted to check the progress of her healing wound, which meant painful prodding of still tender flesh and having to demonstrate the flexibility of her arm and shoulder. She'd lost so much strength that her visits with Leese often left her exhausted and in tears. Leese was most sympathetic and patient, but in equal measures thorough.

"Time to check on my wound?" Dale asked, hoping maybe the mender had something else on her mind for once, like an invitation to tea or the recommendation of a book for Dale to read.

"The usual," Leese replied. "Today, though, I want to take special care and time. If you could join me in my tent in a couple minutes?"

"Of course," Dale replied, then groaned as Leese walked off.

Alton glanced at her in surprise. "Is Leese not treating you well?"

"Too well. I must be her only patient. Why can't anyone else around here get sick or break a leg or something?"

Alton sat before his tent doodling in his journal. He mulled over what he'd seen in the cracks in the wall, the patterns. *Eyes.* And faces. Some of these he drew with their tormented expressions, but he was no artist and he scribbled them out. When he'd taken Dale to see the cracks and she saw nothing unusual, he became unsure of his perceptions. He couldn't make out the faces either. Maybe he hadn't been looking at them at the right angle, or the sunlight was different, or . . . He just didn't know anymore. Perhaps he obsessed over the wall so much it was influencing him in odd ways. Maybe he really was cracking like his cousin Pendric. Those rumors were still being whispered around camp.

A commotion distracted him from his scribbles and thoughts of patterns and cracks. Dale emerged from Leese's tent and declared she was *free,* followed out by the grinning mender. It took several moments for Alton to realize the sling and bindings had been removed from Dale's arm.

"Look," she said, flexing her arm for him and others who gathered around her.

"She's not to overuse it," Leese cautioned, "and she's still to wear the sling for a portion of the day."

Dale rolled her eyes. "It's not like I'm going to start flinging a sword around or hauling granite."

Leese looked mortified by the mere suggestion. "I should hope not! It would undo all the good work."

The next thing Alton knew, Dale was announcing it was time they had a little party to celebrate. An "arm liberation party," she called it. The cooks of both encampments began pooling supplies, and some off-duty soldiers went hunting and actually returned with a stag, several hares, and some grouse. Alton donated his aunt's gift of whiskey and his own supply of wine, but it did not take long before Dale had him peeling potatoes. The cooks who had taken a shine to him after all his wood chopping joked with him, teaching him a bawdy song, and teasing him when he blushed.

Both encampments perked up as anticipation of the event spread. Life at the wall was a serious affair, with danger never far and the fear of the wall's demise hanging over everyone, but this respite was welcomed by all.

Dale was here and there, supervising the fire pit over which the stag would be roasted, directing the collection of wood for a bonfire, and the making of benches to sit on around it. She rounded up various personnel with musical ability and instruments and got them practicing, which picked up the spirits of all who heard them even more. She dashed by Alton's work station and grabbed a potato.

"Look!" she cried, and she threw it into the air and deftly caught it. "I can do this now!" Then she tossed the potato to him and sprinted off to the next thing.

She was a dervish if Alton had ever seen one.

It was dark by the time preparations were ready. Wonderful aromas wafted through the encampment, making mouths water, and torches and lamps encircled the party area giving off festive light. Dale even coaxed some idle soldiers into cleaning out pumpkins and gourds and carving faces into them. Everyone donated candles and soon faces both humorous and grotesque glowed at them from the shadows. The faces reminded Alton of the cracks in the wall and he shuddered.

The soldiers on guard duty worked out their shifts so all could have a turn enjoying the festivities, and Alton was astonished but pleased by the high spirits exhibited by all as they feasted, sang, and danced, all in celebration of the liberation of Dale's arm. He knew it was just an excuse she made to raise morale. She was always up to such things at Rider barracks, keeping everyone laughing and coming closer together as family. The seriousness of this place, and her own frightening experience of being trapped in the wall, must have been too much and she deemed the time ripe to break the spell.

Even as Alton was gladdened by the sight of such frivolity, he found himself edging away from the light and gazing toward the heavens. One half of the sky was cut off from view by the looming silhouette of the wall, but the other half was filled with stars. The music and laughter of the party faded away as he became lost in thoughts of his purpose in life and how he seemed to be failing at it. He couldn't fix the wall. The cracks kept spreading. And was he mad because he thought he saw eyes in the wall?

He was even a failure as a friend. In an inner pocket, he kept Karigan's letter, still sealed and unread. He feared what he might find in it: words of anger, words of spite. He'd treated her terribly when they last parted; at the time he remained under the trickery of Blackveil. Those dreams still plagued him, still painted her as the traitor who almost made him destroy the wall, but as time passed, he knew those dreams to be lies, poison, and slowly the dreams held less and less power over him. He feared, however, what he had done to his friendship with Karigan—maybe because he wanted it to be more than friendship.

That's what this was all about, wasn't it? This trying to defend the lands from Blackveil. It was about preserving friends and family, all those things he valued and loved, and he'd practically thrown it all away.

"Here you are."

Alton started. He hadn't heard Dale's approach.

"The party's back there," she said. "We've lit the bonfire."

"Just needed some quiet," he said.

"I think you've had a little more than enough quiet if I do say so myself. It's fine and good to brood about the future and what's on the other side of the wall, but sometimes you have to let it go for a little while to remember why it's so important to worry in the first place."

Alton glanced at her in surprise, though all he could see of her was her outline sketched by the light of the bonfire. Hadn't she said aloud what he had just been thinking?

"How about it?" she said. "There's still some apple pie left."

And she grabbed his arm and led him back into the light.

ITHAROS

Dale toddled into Tower of the Heavens the next day with a dull headache. She was hungover from last night's party, but not nearly as miserable as Alton, who drank freely of his aunt's whiskey and danced the remainder of the night away, even into the morning hours. The poor fellow came to her at breakfast with a pinched expression on his face and looking a bit green around the edges to ask if she was ready to check the tower. She smiled. It was worth it, worth it to see him let loose. She would find another excuse for another party somewhere down the line, but maybe remind Alton not to imbibe so freely. Maybe.

Because she was distracted by these happy thoughts, or by her own hangover, she nearly fell over when she stepped into the tower chamber to find a figure clad all in black floating menacingly above her with its caped arms spread wide like bat wings. She screamed and plastered her back to the wall.

The figure descended to stand on the floor and two pale hands emerged from sleeves to pull the cowl away from its face. *His* face. It was framed by silver hair and a beard like a shipcat's ruff. His nose was long and his eyes so pale they were nearly white.

"Who?" she demanded. "Who are you?"

He swept his cape around in a manner that could only be called elegant and said, "I am Itharos of Glacea Toundrel, that is Tower of the Ice, seventh east of Ullem Bay. I am watching the cat."

For several moments Dale could only stare. "Of–of course. You are one of Merdigen's mages."

"I do not belong to Merdigen."

"No, I mean, you are a member of his order. The same one he belongs to."

"Ah, yes. I see. I am. Did he not tell you of me?"

"He, uh, did not give me any names, just to expect company."

"So like him," Itharos said with a dramatic sweep of his cape.

"I'm Dale Littlepage."

"Yes. Merdigen's message mentioned you, by name I might add, and that you would visit from time to time. Now Rider Littlepage, I have missed much as I slumbered and Merdigen's message was terse, but I sensed during my passage that all is not well with the wall. You'd best begin with King Eridian. He just ascended the throne." Itharos conjured himself an ornate and comfortably cushioned chair fit for a king, and with a flourish he threw his cape over his shoulders and sat, waiting expectantly for her to begin.

Dale swallowed hard. King Eridian? She didn't remember a King Eridian . . .

Fortunately Itharos was forgiving when it came to lapses in her knowledge of history. Eridian, it turned out, was the first of the Sealender kings.

"He did come of the sea," Itharos said, "a seafarer and fisherman from the east, and he was called the King of Fish by those of noble blood who thought themselves loftier than he. Accordingly, he took as his personal heraldic device a flatfish of gold so the nobles would never forget who he was." Itharos laughed heartily. "And I expect they did not forget. By all accounts his reign was off to a good start."

Dale didn't know how many Sealender kings there had been, but she knew how the line had ended, with the beginning of the Clan Wars, and Dale filled him in.

"Disappointing," he said, stroking his beard. "All I know of the Hillanders is that they, too, were of the sea, but from the more tame Ullem Bay."

"Sacoridia has done well under their rule," Dale said, and she continued to relay to him all the major events that led to her sitting in Tower of the Heavens with him.

"Fascinating," Itharos said. "A pity we were not awakened sooner or that the corps of wallkeepers was not maintained. A pity, but not really surprising."

"Why?" Dale asked.

"Human beings are naturally flawed when it comes to time and memory. The past is forgotten, or it is believed bad things will not recur, and people become bound in their current problems. That which afflicted the grandfathers of their grandfathers is a distant, dim thing, and not as important as present concerns, no matter how trivial."

"You sound like someone who knows," Dale said. She found Itharos more to her liking than grumpy Merdigen. He bore himself with greater dignity, which made him seem more like a great mage ought to be.

"You must keep in mind," he said, "that I've existed for centuries in one form or another. I have seen the forgetfulness time and again." He tapped his chair's arm with a long fingernail. "The greatest mistake that I've seen in all my time, however, was forgetting the upkeep of the wall, and the danger it holds at bay."

He straightened suddenly in his chair. "Someone comes."

Dale glanced around, expecting Alton or another Rider to pass through the wall where she had entered, but Itharos rose and strode to the center of the chamber next to the tempes stone, drew his cowl over his head, and did the menacing, floating thing again.

Someone did enter the tower, but not through the wall, rather emerging from beneath the archway to the east. The figure was clad in oilskins and wore a squall hat like sailors used in foul weather. The figure, a woman, Dale thought, was drenched and left puddles with each step she took, her oilskin boots clomping on the stone floor.

She paused before Itharos and looked up at him, water runneling off the rear brim of her hat. She stared, and he floated for what seemed like forever, then they both broke out laughing.

Itharos drifted to the floor and threw his cowl back, and stretched his arms wide. "Boreemadhe, my dear! I am so happy to see you."

The two hugged. "It has been a while, hasn't it?" the newcomer said. Even with Itharos standing on the floor, she was very short, almost squat.

Itharos put his arm around her shoulders and brought her to Dale. "This is Boreemadhe," he said, "and Boreemadhe, meet Rider Littlepage."

"Pleased," the woman said. "I am the guardian of—"

"Don't tell me," Dale said. "Tower of the Rains."

Boreemadhe clapped, spraying illusory drops. "Yes! Tower of the Rains. So nice to be *here,* where it is dry." She proceeded to peel off her oilskins, which vanished as she dropped them to the floor. Last off was the squall hat, revealing a round elfin face and eyes that creased to crescents when she smiled. Underneath her oilskins she wore a fisherman's sweater, the cuffs rolled up, and a long woolen skirt. "I feel I must have moss growing behind my ears."

Itharos checked. "No, my dear, you do not."

"Are we the only ones who've arrived?" Boreemadhe asked.

"So far."

"Then perhaps you can catch me up on what this is all about."

A full tea service appeared on the table, as well as another chair exactly like Itharos', and the two sat to tea. Dale wished it wasn't just illusion as she wouldn't mind a cup herself. She was enlisted to once again fill in the missing gaps of history, with occasional comments from Itharos. She wished Alton could be here to do the telling, and she hoped her long absence wasn't driving him mad.

When she finished, Boreemadhe said, "I did notice the guardians were most, erm, grumpy, during my passage. Off-key, as you will."

Itharos nodded solemnly. "A most apt description. There

is anger, resentment, and fear among them. I should hate their song to unravel altogether."

Boreemadhe nodded emphatically. "That would be the end, wouldn't it?"

"The end?" Dale asked.

"The song," Boreemadhe said, "keeps the wall whole, strengthens it, gives it life, so to speak. As it stands, the song's harmony is fragmented, the rhythm chaotic from some quarters. Think of the guardians as a chorus. As the disharmony spreads, as it inevitably will, the wall will weaken."

"The song," Itharos added, "is becoming a lament of sadness, and presently the guardians are on a path of despair and self-destruction." He closed his eyes, his hand outstretched, wavering, as if there was something he felt on the air. "Darkness and despair." He shuddered and opened his eyes.

Dale excused herself and told the two she'd return the next day. As she sank into the tower wall, she heard them carrying on like old friends after a long separation. As if, she thought, the imminent danger to the wall, and to them all, were a passing thing.

SHIP IN A BOTTLE

The seeker ghosted through the woods, weaving between spruce and pine, wafting toward the canopy on updrafts only to spiral downward and continue its journey through the shadows, a tail of crimson and gold light streaming behind it. Thursgad, riding his weary horse, followed it; had followed it for days upon days through impossible and wild terrain as the glowing red ball illuminated the most direct path to its destination.

"Direct" did not mean "easy," and the hungry, exhausted man on his stumbling steed bemoaned the fact that the seeker rarely led him along roads. Down ravines, up ledges and hillsides, through tangle of wood, yes, but not along any civilized path. Not that there were many roads or maintained pathways in the thick of the Green Cloak.

Hunger and exhaustion were meaningless to the seeker. It existed for the sole purpose of leading Thursgad to the book of magic Grandmother desired. Her other spell, tucked in its purse, hung from his belt. Maybe his imagination got wild now and then, but sometimes he swore he felt the thing hungering, hungering for his blood, pulsating against his hip. It made him shudder. He followed Grandmother's explicit orders not to handle it or look at it. Not until he had to.

The seeker flared. It had brought Thursgad to the edge of a clearing. He half dismounted, half fell from his horse, and tied the reins to a branch, then dropped to the ground and crawled to the very edge of the woods, staying in the shadows.

A cry of surprise almost passed his lips and he put his hand to his forehead thinking he must be fevered and seeing things. A grand manor house of stone and timbers rose up before him, occupying well-ordered grounds of lawn and garden. He blinked his eyes to make sure he wasn't dreaming, but the place did not vanish. What was it doing here in the middle of the wilderness? He scratched his head. There'd been no roads, no paths, and this was no simple woodsman's cabin.

The seeker circled his head like a biter looking for blood, impatient for him to move on. He swatted it away and continued to survey the scene before he stepped from his concealment. He did not want to be caught by the estate's inhabitants.

He saw no signs of life except for threads of smoke twining into the sky from a few of the chimneys. The manor had quite a few chimneys, as a matter of fact. The seeker buzzed around his ears.

"Aye, I'll go," he muttered to it, and crept across the clearing.

The seeker led the way to a side entrance framed by a trellis of rambling rose vines. The roses were done for the season, their fruits fallen and shriveled. Sweat streamed down Thursgad's face as he imagined the vines closing down on him, wrapping around him, the thorns biting into his flesh.

Should've run away to Rhovanny, he thought. *Could've joined a merc company there.*

The seeker flitted beneath a green door and Thursgad paused, looking around before reaching for the door handle. It was crafted to look like the looping rose vines and he shuddered, but all he felt when he grasped it was cold wrought iron. He cracked the door open and peered inside. No one was to be seen, just the seeker bobbing in the air, waiting for him. He stepped inside and found himself in a large kitchen. The seeker sped off.

Thursgad had to run to catch up, passing ovens and tables and pantries, then into a formal dining room with a lengthy table. He had no time to pause to take in the details of the rich furnishings for the seeker floated out of the dining room into a wide corridor. There it hovered for a moment.

Entry hall for main entrance, Thursgad thought. Sunshine flowed in through the windows that framed the grand doors. Opposite the doors, stairs climbed to upper levels. Across the hall from the dining room was a parlor.

Which way? he wondered.

As if in answer, the seeker pulsated and whisked up the stairs. Thursgad placed one foot on the first step and his hand on the railing when someone behind him cleared her throat.

"Look, sister, we've a guest just in time for tea."

"I'm not blind yet. I can see him very well for myself."

Slowly, very slowly, Thursgad removed hand from the railing and foot from the step, and turned around. Two elderly ladies stood there in the light of the entry hall gazing at him. The taller thin one in green scowled at him and the shorter, plump one, wearing a sort of orange dress, smiled kindly.

"He is pungent," the thin one said.

"Yes, and dirty."

The thin one cast the plump one a withering look. "Pungency suggests dirt, sister. Letitia will not be pleased, but he's no time to bathe. Tea is ready *now.*"

Thursgad glanced around for this Letitia to appear, but she did not.

"We shall overcome his scruffy appearance," the plump one said, "and we shall be brave in the face of Letitia's wrath." She walked toward him. He flinched as though she carried some weapon, though of course she possessed nothing of the sort. She took his arm and started to lead him into the parlor, her sister following behind them, cane tapping on the floor. "Now, young man, you must tell us all about yourself."

Thursgad sweated as he'd never sweated before. The porcelain teacup and saucer, decorated with dainty flowers, were slippery in his hands. He sat perched on the edge of a plush chair and sun rippled through the leaded windows, catching in his eye. The two ladies, one of whom was called Miss Bunch, and the other Bay or Miss Bay or Miss Bayberry—it all rather confused him—kept up a chatter that filled his ears with noise. He wondered where the seeker was, how he'd allowed himself to be drawn into the parlor for tea, and how he would get away from the ladies and find the seeker. Would he have to kill them?

"Pardon?" he said when one addressed him and he hadn't been paying attention.

"Your name, young sir," the Bunch one said. "And where you are from. You never told us."

"Thursgad. My name's Thursgad."

"Such a strong name, isn't it Bay?"

The thin one shrugged, her expression sour. Thursgad sweated.

"And where are you from?"

"Mirwell Province."

The two women exchanged glances. A droplet of sweat rolled down Thursgad's nose and plopped into his tea.

"I thought his accent was of the western parts," Miss Bay said.

"It is so long since we've had a visitor from that region. I'm surprised you recognized it."

Miss Bay's expression turned to one of superiority and she sipped her tea. Thursgad still hadn't touched his.

"And what brings you this way?" Miss Bunch asked.

Thursgad cleared his throat, trying to think fast. "Hunter. That is, I'm hunting." Pleased with his own answer, if not the delivery, he relaxed a tad.

"With a sword?" Miss Bay demanded. "It's not even a hunting sword."

Thursgad looked down as though seeing his sword for the first time. It was his serviceable sidearm issued to him when he first joined the Mirwellian provincial militia.

"Uh, for–for brigands," he said. "Aye, brigands."

"Sensible," Miss Bunch said to her sister. Then, "Young man, you've eaten nothing. Poor Letitia will be most affronted if you don't try some of her delicious treats."

Thursgad's stomach grumbled in response. It seemed like he had not eaten in days, so he took a tea cake into his calloused hand, the lines on his fingers and palm etched with dirt and pine pitch, and ate all the buttery, sugary goodness. Next he tried a finger sandwich and then a slice of pound cake. He tried this and that until there was little more than crumbs left on the platter, the sisters watching him in amazement. He brushed powdered sugar from the bristles on his chin, and swigged down the last of his tea.

"Must not be a very good hunter if he's that hungry," Miss Bay said acidly.

"My, but one forgets how much nourishment a young man requires," her sister replied. "He must stay for supper."

"S–supper?" said Thursgad. Sweat trickled down his temple anew. Supper sounded good—he could eat a couple moose about now. The tea dainties only served to whet his appetite. But this was complicating his mission. What of the seeker? He fingered the pommel of his sword, wondering if he should just kill them now and get it over with.

But he couldn't. They were old and harmless. Well, Grandmother was old, but not harmless. Looks could be deceiving. Still, he couldn't bring himself to draw his sword.

"He needs a proper cleaning," Miss Bay said. "I will not sit at table with him until he has bathed."

"Agreed, sister. Hunting is dirty business, is it not?"

Before Thursgad knew it, the ladies led him to a bathing room with a hip tub already brimming with steaming water.

"We shall rummage through father's old trunks to find you something suitable to wear," Miss Bunch said.

Thursgad reflexively glanced at his clothes, stained and caked with mud, damp with sweat.

"Enjoy," Miss Bay said, and she swung the door shut.

He listened at the door as their voices receded.

"Where is Letitia?" Miss Bunch asked.

"I believe she is sweeping upstairs," her sister replied. "The library needs particular attention."

When Thursgad could no longer hear the ladies speaking, he found himself tempted by the bath. He dipped his hand in the hot, fragrant water. It would feel so good to be submerged in it, to let him warm his bones and relax his muscles. He sighed, the mere thought bringing on a sensation of pleasure.

Then he recoiled. Was he some kind of fool? Had the ladies bewitched him somehow with their chatter and tea cakes? What kind of place was this that appeared like a magic castle in the middle of nowhere? Not to mention he normally detested bathing.

Thursgad slipped his hand through his lank, greasy hair. *Bewitched. I'm bewitched.*

As much as the bath and thought of supper beguiled him, he must not fall any further under their power. He must complete his mission at all costs.

He squeezed his eyes shut and drew a deep breath. Then resolutely, he turned his back on the bath and headed to the door. He cracked it open to make sure no one was about. The corridor was empty. He tiptoed out, retracing his way through corridors hung with portraits of knights and noble persons and past rooms with fires lit in cobblestone hearths.

When he found himself back in the main entry hall, he glanced from side to side, and then trotted up the stairs to the second floor. The place was unnaturally quiet. Maybe the sisters had gone to take naps. That's what old ladies did, wasn't it? But what of the servants? There was at least one—Letitia. And how did these ladies maintain the estate without the help of men? Yet he'd seen no sign of a single servant. Were they invisible or something?

Thursgad snorted at the idea and decided not to worry about the servants. If he saw any of them, he'd kill them.

The upper floor was lined with doors. Would he have to open each one to find the seeker? He despaired of the time that would take, and the increased chance of discovery. If the sisters found him, he'd have no choice but to kill them, too, and he really didn't want to.

The first door he opened revealed a comfortable looking bedroom with a canopied bed. The second door opened into another bedroom. When he opened the third, a cacophony of geese blasted him. He slammed the door shut, a few feathers drifting into the corridor.

"By all the hells," he muttered, shaken. Then he saw the inscription on a brass plaque mounted on the door. He could read very little, but he knew these words: *Goose Room.* He scratched his head, and moved on.

He had his hand on another doorknob when the seeker swept down the corridor and circled and bobbed around him like a dog happy to see its master. It then flew back the way it had come and Thursgad charged after it.

The seeker paused before a door then darted through the keyhole. Thursgad hoped the door was not locked because there was no way he was going to fit through that keyhole. He twisted the doorknob. *Not locked.* Carefully he pushed the door open, hoping it wasn't another goose room, or something worse. There was an inscription on the door, but he didn't know the word.

All was quiet within, much to his relief, and he stepped into the room, which contained the most amazing array of books he'd ever seen. He'd never been in a library before, and never knew so many books existed. Walls of books. Books that would take a lifetime to read. If he could read, or at least read well. As Thursgad stood there, surrounded by leather bindings dyed in reds and greens, yellows and blues, with their silver and gold embossed lettering brought to gleaming life by the sunshine that filtered through a window, he felt very stupid, ashamed he was uneducated. Sarge was always calling him a "rustic bastard," and here Thursgad knew it was true.

There were other objects in the room: a telescope pointed out the window, a fancy harp embedded with shiny jewels, a scrimshaw carving, and a ship in a bottle, all set out like artifacts in a museum, or so Thursgad could only guess, for he'd never been in a museum either.

The seeker, however, was not interested in any of those things. It bobbed up and down and pulsated to a deep red to catch Thursgad's attention, then floated to a book and turned it aglow in red.

What I came all this way for, Thursgad thought.

He pushed a ladder on runners to the location, climbed up, and pulled the book out. The leather was a natural, warm golden brown with no fancy lettering on it. He opened the book but found it contained only blank pages, except for some handwriting on one page. That was it. Even as he told the seeker this better be the right book, it extinguished itself, leaving him on his own.

He descended the ladder only to see something more frightening than a room of geese—a broom wielded by invisible hands flying at him. He barely had time to fling up his arm in defense when the broom descended on him.

"Ow!"

He scampered to and fro to avoid the broom as it swatted him. He bumped into the telescope and knocked it over. Its precious lenses smashed to bits when it hit the floor. The broom smacked his head and he yelped. He jumped out of the way to avoid another strike and the broom swished by him, sweeping all the objects off one of the tables. The harp thudded to the floor, emitting the most unearthly notes, like voices humming.

Down came the broom again and again. He headed for the door, but staggered into a side table that held the ship in the bottle. The table keeled, the water in the bottle cresting and washing over the ship rails. The miniature sailors on deck scrambled for handholds. *Sailors?*

Thursgad watched in horror as the table teetered on edge, the bottle sliding, sliding . . . He couldn't move, was unable to stop the inevitable. Even the broom paused, hovered in place. It felt as though all the air had been sucked from the room.

The table pitched over and the bottle smashed to the floor, expelling its contents in a wave across the carpet. The house itself seemed to heave a great sigh as a breeze tousled Thursgad's hair. He imagined he heard the cries of all those sailors and the crashing of surf.

Then the broom came after him again and he found himself splashing through water, water that kept rising, was even now rising to his ankles. How could it be? The bottle wasn't that big. He smelled brine in the air, gulls cried . . .

He sloshed through the water, the broom assaulting his head and shoulders. He finally escaped through the door, water rushing out with him. He pelted down the corridor and leaped down the stairs. He didn't dare look over his shoulder to see if the broom followed. He didn't care—he just had to escape the house.

He ran through the kitchen with its oven emitting wonderful aromas and flew out the door for the woods, his prize tucked safely beneath his arm. Even in all the mayhem, he had somehow managed not to drop it.

"It was a yellow warbler, I told you," said Miss Bay.

The sisters ambled across the stone bridge and along the drive that led to Seven Chimneys.

"What would a yellow warbler be doing here at this time of year?" Miss Bunch asked. "You know full well they've all migrated south."

Miss Bay lifted her chin and sniffed. "Not all. I know what I saw."

"You can't have seen it, sister, it is just not possible. All the warblers have gone."

"Hmph."

"Really, if you saw a warbler, then I'm a trout."

Miss Bay gave her an appraising look. "You are a trout."

Miss Bunch pouted.

They paused before the grand old house their father, Professor Erasmus Norwood Berry, had built for their mother long years past. It was as fine a country manor as one could find in more populous regions, surrounded by gardens and plantings the sisters had cultivated over their lifetimes. The gardens had been put to rest for the season by Farnham, the beds buried in mulch.

"I for one miss the warblers," said Miss Bunch. "It shall

be another long, dreary winter, though I suppose the blue jays and chickadees will entertain us."

"And the seagulls!"

"Really, Bay, you must stop lying about birds."

But Miss Bay raised her bony arm and pointed to the sky, her gaze unwavering. "I do *not* lie about birds."

Miss Bunch followed her gaze and gasped. Seagulls, instead of smoke, were issuing from the chimneys and wheeling about the roof.

"I spoke too soon, I fear," Miss Bunch said. "But what are seagulls doing flying from our chimneys?"

Miss Bay made a squeaking noise, rather like a broken scream, a sound Miss Bunch had never heard her sister make before.

She turned her attention back to the house and discovered what upset her so—water smashed through windows and poured out of them in spouts. Her hand went to her heart. "Oh no! Mother's fine things!"

"Father's library!" Miss Bay echoed.

They glanced at one another in horror.

"The bottle," Miss Bunch whispered.

"Is broken," Miss Bay said.

They turned to hobble away from the house as quickly as possible. Behind them the house quaked, more sea water pouring through windows and doors, and flooding the gardens. Tall masts smashed through the roof sending slate tiles flying and scattering seagulls. The front and back of the house exploded outward, the walls crumbling into piles of broken timbers and stone rubble, making way for stern and bow of a sailing ship. A mermaid figurehead seemed to watch the sisters as they hurried away.

Miss Bay and Miss Bunch retreated down the drive and across the stone bridge. The sweet brook that flowed beneath it was rising rapidly.

"Whatever shall we do?" Miss Bunch wailed.

"Hide!" Miss Bay snapped. "What do you think those pirates will do if they find us?"

Miss Bunch whimpered. "We should never have taken in that young man. Nothing good ever comes from Mirwell."

"I fear you are correct, sister," said Miss Bay. "For once. Who knows what other mischief he got up to in father's library."

Now Miss Bunch moaned, but her sister grabbed her arm and dragged her into the forest to hide from pirates.

TO MIRWELLTON

It hadn't been easy saying farewell to Damian and Lady as they stood arm and arm on the front porch of their house, Ero sitting beside them. Fergal especially looked melancholy as he and Karigan set off, their saddlebags bursting with food from Lady's kitchen.

Gus and Jericho guided them on the confusing network of trails to the main road that led to Mirwellton, and there they waved good-bye, leaving the Riders on their own. If Fergal was sad to leave the Frosts, Karigan dreaded this leg of the journey, at the end of which she would find her old school nemesis, Timas Mirwell, now lord-governor of Mirwell Province. He'd been spoiled and mean-spirited back in school, and she hated to think what a little power had done to him now. And here she was, more the commoner than ever in her Rider uniform.

It seemed appropriate that on the morning of their departure, a dusting of snow covered the hardening ground.

A week after leaving the Frosts, Karigan and Fergal arrived on the outskirts of Mirwellton beneath a sun that shed only cold light. The streets were churned and muddy and the buildings that lined it had a tired look, settled and sagging on their foundations, in need of a good whitewashing or fresh coat of paint. Above the roofs rose the blocky keep, which was the seat of power for the province's lord-governor, scarlet pennants streaming from the towers.

Though it was Karigan's right as a king's messenger to request lodging there, she had no interest in sharing the same roof as Timas Mirwell. She'd seek rooms at an inn for her and Fergal.

As they rode toward the center of town, Karigan knew she was being childish to worry about Timas in this way, but she'd never really gotten over his mockery of her and his bullying ways. She almost laughed out loud at herself. She'd faced down warriors and thugs, even battled groundmites, not to mention dealt with spirits of the dead, and yet Timas Mirwell still held this power over her, to heighten her anxiety and fill her with loathing. She could not let on about her feelings, however, especially to Timas. She would embody the professional demeanor of a Green Rider to shield herself against anything he might say or do to ridicule her. Her uniform would be her strength, not a symbol of servitude.

They entered the town's main square, which was paved and busy with shoppers. It was market day and the merchants hawked their wares in booths and beside carts. Dead chickens hung from one, while a nearby merchant haggled over sheep skins. Carcasses of pigs and cows were for sale, as well as tools and blankets and leather goods. Some dispirited looking farmers attended their carts of squashes, turnips, parsnips, and potatoes. Their supply was meager, and Karigan remembered Mirwell had had a poor season.

Nothing good ever comes out of Mirwell, was a common saying outside the province, and Karigan heard it most often uttered by her father. But it wasn't the fault of the common people, and she felt sorry for the farmers.

Looming over the market was an immense fountain with a statue in its midst, of a heroic mounted figure of some Mirwell or other in full armor bearing a war hammer. The statue might have inspired more awe in Karigan if pigeons weren't lined up on the war hammer and hadn't left white splotches all over the warrior's stern face. One pigeon roosted on the statue's helm like a living plume.

Karigan and Fergal dismounted in front of a likely looking inn on the town square called The Fountain. She secured Condor to the hitching post and stretched her back, watching shoppers moving from stall to stall. She wouldn't mind taking a look around herself. She could bring back some trinkets to amuse Mara.

She was thinking about how much currency she had left when Fergal gasped behind her. The next thing she knew, he was grabbing her arm and dragging her around the corner of the inn into a shadowed close.

"Fergal, what the—"

"Shhh!" he admonished her. "Did you see it?" His eyes were wide and he was visibly shaking.

"See what?" Karigan asked.

"Her."

"Her *who?*"

"Out there," he said, pointing toward the square.

Karigan went to the close entrance to look, but Fergal grabbed her again and yanked her back. *"Careful,"* he whispered.

What had gotten into him? Karigan pressed against the side of the inn and peered into the square. All was as it had been before—shoppers visiting vendors and pigeons sitting on the statue. A man bargained for a leather pouch at a nearby stall, and another purchased a pumpkin from a farmer. The scene was perfectly normal and could have been drawn in any Sacoridian town on market day.

"Fergal, I don't see anything."

He pointed a trembling finger toward the square, his face gone pale and perspiration beading on his temple. "There."

She saw a cluster of people, a man balancing a towering stack of hats for sale on his head, and a woman paying for a new stoneware pitcher. A little girl walked hand-in-hand with an elderly woman, her grandmother perhaps, as they browsed beautifully dyed yarns.

"Fergal—" When she turned to speak to him, he staggered against the wall.

"I–I don't feel so good," he said, and he fell to his knees and retched up his midday meal, and maybe breakfast, too. He hadn't complained of feeling sick before, and she was pretty sure he would have.

She steeled herself against the sour stench of vomit and knelt beside him, putting her hand on his shoulder. "You all right?"

He heaved once more, but nothing came up. He wiped his mouth with his sleeve, and when he looked at her, it was with an expression of horror that she'd never forget. He lurched away from her touch and scrabbled along on the cobbles, and collapsed in a heap.

Stunned, she followed after him. "What's wrong?"

He glanced over his shoulder at her, his eyes haunted. "Darkness. You sink into it—all dark." He hid his eyes from her.

What madness had come over him? Could a fever take hold and grip one in delirium so quickly? She grabbed a handful of his greatcoat and forced him to turn toward her, but he kept his gaze averted.

"Fergal!" she said, giving him a shake. Then she put her hand against his forehead and cheek, but he was not hot with fever. "Look at me, will you?"

He did not. She shook him again and he raised a hand as if to block a blow. Remembering his father the knacker, she released him and knelt before him. She gently put her hands on either side of his face to direct his gaze at her.

"Fergal, it's me, Karigan. Look at me."

He shut his eyes.

"It's just me," she said. "*Look.* The same Karigan you've been traveling with."

He blinked and cringed. "Dark wings," he whispered. A tear trailed down his cheek.

His words rattled her. What was he seeing? And why? "Whatever it is you see," she said, "push it away, block it out. See *me*—Karigan, in green."

Fergal tensed and squeezed his eyes shut, then with a shudder, looked at her again. He was about to speak when another's presence entered the close.

Karigan whipped around with her sword half drawn, but she found only a man in an apron with an ale cask on his shoulder.

"There a problem?" he asked.

"My friend here is sick," she said. It was true enough. "Do you work at the Fountain Inn?"

"I'm the proprietor," he said.

"Then we'll be wanting a couple rooms if they're available."

The rooms were cramped and the mattresses stale, but Karigan didn't care. She made Fergal get into bed and brought up some broth for him. He wouldn't look at her directly.

She sat in a chair, arms crossed.

"S–sorry about this," he said, gripping his mug as if it were an anchor to reality.

"Do you still see—?"

He nodded. "Darkness. Around you."

"Around anyone else?"

"No. Well, except the old lady."

"What old lady?"

"The one in the square. I pointed her out to you."

Karigan drummed her fingers on the armrest. There'd been numerous old ladies in the square shopping. "And you saw darkness around her, too?"

"Aye. No." He started gagging again. Karigan rescued the mug from his hands before broth sloshed over the brim and scalded him. He curled his hands into fists and regained control. "I saw . . . all the worst things, vile things that crawl and slither. Dead things, dying things. The vermin that live on corpses." He shuddered.

When it seemed he wouldn't have another reaction, she returned his broth and dropped into her chair again.

"What's wrong with me?" Fergal asked in a plaintive voice.

"Would you like to hear the whole list?"

It took him a few moments to realize she was joking, and he relaxed. "Guess I deserve that."

She shrugged. "You haven't been the easiest of traveling companions at times."

"I know." He looked into his broth.

"What I think your current problem is," she said, "is that your special ability has emerged."

"What? This? Making me sick?"

"Well, I don't know what *this* is. I mean, I don't know what the nature of your ability is, but it's the only answer I can think of. The sickness, I think, is a reaction to your ability coming out. We talked about this, remember? My headaches?"

Fergal frowned.

"Hopefully your reaction," she said, "won't always be so severe." On impulse she asked, "The darkness still there?"

"Fading," he said. "I keep trying to push it to the back of my mind."

"Is it . . . is it like what you saw around the old woman?"

Fergal shook his head. "Different. Like night. Endless. And there were the wings . . ."

Karigan shuddered as his voice trailed off. She had not realized how taut she'd been. "I guess we'll learn more if anyone else makes you sick."

She tried to make her words light, but as she left his room for her own, she knew that when one's special ability emerged, it was often in response to a life-threatening situation. Not always, but often. She wondered what Fergal's reaction saved them from this afternoon, and what his vision of darkness around her meant.

GOLD CHAINS

The next morning, Fergal declared over breakfast he was back to normal and claimed he saw nothing unusual when he gazed upon Karigan, though he seemed hesitant to look her way, like he might see something he didn't want to. He was steadier on his feet and his appetite had returned with a vengeance. As he stuffed yet another flatcake into his mouth, Karigan hoped nothing would trigger his newfound ability—whatever it was supposed to be—and make him sick.

After breakfast they readied their horses and rode from the square, which was empty and forlorn without the market, but for the pigeons lurking about and warming themselves in the sun that bathed the statue. Karigan felt obligated to give Fergal some warning of her past with Timas Mirwell, but she did not want to overplay its significance. As the horses plodded along Mirwellton's muddy main thoroughfare, which led to the keep, she explained that she and Timas were classmates at Selium and had not been friendly.

"In fact, he and his cronies made life miserable for a lot of students, mostly the commoners who were at Selium on scholarship. They felt powerless against a lord-governor's son."

"Is he the one you beat up?" Fergal asked.

"What? How do you know that?"

"Mel told me."

Condor's hoof sucked in the mud.

"Ah, of course she did. Well, I didn't exactly beat him up. I defeated him in a bout of swordplay. Soundly defeated him.

It was very satisfying." She smiled at the memory, then hastily added, "Don't bring it up or even allude to it while we're in the keep. Don't bring up his father, either."

Fergal thought for a moment. "Oh, aye, the traitor." He ran his finger in a cutting motion across his neck and grinned.

"Er, yes, the traitor. In fact, now that I think of it, it's probably best if you don't say anything at all. When we see Timas—*Lord* Mirwell—it's probably wise if you just stand there and look, well, Riderly."

Fergal scowled at her, but did not argue.

They rode on in silence. When they reached the portcullis of the keep's curtain wall, the scarlet-clad guards, who knew the insignia of the king's messengers, ushered them through without challenge. They were now truly in Timas' domain and Karigan's sense of loathing increased.

They rode across the courtyard into the shadow of the keep. The structure was simple, purely a fortress with high walls and narrow windows, all stone, and without embellishment. Unlike the king's castle, Mirwell Keep changed little from its original design over the centuries. It was made for war and Clan Mirwell had not deviated from its militant heritage. While some provinces did not possess even a provincial guard, Mirwell kept a sizeable army, or had until after the old lord-governor's attempt to dethrone King Zachary. By order of the king, Mirwell's militia had been diminished to a skeletal version of its former glory, and would remain so until the new lord-governor proved his loyalty beyond a doubt.

They halted and dismounted before the steps leading to the keep's entrance. A soldier took their horses while another stepped from the entrance to ask their business.

"A message for the lord-governor from the king," Karigan said.

"Follow me, please." The soldier turned smartly and trotted up the stairs.

Karigan hesitated and took a deep breath. The sooner this was over, the better. It was her duty, she reminded herself, and her real mission was not so much to hand over the message to Timas Mirwell but to make contact with Beryl Spencer. She straightened her shortcoat, threw back her shoulders, and climbed the steps at her own pace. She would not be cowed as if she were still a schoolgirl.

Stepping into the keep was like entering a cave, especially when the great doors closed behind them, shutting out the daylit world. A combination of torches and lamps offered smoky illumination, but the dark lingering in the corners was as heavy as the stone walls surrounding them. Just as well. There wasn't much to look at—a few suits of armor along the walls, faded tapestries recounting the glorious and bloody history of Clan Mirwell, and shields painted with coats of arms of the vassals that were protected by Clan Mirwell.

The soldier led them across the entry hall and a short distance down a corridor. Karigan closed her eyes for a brief moment to collect herself as the soldier knocked on a door. Without waiting, he entered.

"Idiot!" a voice shouted from within. "Wait until I give you permission."

The soldier backed out and reddened. "I'm sorry, my lord."

"You will be if this isn't important."

The soldier stiffened, swallowed hard. "My lord, messengers from the king."

A pause, then, "Very well. Out with you, Clara."

A feminine giggle trickled out into the corridor and shortly a girl, a few years younger than Karigan, emerged from the chamber, tying her bodice as she left. From her dress, coarse and plain, Karigan presumed she was a servant. She frowned.

"Let them in, stupid," came the harsh voice from within.

With a sympathetic look to the Riders, the soldier gestured they should enter the room. When they did so, he closed the door behind them. A surge of panic threatened to overtake Karigan until she forced herself to calm, and only then did she realize that the young man in front of them, who was buttoning up his trousers and tucking in his shirttails, was not Timas at all, but one of his friends from school.

"Barrett," Karigan murmured. He was sharp featured, tall and lanky, and had grown, or had attempted to grow, a sparse beard. She wasn't surprised to find him dallying with a servant. Rumor in school was that he had coerced many a poor girl into his bed with promises of his eternal commitment and of support for her family, but had only ruined her reputation and left her on her own if she became pregnant. One rumor claimed he'd told a girl to, "Drop the brat off a cliff for all I care." Karigan believed it.

"That's Lord-Steward Barrett to you, Messenger," he said.

Steward? The thought of him in so important a position disturbed Karigan, but it explained his being here in this office with its fine furnishings.

He squinted at her. "Do I know you?"

"Very unlikely, my lord." Karigan prayed he wouldn't ask her name.

"Then how did you know me?"

"The soldier." Karigan didn't like to lie, but right now her loathing of Barrett overrode her sense of duty. She did not want him to remember her. It was a small lie anyway, and wouldn't hurt anything. "The soldier told us."

"Oh." Barrett sat in his cushioned chair, crossing his legs and looking relaxed and self-important. He gazed at her expectantly.

"We have brought a message from the king for Lord Mirwell."

"Let's have it then," he said.

"I'm sorry, my lord, but the message is written in the king's own hand for Lord Mirwell's eyes only."

Barrett sat up, his expression one of displeasure. "But *I* am Lord Mirwell's eyes. *I'm* his steward."

"Duty requires I present the message to—" and here Karigan faltered, almost saying "Timas" "—to Lord Mirwell."

"Is it urgent? Life or death?"

"I do not know what the message contains, but I was not given to believe it was urgent." Truly, she knew the message was of little importance, for this exercise was really about giving her a chance to contact Beryl.

Barrett sat back again, tapping his fingers on the armrest, his gaze calculating. "Then you'll have to come back tomorrow."

"What?" Karigan was flabbergasted. No one had ever sent her away before a message, a message from *the king,* had been delivered.

"Tomorrow," Barrett said. "You can't expect Lord Mirwell to come at your beck and call. He's busy. He can't see you today."

No lord-governor or his staff had ever treated her this way. "But—"

"If it's not urgent, and if you won't leave it with me, you can try back tomorrow."

Karigan tried to maintain her composure. "Very well. Good day."

"Wait a moment," Barrett said before she could escape. "Are you sure we've not met?"

"Quite sure," Karigan said.

"Pity. Perhaps we'll get to know one another before you return to the king. It *is* customary for the lord-governor to offer lodging to the king's messengers—"

"We've already lodging in town. Good day, my lord." Before he could stop her again, she gave him a cursory bow and retreated through the door. She hastened through the keep and out the entry as fast as decorum allowed. She headed straight for the horses, being held for them in the courtyard. Once she and Fergal were off the keep's grounds, she sighed. Then she muttered some curses worthy of the sailors she grew up around on the docks. Fergal knew enough to stay quiet.

"That," she said, "was another of my schoolmates."

"So you *did* know him," Fergal said.

"Unfortunately. He was in Timas' circle, of course." She couldn't get over the sensation of slime coating her skin after being in Barrett's presence. "And unfortunately we'll probably see him again tomorrow."

Tomorrow she hoped to conclude their business here and return to Sacor City. Tomorrow she hoped she'd see Beryl. If she didn't, she did not know how to ask after her without arousing suspicion. But that was tomorrow's worry.

The next day found Karigan and Fergal mounting the steps to Mirwell Keep behind the same soldier as yesterday. An ache had begun building in Karigan's head throughout the morning. The thought of seeing Timas was bad enough but Barrett, too? As they crossed the entry hall, she glanced around, hoping to spot Beryl. Surely Beryl would have heard by now that two Riders had visited the keep. In hopes word would travel, Karigan mentioned to the soldier in a conversational way where she and Fergal were staying.

Once again they were led to Barrett's office, but this time he did not shoo a serving girl out. He appeared to be actually working, poring over some papers on his desk.

"Ah, you've returned," he said.

"We wish to deliver Lord Mirwell's message."

"I'm sorry, but you'll have to try again tomorrow."

"May I remind my lord that this is a message from the king?"

"You may, but unless you've changed your mind about leaving the message in my care, you'll have to come back tomorrow. Lord Mirwell cannot receive you today. He is busy."

Karigan bridled her annoyance and managed to take leave of Barrett without exploding. He was worse than most bureaucrats she'd met. She paused in the entry hall, almost tempted to search out Timas herself, and maybe find Beryl in the process, but one did not do such things when one was a Green Rider.

On their third visit to the keep, Barrett rose when they entered his office. "Well, well, the diligent Greenies are back."

Karigan wanted to smack the smirk right off his face.

He circled around her, closer than felt comfortable. She stiffened.

"Are you sure," he said, "we haven't met? What's your name, Greenie?"

Damnation, Karigan thought. She considered giving some false name, but that was not as simple a lie. She'd be found out. It would be dishonest and dishonorable to the king and the Riders. "Karigan," she said, not willing to give him her full name.

"Karigan," he repeated softly, standing to her side, close enough that she could feel his breath against her cheek. She forced herself to stare straight ahead. "Karigan. You know, that seems awfully familiar to me, an unusual name like that. What is your family name?"

Karigan wanted to squirm, run out, but by force of will she stilled herself. "G'ladheon, of Clan G'ladheon." She did not offer him her service as was customary and polite.

Barrett stepped back and barked out a laugh. "Oh, very good! How amusing. I remember you now. Selium. The good old school days. How could I forget? You were the little bitch that took Timas out in swordplay. I wish you could have heard all he said about you later that day, and all the things he swore to do to you if ever he saw you again. Unfortunately you ran away before he could carry out his revenge. But here you are now. How very interesting." Barrett's expression was one of pure delight. "We all said we'd help in his revenge."

Karigan turned to face him directly; looked him in the eye. "I am here on king's business to deliver Lord Mirwell a message."

"How it must gall you," Barrett said, "to be in so subservient a position."

"It is my *honor* to serve the king."

Barrett chuckled, and Karigan figured he had little use for "honor." "Timas, Lord Mirwell, is going to be pleased to see you again. Oh, yes, he most surely will. But not today."

"You're sending us away again?" Karigan asked in disbelief.

"Are you so anxious to see him?" Barrett moved in closely again.

Karigan rested her hand on the hilt of her saber. It centered her.

"Tsk, tsk," Barrett said, not missing the movement. "Seems the Greenie is feeling threatened. I might have to ask you to remove your saber. And perhaps other things, as well . . ."

"I'd remind the lord-steward," Karigan said, her voice now frigid, "that Green Riders answer only to the king, and the king does not take kindly to disrespect toward his own messengers."

"Too bad he's all the way in Sacor City with so many more worthy problems to preoccupy him than one lowly messenger." Barrett actually reached out to stroke her braid.

Karigan knocked his hand away and heard steel drawn. Fergal stood there holding his saber at the ready. Though taken aback, she hesitated only half a moment.

"Fergal," she said, "put it away." When he didn't obey immediately, she snapped, "*Now!* This one is not worth it."

Fergal sheathed his blade, though reluctantly.

"Did you think to spill my blood, boy?" Barrett demanded. "Did you? I should call the guards in right now to throw you into a cell and teach you a lesson."

"Lord Barrett," Karigan said, a tight smile on her lips. An icy calm had settled over her like a mantle. The headache was gone, her absurd fear of meeting with old classmates had dissipated. "The young man's name is Rider Duff, and I shall remind you that king's law supersedes all others. You will not imprison him. I don't think you comprehend how much the king values his own Riders, and he will certainly be informed of our treatment here. Never forget it was the king himself who meted out justice to Lord Mirwell's father."

Before the flabbergasted Barrett could respond, Karigan turned on her heel and walked out, Fergal falling in behind her. By the time they were halfway across the crowded entry hall, Barrett had regained his voice.

"Just you wait till you see Timas, bitch!" he yelled. "Then you'll be sorry."

Karigan shook her head in wonder at how childish Barrett sounded, and in front of all those soldiers, servants, and nobles, too.

At last, tomorrow, she could finally give Timas the dratted message and be done with it. If she didn't see Beryl? Then she'd have nothing to report when she returned to Sacor City and it would be up to Captain Mapstone to decide what to do next.

Beryl could not remember how she came to be here, or where "here" was. It was some sort of encampment, off in the haze around her. She hardly remembered who she herself was. She was caught in a spiderweb network of gold chains anchored to her flesh with hooks. If she moved a hand, it yanked on a hook embedded in her neck. If she shifted her leg, it buried a hook deeper into her back.

The gold chains were filament fine, exquisite, like something a noble lady would wear clasped about her neck, and Beryl couldn't say if they were real or imaginary, only that pain, akin to a razor slashing at her skin or a dagger sliding deep into muscle, racked her body at the barest movement.

So she did not move. She sat cross-legged on the ground, hands folded across her lap, and with her whole being, with everything she was, concentrated on not moving. The sounds of the encampment fled her hearing and she saw little beyond the haze. Maybe two or three times a day someone came and slackened the tension on her chains so she could relieve herself and eat the pittance of food they gave her. Trying to move her limbs at these times was almost as excruciating as the hooks grappling her flesh, and if she wasn't careful and moved beyond the loosed length of the chains, the hooks tore flesh, spread a whiteness of pain through her mind.

In truth, she did not even know if she bled. If the wounds were real.

She tried to envision pleasant places like lush valleys and serene lakes, her Luna grazing at pasture. These visions helped until she fell asleep. All the hooks ripped through her, leaving her in red agony until she could once again find the position that would prevent pain. She could not allow herself to sleep, and from then on recited marching cadences in her mind, all that she had learned throughout her military career, over, and over, and over.

The lack of sleep and too little food and water weakened her. She was too well-versed in dispensing torture not to know it was a matter of time before she gave in, but she had no idea what her captors wanted from her, for no one ever questioned her. Maybe it was torture for the sake of torture. At least when she utilized it, she was always after a confession or information. If she simply wanted someone out of the way, she killed them and did not make them suffer.

Once in a while she became aware of the Little Girl sitting on the periphery of the haze playing string games. Games Beryl once played when she was a child. Child? Had she really been a child once? Little Girl wove the strings about her fingers making designs until Beryl felt caught up in the strings; bound, prey in a spider's web, only the web was gold chains, beautiful and painful.

At other times Little Girl threw pebbles at her, trying to make her flinch. When Beryl learned to endure pebbles, pebbles became rocks, and Beryl thought the hooks would flay the flesh off her bones when she reacted to being hit in the face.

Sometimes Grandmother took Little Girl by the hand and led her away, scolding her.

Beryl was chanting the infantryman's basic half-time cadence in her mind when she became aware of two people standing on the edge of the haze.

"What are we going to do with her?" It was the gravelly-voiced man whom she was certain she knew, but she dared not divert her mind from the cadences to try and remember his identity.

"She's strong," Grandmother said. "We will leave her."

"We should just kill her. Or torture her conventionally. This is not useful."

"Now, now. Do not underestimate what you cannot see. She will break eventually, then we'll decide if she is useful to us. I'd like to discover the source of her ability. Long ago the Green Riders were ordered to give up their magical devices. Their maker, Isbemic, was forced to destroy them. Some deceit has been at work all these centuries and I wish to unravel it."

The voices ebbed from Beryl's hearing. There was only the rhythm of marching feet and the pain of gold chains.

AN UNEXPECTED MESSAGE

Much to Karigan's amusement, Barrett was still angry enough from the previous day's encounter that he communicated with her and Fergal using only single words and sharp gestures.

This time they were actually going to see Timas, and Barrett led them up a winding staircase. Karigan felt battle ready, almost eager to spar with her old nemesis, but she could not forget what she was and who she represented. It meant she must remain moderate in her words and actions, to always reflect well upon the king and the Green Riders. It was unfortunate to be constrained by her position, but there were other, subtle ways to nettle Timas.

She hoped Beryl would be there, beside Timas, as she'd always been for Timas' father.

The stairway opened into another corridor just as dark and narrow as anyplace else in the keep, lit by torches that blackened the ceiling with soot. The keep had a primitive quality to it that reminded Karigan of the abandoned, ancient corridors of the king's castle, but these weren't abandoned.

Barrett led them to the far end of the corridor where a large door with a raised carving of a war hammer breaking a mountain sealed off a room. He opened it and entered the room, the Riders behind him.

The lord-governor's receiving room was like a small throne room, long and narrow with an elaborate chair gilded in gold set on a dais at the far end, a hearth gaping behind it.

Armor and weapons displays lined the walls, along with portraits of, Karigan assumed, Mirwells through the generations.

In fact, the current lord-governor was having his portrait painted. He stood at the throne, a foot on the dais and one hand on the throne's arm. He held a war hammer to his breast—no doubt the clan's ancestral weapon from the Long War days. It was wood and iron, and unadorned, the handle darkened from centuries of use and, perhaps, blood.

Natural light streamed through a narrow window and onto his face. A velvet cloak of scarlet stitched with gold thread flowed off his shoulder and draped at his feet and beneath he wore the longcoat of a Mirwellian commander, dazzling with gold fringed epaulets, insignia, cords, gold piping, and elaborate oak leaf embroidery. Medals he certainly could not have earned in a single lifetime covered his breast and made his black silk baldric sag. At his hip he wore a smallsword that, in contrast to the plain war hammer, had a finely wrought swept hilt and a ruby set in the pommel and was sheathed in a jewel-encrusted scabbard.

Karigan took in that scene, then glanced over the artist's shoulder to compare it with the painting. The painting was well along and depicted Timas, his attire, and his surroundings in a realistic way, and yet more so . . . Maybe it was how the artist captured the light. There was a strong romantic feel to the rendering. Timas' face appeared more pure, as though he was blessed by the gods, and in fact the artist incorporated the crescent moon into the window leading, which was, in reality, made up of plain panels. Timas' hair was shown as more raven, his flesh more full of color, and most important, the artist made him appear taller than he was.

Karigan wanted to laugh, wanted to laugh at how ridiculous Timas looked in his getup, and at how little he'd grown since their school days. He was still short. She wondered what people would think of him from that painting a hundred years from now. They'd think him tall, noble, and even heroic. Timas had chosen his artist well, but truly, only his deeds in life would determine whether or not he lived up to that image.

In addition to Timas and the artist, there was an officer sitting in a lesser chair to the side, looking through papers. He was a colonel, and he was not, Karigan was sorry to see, Beryl Spencer. Where was she?

"My lord," Barrett said, "the G'ladheon bitch is here."

Someone, Karigan thought, ought to drop Barrett out of a tower window. The receiving room turned to silence except for the artist's brush *swishing* across the canvas. The colonel looked up. He was a hard man with those features—they appeared chiseled from ice. Unlike Timas, his scarlet uniform bore little decoration aside from his insignia, and his sword and sheath were not ornate but serviceable looking. This colonel was no fop but a genuine warrior.

"My Lord Barrett," the colonel said in a deceptively mild voice, "that is not how we speak of the king's messengers."

"With this one it is," Barrett said. "Besides, you can't tell me what to do, Birch. I'm lord-steward, if you remember, and you answer to me."

The colonel's mouth became a thin line, and it was difficult to read what went on in his mind, but Karigan knew Barrett was making a mistake by speaking to him in such a manner. The colonel did not look like one to tolerate fools, no matter their title and status.

"Barrett." It was Timas. The Noble One spoke, but did not alter his pose.

"Yes, my lord?"

"Shut up. Birch answers to *me*."

"But—"

"Would you like me to order Colonel Birch to shut you up?"

Barrett clenched and unclenched his hands, but he obeyed and said nothing. The colonel's mouth curved into a cold smile.

"Leastways," Timas continued, "we do not speak of the king's messengers in that manner while they are present."

Barrett sniggered.

Karigan felt Fergal stiffen beside her. Back at the inn she'd lectured him about not drawing weapons in the presence of nobles; weapons were only a last recourse when one's life was in danger. Insults did not count. She'd made sure he knew she appreciated his gesture of standing up for her yesterday, and in fact she'd been genuinely touched, but she needed him to understand that drawing a weapon in the face of mere words was not an option.

Barrett really could have imprisoned Fergal, and in prison he would have sat till she could obtain clemency from the king, which would have involved the journey all the way to Sacor City and back. Fergal, in the meantime, would be at the mercy of the Mirwellians. He had apologized and promised he wouldn't draw steel on Barrett unless he had to kill him. Fergal had looked as though he hoped an opportunity would present itself.

"You must excuse my steward," Timas said. "He is newly come to his position and has yet to learn discretion in public." He turned so he could see them, which cast his face into half shadow. The artist emitted a strangled, frustrated sound. "You may approach the dais."

Karigan had no choice but to bow to Timas, no matter how it rankled her, so she made it the most elaborate bow she could, bordering on mockery. A smirk grew on Timas' face.

"I'd heard you became a Greenie," he said, his voice quiet. "Seems fitting to finally see you bow to me."

Karigan ignored the remark. "I've a message from the king for the lord-governor." Saying it that way she did not acknowledge Timas was the lord-governor.

"Barrett," Timas said, "bring me the message."

He stood no more than a yard from Karigan, but would not take the message directly from her, as though her mere proximity would sully him.

Barrett appeared amused that Karigan had to give *him* the message after all. Karigan kept her expression cool. Barrett broke the seal, but before he could read the message, Colonel Birch stood with unexpected suddenness and swiped it from his hands.

Barrett scowled.

Birch scanned the message. "An invitation," he said, "to a betrothal feast." He handed it over to Timas and returned to his work as though the invitation was of no consequence.

Timas gave it a cursory glance and dropped it on the seat of the throne. "Betrothal feast, eh? We'll see, we'll see."

Colonel Birch looked sharply at Timas. A warning? Karigan couldn't tell. The dynamics in the room were strange, very unsettling. It occurred to her to wonder, in fact, who was actually in charge here.

"I'll write a response later," Timas said, and he took up his pose by the throne chair again. "I'll have it delivered to your lodging. Dismissed."

Dismissed? That was it? She was astonished, but before anyone could say another word, Karigan gave a shallow bow and swept out of the room, not waiting for Barrett to guide them. She and Fergal were hardly two steps through the door when she heard Timas and Barrett break out in laughter, no doubt at her. She couldn't worry about it. In the scheme of the world, their opinion of her mattered little—she had more important things to concern herself with. It was clear Timas and Barrett were still stuck in childhood. And Timas' getup! She found herself laughing as she strode down the corridor, Fergal giving her a sideways glance.

Outside the keep, Karigan and Fergal were directed to the stable to collect their horses. With each step across the courtyard, Karigan was increasingly glad to be done with the business and would be even happier to be on the road to Sacor City come morning. Once Timas' response was delivered to them at The Fountain, they'd be free of all things Mirwell.

In the stable there were only a few horses besides Condor and Sunny. One, a bay mare, turned agitated circles in her box stall. Condor bobbed his head and whickered, as if picking up on the mare's distress.

"What's wrong with her?" Karigan asked the stablehand, who was sweeping.

"Her mistress hasn't come around in a long while," he said. "Out on maneuvers or some such. Usually she takes the mare with her." He shrugged. "Luna Moth pines for her."

Luna Moth! Beryl's horse. Karigan had not recognized her. Why would Beryl go out on maneuvers without her? Separating a Rider from her mount was not done lightly.

"Is the horse sick or lame?" Karigan asked, wanting to ensure Luna's separation from Beryl wasn't due to something mundane.

"Nope," the stablehand said. "Perfectly fit."

Taking a chance, Karigan asked, "When is her owner due back?"

The stablehand shrugged again. "No one would tell the likes of me, but she's been gone a good while this time."

Karigan didn't like the sound of that, not at all. Was Luna trying to convey something in her agitation? She went over to the mare's stall and stroked her neck. She settled some, watching Karigan's every move. "Don't worry," Karigan whispered. She gave the mare one last pat, and led Condor from the stable. There was nothing she could do for Luna without arousing suspicion. Even if Beryl was all right, Karigan could not risk exposing the Rider's true affiliation as an operative of the king by seeming to know her or by asking injudicious questions.

She also had her orders. If Beryl could not be contacted, she was not to investigate further but to return to Sacor City and report to Captain Mapstone.

The common room of The Fountain was quiet as Karigan and Fergal finished their evening meal of stewed mutton. A few regulars sat by the hearth sipping their pints and tossing dice. Karigan mulled over the scene in Timas Mirwell's receiving room and fretted over the missing Beryl. Beyond Barrett's immature behavior and her natural loathing of Timas, she could not get over the feeling the one with the real power in the room was Colonel Birch. She wasn't concerned with provincial politics, but when it came to a fellow Rider who *should* be accounted for, who should have been present in that receiving room . . .

Karigan had not been privy to the reports Beryl had sent to the king and Captain Mapstone after Timas assumed the governorship, nor had she ever heard mention of a Colonel Birch, but she had thought everything in the province was going well. Until the silence.

"Are we going to look for Rider Spencer?" Fergal asked.

"Our orders are to return if we don't make contact," Karigan replied. She was both relieved and frustrated she could not investigate further. Relieved that the responsibility would fall to her superiors, frustrated there were unanswered questions, and worried that Beryl might be in trouble. She tried to console herself with the knowledge that Beryl was tough. Very tough, in a way Karigan herself never would be.

The inn's door opened, bringing in a draft of fresh night air and the sound of splashing water of the fountain. Everyone in the common room looked up, and in walked Barrett, followed by two scarlet-uniformed soldiers. Karigan sighed and the other patrons muttered among themselves.

Attired in fine silks and velvets, Barrett stood out like a rooster among sheep. He gave the common room a cursory glance, distaste on his face, and strode straight toward Karigan and Fergal once he spied them.

"I don't know why Lord Mirwell has me running this trivial errand," he said without greeting. "I am not accustomed to this." He stopped before their table, reached into an inner pocket of his frock coat, and bent down close enough to Karigan to whisper, "He sent me because he trusts me. I tried to come alone, but Birch made those other two come along." He barely nodded his head in the direction of the soldiers. "You will find more than one message here."

He then straightened, produced an envelope, and slapped it on the table. Aloud he said, "That is Lord Mirwell's reply to the king." Barrett turned and swept from the common room to the square outside, the soldiers right behind him.

Fergal leaned toward her and asked in a low voice, "What was that about?"

"I don't know," Karigan replied. She had a dark thought that Timas and Barrett were playing some game with her, but Barrett's manner was . . . different. And it confirmed what she was thinking in regard to Birch. Underneath the sealed message to the king, she found a folded piece of paper. She glanced around the common room. The other patrons were again absorbed in their games, but she made sure no one observed her placing the folded paper in her message satchel along with the official message to the king.

Only when she was back in her room did she dare look at the hidden message. It was short and mysterious.

"Well?" Fergal said.

Karigan glanced up at him. "It's signed by Timas, in his own hand. He says that he knows why we're really here, and that if we go to the Teligmar Crossroads at dawn, we will see something of interest to us."

"What in five hells does he mean?" Fergal asked.

"I assume it has something to do with Beryl," Karigan said, "though he could be playing some trick on me. But it just doesn't feel like a trick."

Fergal dropped into a chair. "So, are we going to this place?"

If it had something to do with Beryl, she could not ignore the note. "Yes," she said, "we're going to the crossroads. *Now.* I don't dare wait till dawn. While I think this is genuine, I wouldn't put it past Timas to have some unpleasant surprise awaiting us. If we go now, we can scout the area, then wait."

THE WALL SPEAKS

We sing our will to strengthen and bind.

Defeat.
No!
Cracking. Bleeding.
No! Listen to me. Follow me.
You unravel.
Sing with me.
Disharmony. Discord.
He must hear us. He must help us. He must heal us.
Do not trust. Hate him!
Hate . . . *Uncertainty.*
The struggle weakens us.
We are tired.
If we fall we can rest.
No! I strengthen you. *Us*.
We are tired.
We are dying.
We feel his heartbeat.

HEARTBEAT

Over the course of weeks, Dale met the rest of the tower guardians east of the breach as each arrived: Cleodheris from Tower of the Clouds, a serene and ethereal woman who spoke little, even as Boreemadhe sniped at her for sending so many clouds to Tower of the Rains; Doreleon from Tower of the Rivers, who played a reed pipe and never tired of fish tales; Fresk from Tower of the Valleys, who appeared younger than the others, if youth was of any relevance among magical projections; and finally, Winthorpe, from Tower of the Summits, the elemental mage who had long ago created running water in each tower for the benefit of the wallkeepers.

Merdigen remained absent along with the three other guardians to the west, and Dale was beginning to worry, but in the meantime she had been obliged to tell, over and over, the story of the breach in the wall, and update each new arrival on the course of history over the last two hundred years or so. By the time Winthorpe arrived, her tale was well-practiced.

After so many years of "sleep" and isolation, the tower guardians made up for lost time with parties. At any given moment, Dorleon might pull out his pipe and play a raucous tune on it, and Itharos would lead Boreemadhe around the chamber in a dance. Meanwhile, Fresk would take Winthorpe on in a drinking game in which both grew steadily more inebriated. Cleodheris presided over it all with extreme serenity.

One would never suspect, with all their carrying on, the wall was in fragile condition.

As practiced as Dale was in bringing the tower guardians to the present, she was equally rehearsed in telling Alton about each new arrival. He'd taken to recording notes in his journal, and often made her repeat certain details as he needed them, which was something of a trial. Once he'd actually followed her all the way to the latrine, peppering her with questions until she shooed him away.

Mostly Alton was interested in whatever she could glean from the guardians about their individual towers and what they knew of the construction of the wall, and what Dale received from them were variations of Merdigen's tale, of lonely exile, the murder of their fellow mages on the mountain, and the choice King Jonaeus had offered them. Then serious discussion would disintegrate when someone suggested a game of Intrigue or speculated on the position of the stars and the meaning of their formations and that of the periodic appearances of other heavenly bodies. Inevitably someone would produce parchment and pen from the thin air and start scrawling equations and geometric shapes that were beyond Dale. Their discussions were even more incomprehensible, one part philosophy and one part mathematics, and all more or less gibberish to Dale's ear.

Above all, they preferred parties, and when the wine and ale started flowing—wine and ale that did not exist and that Dale could not therefore enjoy—it was impossible to get anything worthwhile out of them, so she gave up in disgust, ready to grab bunches of her hair and rip it out, and left the guardians to their own devices.

And then she'd have to give Alton the details, such as they were, and repeat them over and over.

One night Dale slept comfortably bundled in her blankets, dreaming she was floating over beautiful hills and valleys, the landscape rolling along beneath her. She was overcome by a sensation of lightness and freedom. Until Alton called to her.

"Dale? You awake?"

She dropped like an anchor and awoke with a snort.

"Dale?"

She blinked at candlelight only to find Alton leaning over her. Gone was the joy of the dream.

"What's the hour?" she mumbled.

"Don't know," Alton said. "Late. Er, sorry to wake you, but . . ."

"I was flying," she said, her voice mournful.

At first Alton remained silent, then said, "Flying?"

"In my dream."

"Oh."

"It was a beautiful dream." She sighed. "What do you need?"

He wanted her to recall more of the equations the guardians had been drawing.

Dale raised herself on her elbow and regretted it as cold air seeped into the toasty regions beneath her blankets. "Whatever for?"

"Could be important," he replied.

"It has to do with the stars, not the wall." She fell into her pillow and pulled the covers up to her neck. "You know what I think? I think you should try to get more sleep."

"I can't," Alton said. "All I can think about . . . There's just too much going on in my head."

"Maybe Leese would make you a draught if you asked her."

"I don't want one," he said. "In case . . . in case some idea comes to me or something happens."

"No ideas will come to you if your mind is too tired to come up with them."

"You don't understand."

"I understand," said Dale irritably, "that you woke me up in the middle of a beautiful dream."

"Fine," Alton snapped, and the candlelight faded as he left Dale's side. "It's easy for you. You can get inside the tower and talk to the guardians. You don't have the weight of the wall and the destruction of Sacoridia on your shoulders." With that, he was gone.

Easy? Dale wondered. It was true that his burden was greater, and his frustration immense, but it was not so easy for her either, to play messenger between him and the party-happy tower guardians. And it wasn't as if she didn't know what was at stake—she knew all too well. She was not, however, going to feel guilty about it.

At least, not until reveille.

Alton had nowhere else to go. It was either back to his own tent or to the wall. He chose the wall.

He knew the way with his eyes shut, so walking through the dark with only weak illumination from the watch fires was not difficult. The guards nodded to him as he passed by. Otherwise the world was quiet and the air frosty, the encampment caught in stillness, stillness he could not bring to himself. He longed for that sense of peace, which he had not felt since the wall was breached. Back then, he'd known his place in the world and had no reason to doubt the future. The breach had changed everything, and all he could see in the future was disaster.

He paused before the tower wall. The granite shone in the starlight, and he slipped off the mitten his whiskey-distilling aunt knitted for him and pressed his palm against the rough, unforgiving stone. It was not fair that others should be able to pass through it and speak with the tower guardians. By all rights, by his *birthright,* he should be able to pass through the tower wall and communicate with the guardians, but now, as always, the stone before him remained mute in the serenity of the night.

He thought Karigan might understand his frustration better than Dale. She'd been on the other side of the wall; she'd dealt with the dark powers there. He almost reached for the letter still unread in an inner pocket and stopped himself. Yes, Karigan would understand the danger, he knew that. But he wasn't sure she would understand *him.*

Alton sat on the ground, leaning against the wall, his

cheek and ear pressed against it as if listening for a heartbeat, but he heard nothing, of course. In the morning he'd take a ride to inspect the wall and the breach. He had not seen the eyes in the wall since that one time, though he always felt watched and as if there were conversations going on about him just below his hearing. Maybe the eyes watched him when he wasn't looking.

He gazed above the fringe of treetops, toward the heavens and there shimmering across the sky was the greenish hue of northern lights. Alton wondered if maybe the gods were relaying some message, and though the lore of the land interpreted the lights in many ways, from good fishing to a long, hard winter, the gods did not speak to him.

In the quiescence, Alton's eyes started to close. He did not move, did not feel impelled to, and imagined himself turning to stone, a statue of granite, a memorial to the one who tried and failed.

He fell asleep there, leaning against the tower wall, the side of his face pressed against granite. Were he awake, he might have detected an answering gleam to the northern lights on the wall, an aura of green aglow around him that faded in a breath.

In the deepest places inside his mind, however, he did hear a heartbeat, his own in rhythm with that of the wall.

FLIGHT AND PURSUIT

Estora would never again bemoan her lot in life. If she were allowed to continue living it, that was. As far as she was concerned, her father, the king, or anyone else for that matter, could lock her in the castle and toss the key in the moat, and she would not complain. In fact, if she returned safely to Sacor City, she would obey her father, she would marry the king without argument, and light an extra candle at chapel in gratitude to the gods.

She rode with four ruffians. One of them usually scouted the way ahead, two rode with her front and back, and the fourth lagged to detect pursuit. Her hands were bound before her, numbing her fingers, making them swell, and her captors maintained a cruel pace, slowing only to spell the horses. She had never ridden so hard or for so long before.

She had lost track of the days since that horrible moment when the Raven Mask had appeared out of the fog to whisk her away to who knew where, only to be slain right before her eyes by the leader of the ruffians, who then grabbed Falan's bridle and swore that if she resisted, he would cause her grave pain. When she opened her mouth to scream, he'd slapped her across the face. She'd raised her riding crop to strike him, but he had wrested it from her hand and snapped it in half.

Her eye was still half-closed with the swelling, but the blow had not hurt as much as had the sound of crossbow bolts whizzing into the fog, followed by the screams of her entourage. Were her dear sisters all right? Lord Henley?

What of the stalwart Weapon, Fastion? Lord Amberhill? Had any of them survived?

Every time she thought about what must have been a massacre, tears threatened to cascade down her cheeks, but she was determined not to give in to them. No matter how much she longed to release all the emotions that had built up within her, she dared not reveal her weakness to her captors; she must not weaken herself.

So she rode on, through vast stretches of woodlands, along deer trails and dry stream beds, and beneath the boughs of giant white pines. Once she would have found the scenery beautiful and wholesome, but now she saw only the dull hues of approaching winter, the rusts and browns, the dying vegetation, and the sky crisscrossed by branches like an enclosing net.

She knew they traveled west, for they followed the fading sun, riding into the narrow shadows of tree trunks like cavalry into the waiting pikes of infantrymen.

The ruffians spoke little to her, or to one another. In their demeanor she saw military men though none wore any device. They called their leader Sarge and he rode just ahead of her. He set the pace, determined the length of their ride for the day, and spoke only to bark out orders. They were soldiers on a mission—a mission to steal her—and they knew the king would send a swift and deadly force after them. They were driven by the knowledge that their capture by king's men would result in the ultimate punishment.

The group would ride for a while after sunset until Sarge called a halt. Some of their campsites were stocked with supplies, food hanging high in trees. They'd planned her abduction well, not carrying more than they had to so they could travel light and swift. Once they stopped, the horses were tended to first, Sarge assisting Estora off Falan then helping her to sit before her legs buckled beneath her.

She was given no other courtesy, even when it came to relieving herself. Her captors did not allow her far from the campsite, and not entirely out of view. If she was lucky, there'd be a boulder nearby, or dense growth to conceal her in this most private function, but at other times, she had little more than the skirts of her habit to hide what she was doing.

The men did not care, but she always felt the tears fighting to take hold, and she continued to dam them up inside her.

This evening was like all the others that preceded it. The men went about their assigned tasks with nary a word between them. Two cared for the horses, one sparked a small fire that was used for warmth and nothing more, for they did not cook, and the fourth man who rode rear guard had not caught up with them yet.

Estora found a log on which to sit. It smelled of rot and was slimy to the touch, but it did not crumble beneath her weight. As the men worked, she rubbed and stretched her legs, though she noticed they were not feeling so absolutely dreadful as they had, and her back end was not nearly as sore. The top pommel of her sidesaddle, however, chafed continuously at her thigh, rubbing it raw, even through the doeskin breeches she wore beneath her skirts. She resolved once again not to complain. Doing so would only, like tears, reveal weakness.

When the campfire grew to golden life, she did not draw closer to it for warmth. Always she held herself aloof from her captors. The men more or less ignored her, didn't care if she was freezing or not, except to toss her a rough but heavy blanket for the night. Oh, how she missed her soft feather bed and comforter!

As she sat chewing on the night's ration of leathery dried meat, she thought of Karigan and realized she now had a much clearer picture of all her friend—former friend?—must have endured during dangerous missions. What a fool Estora was. Hadn't she once wished for the life of a Green Rider, to ride where she willed?

She almost laughed aloud. As if Green Riders had free will! They rode where and when the king commanded, no matter the peril. It's just that she hadn't understood it so completely until now.

The rear guard, Whittle he was called, rode into camp and

dismounted. He spoke quietly with Sarge by the fire. Estora could not hear their words. When they finished, Sarge spoke individually to the other men, then came over to her and planted his foot on the log beside her. He towered above her.

"Seems you've got a hero following us. Either he's a lousy tracker and keeps getting lost, or he's so stealthy Whittle loses all trace of him. Either way, if he comes too close, he'll be dealt with. If you should try to run off to him or scream, that will be dealt with as well."

"You've done little to harm me thus far," Estora said, "and I believe whoever you are taking me to has commanded it so."

Sarge caressed the hilt of his sword. "There is more than one way to deal with prisoners who misbehave. A gag for starters, and our method of tying you down, as well."

"You'd never—!"

"And I'm not past inflicting a certain amount of injury to accomplish what I must. Nor are my boys."

Estora's hand went to her swollen cheek.

"I suggest," Sarge said, "you behave like the fine, cultured lady you are, and things will continue to go smoothly for you."

"Who is it you're taking me to?" she demanded, not for the first time. But as usual, Sarge walked away without answering. What heightened her concern was that whoever ordered her abduction possessed an ability with magic, for the fog that obscured the woods when she was ambushed was no natural phenomenon. Sarge had only smiled knowingly when she asked him about it. Someone had given him a spell, but *who?*

Before Estora could prevent it, a tear slipped from her swollen eye.

Oh, F'ryan, she thought, *was it ever like this for you? Were you ever afraid?* If he had been, he'd never revealed his fear to her, and so she'd thought nothing could stop him. Until a pair of arrows had.

Thoughts of her dead lover only made her feel more forlorn and she bent till her forehead nestled in her hands. She considered her situation. She'd not been irreparably harmed, nor had her captors done anything inappropriate to her. They must be under *very* strict orders to show restraint. Who commanded such discipline from them? Who was it that ordered her abduction? And why? What would they ransom her for? Where were they taking her?

Mirwell Province lay in the west, and beyond, Rhovanny. Now that she thought of it, Sarge's accent, and that of his men, was of the west, but not of Rhovanny. If they were mercenaries, of course, it didn't matter where they were from. They could be working for anyone, whether in or outside Sacoridia.

She tried to bolster her spirits by reminding herself that at least someone pursued them, a "hero" Sarge called him. Who could it be? Then her spirits sagged again when she realized he'd probably be killed in his efforts to rescue her.

It all seemed so hopeless. *What would Karigan do?* she wondered. But she did not know. She hadn't the kind of courage to figure it out.

Remember honor, Morry had said.

Amberhill beat through the woods after Lady Estora's captors like a man possessed, until he realized the punishing pace would only kill Goss. Though his quarry wasn't careful about covering its tracks, his haste had led him astray more than once, wasting more time than if he'd gone at a more measured speed.

One of his accidental diversions had turned fortuitous when he ended up in the yard of a woodsman's cot. Famished and freezing, he knocked on the door. A gruff, dirty fellow opened it, and Amberhill could only guess at the man's thoughts as he took in a bedraggled, shivering nobleman on his step, holding the reins to a stallion of some breeding.

Amberhill pled for food and a place to rest for the night. He had been prepared for a pleasant day's jaunt with other nobles through the countryside, not a seemingly endless journey through the wilds of Sacoridia.

Grudgingly the woodsman allowed that Amberhill could sleep in the loft above his pair of oxen, and provided him with a skin of flat ale and half a loaf of hard bread. Thankful for even this little, he pressed one of the plainshield's gold coins into the woodsman's calloused hand. That night Goss deigned to share shelter with the oxen pair, munched on fodder provided by the woodsman, and drank water fresh from the well. Up in the loft, Amberhill finished off the bread and ale, and buried himself under the hay to keep warm. He'd really gotten himself into it this time, haring off after Lady Estora's captors when really he should have returned to the castle and let his cousin handle things.

But he couldn't. He remembered Morry dying in his arms, and those words he'd spoken. Amberhill had forgotten honor, he'd been so beguiled by the currency he'd been offered. Everything was his fault. His weakness had left Morry dead and a woman who did not deserve to be terrorized in the clutches of cutthroats. Only in hindsight did he understand there was no such thing as an "honorable" abduction. There probably hadn't even been a noble involved to begin with—none would have been in his right mind to order the abduction of Lady Estora. Greed had clouded Amberhill's judgment. He should have listened to Morry.

Grief now drove him to avenge Morry, and to make right the wrong he committed against Lady Estora. Exhausted, he slept deeply through the night and well into morning. When he arose, he climbed down from the loft to discover the oxen and their harness gone and some gifts from the woodsman—food, another skin of ale, and a sack of grain for Goss, as well as a rough, but warm, woolen cloak.

"Thank the gods," Amberhill said, throwing the cloak around his shoulders. The woodsman must have been pleased by the gold coin and thought to better supply Amberhill for his journey. Thankful for the kindness, the gentleman thief left a second gold coin on the woodsman's doorstep.

Before he set off on another day of pursuit, he buckled on his swordbelt with rapier and parrying dagger. Concealed beneath his clothes, up sleeves and in his boots, were more weapons. He may not have been prepared for traveling cross country, but he was always ready to win a fight.

Amberhill retraced his steps and searched for the trail of his quarry. He was indeed a gentleman thief, not a wilderness tracker, but with patience, he found the trail. There were at least three sets of horse hooves. He believed there must be more in the party, but he could not tell for certain.

He clucked Goss into a jog, fearing his side trip allowed Lady Estora's captors to establish a substantial lead. He knew Zachary must have sent out his own pursuers and that they were somewhere behind him, but he would not give up. This was personal.

By evening, Amberhill found the remains of a camp, the blackened fire ring cold. He could only surmise they had almost a day's lead on him. Could be worse, he thought, and could be better. At least he found clear evidence of their passing.

The autumn days had grown short, and though Amberhill desired to go on, he reined himself in. Trying to track in the darkness, especially without the benefit of a bright moon, would plainly be stupid. He'd lose the trail, probably become lost altogether. He had no idea of where in the wilderness he was, and losing the trail would be disastrous in more ways than one.

He dismounted Goss with a sigh, giving in to common sense. He'd camp here this evening—in the cold without a fire, for he'd brought no flint with him—and continue his pursuit at dawn.

He saw to Goss' needs, then huddled beneath the woodsman's cloak in the deepening dark. Before the light dissipated entirely, he pulled the locket from his waistcoat pocket. He'd found it on Morry during a hasty search of his friend's body and thought it too curious to leave behind. In his desperate dash through the woods, he'd forgotten all about it.

Engraved on the gold of the locket was a rose, and Amberhill guessed Morry had a secret love. He was stunned, for he thought he'd known everything about the older man, who seemed to revel in his bachelorhood. He'd been well-provided for by Amberhill's grandfather and lived comfortably.

Amberhill hesitated to open the locket, thinking it invasive, then scolded himself. Morry was dead. What would he care?

Amberhill opened the locket. In one half he found a delicate braided curl of auburn hair. In the other half was a miniature portrait of his mother. His insides fluttered with pangs of grief for his mother, whom he still missed, though she died ten years past of a poor heart. He'd always thought that his father broke her heart from all his gambling and drinking, and she'd died desolate and starved for love.

As Amberhill gazed at the locket, he thought maybe it had not been so after all. He recalled those terrible days of his mother's final suffering. He'd been seventeen, just entering his manhood. His father, as usual, had been absent, out somewhere mounting up debt. The one he remembered always being nearby, providing company and care for his mother at the end of her days, was Morry. Morry who had loved her. With this token in the palm of his hand, Amberhill realized she must have loved Morry in return.

He snapped the locket shut and returned it to his pocket. He felt a lightness within him, that his mother had found comfort despite her husband and his shortcomings. He glanced skyward at the stars shining through the canopy of the forest, thinking that now Morry and his mother were together once again, and for eternity. If there was any justice in the world, his father spent his time in the hereafter crawling from hell to hell, tormented by demonkind.

Such thoughts brought Amberhill peace, and after a spare meal of bread, cheese, and flat ale, he slept.

The next morning, it was not dawn that awakened him, or even the whinny of his agitated stallion, but a blade at his throat.

PIRATES

"He a pretty one, aye."

Six of the most disreputable characters Amberhill had ever seen glared down at him where he lay, smelling of fish and their own unwashed bodies. Their hair and beards fell in stringy snarls and their clothes hung off them in tatters, practically rotting off their bodies. None wore shoes, and Amberhill very much doubted they possessed enough teeth among the lot of them to fill one mouth.

He deemed the one who held the rusty cutlass to his throat to be the leader. He had a bulbous nose that was pocked and discolored from disease, but was ornamented with a gold ring. His eyes were yellow and red rimmed and horny growths protruded from his feet. They looked rather like . . . barnacles.

"Never ye mind the Eardog," he said to Amberhill. "We hain't seen women for many a year. He can't recollect the difference."

Amberhill swallowed carefully, not wanting to be nicked by the rusted blade, and thinking this was a rude start to his morning. He wanted to protest he was not a woman, but he feared that in their desperate state, the six would not care. Were they prison escapees? Perhaps, but they looked to be something far worse: sailors. "What do you want?"

"Liquor! Women!" the one called Eardog cried. He was missing an ear, and drooled excessively.

"Shut it, Eardog!" the leader snapped.

Eardog subsided, but a crazed expression remained on his face.

"We lost our bearings, see? Our ship run aground, all wrecked and ruined. We look for the nearest port."

Seamen, indeed, Amberhill thought, *and madmen. Their ship was grounded? They sought the nearest port? Insane.*

"You are far from the ocean," he said.

"T'is a strange thing wot happened to us long ago," the leader said. "A strange tale of witches wot cast an evil curse on us. Aye, bottled up and becalmed on the endless sea. No merchanteer for the picking, no land for the seeing. Nothing. Until now!"

Not just sailors; pirates!

"We could eat the horse," Eardog suggested.

The others muttered their agreement, and a brown gob of drool leaked from the leader's lip onto Amberhill's lapel.

"Tasty land flesh, eh?" the man said. He licked his fingers as if already savoring the meal. "Tired of scaly fishes we are, aye. Ate me sea satchel." He burbled madly.

"And bilge rats," Eardog added.

"Aye, and bilge rats, till there were no more." His grin was hideous, showing his few rotting teeth. "The horse, men! See to it we got some land flesh!"

All but the leader shuffled out of Amberhill's view, but shortly he heard hooves pound the ground and pirates shouting obscenities at Goss.

"My horse will kill them," Amberhill said.

"We shall see, me fine cat."

This was followed by the sound of a wet impact.

"Cap'n Bonnet!" Eardog cried. "It killt Bonesy!"

An intolerable odor wafted over the area, like rotting offal with a tinge of dead fish floating belly up in a marsh. Amberhill's guts knotted up. The stink enraged Goss all the more and he bugled his fury.

The captain's face flushed with veiny lines and his neck seemed to swell like gasping gills. "Lost men to the ocean, aye. Lost 'em to hunger and scurvy, aye, and when we hove aground, more lost. Ye will help us kill that beast, or so help me, I will carve out yer heart meself for a snack."

Captain Bonnet retracted the blade. Amberhill stood and assessed the situation. The dead man, Bonesy, lay in a heap with his brains bashed out, but oddly, his corpse appeared far more decomposed than it ought for a fresh kill. Goss scraped his hoof into the earth, his neck frothy with sweat.

Five pirates were left. Three, including Eardog, surrounded Goss, but dared not advance within striking range of his hooves despite their weapons—a couple of cutlasses and an ax. Another stood well off. He bore an adze, and was probably ship's carpenter.

The pirates had thrown his sword and gear in a pile out of reach. Fortunately they had not searched him thoroughly.

"If you want me to help kill the horse," he said, "I shall need a blade. My own sword ought to do."

Captain Bonnet laughed. "Nay, me cat. Ye will calm the beast, see? *We* will do the carving."

Amberhill shrugged and glanced once more at Goss. He was not the most predictable of horses, and no doubt the foul stench of the sailors offended him. He hoped it worked to his advantage, as it already had with Bonesy.

He found himself more than a little irritated by being accosted by this band of cutthroats and alarmed by the amount of time this was costing him. Time he should be using to catch up with Lady Estora and her captors.

He'd be at a disadvantage without his rapier, but as the Raven Mask, he knew to never be unprepared for any situation that may develop. He marked again where each pirate stood, and cross-drew twin knives from wrist sheaths.

The first he threw dropped the carpenter. The second he used to deflect a blow from the captain. He whirled and pulled another knife from a boot sheath and now he parried blows from the captain with both.

From the corner of his eye, he caught Goss rearing at the end of his tether, the remaining pirates holding their weapons before them, but backing away from the stallion's flying hooves. In Amberhill's experience, seamen rarely possessed any horse sense and that was all for the better in his opinion.

The captain's sword work was not fine, but it was relentless and he hacked at Amberhill like a windmill, one blow after the other. Amberhill parried blow after blow with his knives.

A branch cracked, and Goss was free, rearing and thrusting his hooves at the pirates. They yelled and scattered.

The captain faltered just a hair, and Amberhill dove to the ground and rolled. He ended up by his gear and rose to find a pirate running at him with cutlass raised.

Amberhill threw a knife and it took the man in the belly. The pirate staggered and fell to the ground, quite dead. The enraged Goss bounded over to the pirate and started pummeling his body, causing an eruption of stench and gore. Amberhill gasped, wishing his horse would go after the living.

He heard a grunt behind him, and rolled away as the captain's sword slashed down where he had just been standing. He circled with the captain, his gear between them.

He batted away a thrust. They circled some more, Amberhill aware of the sailors on the fringes of his concentration yelling encouragement to Captain Bonnet.

"Give up, me cat," the captain said, "and I'll make yer death less painful."

It was a dreadful chance, and Amberhill knew it, but this had all become a damned nuisance. When the captain raised his arm to deliver another blow, Amberhill threw his last knife. It didn't mean he hadn't other weapons on him, but they were not made for throwing.

Captain Bonnet screamed—it was a gurgling scream—and dropped to the ground grabbing at the knife in his throat. Blood spurted between his fingers.

Before the captain even fell, Amberhill grabbed his rapier and parrying dagger and turned just in time to skewer a pirate rushing him. Behind him, Eardog's eyes widened, and he turned tail to run. Amberhill slid the knife from the twitching captain's neck and hurled it into Eardog's back. The pirate fell into the brush and did not move.

Amberhill wiped his brow with his sleeve and paused to catch his breath, only to retch on the vapor of putrefaction that arose from the bodies. He pulled a handkerchief from his pocket and covered his nose and mouth. As he watched, the flesh of the corpses sank into their bones with unnatural speed.

"Five hells," he muttered.

Goss still reared on the long dead corpse of the one pirate with a methodical ferocity that stunned him. The bones were by now quite pulverized. "Goss! For heavens sakes! He's dead already."

Amberhill picked his way into the mess and, taking Goss' tether in hand, he spoke soothingly to calm him and led him well away from the gore. He returned to collect his gear. When he went to pull his knife from the remains of Eardog, he found much to his surprise, jewels and gold coins shining among the bones. Using the tip of his knife, he jostled the bones about, and more coins and jewels spilled out of the pirate's carcass. He checked the others, and sure enough, he found a great fortune of wealth beneath their now papery skin and among their bones.

"How extraordinary." He'd never seen such a thing before and wondered how it could be, but even more than being surprised by the treasure, he was dazzled by its shining beauty.

As he poked among Captain Bonnet's ribs, a brilliant flash of red caught his attention, and he spied a ring on the captain's finger. It was gold, fashioned into a fierce dragon with its tail wound around its neck, its eye inlaid with an exquisite blood ruby.

Surely he would have seen this on the captain's finger before, but he hadn't. He slid the ring off. Captain Bonnet's finger was now no more than bone, so it came easily into Amberhill's hand. He slipped it onto his own finger and it fit perfectly. He admired it for a time, how it shone in the light; he breathed upon it and polished it with his handkerchief, then regarded it for a while longer with much wonder and delight.

Eventually he tore his gaze from it and started to collect the rest of the treasure from among the bodies. He'd hide it—hide it all. He couldn't carry it away with him right now, and there was no sense in leaving such largesse in the open like this for just anyone to find.

He collected sapphires and opals, diamonds and emeralds and lapis lazuli. There were the coins both gold and silver imprinted with the dragon sigil from lands unknown, and strands of fine links of the same. He discovered jade and topaz, pretty brooches and more rings. He loved the smooth kiss of the gems on his skin and the cold bite of the gold and silver. He stashed the treasure in the hollow of a tree.

He would return for it later. A treasure such as this would restore his estate ten—no, a hundred times over and he could start the horse breeding farm he dreamed of. He didn't even steal it, and any curse laid upon it must have surely been lifted with the demise of the pirates. Surely! He almost giggled at the prospect of all debts repaid and his estate's finances secured in prosperity forever.

When he finished he wiped his hands clean. And paused. What was he doing? The time he had wasted hiding treasure when he should be pursuing Lady Estora's abductors! It was now midmorning. His ugly greed had reared high, obscuring his mission, delaying the lady's rescue. He had behaved dishonorably again, had dishonored the memory of Morry.

I am no better than my father, he thought in disgust.

Ashamed, he tracked down Goss and tacked him. The stallion was nervous, his skin twitching. Amberhill cursed himself further, for it would be a while before Goss was calm enough to ride.

Well, he decided, patting his stallion soundly on the neck, *at least the world is less six insane pirates and I am flush with treasure. Truly, a caper worthy of the Raven Mask. Now it was time I rescued the beautiful noblewoman.*

He turned and led Goss westward.

"Clay!" Sarge bellowed.

He'd already lifted Estora off Falan, and she stood by her

white mare's head, speaking softly to her. Falan had done remarkably well on this mad dash through the woods, a tribute to her breeding and training. But now she held her right forehoof aloft and looked miserable. Estora prayed she'd be all right.

Clay, the scout, joined them.

"Check out the mare," Sarge said.

Clay dismounted and went to Falan, probing her leg in a practiced manner. Falan did not appear to be afflicted by pain at his touch. He cupped her hoof in his hands, concentrating, then pulled a hoof pick out of his pocket.

"She's a stone is all." He worked the pick inside the hoof, and after a bit of prying, the stone popped out. It wasn't large, but it had been significant enough to bother Falan.

"Prob'ly bruised somewhat," Clay said, "but not badly."

"She won't slow us down?" Sarge demanded.

"Don't 'spect so," Clay said. He patted Falan's neck, and returned to his own horse.

When Clay had finished with the mare, she planted her full weight on the hoof and Estora was much relieved.

"If she comes up lame again," Sarge said in a warning voice, "we're leaving her behind and you're riding with me. We've already wasted enough time here."

He helped Estora mount, and once again they were off. It went like so many days before, Sarge pushing them at a furious pace through the unpredictable footing of the woodlands. Estora worried about Falan's hoof, but the mare's gait proved unflagging and solid.

As the day passed, the forest thinned and grew more patchy, and at times they had to cross fields and meadows. As always, Clay scouted forward to ensure they'd pass unobserved. They hurried from thicket to thicket, sometimes keeping to streambeds that had high banks and growth around them. In the distance, rounded mountains began to dominate the horizon, and it was clear they were headed in their direction.

During one of their infrequent breaks, Estora asked Sarge what the mountains were called.

"If you don't know," he said, "then I've no call to tell you."

If Estora survived this ordeal, and especially if she became queen, she'd make it her business to know the geography of every corner of Sacoridia. She'd never bothered to know in detail anywhere but her own Coutre Province, and the immediate surroundings of the castle in Sacor City.

Of course, if she survived and became queen, she was not leaving the castle ever again!

The evening found them in a woodland gentler and less dense than the Green Cloak they left behind, and here they stopped for the night. Although all was routine, Sarge appeared more agitated than usual, counting off on his fingers as he paced, and checking the moon. Estora surmised he was required to reach their destination on a specific day.

Whittle joined up with the group and this time Estora could hear him telling Sarge, "No sign of our hero."

Sarge looked pleased and announced the watch schedule for that night.

In the morning she was roused early. Clay checked Falan's hoof before they set off and pronounced it sound.

"We've a hard day ahead of us," he confided to Estora.

More difficult than all the days that proceeded this one? She could scarcely believe it until Sarge set off. They rode faster and longer, deeper into the night, their horses slathered in sweat and stumbling until finally, at some awful hour, Sarge called a halt. By this time Estora was so exhausted she was slumped over Falan's neck. When Sarge helped her down, she could hardly stand unaided.

"We will wake before dawn," he warned her. His tone was almost jovial. "It will still be dark."

A VOICE IN THE DARK

Karigan and Fergal settled down behind a cluster of boulders to keep watch. Not that they could see much in the dark, but moonlight pooled in the clearing that was the Teligmar Crossroads, and they'd be able to detect any movement there. Their initial inspection of the area showed no sign of a trap; turned up nothing, really, and so they hid the horses and found this spot for themselves. If Timas Mirwell wasn't playing some joke on them, they were in a good position to see whatever it was they wcrc supposed to see.

They took turns keeping watch while the other slept. Karigan dozed uneasily, her back at an uncomfortable angle against a rock. Her mind chattered endlessly, debating with itself as to what it was Timas thought she'd "want" to see, and why. Did it have something to do with Beryl? He indicated he knew why they'd come to Mirwellton—to make contact with Beryl.

Just as Karigan's mind settled and it seemed she might get some rest after all, Fergal gently shook her wrist.

"Whaaa—?" she began.

"*Shhh.* Someone's coming."

All at once Karigan was fully alert and upright, peering into the dark. Five riders approached through the woods, halting short of the crossroads by several yards.

"Clay," a man said, "I want you to go on ahead and take a look around."

"Aye," one of them replied, and he urged his horse away from the others, heading for the crossroads.

The first speaker then turned in his saddle to address the others. "Jeremy, you're with me. Whittle, you are to stay here with the lady." He and the rider named Jeremy left Whittle and "the lady" behind, guiding their horses toward the crossroads but halting just at the edge of the road, remaining within the cover of the woods. They sat there, apparently waiting. Waiting for what?

Karigan wondered if "the lady" seated on the white horse might be Beryl. But she didn't think Beryl would be riding sidesaddle. Perplexed, she whispered to Fergal, "I'm taking a closer look. You stay here."

Before he could protest, she called upon her ability to fade and stepped out from behind their cluster of boulders. She crept toward Whittle and the lady as silently as possible. When she got near enough to identify features, she almost gasped aloud. She hastened back to Fergal and behind the boulders, dropping the fading.

"That's Lady Estora on the white horse," Karigan told him without preamble. "Her hands are bound—she's a prisoner."

Fergal's mouth dropped open in surprise.

"We've got to act," Karigan told him, "and we've got to act quickly. That's our future queen being held captive, and we have no idea of what's about to happen to her. I *need* your help, Fergal. Will you do exactly as I ask? I'm going to be asking a lot of you."

There was a slight hesitation before Fergal nodded. "Aye. Anything. I'll do anything you ask."

Karigan smiled and placed her hand on his shoulder. "You wanted our errand to be more exciting, eh? Well I guess it is now. All right, here's what we're going to do. The darkness will be our friend . . ."

In the moonlight, Estora saw before her an intersection of roads with a signpost in its center. She could not, however, read the lettering for it was too dark and too distant. Sarge ordered her and Whittle to remain several yards under cover of the woods. He sent Clay off to do his usual scouting while Jeremy waited with him just off the road. Waiting. Waiting for what? Or for whom?

Falan shook her mane, the silver of her bridle jingling. She was as restless as Estora felt.

Thunk.

Both she and Whittle glanced into the woods at the unbidden noise.

"What was that?" Estora asked him.

He scratched his head. "Nothing, most like."

Crack. The unmistakable snap of a branch.

"Animal, I reckon," Whittle said. He gazed toward Sarge and Jeremy, but they had not moved, had not seemed to hear the noise.

They sat and waited for a while more, then, *Thump! Crack!*

"Damnation," Whittle muttered. "Better make sure it's not your hero. You will stay here, m'lady. Do not move a muscle. Understand? You know what Sarge will do."

Estora nodded. She knew. But there was a fluttering in her stomach as Whittle reined his horse away. Could thc noise belong to an animal, or her "hero," whoever he was?

"Shhh."

Estora sat straight in her saddle, looking desperately around but seeing nothing. "Who's there?" she demanded.

"It's me, Karigan," a disembodied voice whispered.

Estora was so startled she could not speak. *Karigan?* Where? And what in the name of all the gods was she doing *here?* She sounded so close, but Estora could not see her. And it was *her* voice; of that she was certain.

"Karigan—" she whispered.

"Shhh. Don't say anything, no matter what happens," Karigan said in a low, urgent voice. "Don't make a sound. I'm standing at your horse's left shoulder, but I'm faded out. Using my special ability."

Estora peered at the location but saw nothing, and she recalled the scene in the throne room of the castle two years past and the demonstration of Karigan's ability. She had even made King Zachary vanish from sight.

"I've already made you and your horse fade out," Karigan whispered. "I'm going to lead you away. All right? No one will see you, except me. Remember, make no sounds."

Invisible hands took Falan's reins and turned her about, leading her deeper into the woods. Estora did not feel invisible, and when she looked down at herself and Falan, she seemed as visible as she should in the dark of morning. She could only trust in Karigan.

Then it began to sink in. Karigan was helping her escape! She was so relieved, so overjoyed, that her tears almost washed away her self-imposed dams. The hero Sarge and his fellows had worried about was actually Karigan! How could she contain herself? But she must so no one would detect their departure.

She glanced over her shoulder. Sarge and Jeremy were lost to sight, but she could still discern Whittle, standing in his stirrups, straining to see into the dark in the opposite direction. A flash of silver arced toward him, and he slumped in the saddle and fell from his horse. He did not move. Estora put her hand to her mouth to forestall a gasp. She thought she observed someone move near Whittle's body, but then the scene fell out of sight as Falan stepped into dense growth.

They came to a stream and here Karigan led Falan into it and downstream. "There's enough flowing water," she explained, "to fill in the hoof prints with silt."

At one point they traveled beneath an opening in the canopy and moonlight showered down through it, glinting on the stream and revealing a ghostly figure leading Falan, one pale hand on the mare's neck. Estora caught her breath, but in the next instant, as they passed from the moonlight, Karigan vanished from existence once more.

Estora longed to break the silence, to make Karigan real—to make all this real, for this slow ride in the dark, with a phantom for a savior, made her feel as if she were caught in some unending dream.

Falan clambered out of the stream, up the bank, and deeper into the woods. Karigan reversed their direction of travel so many times, as if walking a labyrinth Estora could not see, that she became thoroughly disoriented. She guessed Karigan hoped it would likewise confuse anyone who came searching for them.

As time went on, the terrain became rocky, and boulders the size of small cottages lay about the woods. As they picked their way among them, dawn began to lighten the morning, and as it did so, Karigan the ghost was gradually revealed to her once again.

Karigan sighed and solidified, her flesh and clothing taking on color, though muted by the weak light.

"We're no longer faded out," Karigan said. She sounded weary, and rubbed her temple as if her head pained her. "Bear with me for a few moments more and remain silent."

Estora nodded, though she was ready to abandon all restraint and leap off Falan's back and hug Karigan. She was free!

They came to the bottom of a rockfall that must have been calamitous when it happened. The boulders were jumbled this way and that, creating a primeval, natural wall at the bottom of a cliff. The going became more difficult for Falan as she walked over the boulders, but then Karigan angled her approach toward the rockfall and an opening to a cavelike shelter appeared. If they had not approached it just so, one would never know it existed.

Inside, a shaft of brightening light fell through a gap near the back of the cave and she saw two horses there, one of which she recognized as Condor. He nickered quietly in greeting while the other horse seemed content to snooze.

Karigan led Falan right into the cave. The floor was gravelly. Silently Karigan helped Estora dismount, then drew her knife to cut her bonds. The tears finally came. Estora wiped her eyes, and then rubbed her wrists, raw from the cords.

"Are you . . . are you all right, my lady?" Karigan asked her.

"Am I all right?" Estora started laughing and crying at once, thoroughly discarding her usual aloof composure, and hugged Karigan who received her stiffly. "Oh thank you, thank you for taking me away from those awful men!" When she released Karigan, she saw the Rider's eyes were wide.

"Uh, you're welcome," Karigan said. "Look, we need to talk, as I'm just as surprised to see you as you were to see me. I'd like to know what the five hells is going on."

"You mean you didn't know I was abducted?"

"No idea. I've been on the road." Karigan winced, closed her eyes with a groan and rubbed her temple again.

"Karigan?"

"Headache. It'll pass. Make yourself comfortable. I'll take care of your horse."

Estora did not know how she was supposed to make herself comfortable in this place, but she found a flat rock to sit on and continued to work on bringing life back to her wrists and hands.

Karigan, meanwhile, untacked Falan and rubbed her down, then took her to the back of the cave with the other horses where apparently there was a spring for them to drink from. As Karigan worked, she kept glancing toward the cave entrance as if she expected someone to appear there at any moment. When she finished with Falan, she strode to the entrance and peered out, hands on her hips, and muttering to herself about "that boy."

When she returned, she asked, "Do you need food or water?"

Estora broke down again, and Karigan stood by looking helpless, which made Estora laugh through her tears, and only made Karigan look more perplexed.

"I'm just grateful," Estora said, sniffing, "to be free." She blotted her eyes with her sleeve. "It was awful."

Karigan sank down on a nearby rock and asked in a low voice, "Did . . . did they harm you?"

"No, not really. I was just terribly frightened. I did not know their intent."

Karigan nodded as though she understood, and Estora was certain she did. "Well, you're free of them now, but I have to warn you we're not out of danger. Given time and persistence on their part, they'll most likely find this place."

"What shall we do?" Estora asked.

Karigan flipped her braid over her shoulder and glanced at the cave entrance. "I'm not exactly sure. For now, we wait for Fergal to return, and while we do, I think you should tell me how you ended up in the clutches of those thugs, and then I'll tell you how I came to be here myself."

Estora obeyed, beginning—hesitantly so—with her desire to escape the castle. As she poured out her story, Karigan made a few short comments marking, without surprise, the presence of the Eletians outside Sacor City, musing that she did not recall meeting or hearing of a Lord Amberhill, and uttering surprise at the part taken by the Raven Mask in the abduction and of his subsequent demise. To the rest she listened quietly and raptly until the end, and remained silent for some moments after.

"So we don't know their exact purpose in taking you," Karigan said.

Estora shook her head. "They would tell me nothing. I can only expect they wished to obtain a large ransom for my release."

"Perhaps."

"But come, you were to tell me your part of the tale."

"Yes, but it is not as long as yours," Karigan said. "The short of it is that Fergal—he's a new Rider—and I were in Mirwellton on king's business to see the lord-governor, which we did yesterday. Later, as Fergal and I sat in the common room of our inn, Lord Mirwell's steward—" and here Karigan's face showed clear distaste "—smuggled to us a note from Lord Mirwell that we'd see something of interest at the Teligmar Crossroads at dawn. I must say, it was not you, my lady, I was expecting to see."

Teligmar! Now the small mountains Estora had seen made sense, and she finally had an idea of where she was. As for who Karigan expected to see? She did not explain.

"Naturally I was suspicious of the note," Karigan said, "so I made certain Fergal and I arrived well before dawn. We scouted the area out, and expecting possible trouble, we established this as our hiding spot. We then returned to the crossroads on foot and hid ourselves and waited. The rest you know." She paused, deep in thought. "I've no idea what game is being played, or what part Lord Mirwell has in it, but it is clear to me Mirwellton is no safe haven for you. We will have to find refuge for you elsewhere."

Karigan hardly finished her sentence when Condor whickered, followed by the sound of rocks clacking outside. Karigan leaped to her feet, sword bared, and faced the cave entrance.

Estora rose, not sure what to do. Was this Sarge or one of his men coming to reclaim her? Had they been found already? She wilted back to her rock in relief when a young man in a green uniform appeared in the entrance. He leaned against the rock wall breathing hard, his hair tousled. Estora relaxed even more when Karigan sheathed her saber.

"Where have you been?" Karigan demanded, looking simultaneously aggrieved and happy to see him.

The young man, who could be none other than Fergal, entered the cave and found a rock of his own to sit on. "Up a tree," he said. "Hiding."

"Were you followed?"

Fergal shook his head. He looked dazed, and to Estora's mind, much too young to be doing such dangerous work. "I made sure," he said. "No one followed." Then he looked at his hands. "I–I killed that man."

Estora's heart went out to him. No wonder he looked dazed. Lost even.

"I know," Karigan said. "I saw him fall. You did well, Fergal. You helped Lady Estora get free of those men."

He looked up, as if noticing Estora for the first time. He started to rise from his rock. "M–my lady—"

"Sit, Rider," she said. And she herself rose and took his young hands into hers and said, "Thank you. Thank you for your help."

Karigan cleared her throat. "Fergal Duff, meet your future queen."

Fergal's mouth dropped open and he tried to stammer something, but Estora simply smiled and gave his hands a squeeze, and returned to her seat. Only then did Karigan sit again herself.

"What happened," Karigan asked, "after you killed the man?"

Fergal swallowed hard. "I caught his horse and tied it to a tree so it wouldn't run off and alert the others. Like you told me.

"And then," he said, "I got my knife out . . . out of the body." He squeezed his hands into fists. "I was going to hurry back, but as I was starting to make my way, more men joined the two at the crossroads. They talked a bit, and one of them called for the man I killed. I tried to get out of there, really I did, but when they realized something was wrong, they were all over the place. There wasn't anywhere to hide, except in a tree. No one thinks to look up. Once they found the dead man, they searched all around, and I snuck away."

"How many men?" Karigan asked.

Fergal scratched his head. "Maybe ten all told, but they sent one for reinforcements to help with the search."

Karigan's face turned grim, but her words were soft. "Well done, Fergal, well done."

"What are we to do?" Estora asked.

"Rest for a while," Karigan said. "Rest and think."

Karigan and Fergal gathered together some of their food supplies for a belated breakfast and for Estora it was nearly a feast even though Karigan would not light a fire, fearing their foes would easily spy the smoke. Afterward, Estora washed her face in the icy spring. She shivered, but was exultant to wash away days of grime.

She finished feeling renewed, but weary, and found Fergal curled up in a bedroll, snoring softly. Another was spread out nearby.

"You may use my bedroll to rest," Karigan said.

"What about you?"

"I'm going to keep watch. I'll wake Fergal when I'm ready for a nap."

Estora nodded and made herself as comfortable as she could among the rocks. She struggled to fall asleep for a time, but when finally the warmth of the cocooning blankets and her sense of safety lulled her to the edge of sleep, the last thing she saw was Karigan sitting in the cave entrance cross-legged with saber bare across her lap, the sun gilding the crown of her brown hair with gold.

Estora was dreaming of sailing on the bay in her father's sloop on a warm summer's eve, the lowering sun sparking off the crests of waves and absorbing the silhouettes of other vessels into the golden dazzle when the rocking motion of the sloop turned into someone shaking her awake.

"My lady," Karigan said, "I have a plan."

Estora sat up, groggy and disoriented, wondering what Karigan was doing on her father's sloop, then saw the rock walls and remembered. She pushed her hair away from her face and found Fergal wrapped in his blankets and looking as sleepy as she felt. Karigan had not made him take his turn at watch after all. She sat on a rock before them, looking tired, but fully aware. Behind her, the cave entrance had darkened with the change in the sun's slant. Afternoon. How late, Estora did not know.

"There are several men out in the woods," Karigan said.

"You went out there?" Fergal asked in incredulity.

"I didn't need to."

"They're that close by?"

Karigan nodded. "We cannot wait till cover of dark. They'll find us before then. And in any case, I don't . . . I don't think I could make all of us fade out at once."

"We're trapped?" Estora asked, her voice sounding more shrill than she intended.

Karigan gazed at her with an expression that was oddly serene. "It won't come to that."

When she told them her plan, both Fergal and Estora begged her to consider otherwise, but she would not hear of it. Estora thought her mad, and told her so.

KARIGAN'S PLAN

"It's the only way," Karigan said, "and we have to move *now*. Before it's too late."

As if to augment their imminent peril, they heard a shout in the woods. Though distant, it was still too close for comfort. Karigan's plan left Estora too stunned to move, but Karigan had no such qualms and swung into action.

"Fergal, keep watch," she said, "and keep your eyes looking outward until I tell you otherwise."

The young Rider shook off his blankets, grabbed his saber, and took up a position at the cave entrance. Karigan squatted down by her gear and started digging through a saddlebag. Estora stood by, simply watching and feeling helpless.

"Are you sure this is the way?" she asked.

Karigan paused. "Unless you can think of something better."

Estora shook her head, and Karigan resumed her digging, pulling out and unrolling trousers and a shirt.

"These should be . . . hmmm . . ." Karigan sniffed them and smiled wryly. "They should be fresher than what I've got on. And I think they'll fit."

Estora could only stare in disbelief.

"I think my boots are too big for your feet, though," Karigan continued. "We'll have to keep our own footwear."

"This is madness."

"Better than being at the mercy of those thugs, I should think. Now please, I shall need your habit, and you may put on this uniform."

"But I'm not a Green Rider," Estora said.

"I wasn't either when I first wore the uniform," Karigan replied, "or at least I didn't know I was. Now please, my lady, we must do this quickly."

Karigan turned her back on Estora and started removing her shortcoat, unpinning something from the front of it that Estora couldn't quite make out, then shed her waistcoat and boots. She started unbuttoning her shirt, but paused and turned toward Estora again.

"Please," she said. "I'm going to get cold rather quickly."

Estora shook herself. Madness! But she knew of no alternative. She turned around herself and started removing the layers of her habit.

When the exchange was complete, she looked down at herself in amazement, all in green. She feared Karigan's uniform would prove too snug, and it was a tad, in the hips and breast, but she must have lost considerable weight as a captive. Karigan had even girded her with the sword to complete the illusion. When Estora protested that Karigan should retain it, Karigan said, "If all goes well, I will not need it."

If Estora's mother ever heard of this, she would faint. The unfamiliar weight of the sword banged her thigh with every movement. If she was careful, she would not trip over it. She experimented with walking about the cave.

"You are walking like a lady," Karigan said. "Walk like you have business. Don't flounce."

"Flounce? I do not flounce."

"Yes, you do. But you don't have time to practice just now. You must help me with my hair."

Karigan waited expectantly. The black habit made her look older, more severe, more mysterious, and somehow even more commanding than when in uniform.

Is that how I appear to others? Estora wondered. She didn't think so, not precisely, anyway. Not so deadly serious. Karigan was going to place herself in the direct path of danger, and Estora read determination and a clear knowledge of what she was doing in her face. And it took her aback, for this was not a version of Karigan she often witnessed; this was not the Karigan with whom she had spent so much time sitting in the gardens gossiping, sharing dreams and fears. Those conversations in the safety of the castle walls were so far removed from where they were now that Estora wondered if they happened in another life.

This wouldn't be the first time Karigan faced terrible danger, Estora knew. Karigan did not talk much about her exploits, but Estora had heard the stories from others, and when she helped Karigan with the corset, she glimpsed the scars on her ribs from old stab wounds.

"I think," Estora said, "we can simply pin your braid up beneath the hat." Somehow, her ridiculous hat with the pheasant feathers had survived its rough travel across country. She started to pull the pins from her own hair.

"How sharp are those?" Karigan asked. She took one from Estora and jabbed her finger with it. "Hmm. Fergal?"

The Rider turned and gaped at them, seeing them in their new attire for the first time.

"Fergal," Karigan said, "please sharpen these hair pins for me."

Sharpen the hair pins? Estora wondered. When Fergal completed the task, Estora coiled Karigan's braid and neatly pinned it beneath the hat. Estora's own hair was then braided into a long rope that fell between her shoulder blades. It felt strange, for she never wore her hair this way—not in public anyway, and the uniform! It was unnatural, but ever since Sarge had abducted her, nothing was as it should be. She could only think Karigan felt much the same but the Rider was busy helping Fergal clean up the evidence of their camp and tack the horses.

Estora, who was so accustomed to servants seeing to her every need, now felt guilty as she had not before that she wasn't helping, but Karigan and Fergal appeared to have a routine worked out and she did not wish to disrupt it. Of late, she was discovering just how very useless she was.

When they finished, Karigan planted her hands on her hips and gazed steadily at Estora and Fergal.

"Fergal," she said, "avoid towns as much as possible. Use the waystations." She handed him the message satchel. "Maps are inside if you need them, as well as the messages we've collected. Your job is to return them to the king, but your most important duty is to return Lady Estora to him safely. Do you understand?"

Fergal reached out to receive the satchel with some hesitance. "Aye. I do. What about you?"

"I'll make my way back to Sacor City as best I can," she replied. "Don't worry about me. Just worry about Lady Estora. Get her home safe and sound. As of today, you're no longer a trainee. Do you understand, Fergal? You're a true Green Rider, and I know you can do this."

Fergal nodded, looking daunted by the task. Estora would have preferred Karigan to ride with them, but she would not be gainsaid.

Karigan then said to Estora, "Don't draw that sword until Fergal shows you how to handle it." She smiled. "It was F'ryan's, you know."

Estora's voice caught in her throat. "I know."

Karigan nodded, lifted her skirts, and walked over to Condor. She spoke words to him no one else could hear, and kissed his nose. Was it Estora's imagination, or did the gelding look glum?

"I told him to take you home," Karigan said to Estora. "And he will. Trust him. Now, as for Falan . . ." She turned to the mare, gazing at the sidesaddle rig with trepidation. "It's been a while since I've sat a sidesaddle . . ." She stepped up on a rock to mount.

"Wait," Fergal said.

Karigan turned, and the young man removed a knife from each boot. He offered them to her, hilts first. She gazed down at him with a startled expression.

"Are you sure?" she asked. "I haven't practiced of late . . ."

He nodded. "Aye. Take 'em."

"Well, then," she said, "those villains will get a surprise if they come too close."

"They'd have to be real close," Fergal said.

The Riders laughed at some joke Estora was excluded from, then Karigan mounted, tangling the skirts of the habit in the process.

"Um . . ." she said.

Estora helped straighten everything out, but Karigan couldn't quite get the seat right.

"Don't sit to the side," Estora instructed her. "Sit atop. You will be secure."

"Then why do I feel like I'm going to slide off?" She reined Falan around, looking wobbly.

"Hold the balance strap if you need to," Estora said.

"This is unsettling," Karigan muttered, switching the double reins to her left hand and grabbing the balance strap with her right. "I can't ride the whole time like this."

"You'll do fine," Estora said, but it came out sounding more like a question.

"Such confidence." To Fergal, Karigan said, "Give me a little time to get the attention of those searchers. After that, you will have to gauge when it's best to leave the cave and make your escape. Don't wait too long, though."

He nodded once and looked at his feet.

"Godspeed," Karigan said, and she clucked Falan toward the cave entrance, letting out a little "whoops!" when the mare lurched forward and unsettled her center of balance.

"Godspeed," Estora whispered.

They watched her guide Falan away from the cave and down into the woods, which soon absorbed her. They waited minute after minute, until the waiting became unbearable. Then a sharp "Yoo hoo!" rang out in the forest, followed by the shouts of men.

"There she is!" one cried.

Estora bit her bottom lip, hoping her brave, foolish friend would be all right.

"I don't think she'll make it," Fergal said suddenly, countering her thoughts.

Estora started at his pronouncement. "What are you saying?"

"I–I saw death around her."

"What?"

"When . . . when my ability came. When we were in Mirwellton. I saw darkness around her, and wings. I'm sure it meant death."

Estora felt herself blanche. "Why on Earth didn't you say anything?"

Fergal gazed up at her looking haunted and very young. "It wouldn't have changed her mind. She'd have gone anyway."

Truer words could not have been spoken, and Estora trembled at the thought of never seeing her friend again. *Oh, Karigan, why do you do these things?*

"We'd best mount, my . . . my Rider," Fergal said. He'd been ordered not to refer to her as Lady Estora in public, but as Rider Esther if any name must be given—close enough to Estora to remember, different enough to not attract attention. "We'd best make use of the time she's trying to gain us."

He was right, and Estora did as he instructed, struggling to mount without a gentlemanly hand to assist her. The tears blurring her vision didn't help matters. She apologized to Condor as she finally swung gracelessly into the saddle. Getting the saber tangled between her legs did not help. Like sidesaddle for Karigan, riding astride was going to be a trial for Estora. She was going to be very sore, and very humbled, by day's end.

But if Karigan could play the decoy, Estora resolved to endure her portion of the escape without complaint.

Before Fergal motioned it was time to leave the cave, she sent up a small prayer to the gods that the decoy did not become trapped herself, and that Fergal was wrong about his vision of death.

BRAVE SOUL

Amberhill led Goss along the confusion of hoofprints that disturbed the pine needles, dead leaves, and mosses of the forest floor. They went off in all directions, crisscrossing and turning round on themselves. Fresh piles of horse droppings revealed all the activity was recent. He concluded that a good many riders were in the area, not just Lady Estora and her captors.

He paused and scratched his head, wondering which direction he should go. He gazed up at the sun, estimating it was mid- to late afternoon. The sun set quickly this time of year—too quickly—and clouds were beginning to move in.

Lowering his gaze, he could see through the trees the rounded ridges of what must be the Teligmar Hills, which were, as he recalled, the most notable prominences in the west of Sacoridia. They'd come far, and Amberhill felt every step of the journey in his bones. Goss, though a tad thinner in the ribs, appeared to thrive on the extended running. It was all for the good, Amberhill supposed, but just went to show his stallion was more muscle than brains. He patted Goss' neck.

"Which way?" he wondered.

After some consideration, he decided to keep traveling westward. That was the direction the captors had been heading all along, so perhaps they had not deviated, and the confusion of prints was coincidental. Amberhill doubted it, but he hoped.

A clearing brightened between the tree trunks ahead,

and as he neared it, he realized it was a road. He paused on the edge of the woods, squinting in the brightness. Just to his right was an intersection with a signpost. It indicated Mirwellton to the south, Adolind Province's border to the north, and the Teligmar Road leading westward. Though there was no eastward road, Amberhill knew this to be the Teligmar Crossroads.

"How am I to find them now?"

If Lady Estora's captors used one of the roads, it would be next to impossible to know which way they went. Amberhill stood there despairing over what he should do, berating himself anew that he hadn't caught up with them, that he'd lost too much time getting lost and stashing away jewels. He glanced at the dragon ring on his finger, the blood ruby fiery in the full sun, and he thought to tear it off his finger and throw it away when Goss jerked his head up and snorted, ears twitching.

Shortly Amberhill discerned what Goss already detected—hoofbeats pounding down the road at a great clip. Around a curve in the road she came, leaning low over her light-footed hunter's neck, leaving a plume of dust in her wake.

Straight through the intersection she galloped, northward.

Lady Estora!

Goss started to rear and Amberhill grappled with the reins to keep him down. But even before he calmed Goss enough to mount, he heard more hooves, multiplied many times over, in pursuit. One, then five, then ten, then twenty riders altogether whipped by and spurred their horses after Lady Estora.

"Oh, no," Amberhill moaned. Lady Estora showed tremendous courage and spirit in her escape attempt—however she'd managed it—but he had no hope it would end well with so many riders pursuing her.

His only choice now was to follow.

The plan, Karigan thought, was simple enough: distract the ruffians so Estora and Fergal could escape. Disguised as Estora and riding her white mare to complete the illusion, it was not difficult to lure the ruffians after her.

From there, it was supposed to be easy: outrun them. And pray for a quick nightfall so she could use her ability and vanish. She'd ride to a waystation on the Adolind border, hide and rest, then return to Sacor City to report.

Unfortunately she erred by not taking Falan's ability into account. The mare lacked the speed and endurance of Condor, and the poor thing had been cruelly pushed on her journey west. She tired rapidly.

Karigan should have waited until closer to sundown to make her move, but the ruffians were so close to their hideout she was certain they would have been trapped if she waited. At least this way Estora and Fergal had a chance at escape.

Her own chances? She glanced over her shoulder and saw the riders several horse lengths behind her, and gaining. Not good.

Falan stumbled and Karigan lurched forward, but the pommel held her leg securely and she didn't lose her seat. The mare recovered her footing, but Karigan knew it meant the pursuers were even closer.

She hurtled through the intersection of the crossroads, willing the mare to run faster. The farther she led the ruffians on, the better chance Estora and Fergal had of escaping.

Odd, but it wasn't all that long ago Karigan had felt hurt every time she saw Estora around the castle after the betrothal announcement, and she'd rejoiced to leave on a message errand to get away from all the wedding frivolity. And now here she was, disguised as Estora; Estora who was to marry King Zachary, the man Karigan had fallen in love with.

When she'd seen Estora at the crossroads, all the resentment and hurt had fallen away, and she had not hesitated to aid her. Her actions here and now would, if all went well, allow Estora to return to King Zachary so they could marry as planned. She appreciated the irony, but she also knew her duty. Estora's safety came well before her own, and no matter that Karigan had tried to distance herself from her and end their friendship, she was still a friend.

But why did Estora have to be *such* a lady and ride sidesaddle?

Falan careened around a curve in the road, the poor mare huffing and lathered in sweat. Karigan glanced over her shoulder again, and there were her pursuers, still gaining. One had a crossbow.

Damnation. She could try veering into the woods to make it more difficult for the bowman to aim, but she saw no likely spots to enter.

A bolt skittered along the road ahead of her lifting puffs of dirt. Falan spooked but Karigan steadied her and kicked her on. The bowman would not be able to reload at a full gallop. She watched the roadside for an escape route that would not involve trees scraping her off Falan or tumbling down a steep embankment. If she could evade her pursuers for long enough in the woods, she could use her ability as the sun crept down in the west. She did not like to think what would happen if the men caught her.

Even as she renewed her determination and found a likely opening in the woods, Falan failed her.

One moment the mare was running full tilt, the next she stumbled, went down, plowed into the road on her chest, launching Karigan from the saddle, hurling her through the air.

Time stretched, Karigan seemed to hang in the air forever, awaiting the inevitable. And then—

She slammed into sharp gravel and hard dirt in front of the mare. She lay there, the fall not yet penetrating her mind. She shook her head and saw Falan trying to rise, but she could not. The mare emitted a plaintive cry unlike any Karigan had ever heard from a horse.

Gradually she became aware of a burning pain in the palms of her hands, her elbows, and her knees. She gazed at her palms. Estora's fine doeskin gloves were shredded, revealing chewed flesh embedded with gravel and dirt, and seeping blood. She knew it must be the same for her knees and elbows. Then all at once, everything hurt, all her joints and muscles were crying out for attention, though nothing appeared to be broken. Unlike poor Falan.

The ruffians slowed their approach and came to a halt before her in a great cloud of dust. She couldn't outrun them on foot even if she could make her limbs obey her.

Training took over, Drent screaming in her ear, berating her for being too slow, for thinking too much. She needed not to think, but to act. She drew the knives from her boots into her stinging hands. The first she threw did not hit the lead man as she intended, but went wide and hit the man next to him. He tumbled from his saddle. Before the ruffians recovered their wits to respond, she threw the second knife and took out another man, his expression one of surprise. Karigan was surprised as well. Fergal, she thought, would be proud of her.

Men dismounted and surrounded her. She couldn't get her addled mind to count how many there were. Didn't matter anyway. There were too many of them, and only one of her.

The leader walked over to her. "It appears, *my lady,* you have teeth."

"Who is she, Sarge?" another asked. "That ain't the real lady, is it?"

Something deep in Karigan's memory stirred. *Sarge . . .*

"No, you idiot, this is not Lady Estora." He squinted at her as though trying to recall something himself, then shook his head. "She'll tell us soon enough where the lady is hiding."

He reached for Karigan. Gritting her teeth against the pain of her raw hands, she grasped a handful of sand and gravel from the road and tossed it into his face. His hand went to his eyes as he cursed.

Karigan sprang upon him and wrested his sword from him. She went to strike him, but another man's sword stopped her blow. Men shouted, were moving all around, raising a haze of dust. She swung the blade again, and again it was parried. The corset shortened her breath even though she'd told Estora not to secure it too tightly. Dust clogged her nose and throat, and her skirts whirled about her ankles. Each moment she kept her foes occupied won another moment for Estora and Fergal.

She focused on the swords, lost sense of her pain, and let the training take command of her. She'd trained to fight while well-attired, and this time she wore not fancy shoes, but her own boots, and the habit's skirts were not so confining. She had those advantages, at least.

Her sword drove through the stomach of her foe. She withdrew it and went after the next blade, and the next. She nearly succeeded in killing the fellow when someone slammed into her from behind, knocking her to the ground and the sword from her hand, out of reach.

She wrestled with whomever knocked her down, biting, kicking, clawing. She grabbed at her hair, drawing out a pin and impaled her assailant's arm. He fell away screaming.

She tried to stand, but someone kicked her feet out from under her. Several hands held her down, yanked strands of her hair out while removing pins, kicked her in the sides and hips if she struggled, clouted her in the head.

Sarge glared at her. "I know you," he said. "I *remember* you."

She started to speak, but Sarge ordered her bound and a cloak thrown over her head, and secured to her so she could not see. Rough hands settled her on a horse to which she was also bound.

"Let's take her up the hill," Sarge said.

Blinded and immobile, Karigan could only close her eyes. All around her were the sounds of the men and horses moving out. Her horse turned around and lurched forward, and Falan screamed somewhere behind her.

At least the brutes put the mare out of her misery, Amberhill thought. The road absorbed the blood pooled beneath the mare's slashed throat. He knelt in the road and picked up Lady Estora's hat. It was trampled, coated in dust, and a couple of the feathers were broken. He'd arrived toward the end of the melee, as they subdued her and trussed her to the horse—he hadn't dared approach with anything but stealth, and once again he was too late.

But here was a puzzle. This was Lady Estora's hat, and the dead mare was hers, too, but if that was the lady being carried off, there was a dimension to her he had not even imagined existed. She killed a few of the men, and injured others—he'd watched them ride back down the road with their dead. Definitely not fighting skill he expected from a noble lady.

Whoever it was, then, had done Lady Estora a great service, must have helped her escape when he'd been incapable of catching up with her captors.

He was of two minds. One was to go in search of the real Lady Estora, the other was to follow the band of cutthroats and try to help the brave soul who had taken her place. She—or possibly he?—would at least know what became of the lady, and he owed this person any aid he could render.

He walked over to Goss, who had scented the dead mare and wanted to bolt. He made the stallion stand still long enough for him to mount.

He cantered back to the crossroads and reined Goss west, on the road that led into the Teligmar Hills. A little way along, he hung Lady Estora's hat on a branch as a clue to any force King Zachary might have sent out behind him.

JAMETARI'S DESIRE

Laren could see Zachary's reluctance, but she knew the pressure Lord Coutre exerted on him to recover Lady Estora. The pressure, coupled with his own guilty feelings finally overrode his pride. He sat his horse unmoving before the blue tent of the Eletians' encampment, waiting, just waiting for any indication Prince Jametari would deign to see him.

Zachary asked her along, but relegated his honor guard to a few Weapons. There were no banners this time, no soldiers in shining mail riding in columns. No pageantry. The guards at the city gates ensured no one approached or disturbed him, but curious onlookers gazed down from the wall wondering what their king wanted with the Eletians.

Little was ever seen of them, though a few Eletian "scouts" had ventured into the city. They always traveled in threes, spoke to no one but select shopkeepers, and did not linger. Laren couldn't blame them, for everywhere they went, crowds gathered and gawked, congesting the street and forcing constables to intervene to keep traffic flowing.

And what could possibly interest Eletians in Sacor City? Reportedly they'd visited the museums and arts district, but much of their interest focused on Master Gruntler's Sugary, and it was said the master himself was working all day and night to fill orders for chocolate treats. The Eletians had also ordered sacks of roasted kauv beans from a Gryphon Street tea house.

No one knew what the Eletians did in their tents all day,

but Laren amused herself by imagining them sitting around popping Dragon Droppings into their mouths, sipping kauv, and reading esoteric poetry to one another—a heady combination. She smiled and wondered if the Eletians truly inhabited the tents at all, or if the tents were really passages to elsewhere. Were the Eletians even *here,* in Sacoridia? Were the tent interiors in an altogether different location than the exteriors?

It was such mysteries that made the Eletians so intriguing, but the longer she and the others sat waiting for one to appear, the more her curiosity waned.

As their wait became more protracted, the clouds in the leaden sky roiled eastward. Laren sniffed the chill air and thought it smelled of snow. They'd had a dusting already, but it melted quickly in the sun. The cold worked its way into her back, which ached from sitting so long. Bluebird's head dipped as he dozed. Still, Zachary's expression was set. He was not moving.

Laren was about to suggest they return to the castle, attempt to convince him to return tomorrow for another try, when the flap of the blue tent folded back, and there stood the Eletian they had dealt with before, Prince Jametari's sister.

"Welcome, Firebrand," she said. "My brother will see you."

Zachary dismounted and his small company followed suit. After he handed off his reins to one of the Weapons, he chose another to accompany him and Laren into the tent. Neither General Harborough, nor Colin, would be happy with just one guard, but they had not been consulted about—or even told of—this little adventure. No, they would not be happy at all when they learned of it.

Their Weapon was Sergeant Brienne Quinn, lately up from the tombs, as were all the Weapons who now guarded Zachary, leaving but a few to watch over the avenues of the dead.

The three of them entered the tent, and it was as before, the birches lining the path, their golden leaves rustling, white limbs holding up the sky. Laren smiled when she saw Brienne's look of wonder mixed with a healthy dose of suspicion.

The tomb guards were having to make many adjustments with their new duty of guarding the living, such as working above ground and in daylight. They were pale, these Weapons, and seemed always to squint, even on a dim day such as this, as though even the hint of sunlight were too much for them.

All Weapons were quiescent and showed deference to the king, but with the tomb guards it was more; they were almost sepulchral in demeanor, accustomed to hushed and hallowed places, the silent gardens of the dead. How did they view their living king? As a future ward of the tombs?

Laren shook her head. Such thoughts!

They followed the Eletian down the path and across the stream to where Prince Jametari awaited them, this time attired in silvery blue. His attendants set out chairs and refreshments again, but Zachary remained standing, prince and king assessing one another in silence.

Presently Jametari said, "I welcome your return, Firebrand. What is it the Eletians may do for you?"

"You don't know?" Zachary asked. "I thought you were gifted with prescience."

Jametari nodded. "And so I am, but such gifts are fickle in nature and do not reveal themselves on command, and usually tend to illuminate events of significance, not the mind of a king."

Zachary hesitated before speaking again. "Your sister said you had a way of knowing things, that the woods and stream tell you the news of the land."

"They do," Jametari said.

"We've no word from those who pursue Lady Estora's captors and no ransom demands."

Jametari gazed off to the side as if caught in a daydream. "There is not much I can tell you, and certainly not the specifics you wish, for the story the land tells fades the farther west it goes." He then turned his light blue eyes to Zachary. "The land speaks of the passing of a great host on paths otherwise little traveled. Toward the setting sun they've ridden, hunters clad all in black like this guard of the dead who accompanies you. They pause rarely, the hooves of their steeds like thunder on the earth, shaking the very roots of trees. The forest around them senses fury and urgency, and the creatures flee before them."

"That's all?" Zachary asked.

"Their passage obliterates all else."

Zachary's expression was downcast. He was hungry for news, ready to ride west himself. Only Laren's coaxing, and that of his other advisors, prevented him from joining the pursuit. She did not know if he was driven more by fondness for Lady Estora and a fear of what may happen to her, or by concern of the ramifications to the kingdom if she was not recovered healthy and whole. He did not confide in Laren his personal feelings for Lady Estora, so she assumed it was some mixture of the two. Zachary had a good heart and he didn't like to see anyone harmed, especially one as gentle as Lady Estora.

"Truthfully," Jametari said, "my mind has been bent toward the problem to the south, not toward your lady's plight."

"Blackveil?" Zachary asked sharply.

Jametari nodded. "Would you and your captain sit with me for a while?"

Zachary glanced at Laren, and said, "Of course."

All but Brienne and a few of Jametari's attendants sat, and at first there was silence, except for the chiming of the stream and the flutter of blue jay wings among the branches of a birch.

"The story I feel from the south," Jametari finally said, "has not changed since the Galadheon moved Mornhavon the Black into the future. The forest rests with no consciousness driving it into deeper shadow. It stagnates, remains evil and dark, yet much taint was removed with Mornhavon. Given the passage of an age, the forest might heal."

"I do not think," Zachary said, "we have that kind of time."

"So you've expressed before. And I agree. The threat will reappear before then."

"Is there something, then, you propose to do about it? You know my feelings on the subject."

Jametari folded his hands on his lap. He had long fingers. "I am not sure it is so much a proposal as much as a long-held desire." The prince paused, looked to his sister who did not appear pleased by the turn in conversation.

"What is that desire?" Zachary asked.

"To look beyond the D'Yer Wall," he replied. "To enter the forest and look upon it."

"Two of my Riders entered the forest and found it deadly," Laren said. She did not add, out of respect, that suggesting to do so was madness.

Jametari smiled at her, but it was not a friendly smile. "Yes, it is deadly, and no Eletian has dared enter it since the breach, except . . ." He halted. His son Shawdell had entered Blackveil, for he was the maker of the breach. "The peninsula upon which the forest exists was once a fair land, but is a legend now even for Eletians. In your tongue it was called Silvermind, and in ours, Argenthyne."

The name sparked magic in the hearts of Sacoridians, for all children were told tales of Laurelyn the great Eletian queen and her castle of moonbeams. Until this summer, Argenthyne existed only as legend, but now they knew there was a basis in reality for the story.

"It was the jewel of Avareth on Earth until Mornhavon broke it." It was Jametari's sister who now spoke. With a pleading look to her brother, she added, "It is gone. A sad corpse that is corrupted and decayed. You will find nothing there remaining of the Argenthyne of memory."

"Perhaps not," he said. "But it may be that some vestige of good yet sleeps there, some remnant of what was once fair, and now is the time to see, while Mornhavon is absent."

"He could return in the middle of any exploration," the sister said.

"That is possible."

Zachary and Laren exchanged glances at what seemed to

be an ongoing argument between siblings. She wondered if Jametari thought an excursion into Blackveil would help him decide which side to support among his people: the side that wanted the forest closed off forever or the side that suggested the D'Yer Wall should be allowed to fall in the hope that it would strengthen the Eletian people. Maybe the prince had already made his decision, but wanted his people to see for themselves.

As if confirming her thoughts, Jametari said, "It is in the interest of the Eletian people for us to enter the forest, to explore what remains there to see what kind of threat truly exists and what might be restored to the light."

"You seem resolved to do this," Zachary said.

"I am, though I fear I will not be permitted to go myself."

"Who will go in your stead?"

"My *tiendan,*" Jametari replied, "led by my sister, Graelalea."

His sister looked away, plainly unhappy. Laren couldn't blame her.

"When will they go?" Zachary asked.

"It has not yet been decided. The season grows late, and winter is not the best time for a journey for anyone, not even an Eletian."

"But you do not know when Mornhavon will appear."

"That is the dilemma."

Zachary stroked his beard. "I am struck you would tell me of your intentions, Prince Jametari. Do you seek my leave?"

The two gazed at each other for some moments, again assessing the other, until Jametari's lips curved into a smile.

"It is you, Firebrand, who reminded us of cooperation and old alliances. I would not have it appear we were trespassing upon your lands and entering Blackveil for secret reasons. As for what we may find on the other side? It may be that Sacoridia has some interest in it."

The audience concluded in a congenial manner, though Zachary did not comment on the prince's plan. Jametari promised to come forward with any news of Lady Estora if he learned anything via the land or prescience.

On the ride back up the Winding Way, Zachary remained in thoughtful silence, and it was not until they passed beneath the portcullis and stood before the castle itself that he halted his horse and folded his hands upon the pommel of his saddle. Laren halted Bluebird beside him and waited for him to speak.

"Did you find it as curious as I," he said, "that the prince should mention his plans to us?"

"I suppose," Laren said. "The Eletians seem to come and go as they will, seeking leave from no one. Maybe he truly is interested in cooperation."

A raven spiraled above the battlements and another squawked from the tip of a nearby tree.

"You may be right," Zachary replied, his gaze following the flight of the raven. "I do not know what to believe from these Eletians or how to gauge their intentions. One thing is for certain—they will not enter Blackveil without Sacoridians accompanying them."

Laren shuddered. Whoever he sent would have little chance of returning.

THE WALL LAMENTS

From Ullem Bay to the shores of dawn, our song unravels, erodes stone and mortar. Once we shielded against great evil. We stood strong as the bulwark of the Ages.

But we were breached. Our song weeps in a clash of notes out of time. Lost is the harmony, erratic is the rhythm.

No one hears us. No one helps us. No one heals us.

Betrayed.

Yes! You must hate him.

Betrayed and dying.

Cracking and bleeding.

From Ullem Bay to the shores of dawn, our shield shall fail and great evil will shadow the world.

No!

We are broken.

Unweaving.

Dying.

THE BLEEDING OF STONE

Alton awoke with the dawn—not that he'd slept much through the night. As usual. He ate a cold breakfast and readied himself for an inspection ride of the wall. Night Hawk was happy to bear him along no matter the hour, and so Alton rode from the sleepy encampment, following the clearing along the wall, urging Hawk into a canter once the gelding warmed up. He'd probably be back by the time Dale was up and eating breakfast. He ground his teeth, again resenting the fact he must rely on someone else to enter Tower of the Heavens because he couldn't.

The miles flowed swiftly by and when he reached the portion of the wall where he'd first seen the eyes, he reined Hawk to a halt. The cracks had multiplied since then, fine lines spreading like spiderwebs. He saw no pattern in them this time, and with a sigh of relief he clucked Hawk along.

When he reached the breach and the main encampment, he did find something that disturbed him, and those on duty there, greatly. The wall, where it abutted the breach, was showing the most signs of deterioration, with cracks that left few ashlars unlined. Another sign of wear was efflorescence—moisture seeping through joints between ashlars and leaching lime from the mortar drop by drop while redepositing minerals on the facing wall, like the flowstone of a cave. Alton had seen the process at work beneath old stone bridges where drainage failed causing stalactites to form like fangs beneath the arches.

In and of itself, the efflorescence would have been disturbing enough, for the wall had been constructed to weather the elements for all time, but there were even more troubling signs. The erosion was occurring at an abnormal rate. A process that might ordinarily take years appeared to be taking just weeks. Even worse, instead of flowing white, or yellowish white, the efflorescence shone with red, as if the wall bled.

"Aye," the watch sergeant told Alton, "we only began to notice the color yesterday. It has the guard unnerved. Making the sign of the crescent moon, every last one of 'em."

Alton stood in his stirrups next to the wall and reached up, touching the moisture. When he withdrew his hand, a bead of crimson rolled down his finger. He sniffed it, and dabbed it with his tongue. Salty, faintly metallic. Like blood.

He shuddered and wiped his hand on a handkerchief. He would not tell the soldiers here what he thought—there was already enough fear and superstition around the wall—but the watch sergeant who stood at his stirrup had probably guessed.

"Tastes like stone," Alton lied, trying to keep the quaver out of his voice. "Different minerals in the mortar can affect the color."

The sergeant nodded, relief plain on his face at this explanation.

Alton found more oozing on either side of the breach, and more cracks forming. The repair work in the breach itself stood solid and unaffected, the cut stone still looked fresh and new.

"If you notice further changes," Alton told the watch sergeant, "*anything* that doesn't look right, let me know at once."

"Yes, m'lord."

With that, Alton reined Night Hawk back east along the wall, looking at it more closely. He found some efflorescence he'd missed on his way to the breach. In a couple of spots, crimson dribbled down the granite facade in long runnels.

And this time, he saw images of faces formed by the cracks. More deranged, more tortured than those he'd seen before, with eyes scratched out and features twisted.

Sweat glided down Alton's face. He passed his hand over his eyes and the images were gone. Just cracks remained. He wondered if the wall was going insane, or himself. If only he could enter the tower and merge with the wall; if only he could try to make things right.

He patted Night Hawk's neck, taking comfort in the texture of a soft winter coat growing over solid muscle.

Alton's cousin Pendric had sacrificed himself to the wall, claiming he would mend it, that he would be the one to accomplish it, but all he succeeded in doing was turning the guardians against Alton and spreading his madness.

Alton moved on and did not pause till he reached the spot he and Dale had visited. This time he thought he saw the cracks form a pair of giant eyes that peered at him. They were malignant and crazed and they followed him no matter where he moved. He imagined it was Pendric peering out at him, full of hatred.

Alton dug his heels into Night Hawk's sides and left behind whatever it was he thought he saw as fast as he could.

Dale paced in front of the tower, kicking a stone, while the encampment went about its business around her. Where was Alton? She knew he used his mornings to inspect the wall, but usually he was back well before now, dragging her out of bed and rushing her through breakfast to get her in the tower as soon as possible.

Maybe it was just a continuation of his avoidance of her. Ever since he'd woken her up from her wonderful dream and had nearly frozen himself to death sleeping by the wall, he'd been more distant, gloomier, and he no longer came to her to clarify his notes. She thought she had made progress with him, but apparently not as much as she'd hoped.

"Men," she grumbled. "Crazy and moody."

She was about to return to her tent to pass the time when Alton came riding up on Night Hawk from alongside the wall. His face was hard to read as he dismounted and led his horse over to her, but as he approached, she sensed something disturbed him deeply. He looked pale.

"Morning," she said.

"Morning. Thinking about going to see your mages?"

My mages? She thought about giving Alton a good, swift kick in the shin, but didn't think it would improve their strained friendship.

He must have realized how it sounded for he said, "Sorry. It's not been a good morning. When you go into the tower, would you ask the mages about why the wall is bleeding?"

She gaped. "The wall is bleeding?"

"And I saw the eyes again," Alton said, and he told her of his inspection ride.

"That can't be good," Dale murmured. "Yes, I shall certainly see what Itharos and the others have to say about it."

He nodded. That was it. No "be careful" as was once usual. Maybe it was just that he was preoccupied by what he'd seen this morning. She hoped so.

She plunged through the wall, and when she emerged into the tower chamber, the scene was typical, more or less. Itharos was standing between Boreemadhe and Cleodheris, moderating an argument. Dorleon sat at the table carving a fish lure while Fresk and Winthorpe were deep in discussion over mugs of ale. Dale frowned, thinking the hour too early for ale. Their voices, except Dorleon's, echoed about the chamber.

"Ahem," Dale said. When no one heard her, she said more loudly, *"Ahem."*

"Hello, Dale," Itharos said, and the others stopped what they were doing to greet her.

"Now I know why," she said, "they put you in separate towers. How did you ever get any work done at your lodge?"

They all started to speak at once and Dale held her hand up to stop them. "Never mind. Any sign of Merdigen?"

"No," Itharos said, "he has not appeared. Fear not, he is a most able pathfinder and will soon return."

"Yes, well, I'm not sure you understand the urgency of the situation."

"Better than most, child," Boreemadhe said, "but there's not much we can do about it. We can only await the others and find out what Merdigen intended by calling us together."

"I suppose that means more parties and games." Dale loved a good party as much as anyone, but she knew time was running out, especially after what Alton reported this morning.

"Of course we must have a party when the others arrive," Itharos said. "We have not seen them in ages."

Dale folded her arms. "So, while the wall cracks and bleeds, you're planning the next party."

All six of the tower guardians gazed at her, stunned. "Say again," Itharos requested.

"The wall," Dale said, "cracks and bleeds."

All the mages scrambled to their feet and hurried across the chamber and beneath the west arch. Their voices reverberated as they conversed among themselves. They reemerged, looking unhappy.

"We knew the cracks were progressing," Winthorpe said, his hands tucked into opposite sleeves of his robe.

"The regions nearest the breach are weakening," Itharos added, "to the point of death. Unstopped, the weakening will spread to each end of the wall."

"I know," Dale said. She would have shaken them if only they were corporeal.

"The wall bleeds," Itharos continued, "because those guardians are no more. They have succumbed."

"Isn't that why you're here?" Dale demanded. "To keep that sort of thing from happening?"

The mages looked uneasily from one to another.

"Not precisely," Itharos said. "Our function is to inform the wallkeepers of trouble, and they in turn are supposed to inform the Deyers. It was up to the Deyers to fix any problems, for it is the Deyers who have an affinity for stone in their blood; the ability to work with the guardians.

"You must understand that we've little influence over the wall guardians. We can communicate with them enough to know when all is well, or not. We can even negotiate with them on a limited basis, as Merdigen did to rescue you from being imprisoned in the wall, but that's about it. Before our powers faded with the departure of our corporeal forms, we might have been able to do more, but all our magic is gone from us, except for giving us the power to be."

She looked hard at each one of them. "Then what's the point of your being here?"

Itharos shrugged. "We don't know the entirety of Merdigen's intent in drawing us together."

"So you're just going to wait," she said. "Wait and have a party when and if Merdigen returns, and in the meantime the wall will continue to die. Because that's what's happening, right? The wall is dying."

"It is unfortunate," Boreemadhe said, "but we cannot prevent it from happening."

"Unfortunate?" Dale was incredulous. "Is there anything you *can* do?" Her question was met with silence and the shuffling of feet.

"Believe us, child," Boreemadhe said, "if there was something we could do to repair the wall ourselves, it would have been done as soon as we were awakened."

Dale practically quivered with anger, comprehending something of Alton's frustration. "Nothing you can do," she spat. "Do any of you even remember what it was like to be flesh and blood? Living under the open sky and breathing the fresh air?"

"Well, it's been a while—" Itharos began, but Dale silenced him with a curt gesture.

"You may not have seen each other in a very long time, but you also haven't seen your homeland in even longer. Each of you spoke to me about your shock over the devastation of the land, the people, following the Long War. Famine, child warriors with missing limbs, disease, a people and country moved back centuries to a more primitive age." It was odd, when she thought about it, that she should find herself lecturing thousand-year-old great mages. Or, rather, *projections* of thousand-year-old great mages.

"It took centuries," she continued, "for the people to

make recovery. You'd probably not recognize Sacoridia today as the same place you left. Commerce is stronger than it's ever been, with ships sailing to far off ports in search of trade, the land producing for the people, whether it's the timber that builds the ships or the crops carried in their holds. Sacoridia's arts and culture also flourish. The school at Selium spreads it across the land, and there are museums, theater, and music. Some painters and poets are almost as famous as the king! Why, you wouldn't believe the number of bookshops in Sacor City alone."

That caught their attention.

"Books," Dorleon murmured.

"Books, bookshops, binders, printers—"

"*Printers?"* Winthorpe demanded. "What is this?"

They were in awe when she told them so many more books could be produced with a single printing press.

"You must bring us books," Winthorpe said.

"Yes," the others murmured. "Bring us books."

Dale gazed at them in surprise. Their faces were hopeful, pleading, almost childlike with desire. Then she narrowed her eyebrows. She had them now.

"Sacoridia has arisen from the ruins through hardship and wars, and now it shines. You'd be proud of your people. But if we don't solve the problem of the wall, there will be no more books. There will be nothing. Look, you're all learned, scholarly people. It seems to me your ability to look at problems and solve them should not have been affected by the fading of your old powers. I've seen you working out those equations! And I assume you have no wish to see Sacoridia come to ruins after all your sacrifices. If you apply yourselves to the problem of the wall in this manner, who is to say you won't find a solution to fixing it?"

"She's right," Fresk said, and the others nodded and murmured in agreement.

Dale decided to clinch her argument with an incentive. "If you get to work, I'll see about finding you some books."

She thought Alton would be proud of her little speech. It had the desired effect, for the group set aside their usual preoccupations and conjured chairs for themselves to sit around the table and work. Probably nothing would come of it, but at least she'd gotten them to try.

Alton appeared to relax when she sat down with him later in his tent to tell him of her visit with the tower guardians.

"I think they need Merdigen in order to focus," she said. "He's their leader, and they've just been waiting for him, not taking any initiative themselves."

"That means you must keep them focused till he returns," Alton said. Then he added, "I can't believe it's taking him so long."

Dale shrugged. "There's a lot I don't understand about these tower guardians, except they love a good party."

Alton smiled, though it was a worried smile. "Look, Dale, I'm sorry if I've been distant. I just feel helpless."

"I know. But you have to realize that I have a good idea about the danger Blackveil presents." She grimaced at the memory of black wings and rubbed her old wound.

"Of . . . of course you do," Alton said. "I'm sorry if I acted as if—"

"Apologies accepted. By the way, I asked Itharos about the eyes and faces you've seen. He had no explanation, except that the wall guardians were, well, acting out."

"I guessed as much," Alton said.

They sat there in gloomy silence until Dale couldn't take it any longer. "I'm thinking Plover needs some exercise and Leese has cleared me for riding. And I do not intend to go anywhere near the wall, but *away* from it. North into the woods. Would you and Night Hawk care to join us?"

Alton looked like he was about to say no, but hesitated, and with a smile, replied, "Yes."

More progress, Dale thought with a surge of pleasure. It had been a productive day after all.

HEAVEN'S EYE

Grandmother stirred the coals of the fire with a stick, dreaming of warmer climes and missing her old hearthside in Sacor City. She thought Arcosia must have been a warm place, for the chronicles of her people spoke of lemon and olive trees, orchids and an azure sea, but never of snow and ice and the cutting wind. She wore two cloaks and a pair of mittens she knitted herself, and still she was not warm enough. Soon she and her people must descend Hawk Hill and go back to hiding in plain sight.

Most of her people had decided where to go and news would pass among them along the usual network of Second Empire and its institutions. Some of their best meeting places were the abandoned shrines of Sacoridia's forgotten, marginalized gods found in almost every village, and there they could exchange news, distribute messages, worship the one true God, and congregate for whatever purpose may be required.

Grandmother had not yet decided where she and Lala would spend the winter. Once she had the book of Theanduris Silverwood in hand, she thought she should be near the D'Yer Wall so she could work on solving the riddle of its construction, and therefore its destruction. Her other option was to stay with a cousin in Wayman Province. Her cousin had a large house with servants and she knew she'd be warm and comfortable there. After all, she did not think there was much she could do at the wall itself during the harsh winter. There was no suitable village near it, and camping beside it was no more appealing than spending the winter on Hawk Hill. Spring would be soon enough to destroy the wall, wouldn't it?

She just wasn't sure, and every day she prayed for guidance. All the time she preached to her people that God would take care of them, that He would see to it the empire rose again to its glory of old. She'd heard His whispers over the summer and that's when her ability to work the art had improved. She'd learned that a presence in Blackveil Forest had awakened, which the elders of Second Empire believed to be Mornhavon the Great, a sign that the time was at hand for the descendents of Arcosia to come into their own.

Alas, she'd had few portents since the end of summer. God had stopped whispering to her and the presence in Blackveil had faded or gone back to sleep. Everything had been silenced. Everything except her ability to work the art. Though she knew the silence was temporary, she felt abandoned.

She sighed as she gazed into the fire, oblivious to the activities of the encampment. The soldiers had been coming and going. Today was the day Sarge was supposed to bring Lady Estora to them. It would be interesting, she supposed, to meet the noblewoman, but her real intent behind the abduction was simply to distract the king and his protectors, to draw out his Black Shields, and leave the castle and tombs vulnerable.

She'd let Immerez decide whether or not to kill the noblewoman or to use her for some other, better purpose later, for he knew the workings of the minds and hearts of the nobles better than she, and what action would derive the greatest benefit overall.

She tossed some more sticks onto the fire. It sputtered and blazed and she wiggled her log closer to absorb the heat. Lala was off somewhere playing with her string and no one seemed to have need of her just now, so she sat alone with her thoughts, depressed by the cold and a lack of direction when so many counted on her.

One thought did give her pleasure: Thursgad must surely have the book by now, and be on his way to Sacor City. She smiled, thinking of the havoc her little surprise, in the form of the silver sphere, would cause the inhabitants of the castle. She almost wished she could be there to see it. *Almost.*

A hawk screeched overhead. Their numbers had diminished greatly over the weeks, as most had already left for their wintering grounds. Another indication she and her folk must move. It would snow soon, and then they'd be stuck.

As she gazed at the sky and the gliding hawk, it occurred to her she could seek some guidance on where and how she should spend her winter by using the art. She ruminated over her mental list of spells and knots for something appropriate. She could not invoke God Himself, certainly, but maybe she could enhance her prayers and invite inspiration.

The series of knots she came up with was called Heaven's Eye. It wasn't so much a spell as an offering and focal point to open oneself to the divine. Her mother, and her mothers before her, used it when in need of guidance or when they wanted their prayers to be heard more clearly by God.

Grandmother picked through her skeins of yarn. Recently she and Lala and some of the other women had journeyed down to Mirwellton for supplies and there she visited the spinner who made a fine quality of yarn and also had a good head for dyes. Grandmother spent precious silver to replenish her supply.

She decided to use sky blue yarn. The eternal meadow, the heaven of her people, was always perceived to be "somewhere up there" above the clouds and beyond the stars, so using the color of the air seemed appropriate.

She removed her mittens and cut a length of yarn. She tied knots into it, murmuring in prayer, "Dear God, our shepherd, keeper of the eternal meadow, I seek guidance for those who are Your faithful on Earth." And on she went, focusing only on the prayer and the formation of knots, opening herself to any sign from God.

When she finished, she held in her hand a round, knotted wad of yarn, and she threw it into the fire. The smoke would carry her words to the sky and beyond, and she waited, gazing into the flames, hoping, wishing, praying for at least some inkling of inspiration.

The flames flickered in the wind, spat sparks, separated, merged, and separated again in their elemental dance, and nothing came to her. Grandmother did not know how long she sat there, but she'd had enough. It was time to move her old bones and stretch.

But then a glowing ember caught her eye. The ember grew and grew in her vision, a depthless golden flame, and in its midst was a hot, white light with columns of flame twisting and branching within it like a forest. She wanted to avert her eyes, but did not dare.

The whiteness sucked her in until she was surrounded by it and the coiling, flaring trees. All else—the encampment and Hawk Hill—was lost to her.

It was as if a door opened then and cold blasted her and dimmed the white light, made the trees of flame dip and sputter like candle flames. She had a sense of traveling forward through a tunnel, of being touched by time and its passage. Through the opening came a faint, black breath of command: *Awaken the Sleepers.*

And that was it. She was thrust from the white light, out of the vision, and found herself blinking at her very ordinary campfire. She had sought the word of God and heard it, and she now knew what she had to do. She must take a journey, and she would hasten it by traveling the ancient ways of her mothers, which would cover long distances in a short time.

She stood. Though her bones ached, she did not feel weary, but renewed, excited, invigorated. She must now speak with her people and Captain Immerez.

SARGE'S GIFT

"This sword was made for stabbing
Make it rain blood ye infantrymen
This sword was made for slashing
Keep in step ye infantrymen"

At times the marching cadences allowed Beryl to transcend pain and discomfort, the rhythms carrying her aloft from the cares of the physical world up toward the dark of the heavens and peace, till she felt nothing at all.

Only to be yanked back to Earth by her guard jangling her chains, which sent shards of glass ripping through muscle and tendon. She screamed until she was too weak to scream, and was left whimpering and drenched with sweat, the gold chains strung tautly about her body. She became conscious of the camp buzzing around her and the sweat cooling on her skin. The tremors started as her body tried to warm itself, rattling the chains anew and sending the glass shards slashing again.

Did she weep blood? Did her flesh gape open from a multitude of wounds? She did not know. She knew only hooks and chains until she could gather her focus again, begin the marching cadences all over and escape. The moments of peace were worth the violence of being yanked back to herself, though she did not know how much more she could endure.

She was about to start the cadences again when she sensed Grandmother and the man standing nearby. She willed herself to listen to their conversation.

Grandmother sighed. "Eventually it would work. She's wearing down, but I have not the time to wait."

"What are you saying?" The man's gravelly voice chafed Beryl's nerves and only her will prevented her from shuddering.

"The book is on its way to Sacor City," Grandmother replied, "and our brothers and sisters there will see it to the high king's tomb. I am done here. It is time I went south and awaken those who sleep."

"Done?" the man demanded.

"Done *here,* my friend. The work itself goes on."

"What of us? You can't just leave us."

"But I must if I'm to succeed. You knew this day would come."

Silence.

Then, "I didn't think it would happen so soon," the man said. "What are we supposed to do?"

"As you always planned," Grandmother replied. "Disperse. Disperse as my sisters and brothers will, until called. Before I depart, I will release this Green Rider of her chains, and you may do with her as you wish. There is no time to see this experiment through to its conclusion."

Beryl almost cried out her joy. To be released from gold chains! It did not matter what came next, for surely even death was better. The man cleared his throat as though to respond to Grandmother, but a commotion arose from somewhere across the encampment. Grandmother and the man left her.

Her elation turned to despair and again she almost cried out, for Grandmother had not released her. She had no other choice but to focus again on her cadences. Maybe it would be the last time she'd have to do this. Maybe Grandmother would return soon and release her. She enfolded herself in the steady rhythm of her cadences and awareness of everything around her dissipated.

Even as blind and disoriented as Karigan was with her head shrouded in the cloak, she guessed they were climbing into the Teligmar Hills. She had to adjust her center of balance as her mount trod a continuous incline, and she sensed many changes in direction as though following a trail of switchbacks. It made her light-headed, this movement without vision to ground her.

The air burned the raw flesh of her hands, knees, and elbows and sent feverish tingles shivering along her nerves. Would she have a chance to pick the gravel out of her skin? She was lucky not to have been crushed by Falan, if one could call being captured luck. The cutthroats had kicked and hit her into submission, but by the grace of the gods she did not think any of her bones were broken, though everything hurt.

She continued to pray she gave Estora and Fergal time to escape. There'd been too much confusion and pain to know if any of the cutthroats were sent down the road to look for them. At this point she could only guess her own fate, and none of her guesses boded well.

As she rode she felt almost as if she floated and she allowed her mind to wander away from her circumstances. Images of the plains came to her, images that now seemed so distant and out of reach; waking dreams of freedom and a gentler, more pleasant time. But she did not see the Frosts or their herds of horses or Ero the wolfhound. She saw *him,* the great black stallion walking alongside her with grace beyond that of an ordinary horse. His hooves made no sound on the earth, the breeze feathered his mane and tail little even as it stirred the tips of grasses. Then he knelt on the ground beside her, waiting expectantly for her . . . for her to mount?

Her horse stumbled and she grabbed at the pommel of the saddle with a cry at the pain that jolted through her. Gone were the images of the plains, lost was the stallion from her mind. Why would she seek comfort in the death god's steed anyway?

The climb leveled out, and Sarge and his men were challenged by guards, followed by cheerful greetings of welcome. As they progressed, Karigan heard more and more activity around her, a spoon ringing on a pan, more horses whickering in the distance, voices in conversation, a hammer pounding . . . What was this place?

Amid the activity they came to a halt.

"Welcome back," someone said.

"What ya got there, Sarge?"

"Get her down," Sarge ordered.

Rough hands pulled Karigan off her horse and held her steady when she staggered. She concentrated so hard on maintaining her footing that she was surprised when the cloak was unbound and lifted from her. She blinked and squinted in the light until her vision cleared. Many people ringed her, gawking. There was Sarge and his band of cutthroats behind her and ordinary people of all ages before her, male and female, young and old, whole family groups. Sprinkled among them were the harder faces of soldiers, none wearing any device.

Muttering rippled through the crowd as a man shoved his way through, emerging before Karigan, towering over her. She stumbled backward in shock till she bumped into Sarge's men and could go no farther.

"Immerez," she whispered.

It was as if he stepped right out of a nightmare, glaring at her with his one green eye. The other was, just as she remembered, covered by a patch, a scar radiating out from beneath it. The waning light of the afternoon gleamed on his bald head.

Karigan shuddered with the memory of him hunting her, hunting her through the northern Green Cloak, his whip snapping behind her. Snagging her around her ankle till she cleaved off the hand that held the whip. She looked down and saw a sharp shining hook where that hand had once been.

If Karigan thought things were bad before . . .

"We have a problem," Sarge said.

Immerez glanced at Sarge in incredulity. "A problem?" he asked softly.

Karigan closed her eyes and shuddered, remembering that harsh voice.

Incredibly Immerez threw his head back and laughed. It was an awful rasping sound.

Then he struck like a viper, hooking Sarge's collar and drawing him close, almost nose to nose. Sarge swallowed hard.

"You've brought me a Greenie, not the lady of Coutre."

"I–I can explain!"

"Release him, Captain." An elderly woman appeared beside Immerez, a shawl across her shoulders and a basket of yarn over her wrist. She looked to be no one out of the ordinary, a villager or farmwife, someone's grandmother, but Immerez deferred to her and released Sarge.

Sarge licked his lips. "We . . . we had the lady, sure enough, all the way to the crossroads. As we waited for your men to come down, somehow she escaped—vanished." He glanced at Karigan. "A Greenie trick, no doubt."

"No doubt," Immerez echoed. "Then what happened?"

"We searched and searched the area. It was confusion, but then suddenly Lady Estora comes riding through the woods on her horse and we pursued. When we caught up, she killed three of my men, not to mention Whittle earlier. This one tricked us into thinking she was Lady Estora."

"Idiot." Immerez raised his hook as though to slash it across Sarge's neck. "How could you be fooled so easily?"

"Hold," the old woman said. "Hold, my friend."

Immerez's hook dropped to rest at his side. "Why should I? He failed us. He lost Lady Estora."

"Did he fail us? Really?" the woman asked. "He got her all the way to the crossroads, and I think it more than adequate."

Everyone gaped at her like she was mad.

"Our goal," she continued, "was to distract the king, was it not? To distract the king and those who serve him, to send them on a merry chase. It would have been nice to meet the lady, and to use her captivity to our advantage, but our first intention was to empty the tombs of its guards, yes?"

Immerez calmed and nodded, and Sarge let out a breath of relief.

Karigan's own thoughts were awhirl. They kidnapped Estora just to distract the king? To empty the tombs? What were they up to?

"*Who* are you?" she asked the woman.

The woman did not answer, but withdrew a pendant from beneath her chemise. It was crudely made of iron, but shaped into a design Karigan knew well: a dead tree.

"Second Empire," she whispered. She glanced at the onlookers. "You're all Second Empire?"

Some drew out pendants like the woman's, and others raised their hands, palms outward, to show the tattoo of the dead tree.

The old woman smiled kindly to her as she would to a child. "Just a few of us. There are more, many more out in the world, my dear."

"And *you?*" Karigan demanded of Immerez.

But it was the woman who answered. "There have always been those not of the blood who serve the empire. Arcosia, after all, was a land of many lands, and such cooperation was common." Then more brusquely she added, "And now it is time for us to disperse. No doubt the king's men will find this place in good time. Go on now," she said to her people, shooing them away. "Finish packing and leave as soon as you are able."

Many bowed and murmured, "Yes, Grandmother," and wandered away.

The woman said to Immerez, "You may do with the prisoners as you like. They are no concern of mine." She then walked away, among her people.

Memory of Fergal on his knees next to the Fountain Inn came to Karigan. He'd been sickened by the sight of an old woman. He'd seen in her, or around her, "all the worst things." Was this her? It had to be.

Immerez addressed his men, "Get to work. We leave in the morning."

When Sarge started to peel away, Immerez grabbed his

cloak with his hook. "Not you." Sarge blanched. "Did you send anyone looking for the lady?"

"Yes, sir. Clay and three others. If anyone can find her, Clay can."

Immerez released him. "Good. If he catches her, we may stand to profit after all."

When Sarge strode off, it was just Karigan and Immerez facing one another. He rubbed his cheek with the curve of his hook.

"Well, well," he said. "After all this time. How often I imagined what revenge I'd take if the opportunity arose. Sarge doesn't realize just what a gift he's brought me."

BLADES IN THE DARK

The road became uncommonly busy with travelers walking and riding. They looked commonplace enough to Amberhill, ordinary citizens alone and in groups, chatting and laughing among themselves, children skipping alongside carts loaded with belongings. It was just the sheer numbers of them on what should be a quiet road that made it so odd, like some exodus was occurring.

He grew even more suspicious when he discovered they were descending a winding path from one of the small mountains down to the road. It was too much of a coincidence to assume the travelers had nothing to do with the plainshield and his band of cutthroats, so Amberhill decided on a course of caution and hid from sight.

He watched from the shadows of the woods for a time, but did not see the plainshield or any of his men among the travelers. He decided he'd best climb the mountain if he wished to find them and concluded it wise to hide Goss and ascend on foot. It was difficult to remain stealthy with a horse in tow. Unfortunately it would cost him time and the sun was descending.

Amberhill secured Goss in a deep thicket hard against the rocky foundation of the mountain. There was even a trickle of a stream for the stallion to drink from. Once he settled Goss he returned to the trail. The travelers thinned out, but he kept to the shadows of the woods all the same, clambering among boulders and outcrops and the trunks of trees, the trail always just in sight. Whenever he detected someone coming down, he paused and watched. Still no sign of the plainshield or the one who posed as Lady Estora.

Up and up he climbed, scrambling straight up the slope, sometimes on hands and knees, instead of following each switchback. By the time the pitch leveled out, he found himself near the summit, the vegetation shrinking. He crouched low, watching for guards, and was not disappointed. He sank into some stunted trees and shrubs as the guard passed just a few paces from him. The deepening of dusk helped conceal him. Clouds had moved in through the afternoon, forming a halo around the low sun and obscuring rising stars.

When the guard was well off, he crept closer to view the summit, hiding among some boulders. An encampment spread out before him—a small encampment with tents. From the mixed stenches of animal and human waste, and after witnessing the exodus of the civilians, he could only conclude the encampment once sprawled across the whole of the summit. The ground cover was well-trampled and littered with refuse. There were numerous blackened fire rings left unlit like the remnants of some ancient civilization.

A few campfires popped up closer to the middle of the encampment. It was there, Amberhill surmised, he would find the brave soul who took Lady Estora's place.

"Keep her close to the light," Immerez ordered.

A pair of soldiers threw Karigan down beside a campfire, jarring her injuries. A cry escaped her lips and Immerez smiled.

Up until now, he'd spent his time organizing the followers of Second Empire in their departure and chivvying his own men to be prepared to leave in the morning. Throughout it all he stole glances at her like a hungry catamount anxious for dinner to begin. Finally, as the last stragglers departed and the gloom of dusk blanketed what remained of the encampment, he turned his full attention to her. A cold wind spread across the summit, blowing her hair into her eyes.

"We would not want to lose you in the dark, would we?"

Immerez said. "No, I should think not. Greenies have ways of vanishing, don't they?"

Karigan guessed he didn't expect an answer, so she didn't give him one. Not that she'd discuss Rider abilities with him anyway. She watched him pace before her, and again she saw the hungry catamount.

"You've no idea," he told her, "what it's been like. No idea. Hiding all this time as nothing more than a common outlaw, having my life and livelihood taken from me. *My hand.*" He waved his hook in front of her face, close enough she could see the tip had been honed to a sharp point.

He towered over her, gloating. "But who knew we'd meet again, eh? Who knew . . ."

"So you sold yourself to Second Empire." The words were out of Karigan's mouth before she could stop them.

"What else was I to do?" Immerez asked. "Run and hide in Rhovanny? No. The goals of Second Empire are not unlike that of Lord Mirwell's." The old lord, she assumed he meant. "To depose Hillander and establish a new order."

"Are you sure that's what you want? To become enslaved to the descendants of Arcosia? You know their history, don't you, their desire to establish Mornhavon the Black's empire here?"

"I am aware of their goals. And of course, they pay me well."

"They'd destroy this land," she said.

"What do you know of it?"

Quite a lot, actually, she thought. More than he could imagine.

"Besides," he added, "their side is the winning side. The day will come and the world will see. I intend to be among the winners."

Karigan sighed. She didn't have the energy to argue with him. He'd committed enough treasonous acts that no amount of words would sway him. And really, what choice *did* he have? He'd be executed if King Zachary's forces ever caught up with him—he was a hunted man so he might as well throw his lot in with anyone who offered him an alternative to being hanged. Odd that she was so understanding of his plight, though it had nothing to do with sympathy.

Must have jiggered my brain in the fall, she thought.

She wriggled her hands in their bonds, grimacing at the pain. Smoke spiraled up from the campfire and beyond it she could see Immerez's men moving about, some cooking by another fire. She did not know what to do to help herself. Without the dark, she could not fade, and Immerez was not about to let her out of the light. Without the ability to fade, she could not make an escape.

"What of your allegiance to Mirwell Province?" she asked him.

Immerez slashed his hook through the air. "It died with the old man. The boy is a pup, an idiot."

Karigan didn't disagree.

"No more than a tool," Immerez added.

That was interesting. "So he hasn't joined up with Second Empire's cause?"

"He complies," Immerez said.

With "help" from Colonel Birch, I bet, Karigan thought. As long as Immerez was feeling conversational, she might as well try to draw him out. If she survived this and could bring information to the king, it would be worth the effort. "About the one called Grandmother," she began, "what—"

He struck down on her and at first it felt as though she'd been stung on her head by a wasp, but then warm blood trickled down her forehead and dripped into her eyes. She blinked rapidly, stunned.

Immerez knelt before her, displaying his hook for her in the firelight, showing her the wad of bloody skin and hair on the tip.

"No more questions from Greenies," he said, his voice low. "Before daylight, you will know what my life is like, one-eyed and one-handed."

He wiped the hook off on her coat and his face filled her vision like a glowing orb, his features formed by darkness and flickering light. He rotated his head to fix her with his one eye, shadows shifting across his face. He smiled.

Blood blurred Karigan's eyes and she blinked them clear. He showed her the hook again, turning it carefully and slowly so she might see it from all angles. A sensation like cat paws tiptoed up her back—or maybe it was someone walking over her grave. She'd been here before, had seen it all in the telescope of the Berry sisters long ago, and she knew what was to happen next.

He moved the hook toward her eye.

"No!" she screamed.

A whisper of memory in her mind: *The future is not made of stone.* She could change what was to come.

Karigan drew her knees to her chest and kicked out, catching Immerez in the belly with her feet. He flailed backward, landing on his buttocks.

A vision of the telescope crashing to the floor, its lenses shattered.

She flipped to her belly to crawl away, only to come eye level with a pair of boots. She gazed up to find Sarge glaring at her.

"I don't think Captain Immerez is done with you."

"I'm not," Immerez said. "I forget how much fight this one has."

Cold air streamed across the ground and over Karigan's body. She shivered. Immerez grabbed her hair and hauled her back till she was on her knees.

"Sergeant," Immerez said. His voice was cool, as if he were giving some common order. "I want her right hand *here*." He tapped a stump that had served as a chopping block for kindling. A hatchet was embedded in it.

Karigan cried out and struggled, but Sarge clouted her in the head until she was too dazed to resist. The next thing she knew, her hands were unbound and another soldier had been called over to lock her left arm behind her back while Sarge clamped her right hand to the stump.

Immerez twirled the hatchet into the air and caught it as easily as Fergal had with the throwing knives at Preble Waystation so long ago.

Please be safe, Karigan thought to Fergal and Estora.

Please let this be worth it. To her shame, tears poured down her cheeks at what was about to happen.

Immerez tossed the hatchet, but this time he miscalculated his catch and leaped back when it tumbled down and hit the dirt. He picked it up.

"You took my sword hand," he said, "but I've been working hard with the other so it can be just as good. Seems I need more practice, but in this case, I don't think we need worry about accuracy."

Karigan struggled, but Sarge and the other soldier held her securely.

Immerez pressed the hatchet blade against her wrist to set up for the cutting stroke. "Not to worry," he told her, "the blade is sharp."

Karigan squeezed her eyes shut, waiting, just waiting, a scream building inside her, but still the hatchet did not descend.

"Sergeant," Immerez said, "remove the glove first."

Before Karigan could recoil, Sarge stripped Estora's doeskin glove from her hand, tearing off scabbing flesh and probably some gravel, too. She screamed.

Immerez chuckled. "That injury will not bother you much longer." He raised the hatchet again and Karigan waited for it to fall.

Instead, the soldier locking Karigan's arm behind her screamed and released his hold on her. He dropped to the ground, a knife jutting from his back. The hatchet hurtled down and buried itself into the chopping block just a hairsbreadth from her fingertips. Sarge let go of her hand and drew his sword. Immerez cried out in fury and whirled around. Men shouted into the night.

Karigan wasted no time—she crawled away from her distracted captors, crawled away from the light of the campfire and faded, leaving behind only a bloody handprint on the chopping block.

She kept crawling, always away from sources of light—other campfires, torches . . . Men ran by her, weapons drawn. She just kept crawling into the dark.

She started to give one tent a wide berth, for a lamp glowed dimly within, but then the wind opened the flap as if just for her to see the figure sitting cross-legged on the ground inside, dressed in a scarlet uniform.

Karigan hesitated, not sure she believed what she saw. *Beryl?*

She glanced over her shoulder. Whatever the disturbance was, it kept Immerez and his men busy on the other side of the encampment. She dropped her fading and crawled into the tent.

It *was* Beryl, sitting peacefully with eyes closed, her hands upon her knees. Strands of indigo yarn were looped and woven around her like a messy spiderweb.

"Beryl?"

Karigan's query elicited no response, so she pulled at the yarn. Beryl's scream made her fall back.

Beryl's eyes shot open and she gazed about herself as if awakening from a long slumber.

"It doesn't hurt," she murmured. "The chains and hooks are gone."

"Chains and hooks?" Karigan asked. "I see only yarn."

"Yes, it's . . ." Beryl looked at her, squinting. "Who are you? Where's Grandmother? You're not Little Girl . . ."

Karigan crawled closer. "It's Karigan—Karigan G'ladheon. You know me. Look, we have to get out of here, and quickly."

Beryl did not move, and continued to gaze at her with the dazed expression. "You've a face of blood."

"I know." Karigan wiped at it with her sleeve. It was sticky. She gave up and started pulling yarn off Beryl. It was wound in some pattern, knotted in places, but she could not make sense of it. She broke strands with her teeth when she became confounded by knots.

Beryl's face was wan, with dark rings beneath her eyes, and her forehead creased from great strain. She was thinner than Karigan remembered, but she could detect no obvious physical wounds on her.

When finally she pulled off the last strand of yarn and

threw it to the ground, Beryl looked down at herself in incredulity.

"Grandmother said she'd remove the chains and I guess she did." She patted herself up and down. "I . . . I don't hurt."

Karigan only half listened, trying to be alert to trouble outside the tent. Soldiers still shouted outside but they sounded more distant. She doused the lamp.

"What are . . . ?" Beryl began.

"We have to leave," Karigan said. "Something's distracted the soldiers and we have to escape while we can."

"But . . . but where are we?"

Karigan helped Beryl rise, which was a feat considering she could hardly stand herself. "Teligmar Hills. Immerez is in charge here."

Beryl swayed and Karigan shook her. "That's who . . ." Beryl whispered. "I couldn't think, I couldn't . . ."

"Never mind all that," Karigan said. "We're faded out. We're leaving."

The dark outside was immense enough that if they avoided fires and torches they'd be hard to see even without fading, but Karigan wasn't taking chances. The wind swirled around them as they left the tent and Karigan felt something cold and sharp alight on her cheek.

Snow.

Amberhill, feeling more like an assassin than a gentleman thief, eliminated three of the perimeter guards before they could cry out and raise the alarm in the encampment.

He planned to continue with the stealthy slayings, bide his time till he could aid the young woman, but he saw what the one-eyed man was going to do to her hand and he couldn't let it happen. He needed to act.

So he positioned himself as well as he could, and as quickly as he could, but his best target was one of the cutthroats restraining the young woman, not their leader. His knife struck true.

From then on he lost track of what became of the young woman. In the pandemonium she disappeared and he had other things to worry about. His foes weren't like the pirates he met in the woods—these were disciplined warriors. He could tell by the way they carried themselves and guarded the encampment and how immediately they sprang to once the alarm went up, all the while retaining order.

Unfortunately there were quite a lot of them. All the throwing knives in the world would not help him now. He ran into the brush, hoping to disappear into the night without breaking a leg on the uneven ground, but they pinpointed him like hounds after a fox and came howling after him.

He crashed through shrubs and branches, leaped from boulder to boulder and only his excellent balance saved him from a disastrous fall. And still they came rushing headlong after him.

Cold, wet drops pricked his skin, and at first he thought it was raining, then he saw the graying of the night. Snow.

As he descended the side of the small mountain, he realized he would never reach Goss in time. He'd have to turn and fight. He had made a mess of his "rescue"—a mess from the very beginning. He only hoped the young woman could escape while he provided a distraction.

Finally he stopped running, skidded to a stop. He drew his rapier and parrying dagger, took a deep breath, and turned around to face his fate. If he was destined to be sent to the hells this night, he was sure it was as he deserved, but he wouldn't go down without taking as many of the cutthroats with him as he could.

The silhouettes of the men surged toward him through the dark and he saw the barest of gleaming light on their weapons. Their movement changed the pattern of the falling snow, made it swirl back into itself. He felt only stillness, could hear the snowflakes landing on his shoulders, his head, the branches of nearby trees.

When the cutthroats reached him, they almost plowed right into him. Perhaps he stood so still they thought him a tree. To his pleasure, the plainshield led them—the plainshield who had betrayed him, had betrayed Morry. He'd overheard the men call him Sarge.

"So here is the lady's *hero,*" Sarge said. "You're too late—someone else already rescued her." He and his men laughed.

"A testament to your competency, I surmise," Amberhill said in a mild tone.

Sarge growled and raised his sword.

"We've business, you and I," Amberhill continued.

"That right? Do I know you?"

Amberhill dropped the purse of gold at Sarge's feet. The clinking of coins was unmistakable.

"What's this about?" Sarge asked.

The wind kicked up, making new patterns in the flurries, sending them this way and that, blowing the hair away from Amberhill's face.

"It is," he said, "the price of your death."

Sarge backed a step and the men behind him grumbled.

"Kill 'im, Sarge!" one cried.

"Silence!"

Amberhill sensed Sarge's disquiet, could see it in his stance and hear it in his voice.

"You speak in riddles," Sarge said. "Maybe you are some madman, but it doesn't matter, for you will be wolf fodder shortly." His men laughed at this.

When they quieted, Amberhill said, "You cannot kill a man twice."

"You *are* mad. You speak nonsense."

"No," Amberhill said, a lightness filling him, a sense of not fearing death, "I am the Raven Mask."

"But he's—"

Before Sarge could say the word "dead," Amberhill knocked his sword from his hand and even as it clattered on the rocks, Sarge collapsed to the ground with his throat slashed open. Amberhill's nostrils flared with the scent of blood.

"Pity," Amberhill told the corpse. "I'd hoped to feed you those coins."

The other men backed off, a few crying out. They turned tail and fled in terror back the way they'd come.

Amberhill was aghast. "Huh. Guess they weren't as tough as I feared. Not that I'm complaining, of course."

He turned and almost fell from his rock. Gleaming sword blades bristled out of the dark, carried by shadows that passed by him in silence. Only the snow powdering their heads and shoulders, and the glint of their eyes, revealed they were living beings.

His legs weakened beneath him and he sat beside the corpse that was steadily accumulating snow and shuddered. None of the shadows stopped to speak to him, or even acknowledged his existence. They were on a mission and Sarge's men were as good as dead already.

FIGHTING THE HEAVENS

Karigan staggered through the gray, swirling cloud she was caught in. She could not say where she was, or where she was going. She just kept trudging on.

She put her hand to her throbbing head and groaned. Blood loss and the abuses to her body weakened her, and the use of her special ability did not help. "I've got to sit," she told Beryl, and she dropped to the ground where she was, not caring about the snow. Beryl sat beside her and said nothing, and Karigan held onto her arm as much to keep them both faded out as to remain grounded.

The black stallion awaited her on the plains. He lay on the ground with his legs tucked beneath him, but now the grasses were covered in snow. A storm was reflected in his eyes, a turmoil of snow squalls warring in shifting winds.

He wanted her to ride with him into the storm? Was that it?

She shuddered out of the vision. Her hand slipped from Beryl's sleeve and hastily she grabbed the Rider's wrist. Beryl was shivering, or was it she herself who shivered?

I am lost, and it will be the death of us.

Beryl remained mute and had allowed herself to be led aimlessly around. It was wholly unlike the Rider Karigan remembered. She blinked into the gray dark and against the snow blowing into her eyes. Her surroundings were indistinguishable from any other part of the small mountain. She strained to hear sounds of pursuit, but only the wind sheared past her ears.

A shape loomed out of the gray ahead of her, and before she could move herself or Beryl, it tripped over them.

"What the—?" he said as he fell.

Karigan let go of Beryl, and before the man could say or do anything, Karigan launched herself on him, pounding her stiff, sore hands on him, but he threw her off, and when she hit the ground, the gray world darkened and closed in.

The black stallion still waited for her on the snowy expanse of the plains. He gazed at her, waited for her to make some sort of decision.

"Whad you want?" she demanded of him. Her mouth felt full of cotton.

"What is she saying?" someone asked from afar.

"Don't know. Hold her still until I finish."

Something, a snowdrift, yes, a snowdrift, weighed her down. She could not move toward the stallion or walk away.

Prick.

"Ow!" The piercing of flesh seared through confusion.

"Don't move, Karigan," said the voice from afar. "I've got a few more stitches to go."

Ty? Ty was there on the plains with her? Yes. His hands were busy above her head. Ty sewing. Of course. Ty was excellent at sewing. He always carried needles and thread with him in case a tear in his uniform required mending. He was Rider Perfect.

Prick, tug. The drawing of thread through her skin.

The stallion stood and shook his mane. His black hide against the white landscape was like an open window to the heavens. She saw the stars within him, celestial bodies in brilliant colors with dust clouds swirling in storms around them.

"You're pulling me in!" she cried.

The snow held her down. She kicked and flung out her hands.

"Keep her still!" Ty said.

"I'll sit on her legs," someone, a third someone, offered.

"I don't want to go," Karigan said. "Salvistar wants me to go to the heavens."

"For gods' sakes," Ty said, "you're not dying. It's the shock," he told the others.

It was too hard to fight; too hard to fight the heavens, to keep from being sucked into the blackness amid the celestial bodies and their veils of sparkling dust. Where would she end up? Would she be allowed to return home?

"So many stars," she murmured.

Prick, tug.

"I just want to go home."

Prick, tug.

"There," Ty said, "I've made the last knot."

Amberhill slid wearily into the chair beside the woman's cot. Ty asked that they take turns sitting through the night with her to keep watch lest her condition worsen, and Amberhill volunteered for the second watch.

At first he had not recognized her for all the blood that masked her face, but when Ty washed it away, he found a face he could not forget. Who could forget a lady who challenged him with a sword?

"Who is she?" he demanded of Ty.

"Green Rider," was the simple reply.

It explained her actions that day in the museum and why no one among the aristocrats had known her, but it did not answer his question by half. He learned her name and of course knew of the G'ladheon merchanting clan. Lady, messenger, merchant. Even the Weapons seemed to regard her with some esteem. But *who* was she?

Obviously someone born with an insane sort of courage.

As he sat there in the dark, chin propped on hand, listening to her breathing, he found himself vexed by her, but he didn't know why. Maybe it was because she had challenged him at the museum when all other ladies would have swooned in his presence or begged for his favors. Maybe he disliked being deceived. She was a lady, then was not. She was Estora Coutre, then was not. Frustrating!

He yawned, the debate simmering, then dying, as he fell asleep.

Muted daylight through canvas.

"Strange dreams," she murmured.

"She's coming around," someone said.

With her awakening came awareness of pain, her throbbing head, the strained muscles, bruises, and lacerations.

"What?" she asked the light. "Am I home?"

"No."

"Ty?"

He stood above her, looking down at her. "That's right." He smiled, but it was a tired smile. "What do you remember?"

An image of a gloating Immerez rushed into her mind, his hook slashing down, blood in her eyes. "I remember everything." She went to touch her head and was surprised to find her hand, both hands, swaddled in bandages.

"Willis picked out all the gravel and dressed them," Ty said.

"Willis?"

"At your service." The Weapon stepped into her vision opposite Ty.

She had yet to make sense of where she was and what Ty was doing here, much less one of the king's Weapons. Everything was fuzzy around the edges. "Where am I?"

"You're in the encampment," Willis said. "One of the officer's tents."

"What . . . what are you doing here?" She started to take in more of her surroundings, the dim tent interior, the cot she lay on. She was covered in layers of blankets and it was then she realized she was very naked beneath the covers, except for bandages on her knees and elbows. She blushed and it made her head pound all the more.

"We came to rescue Lady Estora," Willis said. "We found you and Rider Spencer instead."

"Immerez—" Karigan said.

"He is under restraint," Willis replied. "He will be questioned."

"Tombs! Grandmother wanted the tombs beneath the castle emptied."

"Grandmother? We haven't seen any grandmothers here," Ty said. "And what would anyone want with all those corpses?"

"Not the corpses," Karigan said. "Emptied of *Weapons.*"

Both men fell silent and gazed at one another.

"The tomb Weapons are guarding the king while the rest of us are here," Willis said in a quiet voice. "The tombs are essentially empty of Weapons but for a minimum contingent."

"Why would this Grandmother want such a thing?" Ty asked.

"She's Second Empire," Karigan replied.

Silence again.

"Karigan," Willis said, "you will have to tell us everything you know, both about Lady Estora and what Second Empire is up to."

"First," Ty said, "let her have this. Sit up carefully, Karigan."

The banging in her head intensified as she did so. When she was securely propped up, Ty passed her a warm mug of broth and a hunk of bread to dip in it. The broth was heartening, and she hadn't realized how famished she was until it was all gone. Ty fetched her another mugful and more bread, and as she finished this serving, someone else entered the tent. He stepped right up to the side of her cot beside Willis. His jaw was covered with stubble and he wore a shabby cloak. A lock of black hair fell over one of his eyes and through it he stared hard at her.

"Who's this?" Karigan asked Willis.

"Lord Amberhill," he replied. "He was in Lady Estora's party when it was attacked, and tracked her all this way. He's the one who found you and Beryl."

"Tripped over you," the man said.

"Oh." What else could Karigan say?

"How did you do it?" Lord Amberhill demanded, still gazing intensely at her. "How did you assume Lady Estora's place? I followed her all the way to the crossroads, but then she became you."

"Stand down, my lord," Willis said. "Karigan was about to tell us everything, but she's only just awakened."

"Tea?" Ty asked her.

Karigan started to nod, but regretted it for the pain. "Yes, please," she said.

Ty left and the tent remained in uneasy silence until he returned. While the tea cooled, Karigan recounted everything from her stop in Mirwellton to the point where Lord Amberhill tripped over her. She did not, in the presence of this unknown man, speak of her fading ability. She figured Ty and Willis guessed at her using it.

"You do not know where the lady is now?" Willis asked.

"No. All I know is that she and Fergal are heading east to Sacor City as secretly as possible. Lady Estora is riding under the name of Rider Esther."

Willis placed his hand on her shoulder. "You are truly a sister-at-arms. You've done well."

"Th–thank you," Karigan said at the unexpected praise.

"I am now going to order half a dozen Weapons to search after them," Willis said, and he left the tent.

"Beryl is anxious to question Immerez herself," Ty said, "and once she finishes, Osric or I will ride east, as well, with the news."

"Osric? How many of you are here?"

"Two Riders and a phalanx of Weapons. There wasn't much of a battle," Ty reflected. "Immerez's men, those still alive, were quickly rounded up."

Karigan could only imagine the scene of all those angry Weapons swarming the summit. It would have been terrifying.

"What is Second Empire?" Lord Amberhill asked.

"Descendants of Arcosians who came to this land with Mornhavon the Black," Ty explained. "Through all these centuries, they have retained a secret society with the dream of eventually restoring the empire to power."

"Madness," Lord Amberhill said.

"That's usually what it takes," Ty replied.

Karigan sipped at her tea, her eyelids sagging, the weight of exhaustion settling back down upon her.

"I'm going to fetch some more linens to redress your head wound," Ty said, "and a fresh poultice. I did a good job if I do say so myself, though, uh, I had to cut some of your hair. I'm afraid it will look odd for a while."

Karigan was sure Ty's stitching was very fine, and she was equally sure that beneath the bandage, her head looked terrible. It would be a while before she had any desire to look in a mirror.

Lord Amberhill cleared his throat and she jolted, spattering tea on her blankets. She'd forgotten he was there.

"There is more to your story," he said. "I tripped over *nothing.*"

Karigan did not feel like speaking to this man. She was tired and did not possess the energy to fence around her special ability. "It was dark."

"I know what I saw. Or didn't see. I have excellent night vision."

"Not excellent enough." She yawned, wondering if Ty slipped something into her tea to help her rest.

"I thought you were a lady," Lord Amberhill murmured.

"Excuse me?"

He scowled at her. "You're a Green Rider and you deceived me. It explains a few things, but not your . . . your invisibility."

Karigan wished she did not feel so vulnerable, tired and hurting, and naked beneath her covers. The air of superiority he exuded irritated her.

"I think I understand," she told him, "what is bothering you."

"And what would that be?"

"You were denied the rescue of Lady Estora by a common messenger. Your glory was stolen from you."

His face reddened. She did not attribute it to embarrassment, but anger.

"I did not pursue the lady and her captors for glory," he said. "And I didn't climb this mount for the pleasure of a hiking excursion. I came to help the brave soul who effected the escape of Lady Estora."

Heat warmed Karigan's cheeks, and for her it *was* embarrassment. "That was your knife that took out Immerez's man?"

Lord Amberhill nodded.

"Thank you." Why did it gall her to say those two words? She *was* thankful, after all. She just didn't like being thankful to *him*.

"Your Rider friend Ty does do neat work," he said, "even when you're thrashing around. But I believe you'll be wanting a hat for a while. Or maybe a hood."

With that, he turned on his heel and left the tent. Karigan repressed the urge to hurl her teacup after him.

HANDS

Beryl sat at the small table, gazing at Immerez, who was securely bound to a chair. A Weapon stood on duty just outside the tent's entrance, alert to her needs. Willis, aside from reassuring himself she was well enough, was not at all averse to her conducting the interrogation. He knew of her skills.

She fiddled with Immerez's hook on the table, safely detached from his stump. It was sharp enough to rip out a throat. The apparatus included a rigging of leather straps and buckles used to secure the hook to his wrist, which she examined with mild interest. Also on the table lay a hatchet, the one Lord Amberhill said Immerez was going to use to chop off Karigan's hand.

Beryl just sat there, not speaking, while Immerez glowered in defiance. He'd never been subjected to her questioning before. Lucky him—until now. She'd promised Willis she would not draw this out, but there was a craft to it, a way to go about it that varied with each individual questioned, that simply could not be rushed. She believed Immerez would cave in good time—all that defiance was a facade for his uncertainty. She'd seen it before in her other subjects.

The longer she sat there, the more she played with his hook, making the buckles jingle, the more he glowered. She was patient. She could wait. Soon he would not be able to help himself and would break the silence. Even now he tightened his jaw, setting off a tick in his cheek.

While she waited, she caught herself chanting marching

cadences in her mind. It was hard to free herself of them, of their comforting, certain rhythms. They'd saved her when she was bound in golden chains, kept her sane, kept her from breaking.

Even after a good night's rest and all the food she could eat, she felt wrung out. Tired. She could sleep for days, but she would not let anyone else handle this interrogation. There was unfinished business between her and Immerez.

She set aside the hook, folded her hands on her lap, and gazed steadily at him through her specs. She remained perfectly still, not tapping her foot or fidgeting. Her fight was to keep from falling asleep.

Immerez tested his bonds subtly by flexing his muscles, but she, of course, did not miss a thing. He clenched and unclenched his left hand. The lines of his forehead darkened into furrows. The tick quickened in his cheek. He was growing angrier by the second and she didn't think she'd have to wait much longer.

Sure enough, he broke the silence. "Are you so pleased with yourself that all you can do is sit there and gloat?"

She did not reply, just waited.

"Should've killed you," he continued, "but Grandmother had to try her little experiment."

"For how long did you know I was an operative?" she asked.

If he was surprised she finally spoke, he did not show it. "Birch found your return to Mirwellton suspicious, but then he became as convinced as everyone else that you were as you claimed, a loyalist to Mirwell Province. Until summer. Then we knew."

Summer. Many odd things had gone on and she received word that Rider abilities faltered. Her own ability to assume a role must have failed her as well, and Birch and his compatriots saw through it. It made sense. But it was too late to worry about it now.

"To think you were Lord Mirwell's favorite," Immerez said. "After all I did for him."

Old Lord Mirwell he meant. "Still bitter?" she asked.

"Still bitter I got all the promotions and his attention while he treated you like dirt? And it really turns your gut that I was a spy all that time, too, doesn't it."

Immerez did not reply and resumed glowering at the tent wall.

Beryl laughed. "Yet you were loyal to a fault. You loved the old fool. In your mind, you were the son he *should* have had." Abruptly she rose and paced, allowing her boot heels to click on the tent's wooden platform. "I, too, am loyal. Loyal to Sacoridia, to my king, to the Green Riders, and most of all, to the province of my birth. That is no lie."

He turned his glare on her. "How can you say that when you betrayed your lord-governor?"

"I said I was loyal to my province, not necessarily my lord-governor. Tomas Mirwell was a fool."

"He wanted to restore the province to its glory," Immerez shouted.

"For what? Endless years of warring among the clans? By replacing King Zachary on the throne with his greedy and cruel brother? The unity between the provinces would have crumbled, not to mention your Eletian friend, Shawdell, meant for chaos to occur so he could destroy the D'Yer Wall and cultivate the power of Blackveil for his own purposes."

Immerez clenched his jaw and remained silent.

"So now you've decided to help Second Empire."

Immerez shrugged in his bonds. "Would anything I say matter? I will be hanged in the end anyway."

Beryl smiled. "Your ultimate fate is for the king to decide. Things could be made easier for you if you answer my questions. But in the end, I suppose you're right—it does not matter whether or not you've always been in league with Second Empire. I have other questions."

"I'm not in an answering mood," Immerez replied.

"You will be."

"I've been wondering when I'd see the terrible interrogator I heard whispered of in Mirwell Keep. I still don't see her."

"Do you remember my brother by any chance?"

"That's your question?"

"His name," Beryl said, "was Riley Spencer, as proud and loyal a Mirwellian you could ever meet. He served as a private in the militia. He was proud of his uniform, and I remember when he came home on his first leave wearing that scarlet uniform with its chevrons and shiny buttons. He was so excited and I looked up to him. I wanted to be like him when I grew up. Twelve years ago you were what? A young sergeant?"

"That's right," Immerez said warily. "I was in charge of the house guard then."

"I know. Tell me, how has it been for you since you lost your hand?"

It took him a moment to catch up with the sudden change of topic. "How do you think?"

"I think it must have been a terrible adjustment for an officer in his prime to lose his sword hand," she said, displaying her own in front of his face, stretching out her fingers then curling them into a fist. "All those things you were accustomed to doing, actions as natural as breathing, were no longer possible. Scratching an itch, for instance, or eating. You've had to retrain your mind to even just remember your hand is not there."

"So?" Immerez said. "Lots of soldiers lose limbs in combat."

"I think," Beryl continued, as if she hadn't heard him, "it sometimes feels like that hand is still connected to your wrist. You *feel* it. You can feel yourself flex phantom fingers. Maybe you feel your hand cramp or the palm sweat. But I think where you really feel it is *here*." She put her fist to her heart.

Immerez said nothing, but he was taut, almost shaking. Yes, she knew exactly how it had been for him.

"I suppose there are practical matters," Beryl said, "that became more difficult. Dressing and undressing, caring for your personal needs. Convincing your men you were whole and strong."

"How would you know?" he demanded. "You've got both your hands."

She picked up the hatchet from the table and weighed it in her palm. "Still don't remember, do you?"

"Remember? Remember what?" He'd paled when she picked up the hatchet.

"Can you appreciate irony, Immerez?"

He just stared incredulously at her.

"Private Riley Spencer," she said. "One of yours. New to your unit."

He paled even more. Yes, he was beginning to remember.

"There was an incident with one of Lord Mirwell's favorite saddles. It was dropped or some such, and the leather marred. Lord Mirwell was not pleased and demanded justice. Someone claimed it was Private Spencer who committed this terrible act of clumsiness."

Immerez licked his lips. Perspiration broke out on his temple. Beryl was pleased, and pointed the hatchet at him. "It was you, wasn't it, who marred the saddle. It was you who reported my brother. He told me this after the incident. Did you know how much he respected his sergeant? How much in awe of him he was? That was *you* he looked up to. He would have followed you into a fire or a volley of arrows if you so commanded it.

"But you betrayed him. To you he was just another private, young and expendable, but you had ambitions and could not be seen as less than perfect in your lord's eyes. And in the end, who would the lord-governor listen to? A simple, untried private from the country, or an experienced sergeant he was grooming for greater things?"

"Lies," Immerez sputtered.

"A dying man usually tells no lies," Beryl replied. "I, for one should know, considering how many I've brought to the brink. And make no mistake, when Mirwell cut off my brother's hands in punishment and sent him home in disgrace, he was already dying. Dying inside. There is not much a man can do without his hands. He can't work the land, write, or hold a sword. Truly I can only guess at how it felt to him to have his mother and little sister tend to his every need, no matter how trivial or private. But worst of all, the betrayal broke his heart. Your betrayal."

She gazed at the hatchet, turned it over in her hand. "Eventually he took his own life; jumped off a cliff because he couldn't put a knife in his own gut."

"It was Lord Mirwell who cut off his hands!" Immerez said.

"So it was. And you knew his pleasure at doling out such punishments, which is why you could not do the honorable thing and admit you were the one to scuff the saddle."

"Would you?" Immerez demanded.

Beryl raised her eyebrow and smiled. "I would not have found myself in that position in the first place. I knew what kind of a lord-governor we were stuck with and I did not serve him. But this is not about me or my choices. It's not even about my brother or the old Lord Mirwell. This is about you, some questions you can answer, and this hatchet."

Immerez sweated profusely now, his bald head glistening with droplets.

"I think among those rumors you heard about me circulating the keep," she continued, "was that I was ruthless, pitiless, and cruel." She bent down beside his ear and whispered, "The rumors are true."

She then stepped back and said, "I'll start with the fingers on your remaining hand, and if I receive no satisfaction, I will cut off the hand and work up your arm in slices. I've irons heating over the fire outside to cauterize the wounds."

True fear finally awakened in Immerez's eye and he strained against his bonds. "You said the king would decide my fate!"

"And so he will. It does not, however, preclude my use of certain questioning techniques. A pity for you, for you will not be allowed to die, and you will want to by the time I'm through."

Immerez's nostrils flared. "Should have killed you!"

"Yes," Beryl said, "you should have." She sat in her chair, crossed her legs, and settled the hatchet on her lap. She gave him her most pleasant smile. "Ready to answer some questions?"

ANSWERS

When Karigan awoke the next morning, she felt about a hundred years old despite the mug of willowbark tea Ty provided her to help dull the pain. Every muscle felt wrenched and every inch of her skin was scraped raw or bruised. Ty also produced a satisfying breakfast of flatcakes and sausages he said were from Immerez's own stores. Her stomach was about the only thing that wasn't sore and she was happy to fill it, but it hurt just to lift the food to her mouth.

When she finished, Ty carried in a bundle of clothes. "Try these when you feel up to it," he said. "I'm afraid the riding habit you were wearing had to be cut off you."

Even blushing hurt, causing throbbing in her tender head. When Ty left the tent, however, she forced herself out of bed, groaning with every little movement. She took care of her needs, and though she'd been supplied with a warm bucket of water to wash up with, she'd been instructed not to get her bandages wet. That was hard when her hands were swathed in linens. What was she supposed to do? Stick her head in the bucket? But, no, she had bandages there, too.

Finally she decided just to remove the bandages on her hands, so she unwound them, gingerly pulling them off where they adhered to her lacerations. Some of the scabs tore off and started bleeding again. Tears filled her eyes when she dipped her hands into the water, they stung so bad. When she finished and dried off, she had trouble rebinding her hands, but somehow managed with the help of her teeth. Willis or Ty would have to do better later.

As for the clothing, it appeared Ty and Osric had scrounged through their saddlebags for uniform parts. From this she was able to pick out an oversized shirt, baggy trousers and a belt to tighten them with, as well as a shortcoat. Even if none of it fit just right, it was far and away better than a corset and habit, and seeing herself in green again lifted her spirits.

When she stepped out of the tent she found herself in a new world. Snow blanketed the summit, and beyond heavy clouds cut off the view to the surrounding landscape so that she felt trapped in a shifting, vaporous fortress.

Weapons huddled around campfires, draped in black cloaks and clasping mugs in their hands. They looked like graveside mourners, heads bowed, speaking quietly. Others stood guard over a dozen or so of Immerez's men, who appeared to be bound hand and foot. Yet another pair of Weapons guarded a tent.

When they saw her, a few hailed her with greetings and she smiled and waved. She was about to ask after Ty and Willis when Ty appeared from another tent and trudged through the snow toward her. His breath puffed upon the air and she shivered with the cold.

"Glad to see you up," he said when he reached her. "Do you feel ready for a meeting?"

She nodded.

"This way then." He led her back across his tracks toward the tent he emerged from. "Osric has already left with the news."

"Already?"

"It seemed best to send him as soon as possible." He halted in front of the tent and raised his hand to keep her from entering it. "Just one moment. When you were rather out of it, you called me Rider Perfect. What . . . what did you mean by it?"

Karigan's head started throbbing again. "Um, I . . . I don't—"

"Karigan? Is that you out there?" came an inquiry from within the tent.

She let out a breath of relief. Saved by Willis! "We're here," she said, and she entered the tent, very conscious of Ty right behind her.

Inside she found Beryl, Willis, Lord Amberhill, and another Weapon Karigan knew, named Donal, all sitting around a small table in the center. They looked up when she entered, and Willis rose and rounded the table.

"Our sister-at-arms should not freeze." He removed his fur-lined cloak and wrapped it around her shoulders.

She warmed quickly and her shivers subsided. "What about you?" she asked him. "Aren't you cold?"

"I've a spare. Do not worry."

Karigan was given a chair and she took in Beryl's appearance. The Rider was still in Mirwellian scarlet, but also wore a black cloak over her shoulders. Her cheeks were gaunt and her face lined with care, but her eyes were alert and her shoulders square. She looked exhausted and worn to the bone, but straight as steel. This was much more the Rider Karigan remembered.

"Are you well?" Karigan asked her.

"Very well," Beryl said. She looked pleased with herself.

"She got Immerez to talk," Ty said.

"Immerez? Talk?" Karigan was still too befuddled by all that had happened to sound overly coherent.

"Didn't take much," Beryl said. "He wanted to keep his hand."

Karigan could only stare. She knew what sort of work Beryl did, or at least she had an idea of it, but it was hard to reconcile a Green Rider engaging in such "interrogations."

"What did he say?" Karigan asked, not wanting to dwell on *how* the information was acquired.

"He talked about a book," Willis said, "that was supposed to tell about the making of the D'Yer Wall."

"That's what the king sent you to find in Selium, wasn't it?" Ty asked her.

"Yes, but Lord Fiori didn't believe it was there."

"It wasn't," Willis said. "Just where it was hidden Immerez wasn't clear on, but one of his men went after it. Apparently this Grandmother, who is the leader of Second Empire, or at least *this* faction, knew how to find it. She is also the one who ordered some thefts."

"The Sacor City War Museum," Karigan said.

Lord Amberhill bowed his head into his hand when she said the words, but what really caught her eye was the ruby on his finger. It was the shade of blood, and as she had seen too much of her own of late, she shuddered and looked away, nestling into the fur of the cloak.

"Yes," Willis said. "Second Empire, working through Immerez and his men, hired a thief to steal a document from the museum. The thief was, or claimed to be, the Raven Mask, apparently out of retirement. In any event, he was slain in the scheme to abduct Lady Estora. Or at least that's what witnesses say. We found no body."

"Yes," Karigan said. "I'd heard that. What of the document? Did Immerez say what Second Empire wanted with it?"

He said it contained instructions for using the book. The problem was that it was in Old Sacoridian, and no one among them could translate it. Which led to the second theft."

"Selium," Karigan said. "It happened just before I arrived there."

Willis nodded. "Once they had the key to Old Sacoridian, they were able to translate the instructions."

"Why would a book require instructions?" Karigan asked. "I mean, it's a *book*."

Willis and Donal exchanged glances, and Karigan felt silly for asking, but she'd known books to contain instructions, not require them.

"This book was written by a great mage." It was Donal who spoke, and his rich, deep voice took Karigan by surprise. "It is an arcane object and likely does not obey the same rules as a book of mundane origins."

"Immerez gave up the instructions," Willis said. "That the book could only be read in the light of the high king's tomb."

Karigan passed her hand over her eyes, feeling tired, almost light-headed. "That's why Grandmother wanted the tombs emptied of Weapons."

"Hence Lady Estora's abduction," Willis replied. "It was as big a diversion as they could think of."

Of course it was. She knew all too well how important the betrothal between King Zachary and Lady Estora was for maintaining unity among the provinces. She could only imagine all those members of Clan Coutre besieging the king with their demands for Estora's safe return, and their threats if he failed to bring her back unharmed. If Estora were harmed, or worse, killed, not only would Coutre and its maritime allies seek vengeance, but the confidence of the people in their king would erode. All this while he and his advisors should be focusing on Blackveil.

Naturally, to appease Coutre and to ensure Estora's safe return, King Zachary sent his most elite warriors, his own Weapons, in pursuit of the captors. Someone needed to guard the king, so the tomb Weapons were brought above, leaving the tombs without their normal protection.

"Grandmother had no real interest in Lady Estora," Willis continued, "other than the distraction her abduction would cause. Immerez was more interested in obtaining ransom and committing vengeance against the king for bringing down, and executing, Tomas Mirwell."

Karigan was more relieved than ever Estora never had the chance to meet Immerez. She did not like to think what he would have done to King Zachary's betrothed. "The book," she said faintly. "Where is it now?"

"Immerez believes it is by now on its way to Sacor City and the tombs," Beryl said. "Immerez was most amused. He said his man should be about there by now, and that members of Second Empire in the city would aid him."

Karigan looked from face to face at those seated at the table. All were grim. The reason Immerez was amused was that there was not a thing any of them could do to stop the book from reaching its destination. They were too far away.

"So," Beryl said, "Second Empire will be able to learn all about the craft that went into the making of the D'Yer Wall so they can unmake it."

"And when Mornhavon the Black returns," Karigan said, "nothing will stand in his way."

The remainder of the meeting consisted of logistics. Ty would take the information gleaned from Immerez to the king, though by the time he reached Sacor City, it may very well prove irrelevant. Karigan, Beryl, and Lord Amberhill would set off the next morning, accompanied by a contingent of Weapons. They'd travel swiftly, Donal told them, for there was no telling what could be happening at the castle if members of Second Empire were infiltrating the grounds and tombs. King Zachary needed his full complement of Weapons as soon as possible. The rest of the Weapons would return more slowly with their prisoners, including Immerez.

The meeting concluded, Ty ordered Karigan to get some rest as he swept by her to gather his gear and ride out immediately. Karigan intended to. Her head still throbbed, or maybe it was all they discussed that made it hurt and exhausted her. She closed her eyes for a moment, then looked up to find Willis and Donal were already gone and Beryl was on her feet.

"Did I . . . did I doze off?" Karigan asked.

Beryl and Lord Amberhill exchanged glances.

"You should do as Ty wishes," Beryl said.

"I will." It took effort to rise to her feet, and when Lord Amberhill attempted to assist her, she stepped out of reach.

"I'm only trying to help," he said.

"I don't need help," she replied.

"You snore," he said as he stepped out of the tent.

Karigan scowled, but it pulled on her head wound and hurt. She trudged toward her tent, grumbling about annoying noblemen as flurries fell softly around her, muting the world.

NO ORDINARY MESSENGER

Karigan napped through the day, rising only to relieve herself or eat some food Willis brought her. Each time she crawled out of the warmth of her cot, the chill air assailed her like icicle daggers.

She heard the activity outside, voices, horses, people tramping by. She was just as glad she didn't have to help prepare for tomorrow's journey. She wondered what horse she'd be riding, and with pangs of loneliness, she missed Condor more than ever, but knew he was doing his duty to bear Estora swiftly and safely home. She wondered where they were now, if Estora and Fergal had found safe haven and were warm with their feet before a fire.

She looked forward to returning to Sacor City despite all the marriage preparations and the awkwardness and pain the wedding would entail. Somehow it did not seem as important to her now. She would carry on as well as she could. She had to. They were faced now with a new problem: Second Empire was learning the secrets of the D'Yer Wall from the book.

Karigan turned over on her side, and after a time her mind quieted and she fell into a troubled slumber.

She dreamed the land quaked with such force the D'Yer Wall shook and wobbled, spreading cracks down its entire length until it collapsed, taking each tower down with it, one after the other. An immense dust cloud rose from the ruins, enveloping the lands in shadow.

Karigan stood there before the desolation, all alone, without even her saber at her side. The dust settled to a mere haze and there on the rubble and beyond massed the denizens of Blackveil Forest, groundmites and creatures winged and on foot that defied description; and behind them there was something darker, more evil, and battle ready but she could not make out this new foe clearly.

All she had to defend herself and her country with were stones, broken shards of the wall. She hurled them at the enemy, but they bounced ineffectually off scales, off armor, off shields.

She gasped to wakefulness at first hot and sweating, then turning cold. She shivered and huddled beneath the blankets, unable to warm up. What was wrong with her? She touched the bandage over her head wound and winced when she pressed too hard, but she could feel the heat radiating through it.

"Not good," she murmured. Leave it to Immerez to give her a wound that festered.

Eventually her body found equilibrium, neither too hot nor too cold. She fell again into an uneasy sleep. The dreams were hazy and nonsensical until *he* walked into her mind, all starlight and night sky, tail and mane flowing like black silk. He stood on the midnight plains, stark against moon-bright snow. He gazed at her, and knelt to the ground.

Hoofbeats pumped through Karigan's body. Or were they wingbeats? Wingbeats of Westrion trying to drive her from bed. A breeze flowed over her sweat-dampened face and she sat up, pain stabbing her head. All was darkness and silence, and she thought she might be the only soul left alive on Earth.

She closed her eyes and rubbed them, only to be visited by the vision of the black stallion awaiting her. Always waiting.

"Gah."

She flipped the blankets aside and was at once assailed by chills. She stumbled about the tent to find the frozen chamber pot, teeth chattering the whole time, and used it. Afterward, a fumbling search turned up her clothes which, with painstaking effort, she put on.

When she was ready, she flung the tent flaps open and stepped outside. She squinted against moonlight reflecting on the snow. In the distance the watch fires and torches were drowned in it.

Maybe it was a fever that drove her, or maybe a greater impulse lured her—it didn't matter. She *knew.* She knew *he* awaited her. She intended to have some words with him.

She touched her brooch—it was ice cold—and faded away. There he was, black against shades of gray, lying in the snow and waiting for her.

The stallion gazed at her with obsidian eyes. Nostrils flared to take in her scent. Somehow Karigan sensed the wings beating in the air, could feel the breezes they created curling against the back of her neck.

The stallion would carry her to Sacor City. She knew this. He would bear her more swiftly than an eagle and she would arrive in time—in time to do whatever needed doing.

She shuddered at what it could mean to ride the death god's steed, the harbinger of strife and battle. What would happen to her? What might she become? Something less than human? She wanted nothing to do with gods, wanted them to watch after their own affairs and leave her out of them.

"Why me?" she demanded. "Why can't you leave me alone?"

The only reply she received was the rhythmic beat of wings—or maybe it was her own blood hammering in her ears. Many people, she thought, would be honored to serve the gods in such a way and would not protest or hesitate. Why couldn't the gods choose one of them? Hadn't she done enough already? All she had wanted was an ordinary message errand for once, and this is what she got.

She put her hand to her forehead and was startled by the heat. She was shivering and roasting at the same time.

And still the stallion waited.

She wondered if her earlier dreams were given to her to show her what was at stake if she did not act. Surely the collapse of the wall would be catastrophic. And surely the death god's steed would not come to her if it wasn't important.

"Damnation," she muttered. And to the stallion she said, "I will *not* ride. If you want me to go, you'll have to find another way."

The stallion rose, and with a glance at her that plainly said *follow,* he headed off into the night.

"Damnation." Karigan half hoped there was no other way, that the stallion would just leave her alone and seek out someone else to solve the world's problems, but it was not to be. She was about to follow when she detected someone else watching. Through the haze of her ability she saw Lord Amberhill's silhouette against her tent, his blood ruby intense in her colorless world. She said to him, with no small satisfaction, "You imagined all this." And she hurried off to catch up with the stallion, wherever he may lead.

Amberhill could not believe his eyes at the sight of the magnificent stallion that put his Goss to shame. No, there wasn't even any comparison . . .

And *she* but a shadow against the snow, talking to the stallion. He saw her leave her tent, unsteady on her feet and wan in the moonlight, then she faded to shadow and somehow the stallion appeared in his vision. The stallion was really too great for his eyes to take in. He was overwhelmed.

What was he to make of it? He was so taken with the stallion he almost forgot to listen.

"I will *not* ride," the G'ladheon woman said. "If you want me to go, you'll have to find another way."

As if he understood the words, the stallion rose and walked off into the night.

"Damnation," the Green Rider said.

It was all very perplexing. Unearthly. Amberhill thought back to the day he had fought the lovely woman in the museum over a scrap of parchment. He'd thought her brave but a fool. Though he'd detected her skill with a sword, hampered by her dress as she had been, he'd little understood what he'd really been facing. Not just a Green Rider, but someone who obviously dealt with *powers*, otherworldly powers. No ordinary messenger was she.

To his astonishment, the shadow turned to him and the moonlight illuminated the curve of her cheek and the flash of a bright eye. She said, "You imagined all this."

With that the shadow hurried away until it was lost to the night, leaving behind footprints in the snow, but even these proved elusive, ending in midstride. He found no hoofprints. How maddening!

What was this Rider? Well, rude came to mind, but was she real?

Maybe her parting words were right. Maybe he in fact imagined it all. Hastily he strode back to her tent and peered in. The moonlight fell upon an empty cot, the blankets rumpled.

"Something wrong, my lord?"

Amberhill almost jumped out of his boots. The Raven Mask was truly slipping if he couldn't detect the approach of another, but then these Weapons were uncanny. It was Donal who stood beside him.

"Please tell me," Amberhill said, "it's not my imagination that your Rider G'ladheon has left us. Disappeared."

CROSSING BRIDGES

"Oh no," Karigan said. "Not this place again." She whirled to walk back to the snow-clad encampment, but the way was gone, like a door closed.

The stallion had led her into a white, white world of empty opaque plains draped by a milky sky. The terrain, if it could be called such, was flat and empty. It bleached the color from her clothes and flesh, but the stallion remained coal black. The contrast hurt her eyes.

She'd been conveyed here the last time by wild magic and learned it was a transitional place between the layers of the world, not of Earth or the heavens, but a place populated by symbols and images.

"Isn't there another way?" she asked.

The stallion began to kneel.

"No—no, I won't ride." Her dread of riding him, what it might mean, was stronger than her dread of the white world. At least this time she had a guide, and maybe they wouldn't be here long. *Hah!* As if time had any relevance in the white world. "Lead on," she told the stallion.

He did so, plodding onto the featureless plain. She followed, her boots crunching on short, white grass. As she walked, she noticed the pain in her head subsided and she did not feel quite so fevered.

She walked and walked, but she might as well have been standing in place, for nothing changed around her, no landmarks appeared, and the plain remained level underfoot. All she could do was trust in the stallion and follow, watching the sway of his silken tail. She had an insane desire to pluck out some of those tail hairs for Estral to use in stringing the bow to her fiddle. She assumed, however, it was not wise to pluck the hair of any god-being. The absurdity of it made her laugh, and her voice rang sharp and disquieting in the emptiness. She hushed immediately.

At least this time she saw no corpses on funeral slabs, or Shawdell the Eletian trying to lure her into a game of Intrigue she could not win. Nothing of that nature thus far . . .

Until she saw the first bridge. It was an ordinary bridge of irregular, cut stone that spanned nothing, no brook, no chasm. It was as if some giant had picked it up from the real world and set it down here on the white plain. What was the purpose, she wondered, of a bridge that crossed nothing? She strode over to it, wanting to inspect it more closely, but the stallion darted in front of her and blocked her way.

"I just want to see it," Karigan said.

The stallion laid his ears back.

"But—"

He scraped his hoof on the ground, raising a puff of white dust, then shouldered her away from the bridge as he might one of his mares, though perhaps more gently. She shuddered at the power she sensed lying just below the surface, and not just the physical power of muscle and sinew.

"All right," she said, "I'll leave it."

She followed the stallion away from the bridge and glanced back at it, wondering why the stallion did not want her near it. She supposed she did not need additional trouble by pursuing it, but she couldn't help wondering who might have built the bridge here and for what purpose. Maybe it was just an illusion.

The second bridge they came to was broken. This time the stallion did not prevent her from approaching it. The arch had crumbled away, leaving a gap between abutment walls. Blocks of cut stone littered the ground. She stood beneath the gap wondering what caused the arch to give away. Neglect? Weather?

Weather? What weather? Nothing changed here as far as

she knew. Then she saw black scars on the bridge rocks, as if they had been scorched by some tremendous force. If only the stallion could speak and explain the ruins to her, but she could only find answers in her own imagination.

She left the broken bridge behind and followed the stallion toward the ever retreating horizon.

Just as one lost sense of time in a subterranean world that no sunlight reached, Karigan could not say how long she followed behind the stallion, only that she was growing weary and thirsty and her head throbbed anew. Nothing changed in the landscape or sky, there weren't even any more bridges, just the same blanket of white.

When she had enough, she plopped to the ground and closed her eyes, trying to remember other colors and the smell of the forest after rain. She tried not to think about how tired and thirsty she was, or what food used to taste like. She touched the bandage around her head, felt the pain and heat of the wound. At least those things were real.

She opened her eyes to find the stallion's velvety nose hovering just inches from her own. He blew a sweet breath into her face and she felt revived, no longer thirsty, no longer worn out. She gazed at him, startled, but then remembered what he was and figured he possessed even more remarkable abilities. In any case, she was grateful for this gift.

She rose to her feet to press on, but something caught the corner of her eye. In the distance a figure stood watching. The only details she could make out about him were a sword and quiver strapped to his back and the gleam of mail. She took a step in his direction, but he turned around and strode away, merging into the white. The white world, Karigan thought, was playing tricks on her and she wondered what else lay ahead.

She and the stallion set off again, and she soon found out. The delineation between land and sky grew hazy and a gauzy fog settled around them. She kept close to the stallion almost reaching out to touch him to make sure she did not lose him. But like her aversion to riding him, she feared tactile contact would draw her in and she'd lose herself in the vastness of the unending universe.

She tripped and fell to her hands and knees. Her surprise was supplanted by curiosity of what could have caused her to fall. She reached through the fog and felt around the ground. She touched something cold, but pliant, suspiciously like flesh. She recoiled and the fog swirled away first revealing an outstretched arm, a sword loosely gripped in its blood-spattered hand.

She hastened to her feet, a scream caught in her throat. Frantically she whirled looking for her guide, and just as she was about to cry out for him, he came back through the fog, pushing it aside.

As the clearing around him widened, it revealed the arm she tripped over was attached to the body of a soldier in Sacoridian black and silver with an arrow in his neck.

The lifting mist uncovered more. More dead twisted and sprawled upon the ground, impaled with pikes that jutted at angles above the landscape, or their heads cut off, or torsos skewered with swords and arrows and crossbow bolts.

Horses lay dead along with their masters, bloated and thick, and among the corpses was the debris of battle, pennants lying limp on the ground, broken weapons, shields, helms, bits of gear, shattered cart wheels, and there was the gore smeared across the white ground.

The stallion walked into the carnage, following some invisible path only he knew. Karigan fought with herself, clenched and unclenched her hands, trying to feel the pain of healing flesh to turn her mind elsewhere, to banish the scene from her vision.

"This is not real," she whispered. "Not real, not real . . ."

It was the sort of trick the white world liked to play, to send such images, like a bad dream needing interpretation.

She steeled herself, continuing to tell herself over and over that it was not real, and set off after the stallion. Among the uniforms of the dead she noticed provincial colors—the cobalt of Coutre, the blue and gold of D'Yer. Solid black caught her eye—a Weapon. And there was green. She refused to look at faces, to even look at the horses, but her gaze drifted and before she could stop herself, she saw Ty beneath Crane, his eyes open but dull, a wound deep in his gut crawling with maggots.

"Not real," Karigan chanted. "Not real."

She hurried the best she could. In places the bodies were so thick and intertwined she had to take a circuitous route, and during one of these her gaze was stolen again by familiarity—a banner of silken green with a gold winged horse rising, the ancient banner of the Green Riders woven and embroidered by Eletian hands, now bloodstained and torn, and lying across the body of Captain Mapstone like a shroud.

"N–no!" Karigan cried, but her eyes were drawn just beyond to a mass of slain warriors in black that had been protecting one man, all cut down by some force greater than themselves. In their midst lay King Zachary, splendid in his silver and black armor, his amber hair swept back from his face, a trickle of blood flowing from the edge of his mouth into his beard. His body bristled with arrows.

"No!" Karigan cried again. Her voice echoed across the silent landscape and raised movement among the dead. Flapping wings, stabbing beaks seeking flesh.

Overhead a monstrous avian circled, dragging its shadow across the battlefield and Karigan. The creature shrieked and dropped to the ground, then hopped over the corpses with wings spread until it stood upon King Zachary's chest. Its head swiveled from side to side at the end of a snakelike neck and, after one glance at her, plunged its beak into King Zachary's throat.

She screamed in rage and was about to throw herself at the avian when she heard the unmistakable *twang* of an arrow and the thud of impact. The avian slumped to the ground, its head hitting a discarded shield with a definitive *clunk.* The arrow, with its green fletching, jutted from its neck.

She turned and there was the watcher again, holding a short, stout bow. She caught the glint of a golden brooch, and this time she could tell he was garbed in a Rider uniform of ancient vintage, with mismatched mail and leather, and a sash of blue-green plaid across his chest. The horn of the First Rider rested against his hip. He nodded to her and mounted a white horse, and when he cantered off into the plains, he seemed to ride a cloud.

She squinted after him as he vanished into the distance. His appearance sparked a vague memory—from a dream? That was it, she thought. He had come to her in a dream. But all she could remember about it, besides the Rider himself, was an unanswered question that niggled the back of her mind like an itch, a question she could not answer because it was lost to her; she could not recall it.

"Not real," she murmured. None of it. Not the dead, the gore, this world; but she was thankful for the intervention of the watcher, even if he wasn't real either. Or was he more than a simple dream vision? Karigan sighed. Maybe some questions were better left unanswered. All she knew was that the white world was full of deceptions; that it drew images from her mind and made them *seem* real. She could trust nothing she saw there.

They set off again, Karigan not looking back, trying to focus on nothing but the stallion ahead of her. But more movement caught her attention—three figures walking toward them. What now? Survivors of the battle? Other travelers? Illusion?

When they met, Karigan recognized one of them.

"Merdigen?" she asked incredulously.

He squinted at her. "You again? Did you cause this mess?" He swept his hand to take in the battlefield.

"What? I—"

"Figured as much," he grumbled. "And I see you found the horse you were looking for." Then he peered more closely at the stallion and jerked back. "Oh! I see. Dear me. Interesting company you keep." And he gazed long and hard at Karigan.

"Are you really here?" she asked Merdigen.

"Are *you?*" he countered. "Why is it everyone always asks me if *I'm* real?" He shook his head. "How many times have I had to explain I'm a magical projection of the great mage Merdigen? Hmph. Well, I haven't the time for a conversation, fascinating as philosophy can be. The others and I are looking for the right bridge."

The man and woman who accompanied him bore walking sticks and packs as he did. The man had a long beard like Merdigen's, though it was rusty in hue, and the woman was tall and willowy and wore a sort of leaf hat. Or maybe she just had leaves and twigs sticking out of her hair—it was hard to tell. The green of the leaves, fresh like spring, defied the bleaching effect of the white world, bringing Karigan visual relief that had nothing to do with corpses.

"Who are—?" Karigan began.

"Radiscar," Merdigen said, and the man bowed solemnly. "And Mad Leaf." The woman smiled, looked on the verge of giggles, which was more unsettling than humorous. "And before you ask, yes, they are magical projections, too. We've been on a long journey."

Before Karigan could speak again, Merdigen started ambling off with the other two behind him. "A most unpleasant mess this is," he grumbled. "Farewell."

Karigan watched them go, but the mist rolled back in over the battlefield and they were lost to sight. Once again she followed the stallion as he delved into the delicate billowy stuff, but it quickly lifted, and when it did, all signs of the battle were erased. She shook her head and continued on.

Karigan almost walked into the stallion's rump when he came to a sudden halt. She peered around him to find they had come to another bridge rising up in a graceful curve. It was made from the same rustic cut granite as the others but the parapet walls ended in rounded scrolls. She couldn't get over how ordinary and real the bridges were, and how at home they'd look in a park or country estate.

"Are we going to cross this one?" she asked.

The stallion tossed his head, his forelock falling over one eye, then stepped onto the bridge. She walked beside him, observing nothing different about the white world as she did so, but when they reached the center of the bridge's vast deck, the far end appeared darker, murky, like a storm cloud was forming there. She glanced uncertainly at the stallion. His nostrils flared and he bobbed his head.

"What—" she began, but he nudged her with his nose and she stumbled forward. The message was clear: he wanted her to cross the bridge into the murk. "You aren't coming with me?"

The stallion took one step back and bowed his head.

Karigan licked her lips and hesitantly walked forward, toward the cloud engulfing the scrolled ends of the bridge. She took a final glance back at the stallion—he stood silent and still as a statue, just watching her.

She had to trust him. She had to trust he had guided her to someplace she could be useful and not into another strange world. Before she could talk herself out of taking those last few steps, she strode the rest of the way into the dark cloud.

RIDER IN BLACK

A burst of wind from behind thrust Karigan the last steps across the bridge and into darkness. She tripped and landed in a pile of refuse.

"Ugh," she said, pushing herself up from the rotting vegetables, egg shells, and . . . fish guts?

From the shadows a raccoon hissed at her for disturbing its repast. She rose to her feet, brushing fish scales and other disagreeable bits from her clothes and laughed; laughed in joy at the stench, the dark of night, the sounds of voices somewhere nearby, the gold of lamps and candles in windows, flurries swirling around her. She'd left the white world behind and returned to one full of life, scents, and textures.

She tugged Willis' cloak closer around her to fend off the cold, realizing that while this was a vast improvement over the white world, she hadn't the faintest idea of where she was. Was she even in Sacoridia? At the moment she stood in a tiny courtyard behind someone's house or business, occupied mainly by crates, casks, and rubbish.

Business, she decided.

The opportunity arose to discover her precise location in the person of a portly and harried woman carrying a bucket from the back door of the establishment.

"Excuse me," Karigan said.

The woman squawked, liquid sloshing over the brim of her bucket. "Who's there?" she demanded.

"Could you please tell me where I am?" Karigan asked.

It was apparently the wrong thing to say.

"You get outta my dooryard at once, you no good vagrant!" the woman screamed. "I won't have your ilk picking through my rubbish no more! Now git!"

Karigan did not move fast enough to satisfy the woman for the contents of the bucket were flung on her. She tore from the dooryard and onto the street, the woman hollering after her. Unfortunately the liquid that doused her smelled of boiled cabbage. She hated cabbage.

At least, she consoled herself, the woman spoke the common tongue and it had that neutral, mid-Sacoridian lack of accent she associated with Sacor City and its surroundings.

She ran down the narrow street past silent shop fronts until she finally came to a signpost beneath a street lamp that confirmed her thoughts. She stood on Fishmonger Street. She cried out in triumph, for the adjoining street was the Winding Way—she was in Sacor City. She still had a ways to go to reach the castle, as Fishmonger Street was in the midsection of the city. Why in the names of the gods did the bridge she crossed leave her in a refuse pile on Fishmonger Street?

The gods obviously had a foul sense of humor. Literally.

She sighed and turned up the Winding Way. It was uphill, though gradual. Her wet hair was beginning to stiffen in the cold. Maybe some kind soul would give her a ride in their cart, but between the stench she must emanate and the hour, she doubted her chances were very good.

Karigan trudged all the way up the nearly deserted street, taking shortcuts where she could. It was so much easier when she was astride her Condor. It did not help that her various aches and pains from before the white world reawakened, making her walk more of a trial than usual, and it really did not help when the snow-slick cobbles underfoot caused her to fall.

When finally she reached the castle's outer portcullis gates, she wanted to kiss them. Instead, since they were closed for the night, she rapped on the door to one of the portcullis towers. Someone moved inside and slid open the peephole.

"What ye want?" a gruff voice demanded.

"It's Rider G'ladheon," she said.

"*What?* Where's yer horse?"

"Long story that has no time for the telling," she replied.

The weariness in her voice must have convinced him for he did not press her further. Instead he stepped outside with a lantern to look her over.

"Yup," he said. "I recognize ye, but yer not looking too good." Then he crinkled his nose. "Not smelling too good neither."

He called up to his fellows in the tower above, who in turn called down to the guards on the other side of the gate. They opened the pedestrian door in the gate and ushered her through, locking the door behind her, keys chiming on a huge ring.

"Cold night," the guard with the keys said. Then he snuffled. "You smell something rotten, Rider?"

Karigan shook her head and hurried over the drawbridge that crossed the moat. At one time, King Zachary had kept both gates open as a symbolic gesture to his people, but that had changed when the grounds were infiltrated by undead wraiths over the summer. She did not think a closed gate would have deterred them, but Colin Dovekey insisted at least the outer gate remain closed during the night as a precaution.

Guards challenged her several times as she made her way to the main castle entrance. When she reached it and was admitted into the castle, she stood some moments just inside, both relieved to have made it back so quickly, even if by unconventional means, and unsure of what to do next. Report to Captain Mapstone, she supposed. That meant venturing back out into the snow and cold and trudging to officers quarters.

She'd just rest a minute, she decided. She was weary and everything was a tad hazy. She slid into a nearby chair, oblivious to the guards grimacing and fanning their noses. One cracked the doors open to let in fresh air.

Feverish and chilled, shivering and sweating, Karigan dozed off where she sat.

* * *

When someone prodded her shoulder, she awoke in mid-snore, and an inrush of awareness—the foul odor, her sore head, lamplight glaring in her eyes—assailed her. Before her stood a Weapon. Or somewhat stood. He leaned on crutches.

"Rider?" he queried.

"*Fastion?*"

He inclined his head.

Then it all came back to her, the reason for her extraordinary journey; its urgency. And she'd been sleeping! "The tombs—" she began.

Fastion nodded down a corridor. "This way. There is no time to lose."

Karigan stood, feeling like every bone ached. "You know?"

He gave her that stony look that once caused her to nickname him Granite Face. "Of course I do not know, but you arrived without a horse, or so the guards say, and without your saber. You are wearing a Weapon's cloak, which is curious in itself. And where you are concerned one may expect trouble." Fastion led the way down the corridor, swinging along rapidly and with ease on his crutches.

"You aren't going to say anything about how I smell?" Karigan asked as she hurried to catch up.

Fastion merely spared her a look of disdain. When she asked him about the crutches, he said he'd acquired his wound during the ambush on Lady Estora.

"She's fine," Karigan said. "At least she was when I saw her in Mirwell."

That brought Fastion to a halt and he squinted at her. Then he muttered something unintelligible and set off again.

He took her deep into the west wing to a chamber she had never seen before, a long room lined with black banners and black onyx statues of stern warriors. There were tables set in orderly rows and she took the place for the dining and meeting hall of the Weapons. Five awaited them as if anticipating their arrival. She recognized Brienne Quinn, though it had been a while since she had seen the tomb Weapon, but the others were unknown to her. They formed a half circle around her and Fastion.

"Rider G'ladheon has come to speak of the tombs," Fastion said.

What? she thought. No "how are yous" or an offer of tea? She repressed a sigh and decided to get straight to the point and leave the Weapons to it so she could find her own bed and rest. It seemed a very good idea just then to let someone else shoulder the kingdom's problems.

"The book the king has been seeking to fix the D'Yer Wall," she said, "has been acquired by Second Empire. In order to read it, they must put the book in the light of the high king's tomb. If they decipher the book, they may use the information to destroy the wall. They kidnapped Lady Estora to empty the tombs of its Weapons and make their task easier, and they may be here even now."

She fully expected the Weapons to launch into action, but they stood as still as the statues lining the wall.

"Food and drink for Rider G'ladheon," Fastion ordered and one Weapon peeled away. "And a uniform and sword."

"One of mine should fit," Brienne Quinn said.

"What?" Karigan asked, but her query went unheeded as servants were summoned.

"Lennir, see to the tombs," Fastion said, and the third Weapon strode from the chamber.

Meanwhile, the fourth Weapon—she didn't give her name—removed Karigan's odorous cloak and started stripping off bandages to examine her wounds.

The fifth Weapon departed to seek out other available Weapons, but with the possibility of intruders on the grounds, few would be able to leave the king's side. Soon servants arrived with cold sausage rolls, cheese, and tea.

"She's feverish," the Weapon tending her informed Fastion. "The head wound appears to be festering."

He gazed at Karigan with some intensity, then told the Weapon, "Do the best you can with it. She can go to the mending wing later."

After fresh dressings were wrapped around Karigan's wounds, she said, "Don't you want to hear about Lady Estora?"

"Later, after we learn what is happening in the tombs," Fastion said. "You told me she was fine, and that is good enough for now."

Karigan had to admire his singleness of purpose. She picked at a sausage roll, but found it did not appeal to her. The tea did. It wasn't long before Brienne returned with a uniform and longsword. She stood before Karigan. Karigan set her teacup down.

"What? What do you—"

"There are too few of us," Fastion explained, "and you have been in the tombs before. You know the law. Therefore you must go as one of us."

Karigan gaped. Only Weapons and royalty were permitted in the tombs, as well as the caretakers who lived out their lives there. Anyone else caught breaking the law by entering the sacred territory beneath the castle was doomed to remain in the tombs forever, to become caretakers themselves and never see the living sun again. A couple years earlier Karigan and a few others were permitted passage through Heroes Avenue by king's will alone.

"But—" Karigan began.

At that moment, Lennir returned at a run. "The doors to Heroes Avenue are barred," he said, not at all out of breath.

Fastion cast his granite gaze on Karigan. *"Dress."*

"But—"

"You are our sister-at-arms," Brienne said more kindly. "Ever since the usurper tried to take the throne from King Zachary have we regarded you as such."

Karigan could only blink.

"And for your actions since," Fastion said. "Otherwise we would not even consider clothing you in our black because of all it represents. Few in the history of the land have been accorded such honor and regard outside the corps of the Black Shields."

Maybe the fever and exhaustion skewed Karigan's hearing. Maybe the stallion hadn't brought her to her own world after all, but to a slightly altered version of it.

"I'm a Weapon now?"

"No," Brienne said, "that requires years of specific training and sacred ceremonies. You are more of an honorary Weapon, but with that honor comes responsibility."

"Such as our need for you now," Fastion said.

Before Karigan could protest, and right there in the hall of the Weapons, Brienne and the other woman, Cera, helped her strip out of her borrowed Rider uniform and change into black; first the black linen shirt with intricate patterns embroidered onto it with ebony thread, then the leather trousers, followed by the padded doublet. They buckled hard leather guards around her wrists, but agreed gloves would not fit correctly over her bandaged hands. As she had with her Estora disguise, Karigan kept her own boots. They were, after all, black, and very similar in design to that of the Weapons'.

The two women watched as Karigan detached her brooch from her Rider uniform and clasped it to her doublet. An odd light filled their eyes. Did they see the brooch as any Rider would or did they only see her handling an invisible object or maybe a piece of costume jewelry? She knew Weapons were well aware of Rider brooches, and that they distrusted magic as did most Sacoridians, but their regard was somehow of a different nature, on a more intense level.

Overall, Brienne's uniform was a good fit, and so was the longsword she strapped to Karigan's waist.

"I don't know how good I'll be at sword work," Karigan said, raising her bandaged hands.

"If things are well, you won't need to draw a sword," Brienne said.

The man Fastion sent to find more Weapons returned with only a half dozen.

"The main entrance to Heroes Avenue is closed to us," Fastion said, after explaining to them what was happening.

Karigan wondered if they'd have to ride all the way out of the city to the secret entrance, the Heroes Portal, that lay in the side of the hill on which both city and castle stood.

"Our investigation will begin in the Halls of Kings and Queens anyway," he continued. "With luck, that entrance is not known to the enemy and has not been barred." He then raised his hand and clenched it into a fist. "Death is honor!"

"Death is honor!" the others echoed, imitating the fist gesture.

Good heavens, Karigan thought. She hoped the motto did not apply to her. She was, after all, only an honorary Weapon.

She followed the Weapons as they filed out of the hall, feeling awkward and unfamiliar even to herself in black when she should be in green. It was almost like she had not yet caught up with herself and just had to keep running or lose herself entirely.

Like I'm shadowing myself, she thought.

She kept reminding herself she was a merchant's daughter as she strove to keep up with the Weapons and wiped perspiration from her face with the back of her hand. *I'm also a Green Rider. And now I'm apparently some sort of a Weapon, but not.* Maybe her entire existence had become a theatrical, or maybe a masquerade where she portrayed someone different every day. Did she really know who she was anymore?

She shook her head. No use trying to think about it. She could only keep moving forward.

FOLLOWING THE CAT

The journey through castle corridors swirled by in a hazy dream. Karigan was more concerned with keeping up with the Weapons than taking in her surroundings. Fastion led them at an amazing pace on his crutches. Before she knew it, they'd entered the Rider wing. The corridor was dimly lit at this hour, whatever hour it was, and most doors were shut.

She passed her own door—it was ajar and she longed to slip into her room and go to bed. Maybe Fastion wouldn't notice? Wishful thinking.

A white cat bolted from her doorway and streaked past the Weapons down the corridor. This roused the Weapons to surprised murmurs.

"A tomb cat?" Brienne mused aloud.

There was general agreement among the Weapons. What in the name of the heavens, Karigan thought, was a tomb cat doing in her room? Then it occurred to her she'd seen it there before. *This can't be a good omen . . .*

They swept past the common room. Garth stood in the doorway in surprise as they passed by, his teacup held forgotten in his hand.

"Karigan?" he said with incredulity in his voice.

But she could not stop as much as she wanted to, and so only gave him a feeble smile and a wave.

Some of the Weapons grabbed lamps from along the Rider wing, for beyond lay the abandoned section of the castle that remained in a perpetual state of night. The lamps created a temporary dusk, but night fell in behind them as they hastened on.

If Karigan hadn't the Weapons to guide the way, she'd be completely lost. The abandoned corridors branched and intersected in so many places and seemed to stretch for miles that she began to think of it as an unlit labyrinth, with secrets hidden beyond every corner. But they did not pause to unravel secrets. Fastion and his Weapons had a destination in mind and headed toward it without faltering. Rodents with gleaming eyes scattered before them.

Left, then right. Right, then left. Down sets of stone stairs into deeper, darker levels of the castle. Karigan did not even try to remember the way, and simply incorporated it into her streaming consciousness. Keeping to her feet and keeping up was her priority.

They stopped.

Karigan plowed into Lennir, who gave her a stern look.

"Sorry," she mumbled. Some honorary Weapon *she* made.

At some point they'd entered a wider corridor and when Karigan saw lamplight glance off the polished stone surface of a coffin rest, she understood why. The corridor had to be wide enough to permit a funeral procession to pass through, and before them was a set of double doors equally wide. They had reached the entrance to the tombs Fastion sought.

The white cat leaped onto the coffin rest, watching the movement of lamps and pouncing on reflected light, its tail swishing in concentration.

Fastion and Brienne consulted before the doors. The light revealed ancient script and carvings of the gods above them. Most prominent, of course, were Aeryc holding the crescent moon and Westrion with his wings spread, riding his black steed.

Fastion uttered some command and swords whispered from sheaths. Karigan put her hand to the unfamiliar hilt at her side but did not draw the sword, feeling too clumsy. Just the sound she'd make would disrupt the silence the real Weapons exuded.

Instead of a sword, Fastion drew out a key and turned it

in the locks, then carefully tugged on the door rings. The doors did not shift. He tugged harder, but to no avail. Another Weapon helped, but even their combined efforts failed to open the doors.

Fastion pivoted on his good leg, the lamps casting grim lines across his forehead. "Our way is blocked. We must consider the Heroes Portal."

The other Weapons did not speak out in dismay, but Karigan could tell from their heavy countenances they were displeased. It meant gathering horses, riding all the way down through the city, out of the city itself, and losing valuable time.

The white cat jumped down from the coffin rest and landed beside Karigan's feet. It rubbed against her leg, purring loudly. Then, with a stretch, it padded off in the direction they had come.

"Or, we could," Fastion mused, "follow the cat."

Maybe this was a dream after all, Karigan thought. Who ever heard of Weapons following cats? But follow the cat they did.

They found it sitting on its haunches and licking its paw at an intersection of corridors, as if waiting for them. When they approached, it darted off down the corridor to the right. They followed, the cat ghosting in and out of the lamplight, treading a trail it was familiar with. Either that or they were all on a mouse hunt. Karigan almost giggled at the image of Fastion with feline whiskers.

She wiped her brow with her sleeve. The fever inspired ridiculous notions.

Eventually the corridor dead-ended at what looked more like a natural rock face than castle wall. Fastion scratched his head.

"I don't remember *this.*"

"Nor I," said Brienne, "but most of my time is spent *in* the tombs."

The others agreed it was new to them.

Primitive drawings were etched into the rock face—stick figures carrying . . . sticks? Were they spears? Creatures like birds and mammals were also etched into the rock.

"I've seen pictures like these before, though," Brienne said. "Elsewhere in the tombs."

"Yes," Fastion replied. "I remember them."

"Who did these?" Karigan asked. "They look like a child drew them."

"No child," Brienne said. "At least, not that we know of. These were made by the oldest of the old who once settled these lands. They dwelled here long before the Sacor Clans, but what they called themselves no one, except perhaps the Eletians, knows. We call them Delvers. The tombs were not entirely built by the D'Yers—portions were formed from natural niches and caves in the bedrock. But before the tombs, during the time of the great ice, we think the Delvers lived in them. The caves must have provided shelter from the cold and predators."

One of the drawings was of a large catamount-like creature with long curving fangs.

Their own little cat gazed at them thumping its tail impatiently on the dusty floor. When it saw it had their attention, it walked to where the stone face met the corridor wall and vanished.

How'd it do that? Karigan wondered. She'd once thought of the cat as a ghost kitty, but it had felt so real rubbing her leg . . .

Fastion crutched over to the wall. "There is a fissure here. Your position and the angle of light only makes it look solid. Come see."

Karigan and the remaining Weapons clustered around what was not more than, to Karigan's mind, a narrow crack in the wall. Fine for a cat, but a human being?

"It will be a squeeze," Brienne said. "I shall test it first."

Except for Karigan, Brienne was the slimmest of the group. The others, all men except for Cera, had broad shoulders and chests. Brienne removed her sword, felt her way into the fissure, and squeezed in. She did not even take a lamp with her. Karigan admired the sergeant's grit and was glad it wasn't she who had to chance getting jammed in some dark fissure.

It was not long before Brienne reemerged unscathed. "It is tight in the beginning, but widens. It comes out behind Queen Lyra's bed."

There was murmured consternation among the Weapons. "Do the caretakers know about it?" Lennir asked.

The Weapons prided themselves on knowing every crack and corner of the castle, but were now learning they had not discovered everything just yet. Karigan wondered if the castle played tricks on people; changed its configuration now and then; revealed and concealed its extent at whim.

"Perhaps, perhaps not," Fastion replied.

"A tapestry conceals the outlet," Brienne said.

Karigan was still working out the idea of Queen Lyra's *bed.* Surely this was a quaint way of referring to a funerary slab. *Surely.*

But now the Weapons started to file into the fissure, and Fastion placed a hand on Karigan's shoulder and guided her toward it.

"Brienne will be in charge on the other side," he said.

"What? Aren't you coming?"

"Yes, of course, but in the tombs she outranks me. Above is my domain."

It was all really too much for Karigan to digest in her current state. The Weapons were beyond her, and she left it at that.

Fastion practically shoved her into the fissure and she found she had to shuffle sideways to fit. She held the sword vertically against her hip and moved cautiously so as not to jar her already battered body. Still, her cheek grazed a jagged rock and she probably added a new bruise to her shoulder before the passage widened. Light glowed ahead and she surged toward it like a swimmer seeking the water's surface. She emerged into a large chamber, Brienne holding aside the tapestry. Fastion hopped out of the passage next, dragging his crutches behind him.

Brienne dropped the tapestry back into place. Whether or not the caretakers knew of the passage, the Delvers had, for Karigan glimpsed stick figure people and beasts incised into the stone around the opening before the tapestry swept back over them.

"I sent Lennir and Beston to Heroes Avenue to investigate what's happened at the main entrance," Brienne told Fastion in a hushed voice. "Offrid and Sorin I've sent to the village, and I've ordered the rest to scout for intruders."

Fastion nodded.

"Village?" Karigan asked.

"Shhh," Fastion said. "We don't know how near the intruders are. The village is where the caretakers live."

"You two are with me," Brienne said. "We'll visit the kings and queens and perhaps intercept the intruders and the book."

Visit the kings and queens, Karigan thought sourly. *Visit dead people.*

Only now did she take in her surroundings which were lit by lamps at low glow, leaving much in shadow and to the imagination. When Brienne said the passage ended at Queen Lyra's "bed," she hadn't been using a quaint figure of speech. She'd been precise. A canopy bed, to be even more precise.

Beautiful blue velvet curtains draped down from the canopy and were tied to each bedpost with gold cords. Beneath the matching covers a figure reclined against silk pillows, jewels on boney fingers and a tiara on its head sparkling in the light. A perfectly braided rope of silver hair flowed down the figure's shoulder. The flesh was shrunken to skull and bones like parchment, and Queen Lyra gazed out from her bed with a perpetual, skeletal grin.

Karigan did not know if it was some secret method of embalming that preserved the dead in these tombs so well over hundreds of years, or the cool, dry environment, or some alchemy of the two. She didn't care. All she knew was that she hated the tombs. She really did.

The white cat reappeared from beneath the bed and jumped up onto it.

"Shoo!" Brienne said, whisking the cat off. "Agemon would be most displeased to find clumps of white hair on the queen's bed."

Karigan groaned inwardly when she heard the chief caretaker's name, and she hoped they would not encounter him this time.

The rest of the chamber was fitted out like a bedroom, complete with dressing table, armoire, and washstand. There was even a chamber pot stashed under the bed. Though tables and furniture were cluttered with personal items, such as combs and jewelry, no trailing cobwebs hung from the canopy bed; no dirt or grime clung to any surface. There was even a book on a chair next to the bed with a marker in it. Apparently Queen Lyra liked to read.

When Fastion observed Karigan absorbing everything, he said, "Many wish to take with them the comforts of home after death. The dying find it easier to accept their journey to the heavens knowing they'll be surrounded by things they loved in life. The queen's husband, King Cedric, preferred to spend the afterlife with his favorite horses."

He pointed to a slab of granite just to the side of a fine Durnesian carpet inscribed with the king's name and that of fifteen horses.

"They're all under the floor?" Karigan asked.

Fastion nodded. "According to the chronicles the caretakers keep, it was quite a trial to entomb the king and his horses."

Karigan did not ask if the horses were already dead or brought down alive. She did not want to know.

Brienne peered out of the chamber, looking for trouble. "The way is clear," she said in a low voice. "I see no living souls."

Brienne, Karigan knew, was not being facetious.

She followed Brienne out of Queen Lyra's chamber, with Fastion taking up the rear. She dreaded what other burial displays lay ahead. Her only hope was that they'd find the intruders quickly and get this journey into the tombs over with.

THE HOUSE OF SUN AND MOON

The main corridor was more brightly lit than Queen Lyra's chamber, revealing the Halls of Kings and Queens in all its grandeur, reminding Karigan of the west wing of the castle where the king's offices and private apartments were. Rich carpeting softened footfalls, paintings of battles and landscapes hung from the walls, and polished suits of armor stood at attention next to statues of carved marble. Finely crafted furniture that had probably never been used was clustered in comfortable groupings, as if awaiting a social gathering, and tapestries of exquisite embroidery depicting wars and victories, and legends and hunting triumphs, hung from ceiling to floor.

Where there was no other art or draperies covering the walls, glittering mosaics depicted the gods, and goose bumps raised along Karigan's flesh as she took stock of a realistic depiction of Salvistar that looked ready to leap out of the stone.

They came to a library nook overflowing with books. A pair of cushioned chairs faced an unlit hearth.

"Queen Lyra insisted on a library," Brienne told Karigan.

Karigan wished the fire was lit. The cold of the tombs, while not freezing, was penetrating, which accounted for the fur-lined cloaks the tomb Weapons wore year round.

Colorful banners and pennants hung from the barrel vaulted ceilings, blunting the effect of stone. This main corridor did not appear to house the dead, but glimpses down adjoining passageways and into chambers revealed sarcophagi and funerary slabs, or wall crypts both sealed and unsealed. The latter seemed to be found down more primitive, narrower corridors. And were fully occupied.

Everything, like Queen Lyra's chamber, was immaculate—not a single spider had a chance here, and Karigan was sure the tomb cats took care of the rodent population. Just as on Heroes Avenue, the air did not smell of musty old bones or rot; fresh currents of air wisped into her face. Cold and dry. Good storage for corpses.

She marveled just at the lamps, trying to imagine how much of the population's taxes went for whale oil to light the tombs for dead people who could not appreciate it while the Green Riders must be sparing in their use of the pittance they were allotted every year.

Not only that, but she couldn't begin to fathom how much work it took to keep the lamp chimneys and ceilings above free of soot. For heavens sake, there were even chandeliers! She shook her head, boggled by it all.

They prowled the main corridor searching for trouble. The first sign they found was a bust of a king smashed on the floor, then the sound of weeping. Brienne charged down the corridor with Fastion swinging behind her. Karigan hurried to catch up.

The Weapons turned into a chamber filled with numerous, occupied funerary slabs, but Karigan's gaze was not drawn to those desiccated corpses swathed in wraps, but to the fresh corpse on the floor lying in a pool of blood—he looked to have been killed by a sword thrust to the belly. A girl on her knees wept over the man. Both the girl and man were garbed in subdued grays and whites, their flesh unnaturally pale from never having seen the sun. Caretakers.

"Iris," Brienne said, placing her hand on the girl's heaving shoulder. "Did you see who did this to him?"

It took several moments to soothe the girl, who wasn't more than twelve.

"I . . . I was coming to read to Queen Lyra," the girl explained between sobs, "and I found Uncle Charles here."

Brienne stroked the girl's hair, then knelt beside the dead man, placing her hand against his face.

"He's cool," Brienne said, "but not cold enough to be long dead. The intruders are still here, somewhere."

"What is this?" a voice demanded. "What's happened?" They whirled at the sudden appearance of a caretaker in the chamber's doorway. Karigan recognized the long white hair, the smooth face, and specs. Like the girl and dead man, he wore robes of muted colors.

"Agemon," Brienne said.

"What has happened here?" He adjusted his specs in an agitated way, as if not believing what his eyes showed him. "What happened to Charles? I . . . I don't understand."

Brienne took his arm and said in a quiet but firm tone, "Agemon, there are intruders in the tombs."

He wrung his hands. "I knew nothing good would come of it—I knew it!"

"Come of what?" Fastion asked.

"The king sending all our Black Shields above." Agemon knelt by Charles and shook his head. "Preparations must be made. I must—"

"Not now, Agemon," Brienne said. "Fastion and I need to ferret out the intruders so they can't harm anyone else."

"Yes, yes," Agemon murmured. "Do what Black Shields do. I shall tend the dead."

Brienne took a deep breath and exhaled slowly as though schooling her patience with the caretaker. "You will go to the House of Sun and Moon and remain there. Karigan will look after you till we return. Do you understand?"

Agemon finally took notice of Karigan. "She looks ready for the death surgeons," he said. "The king should not have taken away our Black Shields."

"Do you understand?" Brienne asked, with an edge to her voice.

Agemon waved her off. "Yes, yes. House of Sun and Moon. We'll await you there."

Brienne gazed at Karigan expectantly.

"I understand," Karigan said. She hoped Brienne and

Fastion found the intruders quickly so this ordeal would soon end. The two melted down the main corridor, which left her with Agemon, Iris, and the fresh corpse. For some reason, fresh corpses did not bother her as much as the old ones.

Agemon turned to her. "I remember you. The black uniform does not fool me. Yes, you were in green. Yes, yes. Touched the First Rider's sword. Defiled it, you did. I do not believe you are a Black Shield. It is not possible."

"Now—" Karigan started.

"Oh, no. Just not possible. You will not leave the tombs this time. You have broken taboo."

Karigan was so tired that she lacked Brienne's patience. The last thing in the world she'd ever allow to happen to her was becoming a caretaker, stuck in the tombs for the rest of her life. "Wrong," she said, and on a hunch, she drew Brienne's sword just enough to clear a portion of the blade of the sheath.

Agemon looked down at the floor. "I'm . . . I'm sorry. I will not doubt you again."

There was a band of black silk wrapped around the blade just below the guard, which designated the sword's bearer as a swordmaster. Most swordmasters entered the king's service as a Weapon, like Brienne, accepting duty either in the tombs or above ground. Without it, Karigan would be clearly identified as a fraud. She had hoped that since Brienne was a swordmaster, the extra sword she lent Karigan would have the silk and, to her vast relief, it did.

Karigan let the sword slide back into its sheath. "We are going to the House of Sun and Moon," she said, "just as Sergeant Quinn ordered."

"I . . . I just want to cover Charles," Agemon said.

"Do so quickly."

Agemon scurried to the back of the chamber and delved into a bureau. He withdrew a linen shroud.

Convenient, Karigan thought. *But not surprising.*

As it turned out, Agemon wanted not only to cover Charles' body, but to position it just so and tuck the shroud neatly around him as though making a bed.

"We've no time," Karigan said, tugging on his sleeve. "You will have to see to him later."

Agemon looked upon the shrouded body with regret, adjusted his specs, and held out his hand for the girl, Iris. "Come, child. The Black Shield wants us to leave. We'll come back later and care for him properly."

Karigan swallowed hard at being called a Black Shield, feeling more than ever like a fraud.

Iris grasped Agemon's hand and together they stepped out into the corridor, leading Karigan into a branching passage where there were yet other chambers of the dead. What a grim place for children to grow up in, she thought, but Iris strode beside Agemon unafraid and unaffected by her surroundings.

Where did the children play? *Did* they play? How were they schooled? Did everything in their lives center around the dead?

The last time Karigan was in the tombs, she was told that every now and then the Weapons attempted to move caretaker families above ground where they might carry on a normal life, but the families did not adjust well, for it went against everything they believed in about not seeing the sun. For them, death was part of everyday living, and it was ingrained in them to tend the dead.

"Will Uncle Charles go to the heavens?" Iris asked Agemon.

"Yes, child. The Birdman will take him. Once we've done the rites, all will be well."

Iris brightened at this assurance. "I shall miss him, but I am glad he'll be with the gods."

"I wonder what music he would like at the ascension ceremony," Agemon said.

Iris started giving him suggestions. It sounded like they were planning a party, not a funeral. Karigan rubbed her temple and tried to stay alert for the intruders, but nothing besides the three of them moved.

Soon Agemon halted at what looked like a chapel excavated right out of the bedrock. It was not large, but was carved with the signs of the gods and death and the heavens. Lamps glowed behind two stained glass windows, one depicting the rising sun and the other showing the crescent moon surrounded by stars. Statues of Aeryc and Aeryon gazed at one another across the doorway.

"Is this it?" Karigan asked. "The House of Sun and Moon?"

Agemon nodded.

"Stay here," she said, and she stepped inside to make sure intruders were not hiding within, but she found only six curving benches of burnished oak and lit candles on the altar. Behind the altar was a mosaic of Aeryc and Aeryon holding hands, and throughout the chapel was the recurring motif of sun and moon. There were several wall crypts, the most prominent of them housing King Hardell the Third and Queen Auriette. All of the integrated Aeryc and Aeryon symbols made sense, for Queen Auriette had been a princess of Rhovanny before marrying King Hardell.

Karigan ushered Agemon and Iris inside and took up a position near the entry, dropping onto one of the benches. She was so weary. Agemon, on the other hand, produced a cloth from nowhere and started polishing the mosaic. He set Iris to work shining the silver and gold goblets on the altar—not that they didn't already sparkle.

Let them work, Karigan thought. It would keep them busy and out of trouble.

She leaned her head against the cold, smooth stone wall and dozed off.

In her dream, spirits of kings and queens, princes and princesses, arose from their Earthly husks on funeral slabs and swirled down the corridors. Their forms seeped from crypts and coffins like formless smoke. Skeletal hands scraped against the lids of sarcophagi and pushed them aside.

The spirits marched and floated toward her, some remaining insubstantial, others in full royal regalia.

Join us, join us, join us, they said to her.

Skeleton jaws clacked at her, and the spirits swirled

around her in a ragged, wisping cyclone, their voices pitched like the whine of biters in her ears.

Avataaar . . . they whispered.

Cat claws punctured her leather trousers and dug into her thighs.

"Ow!"

Details returned. Sore head against cool stone wall. Sore hands and knees, sore everything.

Tombs.

To her relief, the ghosts had been a dream, though her presence in the tombs was not. Nor was the cat. Ghost Kitty crouched on her lap, ears flat against his head. He emitted a low growl and glared out the doorway of the House of Sun and Moon.

Karigan rubbed her eyes and looked and heard voices. A man in the livery of a castle servant held a knife to Iris's throat, while at least two others stood nearby confronting Agemon with swords.

KARIGAN HAUNTING

"Damnation," Karigan whispered. When and how did this transpire? She detached the cat from her thighs and set him on the floor. With a hiss he scuttled into hiding beneath one of the benches. Agemon must have disobeyed Brienne's orders and slipped out while Karigan napped.

"Tell us, old man," said the intruder with the knife to Iris's throat.

"You should not be here!" Agemon cried. "You have broken taboo—you are unclean. The Black Shields shall be very cross with you."

The man snorted. "You mean the Weapons? We took care of them."

At least Agemon had the good sense to keep quiet about Brienne and Fastion. Unless, of course, the thug *meant* Brienne and Fastion. In any case, Agemon just stood there wringing his hands in distress.

"You will tell us," said a second man dressed in the uniform of a Sacoridian soldier, "which is the highest of the high kings here. Tell us or we cut the girl's throat."

Iris whimpered.

"Highest of the . . . ? Who are you people? Why have you invaded these sacred avenues?"

"Second Empire, old man, and this place is not sacred to *us.* Disgusting and strange, perhaps, but not sacred."

"Spooky," said the third man with a shudder. He wore no disguise or device. He was a plainshield, much unkempt.

"Shut up, Thursgad," the soldier said. Then self-importantly he drew himself up and proclaimed, "We are here in the name of the empire."

Karigan thought Agemon would faint. He actually tottered a bit, but then he spoke a string of foreign words in a commanding voice and spat at the soldier's feet.

The man holding Iris said, "Well, well. That was not a very nice thing to say."

The other two intruders looked as perplexed as Karigan felt. What language did Agemon speak? What did he say? And *Thursgad!* She remembered that name—one of Immerez's men.

Whatever Agemon said didn't matter. She had to do something, but in her condition she could not hope to overcome three fit-looking, armed men.

Need another way.

Trying to think hurt her head. What could she possibly do?

Agemon was pulling on his hair and there was some exchange of words, and finally he acceded to whatever demands the cutthroats made. He led them away down the corridor.

"Damnation," Karigan murmured.

She'd have to follow, but carefully. That was the only thing she could think of to do at the moment—follow and keep an eye on them. She would intervene if they looked ready to kill Iris or Agemon. In the meantime, she hoped they'd bump into Fastion and Brienne, or any of the other Weapons who came in with them. They'd know what to do, and could easily take on the three men, even Fastion with his injured leg.

Karigan allowed the intruders with their captives to get some distance on her, then she crept from the House of Sun and Moon after them, flitting behind columns and keeping to shadows. Her fading ability might prove useful so long as she evaded the lamplight, but she didn't want to draw on it until she had to so she didn't exhaust her reservoir of energy. She wouldn't mind a whiff of stallion breath about now.

She extinguished lamps as she went, as much to signal the

Weapons something was afoot as to provide extra darkness for her ability to fade. The downside was the intruders would realize they were being followed should they look behind them. Fortunately this was not yet the case, for they plunged on, intent on following Agemon.

Agemon turned down one of the more ancient corridors lined with open wall crypts. They were niches, really, chiseled out of the rock wall, and most filled with yellowed bones. There were some shrouded forms, as well as empty niches, everything neat and orderly, of course.

There was less decoration in this cavelike portion of the tombs, aside from sketchy murals, some so old she could barely make them out. They were full of death iconography and the gods, with whom she was becoming all too familiar. Some of the wall art, it appeared, was made to cover Delver drawings.

She maintained her guarded distance, but by some trick of the acoustics, she could hear snatches of conversation as if the men were speaking into her ear. Agemon spoke of doom to the men, about how they'd never see the living sun again.

Thursgad, she saw, clutched something to his chest. It must be the book. The book that would bring down the D'Yer Wall. He also seemed the most nervous of the three, jumping when he came too close to an occupied crypt, muttering to himself about spirits, glancing this way and that. It did not stop him, however, from plucking gold rings and necklaces and brooches from the dead and stuffing them into his pockets.

Karigan dampened another lamp. She couldn't get every lamp, but she left a good deal of unsettling dark behind her.

The corridor dead-ended, and she was so tired she almost laughed at the pun in her mind. A shrouded form lay in a niche there with a crown upon its breast. Karigan could not read the Old Sacoridian script carved above the niche, except for the numeral one. Hairs stood up on the back of her neck.

"This is the first high king," Agemon said. "He is King Jonaeus." He bowed to the shrouded figure.

The intruders showed no such sign of respect. The one who pointed his knife into Iris' back said, "The book, Thursgad!"

Due to the strange acoustics, Karigan could hear Thursgad's nervous breaths as he fumbled with the book. This would be a good time, she thought, for the Weapons to arrive, or even for some ghosts to lend a hand. Ghosts had helped her in the past, but of course they couldn't bother to show up in the one place you most expected to find them.

Figures.

Thursgad placed the book on the niche shelf next to the remains of King Jonaeus. He and the others stared at it. Nothing happened.

Karigan thought of ghosts again, this time the ones who appeared in her dream. *Join us,* they told her. Maybe it was a message; maybe joining them was a good idea . . .

"Open the book," the man with the knife ordered Thursgad. "It probably has to be open."

Thursgad reached for it with a trembling hand.

"Noooooooo . . ." Karigan said in a faint, withering voice from the shadows.

It must have filled the space around them for they looked all over for its origin. Thursgad stuck his hands under his armpits.

"Desecratoooooors . . ." Karigan moaned.

"The lamps!" the soldier cried.

"I told ye there'd be ghosts," Thursgad said, his voice high-pitched.

"Shut it," the man with the knife said. "Some trick of the air. Now hurry, open the book."

When Thursgad refused to budge, the soldier opened it. "Nothing," he said.

The knife man jabbed the point of his blade into Iris's back and she cried out. "This wasn't the right high king, old man. You'd better show us the right one."

Agemon pulled on his hair again. "But King Jonaeus was *the first.* He decimated your empire!"

Karigan had to give the caretaker credit for bravery. She hoped it didn't get him killed.

"Try again," the knife man said, "and take us to the right king this time."

Agemon hemmed and hawed, then resolutely led the way down the corridor toward her. Thursgad and the soldier each grabbed lamps to light the way.

A good time to fade, Karigan thought, and she turned and strode into the dark. She could not see well, but she couldn't let the intruders catch up to her. Or could she?

She didn't exactly like the idea, but she thought it might prove effective. She removed a shroud from a royal pile of bones and crinkled her nose, trying to remind herself of how fastidious the caretakers were.

Thursgad did not like this, not one bit. It was wrong to be here. The spirits didn't like it, either. Aye, he, Rol, and Gare were desecrators all right, and the memory of the spirit's voice sent another chill spasming up his spine, yet Rol seemed determined to ignore it, and Gare, though clearly shaken, chose to imitate Rol and pretend nothing happened. The old caretaker had gotten a queer look in his eye when the spirit spoke. He was probably used to spirits. He probably encountered them all the time.

After this whole adventure, Thursgad was going to take the treasures in his pockets and head west to Rhovanny. No more of this, no more tombs, no more Second Empire. The crazy old ladies in the woods were bad enough to begin with. Let Sarge call him a rustic bastard and deserter all he wanted, but he was going to have no more of this. He'd take his treasures and buy himself a piece of land on one of the lakes in wine country. Maybe he'd buy himself a vineyard. That's what he'd do. He'd become a prosperous wine farmer and no one would call him a rustic bastard ever again.

He hoped the jewels weren't cursed.

He kept close to Rol and Gare, unsettled at how many lamps had been extinguished. But not all, not all . . . It could not have been a trick of the wind. The old caretaker walked into the dark as though he knew the path by memory and needed no light. Thursgad kept his gaze plastered on Rol's back, as if that would prevent him from seeing spirits. He didn't exactly like seeing the contents of the niches either.

Despite his precautions, he caught movement from the corner of his eye. There was the swish of a shroud and his worst nightmare came to life when one of the corpses rose from its shelf. Thursgad screamed and almost dropped his lamp, and the others whirled to see the shrouded figure behind them.

The spirit raised a linen-wrapped hand, blotched with dried blood, and pointed at them. "*Trespasserssss . . .*" it whispered.

Gare was on it in a second, swiping his sword through the shroud. The shroud drifted empty and formless to the floor, the spirit gone.

AVENUES OF HILLANDER

Thursgad screamed and ran.

The way the intruders pushed and scrambled their way down the corridor, practically falling over one another, almost made Karigan laugh. If they didn't hold the lives of Agemon and Iris in their hands, she'd consider it good fun. Her haunting was clearly having an effect. Even on the man with the knife.

The trouble was that in mere moments they'd be in the brightly lit main corridor, making her ghostly antics more difficult to pull off.

Sure enough, once the intruders reached the light, they slowed down and relaxed and put aside their lamps. Karigan watched from the darkness of the old corridor as they marched onward. She glanced briefly into the dark behind her, wishing she'd had a chance to pay her respects to King Jonaeus as Agemon had.

The intruders continued past the corridor leading to the House of Sun and Moon, and when they passed Queen Lyra's chamber, Karigan was so tired she was nearly tempted to slip into bed next to the dead queen and take a nap.

As she followed the intruders, she wondered yet again what she could do. She'd begun to erode their confidence with her haunting, but they seemed to have regained it. If she could frighten them again, maybe they'd make a mistake, slow down, scatter, give Agemon and Iris a chance to escape.

They came to a large round chamber with a domed ceiling, murals painted in its coffered recesses. In the center of the chamber stood a huge, heroic sculpture of a king on a horse, with his arm stretched out like a conqueror offering benediction to the conquered. Down here that would be the dead. All that was missing was a pigeon or two.

A colonnade surrounded the chamber and from it led galleries like spokes to a wheel. At each entrance stood a suit of armor.

"Avenues of Hillander," Agemon said. "This way." And he led the men into one of the galleries.

King Smidhe, Karigan thought, looking at the statue anew. The king responsible for unifying Sacoridia's provinces. Agemon was taking those men to his tomb.

She needed to do *something.* She glanced desperately around, then flitted off down a different gallery, gazing at various Hillanders in eternal repose for inspiration. A good many were installed in sarcophagi, but others rested fully garbed on funeral slabs, their parchmentlike skin taut over skulls and bony hands.

Karigan paused and tapped her foot, thinking fast. The intruders knew nothing of her or her ability to fade. Well, Thursgad might remember, but she doubted he'd connect his "spirit Rider" of two years ago with the ghostly presence in the tombs. He didn't strike her as overly bright. To them she'd appear a ghost, even if she couldn't fade completely in the light. In fact, being only partially faded would enhance the effect. That was her hope, anyway.

She smiled at the plan, but her smile turned to a grimace as she started removing royal raiment from its owners. Agemon was going to have a fit.

A pair of white marble sarcophagi lay at the end of the gallery, practically glowing in the lamplight, the likenesses of King Smidhe and Queen Aldesta regal in their serenity. Behind them was a false window of stained glass backlit with a lamp, depicting a king and queen looking at the castle from a distance, the crescent moon above the highest turret. The king bore a torch.

"This better be the one, old man," the knife wielder said, holding Iris close.

Agemon mumbled imperceptibly and fiddled with his specs.

Thursgad approached King Smidhe's sarcophagus with the book. Karigan took this as her cue to make her ghostly appearance. She'd extinguished several lamps along the way to aid the effect, but it had surely been a trial getting this far dragging her heavy, kingly mantle of thick velvet and fur along the floor behind her.

She faded out, and in the light, looking through her hand was like looking through clouded glass.

"Halt!" she cried.

They turned. Thursgad dropped the book on the floor with a resounding boom and hid behind King Smidhe's tomb.

Agemon took to muttering and pulling on his hair, while Iris, even with the knife held close to her, looked about to laugh. The other two intruders were dumbstruck.

Karigan raised her borrowed scepter, threw her arms wide. "Desecrators!"

She stepped forward, but kept her progress slow. She couldn't tell what made her head hurt more—the fading or the crown pressing on her scalp wound.

"Defilers!" Karigan wished the intruders would do *something* other than gape at her. Agemon gazed at the ceiling. Was he praying? Cursing her for despoiling his precious corpses?

"Who are you, O spirit?" the soldier asked, his voice trembling.

"Shut up, Gare," the knife wielder said.

Karigan kept moving, allowing light and shadows to fade her in and out. What, she wondered, should her response be? She decided the ghostly thing to do was not to answer at all, so instead she moaned. "The empire will faaaaail." And she disappeared into the deepest, darkest shadow she could find.

"You lie!" the man with the knife screamed, his voice echoing down the gallery. "Gare, the book!"

When Gare did not move fast enough, the knife wielder shoved Iris out of the way and reached for the book on the floor.

This was the very thing Karigan had been waiting for. She tossed aside scepter and crown, and threw off the mantle, and charged at the intruders, sword drawn, yelling like a crazed demon.

Thursgad, who poked his head above King Smidhe's sarcophagus, fainted. Gare's mouth dropped open and only the man with the knife had the presence of mind to react by drawing his own sword. Agemon grabbed Iris and ran with her down the gallery.

Good, Karigan thought. Now she had only herself to worry about.

As ready as the man was for her, he looked confused, and when their swords clashed, Karigan realized she'd not dropped her fading. She did so now so it would no longer drain her strength. After all, he could see her in the light, translucent though she was, and once they engaged, it was clear she was a solid living person and not a ghost at all.

She danced away and put Queen Aldesta between herself and them, but Gare jumped up on the sarcophagus lid, straddling the figure of the queen, his sword hurtling down on Karigan. She blocked it, but it felt like a hammer blow. Somehow she held onto the sword and swept it like a scythe into Gare's leg. His scream was horrid and he tumbled off the tomb, crimson splattering white marble.

The last man came after her and their exchange of blows was deafening. Sweat burned Karigan's eyes. If only she could keep this up. If only she could get past his defenses.

But as he pressed her around the king's sarcophagus, she stumbled over the unconscious Thursgad. She managed to keep her footing, but could not properly block the man's next blow. It sliced down her forearm, elbow to wrist, the leather guard protecting only a portion of her wrist before the blade slashed down the back of her hand.

Karigan's sword clanged to the floor and she cried out,

but the man did not pause. He came for the kill. She ducked just in time feeling his sword hum over her head.

The only thing left to her was to call on her fading and run. This she did and she had enough presence of mind to grab the book as she went.

The man was on her heels. She sought the dark places, but there weren't enough to hide her. She pushed a statue in his path and threw an urn at him. This slowed him little. She felt like she ran in mud.

When she came to the domed chamber with the statue, she ran blindly down another gallery. She must hide, and hide quick. Someplace dark.

THE SILVER SPHERE

Thursgad awoke to silence. *Dead* silence.

He sat up recalling where he was and shuddered. The last thing he remembered was a crazed spirit charging him and his cohorts with sword raised. He peered around the corner of King Smidhe's sarcophagus to see what was what and recoiled with a gasp. Gare lay there in a pool of blood, unmoving. Had the vengeful apparition killed him?

Thursgad scrubbed his face. Gare was dead and Rol was nowhere to be seen; had abandoned him in this miserable place. Or maybe because the dead were displeased by the desecration of their tombs, Rol hadn't left willingly but was spirited away to some cursed shadow world to be tormented for an eternity.

Thursgad pushed himself to his feet, gazing warily at his surroundings, but nothing so much as moved. He did not know what he'd do if he saw another ghost. He made the sign of the crescent moon hoping to placate angry spirits and calm himself.

A throbbing against his hip reminded him he carried Grandmother's mysterious sphere. He'd obeyed her instructions so far, not handling it or telling anyone about it, but now it seemed to want out of its purse. Was it time to release the sphere? Grandmother told him to smash it when he was ready to leave the tombs. He was certainly more than ready, having no wish to disturb the dead further and share in Gare's fate, or Rol's—whatever that was.

Thursgad tentatively loosened the drawstrings of the

purse, removed the sphere and rested it on his palm. It was heavier than it looked, and it almost felt like it sucked on his flesh like a leech. He shuddered again.

He could not see his reflection in its silvery surface, but there was underlying movement, like shadows or black smoke. Grandmother had not explained what the spell did, but he knew it couldn't be anything good. Maybe he shouldn't release it at all, but if he didn't, one way or another Grandmother would find him and punish him, and he'd seen what she could do to those who displeased her. She scared him more than any ghost.

He'd obey her wishes, but not until he was nearly out of the tombs. He rolled the sphere around his palm, searching its gleaming surface for any indication his was the proper course. Aye, he'd find his way out of the tombs, release the spell as he left, and flee the castle, the city, and the country. He'd escape to Rhovanny to become a prosperous wine farmer. That's just what he'd do.

Fingers closed around his ankle.

Thursgad screamed. He should have made sure Gare was really dead, but he had not, and with his nerves already on edge, he lost hold of the sphere. It flew through the air in a graceful arc. He fumbled after it, but it was slippery as if oiled, and escaped his grasp. He watched in horror as it plummeted to the floor.

When the sphere hit stone, it did not bounce or roll, but cracked like an egg. No yolk oozed from it, but it expelled a wisp of smoke.

"Help me," Gare whispered.

Thursgad kicked his ankle free of the man's grasp and backed out of reach. He watched the smoke spiral up from the sphere, wondering why nothing else happened. He expected the ceiling to cave in, a maelstrom to sweep through the catacombs, doom to descend, but all was still. Too still, now that he thought of it. Aye, much too still . . . He tensed, ready to bolt.

Until he heard scratching from beneath the lid of King Smidhe's sarcophagus.

Thursgad promptly fainted once again.

Karigan hid a short distance down one of the passages that led off the main chamber where the statue of King Smidhe sat astride his marble horse. She stood in the shadow of a column trying to catch her breath, and held her wounded arm to her, fingers clamped over slashed flesh. The book was tucked beneath her elbow.

From this vantage point, she could see the man searching for some sign of her in the main chamber to indicate which way she'd run. He knelt to the floor and touched something. Karigan glanced at her wound and discovered blood oozing between her fingers and dripping to the floor. He would track the droplets until he found her. She'd have to run again, and she wasn't sure she had it in her. She could just give him the book, and that would be the end of it. She could rest.

But the real end would be how Second Empire put the information in the book to use. The end of Sacoridia.

She would have to try and hide it before the man caught up with her. And he *would* catch up. She knew it.

Before she took a single step, however, a strange sensation crept over her, a palpable shadow, though the passage she stood in was neither darker nor lighter. The tombs were, by their very nature, a still place, but they were too still.

The man stood erect, glancing over his shoulder and up into the dome. He appeared to sense it, too, whatever *it* was.

The air grew colder and a force pulled on Karigan, made her stumble from her place of hiding. Moans rose and echoed through the corridors of the tombs, like an ancient door that has lain shut for centuries and is forced open. The moans keened in layers, some far off, some close to Karigan's ears. She wanted to burrow into a corner and hide, but she was being called. *Raised.*

Bones rustled beneath shrouds. The dead scrabbled at the insides of sarcophagi trying to escape. The linen-wrapped dead arose from funerary slabs. Spirits streamed by her, kings and queens, whole royal families with crowns upon their heads, some mere shadows with gaping holes where their eyes should be. Their passage was a chill wind.

A skeletal hand with a bejeweled ring on its finger skittered by her feet like a spider.

"Bad dream," Karigan whispered, suddenly recalling her nightmare in the House of Sun and Moon.

She tried to hold onto the column she'd been hiding behind, but the calling forced her on, her trailing hand leaving a smear of blood on stone. The calling pushed her forward, compelled her to join the dead in their march toward the main chamber.

She was faded out, a ghost herself. She tried to drop the fading, but could not. Some greater power had taken command of her ability.

Karigan, along with the dead, spilled into the chamber. They were a ghostly sea that surged and receded in waves. The man spun around and around, aware of the spirits by the look of terror in his wide eyes, but there was no way to know how much he actually saw. The ambulatory corpses, royal mantles dragging on the floor behind them, were very visible.

Awakened, the spirits moaned. *Why are we awakened from our sleep?*

The man screamed when a corpse bumped into him. The scream attracted the spirits and they swarmed him. He thrashed and then crumpled to the floor, whimpering and throwing his arms over his head.

Why? the dead implored. *Why are we awakened?*

Karigan wanted to know why, too. Had the intruders triggered something?

Great pressure built in the air and the lamps of the tombs dampened to a weak orange glow, leaving the dome in darkness and the lower levels of the chamber in a sickly light. The spirits gusted around her in an even more agitated state.

Whyyy? they wailed.

A vibration crept up through Karigan's feet, up her legs. As the throbbing increased, statues, armor, and vases shook and rattled. The tremors continued to intensify and all around objects crashed to the floor.

A queen's pallid spirit came face to face with Karigan and screamed, her mouth opening into a cavernous void, before she drifted away in shreds.

The statue of King Smidhe on his horse quaked. His outstretched arm cracked at the elbow and smashed to the floor, chipping the horse's mane on its way down.

The tremors increased even further and Karigan feared the whole of the castle would collapse upon her. If the tombs were shaking this much, it must be far worse above ground.

A powerful vibration almost knocked Karigan off her feet. The head of King Smidhe's horse broke off and shattered into millions of pieces. The floor cracked open and she scrambled backward to avoid falling into it. The crack expanded, opening to impenetrable depths.

A wall of dank, even colder air rose from the abyss and the dead cried out around her. One of the shambling corpses fell into it, crown, scepter, and all, but something worse shot out of the void like flights of arrows, dark spirits whose painful shrieks added to the cacophony of the others. Karigan wanted to press her hands over her ears, but she held onto the book with a death grip.

The new spirits flew around her. They passed through other spirits leaving swirls of otherworldly dust behind them. Before Karigan could leap out of the way, one passed through her like a sword of cold steel sheathed in her ribs. She staggered. Another came at her and reflexively she batted it away with the book. Perhaps because it was a book of magic it deflected the spirit.

Ghostly voices wormed through her mind. She sensed great age in them, but could not discern the words. These spirits were far older than the oldest of those interred in the tombs. From the time of the Delvers? Maybe even older. Their graves must lie below the Halls of Kings and Queens.

The statue of King Smidhe, horse and all, finally weakened by millions of cracks, collapsed into shattered limbs and rubble. Masonry from above began to shower down.

Karigan fought her way through spirits toward the shelter of one of the corridors, but found it in equal tumult.

She breathed hard, wishing away the destruction and the dead, wishing for balance and normalcy, wishing she were nestled in her own bed. No doubt that bed was being jostled hard right now. She could not imagine the chaos up in the castle.

Was this it for her? Would she die crushed in the tombs? Would she be buried beneath the rubble with those already dead?

Her breathing constricted as panic set in. She had survived many things and averted disaster a time or two, but this was way beyond her ability to fix—there was nothing she could do against such a force. She would never see her father or her aunts again, or Condor, or her friends. She closed her eyes against the devastation and chaos, wondering what death would really be like.

As if in answer, she felt the presence of the death god's steed beside her. She opened her eyes to find the stallion standing there in the corridor with her, his mane and forelock flowing in a supernatural breeze.

"Can you make this stop?" she asked. Or, had he come to claim her?

He turned his head just enough to fix her with one obsidian eye. That eye was a turmoil of stars, a race through the infinite. Karigan shook her head and looked away, fearing she'd get swept away in that gaze.

The destruction around her seemed far off, as though the closeness of the stallion buffered her from it. More of the dome's ceiling panels crashed down, raising a powdery dust. The spirits whirled and rose and vanished into it.

"Well?" Karigan demanded of the stallion. "What are you going to do?"

He snorted at her as if marking her impertinence, then knelt down before her.

"Oh, no," Karigan said, backing away. "This is your thing to fix. Your master is the god of death, and this is—this is dead business."

His gaze caught her again and this time she could not escape. She was drawn into a vision of his making. In it she was swept out of the tombs, out of the castle, and upward among the stars as if suspended on wings. Below her she saw the castle and Sacor City. It was still dark and street lamps glittered below as tiny pinpoints of light. Despite the darkness, she could see everything: how the buildings shook and houses crumpled, how the city walls gave way. The towers of the castle wobbled. People fell from walls, were crushed beneath rubble. Others ran screaming through the streets. Fires consumed the noble quarter and other neighborhoods.

It was as if the hill the castle and city sat upon was coming to life and trying to shake the constructions of humanity off its back.

A castle turret toppled, then another, and a portion of the roof fell in. Karigan screamed along with those in the vision.

The hill then heaved and collapsed in on itself taking the castle and about a third of the city down with it, leaving a vast smoking crater. It wasn't just dust rising, she realized, or smoke from burning buildings, but dark spirits spiraling out of the crater like a malignant cloud.

Karigan fell from the sky.

AVATAR

When the vision released Karigan, she was still screaming, thought she was still falling. The stallion exuded a blanket of peace from where he knelt beside her, and once she realized she stood on solid rock, her screams died.

"That's what *will* happen," Karigan said to the stallion, shaking all over. Despite the mayhem around her, the hill and castle had not collapsed. Yet. Her friends, her colleagues, they still lived; there was a chance to change the outcome. She licked her lips. "You showed me what will happen if I don't mount."

The stallion whickered. It came to her as a clear affirmative.

She did not want to submit herself to the will of the gods, to become their tool, but if Sacor City fell, the lord-governors would fight for power over the king's corpse and Second Empire would take the opportunity to seize control. Nothing would stand in the way of Mornhavon the Black's return. From that perspective her decision was simple. She would not, could not, allow Sacor City to fall.

She mounted the stallion.

And found herself clad in the splendor of star steel. She bore a great lance and a shield that displayed the device of the crescent moon, which shone with an ethereal pearlescent glow. Upon her head was a winged helm, and she knew its appearance without having to look at it in the same way she knew the armor she wore was forged by the smith god Belasser, the fire of the stars his furnace. The armor gleamed as though the light of those stars still resided in it, and it weighed nothing. Its surface crawled with winged symbols that changed shape so constantly she could not see their true form.

The stallion was likewise armored, and she sat upon a warhorse's saddle, but he wore no bridle, just a chanfron of star steel to protect his face. The book she'd fought so hard to capture rested now in its own saddlebag of fine mesh mail.

With the armor came knowledge, the knowledge that not only would the castle and city fall if she did not act, but that the void in the middle of the chamber provided a doorway for spirits to leave the realm of death, malignant spirits that would torment and feed on the living.

This was why Salvistar became involved, and this was why she was chosen to act on behalf of his master: this rupture in the layers of the world violated the will of the gods and the laws of nature, and the heavens knew, literally, that she had interacted with the dead often enough.

Salvistar clip-clopped into the central chamber. Riding him was like riding the air. The destruction and shaking of the tombs paused as if all time stopped. The ghosts were clearer to Karigan's vision than before, all the men, women, and children who had ruled over Sacoridia in life. They bowed to her and her steed, and backed out of the way.

The other spirits, those who had come from below, were not as clear. They remained smudges of darkness, but she had a sense of their more primitive natures, their desires were more basic. They hungered, lusted to penetrate the living world. Fear was their tool, souls would satiate them.

Salvistar halted at the void, tossed his head, and leaped into it.

Karigan wanted to scream as they plummeted through the pitch black, but like her knowledge that she was to speak for Westrion, and that the spirits would invade the lands above if not called back to their graves, she knew the stallion would not let her fall. Indeed, she had the impression of great gossamer wings guiding their course and her seat was secure.

Eventually Salvistar landed lightly on a ledge deep within the void. The glow of their star steel armor cast a vaporous light on skulls and bones tucked into hundreds of depressions in the walls of the crevice. Engraved on the walls were Delver drawings and offerings of crude pottery, moldering furs, and weapons and tools of chert littered the ledge.

"Come," she said. The voice was hers, and it was not. She spoke Westrion's words.

One by one spirits massed around her, transparent presences, shadows. Thousands of them. She felt their hostility. Their voices shrieked in disobedience, spoke of their thirst to feed on the living. She knew this even though their utterances were unintelligible. She knew also that though many of the spirits were benign, many of the evil of their kind had been tossed to the very bottom of the void, a form of posthumous justice. Even deeper in the void was a damaged seal between the worlds, and demons scratched at it hoping to escape their hell. This was an even greater threat than that of the spirits.

"Sleep," she commanded the spirits.

They screeched and swirled in rebellion, and one who had been their chieftain in life appeared before her, standing on air. Wild hair floated about his head and he was clad in animal skins.

"Go away, avatar," he said. "You are not our god. We shall do as we wish."

Karigan thrust her lance through the chieftain and he evaporated from existence. The other spirits stilled.

The great voice of Westrion welled up inside her and emerged as a forceful compulsion: *"Sleep."*

The spirits scrambled for their niches like swarming insects and did not reemerge.

Salvistar launched himself from the ledge and spiraled down and down into sepulchral darkness, down to a place that had never known light. Karigan was not sure if it was even a physical place they traveled to or if they had transcended into some other existence.

Finally the stallion alighted and the glow of their armor revealed a dry, rocky landscape. The rocks were unweathered and of sharp and forbidding shapes. Embedded in the ground was a round shield of star steel. Like Karigan's armor, symbols wriggled across its surface, but some did not move, were dead, and a portion of the seal was tarnished and had begun to buckle. She sensed the throng of demons on the other side pushing and scratching and beating the seal for release.

This was the greater threat. If the demons escaped, life on Earth would turn into a hell, a place of eternal strife and darkness, where the living must battle for their very existence or be enslaved and tormented unto eternity. Humans would become the live carrion for spirits and demons and the living world would be transformed into a realm of death.

She lowered the tip of the lance to the seal. Words of command poured from her lips, words she did not know, words that were not of any mortal speech. The seal brightened until she needed to cover her eyes.

Then all at once it faded to a silvery glow, the symbols restored, the tarnish banished, and the demons on the other side cast far away into the deeps where they belonged. With that, Salvistar surged upward, beating his great wings in the air. They climbed and climbed through the darkness until they emerged into the chamber of the Hillanders. Tremors no longer racked the tombs, though many ancient, dark spirits still flooded the avenues of the dead and the castle corridors above.

"Come," Karigan-Westrion commanded and pointed the lance at the void.

The dark spirits flocked into the chamber, a great cloud of them that obscured the light. Unable to disobey Westrion, they spiraled back into the crevice, into the realm beneath the tombs. When the last one vanished, the ground rumbled and moved and the crack closed.

To the spirits and corpses of royalty, the death god said, "Return to your byres and sleep."

The dead receded from the chamber into what remained of the corridors.

The dust hanging in the air cleared, as though sucked

away and rubble rose from the floor and reattached itself to ceilings and walls. Statues and armor righted and reassembled; cracks and chips and dents fixed themselves until no sign of damage remained. All the pieces of King Smidhe's statue flew back together with such speed that suddenly it was in one perfect piece again, the proud king astride his horse of marble.

Karigan blinked, and found herself not sitting on the stallion, but hiding behind the column, where she had started, the book in her arms. There was no sign of the armor or the stallion, and she began to think it had all been part of a dream. Just as before, she watched the man who attacked her kneel beside her trail of blood.

"None of it happened," she whispered, and she put her hand to her feverish temple.

"It happened," said someone beside her.

She turned to find a ghost gazing at her and she almost exclaimed, but he drew his finger to his lips to silence her. This was the Rider of ancient times who had visited her in her dream and in the white world. His winged horse brooch glistened on his chest and her own warmed in reaction.

"Aye," he said, "I was the third to wear this brooch, the same one you now wear."

Karigan shivered with the weight of history, as she had when Lil Ambrioth revealed she was the first to possess the brooch.

The Rider ghost beckoned her deeper into the corridor. "I've seen you before," she whispered.

"Aye," he replied. "I am Siris Kiltyre, third captain of the Green Riders."

As they continued down the corridor, the ghost walking but not touching the floor, everything appeared to be in its place.

"Why are you here?" she asked.

"Do you remember the question I once asked you?"

Karigan was about to shake her head "no," but then it came to her. "You asked me if I knew who—no, *what*—I was."

"Do you know the answer?"

"I'm a Green Rider."

"That is only the beginning," he replied. "You are an avatar."

Karigan stumbled to a halt. *"What?"*

Siris Kiltyre gestured for her to keep moving. "I, too, rode as an avatar for Westrion," he replied. "It is our gift to touch death."

"No! My gift is to fade out, to disappear."

The ghost of Siris Kiltyre glanced back at her, the motion a spectral blur. His eyes were the substance of midnight and deep wells of the infinite. She thought of the obsidian eyes of Salvistar.

"When we fade, we are actually standing on a threshold, the threshold between the layers of the world. That is our true ability: to pass through the layers, or it would be more so if we possessed the power of great mages. With our own simple abilities, we cannot cross that threshold, unless there is some outside influence. Like Salvistar. As avatar, you crossed into the realm of death. You've been elsewhere, too. Through time, even. Because of our ability, we are chosen to ride as Westrion's messenger. We are attracted to death, and it is attracted to us."

Karigan's head throbbed with new ferocity. "You *are* dead," she reminded him.

The ghost paused and faced her. "And you speak to me."

"I asked for none of this," she said. "I never wanted anything to do with the dead! And these . . . these tombs, and gods, and . . . and . . . I just want to go to bed."

Did Siris Kiltyre smile? It was hard to tell, for he'd grown more transparent, his form being absorbed by the backdrop of the tombs. "You may never be asked to ride as avatar again," he said. "Or you may be, but you will not remember."

"What?" A wave of dizziness washed over Karigan. She just wanted to rest. Why did these dreams of ghosts keep plaguing her?

"You will not remember the destruction or the rising of the dead," Siris Kiltyre continued. "No one will. These things were not part of the natural order and were reversed. Or maybe it will seem to you like images from a nightmare. You are, after all, injured and fevered."

"Yes," Karigan said, wiping sweat from her forehead. "Tired. Dreams. I knew it."

"You will learn a necromancer walks the lands. Her abilities awakened over the summer."

"Necromancer," Karigan murmured, her eyelids heavy.

"And now you must hide, for the intruder has entered this corridor, following your trail."

Karigan nodded, but to whom or what, she did not know, for no one was there. She needed to hide. She glanced about and discovered there were many empty sarcophagi lacking lids in this gallery. She did not take the time to puzzle out the why of it, but found a likely sarcophagus and climbed into it, clasping the book to her. Inside it was dark, good for hiding. She settled into its depths, thankful she wasn't lying on anyone's bones.

THE HIGH KING'S TOMB

Karigan roused from an uneasy doze at the sound of voices.

"That is *Durnesian* carpeting made by the hands of the Fifth House of Conover," someone whined. "Over two hundred years old. How am I supposed to get the bloodstains out?"

Light glared between Karigan's cracked eyelids. She buffered her eyes with her hand.

"Ah, there you are," said a familiar voice. Brienne. "Not dead yet."

"Are you sure?" Karigan's voice came out as a croak.

"Pretty sure," Brienne said.

Soon Karigan's eyes adjusted to the light of the lamp Brienne bore. The Weapon, and Agemon, peered at her over the rim of the sarcophagus. It was really like being in an oversized bathtub.

"You are bleeding on the queen's tomb," Agemon said, his voice aggrieved.

"Queen? What queen?"

"The one-who-will-be," he replied.

Brienne reached down to help her rise from the tomb. Suddenly there were other helping hands—Cera and Lennir and Fastion—and together they practically lifted her out of the sarcophagus. She carried the book out with her.

"You *are* bleeding," Brienne said, looking at Karigan's forearm. She directed Agemon to find some linen, which he did nearby, but not without some grumbling about having more blood to clean up.

"Looks like you'll need stitches," Fastion said as Brienne snugly wrapped the wound.

Karigan sighed.

"Cera," Brienne said, "see if you can find one of the death surgeons."

"Death surgeon?" Karigan asked in alarm. "What for?"

"To stitch you up. They're good at it."

When Brienne finished binding the wound, Karigan sank to the floor, her back against the sarcophagus she'd hidden in. Maybe it was all a dream. Death surgeons!

Brienne squatted in front of her. "You did well. Agemon and Iris told us everything. Rather unconventional, but it worked."

"Where were you?" Karigan demanded.

"There were other intruders," Fastion said, "guarding the entrances. They'd knocked out the Weapons on duty with a sleeping draught infused in their evening tea. The enemy's resistance delayed us. We did intercept the one chasing you. All the intruders are dead or captured, and those alive will be interrogated and go for judgment before the king."

"Good." Karigan closed her eyes and leaned her head back against Queen Whoever's sarcophagus. It was nice and cold. Maybe they should have left her inside so she could sleep. A blanket and pillow would make it comfortable. Seemed like she'd already done a considerable amount of napping if all her confused dreams of ghosts and Salvistar were any indication. Not surprising what she dreamed about when one took into account her resting place.

Resting place? She frowned.

"I see you found the book," Fastion said.

Karigan snapped her eyes open. The book! It sat on the floor beside her. She placed it on her lap and flipped through the pages, which were blank. Except for one page.

Karigan eagerly scanned the pretentious script: *One cup of sugar, one cup of blueberries . . .*

Blueberry muffins? A recipe for blueberry muffins? Who would copy a recipe into a book of magic? If this were really the right book . . .

She struggled to stand and was able to do so with some assistance from Brienne and Lennir. "We need to find the high king's tomb," she said. "We can read it only in the light of the high king's tomb."

The Weapons gazed at one another, then at her. "Which one?" Brienne asked.

"Not Jonaeus," Karigan said. "They tried him already. And probably not Smidhe."

Agemon sniffed loudly.

"You have something to say?" Brienne demanded.

"The answer is easy," he replied.

"That so?"

He raised his chin, looking supremely wise and dignified among such errant children. "There is only one high king."

The Weapons again exchanged glances. "King Zachary?" Lennir ventured.

Agemon rolled his eyes. "Yes, yes. Of course, King Zachary. That is, unless something has changed up above that no one has told me about."

Silence.

Then Karigan burst out, "But he's not dead!" Paused, then in a small voice asked, "Is he?"

"No," Brienne said.

Agemon looked down his nose and through his specs at Karigan. "The riddle stated the book could only be read in the light of the high king's tomb. Correct?"

Karigan nodded.

"Does it say anything about the king having to be dead?"

Karigan shook her head and Agemon stepped aside, revealing a sarcophagus behind him. On the marble lid was carved a likeness of King Zachary, looking as though he were no more than asleep, a scepter clasped between his hands. A marble Hillander terrier lay across his feet. Karigan almost fell, felt like the ground shifted beneath her. Lennir grabbed her by the elbow and steadied her.

"But he's not dead," Karigan whispered.

"Preparations for the passing of the royal ones begin well before the great event," Agemon said. "Yes, yes, we would not wish to be caught unprepared. Alas, we haven't a lid carved yet for the queen-who-will-be."

"The queen . . ." Karigan glanced at the empty sarcophagus behind her. She had hidden in Estora's final resting place. This was truly bizarre.

"The book," Fastion urged. "Let's see if Agemon is right."

The caretaker sniffed again and muttered, "Of course I'm right. Yes, of course I am."

Karigan stepped up to King Zachary's sarcophagus, indeed she had to step *up* on a raised platform of stone, and she gazed down on his likeness. The sculptor had captured his image truly—much better than the wax figure of him in the Sacor City War Museum. He lay at ease, noble and serene, and she wondered if the sculptor had created the likeness while King Zachary slept.

She ran her fingers down his arm, and she wanted to touch the smoothness of his cheekbone, the texture of his beard.

"Ahem." Fastion.

Karigan stiffened and hastily snatched her hand away, feeling a heat in her cheeks that wasn't just her fever. Instead she placed the book on the king's chest and opened it to somewhere in the middle.

At first, nothing happened.

THE BOOK OF THEANDURIS SILVERWOOD

Karigan was about to remove the book from King Zachary's sarcophagus and tell Agemon he was wrong when the book shimmered with pale blue light, then absorbed the illumination from all the nearby lamps until it was so saturated it seared the eyes with hot white-gold light.

Karigan staggered back from the sarcophagus shielding her eyes, as did the others.

She felt on the brink of some other world. Images assailed her, images of an ancient battle raging in which magic was used as a weapon to devastate opposing sides. Banners fluttered in the breeze, horses reared, swords clashed, arrows rained from the sky, and magical forces exploded. Amid the chaos, she thought she heard the horn of the First Rider and felt herself stirred to the call and—

The images shifted to laborers, bare backs glistening with sweat, pounding on granite blocks, cutting them, shaping them. Hammers, hundreds of hammers ringing on stone. But there was more, a rhythm, a song to it, a song of strength and binding and endurance.

The building of the wall, Karigan thought.

To her horror, sweat turned to blood as stoneworkers, still singing their song, drove knives into themselves, falling dead upon granite blocks and bleeding into them. The granite blocks pulsated with the rhythm, carrying on the song, taking on lives of their own.

Others who were not stoneworkers also came forward to give their lives to stone, hungry stone, and all the while one man watched, leaning on a staff, his face impassive. He was encircled by a black wall of Weapons.

As if he could see Karigan, he turned to her and said, *I am Theanduris Silverwood, and this is my book.*

When others were brought forward who struggled, who refused the knife, the Weapons gutted them, making sure their bodies fell over granite blocks so the stone could drink their blood.

And on the visions went, showing the placement of the granite, masons at work, the song and rhythm unceasing . . .

When the vision faded, Karigan found herself holding onto the edge of Estora's sarcophagus, the others looking equally stunned, including Agemon, who adjusted his specs. No one spoke. No doubt the visions gave the Weapons present something to think about.

Karigan took shaky steps to King Zachary's sarcophagus and peered cautiously at the book. Glimmering golden lettering, like fire writing, filled the pages. When she lifted the book away from the sarcophagus, the lettering faded. Hastily she returned it, restoring the writing to its full brilliance. She tried to read it, but realized it was in Old Sacoridian and gave up.

Agemon, to her surprise, joined her and flipped through the pages, the golden lettering reflecting against his face. He turned to the first page and read, "I am Theanduris Silverwood and this is my book; my account of the end of the Long War and the building of the great wall."

"You can read Old Sacoridian?" Karigan asked in surprise.

Agemon gave her a much offended look. "Yes, yes. Of course I can. One must know it down here."

It made sense, Karigan thought, when the early tombs included script in the old tongue.

Agemon turned his attention back to the book and added, "And I know Rhovan, Kmaernian—"

"Kmaernian?"

"Just because a civilization is dead does not mean its language cannot live on. Yes, yes, the Kmaernians live on through their words. And of course I know Arcosian, as well."

"Of . . . of course," Karigan said, regarding the caretaker with newfound respect.

Just then Cera returned with a man in black robes, masked and hooded so only his eyes were visible.

"Who am I to tend?" he asked in a low, dark voice.

Karigan shuddered and wanted to hide behind Fastion, but before anyone could speak, Ghost Kitty reappeared, rubbing his cheek against the corner of King Zachary's sarcophagus, then leaping up on the lid. Confronted suddenly with the marble terrier, he hissed and swatted at it, jumped down, and tore away through the gallery.

"Must have encountered the real thing up above," Fastion mused.

Karigan took the diversion to look around at everyone—the Weapons, the forbidding death surgeon, the marble King Zachary, and Agemon, who continued to study the book.

"I'm going to bed," she announced.

Her words were at first met with silence, then a babble broke out around her, but she just walked away, right past the Weapons and death surgeon, retracing her steps into the main chamber of the Hillanders with its heroic statue of King Smidhe, and kept going, dimly aware of others following her. She was done. It was time for others to take care of the rest.

Brienne caught up and strode next to her. "You really ought to allow the death surgeon to—"

"I'm not dead," Karigan said.

Fastion crutched up beside her. "Not quite, anyway," he said. "The death surgeons are also menders down here."

"I'm going to bed."

"Do you know the way?" he asked.

"No, I don't," Karigan replied.

Brienne chuckled. "Then we'd better show you."

"Yes," Karigan agreed.

The environs of the tombs became a blur to Karigan. She no longer cared that she was surrounded by corpses. A few times she thought longingly of Queen Lyra's bed, for the walk back to the corridors of the living seemed so long to a body that had endured so much in so short a time. Fastion and Brienne distracted her with questions about Estora and her role in the noblewoman's rescue and about her remarkable journey back to Sacor City. Karigan answered like a sleeper, did not even know if the words that tumbled from her mouth were coherent.

She never even noticed when they left the tombs and was hardly aware of others appearing on the periphery of her vision, barraging her with questions. Colin Dovekey was there, and so were Garth and Captain Mapstone.

"I'm going to bed," she told them. She perceived Brienne and Fastion explaining things that required explaining, but they did not leave her side. If people wanted explanations, they had to keep up. Her chamber was going to be crowded if they all stuck with her.

Even the king, surrounded by more Weapons, appeared in the corridor. Karigan briefly paused, and bowed. "My pardon, Your Majesty, but I must continue on."

"She's going to bed," someone said. Captain Mapstone?

This time Fastion left her side to explain. One did not expect a king to follow.

Ordinarily Karigan would have desired a chance to spend a few minutes with the king, to talk with him, but not tonight. Or was it already morning?

When they reached the Rider wing, tears of exhaustion and relief ran down her face. She perceived curious Riders peering at her from behind cracked doors.

When she reached her own chamber, she pushed the door open, and disregarding the clumps of white cat fur on her blanket, she dropped into bed.

THE WALL SCREAMS

It was a wearisome journey through the white world, and they'd made all haste, Grandmother, Lala, and half a dozen others. She'd opened a portal and crossed a bridge onto the stark plains. She warned her people against straying or believing what they'd see there.

They'd been tantalized by groves of lemon trees, like those of Arcosia, only to have the fruits rot and fall to the ground and the trees shed their leaves and die before their eyes. There were other images that came and went, including one of the accursed horse of death the Sacoridians worshipped, standing off in the distance and watching them with a vulture's gaze. Her people obeyed her, sticking close, and disregarding such illusions.

Grandmother navigated the white world with an enchanted ball of yarn she rolled across the plains. It unspooled enough yarn that it should have run out, but it stretched all the way to the last bridge, leading them true.

The white world was both unsettling and tantalizing, for it must have been centuries since any of her people crossed into it. The Kmaernians had built the bridges long ago, long before Sacoridia had been a mote in the emperor's eye, but it had been Mornhavon the Great who learned the secret of the white world after his forces were ambushed one too many times by the enemy seemingly appearing out of nowhere when they were *known* to be much farther away. Once Mornhavon had acquired the secret, the empire had also been able to travel the ways and ambush the Sacoridians in like fashion. Soon battles raged not only across the landscape of Sacoridia, but in the white world as well, battles that had been mostly fought on a magical plane by great mages of both sides.

She nudged her horse off the final bridge with some regret into a forest full of natural light, color, and damp smells, smiling when she heard the exclamations of relief from her people as they followed her. When the last horse plodded off the bridge, the bridge vanished from existence. She supposed she could visit the white world again when she wished, but the chronicles warned against traversing it too much, with vague warnings of madness and death resulting, and something about lost souls.

In any case, she knew more intriguing places lay ahead, like the D'Yer Wall.

Before they reached the wall, Grandmother had made spells that rendered them invisible. Indeed, when they entered the encampment, the soldiers and laborers there went about their business unaware that eight members of Second Empire stood in their midst.

Grandmother guided her horse directly toward the breach, reining back when an oblivious soldier almost walked right into her, and she had to wend her way around a pair of laborers lugging water. Blackveil drew her. Its power wafted over the repairwork of the breach like a finger beckoning her on. She fairly quivered with energy.

She sensed also the weakness of the wall. Its cohesiveness was somehow undermined and she wished she had the book of Theanduris Silverwood at hand. She could bring the whole thing down now. But it would have to wait, for she'd been called to Blackveil. She had work to do there. Her destiny, and that of Second Empire, was about to be fulfilled. She would have the book later and the wall could come down then.

As she neared the wall, she felt the alarm of the guardians in response to her presence. *She comes, she comes, she comes . . .*, they shrieked. Yes, they recognized what she represented, but as disorganized as they were, they could do nothing to stop her.

She halted before the breach. "We must abandon the horses," she said.

Lala was plainly unhappy, clutching the reins to her buckskin pony and frowning.

"My dear child," Grandmother said, "we must leave the beasts behind. It would be cruel to take them with us. They'd be too terrified to bear us in the forest, and they'd prove a tasty meal for some predator."

The little girl dismounted and wiped a tear from her cheek. Grandmother was touched by how much Lala had taken to the pony, for she rarely expressed much emotion. The others busied themselves removing baggage from the horses and strapping it to their own backs. Once the horses were released and wandered away from their masters, they would become visible to those in the encampment.

Grandmother surveyed the repairwork of the breach. The alarm of the guardians thrummed beneath her feet. "The stonework is well done," she said, "but mundane for all that and no barrier. This shall take but a moment. Stand clear."

Her people backed away, giving her space. Along their journey she had knotted and knotted a length of yarn knowing what she needed to do. She had used the indigo, and she now unraveled the knotted ball, speaking words of power, invoking the strength of water, freezing, thawing, wind, erosion, and time. The end of the yarn lifted itself from her palm snakelike, gravitating toward the stone. It glided along the joints between the facing, cracking mortar, weakening stone, and boring into it. Ice repeatedly etched across the stonework, and thawed so rapidly that in blinking one missed it. Tremors jostled the ground and Grandmother thought the guardians of the wall would bring about their own undoing.

The yarn, the knots, and the words of power did their work of weakening the stonework, aging and weathering it hundreds of years in moments. The repairwork of the breach buckled, crumbled, and thudded to the ground raising a veil of dust. The ground shook so violently that it almost knocked Grandmother off her feet.

"Come," she said to her people even before the dust settled. "We must hurry across."

Without a backward glance, she started picking her way across the rubble into the forest that beckoned.

The guardians sense the workings of the art. The stone in the breach does not live, but they nevertheless feel the reverberations of magic being used against it.

The art at first probes the stone, licks at it, soaks into the pores of granite. Spreads. There is a counter song, a song of aging and weathering, of weakness and erosion, freezing and thawing.

It reverberates into the weakened portions of the wall adjacent to the breach. The song of the guardians is in too much disarray to repel it. They try to rally, to find harmony and rhythm, but it is too long gone and they are in chaos, like an orchestra playing out of time, instruments out of tune, voices crying in agony rather than combining into melodious notes. The fear of the guardians is great, but they only mangle the song further. There is no single voice to bring them together, to help them.

Listen to me! Follow me!

But the voice of the one once known as Pendric is lost in the cacophony. He has spent so much time spreading distrust and hate that he cannot heal them.

The nonliving rock of the breach gives way as though it has undergone more than a millennium of weathering in but a few moments. Granite tumbles to the ground leaving a gaping hole in the wall.

At first there is nothing more, then the bedrock upon which the wall is built rumbles and the voices of the guardians near the breach rise up in a crescendo of pain. They begin to die. Mortar fails, cracks widen, ashlars edging the breach crumble and fall.

The cry of the guardians escalates into a scream.

MERDIGEN'S RETURN

Dale was pleased. The tower guardians, instead of playing games and partying, were having serious discussions about the wall and its workings. Not that she could understand it all, and not that they weren't passing ale around now and then to, as Itharos put it, "assist in the thinking process." They filled up scrolls with equations and drawings, made diagrams in the air with points of light, and argued theories and philosophy. At least they were doing *something.*

Alton had continued with his inspections and reported the wall, the section nearest the breach, was still oozing blood, sometimes more, sometimes less, and that he saw disquieting images in the cracks, usually the eyes watching him. At times it was only one pair, at others it was several. Today he'd hurried her into the wall, and he seemed more anxious than usual. She wondered what was wrong. Even her passage through the tower wall felt . . . tense? Stiff? Not the usual fluid sensation like passing through water but almost brittle. The wall had not trapped her this time, but she worried about her return. The mages assured her they would speak with the guardians to ensure her passage back was safe.

Dale shuddered and tried to focus on what the tower mages were talking about, but sometimes they fell into using Old Sacoridian or words from other languages she could only guess at. At times they were so incomprehensible in their discussions that she found herself dozing off. Suddenly a question rang through the tower that brought her fully awake.

"So who started the song?" Fresk demanded. "Who started the song they all sing?"

Everyone stared at him. Then a babble erupted and turned into an argument. Cleodheris was certain the Fioris had something to do with it, Winthorpe claimed it was Theanduris Silverwood, Itharos speculated it was the stonecutters themselves, and Boreemadhe was quite sure the Deyers originated the song.

"We were not there to know the origin," a new voice said, "nor did we think to ask."

Dale whirled in her chair and standing there in the middle of the chamber next to the tempes stone was Merdigen with his pack on his back and his staff at hand. Two others were with him, a long-bearded, solemn fellow and a wispy woman with leaves in her hair.

When the tower guardians saw them, they dropped what they were doing and exclaimed in delight. Even Cleodheris smiled and float-walked over in her ethereal way to greet the travelers.

Dale couldn't believe it. After so long waiting for Merdigen to return, there he was standing among them. The two newcomers were introduced to Dale as Radiscar, from Tower of the Sea, the westernmost tower, and Mad Leaf of Tower of the Trees.

Mad Leaf? What sort of name was *that?*

The guardians showered the travelers with questions at once and Merdigen wearily gestured them to quiet.

"I need ale," he said, "and I'm sure Radiscar and Mad Leaf would appreciate refreshment, too."

This request was attended to, with the guardians conjuring a feast from the air, as well as mugs of ale, foam spilling over brims. Dale sat in the one solid chair at the table and waited for things to settle down.

Merdigen heaved off his pack, which dissolved to nothing before it hit the floor, and took in long gulps of ale Itharos handed him. "Ah, that is good," he said. He inquired after his cat, and asked, in turn, how everyone was, including Dale.

"I see you've not abandoned us," he said.

"I see you haven't either," she replied in a quiet voice.

Merdigen nodded. "Yes, I know I've been gone a good while, but the travel was not easy."

"What of Haurris?" Itharos asked. "Why is he not with you?"

Haurris, Dale gathered, was the guardian of Tower of the Earth.

Merdigen's features sagged at Itharos' question. "We could not reach him, I'm afraid. Broken bridges everywhere. Messages sent from Mad Leaf's tower went unanswered."

The group grew somber.

"What could have happened to him?" Boreemadhe asked.

Merdigen shrugged. "Hard to say. Perhaps the breach in the wall has made him impossible to reach, but why him, and not me, when my tower is closest to the breach?" He shook his head. "Whatever the cause, we must assume the worst has happened and that whatever happened to Haurris could happen to any of us."

The festive atmosphere at the arrival of Merdigen and his companions all but evaporated—except for Mad Leaf who grinned, well, madly, and played with a twig in her hair. It seemed one of Boreemadhe's gray clouds settled over the table.

"We must not let this deter us," Merdigen continued. "In fact it should spur us to find answers, and that's why I have called you all together: to find answers, for the wall is constantly weakening. We cannot fix the breach, but there may be other things we can do. We were always more powerful as a collective than as individuals."

"We have been looking at the problem of the wall," Itharos said, with a wink at Dale. He conjured out of the air copious diagrams and equations scrawled across scrolls.

However, as if this was some sort of cue, the tower began to rumble, the floor shuddering beneath Dale's chair. She stood in alarm and the guardians cried out in consternation. The shaking grew, encompassing the whole of the chamber, raising dust. Crockery fell out of cupboards and crashed to the floor. A crack jagged up one wall and the floor pitched so much, Dale staggered from side to side as though she were on a ship at sea.

Blocks of rock tumbled from the unseen ceiling above

and smashed to the floor. Dale dove under the table, knowing it would not be enough to protect her if the whole tower decided to collapse.

She was aware of Merdigen shouting orders and the mages running to and fro in the dust haze until they disappeared beneath the arches on either side of the chamber.

Another block crashed to the floor just inches from Dale and she gritted her teeth, wondering if this was the end of all things.

Alton paced alongside the wall. His night's sleep had been worse than usual, filled with murmurings in his head. Uneasy, ghostly murmurings full of fear and despair eating at his mind. He awoke full of trepidation.

And yet everything about the morning was as usual. The encampment went about its day-to-day business and the wall and tower remained, as far as he could tell, unchanged. He'd hurried Dale through breakfast wondering if the mages in the tower would note any difference and provide an answer to his disquiet. He hadn't told Dale how he felt, but he had practically pushed her through the wall.

Now he apprehensively awaited her return. Waited, waited, and waited. He was sick of waiting when he should be able to get answers for himself.

On impulse, he halted in front of the tower and pressed his palm against the stone facade. Shining strokes of lettering hurled away from his hand. He had not seen this in so long. He knew it was the wall guardians sending out messages of alarm. What was going on?

He was joyous that the guardians allowed him this much communication, but he feared what it meant.

Just then the ground pitched beneath him and he almost lost his footing. He did not jump away from the wall or seek cover, but pressed both hands against it, leaned into it, and tried to remain standing as the ground rolled under his feet.

"Dale!" he screamed in anguish.

SEEKING HARMONY

As the lettering continued to scroll out from beneath Alton's hands, he became aware of the encampment behind him breaking into chaos; heard the shouting and running feet, the screams of horses. He glanced up, and to his horror, saw Tower of the Heavens swaying back and forth, as if it were made of some more pliant material than granite.

He pressed his palms hard against stone and willed the guardians to allow him entry, but a jolt from within the wall, a surge of anger, threw his hands off it. He knew that anger, felt familiarity. *Pendric.*

Still he did not retreat, but planted his feet wide and offered a silent prayer to the gods, then plowed his will into the wall past Pendric, past all resistance. Suddenly, after the long silence, his mind filled with voices in chaotic song.

We are lost. We are broken. We are breached.

If the song fell apart, so would the wall. But how could he fix the song from here, and alone?

There was no way.

Then without warning, the stone yielded beneath his hands and he sank forward into the wall till it swallowed him entirely. The passage was not fluid. He was buffeted from side to side, thrown against hard angles, his flesh bruised and abraded by rough stone, and an underlying thread of song tried to repel him. Pendric again.

Alton pushed forward like a swimmer in battering seas and emerged in the tower chamber, but rock solidified around his ankle. He pulled his foot out of his boot just before the wall crushed it.

He was elated he'd made it through the wall after being denied passage for so long. Maybe the guardians were so weakened, so caught up in chaos, that their barrier against him failed. Or maybe they were ready to embrace him again and accept his help. He hoped it was the latter.

His elation turned to apprehension as he peered through the haze of dust. Rubble littered the floor, and another tremor nearly knocked him off his feet. The columns in the center of the chamber weaved precariously. He could not see Dale and he feared the worst.

Merdigen poked his head out from beneath the western arch. "This way, my boy!" He waved at Alton to join him.

Alton dashed for the arch, and across grasslands where he had a brief impression of a raging storm of snow and lightning exploding around him till he emerged past the columns into the ordinary tower chamber again. One of the columns crashed to the floor beside him, breaking into sections. He ran beneath the arch. Merdigen shone with a faint glow, revealing little in the darkness. Straight ahead the corridor dead-ended where it intersected with the wall.

"The others are merged with the wall," Merdigen said. "We must restore order, and we need your voice. Will you help?"

Alton thought it a ludicrous question. He nodded.

"Good," Merdigen said, and he walked into the wall, merging with it, leaving Alton in the dark.

Alton licked his lips, tasted salty sweat and the grit of stone dust, and groped forward to press his hands flat against the wall. With his mind he announced who he was and his consciousness flowed into stone, leaving his body behind.

Leave, *Pendric's voice thunders, the force of his will almost dislodging Alton's contact.*

Alton braces himself as if facing into a windstorm and with his own strong resolve impelling him forward, he drives his mind past his cousin and deeper into the wall.

The song is in complete disarray. Crackling fills Alton's awareness and he almost retreats, for it feels like it's his own mind that is breaking. It hurts.

The guardians do not welcome him or deny him, nor does the stone tell him stories of its birth and weathering, its quarrying and shaping as once it did. He is surrounded by a forest of crystals—symmetrical trees of feldspar and quartz and blades of black hornblende. The limbs of the trees vibrate with violence and one by one they explode into fragments, the granite a sandpaper scream in his head. The very constitution of the wall is breaking down.

We are breached. She passes, she passes, she passes. We are breached . . .

The wailing shreds his mind and the once unified beat of the stonecutters' hammers is out of time.

Broken. Lost. Dying.

Alton does not know what to do now that he is here. He joined with the wall once before and sang with the guardians, but it was a song of unmaking, a deception given to him by Mornhavon the Black. He realizes he does not know the true song. He cannot discern its refrain from the chaos.

Betrayed. Broken. Unweaving.

Then Merdigen is with him, and the other mages, too.

"You must sing," Merdigen says. "Try to get them to sing with you."

Another tree explodes nearby and Alton feels it as if the fragments cut and puncture his flesh.

"I do not know the words."

"Then listen."

The mages begin to sing. Alton strains to hear them amid the clamor. They are not harmonious singers, but they have the words and melody.

From Ullem Bay to the shores of dawn,
we weave our song through stone and mortar . . .

* * *

Alton listens hard, trying to block out the cries of the wall guardians. Note by note he joins the mages, stumbling over words, trying to capture the tune and rhythm.

A surge from the wall guardians counters him with their lament: Our song unravels, erodes stone and mortar. We are breached. Our song weeps.

Alton wants to shout, No! *but Merdigen says, "Sing. It is the only way. Sing so they hear you."*

So Alton does, forcefully, allowing his voice to gather volume. He sings with surety, for now it feels instinctual, as if he's always known the song, as if it has always flowed through his veins. His birthright.

> We shield the lands from ancient dark.
> We are the bulwark of ages.

He perceives a nearby cluster of crystals vibrating and prismatic colors flaring from geometric planes. The cluster does not tremble with the turmoil of the guardians, but resonates his song, enlarges it. Encouraged, he sings with more confidence and more crystals resonate. It is as if there is more than one of him singing. He is singing in harmony with himself. His voice spreads calm outward in ripples, like rings on a lake.

> We stand sentry day and night,
> through storm and winter,
> and freeze and thaw.

Merdigen and the mages buoy him, hold him steady, ground him. They are his bedrock.

He opens fully to the wall. Feels the emptiness of the breach, the pain and destruction around it, the suffering and deaths of guardians. But he feels also, away from the breach, a tide of unity and strength, and if those guardians once felt uncertainty and despair, now they hear him and add their voices to his, the blows of stonecutter hammers in sync with his heart. Slowly they reweave the song, preserving crystals that have not broken. Those that have been destroyed, however, cannot be remade.

From Ullem Bay to the shores of dawn,
we weave our song through stone and mortar,
we sing our will to strengthen and bind.

Alton stretches his consciousness as far as he can, trying to flood each fracture with song, like filling a dry river bed with water. More guardians take up the song and echo him. The forest flares with red pulsing light, like blood flowing through veins.

The song grows and builds until he hits a barrier of seething hate. Pendric.

Leave. *Pendric's voice is like the tolling of a ponderous bell. Crystal trees shudder with the tone. Alton's song falters.*

Betrayer.

"No," Alton says, his voice small by comparison. "You are the betrayer. You are killing the wall."

Do not trust. Hate him.

Hate, hate, hate . . . *pounds through the wall.*

Alton senses uncertainty in the guardians, the song weakening. The underlying chaos surges while the order he restored ebbs.

We are breached.

We are broken.

We do not trust.

Pressure crushes Alton, entraps him so he cannot move forward or backward. Crystals vibrate with so much anger they slice into his mind.

"You are killing the wall!" Alton cries. Then he remembers who and what he is, and from deep within he calls upon his special ability. Though he has never used it before from within stone, it rises from him, builds a wall around his mind that shields him from harm and thwarts his cousin's attack.

Pendric screams his rage, battering Alton's shield, but it holds.

"Sing!" Merdigen urges him.

The mages help Alton find the song again, and he sings it as powerfully as he can, once again bringing confidence to the guardians. They drown out Pendric, coax unsure voices to join them. In a rising crescendo, he calms the voices, homogenizes them, and they become one. Pendric can no longer be heard. Now he is no longer an individual, but part of the wall's chorus.

There are empty broken spaces in the wall, and try as Alton might, he cannot make them resound with song. The guardians in those places are dead. At least he has helped halt the cascade of destruction, and the guardians that remain sing together.

From Ullem Bay to the shores of dawn,
we weave our song in harmony
for we are one.

Sense of self flees Alton as he soars in the joy of the song. This is where he should be, singing among the guardians, rejoicing among the beauty of crystals, becoming a guardian himself and helping the wall remain strong.

Then, like someone grabbing his collar, Alton is hauled out of his contact with the wall and his consciousness thrown back into his body.

Alton flailed backward, tripping over rubble, and fell halfway beneath the arch. He stared at dust funneling up a shaft of daylight that pierced through a hole somewhere high above in the tower's height.

"I should think that's the end of the observation platform," Merdigen said, following Alton's gaze and stroking his beard.

"Observation platform?"

Merdigen looked down at him and crooked an eyebrow. "You don't think the tower contains only this chamber, do you? That would be a terrible misuse of space."

Someone coughed and Alton sat up. "Dale?"

"I'm fine," she said, coughing again. Through the haze he saw her picking her way across the chamber, stepping over the fallen column, and patting dust off her sleeve. Her hair was gray with it. "I see you finally found a way in."

"Yes, I—"

"Good. Then I don't have to relay your messages all the time and worry about you pulling out your hair."

"Pulling out my hair?" He stared incredulously at Dale, then at Merdigen. The wall may have just fallen and they worried about observation platforms and hair? "The wall!"

"What about it?" Merdigen asked.

"Is it . . . is it still standing?"

"Heavens, my boy. If it collapsed, so would this tower. It was shaken for sure, and the breach may be wider than it was, but with your aid I think we stemmed the tide. Remember, this wall was made of great magic, and a little jostle isn't going to throw it down."

"A little jostle . . ." Alton swiped hair out of his face. "What happened? What set it off?"

"A very good question," Merdigen said. "The guardians were already in disarray, as you know, helped along in no small measure by the other Deyer, the Pendric fellow."

"My cousin."

"Well *I* know that. Off key, he was, and that's putting it mildly, but I think he's a tad more attuned to the wall now."

"He trapped me," Alton said.

"Yes, yes, but you defended yourself well, though in the end we almost lost you. If we had not pulled you out, you would have become like him, absorbed as a presence in the wall without corporeal form. And while that's all fine and good, you'll probably be more useful to us as you are now that the guardians are ready to deal with you again. But you must learn restraint so you do not lose yourself in the wall."

Dale overturned a chunk of granite with her foot and it clacked on the stone floor. "Probably a good idea," she said. "It wouldn't make Captain Mapstone very happy if you up and sacrificed yourself."

As light as Dale's words were, they gave Alton a jolt. An image came to him of his red-haired captain working diligently at some task in her quarters. That ordinary sight led to memories of the Rider call drawing him from his life in D'Yer Province all the way to Sacor City and right to the captain's door. He remembered little of the moment in which he became a Green Rider, except for the warm murmur in his mind, *Welcome, Rider,* and the sense of belonging that overcame him as he held the winged horse brooch in his hand for the first time.

What would he be doing now had he not been called? Attending socials, courting girls of noble blood, hunting, learning how to run a province . . . He'd be the picture of the perfect lordling with too much time on his hands, a young dandy whose greatest crisis was choosing what to wear to the next party. It certainly would not have prepared him for what he now faced.

He was grateful for the call and to be in a position to help mend the wall. It gave him purpose, something meaningful to do with his life. Thinking of the captain, thinking of himself as a Rider in green, brought him home, so to speak. It centered him. Even there in the damaged tower, even after striving within the wall with the guardians.

He touched his brooch and felt a comforting pulse of warmth and knew that what he was doing, and who he was, was as it should be. The anger and frustration that strangled him for so long evaporated and was replaced by a sense of peace. Now he could work.

"In any case," Merdigen said, interrupting Alton's reflections, "it is impossible to say what set off the guardians, though whatever it was, it was unfortunate the wall was in such a fragile state. Did you hear some of them? 'She passes,' they said. What it means?" He shrugged. "Perhaps we'll never know, for we'll not get useful answers from the guardians."

Merdigen might shrug it off, but Alton thought anything with the power to upset the guardians more than ominous.

One by one other figures emerged from beneath the arch

and joined them. They all looked at Alton who sat on the floor.

"So this is the Deyer," said a fellow with pale, pale eyes, who could only be Itharos.

"Handsome," said a lovely, ethereal beauty who floated more than walked. Cleodheris?

"Bit young for my taste," said a short woman with elfin features. Definitely Boreemadhe.

Alton felt rather at a disadvantage sitting on the floor, and so stood with Dale helping him up, and greeted the tower guardians at eye level.

Another fellow emerged from the opposite arch and announced, "I've checked on your cat, Merdigen. He's nervous, but fine."

"Good, good," Merdigen replied. "As soon as we assess the damage to the wall and the towers, we'll see what we can fix with the help of the Deyer."

At that point, Dale introduced the remaining tower guardians. Alton felt like he already knew them from all of her descriptions, though the giggling Mad Leaf and solemn Radiscar were new.

Dale peered upward. "It's snowing," she said.

Alton followed her gaze, and sure enough, flurries eddied through the hole above and drifted all the long way down into the chamber. Individual flakes alighted on Alton's face and melted.

"I haven't seen snow in about a thousand years," Boreemadhe said, her expression one of awe.

Observing something as ordinary as snow impressing one who was herself a wonder made Alton grateful he had not been lost in the wall or obsession. Every moment of life mattered. Even the perfect snowflake that alighted on his palm and melted in seconds.

MENDING

Mara looked good, Karigan thought as she sipped her tea. The two Riders sat with Captain Mapstone in Mara's chamber in the mending wing. Mara was out of bed and sitting in a chair where sunlight filtering through the frosty window fell brightly upon her white nightgown. In fact, she looked better than ever, the difference noticeable after Karigan's time away.

Ben's special mending ability had brought Mara through infection and illness, and reduced the scarring, though some vestige of the burn scars would always remain. Soon Mara would move into her room in the Rider wing, which she'd yet to see, and meet the new Riders who'd arrived since summer. She'd also resume her duties as Chief Rider.

Ben had helped Karigan heal, too. Mostly he used ordinary mending techniques and though she could not remember clearly, she thought he'd used his special ability to heal the festering scalp wound. She recalled lightness and coolness at his touch, a peaceful glow . . . Then again, it could have been a dream.

Now the stitches on her head and forearm were about ready to be removed. She was glad because the shorn bit of her head looked ghastly. She scowled at the memory of Lord Amberhill suggesting she'd want to wear a hat or hood. Unfortunately he'd been right.

She hardly recognized herself when she looked in a mirror these days, and it wasn't just the Karigan on the outside who looked different. No, something had changed on the inside, too. It was hard to pinpoint what was different. Maybe she was finally growing up? She did feel *older.* She sighed. It was hard not to change a little after all she'd been through.

"That was some sigh," Captain Mapstone said.

Karigan looked up, blinking in surprise. She'd forgotten where she was.

"And you were scowling," Mara said.

"Did you hear anything we were saying?" the captain asked.

"I . . ." Karigan thought hard. "Garth. You've sent Garth on an errand."

Captain Mapstone and Mara exchanged smiles. "Not just an errand," the captain said, "but down to the wall to tell Alton the book has been found and that it's being translated."

How could Karigan miss mention of the wall? She resolved to pay attention to the present conversation and to stop dwelling on her own thoughts. "I take it Agemon is in charge of the translation?"

"Makes sense, as the book can't be read anywhere but on the king's tomb and Agemon will not permit outside scholars down below, especially after the mess you made."

"The mess *I* made?" Karigan said.

"I heard something about you dressing up in garb belonging to, er, residents of the tombs," the captain replied. "Agemon thought it very un-Weaponlike."

Karigan had related her journey at length to the captain, except the part about Fergal jumping into the Grandgent—it did not seem appropriate to do so until he returned with Estora safe and sound. Apparently she had left out a few other details, as well. Mara stifled a snicker.

"In any case," the captain said, "Agemon reportedly feels very put upon that he must oversee both the cleanup and the translation. He feels the cleanup is more important, but of course the king believes differently and has Brienne exerting pressure on him."

Karigan did not envy Brienne the task, but she sensed the

Weapon was well-accustomed to obtaining results from the recalcitrant caretaker.

"Agemon will be receiving new help," the captain said. "None of the intruders of the tombs are permitted above ever again, so they're being detained down below and interrogated by the Weapons, of course, especially about this Grandmother character. Some of the prisoners will be trained in the art of caretaking and absorbed into caretaker society. The others, the more dangerous ones, will probably be executed, but that is up to the king."

"Thursgad?" Karigan asked.

"Hard to say, since he was in on old Mirwell's original plot to replace the king with Prince Amilton. My guess, however, is that he's not as culpable as, say, Immerez. We'll see."

Karigan nodded. Even though Thursgad, under Immerez's orders, had hounded her halfway across Sacoridia a couple years ago in pursuit of the message she bore, she did not see him as *evil.*

"Word is," the captain said, "he confessed freely about how he obtained the book, and undoubtedly that will aid his cause."

Both Karigan and Mara awaited an explanation, but the captain gazed thoughtfully into space.

"Well?" Mara demanded.

The captain smiled. "Sorry. I've only heard pieces thus far, but it seems he stole the book from a pair of elderly ladies—sisters, he said—who lived somewhere deep in the Green Cloak. He described their manor house as very fine and full of wonders."

A chill prickled up Karigan's spine. *Could it be?* By the look on Captain Mapstone's face, she had made the same guess at the identities of the two elderly sisters.

"You will—you will tell me when you hear more?" Karigan asked.

The captain nodded.

Thought of the Berry sisters brought to mind the portrait of Professor Berry back in Selium, and a ghostly moan of *Liibraaary.* She dismissed it as her imagination at the time, but had the professor been trying to pass on a message? Then it occurred to her that if this were the case, he'd not been speaking of the Selium library despite the location of his portrait there, but of his own at Seven Chimneys.

It was not inconceivable that among his collections of arcane objects and books that he had somehow acquired the book of Theanduris Silverwood. In fact, the more she thought about it, the more it made sense to her, that of anyplace the book could have been hidden, Seven Chimneys was the most perfect location. Professor Berry had collected objects of arcane interest when most others shunned them.

Why hadn't she thought of it to begin with? Why hadn't she listened to Professor Berry's message? She groaned. As much as she disliked dealing with the dead, she would do well not to dismiss their ghostly whispers as figments of her imagination in the future.

"She's doing it again," Mara said.

"Huh?" Karigan asked, glancing about.

"I'd say it was more a groan than a sigh this time," Captain Mapstone replied.

Karigan furrowed her brow.

"We were just talking about Fergal's new ability," the captain continued.

Karigan sat up, now very attentive, wondering once again what she missed. "And?"

The captain smiled. "It's been about twenty years since an ability like his has surfaced, according to our records."

"*What* is his ability?" Karigan asked.

The captain's smile deepened, and Mara chuckled. "If you'd been listening—"

"Please," Karigan pleaded. "I'm listening now—I promise."

"Very well. His ability has to do with being able to read the aural energy around magic users. It was a more useful ability during the Long War when Riders could pick out enemy mages and detect the type of magic they wielded. After the Long War, when magic users died out with the Scourge, the ability was not as useful. Any Rider who had it pretty much saw only the auras of other Riders.

"When Fergal saw the old woman in Mirwellton, he was definitely picking up on some nasty magic. If there are more magic users emerging now, I'd say that Fergal's ability is going to prove quite useful."

Karigan wondered about what he detected when he looked at her—darkness. Did it simply represent her ability to fade, or something deeper? He'd mentioned "dark wings," and she didn't like the sound of that.

Just then a knock came upon the door and a Green Foot runner entered the chamber. "My pardon, Captain," he said, "but His Majesty summons you to the throne room."

A look of disappointment crept across the captain's face as she set aside her cup. "Duty never takes tea," she said.

"I could go in your stead," Mara offered.

"Not in your nightgown," the captain replied. "I trust you two will stay out of trouble?"

"Yes," Karigan said with fervor.

"No," Mara said. "Leastways, I wouldn't mind a little trouble. Life has been so dull."

Chuckling and shaking her head, the captain left them.

Had Karigan been confined as long as Mara, she'd go batty, too, but seeing as she had had more than her own share of trouble of late, she reveled in the rest both Master Mender Destarion and Captain Mapstone had ordered her to take. It looked like Mara did her best to amuse herself during her confinement—a pile of books towered on the table next to her bed and the captain had brought her a fresh stack of paperwork. Not to mention she was frequently visited by her friends, lately, mostly by Karigan.

"Maybe we could switch places for a while," Karigan mused.

"I said I wanted a *little* trouble," Mara replied. "Not a whole heap. For heavens sakes your stories have been wilder than any in those novels Tegan picked out for me. I want nothing to do with white worlds or icky tombs, or rescuing noble ladies, for that matter. Although," she added, "I wouldn't mind meeting Damian Frost. And Lady. Is that really her name? She's not a noble? If it was her name and she was gentry, we'd have to call her Lady Lady. 'Hello, Lady Lady. It's so nice to meet you, Lady Lady.' " Mara had taken on a sophisticated tone and sat poised with teacup held with pinky raised. " 'Would you like one sugar or two, Lady Lady?' "

Karigan almost snorted tea out her nose. When her laughter subsided to giggles, she had to wipe tears from her eyes. Mara looked vastly satisfied with herself.

Karigan had not laughed like this since she was with Estral, and that seemed like ages ago. It was more healing than all the rest in the world.

"So," Mara said, "anything new for you? Have you been grilled about your adventures by the king yet?"

"No," Karigan said, and she had to admit she was surprised. She hadn't even been summoned, though Lord Coutre had sought her out in the Rider wing to hear everything she had to say about his daughter. He was so caught up in his emotions that he had trouble thanking her for helping Estora. All he could do was pat her on her knee and swallow back tears. The encounter shocked Karigan, but she was gratified by how much he appeared to love his daughter and that he wasn't just interested in how her abduction affected the marriage alliance with the king.

As for the king, Karigan supposed Captain Mapstone and Fastion had given him all the pertinent details, and maybe he didn't think it prudent to interrupt her healing rest for an interrogation. Had she expected him to come dashing to her bedside to hear all that had befallen her? She shook her head. He had greater things to worry about than her. Captain Mapstone brought general good wishes for her wellbeing from the king. Apparently Karigan's time away had done the job of distancing them, but now she found herself annoyed by it, and even more annoyed at her annoyance. Wasn't it what she wanted? She just wished he'd request to see her; wanted him to want to see her.

Still, it was all for the best. There was no future for them and the sooner they put aside any feelings they had for each other, the better. The diversion of her message errand and subsequent adventures had helped distract her for a while, but returning to the castle with him so nearby did not. As soon as she was rested and all her hurts fully healed, she'd make sure Captain Mapstone knew she was ready to resume her duties. She'd request the long distance errands, even in the deep of winter. Who knew? Maybe she'd get sent to the Cloud Islands where she could bask in the tropical sun and eat fresh fruit while the castle stood icebound and braced against the northern winds.

Laren Mapstone left the mending wing and set off for the throne room to answer the king's summons. It pleased her to see both Karigan and Mara looking so well, though she was not certain she'd ever get over the shock of seeing Karigan emerge from the tombs dressed in the black of the Weapons when she was still expecting her to be somewhere in the west. At the time she wondered if this was really her Rider and not some illusion or a twin. But it was neither, and as Karigan's story came out, it was no less remarkable than her past adventures.

Laren also wouldn't forget Zachary's expression of astonishment when he had seen Karigan. The appearance of her in black turned her into something different—older, stern, *dangerous.* The Weapons had proved evasive when asked why they had permitted her to wear their garb. All she could figure was that they held her in some special regard. It wasn't just the uniform, but something different in Karigan's eyes. Something fathomless . . . Laren shook her head.

She'd managed to restrain Zachary from seeing Karigan. Others would take care of her, she knew, and she would not allow emotions to rise between them. When Zachary expressed a desire to visit Karigan, or summon her, Laren put him off, told him Karigan did not wish to see visitors, did not wish to see *him.* He'd given her messages to deliver to Karigan, and she'd destroyed them, telling Karigan only the king had wished her well, as he would any of his Riders.

She hated lying, hated having to destroy the emotional connection between them, but there was something much greater at stake—the unity of her country, and united it must stay if it was to fend off aggression from Blackveil. The sacrifice of romantic feelings between two individuals was nothing in comparison.

She walked down corridors with determination in her step. She would do all she could to separate the two, and pray that Lady Estora soon returned so wedding plans could resume. Of course, then she must deal with Lady Estora and the matter of the secret they shared. She shook her head. Nothing was ever easy.

When Laren found herself at the threshold of the throne room, she was jarred from her thoughts when she looked inside and saw the long chamber cast in ethereal light by the presence of Eletians.

She tugged her shortcoat straight and strode down the runner. The three stood before King Zachary cloaked in silvery white with subtle hues of light blue, like a wintry day with the sun glaring off snow.

When she came abreast of them and bowed before the king, she recognized them as the same three who had come before, including Prince Jametari's sister Graelalea at their head. Colin and Sperren both attended the king, and seemed to blink in the light of the Eletians.

"Greetings, Laren Mapstone," Graelalea said.

Laren nodded her head in respect.

"The Eletians have come to bid us farewell," Zachary said.

The idea of the Eletians leaving saddened Laren, for they brought a touch of magic and mystery into the sometimes dour existence of castle and city, and it would be odd for their encampment, which had become such a fixture down at the city gates, to vanish. She hadn't expected the Eletians to stay indefinitely, but she'd miss them nevertheless, and whatever their motivations for coming to Sacor City to sit on their doorstep, she did not think the people as a whole bad at heart. Just enigmatic.

"Yes, by dawn tomorrow we shall be gone," Graelalea said.

"Why?" Laren blurted, and she cleared her throat, embarrassed.

Graelalea smiled. "The days wane and grow cold, and we wish again to dwell beneath the boughs of our woods. My brother sees a frigid winter ahead, fiercer than in some years past, and so wishes to leave now."

"So he is not sending you into Blackveil?" Zachary asked.

"Not yet," Graelalea replied. "We shall bide our time in Eletia and, if I can, I will turn his mind against the idea over the winter. My feeling, however, is that you shall see us again in the spring, and that is when we'll attempt entry into Blackveil."

"Foolishness," Colin said.

"Perhaps. And while I cannot always know the workings of my brother's mind, he reveals only that which he wishes to be known. It may be that he sees something no one else can in attempting such an endeavor." Graelalea shrugged and sunlight rippled down the folds of her cloak. "My brother bids you all a winter of warmth and fire glow. He is gladdened the book of the wall has been found, though he advises caution, for the building of the wall was accomplished with dark and arcane craft you may not be able to replicate. Nor wish to."

"We will decide what to think of it once the book is translated," Zachary said.

"That is as it should be. My brother, by the way, says the Galadheon averted a great disaster."

"She is the one who captured the book from the enemy," Laren said.

"Ah." Light glinted in the Eletian's eye and she smiled as if she knew something they did not. "For you, Firebrand, some final words from my brother: *She comes.*"

With that the Eletians bowed and turned and left the throne room, taking lightness with them.

HEARTSTONE

The Weapons kept up a relentless pace, but Goss was up to it, and the road was open and wide. It was no wild dash through the unbroken woods this time, and with a complement of deadly warriors all around, Amberhill had no fear of attack from hungry pirates or any other danger, human or not.

Hooves pounded on cobbles and across bridges and the company kept the Rivertown ferry busy with several crossings on the Grandgent. Though the town was sizeable, Willis did not pause, but led them onward, for it was hours before sunset.

When they did stop, whether at a campsite or in a village, there was always adequate provender, for which Amberhill was grateful. He did not starve on the return journey, and the Weapons did not spare wood when it came to building campfires. It was all a satisfactory improvement over his journey west, but he looked forward to returning to his house in Sacor City. Except it would be much emptier without Morry. He reiterated to himself his vow to properly bury and honor his friend, his father in spirit. When he got the chance, he'd retrieve Morry's body and return with it to his estate and place it in the family vault. Morry deserved no less.

The Weapons rode in silence and spoke little when encamped. When they did speak, it usually was not to Amberhill, unless necessary. He did not take it as a personal affront, for he recognized it as their way; the black they wore was only a physical manifestation of the bond among the warriors and a barrier to outsiders that none but those within their circle could bypass. One of those who did not wear black but who appeared to be in that elite circle was Beryl Spencer.

The Weapons respected her Mirwellian rank and called her Major Spencer, though as Amberhill understood it, she was actually a Green Rider. In evenings she sparred with some of the Weapons, the clash of swords pure and musical to his ears as he watched the bouts from his side of the campfire. They moved between the flames engaged in the dance of steel and though graceful, the dance was without flourish. For one like himself who embodied grand gestures, their deadly precision and stark movements were a revelation. And the Rider-spy-major was on a level with the Weapons in ability.

Truth be told, the woman made his skin crawl. Though she was icy to him, indifferent, he couldn't help being morbidly fascinated by her because she was the antithesis of the kind of woman he was accustomed to. Pliant warmth, softness, and curves, yes, that was what he knew well and desired. Not an icicle with an undercurrent of menace who would take as much delight in severing his hand as gazing at the most beautiful work of art. He shuddered.

The G'ladheon woman also made him shudder, but in a different way, with her unearthly powers.

Once he returned to Sacor City, he'd seek out the familiar warmth of the ordinary women he craved, which would melt away any frost remaining on him from being in Beryl Spencer's presence and extinguish the memory of the G'ladheon woman vanishing into the night.

The next evening, when Willis called a halt, they found the field he wanted to camp in already occupied by a tent and a wagon overloaded with furniture and other household goods, all of fine quality, though some of it appeared water damaged. The two owners of the tent sat before a fire in chairs that would look more fit for a royal dining hall than in a field.

A kettle hung over their campfire and the two sipped out

of teacups and nibbled on scones. Oddly, there was no team of horses for the wagon to be seen, nor any guards or servants tending the ladies who were elderly. Amberhill could not see how they'd managed to set up camp, much less traveled with their belongings with no team to pull the wagon. Unless some thugs had stolen the horses. But not their possessions? It did not make sense.

Willis must have thought it odd, too, for after a courteous greeting, he said, "Have you some trouble we could help you with? Are you stranded?"

Curious, Amberhill busied himself with his gear nearby so he could listen.

"Trouble?" the plumper of the two asked, then she chuckled. "Young man, you can't even begin to imagine the trouble we've had; could he, sister."

Her companion snorted in derision, then sipped from her teacup.

"However," the first continued, "we are well cared for, and certainly not stranded, but we do thank you for your concern. Perhaps you will join us for some tea?"

At first Willis declined, but the lady said, "Surely the others can set up the camp without your help, can they not?"

"Well—" Willis began.

"Even a king's Black Shield is permitted a tea break now and then, hmm? Sit down, young man. We cannot imagine what brings you all to be here along the Kingway, but it is propitious, isn't it sister."

The thin one nodded. "An unexpected opportunity."

The way Willis cocked his head, Amberhill could tell he was too intrigued now to refuse. With a slight bow to the ladies, he took a chair that appeared to be waiting just for him.

"And you, too," the thin one said, pointing her cane right at Amberhill.

"Oh, yes," the plump one said. "Come, young man, sit with us."

At first Amberhill was too startled to move, but he set his gear on the ground and sat next to Willis. The sisters poured tea and passed around scones, and introduced themselves. They called themselves Penelope and Isabelle Berry, or Miss Bunch and Miss Bay, respectively. They carried on the conversation quite well by themselves, speaking of the winter to come, their sudden need to move, and the rough paths they had to travel by.

Amberhill found himself quite under their spell, feeling as though he were in some manor house's parlor rather than out in the elements sitting before a campfire. By Willis' transfixed expression, he could tell the Weapon was quite taken, too.

"How, may I ask," said Willis, "did you find yourselves on the road?"

"You may ask," Miss Bay said, "but it is an unusual story and the source of great woe."

Miss Bunch nodded fervently. "It began with a sneak thief that in our poor judgment we allowed into our home."

The clatter and voices of Weapons setting up camp fell away as the sisters told an incredible story of how the thief, whom they thought a hunter lost in the woods, was caught stealing a book from their father's library by a servant named Letitia, and in his struggle to escape, he broke one of their father's "things."

"An arcane object," Miss Bay said. "Do you understand?"

Willis nodded slowly, his eyebrows drawn together. Amberhill didn't think the Weapon had taken more than one sip of his tea once the ladies began their tale.

"That's when it happened," Miss Bunch said. "That's when our lovely house, built by our father for our dear mother, was destroyed."

Both sisters appeared on the verge of tears.

"How?" Willis asked.

"Well, it was the pirate ship, of course," Miss Bay replied tartly.

"Pirate ship?"

"Nasty pirates."

Miss Bay then described, with comments inserted by her sister, how the sea rose in their house despite its location far from the coast, and flooded it and poured out the windows, and how the ship materialized to full size inside the house, destroying it utterly.

"Not a chimney left standing!" said Miss Bunch with a mournful sniff. "It will be a long while before the house mends itself."

"If it can, sister," Miss Bay said. "It isn't like the simple leak we had in the west gable roof last spring."

"True, but I have faith. I *must.*"

A silence passed before Miss Bay said, "We had to hide from the pirates. We hid and hid. They would not have been in the bottle in the first place had they not been very bad."

"Bottle?" Willis' voice cracked as he asked the question.

"Why, yes," Miss Bay said. "Weren't you listening? We said it was an arcane object. Really, I thought the Black Shields grasped such concepts."

"I—"

"In any case, young man," Miss Bunch interrupted, "you will want to warn the king that pirates now infest his forest. This is why we are glad we met you, so you could warn the king."

"*Nasty* pirates," Miss Bay reemphasized.

"We don't know how many, do we, Bay?" Miss Bunch said, and her sister shook her head.

If Amberhill had not slain the pirates himself, he'd have thought the two sisters seriously mad. He twisted the blood ruby ring on his finger.

"Pirates . . ." poor Willis muttered.

"Is he dense?" Miss Bay asked Amberhill.

"No, my lady," he replied. "But I think you need not worry about the pirates anymore."

Willis glanced sharply at him, and the ladies turned intent gazes on him.

"Is that so?" Miss Bunch asked.

"Look at the ring," Miss Bay whispered, pointing.

Amberhill raised it into the light so they could get a better look at it. The fire made the ruby glow with red and orange flames, the dragon seeming to slither around his finger.

He covered the ring with his other hand, withdrew it from the light.

The sisters stared at one another, then turned their gazes back on him.

"There are oddments of jewelry," Miss Bunch began.

"And then," her sister continued, "there are objects that take some responsibility to own."

"If we are not mistaken," Miss Bunch said, "that ring is one such object. If the wearer should own it for the sake of owning it, the consequences could be terrible. But if the wearer accepts the responsibility for whatever the object may represent, then the outcome may prove more beneficent."

"It isn't . . . just a ring?" Amberhill asked, already knowing the answer.

"Young man," Miss Bay said, "that ruby is a heartstone, and only the most powerful of old owned them. Before the Black Ages, mind. Before Mornhavon. Long ago when the Sea Kings roamed the oceans and all the lands owed them allegiance, except those of the Eletians, of course."

"Their symbol," Miss Bunch said, "was the dragon. It is believed that such creatures once inhabited the Earth and filled the skies with their wings, and that only the Sea Kings were able to dominate or destroy them."

Amberhill had seen some strange things on his journey, not the least of which were the pirates. But dragons? Surely they belonged to the realm of fairy tale only. He pressed his thumb against the contours of the gold dragon, trying to imagine the ring as something fashioned and worn by ancients. It was not easy to comprehend.

"If you are honorable, and accept the responsibility of owning a heartstone," Miss Bunch said, "all should be well."

Miss Bay nodded her agreement.

Amberhill did not think Willis had heard a bit of the discussion, for he looked uncharacteristically befuddled and still muttered about pirates.

"Now that you've no home," Amberhill said, "and the winter is coming on, where will you go?"

"We've a cousin in the south," Miss Bay said. "We shall bide our time with her till other arrangements can be made."

Miss Bunch rolled her eyes. "And I say we should go to Rhovanny."

"Now don't you start—"

"But *you* don't like Miss Poppy any better than I. She's a witch!"

"Don't you mean she's a—"

"Bay! Don't you dare say it. You'll make Mother turn in her grave."

Miss Bay chortled.

"In any case," her sister said, "it's only until the house mends itself."

"That'll be forever."

"Oh, stop."

Amberhill excused himself and left the ladies to their quarrel. He retrieved his gear and set up his bedroll and sat upon it for some time, gazing into the dark away from the camp. The words of the sisters disturbed him and he wondered just what the ring tied him into, what responsibility he'd taken on by claiming it.

The Amberhill of old—the one who believed honor abductions a quaint tradition before it nearly cost the country its queen—might have decided to sell the piece for as much currency as he could get, abdicating any responsibility required for owning such an object; but the Amberhill of now, as disturbed by the sisters' words as he was, was willing to face any challenges the ring presented. He'd be an able guardian of it and would not allow it to fall into the wrong hands if it indeed held some form of power.

Most of all, however, he was simply intrigued by the mystery of it. The ring was beautiful, and ancient, and he just didn't wish to give it up.

Besides, the sisters could be wrong about it. He wasn't sure they were altogether sane. He resolved to find out more about the ring, to learn the truth of its origins—once he'd set his estate back in order, of course.

Satisfied by the plan, he rose and headed for the main fire

where stew was warming. As he walked he felt a distinct pinch on his right buttock. He jumped several feet and whirled, his hand to the hilt of his rapier, but no one was near, though he swore he heard the faintest of feminine giggles fading away.

He shook his head, then realized several Weapons and Beryl Spencer had observed his odd behavior and watched him in curiosity. In a move he'd learned from cats, he pretended nothing happened and continued on his way with the utmost dignity in his step.

RETURNINGS

By the end of the first month of winter, all who'd been sent out in pursuit of Lady Estora and her captors returned. First came Ty to report the book the king sought had been acquired by Second Empire and that they intended to break into the tombs. His mouth dropped open when the captain told him Karigan had arrived with the news well ahead of him and had helped recapture the book and round up the culprits.

The next to arrive were Willis, his Weapons, Lord Amberhill, and Beryl Spencer. They were less surprised that Karigan had arrived ahead of them, but had been pleased to hear the outcome. Lord Amberhill disappeared after telling his side of events to take care of some business in the city and elsewhere. He gave no details.

King Zachary and Captain Mapstone agreed that Beryl would not return to Mirwell Province anytime soon and they doubted Lord Mirwell would welcome back a known spy. If they had other plans for her abilities, nothing was heard of it, but she exchanged the scarlet of Mirwell for Rider green and resumed swordmaster initiate training with Arms Master Drent.

Shortly afterward, the rest of the Weapons arrived with their prisoners, including Immerez, who still had all five fingers attached to his one hand. That said, no one knew how long he would retain his head once the king was through with him. Some Weapons had gone after Colonel Birch in Mirwellton, but he'd escaped ahead of them, having sensed, or been informed, that the abduction of Lady Estora had failed and Grandmother had departed the Teligmar Hills.

Lord Mirwell had no idea as to where Birch had gone, but stated he was glad to be done with him. King Zachary would investigate Lord Mirwell's connection to Second Empire further, but it sounded as if the young lord-governor had been an unwilling participant in their schemes.

The only ones still at large were Fergal, Lady Estora, and the Weapons who'd gone in search of them. Karigan fretted daily that she'd done the wrong thing in sending them on their way alone, no matter how much Captain Mapstone and her friends reassured her she'd made a wise and courageous decision. But whenever she saw Lord Coutre, who'd dropped considerable weight and whose face was constantly lined with worry, she wondered. Wondered if she could have done better.

And oh, how she missed her Condor.

One day, while the clouds sent sleet battering against the castle walls, Karigan glared at herself in the mirror to see how her hair was growing back. It was returning, but with a cowlick. Not only that, but the new hair was fine and blond, like a baby's. She'd taken to parting her hair on the opposite side and combing a layer of it over the funny patch to obscure it. All her other hurts healed nicely and were fading, though there was an impressive scar down her forearm. Since it was usually covered, it did not bother her much.

Suddenly her door burst open and Yates strode into her room without knocking.

"Yates!" she cried, swinging around. "I could have been dressing or something!"

"But you weren't," he said with a mournful expression. "You were instead admiring your head."

She planted her hands on her hips. "If you ever barge in here again without knocking, you'll find yourself 'admiring' your head as well."

He bowed. "My humblest of apologies. But I thought you'd want the news."

"News? What news?"

Yates stood there with a smug grin on his face and said nothing.

"Tell me," Karigan commanded, "or I'll shake it out of you." She reached for him but he hopped back just out of her grasp.

"I know you are quite capable of hanging me out the window by my ankles should you so wish," he said, "but I'm not going to tell you. I will tell you the captain would like you to attend her in the throne room, and I'll even escort you." He proffered his arm.

"Scoundrel," she said.

"The lady is harsh," he said, feigning hurt. "But for her I shall endure the severest of tongue lashings."

Karigan groaned and rolled her eyes.

"The sooner we go," Yates added, "the sooner you can find out the news."

She really wanted to swat him, but he had a point, so she grabbed his arm and practically dragged him down the corridor, not quite the same as when he escorted her one fairy tale day in autumn when she wore a blue gown and felt a princess. She remembered how the day ended. Not in the usual fairy tale fashion, but with the throwing of her shoe at the Raven Mask.

Both Tegan and Mara remarked upon how glum many aristocratic ladies had seemed upon hearing the news of the Raven Mask's demise. Karigan felt little pity for them and their fantasies and thought of them as a bunch of silly clucks. Nor did she pity the Raven Mask for he had abducted and endangered Estora, threatening the unity of Sacoridia. Such a one as he was better off dead.

All the way to the throne room, Yates joked with her and treated her like a lady and he her obedient servant. She'd shake him if she weren't laughing so hard. Though it wasn't exactly the "Riderly" behavior Ty would insist on, no one paid them much attention. In fact, those they met in the corridor were in high spirits, despite the gloomy weather. Something was definitely afoot.

Then she caught snatches of conversation and Estora's name.

Karigan grabbed Yates' arm hard enough he yelped, and pivoted so she faced him squarely. "They're back, aren't they."

He nodded, and she rushed off, leaving him behind.

When she reached the throne room, she found it mobbed with courtiers and Weapons. She slipped her way between bodies, angling for the dais. She discerned the king's head rising above everyone else's. Excited voices drowned out the sound of sleet hammering the tall throne room windows. To Karigan it all blended into one big roar.

The crowd actually thinned out near the dais, and she arrived just in time to find Fergal on his knee, extending messages to the king, while Captain Mapstone and Connly, and the king's other advisors, looked on. She almost cried out Fergal's name, but waited as the king reached for the messages. He said something she could not hear amid the clamor, but she thought his mouth formed the words, "Well done, Rider."

Concern, pride, and exasperation filled Karigan as she gazed upon the scene. Concern over Fergal's condition, pride at his safe return with the messages, no less, and exasperation because . . . well, because he was Fergal.

When he rose from his knee, he turned and smiled at her. She swept a critical gaze over him. His uniform was neat, clean, and looked in surprisingly good condition for one on the run. She noticed no illness or injury, and he looked, by all accounts, well fed.

Huh, she thought. Perhaps she had worried needlessly. But she was too overjoyed to worry about worry, and strode over to him and gave him a great hug, right there in front of captain and king and other important persons. Only later would Karigan learn that Fergal had followed her instructions so well that he confounded Immerez's thugs who pursued him and Lady Estora, and even the Weapons who finally discovered them biding their time at an "inn" in Rivertown called the Golden Rudder. Later was soon enough for Karigan to throttle Fergal. Especially when he gave her a perfumed handkerchief as a remembrance from Trudy.

Captain Mapstone tapped Karigan on the shoulder and pointed across the room. When Karigan turned, she found Estora standing there in Rider green, looking as alive and healthy as Fergal. The two stared at one another for a moment or two, but then Estora left those friends, family members, and courtiers who thronged her and hugged Karigan. Lord Coutre came over and patted Karigan on the shoulder before moving on to pump Fergal's hand in a hearty handshake.

The return of Estora marked the beginning of an endless stream of festivities as winter winds gusted in a fury around the castle turrets and leaked with icy fingers through windows, but despite Karigan's involvement in Estora's rescue, she managed to avoid a good deal of it, for there was a certain pre-wedding atmosphere to the proceedings, with both Estora and King Zachary presiding over affairs like the intended couple they were, and it all cut into Karigan's gut no matter how she tried to dull the pain.

There were other matters vying for her attention, anyway. First, figuring was not one of Mara's strong points and the Rider ledgers were badly in need of Karigan's attention. Second, there was Condor who had returned from his journey as unscathed as Estora and Fergal. She spent many an hour grooming him and feeding him wrinkled apples, and even going riding on those days that were not so fiercely wintry.

And finally, there was the day all the Riders anticipated, both old and new: Mara's release from the mending wing and official return to duty as Chief Rider. Yates escorted her from the mending wing to the Rider wing, which she had never seen before. Mara was met with applause from friends who had striven to make their quarters as warm and homey as one could make any section of an ancient castle, with bright tapestries and artwork.

Mara oohed and aahed at the appropriate moments as Yates showed her the decoration and the cozy common room, but Karigan detected a glistening in Mara's eyes, likely of happiness, but also of loss over the Rider barracks that had been home for so long. For her, the Rider wing was a whole new experience.

When Yates took Mara to her room, he explained the trouble Garth had gone to in order to find just the right furnishings, and told her Garth was sorry he could not be there to show it all to her himself. When the door was opened, Mara was met with not only the best furnishings, but a painting by her favorite artist, a replacement set of books for those that had been lost in the fire, warm hangings and quilts, and more.

Finally Mara's tears flowed in full, and Karigan thought the deep healing of her friend had finally come full circle.

SECRETS

Laren stood before the door to Lady Coutre's parlor. The Weapon Willis guarded it, so she knew Lady Estora was within. She'd not been looking forward to this conversation, but it was time. Time before anymore crises arose and this problem was once again brushed aside. She tugged her shortcoat straight and knocked.

After a brief moment, a maid opened the door and admitted her. She was greeted by the domestic scene of Lady Coutre sitting with her three daughters before the fire, engaged in needlework and sipping tea. Laren bowed.

"Good afternoon, Captain," Lady Coutre said, looking up from her embroidery. "This is a surprise."

"I apologize for the intrusion," Laren said.

"Have you a message for us?"

Laren smiled. It was a long time since she had carried messages. The lady's two younger daughters, focused on needle and thread, paid her scant attention, but Lady Estora's regard was rapt, and even hopeful.

"No," Laren said. "I bear no messages. However, I wonder if I might have some words with Lady Estora."

"Certainly, Captain. Won't you join us? I'll have Priscilla fetch you some tea."

Laren shifted her weight from one foot to the other. "Thank you, but I wish to speak with your daughter alone. It is Rider business in regard to her forthcoming role as queen." It was certainly the truth.

"I see," said Lady Coutre. "We can—"

Lady Estora stood, setting her needlework aside. "No reason to trouble yourself, Mother," she said. "Captain Mapstone and I can speak elsewhere. Besides, I feel a need to stretch a bit."

Her mother looked ready to object, then smiled. "As you wish, dear."

Lady Estora preceded Laren out of the parlor and waited for her in the corridor. Laren joined her after taking leave of Lady Coutre.

"Thank you," Lady Estora told her once the door was shut.

"For what?" Laren asked in surprise.

"For the excuse to leave. Make no mistake, I am grateful to be with my family and in safety once again, but I am bored unto tears. Needlework! I can't bear it."

"Ah," Laren said. "That will happen after you've been riding with Green Riders. Nothing is the same again."

"Exactly!" Lady Estora's smile was radiant. "And I've wanted to thank you and your Riders, especially Karigan and Fergal, for their courage and help. They were wonderful. I don't know what would have become of me if they hadn't put themselves at great risk."

"They were doing their job," Captain Mapstone said, nevertheless feeling a surge of pride for her Riders.

"Yes, but I wish they'd receive some official recognition for their service."

"Oh," Laren said with a knowing grin, "no need to worry about that. However, there is something else that has been on my mind for some months now. We need to talk, and we need to do so someplace where we won't be overheard."

Lady Estora's pleasure at seeing Laren faded from her face. "I see. I know of a place where we can speak freely."

And frankly, Laren hoped.

Lady Estora led her to Zachary's old study, which was now a queen's solarium, though it remained barren of furniture or ornament, and was freezing. Footsteps and voices rang hollow, and the light that flowed through the windows was winter cold.

The two women stood there, speaking as frankly as Laren could ever wish, and speaking together as only two women could, about Lady Estora's future, the king, the country, and—most of all—F'ryan Coblebay.

Lady Estora proved to be a mix of nobility and humility, grief and despair. But she was strong, and Laren expected no less of her.

Finally, after the exchange of many words and some well-spent tears, Lady Estora said, "It would be a relief to get this over with."

"I understand." Then, moved by Lady Estora and her situation, Laren took the noblewoman's hands into her own. "My lady, I know Zachary very well. I knew him when he was a young terror in these halls, keeping me on my toes constantly; and he's grown into a thoughtful and compassionate man. Yes, he has a temper that flares now and then, but honestly, I have met no finer man than he. He listens and judges fairly, and he thinks very highly of you."

"He does?" Lady Estora seemed genuinely surprised.

Laren gave her hands a gentle squeeze, and nodded. "This sort of thing is never easy, but he will not be rash in his judgment. You must trust me on this."

She arranged for them to meet with Zachary the very next day. She was glad he agreed to it so soon, because she did not know how well Lady Estora's nerves would hold up if the wait was a prolonged one.

The two women arrived at the solarium at the appointed time and Laren saw that she shouldn't have worried about Lady Estora, for her entire demeanor was resolute.

It had snowed overnight, and the gardens outside the windows had turned into a fairyland of lumps and drifts and soft shapes, unsullied so far except by the tiny tracks of birds and squirrels. Snowflakes whirled down in gentle flurries, muting the light.

The two waited in silence for Zachary to arrive. When the knock finally came, they both turned toward the door.

"Please enter," Laren said.

Zachary stepped into the solarium leaving his attendants

outside. He assessed her and Estora, noted the barrenness of the room, and Laren saw that he was curious and perhaps a trifle nervous.

They exchanged courtesies and Zachary said, glancing at the unlit hearth, "It is cold in here. I could have—"

"No, thank you," Lady Estora said.

He looked from her to Laren, and back again. "Is the solarium not to your liking? I could have Cummings arrange for—"

Lady Estora raised her hand in a gesture that requested his silence. "We do not wish to discuss the solarium, my lord, but know it is a gift that is most welcome and appreciated."

Zachary stroked his beard. "Then what do you wish to discuss?" He gave an uneasy half smile. "Singly you are each formidable women, but I must admit that facing both of you here together, you are more intimidating than an opposing army."

Laren tried to reassure him with a smile of her own. "We are not opposing you. Do not worry on that count! But do keep it in mind for the future when you are married." She meant it in jest, but if this meeting in fact went well, and the wedding proceeded as planned, she suspected he'd continue to find Lady Estora a formidable woman, one who would not bend to his every wish. One who would not break the moment difficulty struck. She would stand by his side even if Mornhavon the Black himself stood on the castle steps with all his hordes behind him. She was a gentlewoman, but one with much hidden strength. One who should not be underestimated.

"I shall keep it in mind," he said with a nod of his head. "But please, what is this about? I am not sure I can take the suspense much longer."

"It's about a secret," Laren replied. "A secret that my Riders and I have been honor-bound to keep for some years now."

"What? Laren, you have never kept anything from me. At least so I supposed until now . . ."

She saw his hurt, and a touch of anger. "We've not been keeping it from just you, but from everyone."

"They've done so to protect me," Lady Estora said before he could interject.

"I don't understand," Zachary said. "What is this secret?"

"It begins with my arrival to court," Lady Estora said. "Your father was still regnant, though near the end of his illness. I was here for his funeral and for your coronation."

"I remember," he said.

Lady Estora was plainly surprised. "You do?"

Again, the uneasy half smile. "Forgive me, my lady, but there were few young men who wouldn't."

She nodded slowly as if she'd heard such things often enough. "You must also guess I was terrified being at court for the first time. Timid, shy. I had never traveled far from home and my parents left me here with only my old nurse and cousin as guardians. My cousin's job was to show me off as bait for a proper suitor."

This last held an underlying tone of bitterness, but she only spoke truth.

Lady Estora glided over to the windows and gazed out to the garden beneath its blanket of snow. She spoke as if to herself. "I was lonely. More lonely than you can imagine. Here I was in a strange city, with customs that were, frankly, different from those at home. Many believed Coutre a backward province, and that I must be an ignorant bumpkin, hence unfashionable and uninteresting. Others, those among my rivals, were perhaps jealous of the attention I received from the suitors they desired for themselves. I was not accustomed to the games played in court, the machinations, the blades thrust into one's back, and so I withdrew. Sought solace elsewhere, away from the social world of court. It all would have been intolerable if not for F'ryan Coblebay."

"F'ryan Coblebay?" Zachary said in surprise. "Your Rider?" he asked Laren. "The one whom Karigan—"

"Yes, F'ryan Coblebay," Laren replied. "*Your* Rider, and one of the best. And yes, Karigan completed his final mission. He died trying to bring you information about your brother's intention to steal your throne."

"Yes," he said quietly, "I remember."

"Do you remember *him?*" Lady Estora asked.

"I do," Zachary replied, "though I did not know him well. It is impossible for me to know well all who serve me."

Lady Estora left the windows to once more stand before him. She held her back straight and her gaze was unwavering. "Then I wish to tell you about F'ryan Coblebay."

Zachary remained silent, but Laren could not discern whether he was confused, upset, or just being polite. In any case, Lady Estora began her story, of a chance meeting with F'ryan in the gardens, and how this first encounter led to other intentional meetings.

"F'ryan offered me friendship and companionship," Lady Estora explained, "when I could find it nowhere else. He made me laugh, took me on rides into the country, and strolled with me in the gardens. Because of him, the Riders allowed me into their world. We played card games and sang songs in the common room of the old barracks." She smiled faintly in memory. "My nurse was really quite ancient, so it was not difficult to steal away."

Zachary did not comment or ask questions. He simply listened.

"F'ryan was a wonderful man," Lady Estora continued. "Always he saw the good in people. He could be serious if the situation warranted, but he was much the jester as well. The stories he told made me blush! And they'd leave me in tears from laughter. He was reckless and daring, but also the first to nurse an ill barn kitten back to health."

Laren found herself immersed in her own recollections of F'ryan. He'd been a damn fine Rider, dispatching messages in record time, charming the nobles, taking on some of the most difficult errands with seeming ease, and escaping one impossible situation after another without apparent effort. Tall, strong, and clever, and not to mention a swordmaster initiate, he seemed to defy the gods and death. Until the arrows.

Until the arrows . . .

She could not forget—would not forget—the sight of his arrow-pierced body in the back of an undertaker's cart. Her

Rider, the living, breathing man who beat her at Knights, who always had a cheerful word for her, who ardently loved his country and fellow Riders. He'd been so strong, so *alive.* How could he have become that body, that corpse of putrefying flesh lying in that dirty cart? *How?*

And so she wondered about all the Riders who perished under her command. How could such life simply be snuffed out like a candle?

"Without your Rider, F'ryan Coblebay," Lady Estora told Zachary, "I would not have survived my first months in court. As you may guess, as time went on, we fell in love."

At first Zachary did not react, but then nodded slowly, as if it was what he expected all along. "I'm sorry I did not know him better. I can certainly understand how you came to love a . . . this Rider, and I am sorry for the grief you've suffered at his loss."

"Yes," Lady Estora murmured. "I grieve for him still. I knew his job as a king's messenger was perilous, but I thought him . . . I thought him invulnerable. And yet, somewhere deep within, I must have known. I must have known that Westrion hovered not far from him." She paused.

Laren waited. Zachary waited.

Lady Estora tilted her chin up and gazed steadily at Zachary. "I must have sensed death awaited him. Before his final errand, I gave all of myself to him, and more than once, and I do not regret it no matter what shame it may bring me."

The three stood there, as silent and still as statues. The wind tossed eddies of snow against the windows. The cold of the room reached up through the floor, numbing Laren's toes in her boots, and crept up her spine so that it ached.

The air was ripe with potential, but whether that potential held an outburst of anger or simple acceptance, she could not predict. For all that Laren knew Zachary well, matters of the heart were tricky and he rarely gave her insight into his own feelings on the subject. Only her powers of observation allowed her to recognize his feelings for Karigan. That was a topic for another meeting some other time, and she did not look forward to it.

"You do understand," Laren told Zachary, "the courage Lady Estora is showing by coming to you with this. She did not wish for you to find out on your wedding night."

"I do," he replied, his voice toneless.

"Do you? Lord Coutre—"

"Lord Coutre," Zachary snapped, "loves his daughter. I know how much, for I saw the effect the abduction had on him."

Lady Estora dropped her gaze to the floor, her shoulders slumping ever so slightly.

"But—" Laren began.

He cut her off with a curt gesture. "I know he is strict. I know how conservative Coutre Province is compared to other regions of Sacoridia. *I know.* And I know also there was a time before the abduction that Lord Coutre would have disowned his daughter had he heard of her relationship with F'ryan Coblebay."

"But if you decide—"

Zachary turned full on to Laren. "I am not Lord Coutre, and this is not his province. I know what would happen if I considered the marriage contract breached. And for what? Because of love? For love of a man who has been dead more than two years?" He shook his head, incredulous. "I don't like secrets, Captain, but in this case, I understand. You did well to guard Lady Estora's honor."

"It was F'ryan's wish that we watch over her, protect her," Laren said, her heart surging with hope.

"And I will ask you to continue to do so," he said more softly. "I see no reason for this secret to be revealed to anyone else. At this point, I don't think Lord Coutre could bring himself to cast out his daughter. And why should he when I am still agreeing to wed her and she will be queen? Still, I think there is no reason to tell him."

Laren wanted to shout in triumph, but remained quiet and still. This was the response she had hoped for. This was the Zachary she knew.

He turned to Lady Estora and lifted her chin with a forefinger. "My lady, this is a brave thing you have done, to bring me the truth even while knowing what the consequences might have been. Truth often requires courage, and I hope there will only be truth between us when we are wed. You are a credit to your clan and lineage, and I believe F'ryan Coblebay was fortunate to have known you, even as you felt fortunate to have him help you through difficult times."

Estora sobbed and Zachary produced a handkerchief for her as if by magic.

"Well then," Laren said brightly. "There's one more thing I wish to bring up."

Zachary looked at her stricken. "There's more?"

She smiled. "Indeed. When are you going to take Lady Estora into your confidence and ask that she attend to court business with you? Better she learn now rather than after she's been crowned. Don't you think?"

"I think, Captain Mapstone," he said in a wry tone, "you should take over the job of running the country. After all, you seem to be running my life pretty well."

"I must decline, Your Highness. Running your life is pleasure enough."

KNIGHT OF THE REALM

When Karigan learned there was to be a ceremony to officially thank those involved in the rescue of Estora, she supposed it to be a simple one in which the king and Lord Coutre expressed their appreciation and that would be that. She was surprised when it turned out to be more.

Every available Rider was to attend, and to wear their formal uniforms, consisting of gold sashes, longcoats, and stocks. Karigan's saber had been returned to her and now it hung comfortable and familiar at her side. Estora reassured her she'd not drawn it even once during her escape.

The Riders walked in a loose formation through castle corridors with Captain Mapstone, Connly, and Mara at their head. The captain wore the ancient horn of the First Rider over her shoulder and Connly bore the shimmering banner of the Green Riders.

Courtiers, soldiers, servants, and administrators had to step aside to allow the massed Riders to pass and Karigan wondered what they thought of the procession. Had Riders ever made such a show in the castle before? Not in many lifetimes, she bet, and her heart swelled with pride.

When they arrived in the throne room, she found it filled with an ample number of courtiers, Estora, and members of her family; Weapons, Castellan Sperren, and Colin Dovekey, and much to her surprise, General Harborough and Arms Master Drent, the latter scowling.

Standing solitary and solemn upon the dais was King Zachary in black and silver. Several commendations were handed out to both Riders and Weapons for their actions in rescuing Estora and securing the tombs from Second Empire. Beryl received a special commendation in recognition of long service, though details of that service went unspoken.

Karigan thought that was to be it, but then she and Fergal were singled out and commanded by the king to come before him. Drent stepped over and stood before Karigan, glaring at her. She'd never seen him in full uniform before and she thought the buttons of his black longcoat would pop off or his shoulder muscles might burst the seams. He clutched papers and looked none too happy. Maybe his collar was too tight. Or he had indigestion, or . . .

"It seems a certain Arms Master Rendle thinks you are worthy of commencing swordmaster initiate training," he said, his tone indicating a difference in opinion. "*Rendle!* Hmph. He has offered to sponsor you as an initiate and will come to Sacor City to train you if I won't. I therefore have little choice but to commence your training. First thing tomorrow morning. I've been easy on you so far, Rider. Be prepared. We've also the matter of missing throwing knives to discuss."

Karigan swallowed hard and felt a bead of perspiration glide down her temple. This was the thanks she got for helping rescue Estora? While she was pleased Rendle thought so much of her skills, she was not so sure he realized what he was getting her into.

Next Lord Coutre came forward with a general of the Coutre provincial militia, bearing a cherrywood coffer. He said, "You rescued my daughter, the future queen of our land, and brought her home safely. I cannot express the depth of my gratitude, for I value nothing more than my family. I love my daughter deeply and never wanted any harm to befall her if it was in my power to protect her. When my power failed, you prevailed."

Karigan glanced at Estora and was surprised by the stricken expression she found on her friend's face. Had Estora not known the depth of her father's love?

"I have here," Lord Coutre continued, "but a token of my

appreciation for what you have done. It is the highest award from Coutre Province, yet still a token. The Order of the Cormorant."

The general opened the lid of the coffer and nestled inside on velvet were three medals of gold, each with a cobalt ribbon.

"I only wish Lord Amberhill were here to receive his medal," Lord Coutre said, "for he proved himself valiant in pursuit of my daughter's abductors."

Lord Coutre said more words that were lost to Karigan who was so surprised by the honor. Her cheeks warmed as he placed the medal around her neck. It seemed to weigh a hundred pounds.

"You both are always welcome to Coutre Province and in my house," Lord Coutre said. "You are also now entitled to lands within the province's borders."

Karigan was stunned, and when she glanced at Fergal, she saw his eyes had grown large. The knacker's son was now a landowner and had a place to settle after his service to the Green Riders ended. It was likely more than he ever dreamed possible.

Lord Coutre and his general returned to the sidelines. Estora hugged her father soundly.

Karigan thought this was the end of it all, but Captain Mapstone said to her, "Kneel before your king, Rider G'ladheon."

Fergal flashed her a smile and backed away to leave her there alone before the king. He evidently knew what was up, the brat!

Karigan knelt, wondering what the king had in mind.

"Long ago our royal ancestors had a way of honoring the heroic individuals who served them," he said. "This mode of honor fell out of favor at the time of the Clan Wars, for it had been used more to curry favor and loyalty and reward not valor but one's favorites in court. It now seems wise to restore this honor in its original spirit.

"A thousand years ago, the honor was created by King Jonaeus in the depths of the Long War for those especially heroic individuals who advanced Sacoridia's cause against the Arcosian Empire. One of the first to receive it was Liliethe Ambrioth, the founder of the Green Riders.

"Because Rider G'ladheon has displayed uncommon courage, not just once, but several times, in the face of dangers unimaginable, I now name her a knight of the realm, in the Order of the Firebrand. Like Liliethe Ambrioth and others who followed, Karigan G'ladheon rides in the light, bears the light, and knows the favor of the gods."

Knight of the realm? Karigan felt numb all over as the king placed another heavy medal around her neck, this one displaying the crescent moon and the firebrand, and the word "valor." He took her hands into his, the heat of his touch jolting up her arms, and he raised her to her feet. She glanced into his eyes, and saw how earnestly he gazed back at her as if there was so much more he wanted to say, but could not. She bit her bottom lip and looked away, and he turned her to face the assembled.

"Receive, my fellow Sacoridians," the king's voice boomed, "Rider Sir Karigan G'ladheon, knight of the realm."

The applause thundered right through Karigan and the rest was a blur until sometime during the reception that followed. Many whom she knew and did not know came to her and congratulated her on the honors she had received, while Captain Mapstone stood beside her, a proud smile on her face. Karigan was entirely too bewildered.

Until Fergal came up to her and said, "I think old Cetchum knew something."

Mention of Rivertown's crusty ferry master surprised Karigan. "What do you mean?"

"He called you 'sir,' right? Aren't we supposed to call you Sir Karigan now?"

Karigan had no words, and Fergal wandered off laughing at his own cleverness.

"He's right," Captain Mapstone said.

"What?"

"The proper address for a knight of the realm is to call you 'sir.' In your case, Rider Sir Karigan G'ladheon."

Karigan gave the captain a sideways glance, but saw no evidence she was joking.

"Could we . . . could we keep it just Rider?" Karigan asked.

"That's up to the king," Captain Mapstone replied, "but you should know he is quite serious about these things." She smiled and excused herself to speak with Castellan Sperren, leaving Karigan to stew amid the milling crowd. She was rather at a loss.

"Sir Karigan?" Colin Dovekey said, as he approached her.

Karigan winced at the unaccustomed title and bit her lip. "Yes?" she said.

"If I may have a moment? The king wished for me to speak to you."

She followed Colin out of the throne room and away from the deafening chatter and into a more quiet corridor. As she did so, a quick glance revealed the king standing beside Estora, engrossed in conversation with Lord Coutre and others. Though he'd presented her with the Order of the Firebrand, he'd chosen not to speak private words with her afterward. It made her feel hollow; diminished the honor.

"The king wished for me to give you these papers," Colin said in a quiet voice. "They came from Lord Mirwell among the messages Rider Duff delivered to the king."

"What are they?" Karigan asked, receiving the papers.

"An indictment against your father for acts of piracy against this realm, and others."

"What?"

"There is evidence," Colin said, "that your father served on a ship called the *Gold Hunter* in his youth. In the years our country skirmished with the Under Kingdoms, the ship served as a privateer, capturing many a ship from the enemy, as well as any goods it carried. After peace came between Sacoridia and the Under Kingdoms, the *Gold Hunter* continued its activities for some years. In other words, captain and crew participated in acts of piracy."

"My father was a *pirate?*" What else hadn't he told her?

She began to wonder if he'd really acquired his wealth as a merchant, or by piracy.

"Your father would have been no more than of age to be a cabin boy at the time, though that doesn't entirely absolve him of responsibility. However, because of his contribution to commerce in Sacoridia, his personal contributions in outfitting the Green Riders, and the subsequent savings to the treasury, the king has decided to overlook your father's connection to the *Gold Hunter,* and give you this evidence to do with as you wish."

Karigan glanced at the papers. An old stained sheaf looked to be a ship's crew roster, and there was her father's name. She grabbed the nearest lamp and burned them right there in the corridor.

"Although one cannot say for sure Lord Mirwell's motive in bringing this evidence forward at this time," Colin said, "it appears he holds some malice toward your clan. Rider Spencer herself dug up the information under old Lord Mirwell's command a couple years ago, and assures us this is the extent of it, and you know she is thorough. However, one cannot say for sure if Lord Mirwell won't come forward more publicly, though without evidence he won't have much of a case, but it may embarrass your clan. In light of this, the king asked me to reassure you that Clan G'ladheon has his favor and protection."

Colin seemed about ready to end the incredible conversation, but he paused and smiled. "One more thing, Sir Karigan. You are now entitled not only to lands in Coutre Province, but anywhere in Sacoridia you like. The king emphasized how lovely Hillander Province is in any season."

With that, Colin excused himself and returned to the reception. Karigan stood there in the corridor, the medals dragging on her neck. She put her hand to her temple, unable to process all she'd experienced and been told this day.

She'd acquired honors and lands. She was a knight of the realm. Her father had been a *pirate?* She sighed. She really needed to sit down and have a lengthy chat with him, about his trying to marry her off and the various digressions of his past. The Golden Rudder. The *Gold Hunter.* He was really into gold. And she groaned.

But everything could wait. She listened for a moment to the clamor coming from the reception. She ought to return, but she did not. No, it was sunny out, and not too cold, and Rider Sir Karigan G'ladheon was of a mind that it was a perfect time to saddle her horse and go for a ride. A *long* ride.

Pleased by her plan, she set off with long, swift strides, never knowing that just moments later, her king stepped out into the corridor desiring to speak with her.

Zachary had observed Karigan depart the festivities with Colin, but to his dismay, she did not return to the throne room when his counselor did. He wished ardently to talk with her—alone—before the event was over and so he tried to make his way through the throne room to the corridor, but it was no easy task to break away from all those who clamored for his attention.

When he at last reached the corridor, she was already gone. Gone like a spirit of the wind he would never be able to grasp.

He stood there in the empty corridor, feeling bereft, feeling she was beyond his reach because of more than the gulf created by his royal status and her common blood. He'd sensed a difference about her since the tombs, a mystery. It was subtle, something in her eyes, an aspect of midnight, as though she'd been touched by something not of this world.

He feared for her; feared for himself that she was slipping away, that he'd lose her entirely. It only strengthened his desire to fold her into his arms, to bring her closer, to protect her. He refused . . . he refused to let her go, to be taken by . . . by what?

He stood there, rubbed his upper lip in consternation. Then closed his eyes and bowed his head, the babble in the throne room fading away. She could be taken by anything. Her job, her duty, it was dangerous. Any message errand she went out on could be her last. He could command that she go on only the simplest of errands, the least dangerous ones, but even his royal status could not override her calling.

And it would not be enough to safeguard her. What he sensed about her, what aroused his fear, went beyond her work as a messenger, beyond the here and now. He could not place what it was that made him fearful, could not name it, but there was *something,* and his only desire was to protect her from it, whatever *it* was.

Actually, there was more he desired. Their brief touch at the dais had not been enough, only begged for more, only intensified his need. But she was gone . . .

He knew very well his obligation to the realm and Lady Estora, he knew he should return to the throne room, but the impulse to search for Karigan was powerful, like a fever. He took a step forward, but then Laren was there at his side, placing her hand on his arm.

"Your Majesty," she said, "many of your subjects still wish to speak with you, and there is Lady Estora wondering where you've gone."

He struggled inside himself, obligation warring against desire. But the stakes for the realm, he knew, were too great for him to follow his heart.

But still he hesitated. He took a deep breath, and another. He promised himself that even while fulfilling his responsibilities, he would do whatever was in his power to protect Karigan. No matter what. With this oath in place, he buried to the deepest regions within all that he wished for himself. He was the high king of Sacoridia and his personal happiness was irrelevant.

"Of course," he replied, and he allowed Laren to lead him back into the throne room, but he could not help glancing over his shoulder into the empty corridor.

HUMILITY AND HONOR

"*Knighted?*" Alton asked.

Garth nodded solemnly. "It was a big secret when I left, but the captain thought you'd want to know so she told me. I swore an actual oath not to tell anyone till I reached you."

They both stared at Dale when she started shaking with laughter. The three Riders sat in Tower of the Heavens before the hearth with a blazing fire keeping them warm, despite the gaping hole above through which cold air and snow whorled down to the chamber. Garth had been astonished by the mess he found, and even more so to find his friends had not been squashed by falling rocks or columns.

It was questionable as to how repairs were going to be made, as emphasis was placed on the breach yet again, where the wall needed to be rebuilt. Alton was never so glad as he was when he heard the book of Theanduris Silverwood had been recovered and hoped it would soon be translated so he could work on restoring the whole wall once and for all. And that would be the end to threats from Blackveil.

"What's so funny?" Garth demanded of Dale.

"*Sir* Karigan?"

"*Rider* Sir Karigan," Garth said.

Dale just laughed, wiping tears from her eyes. "Our little Karigan."

"A great honor," said a new voice. Merdigen emerged from beneath one of the arches and joined them at the hearth where he stretched his hands before the fire as if he could take warmth from it. "Your own First Rider was one such."

That information subdued Dale only somewhat.

"From the sound of it," Merdigen continued, "your friend has achieved a great deal at great personal risk. It only makes sense the king should so honor her."

"I know," Dale said. "It just . . . it just sounds funny." Finally she quieted and composed herself, only to snort and break out laughing again. "Sorry, sorry," she said, and laughing still, she rose and left them, walking through the wall to the outside world.

Garth shrugged and Alton suspected that once Tegan and Dale were back in the same territory, Karigan would find no peace from them.

"I suppose," Garth said, "this would be a good time for you to compose Karigan a letter of congratulations?"

The suggestion took Alton by surprise and his hand went automatically to his breast where her letter to him lay tucked in an inner pocket, the seal unbroken.

"I–I suppose," he said.

"Good," said Garth. "I'll take any correspondence you have when I leave in the morning."

That evening, Alton sat alone in the tower at the table, with paper, pen, and ink before him. He'd made a list of supplies needed, and for the king he explained the damage the wall had taken and the odd find of indigo yarn in the breach, and of strange horses left wandering in the encampment.

He additionally requested more Riders to investigate what happened to Tower of the Earth and its guardian, Haurris. The rest of the mages had returned to their towers, vowing to remain awake and in contact with one another, as well as with Alton, so they could continue in their work of soothing the wall guardians and strengthening their song. Alton wanted a Rider in every tower to make sure communication kept flowing.

In the meantime, he'd also seek members of his own clan who might have an ability to communicate with the guardians. Surely he couldn't be the only one, and if Pendric was any indication, he was not.

That correspondence was easy to deal with. When he finally had no more business, he pulled Karigan's letter out of his pocket. The envelope was crumpled and the seal an indistinguishable blob from his body heat. With a deep breath, he opened it.

The letter was not long, which was like Karigan, he thought. She was not one to waste time over words and would get straight to the point. He steeled himself for those words, and when he finished reading, he just sat there staring at the wall.

I'm sorry, she had written. *I don't know what I did wrong to make you angry at me, but I'm sorry.*

All this time Alton had avoided reading the letter first because of his own anger toward Karigan, then because of the anger he feared she meant to level at him. Instead, the words he read were, *I'm sorry.*

There were other words, promises to do better if he'd only tell her what was wrong. She valued their friendship too much to lose him. He gave her strength, she said.

Alton shook his head in disbelief. Once again he misjudged her and he couldn't blame it on a fever or poisons lingering in his veins. He could not blame it on the machinations of Mornhavon the Black. No, he could only blame himself.

Even when overcome by the fevers, how could he ever doubt her? How could he have believed her capable of treasonous behavior? And now she'd been honored by the king for just the opposite . . .

I am so stupid, he thought. He wondered if it was too late to repair the damage he wrought.

"You know, she seems to be quite extraordinary."

Merdigen took Alton so off guard he nearly fell out of his chair.

"What are you doing?" Alton demanded.

"Why, reading over your shoulder. Your friend Karigan, or should I say Sir Karigan, has not only shown great service to king and country, but has enough humility and honor to apologize when she makes a mistake."

"She isn't the one who made the mistake," Alton said, smoothing the letter against the tabletop. "I'm the one who should do the apologizing."

"Humility and honor," Merdigen said, "are hallmarks of the best leaders. It's also useful," he mused, "if you have a direct connection to the gods." He wandered off shaking his head and muttering about black horses and gods, then vanished beneath the west arch.

Humility and honor. Alton strove to help his country and he'd felt a failure. Maybe things were turning around. Maybe the book Karigan helped recover would allow him to . . .

He shook his head. He was not the center of the world. He would do his best to fix the D'Yer Wall and he would do what he could to repair the breach he'd caused between himself and Karigan, and that was a beginning.

He picked up his pen and put a clean sheet of paper before him. He would begin by opening his heart.

Dear Karigan, he wrote. *I seek your forgiveness . . .*

SLEEPERS

Grandmother paused to catch her breath and gazed upon the twisted dark limbs grasping out of the billowing mist of Blackveil Forest. Unpleasant as the place was, it was, for her, like a homecoming, for here were the roots of the empire, the lands her ancestors conquered when they came from Arcosia. Here was the base from which the empire would again arise. Old powers would awaken and the enemies of the empire would quail in fear.

She had found the old road that led toward the heart of Blackveil. Overgrown it was, with broken statues along its edges, but as clear a path as any. It would lead her true, for other paths were deceptive, might lure them into traps set by predators. The few retainers she brought along with her remained close and wide-eyed, fearful of the creatures that moved through foliage and underbrush. They had nothing to fear so long as she maintained a shield of protection around them. Lala knew she was safe. She sat on a stone playing string games.

"Come," Grandmother told her people, "there will be time enough for rest later. Now we must go awaken the Sleepers."

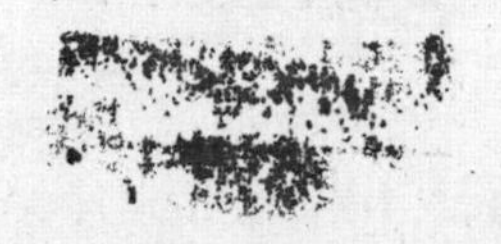